BLAST, CORRUPT,
DISMANTLE, ERASE

BLAST, CORRUPT, DISMANTLE, ERASE

Contemporary North American Dystopian Literature

Brett Josef Grubisic,
Gisèle M. Baxter,
and Tara Lee, *editors*

WILFRID LAURIER
UNIVERSITY PRESS

Wilfrid Laurier University Press acknowledges the support of the Canada Council for the Arts for our publishing program. We acknowledge the financial support of the Government of Canada through the Canada Book Fund for our publishing activities.

Library and Archives Canada Cataloguing in Publication

Blast, corrupt, dismantle, erase : contemporary North American dystopian literature / Brett Josef Grubisic, Gisèle M. Baxter, and Tara Lee, editors.

Includes bibliographical references.
Issued in print and electronic formats.
ISBN 978-1-55458-989-0 (pbk.).—ISBN 978-1-55458-990-6 (epub).—
ISBN 978-1-77112-056-2 (pdf)

1. Dystopias in literature. 2. Utopias in literature. 3. American fiction—History and criticism. 4. Canadian fiction—History and criticism. 5. Mexican fiction—History and criticism. 6. North America—In literature. 7. Literature and society. I. Grubisic, Brett Josef, editor of compilation II. Baxter, Gisèle Marie, editor of compilation III. Lee, Tara, [date], editor of compilation

PN56.D94B63 2014   809'.93372   C2014-900228-9
                                      C2014-900229-7

Cover design by Martyn Schmoll. Cover photo: *Ballroom, American Hotel*, from The Ruins of Detroit Series, by Yves Marchand and Romain Meffre.
Text design by Janette Thompson (Jansom).

© 2014 Wilfrid Laurier University Press

Waterloo, Ontario, Canada

www.wlupress.wlu.ca

This book is printed on FSC recycled paper and is certified Ecologo. It is made from 100% post-consumer fibre, processed chlorine free, and manufactured using biogas energy.

Printed in Canada

Every reasonable effort has been made to acquire permission for copyright material used in this text, and to acknowledge all such indebtedness accurately. Any errors and omissions called to the publisher's attention will be corrected in future printings.

No part of this publication may be reproduced, stored in a retrieval system, or transmitted, in any form or by any means, without the prior written consent of the publisher or a licence from the Canadian Copyright Licensing Agency (Access Copyright). For an Access Copyright licence, visit http://www.accesscopyright.ca or call toll free to 1-800-893-5777.

CONTENTS

Introduction • Brett Josef Grubisic, Gisèle M. Baxter, and Tara Lee   1

PART I   Altered States

The Man in the Klein Blue Suit: Searching for Agency in William Gibson's *Bigend Trilogy* • Janine Tobeck   29

The Cultural Logic of Post-Capitalism: Cormac McCarthy's *The Road* and Popular Dystopia • Carl F. Miller   45

Logical Gaps and Capitalism's Seduction in Larissa Lai's *Salt Fish Girl* • Sharlee Reimer   61

"The Dystopia of the Obsolete": Lisa Robertson's Vancouver and the Poetics of Nostalgia • Paul Stephens   73

Post-Frontier and Re-Definition of Space in *Tropic of Orange* Hande Tekdemir   93

Our Posthuman Adolescence: Dystopia, Information Technologies, and the Construction of Subjectivity in M.T. Anderson's *Feed* Richard Gooding   111

PART II   Plastic Subjectivities

Woman Gave Names to All the Animals: Food, Fauna, and Anorexia in Margaret Atwood's Dystopian Fiction • Annette Lapointe   131

The End of Life as We Knew It: Material Nature and the American Family in Susan Beth Pfeffer's Last Survivors Series • Alexa Weik von Mossner   149

"The Treatment for Stirrings": Dystopian Literature for Adolescents Joseph Campbell   165

Imagining Black Bodies in the Future • Gregory Hampton   181

Brown Girl in the Ring as Urban Policy • Sharon DeGraw   193

PART III Spectral Histories

Archive Failure? *Cielos de la tierra*'s Historical Dystopia • Zac Zimmer 219

Love, War, and *Mal de Amores*: Utopia and Dystopia in the Mexican Revolution
María Odette Canivell 239

Culture of Control / Control of Culture: Anne Legault's *Récits de Médilhault*
Lee Skallerup Bessette 259

The Sublime Simulacrum: Vancouver in Douglas Coupland's Geography of Apocalypse • Robert McGill 275

Neoliberalism and Dystopia in U.S.–Mexico Borderlands Fiction
Lysa Rivera 291

America and Books Are "Never Going to Die": Gary Shteyngart's *Super Sad True Love Story* as a New York Jewish "Ustopia" • Marleen S. Barr 311

In Pursuit of an Outside: Art Spiegelman's *In the Shadow of No Towers* and the Crisis of the Unrepresentable • Thomas Stubblefield 327

Homero Aridjis and Mexico's Eco-Critical Dystopia • Adam Spires 339

PART IV Emancipating Genres

Lost in Grand Central: Dystopia and Transgression in Neil Gaiman's *American Gods* • Robert T. Tally, Jr. 357

Which Way Is Hope? Dystopia into the (Mexican) Borgian Labyrinth
Luis Gómez Romero 373

Dystopia Now: Examining the Rach(a)els in *Automaton Biographies* and *Player One* • Kit Dobson 393

The Romance of the Blazing World: Looking back from CanLit to SF
Owen Percy 409

"It's not power, it's sex": Jeanette Winterson's *The PowerBook* and Nicole Brossard's *Baroque at Dawn* • Helene Staveley 427

Another Novel Is Possible: Muckraking in Chris Bachelder's *U.S.!* and Robert Newman's *The Fountain at the Center of the World*
Lee Konstantinou 453

About the Contributors 475

Introduction

Brett Josef Grubisic, Gisèle M. Baxter, and Tara Lee

The Apocalypse Industry Now

> In these hours of prolific
> doubt, how will we acquit ourselves?
> —Steve McOrmond, "The Good News about Armageddon"

> And meanwhile all over town checks are bouncing and accounts are being automatically closed. Passwords are expiring. And everyone's counting and comparing and predicting. Will it be the best of times? Will it be the worst of times? Or will it just be another one of those times? Show of hands please!
> —Laurie Anderson, "Another Day in America"

Over the course of 2013, four non-fiction works—*Flashpoint 2012*; *Demonomics: Satan's Economy and Your Future*; *The Departure: God's Next Catastrophic Intervention into Earth's History*; and *The American Apocalypse*—represented the total title inventory of the Rapture Ready Bookstore (send cheque or money order to P.O. Box 969, Benton, Arizona). The Bookstore is a peripheral aspect of raptureready.com, "the most popular Rapture-preparedness website in the world" (Savodnik). Founded by Todd Strandberg, the chiliastic enterprise's key features are "Photorama" (click to view a "thumbnail collection of 22 signs of the end times") and a miscellany of op-ed articles and news formats (daily: "End Time Related Events"; weekly: "Nearing Midnight"; ongoing: "The Rapture Index," a regularly updated "Gauge of End Times").[1] With "Donation Depot," Strandberg's undertaking also encourages user philanthropy. Raptureready.com is one among several examples of businesses surveyed by Peter Savodnik in "The Rapture Profiteers." Savodnik explains that a "huge vacuum in the Rapture market" formed upon the failure of Alameda, California–based Harold Camping's 2011 doomsday announcements. As Christopher Goffard notes, the religious leader and Family Radio broadcaster's prediction—for the *spiritual* starting point on May 21, 2011, followed by widespread "'super horror story'" misfortunes culminating five months later in the *physical* Rapture on October 21—had received unprecedented publicity "thanks to a worldwide $100-million campaign of caravans and billboards." Claiming the post-Camping "apocalypse establishment is offering an unprecedented array of doomsday-themed literature, podcasts, survival kits, and other goods and services for navigating the end of times," Savodnik lists diverse commodities—including a "new genre of chick lit called Rapture Erotica" and the bestselling Left Behind series of books and films—that reflect at least one unequivocal fact: the peculiar service sector is "bustling."

Focusing on televangelist DVDs, "Judgement Day–inspired" novelists, and entrepreneurs who are "making more money than they can spend before the world ends," Savodnik's *Businessweek* article bypasses commercial ventures geared primarily toward promoting ideologies instead of consumer goods. For example, endoftheworld2012.net discredits current doomsday predictions while demanding absolute adherence to the Holy Bible and warning of the "coming wrath." Likewise, endoftheworldprophecy.com does sell one book, *America in Prophecy*, but characteristically publishes advice (e.g., "How to Prepare for the End of the World—7 Steps You Can Take Now!")[2] and editorials, such as John Quade's "On the Eve of Armageddon": "Thousands observe the intensity that is taking possession of every earthly element, and they realize that something great and decisive is about to happen—it appears that the world is on the verge of its most tremendous crisis." Adopting a seemingly fringe outlook, Quade shares a commonality with another bullish market segment Savodnik leaves unexamined: non-fiction titles anticipating, in echo of *The Shape of Things to Come*, H.G. Wells' 1933 bestselling novel, eventualities both near ("December 21, 2012" [Joseph, *Apocalypse* 3]) and far ("2060 at the earliest" [Attali, *History* xv]). This diagnostic assortment of volumes represents a burgeoning field, not to mention a zeitgeist definition that furthermore reverberates deeply within popular culture, from recent "apocalypto-porn" alien invasion films (Edelstein) and the "post-apocalyptic theme" (Vena) of Britney Spears' latest world tour, to the dystopian manifesto *2083—A European Declaration of Independence*, self-published, Internet-distributed, and appearing on July 22, 2011, the same day Anders Behring Breivik, its author, bombed a government building and later fatally shot sixty-nine people in Norway.

Between Jacques Attali and Slavoj Žižek, the number of alarm-sounding authors publishing within the past fifteen years is remarkable in and of itself; and, from the end of oil to the sunset years of humanity, the variety of focal points within the genre and the tonal consistency is noteworthy as well.[3] That the perspectives are heterogeneous is no surprise considering that the authors range from evangelical millennialists and interpreters of Mayan[4] prophecy to mathematicians, historians, political scientists, environmentalists, investigative journalists, a former UFC light heavyweight champion, and a "suburban homesteader growing roots (both literally and figuratively) in Southern Maine" ("Wendy Brown"). Nevertheless, their titles broadly correspond in offering analyses of worsening or already "severely dysfunctional" systems (Bello 18) and foreboding contemporary portents that incite pronouncements of "dire scenarios" (Roberts, *End of Food* 305) relating to incipient collapse, apocalypse, extinction, instability, catastrophe, rapid decline, and global warfare. Expressing what Peter Fitting calls a "dystopian mood"[5]—the "sense of a threatened near future" (140)—the publications also provide a mode of public service insofar as they seek to warn, educate, and mobilize readers: to be aware of and prepared for the inevitable on the one hand, or to forestall municipal/regional/national/global disasters and dystopias of authoritarianism, scarcity, tribalism, and so on, by implementing radical systemic changes on the other.

Besides proposing differing theses about specific timelines and locations (not to mention *kinds* of threatened near futures), the authors diverge markedly too about both degree and inevitability: complete annihilation as a *fait accompli* at one extreme and "[c]ivilization as we know it will end sometime in this century unless . . ." (Goodstein 123) at the opposite. For instance, Lawrence E. Joseph adopts a matter-of-fact tone when he states, "2012 is destined to be a year of unprecedented turmoil and upheaval" (*Apocalypse* 15). In *The Long Emergency*, James Howard Kunstler tempers the declaration that humanity is "in for extraordinary hard times" (305) with a call for preparedness: North Americans "will be compelled by the circumstances of the Long Emergency to conduct the activities of daily life on a smaller scale, whether we like it or not, and the only intelligent course of action is to prepare for it" (239). In contrast, Eugene Linden's assertion—that while society may not be able to head off some measure of instability, "humanity has the power to moderate the impact of the coming upheavals" (264)—echoes Daniel Pinchbeck, who warns that the coming decades will present a literally do-or-die choice: since humanity finds itself within a window of opportunity where it can either radically alter its "direction as a species or face devastating consequences," Pinchbeck foresees that humanity will shortly "undergo revolutionary changes ... or it will suffer an apocalypse that may well end humanity's tenure on the planet" (*Notes* 5).

Views about wider geopolitical developments align in a near-identical pattern. While Rapture-ready spiritual leaders and interpreters of Mayan prophecy warn of an imminent and total end (or an imminent and total New Age), political analysts anticipate short-term, empire-wide shifts and ideology or economic system extinction as well as a potential emergence from chaos. In *The End of the World as We Know It*, for instance, Immanuel Wallerstein proclaims that the first half of the twenty-first century will prove "far more difficult, more unsettling, and yet more open to anything we have known in the twentieth century" (1); in like-themed works, he forecasts an "era of transition, of chaotic bifurcations, of choice" (*Decline* 293). Attali's *A Brief History of the Future*, "foremost a meditation on the present" (xvii), outlines the eventual emergence of "hyperdemocracy" (255–78), but not before mapping the arrival of oligarchic "hypernomad" (195) super-empires and, after their collapse, planetary war ("a hyperconflict far more destructive than all previous wars, local or global" [211–212]). In *Living in the End Times*, Žižek declares the "global capitalist system is approaching an apocalyptic zero-point" (x), but suggests the "forthcoming apocalypse" might also offer humanity a chance for an "emancipatory subjectivity" (xi–xii). Roughly commensurate with Attali's vision of long-term strife and clashing, then crashing empires, even Breivik's notably xenophobic and anti-feminist *2083* anticipates the eventual cessation of national and ideological struggles (though not before decades of ethno-religious wars, unparalleled brutality, and countless deaths).

Fin du Globe: End of Days Anxieties in Literature

> Modern man has been diminished and turned into a machine
> Final anarchy of the human race
> America will conquer the earth
> End of the world through the cessation of heat
> —Gustave Flaubert, *Bouvard and Pécuchet*

The small library of premonitory non-fiction appearing within the past two decades has been disseminated in nations where distressing phrases—"debt crisis" and "market volatility"; "extremism," "suicide bomber," and "war on terror"; "climate change" and "species extinction rate"—have become common currency. Inexorable, end-of-decade, -century, and -millennium anxieties—stemming in part from what Bryan D. Palmer calls a "confluence of disintegrations" (3) in the 1990s—became millennial angst; and the post-millennial disquiet in which *Blast, Corrupt, Dismantle, Erase: Contemporary North American Dystopian Literature* now circulates is compounded by ongoing[6] economic, political, and environmental crises.

And though the conviction that humanity will soon face "fundamental transformations of the world-system" (Wallerstein, *Decline* 1) is pervasive, this sense of impending calamity is hardly unique to our era. Commenting on global attentiveness to the Mayan prophecy for 2012, for instance, Matthew Restall and Amara Solari state that such transnational fretfulness is unsurprising because "[c]hiliasm is at the very heart of Western civilization" (116). Moreover, writing in the context of late-nineteenth-century European visual arts, Shearer West remarks, "[d]isasters, catastrophes and fears that the world will come to an end are concerns that have governed human behaviour and have found their expression in art and literature for centuries" (1). West argues further that *fin de siècle* fixations are especially pronounced yet historically specific: the 1490s' "involved religion, whereas those of the 1790s concerned politics," and though those particular acute sensitivities did not entirely disappear in the 1890s, the Victorian worry was "characterized by a greater self-examination and more explicitly psychological perspective" as well as an internationalism made possible by the rise of mass media (15).

The broad point these authors raise is not that there is nothing new under the sun so much as that each era's expression of a preoccupation takes a unique form with distinct foci and intensity. This epochal obsession is by no means limited to a given century's final decade, of course. For example, in his non-fiction companion volume, *Brave New World Revisited*, Aldous Huxley remarks on his heightened pessimism circa 1958: "The prophecies made in 1931 are coming true much sooner than I thought they would.... The nightmare of total organization, which I had situated in the seventh century After Ford, has emerged from the safe, remote future and is now awaiting us, just around the next corner" (1–2). Huxley follows that bleak assessment with a survey of then contemporary harbingers of "permanent crisis" (10), identifying overpopulation and over-organization as well as brainwashing, propaganda, chemical persuasion, and subconscious persuasion; he concludes with a tepid call to arms: "Perhaps the forces that now menace freedom are too strong to be resisted for very long. It is still our duty to do whatever we can to resist them" (97). Situated in the booming middle decade of the twentieth century, Huxley's ample worry corresponds generally with concerns expressed by writers half a century later; and his dire novelistic forecasts of 1931 echo literary depictions that had begun to flood the market a half century before.

Though the general states of dread appear consistent, the areas of acute sensitivity do not. Additionally, the volume of outcry—as measured by publications—supports the notion that while fear about the world's demise may be a constant, there are historical periods in which that constancy garners significant attention. In terms of literary discourse, there is no earlier era with greater volubility about themes pertaining to catastrophe and the dusk of nations than the *fin de siècle* of Decadent artists and Max Nordau's *Degeneration*. Daniel Pick states that the "second half of the nineteenth century is characterised by an enormous output of medical and natural scientific writings on social evolution, degeneration, morbidity, and perversion," and that behind "each of those texts, one discovers an avalanche of similar books, pamphlets, and articles" (20). Conditions beget fiction as readily as non-fiction; and alongside the flourishing of Decadent literature with, as Pick states, "its innumerable lyrical laments and aesthetic discontents" (2), another fretful genre prospered, one filtering widespread cultural currents through peculiar scientific imagery.

While science fiction scholars debate the genre's precise origins and defining characteristics, they do concur concerning a prodigious late-Victorian rate of growth and, generally, the reasons for it: writing as reaction and proactive intervention. In *Scientific Romance in Britain 1890–1950*, Brian Stableford relates the rise of scientific romances in part to the "stimulus of new scientific ideas" (11). Stableford notes, moreover, that after 1890 a society-wide "new pessimism" was signalled by a "massive displacement of Utopian images of the future by dystopian ones" (25). In other words, the "impact of nineteenth-century reality on literary imagery" (Stableford, "Ecology" 263) resulted in conjectural fiction thematizing the anticipated deleterious future effects of class divisions, rampant scientism, urbanization, and industrialization. Building upon I.F. Clarke's calculation that over four hundred "shape of wars-to-come" (ix) stories were published between

1871 and 1914 (xx), Roger Luckhurst similarly states that by 1873 Britain was "awash in invasion and future-war fantasies" (31) expressing a sense of imperial or capitalist vulnerability and an urgent need for militaristic response. Among the conditions enabling the development of this type of forewarning scientific fiction were, in Luckhurst's view, a coherent ideology and emergent profession of science and "everyday experience transformed by machines and mechanical processes, released in a steady stream from the workbenches of inventors and engineers" (29); the quotidian can also be understood as dispiriting, for Luckhurst submits that the "possibilities of biological and entropic decline mark the character of the British scientific romance (23). Like Stableford and Luckhurst, Adam Roberts addresses the influence and popular reception of scientific publications by eminent figures such as Charles Darwin, Charles Lyell, and Bénédict Augustin Morel before proposing a "notional scale" of cultural reaction, with "positivist optimism" at one end and burgeoning "degeneration pessimism" at the other (106–107).[7] Acknowledging that any claim for all early science fiction to fit into this neat schema is a simplification, Roberts nonetheless indicates that the "two ways of responding to the changes in the present, and the possible directions the future might take, do determine much of the fictional speculation" (107) over the 1850–1900 period. Finally, Darko Suvin views this "fin-de-siècle cluster" (*Metamorphoses* 87) of publications as being "historically part of a submerged or 'lower literature' expressing the yearnings of previously repressed or at any rate nonhegemonic social groups," and considers it sensible to conclude that "major breakthroughs to the cultural surface should come about in periods of sudden social convulsion" (*Metamorphoses* 115).[8]

Over a century after the scientific romances of H.G. Wells and the ostensibly scientific methodology of Max Nordau, science fiction has become a well-established, bestselling, quasi-religious (Disch, *On SF* 190; Atwood, *Other Worlds* 64) genre and its formerly unconventional imagery disseminated to the point of ubiquity. If, as Thomas M. Disch claims, the influence of science fiction can be felt "in such diverse realms as industrial design and marketing, military strategy, sexual mores, foreign policy, and practical epistemology—in other words, our basic sense of what is real and what isn't" (*Dreams* 11–12), the question the presence and wide circulation of one of its least escapist branches, dystopian fiction, encourages is: what in general do our literary dystopias reflect about the times? One ready answer is that their very abundance indicates publishers expecting a substantial audience for authors foreseeing threatened near futures and writing cautionary, activist tales in reply. The relationship between historical actuality and literary production delineated by scholars of Victorian science fiction does, after all, correspond to the understanding of purposeful action promulgated by novelists themselves. Huxley's paradigmatic statements about his process and goals—scrutiny of troubling coalescing forces and response with a "prophetic fable" (31) that identifies their malevolent potential—recall statements made by an author influenced by Huxley's "weird tale" (Atwood, "Context" 514). More than seven decades after *Brave New World*, Margaret Atwood situated her dystopian novels in an ideological praxis, telling an audience that literature is "an uttering, or outering, of the human imagination. It puts the shadowy forms of thought and feeling—heaven, hell, monsters, angels, and all—out into the light, where we can take a good look at them and perhaps come to a better understanding of who we are and what we want, and what our limits might be" ("Context" 517). For Atwood, such an understanding is "no longer a pastime or even a duty but a necessity because, increasingly, if we can imagine something, we'll be able to do it" ("Context" 517).[9] Conceived of as vehicles for preemptive political activism, dystopian imaginative extrapolations (from Victorian scientific romances to twenty-first-century speculative fiction) address familiar developments—automation through to authoritarianism—in order to forewarn, illustrate, and dissuade.

In an echo of the literary phenomenon at the turn of the nineteenth century, the recent production spike of cautionary, projected-dark-future diagnosing and dystopia-inhibiting non-fiction runs parallel to the increased visibility of its fiction counterpart, Savodnik's Rapture Erotica representing a single variant of what *Publishing Trends* magazine labels a "dystopian trend" commonly associated with mainstream science fiction and literary fiction rather than niche erotica. The parallel sentiment/productivity of the two eras has not gone unremarked. Luckhurst, for instance, opens a discussion of Anglo-American science fiction—a nebulous genre into which dystopian literature is conventionally placed[10]—of the 1990s with reference to Homi Bhabha's "Anxious Nations, Nervous States" (1994): "As the century nears its end, there emerges a pervasive, even perverse, sense that history repeats itself. Circumstances compel us to regard our own contemporaneity in the language and imagery of a 'past' that turns tradition into turbulent reality" (220). Luckhurst's reference to Bhabha's then-commonplace observation[11] intends to frame a survey of a literary form hyperconscious of the era's awareness of crisis, collapse, and unsteady transformations. For Luckhurst, the twentieth century's end—an "era of accelerated, technologically-driven change" (222)—resulted in the likewise accelerated transnational growth of science fiction subgenres: from escapist space opera revivals to genre hybridization (222). Furthermore, in his view, the 1990s were a "mass commercial vehicle for apocalyptic visions" (231).

Luckhurst is atypical of science fiction scholars insofar as he lists quantifiably distinct emergent trends. Other scholars characteristically pay heed to their particular branch of research or emphasize the irreducibility of the genre. In the introduction to *Future Females, The Next Generation*, for example, Marleen S. Barr charts the development of heretofore separatist feminist science fiction "merging with the mainstream" (1); and within Barr's volume, Jane Donawerth asserts that the "feminist dystopia" was "by far the most popular form women science fiction writers" produced in the 1990s (49). Though making no mention of feminist dystopian literature, Edward James states, "Anglo American sf in the 1990s is too varied to make any predictions about where it is heading" (203), and notes the flourishing of alternative histories, steampunk, and persistent "thinking seriously about the future" (206). Observing the splintering of science fiction into "a variety of subgenres and categories," Darren Harris-Fain's telltale chapter, "Anything Goes, 1993–2000," identifies a "great variety not only in content and in style but also in quality" (167). Adam Roberts, restating the axiom of the "fantastically variegated and multifarious mode" (341) of science fiction, nonetheless points to key texts from the 1990s, including Kim Stanley Robinson's alternative history, *The Years of Rice and Salt*, Douglas Coupland's end-of-the-world novel, *Girlfriend in a Coma*, and David Foster Wallace's *Infinite Jest*, the latter set in the dystopian Organization of North American Nations, a mega-state composed of the former Canada, Mexico, and the United States. In (another) answer to the earlier question, "What do dystopian imaginings suggest about our times?" the fact of impressive growth figures, from feminist dystopias to apocalyptic visions, foremost denotes an avid readership for such generalized anxiety. The enormous assortment, moreover, encourages the conclusion that, to borrow from Stableford, late-twentieth-century and post-millennial global reality has provided bountiful source material for literary imagery; in short, authors have perceived no shortage of everyday indicators about which to express concern.

What *Publishing Trends* highlighted as an escalating market for publishers in 2010 is not *ex nihilo* so much as an evolutionary aspect of a phenomenon beginning a century earlier. Commentators have long noted that dystopian fiction quickly eclipsed its utopian counterpart; with the brutal regimes and massive casualties of the twentieth century, Atwood remarks, depicting awful societies "became much easier" (*Other Worlds* 84). Citing the research of Robert Scholes and Eric S. Rabkin, M. Keith Booker argues in *The Dystopian Impulse in Modern Literature* that "much utopian thought is clearly related to an atavistic desire to return to what is perceived as an earlier better time in history than one's own life" (5). In contrast, the "gradual turn to dystopianism" discernible in twentieth-century literature represented novelistic interventions with contemporaneous historical events and "perceived inadequacies in existing social and political systems" (20), as well as ruminations on the reception and circulation of a "number of developments in nineteenth-century thought" tied to the works of Marx, Darwin, Clausius, and T.H. Huxley (*Dystopian Literature* 5–7). Booker proposes the maturation of a literary genre that is less a fantastical escape from contemporary reality than a political engagement with it. In addition to being "one of the most revealing indexes to the anxieties of our age" (*Dystopian Literature* 4), the turn toward dystopian fiction has produced a contemporary literature whose fundamental purposes are criticism of "specific 'realworld' societies and issues," and provision of "fresh perspectives on problematic social and political practices that might otherwise be taken for granted or considered natural and inevitable" (*Dystopian Impulse* 19).

For Booker, the "growing wave of dystopian visions" (*Dystopian Impulse* 18) suggests a practical activism about headline news on the part of authors, not to mention a greater number of globe-spanning crises requiring attention. Faulting aspects of Booker's methodology, Tom Moylan proposes a dialectical model in "The Dystopian Turn," a key chapter of *Scraps of the Untainted Sky*, surveying modalities within the broad category of dystopian literature. After beginning with E.M. Forster's "The Machine Stops" (1909) and commenting on pivotal texts from the 1950s, 1960s, and 1970s, Moylan applies Lyman Tower Sargent's model of the capitalist power- and conservative-rule-challenging "critical dystopia" to fiction after the mid-1980s, observing in it "a textual mutation that self-reflexively takes on the present system and offers not only astute critiques of the order of things but also explorations of the oppositional spaces and possibilities from which the next round of political activism can derive imaginative sustenance and inspiration" (xv). Moylan perceives in such dystopian literature a reaction to the "present system," and thus a primary function much the same as Booker's, despite differences of nomenclature: diverse political engagements with faulty present-day systems with the growing potentials for widespread harm.

NAFTA, Transnational Discourses, North American Dystopian Literature

> Now it appears we face the prospects of two contradictory dystopias at once—open markets, closed minds—because state surveillance is back again with a vengeance. . . .
>
> [I]t seems that we in the West are tacitly legitimizing the methods of a darker human past, upgraded technologically and sanctified to our own use of course. For the sake of freedom, freedom must be renounced.
> —Margaret Atwood, *In Other Worlds*

The twenty-six essays of *Blast, Corrupt, Dismantle, Erase* focus on works published by North American writers during a notably volatile period: from January 1, 1994, the day NAFTA (the North American Free Trade Agreement) came into effect,[12] to the tenth anniversary of a "moral obscenity" (Eagleton B7) and the "mother of all events" (Sicher and Skradol 164), the suicide attacks of September 11, 2001. As the texts surveyed earlier illustrate, awareness of and deep concern about perceived vulnerabilities— ends of water, oil, food, capitalism, empires, stable climates, ways of life, non-human species, and entire human civilizations—have become central to public discourse over the same period. Even titles of hand-wringing late-twentieth-century non-fiction that can induce amusement, nostalgia, or puzzlement from the vantage point of 2014 have contributed to the contemporary sense of malaise. Dorothy R. Bates' *The Y2K Survival Guide and Cookbook*, an example of an extinct albeit brief and explosive publishing boom, appeared alongside an "orgy" of books representing another "ephemeral" genre (Gould 15) contingent on and responding to the simultaneous conclusion of a century and a millennium. Whether expressing date-specific panic about societies too reliant on technology, or understood as "aggressive millenarianism" indicative of nations awash in "only half-fearful longing for an apocalyptic fulfillment" (Bloom 222), these tense volumes nonetheless influenced the aggregate of cultural consciousness.

While future commodity scarcities and political reformations are predicted to have impacts of varying intensity across the entire globe, NAFTA's three-country limit has unique significance within North America, for its inception has fostered a complex if fraught interconnectivity. Launched two months after the Maastricht Treaty formally brought the European Union into existence, NAFTA, including the "unprecedented" and "overwhelming" (Kay 1–2) controversies its implementation sparked in Mexico, the United States, and Canada, remains divisive, a political reality whose ongoing effects are characteristically discussed at political forums and by scholars of anthropology, economics, political science, and international trade law. Amorphous yet pervasive, and a series of narrowly defined legal "rights and obligations" (Canada) with an indisputable presence in popular culture, NAFTA has an irreducible existence with contested meanings often centred around questions of material loss, gain, and cost for proponents and critics alike. "From Canada to Mexico: 'A Common Future,'" the transcript of former President George H.W. Bush's keynote speech at the "Free Trade @ 10" conference, for instance, presents NAFTA as a "critical cornerstone" (192) in a beneficial trade strategy that will lead to "expanded free trade" as well as "close relations" and "lowering the barriers between our people" (192–93). In contrast, Ann E. Kingsolver views NAFTA as a "symbolic entity" within public space that is commonly "invested with hopes, fears, and agency—the power to change lives and nations" (2). In an echo of Benedict Anderson's definition of a nation as an imagined political community that is "conceived as a deep, horizontal comradeship" (4), Kingsolver's model of NAFTA suggests a duality, a physical and binding transnational legal contract on the one hand and a circulating, ever-evolving public narrative with broad and ongoing socio-political implications on the other.

Then again, despite the promissory rhetoric often tied to the agreement—that of untroubled transparent fraternity—the practical experience may be proving the opposite. In *Borderlands: Riding the Edge of America*, a travelogue recounting two motorcycle trips along northern and southern North American borders in 2009, Derek Lundy declares: "If Canadians want to see the future of their border with the United States, they need only look south to the Mexican" (6). Referring to a thickening or intensifying of border opacity, Lundy observes what Bill Ong Hing calls growing "militarized and racialized enforcement strategies" (166) and Carl Boggs identifies as an unnerving dialectic of increasingly authoritarian governance and "mounting domestic insurgency" (255): airborne surveillance drones, camera-laden balloons, border camera lines, in-ground motion sensors, proliferating Border Patrol agents, vigilante citizen militias, and, in the case of Texas, literally miles of costly, rusting, and unfinished metal fencing.[13] Unlike Bush's utopian rhetoric of dissolving barriers and shared futures of prosperity, Lundy's investigation reveals an emergent isolationism that can only undermine transnational porousness.

Lundy's anecdotal conclusions are supported by extensive research. Asking whether North America "'exist[s]' in any meaningful way economically, politically, culturally, or sociologically" (3), Stephen Clarkson offers a qualified negative. Clarkson acknowledges Robert A. Pastor's *Toward a North American Community* (2001), which contends that "the public is ahead of the politicians in identifying with an integrated North American political community" (qtd. in Clarkson 39), and cites findings that propose a "convergence among citizens of the United States, Canada, and Mexico across a wide range of issues, from beliefs about the importance of economic growth to attitudes towards government, and even patterns of church attendance"; the research seems to affirm the evolution of a "specifically North American consciousness" (39). Clarkson does not, however, accept the idea altogether. Instead, he incorporates data that prompt a less hopeful answer. He surmises: despite the reality that "continuing integration is occurring among the three economies," Canadian, Mexican, and American citizens "have made little progress towards feeling like members of a continental community" (44–45). In short (and in contrast to fictional dystopian North Americas such as Wallace's O.N.A.N. or Panem in Suzanne Collins' *The Hunger Games*), while North America is an identifiable geographical entity, a semi-coherent market, and a weak legal-institutional reality, it cannot as yet be defined as an authentic community (Clarkson 454).

Tied by the facts of continental geography, bilateral political and trilateral economic treaties, disparities of size, population, and economic development, "historical relationships [that] have not been without difficulties" (Johnson 3), and, of course, borders—zones "set up to define the places that are safe and unsafe, to distinguish *us* from *them*" (Anzaldúa 25); complex "sites of contestation" (New 27); entities represented in the arts as contradictory, "polyvalent" (Fox 3)—the North American quasi-community is an unfolding, increasingly militarized entity girded by the "North American security perimeter" (McKay and Swift 280) with which the authors considered in *Blast, Corrupt, Dismantle, Erase* grapple. (And in contrast to the tradition of mapping science fiction and dystopian literature along an Anglo-American axis, moreover, the north-south purview of the essays collected here speaks directly of the particularities of this inchoate community.) Given the complexity of both that historical actuality and literary forms themselves, the filmic and literary engagements analyzed here are necessarily multifarious, and range, for example, from explicit considerations of working class U.S.–Mexican borderlands culture to speculations about the hybridity fostered by border crossings and cultural interpenetrations (at times within one novel). The following discrete sections of *Blast*, then, are neat categories but to a degree an organizational fiction in the sense that, in the works discussed, systems, subjectivity, history, and genre can and do blur and overlap.

Novels investigating the breakdown of systems and the possibility of envisioning (or creating) new spaces are included in "I: Altered States." Janine Tobeck's "The Man in the Klein Blue Suit: Searching for Agency in William Gibson's Bigend Trilogy" analyzes character preoccupation within Gibson's trilogy, and contends that the fixation on the titular villain signals a nostalgia for old ways of conceptualizing power, and that in turn prevents characters from constructing new adaptive behaviours necessary for altered economic conditions. For "The Cultural Logic of Post-Capitalism: Cormac McCarthy's *The Road* and Popular Dystopia," Carl F. Miller utilizes Fredric Jameson's work on postmodernism as a framework to discuss *The Road*'s apparently nihilistic vision, positing that McCarthy depicts not only capitalism taken to an extreme but the end of systems, with no vision of remaking the world. Sharlee Reimer's "Logical Gaps and Capitalism's Seduction in Larissa Lai's *Salt Fish Girl*" situates Lai's novel within a contemporary breed of science fiction that focuses less on science and more on the role of speculation to critique the present. Moreover, she argues that the narrative gaps in this post-catastrophic and dystopian novel compel the reader to consider their own place in global commodification, and the threats to freedom of thought and movement, as well as gendered and racialized expression. Paul Stephens' "'The Dystopia of the Obsolete': Lisa Robertson's Vancouver and the Poetics of Nostalgia" examines Robertson's poetic negotiations with the multiple, conflicted layers of Vancouver's particular local history, and focuses on how nostalgia functions as a spectral critical trope for reimagining the city's urban space in a manner that refuses and disrupts the "useful" narratives of capital and the nation-state. Hande Tekdemir begins "Post-Frontier and Re-Definition of Space in *Tropic of Orange*" with Patricia Nelson Limerick's rereading of Frederick Jackson Turner's "frontier thesis," and discusses Karen Tei Yamashita's novel in relation to its highlighting of the dystopian elements of earlier American West expansion and its depiction of a post-frontier experience for the altered contexts of an increasingly globalized world. Rick Gooding's "Our Posthuman Adolescence: Dystopia, Information Technologies, and the Construction of Subjectivity in M.T. Anderson's *Feed*" maps the difficulties in writing dystopia for a YA audience, especially in terms of critical approaches to YA fiction and the impact of technology on notions of identity.

The essays gathered in "II: Plastic Subjectivities" address works that scrutinize the intricate relationships between social organization, new technologies, and political and economic orders. Annette Lapointe's "Woman Gave Names to All the Animals: Food, Fauna, and Anorexia in Margaret Atwood's Dystopian Fiction" focuses on the tense interplay among food, animals, and gender anxieties thematized in *Oryx and Crake* and its companion-narrative *The Year of the Flood*, in order to argue that Atwood's treatment of the marginalized bodies of women and animals (as a violation and collapse of materiality) nonetheless signals a potential for a return to stable embodiment and the "natural." In "The End of Life as We Knew It: Material Nature and the American Family in Susan Beth Pfeffer's Last Survivors Series," Alexa Weik von Mossner charts problematic representations of agency in a YA series set in a dystopia resulting from non-anthropogenic environmental collapse. "'The Treatment for Stirrings': Dystopian Literature for Adolescents" addresses Lois Lowry's *The Giver*, and in the essay Joseph Campbell employs Foucault, Burke, and Althusser to interrogate dystopian literature as a way of presenting subjectivity in YA fiction. Gregory Hampton's "Imagining Black Bodies in the Future" explores the prophetic qualities of Octavia Butler's science fiction, especially concerning race, and incorporates a discussion of James Cameron's *Avatar* to focus consideration of Butler's contemporary legacy. In "*Brown Girl in the Ring* as Urban Policy" Sharon DeGraw builds upon the work of Jessica Langer on post-colonialism and "anti-dystopia" to analyze Nalo Hopkinson's novel. DeGraw explores Hopkinson's configuring of Toronto as an urban environment facing both decay and renewal, a narrative that also points to renewal through an Afro-Caribbean spirituality mobilizing positive communal change.

The erasure, denial, and rewriting of personal and collective history is a key dystopian trope, and "III: Spectral Histories" collects works applying this complex of ideas to a contemporary North American context. Zac Zimmer's "Archive Failure? *Cielos de la tierra*'s Historical Dystopia" interrogates the locus of stratifications of Carmen Boullosa's novel, simultaneously an evocation of a failed utopia of Mexico's past, Mexico during the time of NAFTA, and a post-apocalyptic outpost reflecting "many of the cultural and political fears surrounding Mexico's embrace of neoliberal globalization." Similarly addressing contemporary Mexico, María Odette Canivell, in "Love, War, and *Mal de Amores*: Utopia and Dystopia in the Mexican Revolution," traces dystopian motifs in Angeles Mastretta's novel and links the novel's depictions of apparently bygone gender and utopian politics to the "nightmare" reality of Mexico in the 1990s. Lee Skallerup Bessette's "Culture of Control/Control of Culture: Anne Legault's *Récits de Médilhault*" views Legault's short story cycle's fragmented representation of dystopian Montreal in the 1990s in reference to the control of culture and post-NAFTA protectionism, a view that does not deny NAFTA's potential for integration in order to overcome cultural fissures and isolationism. Focusing on *Life After God* and *Girlfriend in a Coma*, Robert McGill's "The Sublime Simulacrum: Vancouver in Douglas Coupland's Geography of Apocalypse" charts Coupland's evocation of apocalyptic and dystopian Vancouver in order to "map connections between geography and literature in terms of the accreted apocalyptic valences that Coupland sees in Vancouver specifically and in the North American West Coast as a whole." Juxtaposing "Reaching the Shore," Guillermo Lavín's short story, and *Sleep Dealer*, Alex Rivera's film, in "Neoliberalism and Dystopia in U.S.–Mexico Borderlands Fiction," Lysa Rivera investigates the social geography of futuristic borderlands, linking ostensibly unique developments in neoliberal economic hegemony to the residual effects of colonial power. In "America and Books Are 'Never Going to Die': Gary Shteyngart's *Super Sad True Love Story* as a New York Jewish 'Ustopia,'" Marleen S. Barr presents Shteyngart's novel as a response to the prospect of economic collapse and as an example of Atwood's "ustopia," conjoining dystopia and the possibility of utopia. Thomas Stubblefield's "In Pursuit of an Outside: Art Spiegelman's *In the Shadow of No Towers* and the Crisis of the Unrepresentable" traces the specific characteristics of the graphic novel as a vehicle for response to 9/11 in the context of Jameson's notion of dystopia disjoined from utopia. In "Homero Aridjis and Mexico's Eco-Critical Dystopia," Adam Spires considers the dystopian novels of Homero Aridjis, a prominent Mexican environmental activist. Noting their critique of Mexico's rush to modernize at the expense of the environment and the indigenous mytho-historical past, he situates Aridjis within a body of recent Mexican literature that employs dystopia in order to capture the specificity and immediacy of the post-NAFTA environmental apocalypse.

"IV: Emancipating Genres," the final section of *Blast, Corrupt, Dismantle, Erase*, addresses fiction ruminating on and reworking facets of the dystopian genre, especially those that pertain to North American culture, history, or geography. Robert Tally's "Lost in Grand Central: Dystopia and Transgression in Neil Gaiman's *American Gods*" examines the evolution of dystopian literature and the function of transgression, focusing on Gaiman's use of fantasy as a means of delineating North American millennial anxieties. Luis Romero analyzes Carlos Fuentes' *La Silla del Águila* in "Which Way Is Hope? Dystopia into the (Mexican) Borgian Labyrinth," and proposes that the satire represents a realist variant of dystopian literature that has developed in response to the unique qualities of Latin American politics and daily life. Kit Dobson's "Dystopia Now: Examining the Rach(a)els in *Automaton Biographies* and *Player One*" situates Larissa Lai's poetry and Douglas Coupland's novelistic 2010 Massey Lecture in relation to the NEXUS border-clearing card in order to explore contemporary identity and what role technology plays within a Canadian dystopian context. For "The Romance of the Blazing World: Looking back from CanLit to SF," Owen Percy views Ronald Wright's *A Scientific Romance* and Michael Murphy's *A Description of the Blazing World* in relation to Atwood's ideas about speculative fiction and the deterioration of socially responsible institutions and governments. In "'It's not power, it's sex': Jeanette Winterson's *The PowerBook* and Nicole Brossard's *Baroque at Dawn*," Helene Staveley utilizes Winterson's book as a springboard for an analysis of Brossard. Stavely discusses the utopic possibilities of erotica, wherein blurred distinctions—between reader and writer, seducer and seduced—create a text that can be infinitely re-created, while acknowledging the dystopic interventions of patriarchal assumptions and structures, and especially the specific ways Québéecois culture manifests itself in the embedded narrative of *Baroque d'aube*. And Lee Konstantinou's "Another Novel Is Possible: Muckraking in Chris Bachelder's *U.S.!* and Robert Newman's *The Fountain at the Center of the World*" addresses the proliferation of science fiction texts engaging with the new-millennium issues of "militarism, environmental danger, media manipulation, and global economic exploitation" before valorizing a mode of fiction that places economic class at the forefront of its narrative concern.

Notes

1 In "The Purpose for This Index," Strandberg states: "You could say the Rapture index is a Dow Jones Industrial Average of end time activity, but I think it would be better if you viewed it as [sic] prophetic speedometer. The higher the number, the faster we're moving towards the occurrence of pre-tribulation rapture." Below 100 indicates "Slow prophetic activity," while above 160 means "Fasten your seat belts." The Index stood at 185 on 30 November 2012. The year's high was 186; the low dipped as far as 176.

2 Gardenpool.org, run by the McClungs of Mesa, Arizona, a family featured in TLC's documentary *Livin' for the Apocalypse* (first broadcast on 28 August 2011), features advertisements and items for sale (like "shelfponics" kits in which to grow plants), but much of the site is devoted to sharing information about creating a sustainable and self-contained environment that will feed a family of four when systemic catastrophes render the food-supply infrastructure inoperable in 2012. A similar venture, modernsurvivalonline.com, provides salient information (such as pointing readers to National Geographic Channel's 2011 reality television series *Doomsday Preppers*) and contains ads for businesses like Wise Company, a manufacturer of long-term-emergency food supplies.

3 Consider a sampling—Wendy Brown's *Surviving the Apocalypse in the Suburbs*; Matthew Restall and Amara Solari's *2012 and The End of the World*; Lawrence E. Joseph's *Apocalypse 2012: An Investigation into Civilization's End* and *Aftermath: A Guide to Preparing For and Surviving Apocalypse 2012*; Billy Graham's *Storm Warning*; Joel Levy's *The Doomsday Book: Scenarios for the End of the World*; James Howard Kunstler's *The Long Emergency: Surviving the Converging Catastrophes of the Twenty-First Century*; Christian Parenti's *Tropic of Chaos: Climate Wars and the New Geography of Violence*; Ron Rosenbaum's *How the World Ends: The Road to a Nuclear World War III*; Slavoj Žižek's *Living in the End Times*; Jacques Attali's *Millennium: Winners and Losers in the Coming World Order*; Richard Heinberg's *The End of Growth: Adapting to Our New Economic Reality* and *Peak Everything: Waking Up to the Century of Declines*; Joel Kotkin's *The Next 100 Million: America in 2050*; Eugene Linden's *The Future in Plain Sight: Nine Clues to the Coming Instability* and *The Winds of Change: Climate, Weather, and the Destruction of Civilizations*; John Michael Greer's *The Long Descent: A User's Guide to the End of the Industrial Age*; Paul Roberts' *The End of Oil* and *The End of Food*; David Goodstein's *Out of Gas: The End of the Age of Oil*; Bill McKibben's *The End of Nature*; Benjamin Barber's *Jihad vs McWorld: How Globalism and Tribalism Are Reshaping the World*; Walden F. Bello's *The Food Wars*; Alex Prud'homme's *The Ripple Effect: The Fate of Fresh Water in the Twenty-First Century*; Mark Bauerlein's *The Dumbest Generation: How the Digital Age Stupefies Young Americans and Jeopardizes our*

Future; Alan Weisman's *The World Without Us*; Marq de Villiers' *Our Way Out: Principles for a Post-Apocalyptic World*; Forrest Griffin's *Be Ready When the Sh*t Goes Down: A Survival Guide to the Apocalypse*; Dmitry Orlov's *Reinventing Collapse: The Soviet Experience and American Prospects—Revised and Updated*; Alexis Zeigler's *Culture Change: Civil Liberty, Peak Oil, and the End of Empire*; Mark Steyn's *After America: Get Ready for Armageddon*; and Graeme Taylor's *Evolution's Edge: The Coming Collapse and Transformation of Our World*.

4 Restall and Solari note that the Internet is "packed with blog chatter and websites" dedicated to Mayan prophecy and that scores of books about the 2012 phenomenon are in print (1).

5 Fitting's adjective describing a pervasive sentiment serves to illustrate the complex—or, in Fredric Jameson's view, the "dangerous and misleading" (198)—ambiguity associated with the root-noun dystopia. Whereas the World Economic Forum defines dystopia as an actual (and forthcoming) "place where life is full of hardship and devoid of hope," Margaret Atwood describes dystopias as real or imaginary "Great Bad Places . . . characterized by suffering, tyranny, and oppression of all kinds" (*Other Worlds* 85). Rejecting the word as a descriptor of his fiction, William Gibson implies that it is equally applicable to a fiction genre and the real world: "I suspect people who say I'm dystopian must be living completely sheltered and fortunate lives. The world is filled with much nastier places than my inventions." In contrast to novelists who seem generally uninterested in defining and using dystopia in a consistently strict manner, classificatory scholars—in particular, Lyman Tower Sargent in "The Three Faces of Utopianism Revisited," Tom Moylan in *Scraps of the Untainted Sky*, and Jameson in *Archeologies of the Future*—delineate types of dystopias (dystopia, then, refers to a literary genre—and not to one of Gibson's nasty real places—but also, at times, to states of mind: feeling, dreaming, or desire). Moylan, for instance, proposes a complicated typology of dystopian forms: anti-utopia, pseudo-dystopia, critical dystopia, and, in reference to Atwood's *The Handmaid's Tale*, "'ambiguous dystopia'" (166); and after him, Jameson perceives the need for an additional term, "apocalyptic," in order to differentiate end-of-earth narratives from anti-Utopian ones (199). Working with a variety of definitions (as well as over twenty creative works that bring unique understandings of dystopia/n to their narratives), the twenty-one essays collected in *Blast* accordingly follow no critical orthodoxy.

6 "Faced with inadequate progress on nuclear weapons reduction and proliferation, and continuing inaction on climate change," *Bulletin of the Atomic Scientists* announced on January 10, 2012, that it had moved the hands of the Doomsday Clock one minute closer to midnight. In like fashion, the World Economic Forum's *Global Risks 2012* reports: "Dystopia, the opposite of a utopia, describes a place where life is full of hardship and devoid of hope.

Analysis of linkages across various global risks reveals a constellation of fiscal, demographic and societal risks signalling a dystopian future for much of humanity."

7 Though West and Pick do not focus on scientific romances, their discussions of *fin de siècle* art and culture trace patterns: assertions of progress on the one hand and widespread fears of degeneration on the other. Pick, arguing for the historical specificity of the degeneration model in the latter half of the nineteenth century, views the era's fiction in general as registering the wider social and scientific debate, "sometimes challenging, sometimes simply assuming the stock assumptions of its language" (3).

8 Suvin later states that a "*phase of constitution*" (1848–71) was followed by a "*phase of inception*" (1871–85) (*Victorian* 386). "[A]t the beginning of the 1870s," he explains, science fiction, "always an early warning system, constituted itself, coalesced as a recognizable and henceforth uninterrupted genre"; it was over the 1870s that the sense of a secure society began to be openly and frequently doubted within the wide upper- and middle-class ruling consensus itself (387). In Suvin's view, "ideological instability" and "loss of values" provided the fertile ground for the growth of science fiction (389). See also Evans, Slusser on "paradigm shifts" (28), and James, who views the genre as a natural extension of the ambivalent recognition of the sudden and ongoing transformations wrought by technology (25).

9 Atwood's sentiment, appearing again as an epigraph in *Oryx and Crake*, was also reiterated in a 2006 open letter to a school district in Texas that banned *The Handmaid's Tale*: "[I]f you see a person heading toward a huge hole in the ground, is it not a friendly act to warn him?" (*Other Worlds* 244).

10 Booker draws a qualitative distinction between dystopian literature and science fiction ("But in general dystopian fiction differs from science fiction in the specificity of its attention to social and political critique. In this sense, dystopian fiction is more like the projects of social and cultural critics like Nietzsche, Bakhtin, Adorno, Foucault, Habermas, and many others" [*Impulse* 19]) in much the same way Atwood has controversially defined the line between speculative fiction and science fiction. See also Peter Watts, "Margaret Atwood and the Hierarchy of Contempt," and Atwood's "Context." William Gibson's contribution to the debate, meanwhile, is terse: "Of course, all fiction is speculative." Other scholars refuse the distinction. Peter Y. Paik, for example, states "science fiction and fantasy . . . are capable of achieving profound and probing insights into the principal dilemmas of political life" (1).

11 See Elaine Showalter ("crises of the fin de siècle, then, are more intensely experienced, more emotionally fraught, more weighted with symbolic and historical meaning, because we invest them with the metaphors of death and rebirth that we project onto the final decades and years of a century" [2]), or Asti Hustvedt

("the obsessions of our own culture as the millennium comes to a close seem to resemble those of the last fin de siècle" [10]). Innumerable popular media op-ed pieces indicate that the perception was by no means limited to academic discourse. Travis Charbeneau's article in *The Futurist* is characteristic—"And there is no shortage of decadence as the second millennium winds down. We have endured scandal-ridden preachers and politicians, corporate raiders, militia madmen, and 'the end is nigh' gurus. We have viewed pornography on the Internet and listened to vulgar lyrics on CD. More substantially, we have ravaged the environment, automated both work and play, and invented 'compassion fatigue' as a defense against the incomprehensible scope of suffering in the late twentieth century. We can reasonably expect the list of depravities to lengthen as our millennium approaches its end" (51).

12 This is the same year in which the Peso Crisis brought Mexico "to the point of economic collapse" (Linden 39). Patrick Buchanan's admittedly sectarian editorial in the *New York Times* supplies a popular view of NAFTA, post-Peso Crisis: "One year after Nafta, Mexico devalued the peso, wiping out billions in United States investments. Our trade surplus has vanished. A $17 billion deficit is expected in 1995. Translation: 340,000 lost American jobs. Our winter tomato industry is in ruins. Illegal immigration is rising. Mexico has become the port of entry for America's cocaine."

13 Tu Tranh Ha and John Ibbitson report that the "U.S. Customs and Border Protection Agency put forward the possibility of fencing the border to deter illegal crossings. But a statement from the agency insisted that 'a border fence along the northern border is not being considered at this time.'" A leaked report by the U.S. Customs and Border Protection Agency appeared in September 2011 and outlined methods to help "protect the Northern Border against evolving threats over the next five to seven years," including fencing, increased housing for patrol personnel, and electronic equipment such as "body and container scanners, remote sensors, microphones and cameras and radar."

Works Cited

Anderson, Benedict. *Imagined Communities: Reflections on the Origin and Spread of Nationalism*. Rev. ed. London: Verso, 1991. Print.

Anderson, Laurie. *Homeland*. Nonesuch/Elektra Records, 2010. CD.

Anzaldúa, Gloria. *Borderlands/La Frontera: The New Mestiza*. 3rd ed. San Francisco: Aunt Lute Books, 2007. Print.

Attali, Jacques. *A Brief History of the Future: A Brave and Controversial Look at the Twenty-First Century*. Trans. Jeremy Leggatt. New York: Arcade, 2009. Print.

———. *Millennium: Winners and Losers in the Coming World Order*. Trans. Leila Connors and Nathan Gardels. New York: Random House, 1991. Print.

Atwood, Margaret. "*The Handmaid's Tale* and *Oryx and Crake* in Context." *PMLA* 2004: 513–17. PDF file.

———. *In Other Worlds: SF and the Human Imagination*. Toronto: McClelland and Stewart, 2011. Print.

Barr, Marleen S., ed. *Future Females, The Next Generation: New Voices and Velocities in Feminist Fiction Criticism*. Lanham, MD: Rowman and Littlefield, 2000. Print.

Bello, Walden. *The Food Wars*. London: Verso, 2009. Print.

Bloom, Harold. *Omens of Millennium: The Gnosis of Angels, Dreams, and Resurrection*. New York: Riverhead Books, 1996. Print.

Booker, M. Keith. *The Dystopian Impulse in Modern Literature: Fiction as Social Criticism*. Westport, CT: Greenwood Press, 1994. Print.

———. *Dystopian Literature: A Theory and Research Guide*. Westport, CT: Greenwood Press, 1994. Print.

Boggs, Carl. "Warrior Nightmares: American Reactionary Populism at the Millennium." *Social Register 2000: Necessary and Unnecessary Utopias*. Ed. Leo Panitch and Colin Leys. 243–56. PDF file.

Bould, Mark, et al., ed. *The Routledge Companion to Science Fiction*. London: Routledge, 2009. Print.

Breivik, Anders Behring. *2083—A European Declaration of Independence*. 2011. PDF file.

Brown, David Jay. *Conversations on the Edge of the Apocalypse*. New York: Palgrave Macmillan, 2005. Print.

Brown, Wendy. *Surviving the Apocalypse in the Suburbs: The Thrivalist's Guide to Life Without Oil*. Gabriola Island, BC: New Society, 2011. Print.

Buchanan, Patrick J. "Mexico: Who Was Right?" *New York Times*. 25 August 1995. Web. 10 Sept. 2011.

Bulletin of the Atomic Scientists. "Doomsday Clock Moves 1 Minute Closer to Midnight." 10 Jan. 2012. *Bulletin of the Atomic Scientists*. Web. 18 Jan. 2012.

Bush, George. "From Canada to Mexico: 'A Common Future.'" *Free Trade: Risks and Rewards*. Ed. Ian L. MacDonald. Montreal: McGill-Queen's University Press, 2000. 191–96. Print.

Canada. Foreign Affairs and International Trade Canada. "Article 103: Relation to Other Agreements." *The North American Free Trade Agreement (NAFTA)*. Web. 3 Oct. 2011.

Charbeneau, Travis. "Fin de Millennium." *The Futurist*. 1 March 1998: 51. Print.

Clarke, I.F. "Introduction." *The Battle of Dorking by Chesney George Tomkyns*. Oxford: Oxford UP, 1997. ix–xxii. Print.

Clarkson, Stephen. *Does North America Exist?: Governing the Continent after NAFTA and 9/11*. Toronto: U Toronto P, 2008. Print.

Disch, Thomas M. *The Dreams Our Stuff Is Made Of: How Science Fiction Conquered the World*. New York: Free Press, 1998. Print.

———. *On SF*. Ann Arbor: U Michigan P, 2005. Print.

Donawerth, Jane. "The Feminist Dystopia in the 1990s: Record of Failure, Midwife of Hope." *Future Females, The Next Generation: New Voices and Velocities in Feminist Fiction Criticism*. Ed. Marleen S. Barr. Lanham, MD: Rowman and Littlefield, 2000. 49–66. Print.

Eagleton, Terry. "Evil." *Chronicle Review*. 12 August 2011: B6–7. Print.

Edelstein, David. "The End Is Here." *New York Magazine*. 25 September 2011. Web. 24 Sept. 2011. "The End of the World: Bible Prophecies about the End of the World." endoftheworldprophecy.com. Web. 15 May 2013.

Evans, Arthur B. "Nineteenth-Century SF." *The Routledge Companion to Science Fiction*. Ed. Mark Bould et al. London: Routledge, 2009. 13–22. Print.

Fitting, Peter. "Utopia, Dystopia and Science Fiction." *The Cambridge Companion to Utopian Literature*. Ed. Gregory Claeys. Cambridge: Cambridge UP, 2010. 135–53. Print.

Flaubert, Gustave. *Bouvard and Pécuchet*. Trans. Mark Polizzotti. Champaign, IL: Dalkey Archive Press, 2005. Print.

Fox, Claire F. *The Fence and the River: Culture and Politics at the U.S.–Mexico Border*. Minneapolis: U of Minnesota P, 1999. Print.

Friedman, Thomas L., and Michael Mandelbaum. *That Used to Be Us: How America Fell Behind in the World It Invented and How We Can Come Back*. New York: Farrar, Straus and Giroux, 2011. Print.

Gibson, William. "William Gibson, The Art of Fiction." *Paris Review* 197 (Summer 2011). Web. 3 Aug 2011.

Gleick, James. *The Information: A History, a Theory, a Flood*. New York: Pantheon, 2011. Print.

Goffard, Christopher. "Harold Camping Is at the Heart of a Mediapocalypse." *Los Angeles Times*. 21 May 2011. Web. 24 Sept. 2011.

Goodstein, David. *Out of Gas: The End of the Age of Oil*. New York: W.W. Norton, 2004. Print.

Gould, Stephen Jay. *Questioning the Millennium: A Rationalist's Guide to a Precisely Arbitrary Countdown*. New York: Harmony, 1997. Print.

Graham, Billy. *Storm Warning: Whether Global Recession, Terrorist Threats, or Devastating Natural Disasters, These Ominous Shadows Must Bring Us Back to the Gospel*. Rev. ed. Nashville: Thomas Nelson, 2010. Print.

Greer, John Michael. *The Long Descent: A User's Guide to the End of the Industrial Age*. Gabriola Island, BC: New Society, 2008. Print.

Harris-Fain, Darren. *Understanding Contemporary American Science Fiction: The Age of Maturity 1970–2000*. Columbia, SC: U South Carolina P, 2005. Print.

Heinberg, Richard. *The End of Growth: Adapting to Our New Economic Reality*. Gabriola Island, BC: New Society, 2011. Print.

———. *Peak Everything: Waking Up to the Century of Declines*. Gabriola Island, BC: New Society 2010. Print.

Ha, Tu Thanh, and John Ibbitson. "U.S. Denies Border-Fence Plan, Despite Report." *Globe and Mail*. 29 Sept. 2011. Web. 29 Sept. 2011.

Hing, Bill Ong. *Ethical Borders: NAFTA, Globalization, and Mexican Migration*. Philadelphia: Temple UP, 2010. Print.

Hustvedt, Asti, ed. *The Decadent Reader: Fiction, Fantasy, and Perversion from Fin-de-Siècle France*. New York: Zone Books, 1998. Print.

Huxley, Aldous. *Brave New World & Brave New World Revisited*. New York: Harper & Row, 1965. Print.

James, Edward. *Science Fiction in the Twentieth Century*. Oxford: Oxford UP, 1994. Print.

Jameson, Fredric. *Archeologies of the Future: The Desire Called Utopia and Other Science Fictions*. London: Verso, 2005. Print.

Johnson, Jon R. *The North American Free Trade Agreement: A Comprehensive Guide*. Aurora, ON: Canada Law Book, 1994. Print.

Joseph, Lawrence E. *Aftermath: A Guide to Preparing For and Surviving Apocalypse 2012*. New York: Broadway Books, 2010. Print.

———. *Apocalypse 2012: An Investigation into Civilization's End*. New York: Broadway Books, 2007. Print.

Kay, Tamara. *NAFTA and the Politics of Labor Transformation*. Cambridge: Cambridge UP, 2011. Print.

Kingsolver, Ann E. *NAFTA Stories: Fears and Hopes in Mexico and the United States*. Boulder, CO: Lynne Rienner, 2001. Print.

Kotkin, Joel. *The Next 100 Million: America in 2050*. New York: Penguin, 2010. Print.

Kunstler, James Howard. *The Long Emergency: Surviving the Converging Catastrophes of the Twenty-First Century*. New York: Atlantic Monthly Press, 2005. Print.

Levy, Joel. *The Doomsday Book: Scenarios for the End of the World*. London: Vision, 2005. Print.

Linden, Eugene. *The Future in Plain Sight: Nine Clues to the Coming Instability*. New York: Simon and Schuster, 1998. Print.

Luckhurst, Robert. *Science Fiction*. Cambridge: Polity, 2005. Print.

Lundy, Derek. *Borderlands: Riding the Edge of America*. Toronto: Knopf, 2010. Print.

MacDonald, L. Ian, ed. *Free Trade: Risks and Rewards*. Montreal: McGill-Queen's UP, 2000. Print.

McKay, Ian, and Jamie Swift. *Warrior Nation: Rebranding Canada in the Age of Anxiety*. Toronto: Between the Lines, 2012. Print.

McOrmond, Steve. *The Good News about Armageddon*. London, ON: Brick Books, 2010. Print.

Moylan, Tom: *Scraps of the Untainted Sky: Science Fiction, Utopia, Dystopia*. Boulder, CO: Westview Press, 2000. Print.

Murphy, Graham J. "Dystopia." *The Routledge Companion to Science Fiction*. Ed. Mark Bould et al. London: Routledge, 2009. 473–77. Print.

New, W.H. *Borderlands: How We Talk about Canada*. Vancouver: U British Columbia P, 1998. Print.

Paik, Peter Y. *From Utopia to Apocalypse: Science Fiction and the Politics of Catastrophe*. Minneapolis: U Minnesota P, 2010. Print.

Palmer, Bryan D. *Cultures of Darkness: Night Travels in the Histories of Transgression*. New York: Monthly Review Press, 2000.

Pick, Daniel. *Faces of Degeneration: A European Disorder, c. 1848–c. 1918*. Cambridge: Cambridge UP, 1989. Print.

Pinchbeck, Daniel. *2012: The Return of Quetzalcoatl*. New York: Penguin, 2006. Print.

———. *Notes from Edge Times*. New York: Penguin, 2010. Print.

Publishing Trends. "Now in Hardcover: The Series in 2010." *Publishing Trends*. May 2010. Web. 2 Dec. 2011.

Quade, John. "On the Eve of Armageddon." endoftheworldprophecy.com. Web. 30 Aug. 2011.

Rapture Ready Book Store. raptureready.com. Web. 15 May 2013.

Restall, Matthew, and Amara Solari. *2012 and the End of the World: The Western Roots of the Maya Apocalypse*. Plymouth, UK: Rowman and Littlefield, 2011. Print.

Roberts, Adam. *The History of Science Fiction*. New York: Palgrave Macmillan, 2006. Print.

Roberts, Paul. *The End of Food*. New York: Houghton Mifflin, 2008. Print.

———. *The End of Oil: On the Edge of a Perilous New World*. Boston: Houghton Mifflin, 2004. Print.

Sargent, Lyman Tower. "The Three Faces of Utopianism Revisited." *Utopian Studies* 5.1 (1994): 1–37. Print.

Savodnik, Peter. "The Rapture Profiteers: Is the Debt Ceiling Crisis Resurrecting the Apocalypse Industry?" *Businessweek*. 28 July 2011. Web. 30 Aug. 2011.

Seed, David, ed. *A Companion to Science Fiction*. Oxford: Blackwell, 2005. Print.

Showalter, Elaine. *Sexual Anarchy: Gender and Culture at the Fin de Siècle*. New York: Viking, 1990. Print.

Sicher, Efraim, and Natalia Skradol. "A World Neither Brave nor New: Reading Dystopian Fiction after 9/11." *Partial Answers*. 4/1 (2006): 151–79. Print.

Slusser, George. "The Origins of Science Fiction." *A Companion to Science Fiction*. Ed. David Seed. Oxford: Blackwell, 2005: 27–42. Print.

Stableford, Brian. "Ecology and Dystopia." *The Cambridge Companion to Utopian Literature*. Ed. Gregory Claeys. Cambridge: Cambridge UP, 2010. 259–81. Print.

———. *Scientific Romance in Britain 1890–1950*. London: Fourth Estate, 1985. Print.

Steyn, Mark. *After America: Get Ready for Armageddon*. Washington, DC: Regnery Publishing, 2011. Print.

Suvin, Darko. *Metamorphoses of Science Fiction: On the Poetics and History of a Literary Genre.* New Haven: Yale UP, 1979. Print.

———. *Victorian Science Fiction in the UK: The Discourses of Knowledge and of Power.* Boston: G.K. Hall, 1983. Print.

Taylor, Graeme. *Evolution's Edge: The Coming Collapse and Transformation of Our World.* Gabriola Island, BC: New Society, 2008. Print.

Vena, Jocelyn. "Britney Spears Tour Will Have Post-Apocalyptic Vibe, Manager Says." *MTV News.* 31 March 2011. Web. 26 July 2011.

Wallerstein, Immanuel. *The Decline of American Power.* New York: New Press, 2003.

———. *The End of the World as We Know It: Social Science for the Twenty-First Century.* Minneapolis: U Minnesota P, 1999. Print.

Watts, Peter. "Margaret Atwood and the Hierarchy of Contempt." *On Spec.* 15(2) Summer 2003: 3–5. Print.

"Welcome to the End of the World." endoftheworld.net. Web. 15 May 2013.

"Wendy Brown." *newsociety.com.* New Society Publishers. Web. 4 Oct. 2011.

West, Shearer. *Fin de Siècle.* London: Bloomsbury, 1993. Print.

Žižek, Slavoj. *Living in the End Times.* London: Verso, 2010. Print.

PART I
Altered States

The Man in the Klein Blue Suit
Searching for Agency in William Gibson's Bigend Trilogy

Janine Tobeck

A rash of smart criticism followed the release of William Gibson's *Pattern Recognition*, examining it as a culmination of or break from his earlier work. In this essay, I explore the text instead as the inaugural part of what is now known as Gibson's "Bigend" or "Blue Ant" trilogy, after Hubertus Bigend (the only major character who appears in all three books) or the multinational advertising agency that he fronts. Bigend's singular staying power and the fact that his professional motives underpin most of the plot certainly invite us to study the role that global capital plays in the trilogy's dystopic plausible present. If we accept this invitation, we might think of the trilogy as *The Man in the Gray Flannel Suit* revised and updated for the twenty-first century, with Hollis Henry—the writer protagonist of *Spook Country* and *Zero History*—struggling to hold her ideals of selfhood and expression in the face of her financial dependence on the ad man. Hollis opens *Spook Country* dabbling in freelance writing on assignment for Bigend, ostensibly researching a phenomenon called locative art for a magazine called *Node*. Her unease about this situation starts at not knowing who Bigend really is or whether she will get paid, evolves into a (well-founded) suspicion that she is being used by the advertising magnate for some form of industrial espionage, and ends in full-blown paranoia that Bigend's reach and his hold on her life are inescapable.

From another angle, though, this paranoia is itself an important object of study in the trilogy. While we are narratively limited mostly to plays orchestrated by Bigend, the stories of the novels do exceed this field, with multiple players seeking similar ends for different reasons in a global setting of labour, untraceable capital, and multi-interested agents. At the same time, technological developments alter the fabric of the characters' experiences and habits of perceiving the world in unanticipated ways, and Gibson sets some of these forces to work within and around the relationships that develop between Bigend and other characters. In *Spook Country*, for instance, evolving applications of GPS in the espionage world and the art world actually drive Hollis's actions more consistently than do Bigend's instructions. If we consider Bigend merely as Hollis's doorway to this brave new world, into the "unlegislated future" that Gibson often mentions, we might more accurately read him as an object of her desire for a return to order. Constructing a comprehensible narrative of experience—one that organizes time into an appearance of causal continuity—requires certain limitations on or control over context. In the globalized and technologized world of the trilogy, these limitations are dislodged, and putting Bigend in their place serves as a kind of intermediate coping mechanism for Hollis and others.

The tension between these two readings of Gibson's trilogy reduces its greatest achievement as a dystopia. The allure of seeing Bigend as its villain overshadows its more atmospheric but more consequential conversion of history and context away from our habitual understandings into something strange and new. This, I will argue, is a condition within these novels that provokes characters into nostalgia for an old order, even if it means believing that the Bigends of the world have an inescapable grip on their lives. It is also, however, a condition that provokes adaptation in how they perceive themselves and how they act in the world—and, by extension, in how we look at the world upon our reading. While Gibson is not infrequently criticized for undermining his novels' potential theoretical breakthroughs through a failure of his writing actually to perform them, others have traced the hermeneutic models that emerge through the evolution of his work, as I hope to do in this study of his latest trilogy.[1] Some readers have also complained that Gibson has lost his edge, which was apparently honed on cataclysmic plots driven by intentional characters in a plausible future. It is true that when *Neuromancer*'s Case jacked into the matrix it was a visceral experience—more a *doing* than a *being* online—while, by contrast, readers spend a fair amount of time watching *Pattern Recognition*'s Cayce sit at her computer. I will argue here that the Bigend trilogy marks a turn for Gibson, not just into the present, but into new explorations of humanness, history, and community, and that the perhaps duller edge of its telling is pointedly directed at outdated reading habits that are deeply rooted but lately exposed.

The Paradoxical Antagonist

As the trilogy's ostensible villain, Bigend does little that is concretely sinister, but you never escape the feeling (or, rather, the other characters' feelings) that he *must*. He hovers ubiquitously and, with seemingly bottomless funds, sends people out to hunt and do things, sometimes for professional motives and at other times simply out of curiosity. The threats that Bigend poses to other characters are both familiar and new, ranging from a kind of standard-issue antagonism between artistic expression and corporate purposing to communal paranoia about largely untraceable corporate personhood, once everyone starts talking to each other and discovers how wide-ranging his "interests" are.

In *Zero History*, Bigend provokes such reactions intentionally by wearing (fairly frequently) an International Klein Blue suit, in part because it "unsettles people" (19), and in part because "it couldn't quite be re-created on most computer monitors" (47), making him both unavoidably noticeable and somehow inscrutable or unrepresentable. The suit seems an inescapable nod to Sloan Wilson's 1955 novel *The Man in the Gray Flannel Suit*, wherein World War II survivor Tom Rath searches for a purpose to his conformist life as an advertising agency employee. In *Spook Country* and *Zero History*, Hollis Henry likewise struggles with her financial dependence on Bigend, albeit in an updated fashion. A self-made woman, Hollis was the vocalist for an early-1990s cult band called The Curfew, but lost millions through dot-com investments and now needs to make herself again. In *Spook Country* she rounds out Bigend's freelance assignment to write about locative art with the publication of her own book, but in *Zero History* she is working for him again, trying to track down a "secret brand" of denim clothing called Gabriel Hounds. In her investigative capacity, Hollis is a sort of sequel to *Pattern Recognition*'s protagonist, Cayce Pollard. Cayce is literally allergic to brand names, so although she makes her money as a kind of marketing savant, she is always conflicted about the ends to which her work will be put. This is especially true when what Bigend wants her to help him find is the creator of anonymous film footage released on the Net, whose cult-like fan base includes herself. Hollis is later horrified (as we are no doubt meant to be) to learn that Bigend has ultimately co-opted the footage as a medium to sell shoes (105). Hollis has her own problems with productized art, which are borne out when she and her former bandmates have to decide whether to sell Bigend their biggest hit to use in a Chinese car commercial. Along with a few other minor characters, Cayce and Hollis model a familiar fear about living in a corporate culture: that of having to sell out to survive.

What is new about this story is the extent to which globalism extends the influence and consolidates the power of figures as financially flexible as Bigend, while at the same time making it easier for them to hide in plain sight. War profiteering underpins *Spook Country*'s plot, as all players race to locate a shipping container carrying millions in cash, and *Zero History* comes together around the global workings of the fashion industry and an extra-national attempt to snag coveted military fashion contracts that are legally bound to U.S. territory. And Bigend has his fingers in all of it. It seems everyone has heard of him, but no one is entirely sure who he is, and, as his hilariously able assistant says, this is actually part of his business strategy: "'He doesn't want you to have heard of him. He doesn't want people to have heard of Blue Ant either. We're often described as the first viral agency. Hubertus doesn't like the term. . . . Foregrounding the agency, or its founder, is counterproductive. He says he wishes we could operate as a black hole, an absence, but there's no viable way to get there from here'" (*ZH* 110). In lieu of a viable method, Bigend spreads his shadowy influence through his agents—Hollis, Cayce, and untold others—who do his work under his near-constant surveillance, but are largely unaware of each other. It would also be difficult for anyone who interacted with them to see Bigend's hand in what they do, because they have no way of guessing on the basis of expectation what his intentions might be.

Because they cannot draw the connections between what Bigend orchestrates through them and what they see going on around them, the characters help promote his influence by internalizing and fearing it. This may best be represented in the trilogy through the character Milgrim, whom Bigend essentially purchases by putting him through a pricey experimental drug rehabilitation and then getting him to work on more shadowy assignments. Milgrim is an unmade man—I imagine him as an amalgam of Milgram, the scientist of obedience, and Kurt Vonnegut's haplessly passive Billy Pilgrim—who, fairly predictably, just does as he is told. Initially useful for translating Russian, he is repurposed by Bigend (and, of course, Gibson) for his unique eye for detail. Milgrim's discomfort with Bigend exceeds

Hollis's because his arises from a sense of owing Bigend an unpayable debt: Bigend tells him that his life is "a by-product" of Bigend's curiosity, and the money for the rehabilitation treatment is "the cost" of that curiosity (67). All Milgrim can give, therefore, is his agency, and while he is literally captive to another agent throughout *Spook Country*, he believes himself captive to Bigend throughout *Zero History*. In one of Milgrim's dreams, induced by a recovery treatment substance called a "paradoxical antagonist," he finds himself "stalked by an actual Paradoxical Antagonist, a shadowy figure he somehow associates with the colors in 1950s American advertising illustrations. Perky" (*ZH* 27). We cannot help but read this shadowy figure as the blue-suited Bigend, but if Milgrim's paranoia has a physical stem, Hollis's vision of Bigend in his Klein Blue suit projects a less logical impression of his immeasurability: "He somehow managed always to give her the impression, seeing him again, that he'd grown visibly larger, though without gaining any particular weight. Simply bigger. Perhaps, she thought, as if he grew somehow *closer*" (19). Already in *Spook Country*, though, Hollis has begun to internalize her sense of Bigend's ubiquity and his inescapable agency, "if not yet actual then potential. Once he was established in your life, he'd be there, in some way no ordinary person, no ordinary boss, even, could be. Once she accepted him, past a certain point, there was always going to be the possibility of him ringing her up, to say 'Just checking,' before she could even ask who was calling. Did she want that? Could she afford not to?" (*SC* 281). Moreover, the internalization effect is viral: Hollis's former bandmate later tells her that "'the London PR community are behaving like dogs before an earthquake, and somehow everyone knows, without knowing how, that it's about Bigend.'" He clarifies: "'But the tonality . . . isn't that he's in trouble, or that Blue Ant is in trouble. It's that he's about to become exponentially *bigger*'" (*ZH* 308). Add Bigend's international mobility to the mix, and his threat becomes that of a borderless world in which the only universal language is of brand names.

In that dystopic extreme, Bigend becomes almost an advertising deity, shepherding everyone's purpose into the building of a kind of reverse Tower of Babel. Elsewhere, though, Bigend appears decidedly less threatening, suggesting that he is *not* in fact a prime mover, but perhaps just a particularly resonant node. Hollis even infantilizes him, once saying, "'I haven't actually found him that personally repulsive . . . but I don't like the sense of enormous amounts of money at the service of, of, well, I don't know. He's like a monstrously intelligent giant baby'" (*SC* 156). Nicola Nixon points out that both William James and Frank Norris expressed difficulty in reconciling the understated physical appearances of last-century barons with their reputations as ruthless scoundrels (John D. Rockefeller for James, and the fictive Shelgrim in Norris's *The Octopus*). She shows how both authors used similar "metaphors of immeasurability" in their descriptions of the men, like "inverted skyscrapers, unplumbable depths, vast oceans" (807), which is

> not altogether surprising, for the turn-of-the-century corporate magnate was little more than the collective myth-making that his epistemological elusiveness precipitated. On one hand, [they] were the real figures of the new plutocracy at the end of the nineteenth century, seeming to offer material proof of the success of the American myth of self-making and laissez-faire capitalism. On the other hand, they were, like Shelgrim, only symbols or figureheads for a faceless corporate power that threatened ideals of competitive individualism and republican theories of wealth distribution. (808)

These baronic figures, who stand as "synecdoches for a complex of men and decisions" (808), posed quandaries for those with an individualist understanding of personhood/personality, much as the tension between Bigend the supernatural and Bigend the mundane reflects the confusion of Gibson's other characters in his trilogy. Nixon goes on to read "The Jolly Corner" as a story about turn-of-the-century self-making, wherein Brydon and his spectral alter ego figure a confrontation between the old and new models of the businessman. If we see in this story a parallel to Bigend's elaborate self-fashioning, in his attempts to *make* himself a shadow figure, might we not also see him as a figure just as trapped by last century's thinking as the rest?

The Unlegislatable Future, or History Unhinged

I would like to posit the possibility that other characters' theologically tinged perceptions of Bigend and his influence in *Spook Country* and *Zero History* are remnants of nostalgia for controlled narrative, set in a global context that continually disrupts it. I have argued before that in *Pattern Recognition* Gibson explores the idea of narrative as an object of human desire that, if lost or superceded, might cost more than anticipated.[2] It is not clear whether, ultimately, the drive to narrative (or comprehension) is constitutive of humanity, or merely something that cannot yet be phased out or adapted to fit new circumstances without dire consequences. But while modelling a move away from the stranglehold of conventional narrative understanding over concepts of human agency, Gibson does so through characters who build community around and through a search for conventional narrative completion, in their goal of sequencing, completing, and comprehending "the footage." To Cayce, the appeal of the footage—a disconnected series of anonymously created film clips posted to the Web—is its potentially fulfilling self-contained wholeness, entirely separate from her at-once fractured and increasingly monolithic view of the world (formed as that was at a historical crux of crumbling nationalism and the rise of globalism). Fredric Jameson argues that the footage is so compelling to Cayce and other fans because it is devoid of markers of time or place, providing "an ontological relief" and "an epoch of rest" (114) from the "postmodern nominalism" in which the real world is steeped (109). As such, he argues, the novel "projects the Utopian anticipation of a new art premised on 'semiotic neutrality,' and on the systematic effacement of names, dates, fashions and history itself, within a context irremediably corrupted by all those things" (111–12). Bigend formalizes and funds Cayce's search for the films' maker, and while she hates the thought of his owning the footage in any way, she cannot resist her drive to comprehend it, ultimately fulfilling the job that he hired her to do.

Spook Country and *Zero History* deepen what Gibson starts in *Pattern Recognition* by depriving Hollis of any such attachment to or reverence for her objective, leaving only Bigend as a potential higher power: something or someone on whom to project her need to comprehend a purposeful order in the world that she experiences. She lives in the same time as Cayce, and experiences the same disorienting condition, which is that—as Gibson has said in different ways over a span of years—"in a world characterized by technologically driven change, we necessarily legislate after the fact, perpetually scrambling to catch up, while the core architectures of the future, increasingly, are erected by entities like Google" ("Google's Earth"). I am associating Gibson's "legislated future" here with the concept of narrative, and his dystopic present as the anxious state of disruption in our habituated sense of narrative as a sequence of events bound by time and some controlled realm of context. Two other formulations of this statement help me define Gibson's idea of "legislation" as looking to historical precedent with some assurance of thus controlling for the future—a narrative structure that helped organize the epoch of the Industrial Revolution, perhaps, but one that will not hold up in the face of the information revolution. In 1997, for instance, Gibson explained, "I think that something really big is happening to us again. It's something like what happened when we started doing cities . . . and we just have no way of knowing all of the myriad things that will come out of it. It won't be any sort of approved, legislated future. It never is" ("Clive Barker"). And later, in an interview about *Spook Country*, Gibson suggests that the current revolution will itself be epochal: "The core of how politics and technology work together, for me, is that technology is very seldom legislated into existence. Technology will eventually take us to a point where something will change so much that beyond that point we won't be able to recognize any of it at all. Whatever is left of us, of our species, beyond that point, looking back, won't recognize us as being the same species" ("Spook Country"). It is worth noting that Cayce voices a very similar thought in *Pattern Recognition* (57).

The core elements of any dystopia are history and context, and the very titles of Gibson's latest two novels remind us that that is what we are getting, though in a somehow negated or altered form. In *Spook Country* and *Zero History*, it is the unyoking of time and place from each other that creates the dystopic atmosphere. Or, rather, it is the reinvention of their relationship to each other: in this increasingly globalized and technologized world, time no longer stays in place. The figurative representation of this phenomenon in the novels is locative art or "augmented reality" (*ZH* 163)—what Bigend originally sends Hollis to research. She first experiences it in the opening scene of *Spook Country*, when an artist named Alberto takes her to see his "River Phoenix"—a 3D projection of the actor in his death pose at the exact location where it happened. The art form is a combination of virtual reality and GPS technology, and currently requires an interface device to see, but the suggestion is made that after enough proliferation of and exposure to it, people will internalize the interface (*SC* 65). One of Gibson's bolder predictions in this trilogy, this would amount to a world picture changed so significantly that it could effect his other often-repeated prediction: that to people of the future, we will have become a fiction ("Spook Country" and *PR* 57).

Locative art/augmented reality signals not the end of history, or of narrative, but a saturation of them, to the extent that it enables all events to begin again and again and have the same affective influence on a new observer as they did in their original or authentic moment. As one character explains, it could lead to one giant annotation of "every centimeter of a place," or "spatially tagged hypermedia" (*SC* 22). Gibson's interpretation of what this means, expressed both within the trilogy and in a 2010 *New York Times* editorial, is that

> Cyberspace, not so long ago, was a specific elsewhere, one we visited periodically, peering into it from the familiar physical world. Now cyberspace has everted. Turned itself inside out. Colonized the physical. Making Google a central and evolving structural unit not only of the architecture of cyberspace, but of the world. This is the sort of thing that empires and nation-states did, before. But empires and nation-states weren't organs of global human perception. They had their many eyes, certainly, but they didn't constitute a single multiplex eye for the entire human species. ("Google's Earth")

Given that Gibson constitutes the situation as epochal, as a turning-over of how we perceive the organization of the world, the *dys* in this dystopia is not so much badness as it is a being-uncomfortable in an estranged sense of place. Lauren Berlant, in her reading of *Pattern Recognition*, suggests that what Gibson shows us is "the building of an intuitive sense of the historical present in scenes of ongoing trauma or crisis ordinariness" (846), where "people follow their intuitions and so change the shape of the present, which is not fleeting at all, but a zone of action in a transitioning space" (856). The eversion of cyberspace in *Spook Country* poses this crisis ordinariness literally, as the characters constantly adjust to the dislocation of traditional time and place.[3]

We have to ask whether focusing on Bigend's influence constitutes a productive awareness for these characters, or whether it is a lingering side effect of outdated habits of thought, distracting them from learning positive behaviours of adaptation to a changing world—whether, in a kind of nostalgic suspicion of the postmodern suspicion of metanarratives, they invest Bigend and all that he stands for with more power and significance than they should. I would argue that what Bigend most brings to the table is his intuition about the commodity value of secrets and of searching, which in turn drives more searches. He is really more Google than a god. But he is also Midas: everything that he touches turns to product, and he can search only by proxy. Tom Moylan levels a damning charge at Gibson's first trilogy, arguing that it is a failed dystopia because "oppositional expression is tapped as a necessary source of independent creativity that is capable of ferretting out solutions... to systemic problems" until "the knowledge base of the opposition becomes the knowledge base of the system's own refinement" (193). In Gibson's latest trilogy, the tapper has a name—Bigend—and other characters fret constantly over whether this is precisely what he is doing to them. That he intends to is certainly true: Bigend likens Hollis to "breakbulk," or "'non-containerized freight. Old-fashioned shipping'" (*SC* 201). As he explains, "'I've thought that in terms of information, the most interesting items, for me, usually amount to breakbulk. Traditional human intelligence. Someone knowing something. As opposed to data mining and the rest of it.'" But Bigend is a red herring. Gibson calls him "'an out-of-control trickster,'" a mere author's tool, because "'anything you need to happen can be accounted for by his perversity and endless curiosity'" (Gross). Though Hollis does find what Bigend hires her to find in both *Spook Country* and *Zero History*, she simply withholds the information from him, and hers is not the only successful rebellion. Thus, Bigend is reduced to just another character with just another strategy for adapting to the unlegislatable future: "'risk management. The spinning of the given moment's scenarios. Pattern recognition'" (*PR* 57). His self-fashioning, ultimately, makes him predictable: Garreth (Hollis's extra-legal tactical-expert love interest) exploits Bigend's risk management strategy to help extricate Hollis from his clutches. Bigend *is* escapable—or at least avertable—and if so, maybe so is all he stands for.[4] In light of this important failure, we must see past the characters' paranoia about him before we can judge what the trilogy offers about adaptation to a new world picture.

Rewriting the Protocols

The adaptation demanded by the new world picture might be seen, in Gibson's own terms, as a process of rewriting protocols. I agree with Berlant that what *Pattern Recognition* is doing (and what *Spook Country* and *Zero History* are doing even more dramatically) is "constructing a mode of analysis of the historical present that moves us away from the dialectic of structure... and agency... and toward attending to their embeddedness in scenes that make demands on the sensorium for adjudication, adaptation, improvisation, and new visceral imaginaries for what the present could be" (847). I think that *Spook Country* and *Zero History* do this even more dramatically. In "Discretionary Subjects," I have made the related case that Gibson exposes the conventional crisis/resolution organization of story plots as an outdated organizing principle, and draws our attention to how little information the decision—the mark of agency that theoretically moves that plotline forward—actually contains or conveys in most such stories. It follows that the way we read and tell stories, which both reflects and influences the way we perceive our surroundings, must give way to whatever the new state of "crisis ordinariness" demands. This will be even more literally required of us if, through the proliferation of some version of "augmented reality," our landscape is eventually overrun with everyone's projected truths, in an exposed palimpsest of history and imagination constantly present.

In the terms that *Pattern Recognition* offers, I have suggested that Gibson's model for replacing the decision as the marker of agency lies in the more context-saturated principle of participation. I took the term from Cayce's musings on the film forum's fetishistic need to comprehend the footage and search for its "Maker." It is a "participation mystique" (*PR* 255) and a "[giving oneself] to the dream" (23) that Gibson characterizes as an under-recognized and misunderstood form of agency in itself. As Cayce writes to an address that she thinks belongs to the Maker, "'we have to allow ourselves so far into the investigation of whatever this is, whatever you're doing, that we become part of it. Hack into the system. Merge with it, deep enough that it, not you, begins to talk to us. . . . That we may all seem to just be sitting there, staring at the screen, but really, some of us anyway, we're adventurers. We're out there, seeking, taking risks. In hope . . . of bringing back wonders'" (255). I have also suggested that, in the absence of such an attachment to the object of her search, Hollis at least temporarily displaces the desired "Maker" onto Bigend. She starts *Spook Country*, for instance, telling herself a conventional story about her life: "she knew herself to be that woman of the age and the history that were hers, here, tonight, and was more or less okay with it, all of it" until faced with the crisis point when Bigend "had come calling, the week before, with an offer she could neither refuse nor, really, understand" (37). Through the rest of *Spook Country*, though, she begins to recognize her lack of training in or adeptness at organizing the information that bombards her from multiple overlaid contexts, and that this lack is what makes her attribute causality to Bigend himself. Relatedly, in *Zero History*, Milgrim draws an analogy between his addicted past self and a specialized tracking phone called the "Neo," in that it is prone to something called "'kernel panic,' which caused it to freeze and need to be restarted" (26). Advocating what I take to be another formulation of participation, Milgrim's therapist tells him that the ability to get oneself out of this mode is "a by-product of doing other things, rather than something one could train oneself to do in and of itself" (26). But Hollis is Gibson's best model yet for such adaptation, in part because she embodies an already recognizable condition of the historical or saturated present: celebrity.

Hollis is more open to new arrangements of being and doing than some of the other characters because she has already experienced the "increasingly atemporal nature of music" (23) in the fact that moments from her past, like the breakup of The Curfew, can occur over and over again as if for the first time to every new fan who discovers them. Her experience of history thus coexists with Alberto's "fanboy module," in which that moment "might as well have been yesterday" (23). Bigend calls the celebrity self a "tulpa," a "projected thought-form" (much akin to locative art) that "has a life of its own. It can, under the right circumstances, indefinitely survive the death of its subject. That's what every Elvis sighting is about, literally" (102). Bigend has clearly hired Hollis hoping that her celebrity will get her into places he cannot go. It does. And it is because Hollis "already constitute[s] part of the historical record" that another character uses her as witness to his actions. "'By inviting you to witness what we intend to do,'" he tells her, "'I will be using you, in effect, as a sort of time capsule. You will become the fireplace brick behind which I leave an account, though it will be your account, of what we do here'" (296). Hollis awkwardly comes to accept the role that she plays in the histories and memories of those who recognize her, and starts learning how to use multiplicity in contexts and identities more for her own ends. Such is the case, for instance, when she attempts to gain an interview with a reclusive known fan: "Hollis was about to smile in the direction of the invisible camera, then pretended instead that she was being photographed for a Curfew rerelease. She'd had a trademark semi-frown, in those days. If she invoked the era and sort of relaxed into it, that expression might emerge by default" (*SC* 52). Here she not only exploits her identity but calls the past into the present to increase its potency. Hollis's presence works the same sort of cult magic as does Bigend's absence; her participation is just as effective as Bigend's surveillance, and the information that she gains is ultimately more usable.

To some extent, Gibson emphasizes that the concept of the individual will be an inevitable casualty in the unlegislated future, and this is why we draw back from it, and persist in reading a contextual model of agency, like participation, as being somehow retrograde. Participation mystique, as Jung theorized it, is a primitive or unconscious state of collective relationship, but Gibson seems to want to co-opt something positive from the concept, as Hollis seems to move ably through a world inhabited by multiple refractions of herself. Cayce also ultimately finds freedom from habituated paranoia in the disorienting proliferation of historical selves all present at once that technology's record makes commonplace.[5] But beyond the erosion of individuality, the unlegislated future that Gibson projects in this trilogy will also require that we reassess another concept that we hold dear: authenticity. This is something we already have to do, if we are to account for phenomena like Wikipedia or the fact that the "devoted historians" at a company called History Preservation Associates (historypreservation.com) now include a line of Buzz Rickson's flight jackets called the "William Gibson Collection," thanks to the fact that Cayce sports one in *Pattern Recognition*. But the need for some protocol here will intensify if and as cyberspace keeps "everting" and augmented reality spreads. Here, Gibson's character Bobby Chombo offers a helpful tip by referencing blogs: they all attempt to "describe reality," but "where you're most likely to find the real info is in the links. It's contextual, and not only who the blog's linked to, but who's linked to the blog" (65). This suggests that any sort of authentication of any given version of reality will, of necessity, be a communal endeavour. Laurie Johnson sees in this an upgraded version of Gibson's thought since *Neuromancer*, arguing that "locative art's re-creations of and allusions to significant shared culture moments presume that we very much still inhabit a traditional, fundamentally consensual and therefore reliable virtual reality."

I mention the need for a "protocol" advisedly, as it is a term that functions in the trilogy to deepen what "participation" started to do in *Pattern Recognition*. I have noticed that Gibson often peppers interviews about his writing with terms that play central roles in his stories themselves, and he recently applied "protocol" to the processes of reading and writing. "What I'm really doing when I'm writing a novel," he says, "is I'm making black marks on paper, according to a very, very elaborate cultural protocol, which I've had to learn, and then I give them to you, and you read them, according to a very, very elaborate cultural protocol, which you've had to learn, and you complete the arc" ("William Gibson Discusses"). In this trilogy, Gibson tries to effect his wish that readers "enjoy figuring out what it is these guys he's watching are doing" ("Spook Country") by writing short chapters that follow multiple characters in multiple storylines, interfacing with each other through their own protocols. As such, these novels align even better with Berlant's assessment of how, in *Pattern Recognition*, he "forces readers to be like the protagonists who are also making sense of things without generic or structural guarantees: we are positioned to live the presented present by being in it, touching, tasting, overhearing, and tracking how we are responding to it" (849). Content-wise, in *Spook Country*, the featured "protocol" is a guiding principle used by Tito, a member of a Cuban-Chinese crime family who plays a role in the plot's resolution. Rooted in Santería, and honed by his grandfather into the family's "invisible raft of tradecraft" (*SC* 13), the protocol guides Tito's movements as he carries off his part in the espionage plot—most successfully when he completely gives himself up to it. Even though a protocol is a code of behaviour that persists through time, it seems more adaptable to various contexts than is history as it is currently conceived. Gibson makes it something appealing, something to aspire to. Perhaps, too, the word's common usage in the technological world highlights protocol's potential distinction from a more stultifying tradition or convention, as a communications protocol is definitionally that which allows sharing across contexts. As such, the concept might also help us keep the unlegislated future from degenerating into "situational" morality, which Milgrim at least argues is no viable option for a just society (136).

Notes

1. See especially, for issues cognate to those raised in this essay, Neil Easterbrook's "Recognizing Patterns: Gibson's Hermeneutics from the Bridge Trilogy to *Pattern Recognition*" and "Alternate Presents: The Ambivalent Historicism of *Pattern Recognition*."
2. See Tobeck, "Discretionary Subjects: Decision and Participation in William Gibson's Fiction."
3. Although there are multiple occasions in both *Spook Country* and *Zero History* wherein characters confront things that seem out of place or in the wrong time, perhaps the most obvious "crisis ordinariness" is figured in the kind of perpetual discomfort that Hollis feels inside Cabinet, the curiously decorated non-hotel in which she stays throughout *Zero History*—or in her paranoiac scrutiny of its landscape tapestries, which contain the same folly reproduced in different settings and numbers.
4. As Laurie Johnson writes, "In the neo-Victorian America of *Spook Country*, the middle class is also clearly vanishing, but the disempowered can still accomplish

a lot. They can disrupt the machinations of war profiteers, for instance, by uploading information and smuggling it on iPod drives."

5 As I wrote in "Discretionary Subjects":

> By participating in the forum, Cayce learns through reading . . . that participation can be continuous without requiring a fixed self: when the entire forum has been archived, she finds herself reading early posts she had written without at first recognizing them (Gibson, *Pattern* 267). She encounters her self in a form that is no longer herself, but the record of her participation and what she responded to traces her ongoing emergence, without producing a necessarily deterministic continuity. . . . By allowing herself "so far into the investigation" of the footage and the community that springs up around it, she "become[s] part of it" (255); she exercises, as Foucault writes, "not the curiosity that seeks to assimilate what it is proper for one to know, but that which enables one to get free of oneself" (8). This freedom and "becoming part of it" is neither an evacuation of the self nor an assimilating comprehension of what she finds, but more like a proliferation, a "hack" and "merge" activity (Gibson, *Pattern* 255). Cayce's ego remains, but she "cultivate[s] it on its own special plot," the way her agent father does paranoia. Apart from that plot, she can be "only a part of something larger" (124), not assimilating what she finds to aggrandize herself, or being caught in an eternal feedback loop between particularity and universality. In the forum, Cayce is an agent without being one self. (397)

Works Cited

Berlant, Lauren. "Intuitionists: History and the Affective Event." *American Literary History* 20.4 (2008): 845–60. Print.

Easterbrook, Neil. "Alternate Presents: The Ambivalent Historicism of *Pattern Recognition*." *Science Fiction Studies* 33 (2006): 483–504. Print.

———. "Recognizing Patterns: Gibson's Hermeneutics from the Bridge Trilogy to *Pattern Recognition*." *Beyond Cyberpunk: New Critical Perspectives*. Ed. Graham J. Murphy and Sherryl Vint. New York: Routledge, 2010: 46–64. Print.

Gibson, William. "Clive Barker Interviews William Gibson." *Burning Chrome Live*. Burning City, 13 Dec. 1997. Web. 1 Dec. 2003.

———. "Google's Earth." *New York Times*. *New York Times*, 31 Aug. 2010. Web. 31 Aug. 2010.

———. *Pattern Recognition*. New York: Berkley–Penguin, 2003. Print.

———. "Spook Country." William Gibson Books, n.d. Web. 14 Aug. 2011.

———. *Spook Country*. New York: G. P. Putnam's Sons–Penguin, 2007. Print.

———. "William Gibson Discusses *Spook Country*." FORA.tv. 9 Aug. 2007. Web. 14 Aug. 2011.

———. *Zero History*. New York: G. P. Putnam's Sons–Penguin, 2010. Print.

Gross, Joe. "For Sci-Fi Master William Gibson, It's All about the Here and Now." statesman.com. *The Statesman*, 18 Sept. 2010. Web. 15 Aug. 2011.

Jameson, Fredric. "Fear and Loathing in Globalization." *New Left Review* 23 (2003): 105–14. Print.

Johnson, Laurie. "Upload Now. On William Gibson's Spook Country." *Kritik*. The Unit for Criticism and Interpretive Theory at the U of Illinois, 16 July 2008. Web. 15 Aug. 2011.

Moylan, Tom. "Global Economy, Local Texts: Utopian/Dystopian Tension in William Gibson's Cyberpunk Trilogy." *Minnesota Review* 43–44 (1995): 182–97. Print.

Nixon, Nicola. "'Prismatic and Profitable': Commerce and the Corporate Person in James's 'The Jolly Corner.'" *American Literature: A Journal of Literary History, Criticism, and Bibliography* 76.4 (2004): 807–31. Print.

Tobeck, Janine. "Discretionary Subjects: Decision and Participation in William Gibson's Fiction." *Modern Fiction Studies* 56.2 (2010): 378–400. Print.

The Cultural Logic of Post-Capitalism
Cormac McCarthy's The Road *and Popular Dystopia*

Carl F. Miller

> This Utopian problem ... is supremely social and cultural, involving the task of trying to imagine how a society without hierarchy, a society of free people, a society that has at once repudiated the economic mechanisms of the market, can possibly cohere.
> —Fredric Jameson

The notion of capitalist evolution is central to Fredric Jameson's influential *Postmodernism; or, The Cultural Logic of Late Capitalism* (1991), which thoroughly develops the concept of late capitalism and its conflation with contemporary popular culture. Borrowing the term from Ernst Mandel's 1975 book of the same name, late capitalism is defined by Jameson as the third great stage of capitalism, which becomes the cultural dominant after World War II and is characterized by the collapse of "the cultural and the economic ... back into one another ... in an eclipse of the distinction between base and superstructure" (*P* xxi). As mode of production and mode of existence become indistinguishable from one another, the idea of a world beyond capitalism becomes increasingly difficult to fathom. Rather than signifying the end of the system, Jameson explains, late capitalism represents the more permanent diffusion of commodification and is termed "late" to stress "its continuity with what preceded it [market and monopoly capitalism] rather than the break, rupture, and mutation that concepts like 'postindustrial society' wished to underscore" (*P* xix).

In stark contrast to this evolutionary continuity, Cormac McCarthy's 2007 Pulitzer Prize–winning novel, *The Road*, presents an apocalyptic setting witness to the outright dissolution of our contemporary consumer-oriented culture. Such renunciations of capitalism are decidedly commonplace in utopian literature—stretching all the way to back to Thomas More's archetypal *Utopia* (1516)—with depictions of fresh social systems that eschew materialism and class in favour of an elevated concept of collective humanity.[1] However, rather than offering a utopian outcome that represents an achievement for mankind, *The Road's* depiction of post-capitalism and the loss of a global economy results in a hyper-localized and hopelessly fragmented notion of humanity. In such a way, *The Road* provides a striking theoretical commentary on the legacy of capitalism, and projects an overwhelmingly dystopian view of the loss of popular and consumer culture.

"Shoppers in the Commissaries of Hell"

The logic of late capitalism detailed in *Postmodernism* gives rise to a system of advertising, consumption, and brand recognition that becomes synonymous with both popular and artistic culture; Jameson, for example, suggests that Andy Warhol's "great billboard images of the Coca-Cola bottle . . . explicitly foreground the commodity fetishism of a transition to late capital" (*P* 9). In contrast to this, *The Road* offers a landscape beset by "a pale palimpsest of advertisements for goods which no longer existed" (127–28), as contemporary iconic images and products are unknown to the younger generation and largely irrelevant to the older one. Coca-Cola, in fact, is the only contemporary brand name mentioned in the whole of the book (23, 148), and it is instructive that the boy has not heard of Coke,[2] despite the fact that it is arguably the most recognizable brand name in the world today. Thus, while the commodification of Coca-Cola signals the arrival of late capitalism, the lack of commodification attached to this product in *The Road* is testament to late capitalism's outright dissolution.

McCarthy illustrates a world free of class consumerism in which physical products outlive the brands that produced them. When the man and the boy come upon a roadside gas station, the actual company name is immaterial, and this is also evident with the "anonymous tins of food" for which they search (181). Building on Jameson's work, Michael Hardt and Antonio Negri contend that corporate culture and capitalist marketing are predicated on difference, but take care to include separate segments of society in a project of "diversity management" (153). In *The Road*, by contrast, such difference is replaced by a pervasive corporate anonymity that is predicated on *in*difference. This logic is reflected in the main characters—"the man" and "the boy"—who are given no proper names; in fact, the only character who gives his name in the course of the book—the blind traveller who calls himself Ely—is revealed to have intentionally falsified that name (171).

In contrast to the culture of late capitalism, which Jameson argues has become synonymous with consumerism,[3] the post-capitalist culture of *The Road* instead represents an effective reversion to pre-capitalism.[4] The only acquisition in the book is via theft and scavenging, with characters reduced to "shoppers in the commissaries of hell" (181). Money is rendered non-functional debris: the coins scattered around the soft drink machines are now worthless (23); when the man says he has "found a coin . . . or a button" the distinction is largely irrelevant (204). And the laws of private property are effectively abolished and replaced by the realities of primal force—as demonstrated by the theft of the man's supply cart and the use of his gun to reclaim it (253–58).

Just as significantly, the end of the previous cultural logic signals an accordant loss of value for the products of that period. The man uses magazines to fuel a fire and fan the blaze (208), which becomes the only functional use for such periodical artifacts. The television set the father and son find is worthless because it has nothing to broadcast (22), and the grand piano they come across lacks anyone who knows how to play music (205). Likewise, both the bullets that are not compatible with the gun and the light meter lacking batteries are rendered useless (143, 213), underscoring the interrelated web of contemporary production and economics. Even the simplicity of an agrarian system of production is not afforded to the book's characters; when the man finds packets of begonia and morning glory seeds, he sticks them in his pocket before stopping to rationally ask, "For what?" (132–33).

While any such agricultural production is impossible in the face of indefinite nomadism, his dismissal of the seeds is also predicated on the fact that they will yield only aesthetic beauty—rather than products of sustenance. Many of the former luxury goods the man and the boy come across are now worthless, from an antique pump organ and an old cherry-wood chifforobe (22), to a parlour filled with an imported chandelier and a tall palladian window (205). As a result, items that would previously have been hallmarks of consumer society are reduced to momentary curiosities and remnants of a bygone economic system of values. As the old traveller poignantly states in his conversation with the man and the boy, "It's foolish to ask for luxuries in times like these" (169).

The extent to which one's identity is defined by material markers is confronted in *The Road* when the man chooses what to carry with him and what to discard:

> He'd carried his billfold about till it wore a cornershaped hole in his trousers. Then one day he sat down by the roadside and took it out and went through its contents. Some money, credit cards. His driver's license. A picture of his wife. He spread everything out on the blacktop. Like gaming cards. He pitched the sweatblackened piece of leather into the woods and sat holding the photograph. Then he laid it down in the road also and then he stood and they went on. (51)

Amidst such economic and political reversion, any monetary and administrative possessions become useless and reliquary, while even tools of emotional nostalgia—like the photograph—are irrelevant luxuries. Much as the post-capitalist logic of the road has swallowed up the present, the man's final act is a symbolic gesture that surrenders the past to the road, as well. Instead, the man and the boy carry in their knapsacks what are deemed "essential things. In case they had to abandon the cart and make a run for it" (5): blankets, food, clothing, and a pistol. The only goods of any value are those that can sustain life and those that can end it—and not necessarily in that order—with all other remnants of late capitalist consumer society reduced to decaying, indifferent debris.

Subtraction and Division

Jameson asserts at the end of *Postmodernism* that "the notion of capital stands or falls with the notion of some unified logic of [the] social system itself" (*P* 410). The end of late capitalism, as such, is not simply an event of economic significance, but also correlates directly to the loss of traditional socialization, with the physical mode of production being inextricably tied to intellectual and emotional production. Max Horkheimer and Theodor Adorno argue that, within the culture industry of the twentieth century, "individuation has never really been achieved. Self-preservation in the shape of class has kept everyone at the stage of a mere species being" (155);

Jameson observes that, as a result of this perception, "the only Utopian gratification offered by the category of social class is the latter's abolition" (346). The inherent authoritarianism of late capitalist society and the class system is torn down throughout the course of *The Road*, with this dissolution demonstrating "the frailty of everything revealed at last. Old and troubling issues resolved into nothingness and night. The last instance of a thing takes the class with it" (28).

This is not a glorious class revolution, though, but rather an apocalyptic one. Instead of the utopian abolition of private property giving way to universal social harmony, McCarthy articulates a post-capitalist dystopia that offers a mere reversion to pre-capitalism and gives way to general anarchy. Cannibalism becomes rampant precisely because the mode of production has been halted, with survival necessitating a scavenging of the existing world that eventually filters up to humanity itself. The only seemingly utopian moments are those that offer a nostalgic return to past socialization for the man, such as spending the afternoon with his son sitting wrapped in blankets and eating apples (124), or drinking Coca-Cola out of plastic mugs (148)—both commercial-worthy scenes that prove to be short-lived oases within the new reality of mass chaos. Faced with the seeming inevitability of being raped and eaten, the man's wife says, before she commits suicide, "We're not survivors. We're the walking dead in a horror film" (55).

Just as significantly, the loss of capitalist/corporate structure results in the general loss of popular culture, with each character defined singularly in a disconnectedly local context. Adorno has notably stressed the negative effects that commodification has on humanity, arguing that "the total effect of the culture industry is one of anti-enlightenment . . . and impedes the development of autonomous, independent individuals" (92). However, if the culture industry is responsible for making the individual into part of a mass, it is just as surely responsible for preventing the masses from fracturing into an anarchic sea of disconnected individuals. In *The Road*, when the man asks the stranger, "How would you know if you were the last man on earth?" (169), the question is as poignant as it is pointless.

While Jameson stresses that the possibility of capitalism is predicated on a unified social system, he also warns that "if capital does not exist, then clearly socialism does not exist either. . . . Without a conception of the social totality (and the possibility of transforming a whole social system), no properly socialist politics is possible" (354–55).[5] The oft-repeated utopian calls for capitalism's dissolution are thus tempered by the realization that the late capitalist system—however flawed—provides the contemporary world with its only legitimate mechanism of totalization and collectivity. Per the dystopian onset of post-capitalism, McCarthy does not depict a system simply lacking popular culture, but in fact a world on the verge of forgetting that such a concept ever existed.

"The Richness of a Vanished World"

On the heels of this loss of popular culture, the development of both intellect and artistry are gradually diminished throughout the course of *The Road*, in favour of a present that offers no viable connection to the enlightened past. Education is effectively neglected, to the point where the characters do not worry about the boy's lessons anymore (245); literacy is a dying art, and academicism offers a theoretical exercise in unprecedented contrast to material reality. This is evident when the man remembers standing at the site of a ruined library, and is overcome by the false intellectual promise of the future held within the decaying volumes: "He'd not have thought the value of the smallest thing predicated on the world to come. That the space which these things occupied was itself an expectation" (187).

Such dissolution is just as evident for the fields of artistic production, and *The Road*'s treatment of music is particularly pertinent to the concept of dystopia. Ernst Bloch devotes what is easily the largest segment of his seminal *Spirit of Utopia* to "The Philosophy of Music," and utilizes the development of musical philosophy to map the history of human civilization. (Indeed, Bloch's periodization is reliant on music in the same way that Jameson's is indelibly linked to economics.) In a notable diversion from the daily task of survival in *The Road*, the man "carved the boy a flute from a piece of roadside cane" and offers it to him as an impromptu gift (77). Just as reassuringly, "after a while [the boy] fell back and after a while the man could hear him playing. A formless music for the age to come. Or perhaps the last music on earth called up from out of the ashes of its ruin" (77). This again raises the question of whether the apocalyptic circumstances of *The Road* offer the advent of a new order for mankind or the last gasp of civilization altogether. In this respect, the pair's appreciation of music offers a glimmer of hope; Bloch theorizes that "the *heard* note ... shows us our way without alien means, shows us our historically inner path as a flame" (34), and such production stands in contrast to "the silence" that the man feels will characterize the end of history (274).

However, by the midway point of the novel even this simple preservation of musical artistry has met with rejection. On the heels of their elementary discussion of the emptiness of outer space—which reveals the boy's general lack of education—the man inquires about the boy's musical instrument:

What happened to your flute?
I threw it away.
You threw it away?
Yes.
Okay. (159)

The man's acceptance of his son's act indicates a consensus agreement that such acts of cultural preservation are ultimately futile, a resignation that pushes the book's narrative even deeper into dystopia. While the father and son may still be "carrying the fire" (129)—a phrase they repeatedly use to signify their observance of civilized ethics and order—they have discarded the very thing that will allow them to access that flame in the future.

Rather than in art or in culture, aesthetic beauty and the preservation of civilization in *The Road* are largely witnessed through food. The stark desolation of the world is countered by the man's vivid description of "chile, corn, stew, soup, spaghetti sauce. The richness of a vanished world" (139). In addition to the preservation of the old civilization, food offers the utopian suggestion of the establishment of a new world, with descriptions harkening back five hundred years to the produce of the recently discovered Americas: "Slices of red pepper standing among the ordered rows. Tomatoes. Corn. New Potatoes. Okra" (206).

Part of this interest in food is linked to its role in basic sustenance, as the man admits that "mostly he worried about shoes. That and food. Always food" (17). Immediate survival becomes paramount, and capitalist accumulation is rendered incompatible with the nomadic reality of *The Road*. When the boy asks, "What are we going to do with all this stuff?" his father simply states, "We'll just have to take what we can" (150). As a result, the narrative of the book at times amounts to little more than an inventory of provisions ("Coffee. Ham. Biscuits" [144]) that will keep them filled for another day.

But beyond a mere objective list of supplies, food is also accorded a practically religious reverence by the man and the boy, as evident in the utopian *mise en scène* that they uncover when they are on the verge of starvation:

> Oh my God . . . Crate upon crate of canned goods. Tomatoes, peaches, beans, apricots. Canned hams. Corned beef. Hundreds of gallons of water in ten gallon plastic jerry jugs. . . . He held his forehead in his hand. Oh my God, he said. He looked back at the boy. It's all right, he said . . . I found everything. (138–39)

In this case, it is significant that the man repeatedly says "Oh my God" on either side of this revelation; in a world largely devoid of the hope of religious salvation—as the old traveller states bluntly, "There is no God and we are his prophets" (170)—food is literally the single viable saviour to which the man and his son are witness. This provides an ironic application of Friedrich Schelling's memorable statement that "the souls of those who are entirely preoccupied by earthly matters will simply shrivel up, and approach a condition of annihilation" (qtd. in Bloch 253). Deprived of the capitalist tools of production and accumulation, the man and the boy must forsake any artistic, intellectual, and spiritual pursuits in the interests of day-to-day survival—a concern that grows ever more singular and all-consuming the more the apocalyptic world bears down upon them.

This regression to a hyper-local concept of social welfare and cultural development results in the progressive dwindling of both widespread communication (politics and administration) and local communication (conversation among individuals). This dilemma aligns usefully with Bloch's theory of the intersection of culture and utopia, in which he questions, "What could human history, human culture even mean in and of itself, after not only the individual, the nations repeatedly submerge in them, become unpresent, but their historical summation is also threatened by the possibility of an ultimately disengaged isolation?" (257). While the man and the boy encounter a number of other characters in the course of *The Road*, communication with strangers is most often in the form of threats or physical action, which underlies the inherent distrust generated by the lack of a unified administrative/social system.

Just as significantly, Horkheimer and Adorno contend that "words are trade-marks which are finally all the more firmly linked to the things they denote" (166), and as previously commodified products become blank, so does the general process of communication. Dialogue in *The Road* is generally limited to monosyllabic vignettes between the father and his son, with the topic of conversation most often existential in nature. In fact, the style of dialogue utilized by McCarthy is eerily similar to that used by Samuel

Beckett in *Waiting for Godot* (1953) and *Endgame* (1957)—perhaps the foremost twentieth-century texts on social dystopia and cultural reversion:

> Are we going to die?
> Sometime. Not now.
> And we're still going south.
> Yes.
> So we'll be warm.
> Yes.
> Okay.
> Okay what?
> Nothing. Just okay. (10)

The association with the latter of Beckett's plays—*Endgame*—is particularly intriguing, given the endgame strategy that both texts must employ in the face of unspecified apocalyptic circumstances. However, even in the endgame strategy of chess there is a definitive plan of action grounded in historical precedent, and Beckett's play is accordingly predicated on a structured routine. *The Road* offers no such strategic blueprint—in part because its situation is unprecedented, but also because any such rules have been forgotten. The man's inability to simulate or remember common games is testament to this: "He tried to remember the rules of childhood games. Old Maid. Some version of Whist. He was sure he had them mostly wrong and he made up new games and gave them new names. Abnormal Fescue or Catbarf" (53). Instead, the two of them resort to playing the binary opposite of chess—checkers (153)—a game emblematic of the simplified rules of their world and split-second decisions they must make, with a method of planning that is never more than a few moves ahead.

This simplistic disconnect with past childhood games is symptomatic of a more serious cultural divide. For despite sharing the most prominent and localized social dynamic in *The Road*, and despite their intense dedication to each other, the man and the boy still experience a social disconnect that proves chasmic. When the boy asks his father questions about the ways of the world, they are questions "about [a] world that for him was not even a memory" (53–54). When the man debates how to answer such questions, he stops short of telling his son the reality of the present: "There is no past" (54). It is not simply that the man's cultural referents are different from his son's—as such generation gaps are inescapable within late capitalism—but rather that he has cultural referents and his son does not. Jean-François Lyotard stresses that "the objects and thoughts which originate in scientific knowledge and the capitalist economy convey . . . the rule that there is no reality unless testified by a consensus between partners over a certain knowledge and certain commitments" (77). Accordingly, the man comes to the eventual realization that "to the boy he was himself an alien. A being from a planet that no longer existed" (153).

Life on the Road

Jameson explains that the highest level of contemporary social analysis is that which dialectically views capitalism "at one and the same time [as] the best thing that has ever happened to the human race, and the worst" (*P* 407). The loss of a universal consumer culture limits the supplies of sustenance and fractures all modes of exchange—both economic and otherwise—as a general fragmentation in the global sense gives way to a universal disconnect in the local sense. The man and the boy, for example, often come across "odd things scattered by the side of the world. Electrical appliances, furniture. Tools. Things abandoned long ago by pilgrims en route to their several and collective deaths. Even a year ago the boy might sometimes pick up something and carry it with him for a while but he didn't do that any more" (199–200). While Bloch stresses that it is "the machine" that "make[s] everything as lifeless and subhuman on a small scale as our newer urban developments are on a larger scale" (11), such man-made technology also offers the tools to offset the fragmentation of human culture. In *The Road*, the ultimate disregard of this technology is further suggestive of each character's reduction to a barbaric individual reality. The loss of such physical and cultural connections is crucial, as the characters in *The Road* have subsequently lost the ability to access their collective history, with the man rightly fearing "that was gone that could not be put right again" (136). The past is lost, the present is reduced to nominalism, and the future is an abstract luxury that few people will be afforded.

This loss of historicity in *The Road* again offers an ironic connection with Jameson's *Postmodernism*, which begins by declaring, "It is safest to grasp the concept of the postmodern as an attempt to think the present historically in an age that has forgotten to think historically in the first place" (*P* ix). In the case of postmodernism/late capitalism, this loss of historicity is predicated on the burial of human history beneath the mass of contemporary cultural materials. In *The Road*, these cultural materials are bluntly stripped away, and the accordant loss of history results from a veritable lack—rather than a surplus—of civilization and popular culture. The man and his son are unsure of what month it is, having failed to keep a calendar for several years, and must rely on very primitive tools of navigation to guide their journey south. It is no coincidence that the most compelling object the man encounters in *The Road* is simultaneously tied to obsolete notions of branding, aesthetics, and direction, when he opens the oak box on the abandoned ship:

> He unsnapped the corroding latches and opened it. Inside was a brass sextant, possibly a hundred years old. He lifted it from the fitted case and held it in his hand. Struck by the beauty of it. . . . He wiped the verdigris from the plate at the base. Hezzaninth, London. He held it to his eye and turned the wheel. It was the first thing he'd seen in a long time that stirred him. (228)

In truth, it is likely the promise of orientation that the sextant offers—as much as any physical/aesthetic beauty—that makes it compelling to the man. Jameson observes that, in the history of mapping, "new instruments—compass, sextant, and theodolite— . . . introduce a whole new coordinate: the relationship to the totality" (*P* 52). It is at this point, Jameson says, that the process of mapping "comes to require the coordination of existential data (the empirical position of the subject) with unlived abstract conceptions of the geographic totality" (*P* 52). In contrast to this, *The Road* frames its characters as "pilgrims in a fable swallowed up and lost among the inward parts of some gigantic beast" (3), hopelessly lacking both history and direction.

Bloch theorizes—rather pessimistically—that "We live without knowing what for. We die without knowing where to" (275). In *The Road*, the latter of these statements holds true for both life *and* death, as human existence is characterized by a lack of direction and destination—with the road representing an effective road to nowhere. The book's narrative ironically draws attention to "a log barn in a field with an advertisement in faded ten-foot letters across the roofslope. See Rock City" (21), with the understanding that tourism—much like the defunct consumer goods on other billboards—is a product that no longer exists. Travel has ceased to be a luxury and has instead become an unromantic and permanent way of survival, as the pair's migration south is motivated by sustenance instead of employment, enjoyment, or economics.

The Road consequently offers a world in which tourism has given way to a culture of homelessness. The title of the book—*The Road*—refers to the quintessential medium for travel, with the definite article representative of the fact that all roads are now seen as a single entity. Interestingly, roads have always been a staple of civilization, with nations often being defined as "developed" based on their administrative implementation of roads every bit as much as their economic modes of production. Through the temporary legacy of the road, the book illustrates the gradual reclamation of the world at the expense of man-made institutions, leaving the man to think that "if he lived long enough the world at last would all be lost" (18). Much like the dam they encounter, which the man tells his son "will probably be there for hundreds of years. Thousands even" (20), the roads are a still-functional testament to a system of production they have outlived, as is evident in the boy's questions and the father's explanation:

> These are our roads, the black lines on the map. The state roads.
> Why are they the state roads?
> Because they used to belong to the states. What used to be called the states.
> But there's not any more states?
> No.
> What happened to them?
> I don't know exactly. That's a good question.
> But the roads are still there.
> Yes. For a while. (43)

As such, the remnants of the highway system offer a veritable analogy for past consumer culture: they still exist, but they do not connect anything any more.

Post-Capitalism and Late History

Such longing for a conception of totality—and the recognition of its unrepresentability—is evident in the ending of *The Road*, which concludes with a seemingly mundane yet provocative image:

> Once there were brook trout in the streams in the mountains. . . . On their backs were vermiculate patterns that were maps of the world in its becoming. Maps and mazes. Of a thing that could not be put back. Not be made right again. In the deep glens where they lived all things were older than man and they hummed of mystery. (287)

Ironically, this passage effectively articulates Jameson's seminal method for cultural understanding within *Postmodernism*—cognitive mapping—whose purpose is "to enable a situational representation on the part of the individual subject to that vaster and properly unrepresentable totality" (*P* 51). As the economic and media systems of the world become more expansive, this process becomes increasingly more subjective and conceptual, but this holds equally true for a primitive world as fundamentally regressive as that in *The Road*. Jameson emphasizes that "cognitive mapping cannot . . . involve anything so easy as a map; indeed, once you knew what 'cognitive mapping' was driving at, you were to dismiss all figures of maps and mapping in your mind and try to imagine something else" (*P* 409)—a void that is momentarily filled in *The Road* by the patterns on the backs of the trout.

The search for maps and mazes within nature itself marks a fundamental change from Jameson's cultural/economic model, but it represents the culmination of a trend the man in *The Road* has followed for some time. Instead of simply viewing the apocalyptic events of the book as the choppy transition into an interconnected era, the man has "come to see a message in each such late history, a message and a warning" (91). In contrast to Jameson's late capitalism—which offers an expansive continuity with previous capitalist stages—the late history of *The Road* is the veritable decline and fall of human history. Jameson suggests that postmodernism and late capitalism are "what you have when the modernization process is complete and nature is gone for good"[6] (*P* ix), and considers whether such a completion results in the loss of historicity. *The Road*, on the other hand, presents the question of whether history can survive the inverse triumph of nature over modernization.

As opposed to history being buried under the process of capitalist accumulation, the late history of *The Road* is a last glimpse at the foundational elements of the world as this accumulation is stripped away. The man considers that "perhaps in the world's destruction it would be possible at last to see how it was made. Oceans, mountains. The ponderous counterspectacle of things ceasing to be. The seeping waste, hydroptic, and coldly secular. The silence" (274). Survival is clearly the end objective for the father and son throughout the course of the book, but there also still exists the deeply infused desire to comprehend their individual situation with respect to the new global totality. As Jameson suggests, "Even if we cannot imagine the productions of such an aesthetic, there may, nonetheless, as with the very idea of Utopia itself, be something positive in the attempt to keep alive the possibility of imagining such a thing" ("Cognitive" 356). This kind of faith-based orientation is evident in the man and the boy proudly "carrying the fire" in support of a concept of order and collectivity in the face of economic and social chaos.[7]

However, in spite of such utopian instances of hope, *The Road* is ultimately an apocalyptic panorama of a fractured system of economics and culture that threatens the very existence of humankind. While Horkheimer and Adorno insist that the result of the contemporary culture industry "is a constant reproduction of the same thing" (134), it is the reproduction of something preferable to the regressive dystopia offered in *The Road*. Under the cultural logic of McCarthy's book, the classic anti-materialist mantra—"You can't take it with you"—morphs into an apocalyptic materialist reality: "You can't live without it."

As a result, rather than playing a reduced role, materialism serves a decidedly crucial purpose, and what might initially be viewed as the refutation of late capitalist culture may instead be seen as its validation. Jameson insists that although the system is horribly flawed, "unless the possibility of such an alternate system is grappled with and theorized explicitly, then I would agree that the critique of commodification tends fatally to turn back into a merely moral discussion" (*P* 207). This type of alternate system is precisely what McCarthy offers in *The Road*, which draws blatant attention to man's uncomfortable reliance on commodity culture. With this complex dialectic in mind, Jameson contends in the conclusion to *Postmodernism*:

> Successful spatial representation need not be some uplifting socialist-realist drama of revolutionary triumph but may be equally inscribed in a narrative of defeat, which sometimes, even more effectively, causes the whole architectonic of postmodern global space to rise up in ghostly profile behind itself, as some ultimate dialectical barrier or invisible limit. (*P* 415)

Defeat, in this case, would be characterized by the further expansion of the culture industry, consumer society, and late capitalism—a seemingly dystopian outcome in contrast to the clean break with capitalist society that conceptions of utopia so often advocate. *The Road*, however, effectively reverses this stereotype and theoretically postulates that a world devoid of capitalism just as quickly becomes a world devoid of any human collective. The invisible limit of mankind, accordingly, is challenged in the loss of the world's cultural dominant, and the cognitive mapping through nature at book's end emphasizes "a thing which could not be put back. Not be made right again" (287). Much as the man tries to avoid telling his son, the dystopian loss of commodification and popular culture means there is no past, and leads one to question whether there can be a future.

Notes

1 Jameson himself maintains a dialectical hesitancy toward such extreme models of utopia, stressing that—in its proper sense—Marxist "socialism is not staged as an ideal or a Utopia but on a tendential and emergent set of already existing structures" (*P* 206). In spite of its search from paradigmatic breaks, Jameson's model of social change is decidedly more evolutionary than it is revolutionary.

2 Such product ignorance is the focus of Brian Donnelly's "'Coke Is It?': Placing Coca-Cola in McCarthy's *The Road*" (*The Explicator* 68.1 [2010], 70–73), which draws attention to the way that the boy's response to the Coke ("What is it?" [23]) is actually a pun on the product's classic advertising slogan of "Coke Is It!"

3 This is a point Jameson further articulates in his 1998 collection *The Cultural Turn*, in which he suggests that "the very sphere of culture itself has expanded, becoming coterminous with market society . . . throughout daily life itself, in shopping, in professional activities, in the various often televisual forms of leisure, in the production of the market and in the consumption of these market products" (111).

4 It must be qualified that the setting of *The Road* seems solely descriptive of America, leaving the situation for the rest of the world a matter of speculation. While this article considers McCarthy's regional argument to be a metaphor for humanity in general, it is also worth considering the extent to which *The Road* offers a distinctly American response to such apocalyptic circumstances and the ways that other nations and cultures might confront regional and/or global chaos.

5 This quote is from Jameson's 1988 address "Cognitive Mapping," which—much like his original 1984 article "Postmodernism, or The Cultural Logic of Late Capitalism"—serves as a foundational text for his much larger *Postmodernism*.

6 Hardt and Negri again echo Jameson in defining postmodernization as "the economic process that emerges when mechanical and industrial technologies have expanded to invest the entire world, when the modernization process is complete, and when the formal subsumption of the noncapitalist environment has reached its limit" (272).

7 Of course, this faith-based exercise of "carrying the fire" could just as easily be an act of spiritual faith, given that the loss of consumerism in *The Road* is mirrored by an outright loss of religion—another institutional concept that provides both a sense of community and teleology. As mentioned prior, when deprived of this more long-term sense of spiritual salvation, the characters of the book turn even more inward to material products of sustenance to ensure their immediate survival.

Works Cited

Adorno, Theodor W. *The Culture Industry: Selected Essays on Mass Culture.* Ed. J.M. Bernstein. London: Routledge, 1991. Print.

Bloch, Ernst. *The Spirit of Utopia.* Trans. Anthony A. Nassar. Palo Alto, CA: Stanford UP, 2000. Print.

Donnelly, Brian. "'Coke Is It!': Placing Coca-Cola in McCarthy's *The Road.*" *The Explicator* 68.1 (2010): 70–73. Print.

Hardt, Michael, and Antonio Negri. *Empire.* Cambridge, MA: Harvard UP, 2000. Print.

Horkheimer, Max, and Theodor W. Adorno. *Dialectic of Enlightenment.* Trans. John Cumming. New York: Continuum, 2000. Print.

Jameson, Fredric. "Cognitive Mapping." *Marxism and the Interpretation of Culture.* Ed. Cary Nelson and Lawrence Grossberg. Urbana, IL: U of Illinois P, 1988. 347–60. Print.

———. *The Cultural Turn: Selected Writings on the Postmodern, 1983–1998.* New York: Verso, 1998. Print.

———. *Postmodernism; or, The Cultural Logic of Late Capitalism.* Durham, NC: Duke UP, 1991. Print.

Lyotard, Jean-François. *The Postmodern Condition: A Report on Knowledge.* Trans. Geoff Bennington and Brian Massumi. Minneapolis: U of Minnesota P, 1984. Print.

McCarthy, Cormac. *The Road.* New York: Vintage Books, 2006. Print.

Logical Gaps and Capitalism's Seduction in Larissa Lai's *Salt Fish Girl*

Sharlee Reimer

> "And so all the Workers in the factories . . ."
> "Brown eyes and black hair, every single one."
> "Stuff like that is not supposed to happen any more."
> "Stuff like that never stopped."
> —A conversation between Miranda and Evie, *Salt Fish Girl*

Larissa Lai's *Salt Fish Girl* is a story about many things: it is a love story about two women trying to come together over several lifetimes; it is a complicated dystopian novel that moves quickly between different times and places; it is a novel concerned with capitalist logics. It is also a novel of unanswered questions. This essay, therefore, asks, how do we read the narrative gaps that are scattered throughout the text? And why does Lai stage these questions in a dystopian genre? As I have argued elsewhere,[1] part of the answer to this question has to do with Lai's investment in writing against Enlightenment epistemologies. Robin Morris suggests that "Lai's examination of the textual production of power-based inequalities is a critique of the way in which fixed binaries such as that of creator/created, human/not human, real/not real, works to assure whiteness of its dominance while subjugating and denying the 'other's' movement towards an autonomous identity" (85). While I agree with Morris' reading of Lai's political investments, I want to think more about the discursive function of the narrative gaps in *Salt Fish Girl*.

I will argue that these logical gaps invite us to ask questions about the logical gaps that shape the worlds that the narrator(s) inhabit. We never get a clear sense, for example, of the cause(s) of the dreaming disease. We never know from whom the Sonias originate or why some of them are able to imagine what it might mean to escape. It is unclear how conception happens in relation to the durians, except in Miranda's case. There are many rumours about these things, but no hard evidence. We receive provisional answers, but there is a good deal that remains unexplained. To adapt a phrase of bell hooks', I suggest that the logical gaps in the novel are akin to those that shape and inform the white supremacist capitalist heteropatriarchy[2] that determines the dominant geopolitical worlds that the characters—and readers—of the novel inhabit. The novel takes up questions of race, gender, nation, and labour quite explicitly, asking how these sites of identification converge when total dehumanization is possible. For example, we are never told why it is logical to organize space into corporate cities or the "Unregulated Zone." Neither is it explained why clones are used for cheap labour. And, finally, we never learn why one is not considered human if one is a clone that has 0.03 percent carp DNA. Attention to these gaps is particularly pressing in the increasingly globalized post-NAFTA North America, but the reasons are so mundane that we—both the reader and many of the characters—are meant to take it all for granted.

When thinking about these questions, Paul Lai usefully links these gaps to questions of genre in *Salt Fish Girl*: "The lacuna in the novel around our contemporary moment suggests that a fictional critique of our own time period might best be created in histories about the future" (168). Along similar lines, Pilar Cuder-Domínguez argues that "Lai . . . forcefully points towards the racialization of poverty and the power differential of the First and Third Worlds that make people of some races expendable, a political purpose for which speculative fiction is a peculiarly suitable vehicle" (127). She goes on to say that Lai has "managed to use the speculative form creatively in [her] fictions, bringing together such diverse features as myth, history, SF proper, dystopia, and pioneer writing. The ensuing hybrid form allows [her] to interrogate the representation of Asian women's subjectivity, challenging standards of both gender and genre" (127). Paul Lai, too, sees a range of generic locations: "*Salt Fish Girl*'s juxtaposition of a prehistorical past, historical moments, and a speculative future creates a hybrid narrative that is at once myth, history, fairytale, and science fiction" (169). Paul Lai further elaborates on Lai's project when he suggest that "[b]y deliberately placing freedom and oppression at the center of speculative fiction, Lai forwards science fiction as a project of imagining worlds outside the norms and systems of our contemporary world by reaching back to repressed memories" (175). Robert Zacharias agrees, but he links the genre to nation, suggesting that "historical realism is a mode invested in maintenance of the homogeneous, empty time of the nation" while "the first revolutionary gesture of Lai's *Salt Fish Girl* is its rejection of that normative spatio-temporal paradigm" (15). Furthermore, he suggests that "Lai's challenge to the homogeneous, empty time of the nation complements her use of radically fluid subject identities, myth that intertwines with history, cyborg clones and Chinese goddesses, and a narrative that is deeply fractured—all of which violate the strict order and clear *telos* desired by the nation-state" (16). According to critics, then, science fiction, at least in the case of *Salt Fish Girl*, has significant political potential.

These readings of the genre are supported by genre theorists. Cuder-Domínguez, for example, reads the novel in terms of autoethnography, but uses the work of Patrick Parrinder to think about its generic location, paying particular attention to his suggestion that science fiction is a "metaphor for the present" (27), meaning that the genre is imagining consequences or following current practices to their logical ends in order to make implications of contemporary actions visible. Parrinder goes on to say that "[t]he redefinition of science fiction as metaphor coincided with the politicisation of sf," and suggests that the "[m]etaphorical theory views science fiction not as an alternative to utopia . . . but as one of the contemporary forms of utopian writing" (28). Given the looseness of this genre, then, we can draw connections to other genres, including apocalyptic narrative. Marlene Goldman, in her book on apocalypse in Canadian fiction, for example, argues that "[i]n contrast to the traditional biblical apocalypse, contemporary Canadian fiction refuses to celebrate the destruction of evil and the creation of a new, heavenly world. Instead, these works highlight the devastation wrought by apocalyptic thinking on those accorded the role of the non-elect" (5). Like Zacharias, she also sees connections between genre and nation, suggesting that "the originary apocalyptic violence that engendered the nation-state typically involved the subordination and commodification of women, Native peoples, ethnic minorities, and the landscape" and that "contemporary Canadian writers . . . stress the links between apocalyptic violence and the creation of the Canadian nation-state" (25). To substantiate Goldman's claims in relation to *Salt Fish Girl*, we must ask, though, what the apocalyptic event is. The novel suggests that the catastrophe is the result of capitalism and its effects on space, labour, and the overall value ascribed to some lives, but not others.

Lai demonstrates the ways in which the idea of nation becomes meaningless, one of the key features of globalization and NAFTA in the North American context. There are several mentions of geopolitical spaces in the texts, but they are all denationalized. Indeed, national borders seem to have dissolved completely in the latest time frame. We also hear about the "former municipality of Greenwood, British Columbia" (71). And the latest part of the narrative is set in "Serendipity, a walled city on the west coast of North America, 2044" (11). Brief reference to the cities is made to contextualize their political positionings: Serendipity is, for example, a secular city run by the Saturna corporation in which citizens are "taught to place [their] faith in reason" (61), and Painted Horse, a Nextcorp town that practices "fundamentalist Christianity" (62–63), but these cities are at war. Ian, Miranda's childhood friend, describes, for example, how he has come to live in Serendipity:

> Ian said his parents were intelligence agents for Saturna. They had recently been discovered by the councillors at Painted Horse. They would have received the death sentence if Saturna had not traded them for two of its own, who had recently been charged with espionage in Serendipity. Ian said he thought his parents were double agents, that they were really working for Nextcorp, and were on a mission right this very minute. (63–64)

Now, of course, there is no verification of Ian's story, but that is the point: in this world, we do not know if these are a child's fantasies, or if there is substance to what he says. We do know, however, that when Miranda plays with her father's Business Suit in "Real World," he gets forced into retirement (80), though it is also suggested that this mistake was used as an excuse to oust him based on Miranda's smell. What we find, though, is that the nation, instead of disappearing, becomes rearticulated in a range of ways, such as through the differentiation between the Unregulated Zone and the walled corporate cities, as well as through the policing of embodiment, as we see with the response to Miranda's smell and the fact that she is "the only Asian child in her class" (23).

This rearticulation of boundaries is perhaps not terribly surprising. As Jack Halberstam[3] states in his discussion of non-normative bodies in airport bathrooms, "the policing of gender is . . . intensified in the space of the airport, where people are literally moving through space and time in ways that cause them to want to stabilize some boundaries (like gender) even as they traverse others (like the national)" (20). While these two contexts are vastly different, I am compelled by the suggestion that a destabilization of some significant social boundaries is likely to result simultaneously in a hyper-policing of others.

Complicating a reading of the process by which the nation is replaced by the corporation, however, is Zacharias' convincing demonstration that there is little difference between the operations of the nation and the operations of the corporation. Both are top-down regulatory structures, both impose a range of violences on their "citizenship," and both claim to represent the best interests of all, but, in practice, represent only the best interests of the privileged few, while dehumanizing the many. Indeed, Zacharias draws a connection between *Salt Fish Girl* and Joy Kogawa's *Obasan*, which focuses on the history and politics of the Japanese Internment in Canada. Regardless of the power structure, though, as Joanna Mansbridge demonstrates, regulation of space is never complete: "The alleyways in which the Salt Fish Girl, Nu Wa, Miranda, and Evie move through the cities provide alternative pathways that subvert the flow of global capital. It is these pathways that allow a sense of agency and mobility within a capitalist hegemony" (126). The policing of space and bodies—particularly the deep anxieties about the Unregulated Zone by citied populations, and about Miranda's smell, as well as the need to manage these unruly sites—speak to related anxieties about ideal (corporate) citizenship.[4]

In the age of corporate domination, Mansbridge explains that "[t]he anti-Eden of Serendipity is a walled city in which simulation is reality and everything, including humans, becomes a commodity" (123). Indeed, Lai draws a connection between the histories of labour practices in nineteenth-century China and twenty-first-century North America in terms of factory work. In nineteenth-century China, Salt Fish Girl has no choice but to do work that will adversely affect her health in order to support herself and Nu Wa, the character who will later become Miranda. Like the factory workers in China, the Sonias of 2062 are the workers who do invisible labour, as we see with the Janitors (76), who are also subject to unregulated experimentation because they are not "human": "The Sonias were ambushed . . . [they] were in detention or had disappeared. Without a legal existence to begin with, they could not be reported missing" (249–50).[5] As Mansbridge goes on to say, "Evie rebels and escapes from factory exploitation that kept the Salt Fish Girl imprisoned years before in China" (126). In this context,

Zacharias asks, "[i]f it is true that the autonomy of the Canadian nation-state is giving way to the authority of globalized capital, a wholesale reconsideration of the concepts of sovereignty and citizenship is required. What type of communities will we imagine ourselves belonging to under the banner of transnational corporations? What type of sovereign is the corporation? And what type of citizen is the consumer?" (4). The dominant reading is that corporations are good for all, but in reality, they are good only for the privileged few, and this is what Evie is trying to show Miranda (and the reader).

And, of course, we see the devastation wrought on populations who are not what Sunera Thobani would call "exalted subjects": "[s]uch spaces of abject poverty [as the Unregulated Zone] are causally connected to the unregulated market forces of neoliberal global capitalism" (Morton 94). While not everything is regulated—as many point out, the capitalist economy cannot account for everything—and there is an informal economic barter system, as we see, for example, with Miranda's brother's work (Morton 94), the presence of such a system pales in comparison to the needs of the populations who engage in it. What we see, finally, is the extent to which, as Morton says, "the novel depicts the way in which the social and political rights of migrant workers are determined exclusively by their employment in multinational corporations" (94). There is no room in the definition of fully human for anyone who does not adhere to the social norms as determined by the implicitly white upper-middle-class heteropatriarchy.

These labour relations raise larger questions about whose lives are valued, as demonstrated by the sort of work that marginalized bodies have no option but to do, both in the present and the past. We see consistently that it is women of colour, who are either poor or without any rights, whose lives are disposable. Indeed, it is not even clear where the clones come from, although there are rumours, Evie explains to Miranda, of the clones' "source":

> "Some of the others talk about a woman called Ai, a Chinese woman who married a Japanese man and was interned in the Rockies during the Second World War. She died of cancer right after the war ended. He died of grief. The bodies were sold to science. They say she collected fossils near the Burgess Shale. But it's all rumour. For all I know one of my co-workers made it up. [. . .] Pallas tries to keep it quiet. A nice myth of origins after all, would be a perfect focus for a revolt, don't you think?"
>
> "I don't know."

"I do know that Nextcorp bought out the Diverse Genome Project around the same time as I was born."

"Diverse Genome Project?"

"It focuses on the peoples of the so-called Third World, Aboriginal peoples, and peoples in danger of extinction." (160)

In either case of these potential origins for Evie and the other Sonias, we can see that certain bodies are considered adequate to be exploited in these ways, not just in terms of labour, but on a more basic level in terms of their bodily integrity. And Miranda has no idea about the existence of the clones, never mind having thought about who might be their sources.

The narrative gaps that Lai uses draw our attention to logical gaps that implicate the reader alongside Miranda. As Tara Lee explains, "[c]haracters like Miranda are reduced to submitting to the local manifestations of [the] multinational power network, unable to imagine how they can resist the power grid" (95). However, Evie takes on the question of the inevitability of people's compliance:

"But the newspapers say . . ."

"[. . .] It's all there right in front of you. All you need to do is look. There are thousands of compounds all over the PEU. Don't you ever wonder about them?"

"I was raised to respect private property."

She shook her head. "Is everyone in this town as out of it as you? I don't get it. It's not like you have this comfortable life to protect."

"I'm not out of it," I snapped. But my stomach wavered. My world had suddenly become something quite different from what it had been mere moments ago. (161)

While Miranda is in a defensive position of denial at this point, she later moves to outright resistance to recognizing her class and human status privilege, despite being marginalized in other ways, particularly by race. After breaking her promise never to sell her mother's songs, Miranda elaborately justifies her actions to an extent that is worth quoting at length:

How could I have sold my mother's greatest hit to that shark? And in the service of shoe sales? It wasn't as though I didn't understand where the shoes came from. Evie had described to me in lurid detail the mad, dark factories, the greed that drove pay ever lower as contractors moved their factories to more and more desperate places. Evie, I thought, would be furious. The fat wad of cash burned against my chest. *What the hell, I thought. I didn't personally do anything to those factory women, did I?* What harm could it do for my mother's song to have a second life? It would bring the memory of her to millions, introduce her genius to a new generation who hadn't heard it the first time around. It would put a bit of real glamour into the lives of the women who bought the shoes—bored suburban housewives for whom an evening aerobics class or a morning run through the park was the only time of day they did something for themselves. It would bring a moment of beauty to women who were scared of growing old, women who had worked hard all their lives, women who deserved the beauty they worked for even as time took its toll, loosened their once tight clutches on immortality.... *My imprisonment, I thought, was a kind of martyrdom.* (202–203; emphasis added)

While Tara Lee discusses this scene as one in which "[s]elf-interest, one of the basic tenets of capitalist logic, leads individuals to contribute to the commodification of bodies even when they are not conscious of what they are doing" and goes on to say that "Miranda willingly resubmits to corporate control because capitalist logic is so entrenched in her that she unwittingly replicates it" (103), the lines emphasized above counter this reading. Moreover, we have seen Miranda do this before, both in nineteenth-century China when she abandons the Salt Fish Girl and contemporarily: "I was a sheltered child, living out my parents' utopian dream as though it were reality. They did not show me the cracks. And out of loyalty and love for them, when I sensed the cracks, I refused to see them. But of course this unspoken pact could not last" (71). Miranda is not unwitting in these actions, though she certainly does experience pressures, some external, others selfish. Miranda is working to justify her decisions—she is using what Shannon Sullivan and Nancy Tuana call "epistemologies of ignorance," an active refusal of knowledge in order to maintain the privileges to which she has access.

As many theorists note, under late capitalism, it is easy for people to become dehumanized. The worker increasingly becomes a machine. The citizen increasingly becomes a consumer. Because of corporatization, people become less familiar with daily goings on, such that it becomes easier to hide "unsavoury" forms of labour. Community—as it is traditionally recognized—breaks down. This is not to say, of course, that resistance is futile or impossible, but is, rather, to say that the shape of these things changes. As Lee suggests, "Lai repeatedly writes of the body's potential to destabilize capitalism's normalcy until the futility lies not in the body's inability to escape total control, *but in capitalism's inability to suppress disruptive presences*" (104; emphasis added). Lee is right: capitalism cannot suppress everything, but its lulling and seductive logics reward passivity, while punishing those who notice gaps and ask about them.

In order to draw the reader's attention to these gaps, the novel uses a futuristic setting and a vocal figure, in Evie, to implicate readers. More of Parrinder's work will help here. He says, "science fiction understood as a metaphorical mode no longer has any necessary connection or concern with contemporary scientific developments" (31). That is, despite appearances, science fiction is no longer about science. It is not surprising, then, that Lai does not give us full explanations, but the amount that is left to rumour and speculation is nevertheless unexpected when there is room in the narrative for these elucidations. And so we must consider that Lai leaves these gaps in order to draw attention to other gaps in the narrative, many of which have been highlighted by critics. As Rita Wong, for example, explains, "The people dying in the streets are the logical outcome of the ongoing privatization of public spaces, the corrosion of the social contract, the attrition of diverse communal affiliations. Uncomfortably similar to today's Free Trade Zones, this futuristic Unregulated Zone is the rational extension of policies that exploit and discard labour for the sake of monetary profit" (119). Similarly, Cuder-Domínguez suggests that Lai is "making deep connections between the personal and political, between Miranda's individual body and the way capitalist economies market and exploit human bodies" (122). And, more specifically, as we know is also currently the case, "[i]n Lai's imagined world, Caucasians exploit non-Caucasians" (Cuder-Domínguez 123). Zacharias agrees: Lai shows "the corporation's sovereignty claim to literally dehumanize its subjects [with the Sonias]" (17). As Evie insists, these realities are not a coincidence; they are a part of the system.

Some, however, such as Mansbridge, are optimistic, arguing that "[t]he birth in *Salt Fish Girl* signals a coming into being that is not defined by a racist, heterosexist, paternal order" (131). Along similar lines, Lee reads the final words of the novel—"everything will be all right, until next time" (269)—as "an understanding that continued vigilance is always necessary if the body is to ward off the ever present threat of appropriation" (108).

I would suggest that the ending is more open and ambiguous than that: the statement indicates that there *will* be a next time, and that no amount of vigilance will stave it off. The novel argues, instead, that there will be a continual process of making and remaking in order to move out of this late capitalist system. While I agree with Lee that the novel suggests that self-mutation and self-ownership are valuable, the novel does not fully allow for them. Miranda and Evie will always be subject to their geopolitical circumstances to some extent. And, as we have seen, Miranda in particular is susceptible to the lull of the late capitalist logic, as are many. Instead, the argument that I see is that the text insists on a kind of literacy and a visibility in the form of asking questions of the narratives that we are fed. Evie demonstrates that we must continue to ask how things have come to be the way that they are, and that we must recognize, as she says, that not only have dehumanizing practices long been the norm, but "[s]tuff like that never stopped" (160).

Notes

1. See Sharlee Reimer, "Troubling Origins: Cyborg Politics in Larissa Lai's *Salt Fish Girl*." *Atlantis: A Women's Studies Journal/Revue d'études sur les femmes* 35.1 (Fall 2010): 4–15. Print.
2. In hooks' *Ain't I a Woman: Black Women and Feminism* (Boston: South End Press, 1981) and elsewhere.
3. At the time of publication, Halberstam's first name was Judith.
4. For more on smell, see P. Lai, Oliver, and Phung. For more on multiculturalism as a biopolitical project, see Morton.
5. While the context is different, this circumstance speaks to the ways in which missing and murdered Indigenous women—despite (allegedly) having legal rights—have a long history of being ignored by police when they are reported missing. They, too, are dehumanized.

Works Cited

Cuder-Domínguez, Pilar. "The Politics of Gender and Genre in Asian Canadian Women's Speculative Fiction: Hiromo Goto and Larissa Lai." *Asian Canadian Writing Beyond Autoethnography*. Ed. Eleanor Ty and Christl Verduyn. Waterloo, ON: Wilfrid Laurier UP, 2008. 115–31. Print.

Goldman, Marlene. *Rewriting Apocalypse in Canadian Fiction*. Montreal: McGill-Queen's UP, 2005. Print.

Halberstam, Judith. *Female Masculinity*. Durham: Duke UP, 1998. Print.
Kogawa, Joy. *Obasan*. Toronto: Penguin Canada, 1981. Print.
Lai, Larissa. *Salt Fish Girl*. Toronto: Thomas Allen Publishers, 2002. Print.
Lai, Paul. "Stinky Bodies: Mythological Futures and the Olfactory Sense in Larissa Lai's *Salt Fish Girl*." *MELUS: The Journal of the Society for the Study of the Multi-Ethnic Literature of the United States* 33.4 (2008 Winter): 167–87. Print.
Lee, Tara. "Mutant Bodies in Larissa's Lai's *Salt Fish Girl*: Challenging the Alliance between Science and Capital." *West Coast Line: A Journal of Contemporary Writing & Criticism* 38.2 (2004): 94–109. Print.
Mansbridge, Joanna. "Abject origins: uncanny strangers and figures of fetishism in Larissa Lai's *Salt Fish Girl*." *West Coast Line: A Journal of Contemporary Writing & Criticism* 38.2 (2004): 121–33. Print.
Morris, Robin. "'What Does It Mean to Be Human?': Racing Monsters, Clones and Replicants." *Foundation: The International Review of Science Fiction* 33.91 (2004 Summer): 81–96. Print.
Morton, Stephen. "Multiculturalism and the Formation of a Diasporic Counterpublic in Roy K. Kiyooka's *StoneDGloves*." *Canadian Literature* 201 (2009 Summer): 89–109.
Oliver, Stephanie. "Diffuse Connections: Smell and Diasporic Subjectivity in Larissa Lai's *Salt Fish Girl*." *Canadian Literature* 208 (2011): 85–107. Print.
Parrinder, Patrick. "Science Fiction: Metaphor, Myth, or Prophecy?" *Science Fiction: Critical Frontiers*. Ed. Karen Sayer and John Moore. London: Macmillan, 2000. 23–34. Print.
Phung, Malissa. "The Diasporic Inheritance of Postmemory and Immigrant Shame in the Novels of Larissa Lai." *Postcolonial Text* 7.3 (2012). Web. 13 April 2013.
Reimer, Sharlee. "Troubling Origins: Cyborg Politics in Larissa Lai's *Salt Fish Girl*." *Atlantis: A Women's Studies Journal/Revue d'études sur les femmes* 35.1 (Fall 2010): 4–15. Print.
Sullivan, Shannon, and Nancy Tuana, eds. *Race and Epistemologies of Ignorance*. Albany: SUNY P, 2007. Print.
Thobani, Sunera. *Exalted Subjects: Studies in the Making of Race and Nation in Canada*. Toronto: U Toronto P, 2007. Print.
Wong, Rita. "Troubling Domestic Limits: Reading Border Fictions alongside Larissa Lai's *Salt Fish Girl*." *BC Studies* 140 (2003): 109–24. Print.
Zacharias, Robert. "Citizens of the Exception: *Obasan* Meets *Salt Fish Girl*." *Narratives of Citizenship: Indigenous and Diasporic Peoples Unsettle the Nation-State*. Edmonton, AB: U of Alberta P, 2011. 3–24. Print.

"The Dystopia of the Obsolete"
Lisa Robertson's Vancouver and the Poetics of Nostalgia

Paul Stephens

> What would the utopian land look like if it were not fenced in by the violence of Liberty and the nation? How would my desire for a homeland read if I were to represent it with the moral promiscuity of any plant? These spores and seeds and bits of invasive root are the treasures I fling backward, over my shoulder, into the hokey loam of an old genre.
>
> —Lisa Robertson, *"How Pastoral"*

"I needed a genre," begins Lisa Robertson's *XEclogue*. The phrase is resonant for a critic attempting to survey her eclectic body of work. Like much of her writing, the 2003 *Occasional Work and Seven Walks from the Office for Soft Architecture* defies simple description. The book might be best categorized as a series of prose-poetic essays related to the urban geography of Vancouver, Canada—but this would be reductive at best: it contains photographs, a manifesto, meditations on botany and architecture, as well as a "Value Village Lyric." The book emerges from a local context—and, more specifically, from the context of a particular influential Vancouver-based not-for-profit writers' collective, the Kootenay School of Writing.[1]

In part, it stands as a product of the workshops that the school ran and, arguably, as a result of the school's funding struggles as well.[2] The book describes itself as "an experiment in collaboration with the forms and concerns of my community." Those concerns have largely to do with Vancouver's rapid growth over two decades. Like much Kootenay School writing, Robertson's poetry is deeply cosmopolitan, and yet rooted in the local. Though utopian in its aspirations, her poetry recognizes the failure of an un-self-critical utopianism; though innovative in its use of avant-garde forms, her poetry is frequently concerned with nostalgia.

Problems of genre are frequently transposed onto problems of identity in Robertson's writing. Obsolescent modes (such as the eclogue and the epic) become means by which to counter the inexorable progress of global capitalism. Nostalgia allows Robertson to personalize, as well as to reimagine, historical experience. "Consider your homeland, like all utopias, obsolete," she writes in her introduction to *XEclogue*. Her work refers only obliquely to questions of Canadian nationalism, but is nonetheless strongly concerned with the complexities of Canadian self-identification. Her prose intertwines issues of domestic space, nationalism, and historical injustice: "The horizon pulled me close. It was trying to fulfill a space I thought of as my body. Through the bosco a fleecy blackness revealed the nation as its vapid twin. Yet nostalgia can locate those structured faults our embraces also seek" (n.p.). Having become the "vapid twin" to the space of what is not even precisely the body of the poet, the nation exists at several removes from reality. For Robertson, to engage in practices of nostalgia, or practices of the obsolescent, is to refuse to be useful, particularly to "the old bolstering narratives" of the nation. The angel of history must be assisted by "history's dystopian ghosts" in order to rewrite the past. Such a rewriting refuses to have economic value and challenges our very notion of utility:

> A system is ecological when it consumes its own waste products. But within the capitalist narrative, the utopia of the new asserts itself as the only productive teleology. Therefore, I find it preferable to choose the dystopia of the obsolete. As a tactically uprooted use, deployment of the obsolete could cut short the feckless plot of productivity. When capital marks women as the abject and monstrous ciphers of both reproduction and consumption, our choice can only be to choke out the project of renovation. We must become history's dystopian ghosts, inserting our inconsistencies, demands, misinterpretations, and weedy appetites into the old bolstering narratives: We shall refuse to be useful. ("How Pastoral" 25)

If capitalist societies for most of their histories could be extraordinarily productive while excluding women from full participation in their institutions, then perhaps there is something inherently wrong not only with the political mechanisms of capitalist society, but also with its goals of maximizing production and utility. It is only by challenging the ends, as well as the means, of capitalist production that women can resituate themselves historically. As Robertson writes: "Through gluttony we become historical" (*Office* 145). "Nice girls don't make history," as the bumper sticker would have it. Women's quotidian productive labour is ahistorical; only ruptures within the narrative of production can be registered as meaningful events.

To historicize is in some sense to bring back to life the obsolete—that which is no longer useful. In the following passage from a dream sequence in *XEclogue*, she describes the nation as artifact:

> In deep sleep my ancestress tells me a story:
> "Ontology is the luxury of the landed. Let's pretend you 'had' a land. Then you 'lost' it. Now fondly describe it. That is pastoral. Consider your homeland, like all utopias, obsolete. Your pining rhetoric points to obsolescence. The garden gate shuts firmly. Yet Liberty must remain throned in her posh gazebo. What can the poor Lady do? Beauty, Pride, Envy, the Bounteous Land, The Romance of Citizenship: these mawkish paradigms flesh out the nation, fard its empty gaze. What if, for your new suit, you chose to parade obsolescence? Make a parallel nation, an anagram of the Land. Annex Liberty, absorb her, and recode her: infuse her with your nasty optics. The anagram will surpass and delete the first world, yet, in all its elements, remain identical. Who can afford sincerity? It's an expensive monocle." ("How Pastoral" 22)

This passage typifies Robertson's prose in its compression and complexity. Several arguments are going on at once. "Sincere" nationalism must be recoded—the emptiness of national mythologies must be exposed. Citizenship, in Robertson's terms, is a kind of romance: personal, idealistic, transient. All nations are in some direct or indirect fashion the products of imperial divisions of the world. Robertson's redeployment of Virgil suggests that imperialism must be excavated and reversed through parodic imitation. This would be an imaginative form of decolonization, where no one could take for granted his or her "landed"-ness. "First world" nations "remain identical" to one another in the histories that they exclude, but parallel histories can and must be created. Lady Liberty is a monarch in luxurious surroundings but she is also a monarch in isolation. Lady Liberty cannot help but refer to Canada's southern neighbour, which Robertson seems to suggest cannot simply be ignored, but must be engaged, "recoded," and "absorbed"—made, perhaps, to live up to her self-professed values of freedom and tolerance.

Robertson's critique of nationalism is particularly apparent in her first two full-length books, *XEclogue* and *Debbie: An Epic*, both of which reformulate Virgilian themes in the context of a postmodern feminism that defies any strong sense of region. "The hoaky loam of an old genre" animates her eclogic and epic work, but not in the service of any specific nation, government, location, or party. *Occasional Work and Seven Walks from the Office of Soft Architecture*, although firmly rooted in Vancouver, represents the North American city as something of a global bricolage—a product of conflicting, and often incommensurate, historical influences. Composed in lyrical prose, the book is strongly influenced by Situationism and by Walter Benjamin's *Arcades Project*. The city functions as protagonist, with its suburbs as important supporting characters. The suburb of Burnaby, located east of Vancouver, for example, is brought out of its blandness and made a foil to larger socio-cultural issues surrounding Vancouver's urban development. Nostalgia is central to *The Office for Soft Architecture*'s challenge to Vancouver's growth; the book immediately questions the capitalist processes responsible for that growth:

> The Office for Soft Architecture came into being as I watched the city of Vancouver dissolve in the fluid called money. . . . Here and there money had tarried. The result seemed emotional. I wanted to document this process. I began to research the history of surfaces. I included my own desires in the research. In this way, I became multiple. I became money. (1)

Like the title of Robertson's book *The Weather*, this passage alludes to Walter Benjamin's "Money and rain belong together. The weather is itself an index of the state of this world. Bliss is cloudless, knows no weather. There also comes a cloudless realm of perfect goods, on which no money falls" (481). Robertson makes herself an implicated character within the landscape (or the weatherscape). The old Vancouver may have tragically dissolved in a rain of money but that does not mean that the old Vancouver can be reclaimed through the removal of the corroding influence of money. On the contrary, to understand money's influence on the city, the author must become "money," so as to be able to think from the perspective of capital, rather than to simply dismiss capital's effects. Robertson again personalizes the experience of Vancouver's growth, unashamedly incorporating her "desires in the research." Historical research, the book suggests, cannot be a disinterested undertaking. Desires animate otherwise forgotten histories; desires cannot be dismissed as irrational or feminine. The writer cannot be separated from the metropolis that she inhabits. Vancouver's many changing landscapes (economic, architectural, ethnographic, geographic) must be particularized and experienced rather than pathologized and mourned.

Like Rem Koolhaas' *Delirious New York*, *The Office for Soft Architecture* is a "retroactive manifesto." Inspired by Koolhaas, Robertson performs a *détournement* on the name of his company, "The Office for Metropolitan Architecture." Soft Architecture is deliberately autodidactic and nonprofessional, characterized by the casual walk rather than by the survey and the blueprint. The Office for Soft Architecture is to the Office for Metropolitan Architecture what the Kootenay School is to a conventional M.F.A. program in creative writing. Robertson's architectural writing is proudly improvisatory, and restlessly moves from location to location without any kind of master plan: "This improvisatory ethos is modern. It is proportioned by the utopia of improvised necessity rather than by tradition" (178). Vancouver becomes emblematic of the attempt to create a provisional utopia out of the wilderness.

On the surface, eminently modern in its lack of a long-standing cultural tradition, Vancouver is shown in fact to harbour multiple histories that remain repressed within the city's popular historiography. Vancouver is seen to have been under the influence of globalizing forces since its inception; the city's attempts to present itself to the world come under particular scrutiny:

> The essays . . . reflect Vancouver's changing urban texture during a period of its development roughly bracketed by the sale of the Expo '86 site by the provincial government, and the 2003 acquisition by the province of the 2010 Winter Olympics. In this period of accelerated growth and increasingly globalizing economies, much of what I loved about this city seemed to be disappearing. I thought I should document the physical transitions I was witnessing in my daily life, and in this way question my own nostalgia for the minor, the local, the ruinous; for decay. It was

efficient to become an architect, since the city's economic and aesthetic discourses were increasingly framed in architectural vocabularies. In writing I wanted to make alternative spaces and contexts for the visual culture of this city, sites that could also provide a vigorously idiosyncratic history of surfaces as they fluctuate. ("Acknowledgements")

Documentation provides a means both to preserve and to question Vancouver's past. The book is a loosely organized *dérive* through Vancouver and its environs. Soft Architecture opts for the contemplative walk and the meticulous record of historical events as opposed to the more aggressive *détournement*. In his classic formulation "Theory of the Dérive," Guy Debord writes:

> Among the various Situationist methods is the dérive [literally: "drifting"], a technique of transient passage through various ambiances. The dérive entails playful-constructive behavior and awareness of psychological effects; which completely distinguishes it from the classical notions of the journey and the stroll. (50)

In "psychogeographical" terms, the activity of the *dérive* is more proactive than the activity of the *flâneur*, although in her uncertain drifting, the *dériviste* does not presume to reimagine the city programmatically on the scale of a Baron Haussman or a Le Corbusier. As Joshua Clover points out in his essay on Robertson, "soft architecture" can also be understood "as the body, or as being" (81). As such, "soft architecture" is embodied and receptive—modest in its ambitions to remake the landscape, but immodest in its ambitions to describe the desires and lived histories of the city's inhabitants.

The *dérive* involves an open-ended passivity—which is perhaps also in keeping with the absence of large-scale conflicts or upheavals (attacks, natural disasters) in Vancouver's recent past. The *dérive* may also be well suited to describing the city's perceived historical isolation:

> [O]ur city is persistently soft. We see it like a raw encampment at the edge of the rocks, a camp for a navy vying to return to a place that has disappeared. So the camp is a permanent transience, the buildings or shelters like tents—tents of steel, chipboard, stucco, glass, cement, paper, and various claddings—tents rising and falling in the glittering rhythm which is null rhythm, which is the flux of modern careers. (15)

More like a navy base than a battlefield, the city is typified by the transient careers of its inhabitants. It is a navy base without much of a navy—a nuclear-free zone in a world armed to the teeth. The static wilderness has given way to dynamic urban space. Somehow the specificities of this landscape must be reimagined. This imagining is political:

> The problem of the shape of choice is mainly retrospective. That wild nostalgia leans into the sheer volubility of incompetence. This nostalgia musters symbols with no relation to necessity—civic sequins, apertures that record and tend the fickleness of social gifts. Containing only supple space, nostalgia feeds our imagination's strategic ineptitude. Forget the journals, conferences, salons, textbooks, and media of dissemination. We say thought's object is not knowledge but living. We do not like it elsewhere.
>
> The truly utopian act is to manifest current conditions and dialects. Practice description. Description is mystical. It is afterlife because it is life's reflection or reverse. Place is accident posing as politics. (16)

Robertson offers no pre-lapsarian past for Vancouver, as for instance when she "détourns" the Situationist slogan of May 1968, "*Sous les pavés, la plage*," into "Under the pavement, pavement." "Under the pavement, the beach" might suit Vancouver's False Creek—site of Expo 86 and formerly a highly contaminated industrial space—even better than it would a wall near the Seine. The nostalgia for nature, however, is a form of nostalgia Robertson treats with considerable suspicion. She consistently treats the pastoral not as a genuine form of access to the natural world, but rather as "a nation-making genre" which naturalizes political and social inequality:

> I begin with the premise that pastoral, as a literary genre, is obsolete—originally obsolete. Once a hokey territory sussed by hayseed diction, now the mawkish artificiality of the pastoral poem's constructed surface has settled down to a backyard expressivity. . . . Translate backyard utopia as mythology. . . . I'd call pastoral the nation-making genre: within a hothouse language we force the myth of the Land to act as both political resource and mystic origin. ("How Pastoral" 22–23)

Despite its postmodern attempts to create myths of self-importance—in events like Expo 86 and the 2010 Winter Olympics—Vancouver seems unable to create a singular nation-building pastoral mythology. Expo and the Olympics are emblematic of Vancouver boosterism; they are international events, but it is an internationalism of tourism and spectacle, not an internationalism based on cultural uniqueness. Vancouver may lack a nation-building myth of origin, but Robertson is not arguing that Vancouver needs any such myth of origin. Soft Architecture is practical, and its idealism resides in its senses of possible outcomes, rather than in direct militant action based on a utopian vision of an originary pastoral state or a definitive future identity. The sentence "We say thought's object is not knowledge but living" (16) is a succinct definition of Pragmatism that could have been written by James or Dewey. There is no divine city on a hill, or even a divine city beneath the hills. Myths of origin are implicitly utopian in that they presume a world view; the examination of lived history is not utopian, but pragmatic. Robertson consistently denies the possibility of utopia in Vancouver or elsewhere: "Nothing is utopian. Everything wants to be. Soft Architects face the reaching middle" (17).

In what I take to be one of the book's most important chapters, "Playing House: A Brief Account of the Idea of the Shack," Vancouver is symbolically portrayed as shack-like in terms of its architectural ambitions. Surrounded by wilderness, the city is a haphazard work-in-progress, built from the materials of its own past:

> The landscape includes the material detritus of previous inhabitations and economies. Typically the shack reuses or regroups things with humour and frugality. The boughs of a tree might become a roof. A shack almost always reuses windows, so that looking into or out of the shack is already part of a series, or an ecology, of looking. In this sense a shack is itself a theory: it sees through other eyes. This aspect of the shack's politics prevents shack nostalgia from becoming mere inert propaganda. The layering or abutment of historically contingent economies frames a diction or pressure that is political, political in the sense that the shack dweller is never a pure product of the independent present. He sees himself through other eyes. (177–78)

Most important in this process of reusing is the reuse of windows. The shack must see itself through the glass of others. Not only is ontology a "luxury of the landed," so, too, is epistemology. Vancouver can know itself only through the eyes of others. As a city of immigration, it is a city of borrowed windows and eyes, and cannot be reduced to a simple notion of placeness. Its only authenticity consists in its lack of authenticity. In *Rousseau's Boat*, Robertson offers another vision of flawed utopia:

> I discover a tenuous utopia made from steel, wooden chairs, glass, stone, metal bed frames, tapestry, bones, prosthetic legs, hair, shirt-cuffs, nylon, plaster figurines, perfume bottles and keys. I am confusing art and decay. (21)

Robertson's litany is dominated by the detritus of consumer society but there are also elements like stone, hair, and bones, which remain unaltered features of nature. Utopia is tenuous: a mix, a living being subject to decay. Art may be utopian, but it cannot by itself create everlasting utopia. Like Robertson's other writings, *The Office for Soft Architecture* celebrates the death of the utopian ideal. In *Debbie: An Epic*, she writes: "I celebrate the death of method: the flirting woods call it, the glittering rocks call it—utopia is dead. High Loveliness was born here to cut back prim sublimity. She's a member of the lily tribe whose materials follow themselves. She's a bitch of the inauthentic; her ego's in drag" (n.p.). Utopia, like gender, is a performative erasure of complexity. Power is not a fixed attribute of the just and the good; instead, power is an effect. One can see the deep influence of Michel Foucault and Judith Butler in *Debbie: An Epic* when Robertson writes: "We invented power. Power is a pink prosthesis hidden in the forest. Between black pines we strap it on and dip our pink prosthesis in the pool" (n.p.). Nature is nothing but a pool of abstraction. It is up to humans to fuck in their fashion, and the strap-on prosthesis is inherently no better or worse than the purportedly normative phallus.

Citizenship, class affiliation, and gender roles are all likened to obsolete genres by Robertson—and yet to ignore the role of nation, class, and gender is perhaps to partake of another, more insidious form of nostalgia. Feminism in particular must continually be suspicious of nostalgia:

> I must risk censure and speak of my shimmering girlhood—for the politics of girls cannot refuse nostalgia.
> To be raised as a girl was a language, a system of dreaming fake dreams. In the prickling grass in the afternoon in August, I kept trying to find a place where my blood could rush. That was the obsolete experience of

> hope. But yield to the evidence. And do not decline to interpret. A smooth span of nostalgia dissects the crackling gazebo. (n.p.)

The "gazebo" of power, the official residence of Lady Liberty, reappears as an ambivalent symbol—feminized, vulnerable, unnecessary, open, luxurious. The gazebo is both preserved and demolished by the agency of nostalgia. One must return to "fake dreams"—(a pleonasm?)—before one can dream new dreams. The final chapter of *Debbie: An Epic*, titled "Utopia," is conscious of its own limitations in creating any kind of collective political agenda that would not be constructed out of the failures of the past:

> Now it is necessary to catalogue what, in sadness and tranquility, we have failed to describe in our supple rendering of these tableaux—those objects which stand between our ardent, political address and a new, plural pronoun (inky, dubious, prolix and deluxe): the shining lure of tenderness; the stain of ruddy wildings in a grove; the oblique and quivering kite of eros; history diffused as romance; a genre's camouflaged violence. (n.p.)

The refusal to choose a genre becomes a refusal to camouflage violence. Societies do not function, perhaps, without organizing and limiting violence—but that violence can perhaps be mitigated if it is transparent in structure, or genre.

Seen through the lens of Robertson's Vancouver writings, both urban and suburban development are inescapably violent. In *The Office for Soft Architecture*, Vancouver becomes a kind of failed petit-bourgeois paradise, emblematized by "Vancouver Specials" and "leaky condos." The term "Vancouver Special"—well known to Vancouverites—refers to a boxy, plain, lot-maximizing, two-storey house. Vancouver's "leaky condo" scandal of the 1990s involved lax construction regulation and oversight during a period of spectacular growth. Such localized references serve as regionally specific symbols of the adverse effects of Vancouver's stratospheric postwar building boom. In "The Pure Surface" chapter of the book, four pages are taken up by thumbnail photos of one hundred nearly identical Vancouver Specials. The leaky condos and Vancouver Specials are juxtaposed with a chapter on a turn-of-the-century Arts and Crafts mansion in the suburb, Burnaby. Once the site of profitable strawberry farms and wealthy estates, Burnaby is now a seemingly unremarkable middle-class locale. The mansion represents "an idea of nature as democratic and populist metaphor, the universal paradigm of sincerity and authenticity" (98). As egalitarian and utopian as Arts and Crafts designs might be, they still find their realization in antiquated and elitist methods of construction. The mansion represents the ideal of a suburban development that might have been individualized and artistic—everything the Vancouver Special and the leaky condo are not—and yet the mansion is beyond the grasp of the working-class Debbies who populate Vancouver's less glamorous suburbs.

Debbie herself loves to revel in the nostalgia of times when people of her class would have been servile in ways more apparent than in contemporary society:

> I have loved history's premonitions
> urgencies these parts lovingly I speak
> in the dialect of servility
> and current conditions arms of terror
> and grammar that went into the forest
> motors (n.p.)

Nostalgia enables a false return to paradise, an escape, but it can also permit a reconsideration of the grammar of contemporary social conditions. One must speak "the dialect of servility" in order to understand servitude. History is a kind of mimicking activity for Debbie. Transparency can only be sought, never attained. As she writes: "First all belief was paradise. So pliable a medium. A time not very long. A transparency caused" (n.p.). Instead of seeking paradise, we ought to seek other possible outcomes to the histories that have already taken place. Robertson seems to be speaking about Canadian society as a whole when she uses the word "this" ambiguously: "This was made from Europe, formed from Europe, rant and roar. Fine and grand. Fresh and bright." The ambivalence of the phrases "fine and grand" and "fresh and bright" demonstrates a clear discomfort with an oversimplified Canadian identity "made from Europe" (n.p.).

Debbie is described as "a moot person in a moot place," yet what makes her an epic character is her interaction with world history and with modern empire:

> ... I will discuss perfidy
> with scholars as if spurning kisses, I
> will sip the marble marrow of empire.

Debbie can be a scholar through self-willing; her interactions with historical knowledge take place as erotic experience. She precedes empire just as she perseveres past its demise:

> . . . we were half made when the empire
> died in orgy. Because we are not free
> my work shall be obscure
> as Love! unlinguistic! I
> bludgeon the poem with desire and
> stupidity in the wonderful autumn
> season as
> rosy cars
> ascend (n.p).

Debbie's "Because we are not free / my work shall be obscure / as Love!" is a targeted defence of an avant-garde writing practice. An eroticized language, as in the writing of Gertrude Stein, becomes an effective tool in resisting dominant societal roles. Debbie may be "moot" in the terms of empire, but in her mootness she is better able to observe the operations of empire. From her shack or her "Vancouver Special" or her leaky condo she is able to observe that "Utopia's torn plastic shanties are / moot shells of oscillation." The shack is a spinoff from the continuous movement of empire and of utopia, which—given the dominant coding of language, gender, and economics—amount to nearly the same things from Debbie's perspective.

Robertson's interest in nostalgia shows itself even in her earliest book, *The Apothecary*. The kind of nostalgia that Robertson is thinking of here is sociopolitical but also sexual, and does not necessarily liberate the individual from repression:

> The extreme anxiety of self-disclosure displaces the fantasy of politics with clots of phrase, yet the phantasie gives rise to a curiously useful desperation in the sense that "a house," "a car," or "a field" compensate metonymically. I remember how a house falling reveals an observable structure for an instant, then, through a sexual process, becomes nostalgia. (28)

The house becomes a collective space, the space that feminism has attempted to recover from the patriarchal erasure of domestic labour. Isolation may be necessary for the female to overcome the conditioning of a patriarchal society but isolation is only a strategy along the way to a fuller, more historical socialization. As Robertson writes in *The Apothecary*, memory must be surmounted and rewritten:

> A dexterous genre was available to my thighs only through an aesthetic of scrupulous isolation: aggregative though tentatively emphatic, apt to somatize, dedicated to garnering yet ordinarily engorged—in the burgeoning jargon I surmount memory as if a coppery cigarette toughly sewed the shape of an inclusive object to modulate among luxuries yet I am heard not physical but erring and further inversions clog a kind of nosegay showing how only the systematic is lacking before *copula* translate as "to cure." (19)

The cure the titular "apothecary" seeks is an inclusive new system. The new system requires new genres able to eroticize and to bring pleasure—as well as to somatize and to represent pain. The new system, represented through embodied metaphors, requires the "conspicuous inutility" called for in *Debbie: An Epic*. The adventurous and varied typography of *Debbie: An Epic* could itself be recognized as a conspicuous inutility. Large type and overlaid type make their own semantic arguments, but the book's typography can also be read as a purposeful rejection of the most economical means of conveying a poem. People must travel "vast / itineraries of error" (25) as she writes in *The Weather*. Error is a kind of luxury; revisiting the "errors" of history is a colossal form of luxury that is necessary to resist the depredations of empire. Robertson's epic (or mock epic) is like a palimpsest in reverse. Rather than reusing scarce and expensive paper or vellum out of necessity, Robertson deliberately overwrites what there is no economic need to overwrite. Obsolescence must be sought, not repressed. There is a retrospective joy in understanding the errors of history. In *The Weather*, Robertson writes: "We are watching ourselves being torn. It's gorgeous; we accept the dispersal. It's just beginning; we establish an obsolescence" (33).

Establishing "an obsolescence" is an ongoing process meant in part to counteract the anti-historical pressures of modernity. "The tendency of the age is to forget disturbance," she writes in *Debbie: An Epic*. In other words, as "The Argument" of *Debbie: An Epic* runs, "Slick lyric blocks history" (n.p). Rewriting the pastoral and the epic traditions is a gesture of remembering disturbance. Given the conditions of postmodern life, the only epic possible is an anti-epic. Such an epic, simultaneously materialist and anti-materialist, argues for reorienting social expenditure in a more just manner; it also denies that individuals are merely the products of their material conditions. It preserves some sort of philosophical idealism for poetic subjects: "I want an ingenious fibre to be treated as funny tragedy expressing a classic argument against materialism which runs like this: which changes of costume are bound to be dangerous? what code is honest and practical yet marginally corporate?" (3). To find a "fibre" may not be as ambitious as finding a new method or a new narrative of progress; finding a fibre may be the most "honest and practical" activity under the circumstances. In my epigraph to this essay, Robertson speaks of "The moral promiscuity of any plant" as an alternative to the violence of Liberty and the nation. The "moral promiscuity of any plant" is a call to a non-instrumentalized, non-utilitarian morality; hence, the importance of the echoes of Georges Bataille that run through Robertson's work. The luxury of leisure time or the luxury of the unquantified time spent within the domestic space must not be feminized. Geography, gender, and economics are alike in their performative natures:

> Nostalgia, like hysteria, once commonly treated as a feminine pathology, must now be claimed as a method of reading or of critiquing history—a pointer indicating a potential node of entry. . . . Rather than diagnosing this nostalgia as a symptom of loss (which would only buttress the capitalist fiction of possession), I deploy it as an almanac, planning a tentative landscape in which my inappropriate and disgraceful thoughts may circulate. Nostalgia will locate precisely those gaps or absences in a system we may now redefine as openings, freshly turned plots. ("How Pastoral" 25)

The Soft Architectural approach emphasizes collectivity, as does the urban eclogue. By defining nostalgia as a collective repossession of the past, rather than as an individual loss of the past, Robertson is able to cultivate new cultural possibilities. Not uncoincidentally, she employs agricultural metaphors to describe this reclamation. The collective imaginary she calls upon rejects the possessiveness of the individual lyric ego: "I deplore the enclosure staked out by a poetics of 'place' in which the field of man's discrete ontological geography stands as a wilful displacement, an emptying of a specifically peopled history" ("How Pastoral" 25). Robertson alludes to a time before the Enclosure Movement—to an idyllic pre-capitalist stage, but once again she is skeptical of indulging in Rousseauian fantasies. "Eclogue Three: Liberty" of *XEclogue* is a direct response to Rousseau, and it too plays upon the agrarian origins of the term culture:

> What follows is the interminable journal of culture. This neutral and emotive little word seems, in the operatic dark green woods, so harmless and legal but it's liberty totalized, an incommensurable crime against the girls. To question privilege I'm going to shame this word. I will begin by gathering around my body all the facts. . . . I embody the problem of the free-rider, inconveniencing, the leaf-built, the simple-hearted, the phobic, with the unctuous display of my grief. (n.p.)

To an eighteenth-century audience, *The Social Contract* represented a complete and total assault upon civilization; to a twenty-first-century audience, *The Social Contract*, like *Émile*, cannot help but be a total assault upon civilization that refuses to inquire deeply into the category of gender as a social construct. "Liberty totalized" likewise embodies an oxymoronic contradiction. Even under Rousseau's scathing gaze, culture remains a "crime against the girls." No amount of primitivism, it would seem, can result in full-fledged feminism when mixed with the slightest degree of culture. To return to the problem of utility, if the labour of women goes unrecognized, as it usually does in the pastoral tradition, then women are merely "free-riders." To be a stock pastoral character, a beautiful milkmaid, for instance, is to be the victim of an acculturated nature or of a naturalized culture. Robertson is not content with merely demonstrating that the utility of the milkmaid's labour has been fetishized out of existence—instead Robertson is challenging the definitions of utility both within culture and within language. Consider again Debbie's lines: "Because we are not free / my work shall be obscure / as Love!" The "work" can be writing, but it can also more generally be any kind of labour. In obscurity can be joy, can be meaning, can be the impulse toward liberation.

Although she repeatedly stresses the importance of community in her work, Robertson is wary of utopianism on a grand scale, and she articulates distinct limits and responsibilities for her work. In an email interview with Steve McCaffery, she writes:

> There are traces of unbuildable or unbuilt architectures folded into the texture of the city and our bodies are already moving among them.

> Therefore the exploitation of complicity as a critical trope, an economy of scale. My outlook is not liberatory except by the most minor means, but these tiny, flickering inflections are the only agency I believe—the inflections complicating the crux of a complicity. More and more poetry is becoming for me the urgent description of complicity and delusional space. The description squats within a grammar because there is no other site. Therefore the need for the urgent and incommensurate hopes of accomplices. (Robertson and McCaffery 38)

The impulse is again toward collective action and creation and away from individual imaginative compartmentalization. Just as she reclaims the word "nostalgia," with its pejorative connotations, so too she reclaims the word "complicity." The accomplice is not a criminal but an agent in the creative process, a squatter in the midst of wealth. The "unbuildable" remains as important as what has been built. Room must be set aside for "delusional space," and this space must remain counter-normative within larger shared visions. "A specifically peopled history" must be continually (re)imagined by Robertson and her accomplices.

In the most thoroughly researched chapter of *The Office for Soft Architecture*, "Site Report: New Brighton Park," Robertson attempts to create such "a specifically peopled history." An obscure park in East Vancouver, traditionally one of the city's poorest areas, becomes another kind of palimpsest of lost history.[3] Like Susan Howe's writings on Buffalo, the New Brighton chapter places micro-history in the service of a larger theoretical inquiry. Robertson describes the park as "an inverted utopia" (37), again invoking the Situationist slogan, this time in reverse, "sous la plage, le pavé" (37). The park is surrounded by heavy industry, and yet, in a somewhat challenged form, it offers beach access. Staked out as a town site at the planned terminus of the CPR railway, the park is the site of the first recorded real estate transaction in the city. From this inglorious myth of origin, Robertson goes on to describe the park's many other former uses: site of a hotel, a resort, a prospective steam power facility, and a community pool. The pool is particularly significant in that it was the site of the first racial exclusion policy in a Vancouver park; Japanese Canadians interned nearby during the Second World War were forbidden entry. For Robertson, "the spatio-economic system ... functions as a mutating lens: never a settlement, always already a zone of leisured flows and their minor intensifications, a zone of racialization and morphogenesis" (41).

The park retains traces of many of the major events of Western Canadian history. The settlement colony becomes an industrial producer and a war economy, and then a diversified economy highly reliant on leisure activities. The substitutions imposed on the landscape are not systematic or evolutionary—they are practical and unambitious adaptations to existing conditions. The landscape is unpoetic in the terms of traditional lyric: "Structure here is anti-metaphoric: it disperses convention" (41). Part of the park's unrealized potential is its sheer uselessness in economic terms: "Soft Architects believe that this site demonstrates the best possible use of an urban origin: Change its name repeatedly. Burn it down. From the rubble confect a prosthetic pleasureground; with fluent obviousness, picnic there" (41). New Brighton Park has had its name changed; the New Brighton Hotel did burn down; in comparison to other Vancouver parks, New Brighton is a rubble-filled locale. In a sense, Robertson is creating a kind of urban theodicy out of the park. The best of all possible results has occurred, though hardly by design. Out of a certain degree of randomness has emerged the chaotic celebration of a staccato Steinianism: "picnic there." The park has no reason to be ashamed, nor do those who might go there for pleasure—as opposed to visiting cleaner, larger, better-known parks like the marquee Stanley Park. New Brighton Park is no longer a destination park; it is a neighbourhood park. Robertson's own interest in the park was piqued by its proximity to her home, and its usefulness as a place to walk her dog. New Brighton Park is a perfect subject for the Soft Architectural approach because it is uncategorizable, underappreciated, and diverse. It is a sometime pleasure ground of the lower middle class and of the young artists and writers who have moved to the neighbourhood in the past two decades. Depending on one's perspective, New Brighton is a good example of the reclamation of urban space or it is a spectre of gentrification. It points the way toward a post-industrial, non-discriminatory, transnational Western Canada, but it also points the way to a Western Canada subject to the whims of development—hardly a dystopia and hardly a utopia. As Jennifer Scappetone asks, "Is an inverted Utopia dystopian? Likely not. In describing the capsizing of plots, Lisa Robertson tracks the critical distortion in erecting a multiple pronoun, midway through the condemned hold" (75).

Robertson's work makes her readers intensely conscious of space and of location, and yet, as I have suggested, Robertson herself is not easy to situate. Lytle Shaw observes that she is a "writer whose site specificity exceeds the literal or phenomenological and enters the discursive domain" (44). No location, and no identification with a place, can be taken for granted in her writing. Like much of the work that emerged from the circle of writers involved in the Kootenay School in the 1980s and '90s, Robertson's vision is internationalist in its scope. She maintains strong connections to the American avant-garde. But her writing—like that of other Vancouver poets of her generation such as Kevin Davies, Peter Culley, Dorothy Trujillo Lusk, and Jeff Derksen—is more uncomfortable in its sense of place than that of the 1960s generation of Vancouver poets. Like the pastoral tradition in general, Vancouver may have once been "a hokey territory sussed by a hayseed diction" (*Office* 22), but it is no longer such a territory. Profoundly polyglot and multi-ethnic, Vancouver has outpaced traditional politics of place and identity. Its many identities are overlayed and transient, its histories only partially visible—like New Brighton Park in Robertson's description. Robertson does not disavow a traditional Canadian identity; instead, she encourages us to think of it as a genre among genres. Canada may be a comparatively benign embodiment of the genre of the nation-state—but the nation-state is still a genre that threatens to absorb all genres. The nation-state is an economic, legal, and military construction that subsumes the local and the global. Robertson is suggesting, in other words, that Vancouver encompasses all nostalgias. Vancouver is not a world city in the sense of being a megalopolis—but it is a city of the world, subject both to the benefits and to the costs of globalization.

In effect, Robertson—who has lived in Cambridge, Paris, and Oakland—has written her native city a series of extraordinary love letters, the latest of which, *Magenta Soul Whip*, notes, "This work was completed in Roman Vancouver" (66), and ends with the colophon, "Vancouver—Paris—Oakland 1995–2007." The postscript of the 2006 *The Men: A Lyric Book* reads:

> *(In Vancouver as the dark winter tapered into spring*
> *I undertook to sing*
> *My life my body these words*
> *The men from a perspective.*
>
> *For all those who confuse*
> *Flirtation with monogamy*
> *I drain the golden glass*
>
> *They exit and glance upwards*
> *Adjust their little caps)* (69)

Although perhaps less "located" than her earlier work, the postscript gives a kind of performative grounding to an otherwise non–site specific text. The poem is a product of a vitalist body: "*My life my body*." To confuse flirtation with monogamy is to upset convention, to recognize play among rigorous distinctions, to add nuance to degrees of affiliation. Perhaps one can flirt with identities without losing one's grounding. Robertson has lived in at least three cultural capitals, and yet her writing remains tied to Vancouver. Perhaps her exilic writings should remind us that Vancouver is a site not just of immigration but also of emigration—not simply to the traditional Canadian urban hubs of Toronto and Montreal but to the world as a whole. Utopia is based upon regional exclusion; Vancouver, at its best, is not. As Robertson puts it so well: "we must recognize Utopia as an accretion of nostalgias with no object other than the historiography of the imaginary" ("How Pastoral" 23). *The Office for Soft Architecture* is such an accretion of nostalgias. Perhaps it takes the distance of an expatriate to create such an accretion. Nostalgias cannot be possessed, but they can be shared. Nostalgias show that every project of renovation entails a loss, as does every project of emigration. Likewise, every project of nationalistic self-identification entails a simplification of complex identities and histories. As Robertson writes, "It is too late to be simple" (*Office* 76). Robertson's soft architectural writings show that things were never simple in Vancouver. In the psychogeography of Vancouverites, the "dystopia of the obsolete" and the utopia of the imaginary may never have been all that far apart—somewhere between Surrey to the east and Wreck Beach to the west.

Notes

1 The Kootenay School of Writing (KSW) was founded in 1994 after the forced closure of David Thompson University Centre and its Writing Program in Nelson, British Columbia, Canada. KSW moved to Vancouver with the mandate of providing inexpensive courses, sponsoring critical talks, hosting reading series, and continuing to publish a writing magazine.

2 The seven walks of the book's title emerged from workshops Robertson led at the Kootenay School in 2001. Robertson's 1998 article "Visitations: City of Ziggurats," which provides an account of the Kootenay School's struggle to maintain its funding from the City of Vancouver, in many ways reads like a template for the book as a whole.

3 In recent years East Vancouver has been the centre of more controversy over urban land use than any other neighbourhood in Canada. The Vancouver poetry community and the Kootenay School of Writing have been extensively involved in advocating for affordable housing and in resisting gentrification. See in particular *Woodsquat: A Special Issue of West Coast Line* and "Urban Regeneration: Gentrification as Global Urban Strategy," by Neil Smith, and Jeff Derksen in *Stan Douglas: Every Building on 100 West Hastings*.

Works Cited

Benjamin, Walter. *Selected Writings*. Ed. Marcus Paul Bullock and Michael William Jennings. Vol. 1: 1913–1926. 4 vols. Cambridge: Belknap Press, 1996. Print.

Clover, Joshua. "The Adventures of Lisa Robertson in the Space of Flows." *Chicago Review* 51.4/52.1 (2006): 77–82. Print.

Debord, Guy. "Theory of the Dérive." *Situationist International Anthology*. Ed. Ken Knabb. Berkeley: Bureau of Public Secrets, 1981. 50–54. Print.

Derksen, Jeff, and Neil Smith. "Urban Regeneration: Gentrification as Global Urban Strategy." *Stan Douglas: Every Building on 100 West Hastings Street*. Ed. Reid Sheir. Vancouver: Contemporary Art Gallery/Arsenal Pulp Press, 2003. 63–92. Print.

Koolhaas, Rem. *Delirious New York: A Retroactive Manifesto for Manhattan*. New York: Monacelli Press, 1994. Print.

Robertson, Lisa. *The Apothecary*. Vancouver: Tsunami Editions, 1991. Print.

———. *Debbie: An Epic*. Vancouver: New Star Books, 1997. Print.

———. "How Pastoral: A Manifesto." *Telling It Slant: Avant-Garde Poetics of the 1990s*. Ed. Mark Wallace and Steven Marks. Tuscaloosa: U of Alabama P, 2002. 21–26. Print.

———. *Magenta Soul Whip*. Toronto: Coach House Books, 2009. Print.

———. *The Men*. Toronto: BookThug, 2007. Print.

———"My Eighteenth Century: Draft Towards a Cabinet." *Assembling Alternatives: Reading Postmodern Poetries Transnationally*. Ed. Romana Huk. Middletown: Wesleyan UP, 2003. 389–97. Print.

———. *Occasional Works and Seven Walks from the Office for Soft Architecture*. Astoria: Clear Cut Press, 2003. Print.

———. *Rousseau's Boat*. Vancouver: Nomados, 2004. Print.

———. "Visitations: City of Ziggurats." *Mix: The Magazine of Artist-Run Culture* 24.1 Summer 1998: 33–36. Print.

———. *The Weather*. Vancouver: New Star Books, 2001. Print.

———. *Xeclogue*. Vancouver: Tsunami Editions, 1993. Print.

Robertson, Lisa, and Steve McCaffery. *Philly Talks #17: Featuring Lisa Robertson, Steve McCaffery*. Curated by Louis Cabri. 2002. Slought Foundation. Web. 2010.

Scappetone, Jennifer. "Site Surfeit: Office for Soft Architecture Makes the City Confess." *Chicago Review* 51.4/52.1 (2006): 70–76. Print.

Shaw, Lytle. "Docents of Discourse: The Logic of Dispersed Sites." *boundary 2* 36.3 (2009): 25–37. Print.

Vidaver, Aaron, ed. *Woodsquat: A Special Issue of West Coast Line* 1.37/2–3 (2003/2004). Print.

Post-Frontier and Re-Definition of Space in *Tropic of Orange*

Hande Tekdemir

Widely acknowledged as a pioneering text on the history of the American West, Frederick Jackson Turner's famous 1893 speech, "The Significance of the Frontier in American History," has equally been criticized for championing American exceptionalism. In this controversial speech, which was delivered at the annual meeting of the American Historical Association, Turner articulates his thesis positing the frontier as a continuous westward expansion that has furnished the prototypical American character grounded on individualism and mobility. Turner claims that the census of 1890 "marks the closing of a historic movement" since the report declares that the frontier line of settlement has come to an end. As "the meeting point between savagery and civilization" (19), the frontier lies "at the hither edge of free land" (19–20), carrying a vital importance not only as free and available geography, but also as an open space on which equality and democracy can flourish, in turn promoting individualism and rapid political and economic progress, all of which came to shape the "uniquely" American character. In Turner's thesis, the distinctively American disposition, as practical, egalitarian, and democratic, was considered gradually to come into being with the advance of American settlement westward when the pioneers encountered the wilderness (49–50). Coming from Europe to settle along the Atlantic coast, the first settlers brought with them European ideas, which they then gradually institutionalized and "Americanized" according to the local needs. The progress from primitive to a more advanced society—a "by-product of the Enlightenment," alternately called "the frontier movement, Manifest Destiny, California Dreaming"—necessitated a dialectical relationship between the frontier and the colonist (Lehan 207). As much as the pioneers changed the landscape, the wilderness in turn affected the progressing Europeans:

> The wilderness masters the colonist. It finds him a European in dress, industries, tools, modes of travel, and thought.... It strips off the garments of civilization and arrays him in the hunting shirt and the moccasin.... Moving westward, the frontier became more and more American.... Thus the advance of the frontier has meant a steady movement away from the influence of Europe, a steady growth of independence on American lines. (Turner 20)

Hence, Turner relates the emergence of the American character to the *constant* move from the Atlantic to the Pacific coast and a continuous return to the earliest stages of expansion:

> Thus American development has exhibited not merely advance along a single line, but a return to primitive conditions on a continually advancing frontier line, and a new development for that area. American social development has been continually beginning over again on the frontier. This perennial rebirth, this fluidity of American life, this expansion westward with its new opportunities, its continuous touch with the simplicity of primitive society, furnish the forces dominating American character. The true point of view in the history of this nation is not the Atlantic coast, it is the great West. (19)

Indeed, it is the continuous process and the recurrence of the move that differentiates American social development from others in Europe, where the expanding people either developed within a restrictive area or clashed with other peoples during expansion. In the American case, however, each move westward meant a new beginning rather than closure.

Turner's historiography, briefly outlined above, undoubtedly projects an unabashedly one-sided perspective on American advancement. Instead of questioning the theory itself, however, I will consider Turner's argument as the reflection of the progressive, entrepreneurial spirit of an emerging nation and examine the (ir)relevance of its utopic impulse for the contemporary world. While Turner's thesis has been contested by various historians since the 1960s, recent scholarship on the American West, particularly by New Western historians, such as Patricia Nelson Limerick, has emphasized the complex, non-linear, and multicultural aspect of the frontier experience. In *The Legacy of Conquest,* Limerick argues that Turner's ethnocentric and nationalistic thesis prioritized English-speaking white men while disregarding the contribution of female, non-white, and French-speaking populations to American history (21). His theory, moreover, applied primarily to agrarian settlement, which excluded various other lands, such as deserts, mountains, mines, etc. Rather than discrediting the thesis itself, Limerick offers as a solution the inclusion of twentieth-century events and a rejuvenative reading of the frontier thesis within a more global scale: "Deemphasize the frontier and its supposed end, conceive of the West as a place and not a process, and Western American history has a new look" (26–27).

As an apt illustration of Limerick's revision of the Turner thesis, I would like to focus on Karen Tei Yamashita's 1997 novel *Tropic of Orange,* which lends itself to an exploration of the intersections between historical and contemporary literary representations of the American West, particularly with respect to the politics of space, set against the backdrop of the post-NAFTA landscape. *Tropic of Orange* takes the frontier thesis quite literally and, in doing so, complicates the primarily utopic impulse behind Turner's theory by not only retrospectively displaying dystopic elements associated with the story of expansion, but also revising the post-frontier experience for the renewed conditions of the globalized world. In what follows, I first examine the way the novel can be seen as a parody of the conquest narrative in terms of its caricaturing of land settlement and territorialization. I then consider the influence of the changing conditions of global capitalism on the novel's politics of space, which presents the American West as an exciting place of global connectivity through the region's confluence of people and goods that ultimately serves the exploitation of human capital.

In "The Ends of America, the Ends of Postmodernism," Rachel Adams criticizes the arbitrary periodization of postmodernism as an uninterrupted period of time that extends from World War II to the present. She persuasively argues that the remarkable variety of the different historical contexts during the course of the second half of the twentieth century, particularly the recent outcomes of globalization, render such periodization incoherent. Opting for a more careful distinction between American literary postmodernism and what she calls "globalization of American literature," Adams traces the genealogy of the changing perspective on contemporary

American culture and literature by marking the late 1980s as the transitory phase between the two periods. "[T]he dominant form of avant-garde literary experimentalism during the Cold War" of the former period corresponded to a context "marked by the ascendance of transnational corporations, the upheavals of decolonization, fears of nuclear holocaust, and the partitioning of the globe into ideological spheres" (250). American literary globalism, on the other hand, witnessed an exciting period of transformation and reaction to high postmodernism, marked by an increasing interest in global processes, such as "unprecedented integration of the world's markets, technologies, and systems of governance; surprising and innovative new forms of cultural fusion; and the mobilization of political coalitions across the lines of race, class, and other identitarian categories" (250–51). The move from postmodernism to globalism, as Adams explicates, took place in the form of different treatments of "California and its environs" (251). For instance, while *The Crying of Lot 49*, as a representative text from the former period, portrays the region as the dead end of the westering impulse, the Southern California that appears in Yamashita's novel is an exciting place of dense networking where people and goods constantly move across regional and national boundaries that are nullified through global interconnection.

Taking Rachel Adams' assertions as a starting point, I would like to argue that the confluence of people and global markets in Los Angeles not only presents us with a vital image of a dynamic city, but also displays a place that is teeming with tension. Indeed, *Tropic of Orange* involves various disastrous incidents that are part of a dystopic noir world. The novel's apocalyptic portrayal of Los Angeles is enhanced through disconnected events as diverse as a wide network of child-organ-smuggling, environmental problems because of global warming, a highly dangerous orange scare that turns out to be a global threat, and a serious traffic jam on a Los Angeles freeway that results in the confiscation of abandoned cars by the homeless. The cast of main characters covers a multitude of ethnic communities that inhabit Los Angeles, represented by seven individual figures—Manzanar, Gabriel, Rafaela, Bobby, Emi, Buzzworm, and the partially supernatural character Arcangel—all of whom exemplify a marginal status. Though each incident and character might at first seem irrelevant to the others, the novel, in the final analysis, underlines the subtle connections among people, goods, and events in the globalized world. The title of the novel refers to a contaminated orange, originally grown where the imaginary line of Tropic of Cancer runs through a garden in Mazatlan, which is then transported across Mexico and over the border to Los Angeles. As Arcangel moves northward with a group of Mexicans to meet the allegorical characterization of NAFTA in a wrestling match, the Tropic of Cancer, wrapped around the orange, also moves with them, emphasizing the fragility of maps and borders.

Yamashita's portrayal of the move north as a collision, as much as an expansion of people, insinuates that any story of conquest will inevitably involve conflict among opposing groups. In the globalized world in which nonlinear understandings of time and space dominate, where objects and people constantly cross and recross each other's paths, any theory of progress that merely advocates linearity and unhindered expansion over space is surely doomed to fail. In Turner's vision of the frontier experience, the interaction of people at the front line is maintained through a hierarchical structure. While he saw Native Indians as an intrinsic part of nature—so much so that he faded them into the background—he did not pay attention to the interaction among different ethnic groups as much as he paid attention to the strife between human beings and nature. As Limerick points out, "Only in imagination could virgin lands move smoothly into the hands of new owners, transforming wilderness to farmland, idle men to productive citizens" (60). His story of expansion remains just a "Jeffersonian ideal" when one includes the Native Indians as the deep-rooted residents of the land and the other Europeans as conquerors who settled on the front line before the English (60). Indeed, Turner's thesis rests on a utopic vision that remained only in theory: that all men had equal rights to claim land. Instead, what happened in practice was confiscation of land from the less strong and unarmed. Hence, any claim for "natural rights" quite easily turned into a physical and material display of power.

In the figure of the prophetic artist Arcangel, who alternately appears as a worker, a performance artist reciting political poetry, a professional wrestler, and in various other guises, Yamashita rewrites the "utopic" aspect of the Jeffersonian ideal. By highlighting the violence and injustice behind what appears to be the Manifest Destiny taken over by this enigmatic character, who calls himself a "pilgrim," Yamashita suggests an affinity—albeit one that is persistently negated—with the Mayflower pilgrims who arrived at Plymouth hundreds of years before. Carrying "the beauty of an ancient body" and speaking "a jumble of unknown dialects, guttural and whining, Latin mixed with every aboriginal, colonial, slave, or immigrant tongue," Arcangel seems to give voice to the marginalized and the downtrodden—those who have been cast aside by official history (47). It is noteworthy that the so-called Manifest Destiny in the novel is from the south to the north, rather than from the east to the west. As Sue-Im Lee argues, Arcangel's route towards north is "[a]llegorical of labor's movement from the south to the north, from the Third World to the First" (504). During the course of the novel, it becomes evident that Arcangel has been walking across the southern hemisphere for five hundred years, and performing in an impressive range of genres, such as epics, musicals, and tragedy, for people from all walks of life.

Arcangel thus emerges as a perpetual reminder of a whole continent's bloody history, as he commemorates crucial dates under threat of erasure, such as the Bay of Pigs invasion, the treaty of Guadalupe Hidalgo, and the great "discovery" of the New World, and keeps certain revolutionary names, such as Simón Bolívar, Eva Peron, Che, and Tachito Somoza, alive in his artistic performance. He is also a walking testimony to the ongoing exploitation of the dispossessed: he witnesses Haitian farmers slashing cane, Guatemalans loading trucks with bananas and corn, Indians mining tin in the Cerro Rico—all to be exported north in return for "progress, technology, loans and loaded guns" (145–46). Indeed, he literally embodies the resistance of the south against the oppression and violence of the North American exploitative policy. As the embodiment of extreme corporeality, Arcangel can miraculously move a truck loaded with oranges so that he can release the blocked traffic in a Mexican marketplace, or move a broken bus across the U.S.-Mexican border with the people following him (75, 197). His corporeal resistance is quite evident in a climactic scene at the end of the novel when he appears in the guise of a famous Mexican wrestler, EL GRAN MOJADO, to meet SUPERNAFTA in a professional wrestling match organized at the Pacific Rim Stadium in Los Angeles. By emphasizing the clash of the continent halves after a significant change in land topography, the "unofficial" or "unaccustomed" version of the Manifest Destiny in *Tropic of Orange* posits a counter-discourse to the story of conquest. Arcangel's performance and pilgrimage can be seen as either an enactment of an anti-conquest narrative, or as a return of the repressed. The actual border crossing from Mexico to Los Angeles revives the suppressed memory of South Americans and the damage caused by the European conquerors, such as the elimination of pre-Columbian treasure; the halls of Moctezuma; 40,000 Aztecs; and the spreading of diseases and infection, such as smallpox, TB, meningitis, E. coli, and influenza (200).

In a way that is highly reminiscent of Turner's advancing frontier line, Yamashita re-enacts and subverts the story of westward movement through various other subtle modifications. Both formally and contextually, the novel illustrates disrespect for borders and calls for a retrospective look at the arbitrariness of the land distribution that is intricately connected with the image of the "democratic" American West. As Limerick argues,

> Western history is a story structured by the drawing of lines and the marking of borders. From macrocosm to microcosm, from imperial struggles for territory to the parceling out of townsite claims, Western American history was an effort first to draw lines dividing the West into manageable units of property and then to persuade people to treat those lines with respect. (55)

Contrary to the unquestioning attitude toward fencing in the traditional accounts of land settlement, *Tropic of Orange* questions the fictionality (hence the "fantasy") of the idea behind putting up fences. The grid called "hypertext" that appears at the beginning of the novel, for instance, marks the temporal and spiritual borders of characters' accounts, though the individual stories cannot simply remain confined and, ultimately, transgress their boundaries to impinge on each other's narratives. In terms of content, the move northward of the chaotic crowd, with "its Latin birds and American beers" (134), can be seen as a caricaturing of the unlawful appropriation of land as part of the westward movement.

The story of the gangs and their territorial claim confusion is juxtaposed against the narration of the uncontrollable mob that disturbs geographical boundaries between the northern and southern hemispheres. As a heavy-handed indication of unofficially enforced jurisdiction and the violence connected to it, the gangs are portrayed through their inability to make a truce because of shifting geography. While consulting Buzzworm, an African-American self-appointed social worker who provides assistance to the marginalized, a gang member, ignorant of the displacement of the Tropic of Cancer, recounts the effects of the enigmatic topographical changes that have been happening recently: "We might be dropping out, but the hood's what we know, like the tattoos on our arms. You don't understand the demographics, you don't understand nothing. And someone's movin' it around" (188). Through the gang member's diatribe, Yamashita points at the futility of the idea of territorialization in the rapidly changing world.

In criticizing the misconception that human beings can unproblematically take over and taxonomize land, Yamashita's novel shares a similar approach to Limerick's challenge to the old West's absolutist politics of space:

> White Americans saw the acquisition of property as a cultural imperative, manifestly the right way to go about things. There was one appropriate way to treat land—divide it, distribute it, register it. This relationship to physical matter seems to us so commonplace that we must struggle to avoid taking it for granted, to grasp instead the vastness of the continent and the enormous project of measuring, allocating, and record keeping involved in turning the open expanses of North America into transferable parcels of real estate. Like the settlers themselves, we steadfastly believe in the social fiction that lines on a map and signatures on a deed legitimately divide the earth. (55–56)

In the novel, the only "successful" incident of land acquisition is given as an impractical and romantic enterprise, taken up by the Chicano newspaper reporter Gabriel, whose "spontaneous, sudden passion for the acquisition of land" (5), coupled with his desire to feel close to his roots, results in the purchase of a house in Mexico:

> Still the project continued in alternating states of disarray or progress. He seemed to be building a spacious hacienda, maybe a kind of old style ranchero, circa 1800, with rustic touches, thick adobe-like walls and beams, but with modern appliances. But then again, finishing depended on having money and being able to translate his vision to others. He showed the workers scraps of photos torn from slick architectural magazines: tile work, hot tubs, wet bars, arches, decks, and landscaping. Everyone agreed his ideas were all very beautiful. Old-fashioned, but beautiful. The plans expanded, then diminished; swelled with possibility, then shrank with reality. . . . After eight years, the house—the part that was finally constructed—needed painting again. (6)

As a parody of the pioneering spirit, Gabriel's nostalgic vision functions as an exemplary case of inventing an idyllic past with wooden houses and various other artifacts that no longer exist and are therefore inapplicable to the present. Moreover, in contrast with Turner's agricultural paradise in which "farmers were the central figures of [the] frontier story" (5), Gabriel's useless tilling of land turns into a literal struggle: "Gabriel insisted on planting trees that couldn't survive in this climate" (19). Gabriel's futile attempt shows the unproductive aspect of the human subject's interference with the "natural" environment, and, in doing so, problematizes and complicates the Turnerian treatment of the relationship between space and human beings in arbitrary terms:

> America's hope thus lay in westward expansion—in the extended opportunities for the growing population to acquire property and for the nation to remain at the happy and virtuous stage of agriculture. In America, Thomas Jefferson said, "we have an immensity of land courting the industry of the husbandman. . . . Those who labor in the earth are the chosen people of God, if ever He had a chosen people, whose breasts He has made His peculiar deposit for substantial and genuine virtue." (Limerick 58)

The correlation between the westward expansion and Gabriel's unsuccessful ventures into agriculture might at first seem far-fetched, but the author seems to be highlighting this affinity with the allusion to the oranges brought from elsewhere. As Wallace argues, "While *Tropic of Orange* is clearly global in its contextual reach, its focus is the hemisphere—its colonial history and its neoclassical present. The orange quite explicitly symbolizes this history, oranges having been brought to the continent by Columbus himself" (155). Yamashita recalls and repudiates the story of conquest by conjuring up the image of the orange that, in her story, is brought south from the north. Contrary to the "blooming garden" of Columbus, it pursues a deviant and unnatural development and ends up being dried up as a result of global warming:

> The tree was a sorry one, and so was the orange. Rafaela knew it was an orange that should not have been. It was much too early. Everyone said the weather was changing. The rains came sooner this year. . . . The tree had been fooled, and little pimples of budding flowers began to burst through its branches. And then came a sudden period of dry weather; the flowers withered away, except for this one. (11)

Hence, through various defamiliarization techniques concerning fencing, territorialization, and cultivation of land, the novel caricatures land settlement by underlining the fictionality and arbitrariness of the story of conquest that render its ideology impertinent for contemporary practices.

Wrought with the circumstances of globalization, Yamashita's novel counters the image of the expanding world with that of a highly claustrophobic portrayal of space. More often than not, globalization is defined as a story about the opening up of boundaries, transgression of national territories, interaction among different cultures, accelerated movement of capital, and constant flow of information, goods, and people around the globe. Yet it is, at the same time, the same forces that victimize a certain group of people and subtly condemn them to be even more imprisoned in their local environment. In the novel, this paradoxical reciprocity is most effectively demonstrated in the illustration of freeways. As a twentieth-century innovation and a typical symbolic representation of Los Angeles, the sprawling network of freeways corresponds to fast movement without encumbrance. The cluttered but harmonious vision of the freeways is enhanced by the Japanese-American surgeon, Manzanar, who has quit his job to become a conductor of what he calls "an organic living entity" (37). Standing on an overpass among skyscrapers, he flings his baton to and fro to conduct an imaginative freeway "orchestra" that runs "below and beyond his feet in every direction, pumping and pulsating, the blood connection, the great heartbeat of a great city" (35). Yet, as ensuing events in the novel reveal, it takes only one accident that causes a major SigAlert to disturb the idyllic and allegorical representation of uninterrupted space. Blocked by traffic, drivers are obliged to abandon their cars on the freeway, which are then taken over by the homeless population.

As in the case of the traffic jam on the freeway, space is presented in the novel as both unlimited and blocked, ultimately giving rise to a mob. On the one hand, *Tropic of Orange* is very much a story about rootedness in which characters are immobile to the point of being paralyzed, even trapped, so that they are unable get out of their local community or neighbourhood. On the other hand, the novel, as Rachel Lee also asserts, displays heightened awareness of how America is being transformed by the massive demographic and perspectival shifts wrought by globalization (268). In this way, the new American West becomes part and parcel of the globalized network:

> The novel argues the need to conceive of a new collective subject positioning that can express the accelerated movement of capital and humans traversing the world. Set in Mexico and Los Angeles, the novel

highlights the transnational crisscrossing of labor, goods, resources, languages, and cultures in the late twentieth century, and its characters whose formally disparate lives, separated by oceans and continents, are brought into hitherto unknown proximity and interconnectedness with each other. (S. Lee 502)

Such interconnectivity is clearly brought about by the changing conditions of globalization. Let us now examine those conditions that seem to compress the expanding world so that various goods, people, and cultures are brought together in a single location.

In *The Condition of Postmodernity,* David Harvey describes the "overwhelming sense of *compression* of our spatial and temporal worlds" as the adjustment of what was accepted to be the objective qualities of time and space that were previously considered independently of material processes; yet further analysis reveals "hidden terrains of ambiguity, contradiction, and struggle" behind the contemporary conception of space and time (240, 205). On the one hand, Harvey underlines the relationship between cultural production that is broadly defined as modernist and postmodernist culture, *and* the material practices that appear in different modes of production. On the other hand, he historicizes the conceptualization of time and space according to the evolving nature of this relationship. Arguing that Fordism and flexible accumulation are not merely different forms of production but also distinctive ways of life, Harvey connects the transition from the former to the latter mode of production with the transition from modernist to postmodernist culture that happened in the 1970s. Since then, we have witnessed a speeding up the pace of our lives and an overcoming of spatial boundaries to such an extent that "the world sometimes seems to collapse inward upon us" (240). This collapse corresponds to what Harvey calls the "time-space compression" and interchangeably affects socio-economic conditions: "we have been experiencing, these last two decades, an intense phase of time-space compression that has had a disorienting and disruptive impact upon political-economic practices, the balance of class power, as well as upon cultural and social life" (284).

The crisis of Fordism and the shift to flexible accumulation is an international phenomenon, which, according to Harvey, reflects a crisis on multiple levels: geographical, geopolitical, struggle between classes, and struggle between the state and corporate power (186). By centralizing capital and how it travels across the world, Harvey discusses modernization as a cross-cultural experience based on spatial development. Moreover, as much as conception of time and space changes according to the different material practices of different locations, it is also constantly modified by capitalism's ever-changing mode of production. According to Harvey, the rise of capitalism, due to its "revolutionary mode of production" which is dependent on a constant refinement of material practices and processes, inevitably poses a challenge to the stability of objective qualities of space and time (204). Once it goes through transformation, different conceptions of time and space also change material conditions. What is most "postmodern" about Harvey's methodology is the fact that this collusion does not take place in a linear progression: there is no single and predetermined conception of time or space "against which we can measure the diversity of human conceptions and perceptions" (203).

It is this type of indeterminacy and the sense of speeding up that marks the conception of time and space in *Tropic of Orange*, as opposed to the rational and deterministic approach toward space projected by the Enlightenment thinkers and exemplified, as Harvey aptly demonstrates, in the homesteading system and land settlement:

> The pulverization and fragmentation of the space of the United States along such rationalistic lines was thought to (and in some respects indeed did) imply maximum individual liberty to move and settle in a reasonably egalitarian way in the spirit of a property-owning and agrarian democracy. The Jeffersonian vision was ultimately subverted, but at least up until the Civil War there was enough truth in its practical meaning to give some credence to the idea that the United States, precisely because of its open spatial organization, was the land where the utopian visions of the Enlightenment might be realized. . . . The pulverization of space, which Jeffersonian land politics presumed would open the way to an egalitarian democracy, ended up being a means that facilitated the proliferation of capitalist social relations. It provided a remarkably open framework within which money power could operate with few of the constraints encountered in Europe. (256–57)

The egalitarian vision of the westward expansion thus turns unexpectedly into a system of exploitation, a system that facilitates the free and fast flow of capital in and out of the country, which is effectively portrayed in *Tropic of Orange*. Accompanying the physical movement of the land is the story of the constant flow of commodities and people—or people as commodities—across the border and around the globe. The most dramatic case of the commodification of human beings is the surreal scene of border crossing from south to north when the crossing of thousands of people is accompanied by "the waves of floating paper money: pesos and dollars and reals, all floating across effortlessly—a graceful movement of free capital, at least 45 billion dollars of it, carried across by hidden and cheap labor. Hundreds of thousands of the unemployed surged forward—the blessings of monetary devaluation that thankfully wiped out those nasty international trade deficits" (200). As Adams asserts, Yamashita's novel displays "vast inequities, economic interconnections, and movement of people and goods associated with globalization" (249). The gradual progression of Mexican people toward the north is accompanied by diverse stories of exploitation, ranging from an international organ-smuggling ring to a spiked orange import-export business. Los Angeles is given in such a way that it is the endpoint of all products; yet it also serves as a departure point for the goods to be taken south or across the Pacific. The city thus functions as both the land of promise and a place of disillusionment. Yamashita portrays this dual position with a touch of humour when Raphael asks Gabriel to send some faucets down to Mexico, since she believes that they are cheaper in Los Angeles. When the faucets arrive by mail and Raphael picks them up from the hotel to which they have been delivered, and opens the package right away, the prying hotel manager is amused to point out to her that the faucets are "Hecho en México" (68). This is a dramatic account of the human and labour exploitation behind the ongoing global capitalism. While the faucets are more expensive in Mexico, where they are originally produced, they lose their value as they travel up to Los Angeles for export all around the world.

The constant appearance of oranges and their export and import throughout the narrative also indicate the global connectivity that finds a nodal point in Los Angeles. Yamashita's imagined geographies challenge national territories so that one retrospectively starts perceiving the North American continent as a community, yet one with a wholly different set of interrelationships. In an illuminating conversation, Buzzworm corrects the street peddler Margarita, who claims that the oranges on sale are "imported from Florida": "'If it's Florida, it's not imported. Same country, you see. If it's México, it's imported.' 'Por qué? Florida's more far away than México'" (85). As the conversation implies, the post-NAFTA landscape of the narrative posits the inextricable link between Mexico and Los Angeles—referred to as "the second largest city of Mexico" in the novel. However, the destabilization of the Tropic of Cancer represents interdependency, not only between the United States and Mexico, but also more globally between north and south. Indeed, "the novel draws attention to the divide between north and south that Immanuel Wallerstein has described as one of the great geopolitical polarities of the twenty-first century" (Adams 262). As Wallace points out, it is not through the U.S.–Mexican border, but through the Tropic of Cancer, as a displaced global border, that Yamashita chooses to configure her post-NAFTA landscape (152). In this way, border crossing and challenges posited to it involve more than a national territory: they are located within a larger geopolitical context. In her discussion of the influence of transnationalism in Yamashita's novels, Sue-Im Lee asserts that "Globalization as a force of deterritorialization is a constant interest in all of Yamashita's novels, as she explores the unmooring of fixed ethnic, national, and geographical identities and of established categories by which humans are organized and distinguished" (503). Although NAFTA is a free-trade zone agreement particularly among the United States, Mexico, and Canada, it inevitably transgresses its regional boundaries to be involved with the politics of contemporary transnationalism. Indeed, as it is later found out, the toxic oranges, spiked with a deadly chemical, were imported not from Florida, as Margarita had claimed, but from the south. "Oranges from Brazil via Honduras. Is that the normal route?" asks Gabriel of a legitimate brokerage in El Segundo. This brokerage explicates the complicated transportation network that makes it impossible to trace an original departure location for oranges imported from Mexico under flexible free-trade quotas: "Well, say Brazil's quota for oranges is exhausted, then Brazil exports to Honduras. Honduras to Guatemala, Guatemala to México, and Mexico to the U.S. Then it's cool even though everyone knows the orange harvest is dead in México in June. Keeps everyone in business" (244). Similarly, the infant organ "trade," smuggling infant hearts and kidneys for transplantation, is accelerated by the free trade agreement between the United States and Mexico. Gabriel's efforts to find and report a breaking storyline on the actual origins of these criminal "free trade" organizations are hindered by the subtle networking system based on indeterminate boundaries. NAFTA can no longer be confined to a region: it unavoidably belongs to a complicated network shaped by the ruthless forces of *global* capitalism.

The post-NAFTA landscape that is projected in Yamashita's novel portrays not only the unsettlement of the U.S.–Mexican border, but also the American West's dubious involvement with the Pacific Rim. Referring to Dirlik in her analysis of the organization of capital in the late twentieth century, Rachel Lee posits that "the modern incarnation of the 'Pacific Rim' began as a parallel initiative to the European economic community and anticipated the formalization of the North American Free Trade Agreement (NAFTA)" (234). Indeed, the constant flow of people in the novel involves the Asia-Pacific region as a crucial node of the global confluence. Though Yamashita does not dwell on the economic potential of the region, the novel occasionally underlines the idea that Los Angeles is "the very last point West" but also a new beginning when one takes into consideration the "great Pacific stretching along its great rim, brimming over long coastal shores from one hemisphere to the other" (170). Together with the southern hemisphere and the central Americas, the Pacific Rim thus emerges as what Rachel Lee calls the "extension of the United States' discourse of Manifest Destiny" (235).

The amalgamation of diverse goods, people, regions and cultures in the American West projects an image of the region in general, and the city of Los Angeles in particular, as a place where the globe has condensed. If globalization is indeed a multinoded mixing of "national, cultural, racial components," as Rachel Lee claims, then L.A. is quintessentially a global city (239), "an entrepot to the world," "a true pivot of the four quarters," "a congeries of East, West, North and South" (Soja qtd. in Wallace 154). The novel, however, goes far beyond a naive celebration of cultural diversity in the city—an attitude that frequently reduces the concept of the "melting pot" to nothing more than the co-existence of diverse cuisines. As an appropriate example of this reductionist approach, a white woman dining in a sushi restaurant announces, "I love living in L.A. because I can find anything in the world to eat, right here," calling the city "a meeting place for all sorts of people," "[a] true celebration of an international world" (129). Through giving voice to conflicting opinions about such issues as multiculturalism and global connectivity, the novel's spatial politics ultimately displays great sensitivity toward those who see internationalization as merely extending the wonders of the world's cuisine. As a counterpoint to the argument of the white woman in the sushi restaurant, Yamashita's critical take on cultural and global confluence is most effectively given in the Chinese character Bobby, who is actually a "Chinese from Singapore with a Vietnam name speaking like a Mexican living in Koreatown" (15). His retrospective narration reveals that he secretly joined a camp of Vietnamese refugees who escaped from Vietnam to Singapore after the Vietnam War. Passing for Vietnamese under the name "Ngu" and unnoticed by the American guards who can't distinguish among "Asians," Bobby was taken to America, together with the Vietnamese refugees. As a "model minority," Bobby struggles hard to earn a living and supply for his family, with his inner voice preoccupied with financial matters, such as his mortgage, car payment, and life insurance. Bobby's reluctance to pay a smuggling fee to help out his twelve-year-old cousin stuck in Tijuana presents a caricatured image of a "model minority" who is crudely materialistic. However, the novel urges the reader to take into consideration the coercive social conditions that necessitate financial freedom if one is to be recognized at all as an individual.

The extreme alienation and estrangement of characters are enhanced by the rising significance of cyberspace technologies that are essential for information flow. In the contemporary world, Harvey notes, "[t]he certainty of absolute space and place gave way to the insecurities of a shifting relative space, in which events in one place could have immediate and ramifying effects in several other places" (261). This "instantaneous communicability" is made available through "improved systems of communication and information flow, coupled with rationalizations in techniques of distribution" (288, 285). Indeed, it is with the help of the television producer Emi's multiple monitors and high-tech readability that the homeless encampment on the freeway can be broadcast nationwide. Moreover, through various forms of technical equipment, Emi functions as Gabriel's replacement, keeping track of his multiple storylines and getting in touch with him when he is in Mexico. As in various other cases, the author displays great sensitivity toward including both constructive and debilitating effects of the same phenomenon. The fact that the international organ trade can be conducted and monitored through a kind of satellite tracking system proves the abusive potential of high-tech facilities. Frustrated by his fruitless attempts to find the prime movers of worldwide criminal activity, Gabriel finally gives up: "I no longer looked for a resolution to the loose threads hanging off my storylines. If I had begun to understand anything, I now knew they were simply the warp and woof of a fraying net of conspiracies in *an expanding universe* where the holes only seemed to get larger and larger" (248–49; emphasis added). In scenarios of both positive and negative consequences, what the novel's politics of space is engaged with is much more than a physical location that is conquered, settled, or simply contested.

The overall image of the American West in *Tropic of Orange* is hence far from being the land of wealth, equality, progress, and self-realization. On the one hand, natural phenomena, such as fires, extreme weather conditions, strange mutations in land topography, and appearance of unexpected fauna and flora (such as the accidental presence of crabs inland) are strongly reminiscent of a noir world just about to meet an apocalyptic end. On the other hand, underneath the random interaction of the characters, their lack of communication, or any sort of human connection lies a starkly dystopic urban environment where the globally facilitated flow of human traffic serves the exploitation of human labour, and indeed of the human body itself, i.e. international organ trade. Posited against the surreal atmosphere of the wrestling match, which symbolically puts on stage the politics of NAFTA, the final reunification of the only family at the novel's conclusion might seem to revive the quintessential human relationship. The fragility of the bond between Bobby and Raphael, however, is paradoxically strengthened by the invisible cords/borders that keep them separate from each other. Bobby's unrequited embrace that makes him look "like he's flying" turns him into a ghostly figure, floating in space, never to reach its destination. This is what happens, the novel seems to suggest, when neoliberal politics of global connectivity renders space indeterminate and much less palpable: it prevents basic human touch between individuals who are destined to be close, yet still so far from one another.

Works Cited

Adams, Rachel. "The Ends of America, the Ends of Postmodernism." *Twentieth-Century Literature* 53.3 (2007): 248–72. *JStor*. Web. 15 Sept. 2011.

Harvey, David. *The Condition of Postmodernity*. Cambridge: Blackwell, 1990. Print.

Lee, Rachel. "Asian American Cultural Production in Asian-Pacific Perspective." *Boundary 2* 26.2 (1999): 231–54. *JStor*. Web. 15 Sept. 2011.

Lee, Sue-Im. "'We Are Not the World': Global Village, Universalism, and Karen Tei Yamashita's *Tropic of Orange*." *Modern Fiction Studies* 52.3 (2007): 501–27. *Project MUSE*. Web. 15 Sept. 2011.

Lehan, Richard. *The City in Literature: An Intellectual and Cultural History*. Berkeley: U of California P, 1998. Print.

Limerick, Patricia Nelson. *The Legacy of Conquest: The Unbroken Past of the American West*. New York: W.W. Norton & Company, 1987. Print.

Turner, Frederick Jackson. "The Significance of the Frontier in American History." *Does the Frontier Experience Make America Exceptional?* Ed. Richard W. Etulain. Boston: Bedford/St. Martin's, 1999. 18–43. Print.

Wallace, Molly. "Tropics of Globalization." *Symploké* 9:1-2 (2001): 145–60. *JStor*. Web. 5 Sept. 2011.

Yamashita, Karen Tei. *Tropic of Orange*. Minneapolis: Coffee House Press, 1997. Print.

Our Posthuman Adolescence

Dystopia, Information Technologies, and the Construction of Subjectivity in M.T. Anderson's Feed

Richard Gooding

If the didactic qualities of dystopian fiction, like those of science fiction in its "hard" philosophical tradition, lend themselves to young adult (YA) literature's preoccupation with raising social awareness among youth, dystopias for young readers are not simply less cognitively taxing versions of their adult counterparts. Privileging adolescent points of view, YA fiction inverts power relations between young and old; paradoxically, it also promises young readers that a better life awaits in a world adults have prepared. These qualities resist the inexorable logic of classic dystopian literature, and YA dystopias typically culminate in revolutions and escapes that tax the patience of older readers. While Kazuo Ishiguro's transplantation dystopia *Never Let Me Go* ends with the protagonist resignedly contemplating her future as an organ donor, the closing pages of Neal Shusterman's YA counterpart, *Unwind,* see teen suicide bombers blow up a transplantation facility, allowing the protagonists to escape to a utopian settlement. That this new home is designed and safeguarded by adults discloses YA literature's ambivalence about the world adults have created: that world may be profoundly flawed, but at the same time it offers the young safe harbour.

The difficulty of reconciling dystopian pessimism with the traditional hopefulness of writing for younger readers becomes even more pronounced in imagined societies where technology troubles long-standing assumptions about subjectivity. Here YA literature's perennial concern with identity formation may recoil at assaults to a liberal humanist model of the self as autonomous, self-directing, and rational. In Scott Westerfeld's *Uglies* series, all but the most radical alterations to brain chemistry (those resulting in death) are reversible through sheer effort by the subject who longs to reclaim her former self (that desire indicating a persistent core humanity), and the language of computer hardware is co-opted as an expression of a liberal-humanist ideal of free will as subjects figuratively "rewire" themselves to restore their former identities.

In the 1990s, these narrative outcomes were widely perceived as tenacious and embarrassing testimonials to the inferiority of YA dystopias. Recently, however, attention has shifted to young readers' responses and the genre's constitutive qualities. Maria Nikolajeva contends that the children's dystopia overcomes juvenile literature's habitual hopefulness only insofar as it alienates readers from the focalizing characters' "naiveté or . . . failing morals" (88), while Kay Sambell identifies not simplistic reassurances but "hesitation, oscillation, and ambiguity" ("Presenting the Case" 171) and argues that these qualities may dissuade adolescent readers from "responding with despair or distress" to life's harsh realities ("Carnivalizing the Future" 263). This critical recalibration is underwritten by academic interest in dystopian literature's capacity to recover and regulate utopian elements. For example, in their ambitious study of the utopian impulse in juvenile literature, Bradford et al. posit a model of "transformative utopianism," through which utopian and dystopian tropes alike "promote and advocate transformative possibilities" for society (5). These qualities, they argue, permit YA literature to preserve its habitual hopefulness by treating the dystopia as a way of constituting a better world, whether that world is explicitly realized inside the text or, by implication, outside. In the discussion that follows I continue this revaluation by applying the model of the "critical dystopia" to M.T. Anderson's *Feed*. The term, coined by Lyman Tower Sargent in an influential 1994 essay (10), designates a subgenre that "retrieve[s] the progressive possibilities inherent in dystopian narrative" (Baccolini and Moylan 8) while exhibiting a capacity for blending disparate genres (Donawerth 29–30). The incorporative capacity of the critical dystopia, I argue, allows for an integration of YA and dystopian elements that extends beyond the thematics of any imagined future and opens up new representational possibilities.

One of the most critically acclaimed YA dystopias to appear in recent years, *Feed* belongs to a class of crossover texts that, like Philip Pullman's counterfactual trilogy *His Dark Materials*, reverses the pattern of reception of works like *Nineteen Eighty-Four*, *Brave New World*, and *The Handmaid's*

Tale, which address a primarily adult readership but have become staples of adolescent reading in and beyond the high school curriculum. It achieves this by retaining the relentlessly bleak plot of an adult dystopia while reducing the range of discursive possibilities available to its characters to the point that adolescence becomes the dominant subject position for all ages. Marketed for young readers, Anderson's tale of consumerism in a posthuman information age has nonetheless attracted an extensive adult readership and garnered considerable academic attention, which almost invariably treats *Feed* as a classically dystopian narrative and its focalizer, Titus, as a callow teen irredeemably corrupted by late capitalist consumer culture. Viewed as a critical dystopia, however, *Feed* sustains readings that are considerably less bleak than the critical consensus suggests: the very technologies the novel resists point to the possibility of developing new kinds of ethically mature subject positions in a posthuman world, a possibility that inheres most forcibly in the ways the posthuman condition troubles Titus' narrative style.

Resisting the Feed

Anderson's novel is set several generations hence, when almost three quarters of Americans are interpellated into a culture of frenetic consumerism through brain implants that connect them to the feed, a distant descendent of the Internet. Through the feed, various corporations—American Feedware, Feedlink, OnFeed, and FeedTech—gather information and develop ever more precise consumer profiles. These are used to create and ceaselessly redirect consumer desire through advertising, commercial "feedcasts," and individualized purchasing advice. Set against a backdrop of geopolitical conflict and environmental disaster, the story centres on two teenagers: the fifteen-year-old narrator, Titus, who is a fairly conventional teenage consumer; and his girlfriend, Violet Durn, a home-schooled nonconformist Titus and his friends meet during a Spring Break holiday on the Moon. One night at a dance club, the teens are attacked by the Coalition of Pity, an activist group that hacks people's feeds. Titus and his friends are briefly hospitalized so that their feed connections can be checked for viruses and re-established. Among the teens, only Violet's implant is damaged by the attack, and the novel recounts both Violet's resistance to consumer culture and the decay of her physical and mental abilities as her implant malfunctions and her feed shuts down.

Although the feed is expressly designed to sustain and promote consumer culture, it also infiltrates every aspect of social life. In its most mundane workings, it enables instant messaging, financial transactions, information caching, and instant access to vast stores of on-demand information (troubled, as today, by third-party pop-ups). Movies, children's programming, and popular music are streamed through the feed, thereby modelling consumer behaviour and designating desirable products. Already possessing far-reaching implications for the construction of subjectivity, the feed is "tied in to everything. Your body control, your emotions, your memory. Everything" (170). Its integration into the limbic system is exploited by "malfunction" sites that have replaced illicit drugs, though (not surprisingly, given *Feed*'s young readership, or at least the readers' parents and librarians) the feed's pornographic potential seems to have gone undeveloped. The feed's most sophisticated function, and the one that has the most profound implications for subjectivity, is the "full feed-sim" (245) which, like "simstim" in William Gibson's *Neuromancer*, allows immersion in another's sensory experience.

Like nearly all dystopias, *Feed* is preoccupied with the historical moment that engendered it. Dedicated to those who, like Violet, "resist the feed" (n.p.), it imagines a libertarian America in which information technologies are aggressively promoted by School™, a privatized education system dedicated to whitewashing corporate conduct and teaching, in Titus' words, "how the world can be used, like mainly how to use our feeds" (109–10). The results are as impressive as they are horrifying. Familiar brand names continue to dominate the commercial landscape, and in a Disneyfication of the environment, dying ecosystems have been turned into theme parks and clouds are manufactured and trademarked. In pursuing production efficiencies outside any regulatory regime, industry has ransacked the wilderness for raw materials, replaced farms with factories producing cloned meat, and razed forests to build air factories. Industrial toxins are so widespread that they cause skin lesions in nearly everyone, and high radiation levels force reproduction out of the bedroom and into commercial "conceptionariums." In a land where the pursuit of happiness is equated with the acquisition of consumer goods and engagement in funhouse diversions, this all passes without provoking much notice from the populace, making censorship unnecessary for social control. Nonetheless, the sinister consequences of the corporate agenda leak into the narrative through overheard newsfeeds that soft-pedal international conflict and recount without explanation industrial disasters in Central and South America.

This preoccupation with the intersection of information technologies and consumerism belies *Feed*'s resemblance to recent dystopias—Shusterman's *Unwind*, Atwood's *The Year of the Flood*, Patrick Ness' *Chaos Walking* trilogy—that extrapolate elements of present-day religious fundamentalism into chronotopes that fall just short of being theocracies. In Titus' America, political and social order is sustained through the transfer of religion's regulatory functions to the feed corporations. "Eden," the section chronicling the teens' hospitalization, updates Adam and Eve's expulsion from Paradise for an age in which the feed, rather than God, "knows everything you want and hope for, sometimes before you even know what those things are" (48) and appropriates God's assurance to Julian of Norwich that "*All shall be well . . . and all shall be well . . . and all manner of things shall be well*" (148). The action is set in a sterile environment of sensors and medical monitors, and yet it retains an idyllic quality by virtue of temporarily placing Titus and his friends outside the consumer imperatives that supersede biblical law. As Titus returns to consciousness after the attack, he casts around for connections to the world and realizes he is without "credit" (43) and alone, a single implanted message telling him that he has been disconnected from the feed. He opens his eyes to find Violet, and what follows is in part a series of wry allusions to Genesis 2–3, as Titus tries to see through Violet's hospital gown and Violet offers Titus not forbidden fruit but apple juice. In the chapter "the garden," Violet leads Titus to a destroyed conservatory, out of which "air was rocketing off into space," leaving "the dead vines . . . standing straight up, slapping back and forth, pulled toward the crack in the ceiling where we could see the stars" (62), an impersonal and meaningless firmament. As Edens go, the Moon is pretty sordid, and yet paradisal qualities emerge in the way Titus and his friends interact without the mediation or surveillance of the feed. Here Titus experiences "one of the greatest days" of his life (57) as he and his friends play games and listen to Loga's real-time commentary on an episode of *Oh? Wow! Thing!*, their favourite teen drama. When the feed is restored, the teens are immediately re-immersed in advertising and violent newsfeeds, and, oblivious to the exchange they make, they dance at the prospect of returning to Earth, or, as the title of Part III sardonically puts it, "utopia" (73).

In "utopia," as it turns out, the soft totalitarianism of the feed has nearly completed the transference of religious functions to the corporations. As consumer profiles become more and more expertly tailored to the individual (admittedly, the homogenizing influences of the feed render the term problematic), any outward-looking sense of social justice is undermined by the narcissistic imperative to buy, consume, and discard, a shift that is underscored by distortions in the scant religious language that persists. The President, grasping for an idiom, converts an almost forgotten biblical reminder of original sin into an evasion of responsibility when he reminds Americans of their duty to support the industries responsible for the lesions "*and not cast . . . things at them. Stones, for example. The first stone*" (85; italics and ellipsis in original). In advertisements, the image of "a hand extended toward the lemonade like God's at Creation" (27) turns the gift of life into a gesture of appropriation, and the "eye of the needle" verses from Matthew (19:23–24) are diligently explicated to flog upcars in a promotion that ends, "*The Swarp XE-11: You can take it with you*" (157).

In light of the consumerist parody of religion, it is not surprising that the feed's main resister would assume the dual roles of martyr and apostate. Although Violet is hardly stoic at the prospect of death, she seems less concerned with dying than with protecting her agency from the feed. She may desperately want social acceptance, but her political awareness and near-instinctive aversion to consumerism alienate her from Titus' friends, family (at least his father), and FeedTech, which eventually withdraws technical support because she has stopped being a "*reliable investment*" (247; italics in original). Though clearly not religious in any traditional sense, Violet intuits that, in consumer America, the best expressions of resistance are religious. She alone reads prayers for dying cultures, studies burial rites, and speaks of the soul. Although she feels something like despair when FeedTech succeeds in profiling her tastes in requiem masses, at those moments when she asserts independence most forcefully she is *Feed*'s closest approximation of Milton's Satanic ideal. "It felt good," Violet reports after delivering her jeremiad to Titus' friends, "really good, just to scream finally. I felt like I was singing a hit single. But in Hell" (218).

Although *Feed*'s plot is driven almost entirely by the resistance of activist groups and individuals who, like Violet, have escaped indoctrination by School™, in *Feed*'s America the tipping point has long passed, and individual acts of defiance are futile. The hacker is beaten to death by police, Violet lies dying, and Titus sees in the increasing feed malfunctions the likelihood that others will soon follow. Civil unrest rises as formerly well-regulated citizens riot, for reasons that aren't clear: they may have been hacked by the

Coalition of Pity, or their feeds may have malfunctioned, or they may have belatedly seized for themselves a measure of agency. At the international level, geopolitical tensions with the Global Alliance are ramping up as America annexes the Moon and starts bombing cities in South America. All-out war may never come, but only because the environmental disasters that are making the lesions worse and causing everyone's hair to fall out may make it unnecessary. In a world that is about as dystopian as it gets, it turns out the Coalition of Pity is right: "[w]e enter a time of calamity" (38).

Adolescent America

If *Feed* lacks the social optimism of such YA dystopias as *House of the Scorpion* and *The Hunger Games* trilogy, it nonetheless shares with them a preoccupation with identity formation. Anderson edges toward a posthuman model of identity by dramatizing the discursive effects of the feed to reveal the imbrication of subjectivity, consumer culture, and information technology. Given *Feed*'s genre and primary readership, it is not surprising that Anderson incorporates science fiction neologisms into speech patterns that are youthful enough to engage adolescent readers, and exaggerated enough to make Titus the butt of Anderson's genial satire:

> Marty would be all, "Unit! Just wait one—" and Link would be, "Go for it. Try! Try it!" and Marty would be like, "Unit! You are so—!" And then they would be all big laughing and I felt like a complete bonesprocket for trying to sleep when there was fun. (6)

What *is* surprising, initially at least, is that so many adults adopt a similar register. Even those who have little reason to do so—doctors, corporate investors, government officials—routinely speak like teenagers. It isn't that they are trying to adapt to adolescent culture; they really do think and speak this way. Adolescence thus becomes the main—and, for those fully immersed in the feed, the only—subject position available. The question remains, why would future America be a nation of adolescents?

The answer relates to the conflation of consumer culture and information technologies. For real-world adolescents, the language of advertising can be a powerful tool for expressing individual and collective meanings (see, e.g., Ritson and Elliot), but in *Feed* such language exceeds these functions by instantiating a critique of unreflecting consumerism even as it reduces the range of discursive possibilities. "I would have liked to have been able to take the opportunity to check out these great bargains," Titus awkwardly reports from his hospital bed on the Moon (50), and in a very funny episode that Clare Bradford has deftly explicated ("'Everything must go!'" 131–33), the teens respond to a promotion that awards six-packs to consumers who mention "the great taste of Coca-Cola" a thousand times (158). What ensues is an exercise in aping advertising copy that ends only when Titus and his friends talk themselves into buying the drinks they thought they could get for free. How close such language comes to determining characters' discursive habits becomes clear only later on. As Violet m-chats Titus about what she wants to do before she dies, she suddenly realizes that she has no original thoughts and that her wishes are "*just the opening credits of sitcoms*" (217; emphasis in original). Reducing one's deepest desires to the clichés of consumer culture amounts to a corporation-driven Orwellian Newspeak: as the resources of language dwindle, citizens find it harder to exercise agency, and they become more compliant.

The smooth and facile vocabulary of advertising, however, accounts for only part of the novel's dominant speech patterns, which also tend toward interruption, halting syntax, impoverished diction, and vulgarity. Among teenagers like Marty, this is hardly remarkable (most of us overhear many Martys in the course of a day), but when Titus' father speaks, the effect is striking: "like, whoa, [your mother's] like so stressed out. This is . . . Dude [. . .] Dude, this is some way bad shit" (55). Adults acting as professionals hardly fare better. The physician reconnecting Titus' feed asks, "Could we like get a thingie, a reading on his limbic activity?" (69), and President Trumbull, who is represented with some prescience as a tongue-tied Palinesque demagogue, is prone to meandering utterances like "*What we have today, with the things that are happening in today's society, is . . .*" (71; italics and ellipsis in the original) and calling foreign heads of state "*big shithead*[s]" (119). Evidently, the problem is endemic.

The route from the feed to adolescent speech patterns is less direct than the path to advertising copy, and it begins in distraction. The feed is noisy, and it intrudes at moments that demand the subject's full attention elsewhere, as when it interrupts Titus' attempt at understanding Violet's romantic intentions to promote the seduction software "*Cyranofeed*" (174) or hawks summer fashions as Titus and Violet fly home after their final quarrel. The effect is to create feedback loops that replace outward attention with self-absorption and make the subject "conform to one of [the corporations'] types for easy marketing" (97). Thus, although Titus' friends can name the riots associated with different lines of clothing, they are oblivious to the real-world events that inspired the fashions, and when Violet asks what sparked the Watts Riot, Loga and Calista simply mock her use of "incite" (164). Conversely, wherever the feed's influence is attenuated, a more confident syntax and flexible vocabulary emerges, reflecting a broader perspective and increased capacity for sustained thought. Indeed, one important narrative function of the overheard feedcasts is to imbue the text with a polyphonic quality that militates against the narrowness of Titus' perspective. The reader's awareness of environmental and political conditions comes largely from articulate outsiders who are overheard through the feed but speak from outside it, including the Prime Minister of the Global Alliance, the elderly voices in "... AMURICA: A PORTRAIT IN GEEZERS ..." (94), and the unknown speaker who rhapsodizes on "the age of oneiric culture" (149).

As the Coca-Cola episode suggests, the feed's discursive effects emerge from corporate practices that, in crude Freudian terms, are designed to ensure that the pleasure principle triumphs. Rather than playing the game out to get their free drinks, the teens rush to a store the moment they have convinced themselves they are thirsty. In like manner, fashions come and go within days, and Titus' friends lose interest in their purchases before they even leave the store. By contrast, Violet adopts the more mature position that "everything was better if you delayed it" (143). She becomes the exemplar of restrained consumerism, and her account of her lingering care in choosing, ordering, and finally unwrapping and wearing a new skirt for the first time has the very funny effect of preventing Titus from getting the doughnuts he wants, not because he accepts her lesson, but because he has "complete prong" and is unable to stand up (144).

Among *Feed*'s resisters, Violet's father is most acutely aware of the interplay of technological and economic forces that has turned America into a nation of impatient adolescents. In his climactic confrontation with Titus, however, he identifies only the terminus of consumerism. In a particularly resonant allusion to *The Time Machine*, he accuses Titus of being a "little child" who plays "games" and lives among the eloi in "the land of youth" (290). If, like the childlike eloi in Wells' novel, Americans know only consumption, preferring to ignore how goods are produced or discarded, they seem even less aware of the fate that awaits them. In characterizing Violet as a discarded product (here, too, the allusion to Wells applies), Mr. Durn corroborates the startling accusation Violet directs at Titus' friends: *"You don't have the feed! You are feed! You're feed! You're being eaten! You're raised for food!"* (202). Violet is metaphorically right: submitting to the pleasure principle has its costs, and the Morlocks must eventually be fed.

Technological Anxiety

Squandering one's life, as Violet says, in "tea parties with . . . teddies" (273) may not be the worst fate to befall one in Titus' America. Feed technology itself poses an array of threats to the liberal humanist ideal of the subject as an autonomous, self-aware agent. This is not to say that Anderson denies entirely the liberatory possibilities of such technology, but he does downplay them. To be sure, *Feed* partly confirms a current truism about communications technology: that the totalitarian world presaged by *Nineteen Eighty-Four* has in part been averted because the technologies that enable surveillance also make information monopolies impossible (see, e.g., Fukuyama 4–5). In *Feed*, the extensive communications network limits the corporations' power, forcing them to settle for massaging news stories and exploiting the fashion potential of political unrest and environmental disaster. Although clearly a tool of social and political control, the feed also provides activist groups a conduit to the populace, and through it Violet discovers the effects of industrialization and corporate expansionism and, facing death, finds some consolation in the prayers and requiems she discovers.

Nonetheless, information technology remains a predominantly negative force, even if Titus views the feed as liberating. M-chat—like IM programs today—connects the members of Titus' social group, but it prevents the kinds of pleasure Titus experiences in the unmediated interactions with his friends in the hospital ward. School™ has taught Titus that the principle of retention that once drove education is outmoded because the feed lets us "know everything about everything whenever we want" (49). When he doesn't understand Violet, he consults the "English-to-English wordbook" (23), but the term "dictionary" apparently hasn't been remarkable enough to commit to memory. More tellingly, Titus believes that everyone can be "supersmart without ever working" (47), yet a steady stream of misinformation—chalk and water make nitroglycerine, George Washington fought in the Civil War—reveals his limited capacity for critical reflection.

Technological anxiety, however, extends beyond concern with the feed's effects on memory, critical thinking, or even social cohesion. The narrative instantiates the proposition, recently explored by Katharine Hayles, that humans and intelligent machines are co-evolving in ways that raise the problem of how "the embodied subject and the computational machine can be thought together" (*Electronic Literature* 87). Here too Violet's father best understands what's at stake. Mr. Durn attributes the feed's success to programming developments in the 1990s, specifically the capacity of object-oriented programming to serve "a system of corporate service provision that mirrored the emergent structures of late capitalism" (140). Although he is himself enmeshed in these structures and needs the technology to survive professionally, Mr. Durn understands that the feed's data-mining functions imperil the subject's autonomy. To protect himself from feedback loops that are continuously "streamlining our personalities" (97) by regulating consumer tastes and habits, he renders himself unreadable by "speak[ing] entirely in weird words and irony, so no one can simplify anything he says" (137).

Despite Mr. Durn's precautions, it is not possible for anyone who hosts a fully integrated feed to escape the restructuring of subjectivity, for the corporations are at work even as one sleeps. Awake, Titus overhears the feed piping a "fun-site with talking giraffes" to his sleeping brother (147), but asleep he finds it impossible to distinguish his own dreaming from the operations of others. Soon after returning from the Moon, he reports "something [he] thought was a dream" (92). Whether the episode begins as a dream or a banal advertisement for a gaming site is unclear, both to Titus and the reader, but when Titus feels someone "nudging" his feed (92), he can't determine whether the intruder is the police or the Coalition of Pity, even forgetting the latter possibility until weeks afterwards. Later, he and Violet experience a more sinister "nudging" when they are assailed with violent images of child labour, rioting, and environmental disaster (151). Titus believes he is having nightmares, but Violet understands that they have been hacked and reports the intrusion to an apparently unconcerned FeedTech. A few days later, what appears to have been a widespread attack has been neutralized by the corporations' use of the images to create a fad for riot wear. Chillingly, none of Titus' friends remembers the possible origins of the new fashion.

The liberal humanist model of the subject as an autonomous and self-aware agent has been under attack for at least a century, since the first psychoanalytic constructions of consciousness as an epiphenomenon at the service of unconscious forces. Manipulating the dreaming subject exploits this condition, but the feed corporations render subjectivity even more precarious by making consciousness radically contingent on programming. Agency among Titus' friends is compromised by viruses, malfunction sites, "Nostalgia Feedback" (278), and speech tattoos that make the subject utter product names with Tourette's-like randomness. Seen from this perspective, Violet is merely an extreme example of how programming impinges on subjectivity. Her degenerative illness presents as cascading, technologically induced physical symptoms, memory lapses, and mood disorders, but Violet wonders whether some symptoms stem rather from an essential quality of her self. Under such circumstances there is even the possibility, although the narrative does not explore it, that Violet's resistance to the feed may itself be a programming artifact of the original hacking.

Erosion of the boundaries between biology and technology, dreaming and advertising, agency and programming requires a reconceptualization of identity as "distributed cognition," the condition under which awareness is "located in disparate parts that may be in only tenuous communication with one another" (Hayles, *How We Became Posthuman*, 3–4). While the feed always allows outsiders to invade, under the radar, as it were, Titus also experiences the radical blurring of self and other through the full feed-sims that immerse him in others' sensations, and even more forcefully in a disorienting moment in which he merges with the feed itself. Returning home after seeing the comatose Violet and fighting with Mr. Durn, Titus recoils from consumer culture, spending all his credit on identical pairs of pants and staying up all night to track the shipments. The account unfolds over a remarkable two pages, comprising almost entirely simple sentences beginning with the grammatical subject "I." What Titus expresses, however, is neither teen narcissism nor any assertion of newfound identity as a feed resister, but rather a failed affirmation of autonomy as he simultaneously loses the credit that constitutes his value for the feed corporations and adopts the distributed perspective of the feed:

> I ordered pants after pants. I put tracking orders on them. I tracked each one. I could feel them moving through the system.
>
> Spreading out from me, in the dead of night, I could feel credit deducted, and the warehouse alerted, and packing, I could feel the packing, and the shipment, the distribution, the transition to FedEx, the numbers, each time, the order number, my customer number traded like secret words at a border, and the things all went out, and I could feel them coming to me as the night passed.

I could feel them in orbit.
I could feel them in circulation all around me like blood in my veins.
I had no credit. I had nothing left in my account.
I could feel the pants winging their way toward me through the night.
(293–94)

Feeling credit being deducted falls within the usual range of the subject's experience of the feed, but when Titus also feels the "packing" (the emphatic repetition implying confusion), "shipment," and "distribution," he moves into unfamiliar territory, for these are all actions that the feed controls but normally hides from the consumer. What looks on the surface to be a modifier problem—"[s]preading out from me, in the dead of night, I could feel credit deducted"—suggests instead Titus' perception that he has somehow become dis-integrated and diffused across the feed, while the trading of numbers "like secret words at a border" hints at the processes of encryption. The remark, "I could feel them in circulation all around me like blood in my veins," characterizes the shipments paradoxically as being outside the consumer Titus and inside a Titus who is now coextensive with the feed. If Titus can't quite articulate what is happening to him, his language nonetheless indicates both the disturbing perceptual quality of his experience (something akin to micropsia) and the difficulty of finding a syntax and a vocabulary to articulate a state of diffused subjectivity.

A Heaven of Hell: Posthuman Hope, Critical Dystopia, and the Ending of *Feed*

Although distributed cognition most often entails a nightmarish symbiosis with intelligent machines and programs that promote corporate or insurrectionist agendas, the full feed-sim hints at the feed's potential to create social ties that liberate the subject from the self-absorption of consumer culture. Even here, however, Anderson seems preoccupied with the dangers of accessing the private experiences of others: surveillance is an ever-present threat, and characters routinely "shield" their feeds (147), often imperfectly, to maintain privacy. But characters also freely give one another access to visual, auditory, tactile, and even proprioceptive experiences. At one point, Titus relives his father's whaling expedition; at another, Violet sends Titus a memory of one of her father's college lectures. Although Titus typically reports these experiences in a voice that is recognizably his own, the feed-sim can overwhelm the subject, and on two occasions the distinction between Titus and the other collapses, to be re-established only with considerable effort. At the beginning of the feed-sim in which Violet loses the use of her legs, Titus adopts the first-person pronoun as if Violet herself were reporting, before referring once to "Violet/me" (246), and finally distancing himself from Violet's experience through third-person narration. Throughout, the register remains recognizably Titus', but at the end of the memory, there is a residual effect that leaves Titus experiencing Violet's confusion about whether her physical pain originates in the fall or in the malfunctioning feed. Designed no doubt to allow individuals to communicate the pleasures of consumption, here the full feed-sim militates against the corporate agenda of reconfiguring selves as atomized and self-absorbed consumers.

The subversive potential of the feed-sim is related to a quality of Anderson's novel that has led to critical consternation: the tonal shift that occurs as the novel's dystopian logic becomes evident. Initially lighthearted and very funny, Anderson's satire undoubtedly registers with adolescent and adult readers who recognize in Titus both good nature and immaturity. But when the extent of Violet's plight becomes clear, the tone turns sombre and the harmful potential of Titus' character failings emerges, and most readers take their distance from the narrator. Always prone to reading Violet imperfectly, Titus shifts from concern—diminished in part by Violet's deliberately underplaying the severity of her problem—to defensiveness as Violet becomes needy and importunate. Eventually, Titus ignores Violet's messages, deletes her memories, goes to a malfunction site to avoid thinking about her, and finally casts her off, viciously remarking that her touch is "like being felt up by a zombie" (269). It is true that Titus is an adolescent living in a world where adolescence is nearly the only available subject position, but it is also true that he rejects a responsibility that many present-day adults would find overwhelming, even after years of marriage. Despite this, Titus has attracted widespread condemnation, and academic studies have characterized him at the end of the novel as "gaz[ing] solipsistically at his own reflection," having "failed to mature or learn anything" (Bradford et al., 168) and as "completely unchanged and reduced to the half-robot he was before he met Violet" (Nikolajeva 88). These responses, I think, construe *Feed* too narrowly as a classic dystopian narrative while imagining that Titus could somehow exhibit an agency that is completely independent of the society that shapes him. But there is ample evidence to support quite a different assessment of Titus at novel's end—one made possible by *Feed*'s indebtedness to the critical dystopia—in the capacity for feed technology to shape human sympathies for the better.

The last third of *Feed* is punctuated by increasingly strong challenges to the narrator's adolescent self-absorption, as Titus is compelled to adopt the perspectives of Violet, Mr. Durn, and, finally, the intelligent systems that constitute the feed itself. During the first visit after Violet becomes comatose, Mr. Durn assaults Titus with memories of Violet's final days. As when he experienced Violet's full feed-sim, Titus finds it difficult to maintain an independent identity: "I rolled her over with his hands, I rolled her over, and the back of her pajamas were black and wet with her shit. I started to clean her" (290). The physicality of the experience makes a sentimental response all but impossible, but it also prevents Titus from seeing Violet as a "zombie" (269). Although there's no evidence that Titus accepts Mr. Durn's challenge to learn about the eloi, he clearly takes the criticism to heart, and after squandering his credit as meaninglessly as he can, and learning some things Violet might want to hear, he assumes adult-like responsibility and returns for a final visit.

The novel ends with Titus' second visit to Violet, whose feed function now reads 4.6 percent. That this visit occurs at all is noteworthy, indicating that Titus has been chastened by his disorienting experience of others' subjectivity. The final episode is in fact remarkably nuanced, with Titus imperfectly feeling his way toward the maturity that has eluded him until now, while struggling against the emotional and discursive habits that mark America as "the land of youth" (290). He dresses "real careful, like for a special occasion," but with a teen's maladroitness he cannot decide how far he should roll up his sleeves. He seems aware of Mr. Durn's suffering, repeatedly referring to the man categorically first as "the father" and then as "her father" (295). As he sits by Violet's bedside, struggling to block out what he now identifies as the "noise" of the feed, he tells Violet "little pieces of broken stories," each "only a sentence long" (296). These fragments—decontextualized snippets of news, interspersed with an account of the origins of the iconographic Santa Claus in Coca-Cola advertisements and references to Nero's Rome—are set against a longer account of the Japanese aphorism that "life is like walking from one side of infinite darkness to another, on a bridge of dreams" (296–97), a belief that resonates with Titus's disorientation in the "age of oneiric culture" (149) and his difficulty in identifying the sources of the self. He is, of course, still constrained by the consumer culture he lives in. In language that mimics Violet's earlier in the novel, he imagines a counterfactual version of his relationship with her in terms of the clichés of feedcasts, even assigning the story a PG-13 rating "for language... and mild sexual situations" (298). Nonetheless, both because and in spite of the feed, when Titus looks at Violet and sees himself "crying, in her blank eye," he is more mature than at any other point in the novel (298).

The modest measure of hope that emerges from the very technologies that underpin *Feed*'s dystopian vision allows Anderson to balance, within the narrative itself, the characteristic optimism of YA literature with the grim and unrelenting chains of cause and effect that make dystopias what they are. The need to recover a utopian impetus from the wreckage of Titus' America is characteristic of the critical dystopia, and in other ways than have been discussed here it has made itself felt in sensitive readings of Anderson's novel. In their study of risk society in YA dystopias, Elizabeth Bullen and Elizabeth Parsons ask, "[i]n the absence of a happy ending for western civilisation, what kind of children can survive in dystopia?" Their answer, in the case of *Feed*, is "no one" (134–35). It is a particularly layered claim, since, in a sense, youth is the only subject position the corporations permit. And yet Bullen and Parsons see the narrative as retaining elements of hope, because it presents a model of activism through Violet that can succeed in the world that Anderson's novel has reference to, ours. While I think their analysis is shrewd, and that Anderson's narrative strategy of transferring the reader's sympathies from the narrator to Violet is itself an elegant answer to the question of retaining hope in a genre where hope has tended to cause technical problems for writers, *Feed* remains more open-ended than Anderson's satire of consumer culture might seem to permit. In the end, information technology, for all its destructive tendencies, entails the potential for new and liberating forms of subjectivity, even if that potential is almost drowned out by the noise of the feed.

Works Cited

Anderson, M.T. *Feed*. Somerville, MA: Candlewick, 2002. Print.
Baccolini, Raffaella, and Tom Moylan. "Dystopias and Histories." *Dark Horizons. Science Fiction and the Utopian Imagination*. Ed. Raffaella Baccolini and Tom Moylan. New York: Routledge, 2003. 1–12. Print.
Bradford, Clare. "'Everything must go!' Consumerism and Reader Positioning in M.T. Anderson's *Feed*." *Jeunesse: Young People, Texts, Cultures* 2.2 (2010): 128–37. Print.

Bradford, Clare, Kerry Mallan, John Stephens, and Robyn McCallum. *New World Orders in Contemporary Literature. Utopian Transformations*. Houndsmills, Basingstoke: Palgrave Macmillan, 2008. Print.

Bullen, Elizabeth, and Elizabeth Parsons. "Dystopian Visions of Global Capitalism: Philip Reeve's *Mortal Engines* and M.T Anderson's *Feed*." *Children's Literature in Education* 38 (2007): 127–39. Print.

Donawerth, Jane. "Genre Blending and the Critical Dystopia." *Dark Horizons: Science Fiction and the Utopian Imagination*. Ed. Raffaella Baccolini and Tom Moylan. New York: Routledge, 2003. 29–46. Print.

Fukuyama, Francis. *Our Posthuman Future. Consequences of the Biotechnology Revolution*. New York: Farrar, Straus and Giroux, 2002. Print.

Hayles, N. Katharine. *Electronic Literature: New Horizons for the Literary*. Notre Dame, IN: U of Notre Dame P, 2008. Print.

———. *How We Became Posthuman: Virtual Bodies in Cybernetics, Literature and Informatics*. Chicago: U of Chicago P, 1999. Print.

Nikolajeva, Maria. *Power, Voice and Subjectivity in Literature for Young Readers*. NY: Routledge, 2010. Print.

Ritson, Mark, and Richard Elliott. "The Social Uses of Advertising: An Ethnographic Study of Adolescent Advertising Audiences." *Journal of Consumer Research* 26 (1999): 260–77. Print.

Sambell, Kay. "Carnivalizing the Future: A New Approach to Theorizing Childhood and Adulthood in Science Fiction for Young Readers." *The Lion and the Unicorn* 28 (2004): 247–67. Print.

———. "Presenting the Case for Social Change: The Creative Dilemma of Dystopian Writing for Children." *Utopian and Dystopian Writing for Children and Young Adults*. New York: Routledge, 2003. Print.

Sargent, Lyman Tower. "The Three Faces of Utopianism Revisited." *Utopian Studies* 5 (1994): 1–37. Print.

PART II
Plastic Subjectivities

Woman Gave Names to All the Animals

Food, Fauna, and Anorexia in Margaret Atwood's Dystopian Fiction

Annette Lapointe

Dystopian fictions demand that readers recognize the instability in their own cultures, and the extent to which even very basic cultural elements fail to be politically neutral. Relationships between women and men, between humanity and animals, and even between people and their food are encoded with layers of power. These layers shape much of Margaret Atwood's writing. Atwood's novels *The Edible Woman* and *The Handmaid's Tale*, and particularly her recent mirrored narratives *Oryx and Crake* and *The Year of the Flood*, explore the ways in which eating and awareness of animal kinship shape women's embodiment. The psychic breakdown that accompanies dystopia in these narratives breaks down vulnerable characters' (and especially women's) ability to eat normally; women's return to normal eating is thus less an individual recovery than a sign that the entire culture has shifted to accommodate feminine existence.

Atwood's writing abounds with animals, and with food, and her writing explores how both contribute to women's experiences of embodiment. Food and animals intersect vividly in *The Edible Woman* (1969) when the female protagonist "look[s] down at her own half-eaten steak and suddenly [sees] it as a hunk of muscle. Blood red. Part of a real cow" (167). The terror contained in food persists in later novels; in *The Blind Assassin* (2000), Margaret Atwood distills the intellectual and emotional struggle of self-conscious eating into a series of bathroom-wall epigrams:

> The first sentence is in pencil, in rounded lettering like those on Roman tombs, engraved deeply in the paint: *Don't Eat Anything You Aren't Prepared to Kill.*
> Then, in green marker: *Don't Kill Anything You Aren't Prepared to Eat.*
> Under that, in ballpoint: *Don't Kill.*
> Under that, in purple marker: *Don't Eat.* (105)

This graffiti discourse takes place entirely among women, in the women's washroom of a public restaurant. The blunt language makes explicit the usually sublimated anxieties and demands that underlie both vegetarianism and anorexia. *Don't Kill/Don't Eat* is the fundamental opposition of meat. Potentially, it is the opposition at the heart of all food, the awareness that something living must die in order to sustain each human moment. Though the industrial-agricultural mechanisms of late capitalism obscure the animal-meat relationship, the ethical problems of eating animals, of eating at all, re-insinuate themselves into the culture through its gender anxieties. However, both scenes quoted above take place in late-twentieth-century Canada, a context in which the middle class has historically unprecedented access to food, and equally unprecedented isolation from food production. The protagonists' concern with the origins of their food is distanced. No animals were harmed in the production of this graffiti message.

Atwood's dystopian fiction collapses that distance, making food issues urgent and intense. Even in *The Handmaid's Tale* (1985), food shortages haunt repressively religious Gilead. In Atwood's more recent dystopian near-future novels *Oryx and Crake* (2003) and *The Year of the Flood* (2009), the collapse of the North American food system shapes cultural concerns and individual terrors. *What will I/won't I eat?* ceases to be an abstract question, and becomes a matter of survival for her female protagonists. This chapter explores the ways in which gender shapes Atwood's characters' perceptions of eating animals when all distance has been stripped from the question. Atwood's dystopias emphasize a breakdown at the borders of "humanity," so that some animals crawl into the class of "human," and women slide helplessly into the realm of "animal." Corporate control of both bio-engineering and the crumbling food system exacerbates this border breakdown, leaving Atwood's female characters constantly anxious about the food that they eat, and progressively more terrified that they may *be food* themselves. These women's awareness of their food-chain status marks their ambivalent relationship with the "natural" world, but it also reveals the position of animals and the gender anxieties surrounding food and animals in contemporary culture.

Critical engagement with these ideas in Atwood's fiction has primarily focused on biomedical and ecological themes. In comparison to the crowd of theory and criticism on *The Handmaid's Tale*, criticism of *Oryx and Crake* is still taking its first steps, and that of *The Year of the Flood* is in its infancy. Several authors (Dunning; DiMarco; Cooke) have addressed the spectre of medicine in *Oryx and Crake*. In that novel and its sequel, animals, food, and medicine have overlapping origins, as we shall see presently. Human encounters with nature in *Oryx and Crake* foreground concepts of utopia and dystopia in Jayne Glover's "Human/Nature." Glover notes that much of the novel's devastation is built on "the very cities of today that many ecological philosophers critique because of their sexist, capitalist, and environmentally unsound practices" (54), but pursues the idea of those practices only in an ecological context. Still, her emphasis on present-day systems producing dystopia brings the ethics of contemporary consumption into question. Jovian Parry's suggestion that "[e]ating 'real,' 'natural' meat can be seen as a method of reconnecting to the natural world, as well as a statement about subjugating it" (248) thus demands that food and its origins in *Oryx and Crake* be given extended attention. That demand, coupled with the ideas raised in Jennifer Hobgood's paper "Anti-Edibles: Capitalism and Schizophrenia in Margaret Atwood's *The Edible Woman*," determines much of the course of this discussion.

The intersection of food and sexuality marks an *X* on the female body. Desire and desirability are fundamentally linked for women (or at least for women in a western/patriarchal context) with body image, weight, and eating, so that the female body is the site of ongoing conflict. In his lecture "God and the *Jouissance* of T̶h̶e̶ Woman," Jacques Lacan articulates a pivotal problem in western conceptions of feminine materiality, subjectivity, and desire or enjoyment. Women's *jouissance* (conflicted enjoyments of the body, sexual or otherwise) is never treated as a primary force. Instead, "in being not at all, she has, in relation to the phallic function . . . a supplementary *jouissance*" (144). If we understand *jouissance* as a conflicted space between enjoyment and desire, we recognize its feminine articulation as an unstable site. Bodily desires are understood primarily as sexual, but behind that (phallic) mode, the feminine body's desires are much more complicated.

Food becomes as important or more important than sex. Desire (for food first, for sex only afterward) destabilizes ideas of "normal" behaviour in times of social and personal stress, producing a feminine subject whose desire for survival (containing all other desires) drives her to enact "regular rituals in radically altered ways" (Hobgood 154). This is fundamentally a mark of anorexia, or at least of that mode of anorexia that metamorphoses eating into creative expression, and replaces food with food-related anxiety. Yet anorexia literally means "absence of desire" (155). Though, in fact, most anorexics do not suffer from a lack of appetite, the notion of absent desire allows critics to question "not . . . *what* anorexics want (a question grounded in the concept of lack), but *how* anorexics desire and how the productive mechanisms of anorexic desire work" (155). Whatever the feminine subject wants, her desires are intimately related to her problems of embodiment, and to issues of "doing things normally." The normality, then, of eating, and, particularly, of eating animals, inevitably comes into question, and provokes a crisis in the eating/not eating feminine subject.

The pervasive knowledge among Atwood's feminine subjects that they exist within the same categories as their food marks the characters' awareness of how they are constrained by their status as women. Historically, at least in western/patriarchal discourse, "[t]he categories 'woman' and 'animal' serve the same symbolic function" (Gruen 61). This is particularly true in terms of Platonic constructions of gender, which rely on "the exclusion of women, slaves, children, and animals" (Butler 48). The sense that women and animals overlap, and that men exist distantly and distinct from both, persists. Definitions of "man" summon him precisely as "one who is without a childhood; is not a primate and so is relieved of the necessity of eating, defecating, living and dying; one who is not a slave but always a property holder" (48). This phantasm of masculinity as nearly disembodied effectively separates men not only from women, but also from their food. The anxiety of overlap is subsumed beneath a biological determinism of "man's" social position (Haraway 10).

Within the Abrahamic tradition on which Atwood draws, man's biosocial dominance is established in the Book of Genesis. The story of "naming of the animals" at once establishes patriarchal dominance of ecosystems and blurs the boundary between animals and women. God's assertion that "*It* is not good that the man should be alone; I will make him an help meet for him" (2:18) is immediately followed not by the creation of Eve, but by the naming of the animals, and Adam's dissatisfaction with them:

the Lord God formed every beast of the field, and every fowl of the air; and brought *them* unto Adam to see what he would call them: and whatsoever Adam called every living creature, that *was* the name thereof.

And Adam gave names to all cattle, and to the fowl of the air, and to every beast of the field; but for Adam there was not found an help meet for him. (2:19–20)

Only once the animals have been deemed unsatisfying is woman created from Adam's rib (2:21–23). Woman thus emerges within this cosmology as a tertiary being, ranking below man and functioning as a supplement to the animals. Though contemporary techno-culture repudiates its epistemological relationship with Abrahamic religion, the two systems of knowledge have a common function in justifying ecological and sexual exploitation. Biologist Ruth Hubbard frames this overlap and its ecological implications: "The man-nature antithesis was invented by men. . . . Women have recognized more often than men that we are part of nature and that its fate is in human hands that have not cared for it well" (qtd. in Haraway 80). That recognition drives the feminine anxieties of eco-dystopia.

Late capitalist/corporate culture's focus on commodification reduces the animals to the status of objects and women to the status of animals. In this context, women's empathy with animals demonstrates their awareness that both women and animals are artificially abjected, and that the emancipation of one may be the salvation of the other. As women realize that "[t]he role of women and animals in postindustrial society is to serve/be served up" (Gruen 61), the two groups become natural allies, and feminism necessarily becomes eco-feminism. It is not a coincidence that Gilead, the misogynist theocratic society of *The Handmaid's Tale*, lurches along the edges of ecological disaster, barely surviving. The Handmaids who shop for food know that the sea fisheries have collapsed, and fear that the sea creatures may not simply be few in number, but totally lost: "Sole, I remember, and haddock, swordfish, scallops, tuna; lobsters, stuffed and baked, salmon, pink and fat, grilled in steaks. Could they all be extinct, like the whales?" (154). This fishless theocracy has been poisoned by leaks of nuclear waste and biological-warfare materials. The men who rule have enough to eat. Those most in danger of starvation are the Unwomen (10), exiles whose abjection reduces them to the status of beasts of burden, below the status even of recognizable food.

The Unwoman is a useful figure for understanding the interactions of science/medicine and gender/class outside *The Handmaid's Tale*, as well as within it. Once reduced to subhuman status, women rapidly become acceptable "lab-animals." Lori Gruen suggests that the overlap of the two groups is not accidental: "Because women and animals are judged unable to comprehend science and are thus relegated to the position of passive object, their suffering and deaths are tolerable in the name of profit and progress" (67). However, Unwomen are the products of a theological dystopia; the gendering processes of late capitalism do not produce such overt categories of humanity and subhumanity. Instead, late capitalist feminine subjects function within the most basic cultural logic of postmodernism: an anxiety that flows easily into panic. These women are unable to stabilize their socio-economic status, which leaves them in extreme physical danger, but they are simultaneously subject to a pathological culture which insists on "the *decentering* of . . . [the] subject or psyche" (Jameson 14), perpetuating masculine-oriented and ecologically devastating corporate cultures at the radical expense of the individual.

The terrors of animals and women in the face of medical research underlie Atwood's *Oryx and Crake*. The novel takes place in a series of compounds owned by biomedical corporations, wherein virtually all aspects of human existence have been commodified. The corporations reproduce Platonic constructions of human existence. Their culture is overtly masculine, excluding children, animals, women who perform femininity, and the wide range of slaves that this culture (globalized, late-late-capitalist, corporate-controlled, ecologically poisoned) has produced. The corporations are themselves "bodies" in the same sense that Platonic men are bodies: hyper-rational, non-primate, property-holding. The corporations run on the logic of the Platonic *pharmakon*, a concept which encompasses "medicine, remedy, drug, charm, philtre, recipe, colour, pigment, and, mostly importantly, both poison *and* cure" (Cooke 112). The balance between poison and cure is fundamental. The corporations create both simultaneously, and they do so on the bodies of women and animals.

The bodies of animals are, in *Oryx and Crake*, the more explicit sites of scientific exploitation. In childhood, narrator Jimmy/Snowman is confronted with the possibility that animals have no legitimate existence except in the context of human exploitation. His earliest memory is of thousands of animals, killed by a "hostile bioform," being burned in a quasi-scientific ritual of purification. Jimmy-the-child is "anxious about the animals, because they were being burned and surely that would hurt them" (17). His father, attempting to reassure him, tells Jimmy that "[t]he animals were dead. They were like steaks and sausages, only they still had their skins on" (18). Jimmy is five and a half years old (15), and still coming to terms with the idea that meat is animals, that animals are food. He makes the transition of awareness from "food" to "meat" to "animal parts" individually, as (western, carnivorous) children must do. Jimmy is on some level aware that steaks and sausages come from animals, but the immediacy of animals' individuality and suffering nonetheless takes him aback. His father's remark that the animals simply "still had their skins on" causes Jimmy to add,

> And their heads.... Steaks didn't have heads. The heads made a difference: he thought he could see the animals looking at him reproachfully out of their burning eyes. In some way all of this—the bonfire, the charred smell, but most of all the lit-up, suffering animals—was his fault, because he'd done nothing to rescue them. (18)

His sense that he is morally responsible for the animals' well-being marks Jimmy-the-child as intimately aware of the relationships among the powerless. However, that awareness is retrospectively constructed as absurd. Adult Snowman distances himself from child Jimmy's wild empathy by noting that his sympathy with the burning animals is equal to his sympathy with the "smiling duck's face on each toe" of his rubber boots. The disinfectant through which he walks causes him to worry "that the poison would get into the eyes of the ducks and hurt them. He'd been told the ducks were only like pictures, they weren't real and had no feelings, but he didn't quite believe it" (15). Jimmy's childhood "naïveté," though, is less absurd than Adult Snowman would like. The bonfire takes place within the scientific/corporate culture of the compounds, which is predicated on the assertion that *all* animals "[aren't] real and ha[ve] no feelings" (15). Jimmy thus has no reasonable way of determining the difference between the duck pictures and the burning cattle, or between the animals and himself.

The question of animals' ability to feel pain has lurked at the heart of biotechnological research since the early Enlightenment. More often than the contemporary reader might expect, the assertion that animals lack feelings (or even reality) has been taken as fact. René Descartes established the ethical context for animal-based research when he asserted that

> [t]he capacity of animals for sensation ... was strictly corporeal and mechanical, and hence they were unable to feel real pain.... They just

went through the external motions which in man were symptomatic of pain, but did not experience the mental sensation. Some of his followers denied that animals possessed even the inferior kind of feeling that Descartes attributed to beasts, and they interpreted the cries of an animal during vivisection as the mere creaking of the animal "clockwork." (qtd. in Rudacille 20–21)

Animals, in this construction, are machines without emotion or intellect. Scientists are thus justified in "dismantling" animals to reverse-engineer, as it were, the mechanisms of life. The notion that life itself is a mechanism and that living things not only can but should be engineered in the name of human ingenuity and curiosity underlies the ethical terror of biotechnology. Literary critic Stephen Dunning points to Descartes as well, as an inspiration for the character Crake. Crake's scientific detachment, Dunning suggests, has progressed to the point of total alienation:

[Crake] shares Descartes' rejection of received authority, his desire to work within a comprehensive epistemology founded on ideas as clear and distinct as mathematical proofs, his preference for mechanical models of living beings, his identification of the self as *res cogitans* (the original ghost in the machine), and his misrelation to the feminine, or Nature. (87–88)

The clockwork world that Descartes posits is so explicitly masculine that it reinforces binarisms that make Nature feminine even in critical analysis. Yet, in this context, the binarism is not entirely inappropriate, as it frames *Oryx and Crake*'s interrogation of what constitutes a "real" or "fake" animal.

Jimmy's confusion about the status of "real" animals is compounded by his childhood exposure to a range of transgenic animals. The family works for/lives in OrganInc Farms, where Jimmy's father is "one of the foremost architects" of the pigoons, massive transgenic pigs in whose bodies human-tissue organs are grown for transplant purposes (22). The pigoons defy traditional constructions of food animals. Their overlap with human embodiment makes their porcine edibility uncomfortable. Pigoons can "grow five or six kidneys at a time. Such a host animal could be reaped of its extra kidneys; then, rather than being destroyed, it could keep on living and grow more organs, much as a lobster could grow another claw to replace a missing one" (22–23). The language of harvest applies here to living animals, but the animal-as-food framework persists even as pigoon-grown organs become "spare parts" for human bodies. The pigoons themselves become progressively more malevolent, and more intelligent as they incorporate human nervous tissue into their own bodies.

In spite of their quasi-human biological status, pigoons blur uncomfortably with food. While officially the pigoons are never "processed," that assertion exists largely "to set the queasy at ease . . . no one would want to eat an animal whose cells might be identical with at least some of their own" (23–24). Jimmy "didn't want to eat a pigoon, because he thought of the pigoons as creatures much like himself," but the scientists around him are more inclined simply to engage in dark humour and consume the "back bacon and ham sandwiches and pork pies [that] turned up on the staff café menu" (24). If no other meat is available, then the pigoons become a viable food source through their subhuman status even as they blur with humans biologically.

As the culture becomes more ecologically stressed, adult-Jimmy and Crake debate the fundamental definitions and functions of nature. Crake's pastoral-seeming college campus has been engineered by staff and students. Jimmy's discussion with Crake about the "marvels" of the campus returns, perhaps inevitably, to ideas of a clockwork world, and of women's overlap with animals:

> "So, are the butterflies—are they recent?" Jimmy asked after a while. . . .
>
> "You mean, did they occur in nature or were they created by the hand of man? In other words, are they real or fake? . . . You know when people get their hair dyed or their teeth done? Or when women get their tits enlarged?"
>
> "Yeah?"
>
> "After it happens, that's what they look like in real time. The process is no longer important." (200)

Jimmy cautiously substitutes the term "recent" for "engineered," but still finds himself engaged in a semiotic battle over the legitimacy of bio-alteration. Crake's assertion that "the process is no longer important" negates notions of Nature and even of the real. When Jimmy insists that women, at least, should be subject to traditional ideas of physical legitimacy, Crake mocks him:

"No way fake tits feel like real tits," said Jimmy, who thought he knew a thing or two about that.

"If you could tell they were fake," said Crake, "it was a bad job. These butterflies fly, they mate, they lay eggs, caterpillars come out." (200)

Crake explicitly links women and animals through their beauty and reproductivity. Both may be engineered "by the hand of man," but afterwards, man need not concern himself with the work done. His consumption experience is not affected.

This is a culture which overtly treats women as commodities, closer in rank to animals than to human consumers. Women who seek human status necessarily do so by de-emphasizing their sexuality and refusing animal identification. The female scientist thus becomes the woman who "[isn't] even on offer" (203), whose sexuality is completely subsumed in her work. Effectively, these women gain access to power by identifying as "*homo faber*—he who labours to use every instrument as a means to achieve a particular end in building a world, even when the fabrication of that world necessarily demands a repeated violation of its materiality, including its people" (DiMarco 170). *Homo faber* is implicitly male, and maintains his status through dissociation from the social Other (woman, animal).

This dissociation can produce horrifying results. Women's engagement with the power structure pushes them to efface all empathy and organic kinship. Crake's female colleagues denature animals, creating "a large bulblike object that seemed to be covered with stippled whitish-yellow skin. Out of it came twenty thick fleshy tubes, and at the end of each tube another bulb was growing" (*Oryx and Crake* 202). This "thing" is a chicken, alive but reduced to its parts, where its "parts" are constituted entirely as food. The creature described above produces only breasts; another produces "drumsticks too, twelve to a growth unit" (202). Jimmy is shocked less by the multiplicity of the chicken parts than by a crucial absence: "there aren't any heads" (202). The creature, called a ChickieNob, has no face. The creator informs Jimmy that "they'd removed all the brain functions that had nothing to do with digestion, assimilation, and growth" (203). This, Crake asserts, is a moral victory, as well as a massive improvement in food production, "[a]nd the animal-welfare freaks won't be able to say a word, because this thing feels no pain" (203). In the absence of pain, Crake presumes, the machine has been perfected. The animal problem (a problem of empathy, a problem of identification, a problem of kinship) has been solved.

Crake's global solution to the "animal problem" is both the ultimate creation of *homo faber* and a manifestation of *pharmakon* (both poison and cure): he engineers a version of humanity reduced to what he determines to be its least problematic animal functions. The "Crakers" that he makes are "peace-loving vegetarians, designed to live in harmony with both each other and their environment. There is no rape or sexual abuse, no racial disharmony or dominance/submission culture" (Glover 55). Initially, they appear to embody all the goals of eco-feminism. As an anti-intellectual substitute, however, for humanity (conveniently wiped out by a Crake-engineered super-virus), they are horrific. They reify the belief, pervasive among the characters of *Oryx and Crake*, that the only way to reconcile humanity with nature is to annihilate all that we identify as human, leaving only an engineered, commodified version of the species whose ambivalence regarding animals, eating, and even gender has also been erased. Alienation from nature can, in the techno-capitalist world view that Crake epitomizes, end only when the culture that engendered that alienation has utterly collapsed.

The apocalypse, however, which Crake engineers and Jimmy/Snowman observes is far from absolute. The Crakers take up residence on the beach at the edge of an urban park, and Snowman supposes himself the last man on earth. Humanity, nonetheless, persists precisely by defying the mechanical constructions of culture on which Crake has relied. Within a binary construction of gender and culture, masculine techno-culture has consumed itself and expired, but that techno-culture did not encompass all of humanity. A parallel culture organized on feminine/environmentalist lines survives precisely because it has constructed women, animals, and food in radically different ways. The existence of that parallel culture, then, requires a counter-narrative.

The Year of the Flood provides that necessary counter-narrative. *Oryx and Crake* is recounted in third-person voice by Jimmy/Snowman in mental conversation with the long-dead Oryx, and the novel's scope is restricted by Jimmy's self-pity and reductive notions of gender and humanity. *The Year of the Flood* is a dual narrative, recounted in third-person voice by Toby, a pragmatic middle-aged spa manager, and in first-person voice by Ren, a sex worker and Jimmy/Snowman's ex-lover. Both women form their adult selves within the God's Gardeners' environmentalist community and interact with the larger culture on eco-feminist terms. *The Year of the Flood* inverts Crake's perspective, narrating the last years of western civilization and the first months after the engineered apocalypse ("Flood") through the cosmology of God's Gardeners and the experiences of eco-feminist women. These women interrogate the nature of humanity in a late capitalist culture and the interrelationship of humans, animals, and food.

Food is a constant and complex theme in *The Year of the Flood*. After her family is bankrupted by corporate *pharmakon*, Toby descends through layers of sexual exploitation to the lowest social rung, that of fast-food worker. Initially, she works as a "furzooter," dressing in an animal-mascot suit to advertise different businesses. In this work, she is repeatedly sexually assaulted by fetishists who ignore her but fixate on the complex erotics of the animal suit (31). At the same time, she lives in squalor above a semi-legal "endangered-species luxury couture operation . . . [that] sold Halloween costumes over the counter to fool the animal-righter extremists and cured the skins in the backrooms" (30–31). While Toby does not yet identify herself as an "animal-righter," she remains horrified. The "skin" trade which she observes explicitly harms only animals, but the language of skin and meat blurs feminine status with animal, producing an underclass of women who exist primarily for exploitation.

In an attempt to escape this underclass, Toby confronts and fragments her embodiment. She "donates" (sells) her eggs twice, only to discover on her third attempt that "there were complications, so she could never donate any more eggs, or—incidentally—have any children herself" (32). The revelation causes Toby to spiral into depression. While she has not previously wanted children, the loss of her fertility breaks down much of her identity and most aspects of her sexuality keyed to desire. The categories of woman and animal (bird) overlap: Toby must first cease to be able to "lay" eggs before she can become meat. Her humanity, and her engagement with the future of humanity, collapse at this point, leaving her socially adrift and as alienated from human existence as most of those around her are from animal existence.

The transformation from egg-layer to meat occurs rapidly, and largely as a result of despair. Toby takes a job at a fast-food chain, SecretBurgers, where "no one knew what sort of animal protein was actually in [the burgers]. . . . The meat grinders weren't 100 per cent efficient; you might find a swatch of cat fur in your burger or a fragment of mouse tail. Was there a human fingernail, once?" (33). The language in this passage is insistent and intimate. The repeated "you" in the inventory of meat sources makes the reader complicit with the larger consumer culture in a form of consumption that does not distinguish animal meat from human, so that both fuse into cheerful cannibalism. A third layer of consumption develops as Toby reflects that organized crime runs "corpse disposals, harvesting organs for transplant, then running the gutted carcasses through the SecretBurgers grinders" (33). The restaurant grinds all unwanted meat-sources into marketable commodities.

Toby's role is initially that of a food server, but like the rest of the virtually all-female staff, she is also sexual "meat" for the management. The manager, Blanco, maintains a "beefcake" look of masculinity which is supplemented by the tattoos that redefine his body:

> he sported a full set of arm tattoos: snakes twining his arms, bracelets of skulls around his wrists, *veins and arteries on the backs of his hands so they looked flayed*. Around his neck was a tattooed chain, with a lock on it shaped like a red heart, nestled into the chest hair he displayed in the V of his open shirt. According to rumour, that chain went right down his back, twined around an upside-down woman whose head was stuck in his ass. (36; italics added)

Blanco's "flayed" tattoos make his biological relationship to meat clear. However, his aggressiveness and organized crime connections make him all but invulnerable, and he uses his status to exploit his workers. When he selects Toby as his next victim, she becomes his sexual slave. Her sex work is a supplement to her fast-food work, not a substitute for it, which progressively exhausts her and strips her of her meal breaks, so that she gradually starves.

Toby is "rescued" from her exploitation by a demonstrating group of God's Gardeners, who inform her that "every day [she] stand[s] here selling the mutilated flesh of God's beloved Creatures, it's injuring [her] more" (41). She flees to them more out of sexual terror than moral outrage at SecretBurgers' carnivorism/cannibalism. In the course of her adult life with the Gardeners, however, she transforms from a fast-food cynic into an "Eve," a senior wisewoman whose bio-knowledge strengthens the collective. The Gardeners' theology fuses Christian imagery with evolutionist and scientific knowledge to create a religion that fuses reverence for life with biotechnological facility. Most markedly, the Gardeners have shifted their theology away from the Old Testament dictum that Man should "have dominion over . . . every living thing that moveth upon the earth" (Genesis 1:28). Instead, they assert their biological connection to other life forms. Patriarchal-Christian tradition persists, though, in the choice of the word "Man" to refer to humans, and in the primacy of "Adam" figures over Eves in the Gardener hierarchy. Adam One, the most senior member of the Gardener community, interprets their theology with the authority of a biblical patriarch:

> According to Adam One, the Fall of Man was multidimensional. The ancestral primates fell out of the trees; then they fell from vegetarianism into meat-eating. Then they fell from instinct into reason, and thus into technology; from simple signals into complex grammar, and thus into humanity; from firelessness into fire, and thence into weaponry; and from seasonal mating into an incessant sexual twitching. Then they fell from a joyous life in the moment into the anxious contemplation of the vanished past and the distant future. (188)

While Adam One acknowledges primates as a multi-sex/multi-gender group, he explains the evolution of Man in terms of patriarchal anxiety. He presumes that the progression of food-sex-knowledge has inevitably created an orientation to violence, and thereby reiterates Eve's instigation of the Fall via her appetites. As an Eve, Toby finds that "you could only plummet, learning more and more, but not getting any happier" (188). She remains uncomfortable within the Gardener community, and aware of her limited status and authority as an Eve.

Though Toby survives Crake's engineered plague, she does so in isolation, practising Gardener tenets but living alone. The hierarchy has, by the time of the Flood, utterly collapsed. The Gardeners have become eco-terrorists whose activism is widely perceived as absurdist theatre. As the Flood begins, the corporate news reports on a pathetic failure to "save" the chickens:

> *Do you see that? Unbelievable! Brad, nobody can quite believe it. What we've just seen is a crazed mob of God's Gardeners liberating a ChickieNobs production facility. Brad, this is hilarious, those ChickieNob things can't even walk. (Laughter.) Now, back to the studio.* (*Oryx and Crake* 340; italics in original)

The "crazed" Gardeners are supposedly unable to perceive that ChickieNobs are not animals in any conventional sense, and that dismantling a production facility is at best an act of absurdist theatre. The idea that liberation for ChickieNobs might be death rather than freedom underlies the scene without ever quite surfacing. The spectacle raises the question, though, of what an animal is, and how liberation can function.

The ChickieNobs (in food form) provide background to a more detailed liberation narrative that twines with Toby's. Ren is a young exotic dancer whose conflicts with embodiment have less to do with alienation from the natural world and more to do with alienation from what might be termed "natural eating." She is raised for several years among the Gardeners, then returned to a corporate compound where she briefly functions as adolescent-Jimmy's girlfriend. Just after high school, Ren loses her corporate toehold and and finds refuge in sex work at the Scales & Tails nightclub. There, she semi-miraculously survives the Flood precisely because she has already been isolated for fear of sexually transmitted infection.

Ren works as a "Scalie," an aerial ballet performer whose entire skin is concealed beneath a Biofilm Bodysuit. This is a living second skin, itself in need of feeding, that can be "put on" as a fusion of prophylactic and disguise. The Bodysuits are supplemented with elaborate bird costumes (331), so that the women wearing them are transformed from human to cyberanimal. Ren discovers that her non-human Scalie status gives her access to realms of knowledge that she could not imagine as a woman: "It's amazing what they'll tell you, especially if you're covered with shiny green scales and they can't see your real face. It must be like talking to a fish" (131). However, when her suit tears, she immediately returns to human status and becomes potentially dangerous, a "hot bioform" (with all possible sexual overtones) in need of immediate isolation.

In the "Sticky Zone," Ren subsists by nibbling on ChickieNobs, and forms a habit of eating as little as possible: "I only ever ate half of anything because a girl with my body type can't afford to blimp up" (55). She fasts constantly, first to sustain her childlike appearance for sex work, then for survival. Unable to escape her cocoon, she inventories her food and concludes, "[i]f I ate only a third of every meal instead of half, and saved the rest instead of tossing it down the chute, I'd have enough for at least six weeks" (283). This develops into a mantra: eat less, live longer.

What she does eat tugs at her vegetarian sensibilities. She absolves herself of carnivorous guilt on the grounds that "ChickieNobs were really vegetables because they grew on stems and didn't have faces" (129). In the absence of a face, empathy fades, and the ChickieNob is reduced to the status of an alien, inanimate thing. Ren, however, never takes up the irony of that facelessness. Her own facelessness as a Scalie does not, in her mind, make her a "vegetable" in the same way. One inevitably arrives in this moment at the vegan-activist slogan *fish is not a vegetable*, and the PETAkids[1] appropriation "Fish are friends, not food!"[2] Fish-faced Ren is a generic friend to her clients, but she is also subject to the fish-scent associations of feminine sexuality, and to the food overlap that her sex work creates. On one hand, Ren as fish is both friend and food; on the other hand, in her avian accessories, she is overtly neither fish nor fowl, but some other "thing" which her dying culture cannot identify.

Ren's post-Flood existence exacerbates her problems with "natural" eating. She is a starving woman perceived alternately as an animal and as sexual prey. Ren first appears to Toby as "a huge bird on a leash—no, on a rope—a bird with blue-green iridescent plumes like a peagret.[3] But this bird has the head of a woman" (350). The result is hallucinatory, and suggests a cybernetic gene-splice creation rather than a "real" person. Toby, however, gradually recognizes the spectacle before her as a woman in sexual bondage. Freed from the Sticky Zone, Ren finds herself hunted by Blanco as sexual prey. Ren refuses to recount her rape but the horror of the assault permeates the novel's concluding chapters. The reader's intense, highly subjective investment in Ren's experience brings two novels' worth of anxiety about animals, food, and hunting to a climax. Every consumed animal, no matter how pathetic, returns in the moment that the woman disguised as/mistaken for an animal is raped. In that moment, there is no possible ethical justification for the exploitation of any living creature. The reader sees fully exposed the cultural mechanisms that "[cast] rape as an adaptive strategy dictated by evolution" and assert that "by killing, [the hunter] willingly couples himself into the chain of life and death binding all other predators and prey" (Comninou 141). In a scenario that blends women, animals, and technology, the obscenity and absurdity of masculine bio-domination become apparent. The woman has been "served up," exploited, and consumed almost completely.

The categories of woman, animal, and food, which preserve culture and psyche, and allow stable feminine subjectvity, collapse utterly at this climactic point. The collapse marks the natural end point of late capitalism's logic as well as the culmination of anorexia's gender anxiety. Yet those climaxes are undermined when we realize that the feminine subject persists. Although Ren is temporarily subsumed under Toby's more detached third-person account, she returns to narrative prominence, and then returns again and again, insistently alternating her experience with Toby's. Instead of annihilation, both women gradually experience the return of desire. The possibility of their *jouissance* as a real force, encompassing food and sex, re-emerges. The moment of entire collapse, wherein both the late capitalist culture and the feminine subject are dead, is not an end point, but instead a return to stable embodiment, achieved through eco-political utopianism: "finally undertaking a politics of nature; finally modifying public life so that it takes nature into account; finally adapting our system of production to nature's demands; finally preserving nature from human degradation" (Latour 2). Women eat, and even eat meat. Other Gardener alumni emerge from the park-forest to attest to their own survival, and desire becomes de-problematized. Ren asserts, "[t]he Adams and the Eves used to say, *We are what we eat*, but I prefer to say, *We are what we wish*. Because if you can't wish, why bother?" (400).

While technological collapse does not instantly reconcile women (or, indeed, any human) with their food-chain status, gradual reintegration into the "natural" world eases their anorexic pathologies. The re-establishment of primitive/pre-industrial culture, though, is a largely impracticable utopian fantasy, particularly given that the "cure" is in this case an example of *pharmakon* taken to the extreme (fatalities circa 10 billion). Where patriarchal constructions of femininity persist, food-anxiety will almost certainly also persist, re-manifesting "an ideal of female perfection and moral superiority [achieved] through denial of appetite" (Brumberg 188). The gender binary lingers in the aftermath of advanced technology. The Gardeners' acceptance of gene-spliced fauna as "real" animals, however, supposes that Crake is on some level correct: once the transformation is complete, the process may no longer be (entirely) relevant. If Ren and Toby embody stable femininity "in real time," then their survival may be more important (at least to them) than the process by which they have achieved "normal" eating, and through which they stabilize their individual selves. They functions as "Eves" whose garden is insistently non-utopian but, potentially, functionally feminist. The Eves offer no submission to the Adams, and the women name the animals in a world over which they have no dominion.

Notes

1 Petakids.com is the child-oriented website of vegan-activist group People for the Ethical Treatment of Animals.
2 Cf. *Finding Nemo* (2003).
3 A peacock/egret hybrid. In this context, "natural" animals are almost unknown.

Works Cited

Atwood, Margaret. *The Blind Assassin*. Toronto: Seal, 2000. Print.
———. *The Edible Woman*. Toronto: McClelland & Stewart, 1989. Print.
———. *The Handmaid's Tale*. Toronto: Seal, 1989. Print.
———. *Oryx and Crake*. Toronto: McClelland & Stewart, 2003. Print.
———. *The Year of the Flood*. Toronto: McClelland & Stewart, 2009. Print.
Brumberg, Joan Jacobs. *Fasting Girls: The History of Anorexia Nervosa*. New York: Plume, 1989. Print.
Butler, Judith. *Bodies That Matter: On the Discursive Limits of "Sex."* New York: Routledge, 1993. Print.
Comninou, Maria. "Speech, Pornography, and Hunting." *Animals and Women: Feminist Theoretical Explorations*. Ed. Carol J. Adams and Josephine Donovan. Durham: Duke UP, 1995. 126–48. Print.
Cooke, Grayson. "Technics and the Human at Zero-Hour: Margaret Atwood's *Oryx and Crake*." *Studies in Canadian Literature* 31.2 (2006): 105–25. Print.
DiMarco, Danette. "Paradice Lost, Paradice Regained: *homo faber* and the Makings of a New Beginning in *Oryx and Crake*." *Papers on Language & Literature* 41.2 (2005): 170–95. Print.
Dunning, Stephen. "Margaret Atwood's *Oryx and Crake*: The Terror of the Therapeutic." *Canadian Literature* 186 (2005): 86–101. Print.
Finding Nemo. Dir. Andrew Stanton and Lee Unkrich. Disney/Pixar, 2003. DVD.
Glover, Jayne. "Human/Nature: Ecological Philosophy in Margaret Atwood's *Oryx and Crake*." *English Studies in Africa* 52.2 (2009): 50–62. Print.
Gruen, Lori. "Dismantling Oppression: An Analysis of the Connection Between Women and Animals." *Ecofeminism: Women, Animals, Nature*. Ed. Greta Gaard. Philadelphia: Temple UP, 1993. 60–90. Print.
Haraway, Donna. *Simians, Cyborgs, and Women: The Reinvention of Nature*. New York: Routledge, 1991. Print.
Hobgood, Jennifer. "Anti-Edibles: Capitalism and Schizophrenia in Margaret Atwood's *The Edible Woman*." *Style* 36.1 (2002): 146–68. Print.
Jameson, Fredric. *Postmodernism, or, The Cultural Logic of Late Capitalism*. Durham: Duke UP, 1999. Print.
Lacan, Jacques. *Feminine Sexuality: Jacques Lacan and the école freudienne*. Ed. Juliet Mitchell and Jacqueline Rose. Trans. Jacqueline Rose. London: Macmillan, 1982. Print.
Latour, Bruno. *Politics of Nature: How to Bring the Sciences into Democracy*. Trans. Catherine Porter. Cambridge, MA: Harvard UP, 2004. Print.
Parry, Jovian. "*Oryx and Crake* and the New Nostalgia for Meat." *Society and Animals* 17 (2009): 241–56. Print.
Rudacille, Deborah. *The Scalpel and the Butterfly: The Conflict Between Animal Research and Animal Protection*. Berkeley: U of California P, 2001. Print.

The End of Life as We Knew It

Material Nature and the American Family in Susan Beth Pfeffer's Last Survivors Series

Alexa Weik von Mossner

The dystopian mood, defined by Peter Fitting as "the sense of a threatened near future" (140), has been a dominant feature of much of twentieth- and twenty-first-century American literature, and, in recent years, it has found particularly powerful expression in the young adult novel. Perhaps most remarkable is the flood of publications that turn toward environmental or ecological concerns and their consequences for human existence. Eco-dystopias such as Jacob Sackin's *Islands* (2008) and *Iglu* (2011), Suzanne Weyn's *Empty* (2009), Paolo Bacigalupi's *Ship Breaker* (2010), or Cameron Stracher's *The Water Wars* (2011) speak to the anxieties and desires of a generation that grows up with the vague understanding that by the time they are thirty, the natural world around them will have changed dramatically, and not for the better. That the nightmarish scenarios outlined in these novels resonate with contemporary teenage audiences is evidenced by their phenomenal success in the marketplace. As Karen Springen points out in her review of recent young adult publications for *Publishers Weekly*, "end-of-the-world novels are selling briskly" (Springen). And no end of the flood is in sight.

Susan Beth Pfeffer's Last Survivors series has been especially successful with North American teenagers. In *Life as We Knew It* (2006), *The Dead and the Gone* (2008), and *This World We Live In* (2010), Pfeffer imagines the possible social, political, and personal costs of a sudden, radical environmental change in the very near future. Although she chooses a non-anthropogenic cause for this global disaster—an asteroid hits the moon and knocks it closer in orbit to the earth, thus changing its gravitational pull—Pfeffer offers an intriguing account of its possible local effects in the United States. Whether they live in the rural setting of Howell, Pennsylvania, or in the crowded urban space of New York City, her teenage protagonists not only quickly develop a whole new set of priorities as a result of radically changed ecological conditions, they also learn that their bodies, their thinking, and their very being are inextricably linked to the environment in which they live. When that environment changes radically, so must they and other humans around them. Emphasizing the material aspects of the global ecological crisis she depicts as well as its multifaceted and stratified social outcomes, Pfeffer's novels ask readers to redefine their understanding of what Stacy Alaimo and Susan Hekman have called "the relationships among the natural, the human, and the nonhuman" (7) and remind them that agency is not exclusively or even primarily human.

This, I will argue in the first part of this chapter, is a commendable achievement, although it is not without occasional missteps. What I find more problematic about the series, which made the New York Times bestseller list for Young Adult Literature in 2008, is the nature of the social and personal changes Pfeffer depicts, many of which are meant to soften the blow of the apocalyptic narrative for her young readers and give them a glimmer of hope. As I will show in the second part of the chapter, the Last Survivors series draws on the rich historical mythology of the American frontier in its combination of an environmentalist message about human entanglement in and critical dependence on the natural world with a nostalgic plea for a simpler and more family-oriented life. The material pressures arising from future ecological disasters, Pfeffer's dystopian novels suggest, may beget new kinds of community and new kinds of human-nature relationships that look very much like those of the old American pioneers, with the main difference being that people will eat a lot more canned food.

The Bare Necessities: Material Nature and the Dystopian Struggle for Survival

The Last Survivors series consists of two companion novels and a third book, which functions as a sequel to both of these. While the first novel, *Life as We Knew It*, is set in a rural Pennsylvania town and focuses on sixteen-year-old Miranda Evans and her family, the plot of the companion book, *The Dead and the Gone*, takes place at the same time but in a different location: New York City, where seventeen-year-old Alex Morales and his younger sisters have to fight for survival after enormous tidal waves have taken the lives of both of their parents. *This World We Live In*, finally, brings the two protagonists of the earlier novels together in Pennsylvania and involves them in a complicated love relationship.

Life as We Knew It is told through Miranda's journal entries, which give us a glimpse into her busy life and complicated family relations. Her parents are divorced, her father has remarried a much younger woman, and, in addition to her two brothers, she will soon have a half-sibling from that union. Miranda tries her best to deal with the new situation and with her everyday troubles at home and in school. What bothers her most is that her father is now living in upstate New York, and that her older brother Matt is also far away, having gone to Cornell for his undergraduate studies. The temporal setting of the narrative is undefined. Miranda's journal gives specific weekdays and dates, but she never mentions a year. However, everything in her account—from her suburban environment to consumer goods and technical gadgets she describes—will likely look quite familiar to the average American teenager. The only thing that separates the imaginative world of the novel from a contemporary reader's immediate present—apart from biographical differences—is the fact that we learn early on that an asteroid is on a collision course with the moon, and that scientists are debating the possible consequences of the event.

Tom Moylan has famously argued that dystopian texts have the capability "not only to delight but also to teach" because "discovering and thinking through the logic and consequences of an imagined world" may lead to "an enlightening triangulation between an individual reader's limited perspective, the estranged re-vision of the alternative world on the pages of a given text, and the actually existing society" (xvi–xvii). Pfeffer no doubt wants to provoke just such an enlightening triangulation, but she deliberately starts out with an imagined world that looks deceptively familiar, thus drawing her readers into a narrative about the life of a teenager not unlike themselves. It is only when the asteroid hits the moon that the narrative starts to convey a sense of impending disaster. Observing the spectacle with her mother from the road in front of their house, Miranda is "shocked when the asteroid actually made contact with the moon. With our moon. At that second, I think we all realized it was Our Moon and if it was attacked, then we were attacked" (*Life* 18–19). This is the first time Miranda senses that there is an actual relationship between herself and the moon, and that this unusual cosmic event may have a direct impact on her life. As a result of the collision, she observes, the moon looks "tilted and wrong" and it is "larger, way larger" than it used to be (19). This moment of cognitive estrangement and sudden insight marks the end of the world as Miranda—and the reader—knew it and the beginning of a new and scary era in which the natural environment of the earth changes dramatically, forcing humans around the world to change with it or die.

While the complex relationship between human bodies and minds and their surrounding natural environment is a prominent theme in much dystopian fiction (regardless of whether it is written for young adult or adult audiences), scholarly inquiry has often neglected the material aspects of this exchange. In *Bodily Natures* (2010), Stacy Alaimo rightly bemoans the fact that in our readings of cultural texts, as well as in human readings of nature more generally, "*Matter*, the vast stuff of the world and of ourselves" has too often been "flattened into a 'blank slate' for human inscription. The *environment* has been drained of its blood . . . in order that it become a mere empty space" in which human development takes place (1–2). This is a problem because, as Nicole Boivin argues with reference to the work of environmental psychologist James Gibson, "The environment, or material world, forms the final component of what amounts to a linguistically separated but deeply interpenetrated triad composed of mind, matter, and body" (74). Humans, as Alaimo puts it, "are the very stuff of the material, emergent world" (20) and it is a mistake to think of them as purely socially, culturally, or linguistically constructed subjects. As creators of fictional humans and fictional worlds, writers have always had to "grapple with ways to render murky material forces palpable or recognizably 'real'" (Alaimo 9), and literary scholars would thus do well to pay attention to the representation of such material forces in literary texts.

In the case of speculative or science fiction texts, such attention is particularly vital. Alternative natural environments as well as all kinds of material objects play a central role in what Moylan describes as "worldbuilding": the "ability to generate cognitively substantial yet estranged alternative worlds" (5). In Moylan's view, much of science fiction writing requires the reader to participate in this complex world-building process, because it is necessary to learn "the complexity of the alternative world in order to understand the characters' actions" (6). Readers who are unwilling to do such work will have trouble fully understanding or appreciating the narrative because they have not grasped the fictive world and the influence it exerts on individual characters and their actions. Quite frequently, the alien world to be grasped also includes an estranged natural environment. As eco-critic Patrick D. Murphy has observed, science fiction can be "nature-oriented literature, in the sense of its being an aesthetic text that, on the one hand, directs reader attention toward the natural world and human interaction with other aspects of nature within that world, and, on the other hand, makes specific environmental issues part of [its] plots and themes" (263). Among the examples Murphy offers are full-blooded science fiction novels such as Ursula K. Le Guin's *The Dispossessed* (1974) and Kim Stanley Robinson's *Mars* trilogy (1992–96), which confront readers with complex alien environments whose unfamiliar dynamics they must learn and appreciate in order to understand the narrative. Near-future dystopias set on planet Earth require less effort in this regard, because their worlds tend to be more familiar and are thus more easily grasped. Nevertheless, such novels often introduce natural environments that are quite different from the world in which contemporary readers live and whose difference is central for plot and character development.

The crucial difference Pfeffer introduces into the imaginative world of the Last Survivors series is the changed gravitational pull of the moon, which almost immediately transforms the material living conditions of her protagonists. Literally overnight, the planet on which they live becomes a different one. Changing tides and weather patterns not only kill millions of people the world over, they also make life on the former coastlines impossible. Earthquakes and volcanic eruptions exacerbate the situation, and once the volcanic ash reaches the atmosphere, it begins to slowly block out the sun. Only a few weeks have gone by in Miranda's journal, but the planet on which she lives has now become so strange that it would deserve that somewhat odd name—"eaarth"—that environmentalist Bill McKibben has recently suggested for our actually existing planet because it, too, is on its way to becoming unfamiliar as a result of—in this case anthropogenic—ecological change (1). Pfeffer's novels, however, do not engage with any of the scientific data that inform McKibben's gloomy predictions, and Pfeffer has acknowledged that the natural disasters happening in her fictional world are only vaguely related to scientific principles. Scientific accuracy, she explains, is not really her point.[1] Instead, she is interested in the ways in which humanity would deal with radically new and much less friendly planetary conditions, and in the immediate effects such an ecological change might have on the life of an average American teenager and her family.

The effects are profound. There is an immediate breakdown of nearly all communication systems, including cellphones, land lines, the Internet, and satellite TV. The electricity grid becomes increasingly unreliable and the supply lines for food, gas, and many other essential goods begin to break down. Two days after the collision, Miranda's mother takes her elderly neighbour and her children to the local supermarket, which now has turned into a bizarre consumer battlefield with "people racing for carts, people screaming, and two guys punching each other out" (*Life* 35). The Evans family grab as many canned goods from the half-empty shelves as their carts will hold, throw their hundred dollar bills at one of the "poor terrified cashiers" (36), and drive away with a profound sense that they have been "stocking up for the end of the world" (39). Over the next few weeks, however, they will realize that what they have is not nearly enough. Large parts of the United States are now a disaster zone, and even as the inhabitants of Howell, Pennsylvania, are relatively lucky in being only indirectly affected by the destruction, they will have to prepare for the worst.

The American government, with its police, military, and disaster relief forces, is strangely absent from Pfeffer's first book. Not only is there a complete breakdown in infrastructure, but all governance seems to have been wiped out by the disaster. While the American president—Miranda's mother calls him "the idiot"—does broadcast a brief message from his ranch in Texas, that message only admonishes people to "place [their] faith in God" (*Life* 25). It will take federal relief efforts almost a year before they reach the people in Howell. Until then, Miranda and her family are forced to fend for themselves and to try to somehow survive the bitter-cold winter with "no power and no food coming in and no gas for the car and no oil for the furnace" (123). Her brothers cut wood to keep a small wood stove going, and the two women do their best to control the food reserves. A visit from Miranda's father, who has decided to take his pregnant wife farther west where things are supposed to be better, and the death of the elderly neighbour both result in additional food provisions, but by December Miranda and her mother are down to one small meal per day, and the two brothers are eating only slightly more. Things are getting tough, very tough. People less well prepared than the Evans family are dying of starvation, and many of those who still have food are taken by the flu. Miranda's journal is now focused narrowly on a very small selection of topics: how to get food and water, how not to consume too much of either of them, how to stay warm, how to cure her family members of disease, and how to survive until spring. The natural environment and the biological needs of the human body suddenly gain a significance they never had before in the young girl's life. Without the elaborate infrastructure of the American consumer society, her body and mind are much more vulnerable to the material forces of nature.

Nature, as environmental historian Linda Nash points out, does not have agency in the sense of intentionality or choice. However, Nash suggests, the problem might actually lie with our definition of (human) agency: "Perhaps our narratives should emphasize that . . . so-called human agency cannot be separated from the environments in which that agency emerges" (69). In their introduction to *Material Agency* (2010), Carl Knappett and Lambros Malafouris explain that, in fact, "when agency is linked strictly to consciousness and intentionality, we have very little scope for extending its reach beyond the human" (ix). This, however, we must do if we want to account for the manifold ways in which non-human living things such as trees and seemingly "dead" things such as stones and buildings have significant effects on their environments, including humans. Pfeffer's *Life as We Knew It* chronicles some of these effects. In her desperation, Miranda starts to "hate the moon" as well as "tides and earthquakes and volcanoes." She hates "a world where things that have absolutely nothing to do with me can destroy my life and the lives of people I love" (132). But of course these "things" *do* have something to do with her and always did, only she never before realized just how much. Now that the sun is hidden from the ash cloud, she recognizes how much she—and every living thing around her—*needs* sunlight, and without any oil or running fresh water in the house she develops a totally different relationship to the snow-covered woods.

In such moments, the reader is invited to share Miranda's insights, which is why one reviewer has suggested that this is a book that "everyone should read to help you realize how we take the earth for granted and how one seemingly harmless incident can change everything" (*Two Readers*). Such realization, if it happens, is the result of the "enlightening triangulation between an individual reader's limited perspective, the estranged re-vision of the alternative world on the pages of a given text, and the actually existing society" that Moylan sees at the heart of the dystopian endeavour (xvii). Many reviewers and readers have read *Life as We Knew It* as a cautionary tale warning us to respect and take care of the planet and its life-sustaining systems. The fact that Pfeffer has chosen a non-anthropogenic cause for her future disaster seems to make little difference in this regard. Pfeffer herself has said that until reviewers and readers began to tell her so, she did not even realize that she had written an ecological dystopia.[2] What interested her most when writing the book, she has explained, was "the domestic response to disaster" (*Cynsations*), and it is in this domestic realm that she creates spaces of hope in the middle of an ongoing and unstoppable global catastrophe.

Pfeffer's bleak look into a dystopian future would be difficult to bear for a teenage readership if it were not for the moments in which she offers glimmers of utopian hope. The German philosopher Ernst Bloch saw the "principle of hope" at the heart of the utopian endeavour, which he located not only in literary texts but also in political practice and common daydreaming. And while Ruth Levitas has argued in *The Concept of Utopia* (2010) that "the essential element in utopia is not hope, but desire . . . for a better way of being" (221), scholars and writers tend to agree that in the case of the young adult dystopian text, one cannot in fact write such texts without at least a glimmer of hope. Lois Lowry, author of the best-selling dystopia *The Giver* (1993), firmly believes that her young readers "need to see some hope for [a better] world" and "can't imagine writing a book that doesn't have a hopeful ending" ("Interview" 199). Monica Hughes, author of the Isis trilogy (1980–83), agrees that even the most dystopian young adult text must retain hope in order to be socially responsible. "Dystopian worlds are exciting," she writes, "but the end result must never be nihilism and despair" (156). Given this general agreement that it would be unethical to write a young adult dystopia without utopian moments of hope, it is unsurprising that the first book of the Last Survivor series was marketed as "the heart-pounding story of Miranda's struggle to hold on to the most important resource of all—hope—in an increasingly desperate and unfamiliar world."[3] All three novels are in fact quite typical of young adult dystopian literature in their approach to survival-related hope, and given that Pfeffer is a veteran author who has published more than seventy books in the field, this is perhaps to be expected. What is remarkable, though, is that in *Life as We Knew It*, as well as in the two following books in the series, this hope for a better future rests predominantly, if not exclusively, on the survivor qualities of the American family.

Next of Kin: Self-Reliance and Frontier Mentality in the Last Survivors Series

As a companion novel to *Life as We Knew It*, *The Dead and the Gone* covers the same time span, opening on the evening on which the asteroid hits the moon. The novel makes no reference to the first book of the series and focuses instead on seventeen-year old Alex Morales and his struggle to take care of his two sisters after their parents disappear when enormous tidal waves submerge parts of New York and their native Puerto Rico. The intelligent and highly ambitious son of a nurse and a caretaker not only has to deal with the fact that his parents are missing (they are never officially declared dead) and that his high-flying dreams for the future are destroyed; at the age of seventeen he is also the new head of the Morales household, with almost no money to spend and very little idea what to do. Unlike Miranda, who was raised by an atheist mother and has little understanding of the more fundamentalist form of Christianity she observes in her friend Megan, Alex and his sisters are devout members of the Roman Catholic Church. As such, they are called upon to understand the global ecological disaster as an act of God. While Alex feels increasingly challenged in his faith as human life becomes almost impossible in the slowly decaying New York, his sisters refuse to give up hope that some good will come out of the situation and that their parents will eventually return. However, the narrative does not reward such unwavering belief; at the end of the novel both hopes are shattered.

In his review of the book for the *New York Times*, John Green argues that what makes *The Dead and the Gone* "so riveting is its steadfast resistance to traditional ideas of hope in children's books" (Green). If this were true, Pfeffer would indeed have chosen an unusual way out of what Kay Sambell has called the "significant creative dilemma" faced by all writers of dystopian novels for young adult audiences. "Whereas the 'adult' dystopia's didactic impact relies on the absolute, unswerving nature of its dire warning," writes Sambell, "the expression of moral meaning in the children's dystopia is often characterized by degrees of hesitation, oscillation, and ambiguity" (164). According to Sambell, "In the adult dystopian vision, appealing heroes are unequivocally shown to fail" and "any hope they represent is extinguished in the dystopia's denouement" (164). The authors of young adult dystopias, by contrast, tend to hesitate "to depict the extinction of such hope in the narrative resolution of their stories," a strategy that, in Sambell's view, compromises the imaginative and ideological coherence of their texts (164). The question is, however, whether such complete extinction of hope is really necessary for a successful dystopia. Offering a pessimistic outlook on future developments does not necessarily mean excluding all possibilities for improvement and amelioration. *The Dead and the Gone* is a dark and scary novel, and its appealing hero is shown to fail frequently and tragically as he roams the streets of New York, first for food and later in search of a passage to one of the fabled "safe towns" for himself and his ailing sisters.[4] Like Miranda, Alex is often powerless against the forces of nature and the direct and indirect effects they have on the desperate humans around him. He cannot even prevent his devout sister Briana from dying a horrible and senseless death in a malfunctioning elevator. Kneeling over her emaciated body, he almost finds comfort in the fact that "The moon had killed her, not man" (*Dead* 297).

Despite these tragic moments, however, *The Dead and the Gone* is not entirely without hope. It is what keeps Alex going, and sometimes a most serendipitous coincidence rewards him for his persistence. As in the first book of the series, when federal food rations reach the Evans family just at the right time, not all of these moments seem realistic or probable, but Pfeffer does succeed in portraying a world in which survival depends as much on chance as on anything else. As Green puts it, she "subverts all our expectations of how redemption works in teenage fiction, as Alex learns to live, and have faith, in a world where radical unfairness is the norm" (Green). The source of this faith, however, is not so much his religious beliefs as it is his unwavering commitment to his family.

The mutual responsibilities and expectations between both biological and chosen kin figure prominently in all three of Pfeffer's books. Relying on the members of one's immediate—if sometimes highly patchworked—family is presented as the only chance for survival in an increasingly hostile material environment. As food, water, and fuel are becoming everybody's central concern, the community of those for whom one feels responsible is getting smaller and smaller. In *Life as We Knew It* Miranda is admonished by her mother again and again that "This isn't the time for friendships" and that "We have to watch out only for ourselves" (101). *The Dead and the Gone* continues this theme of self-reliance and the survival of the family, despite its sustained engagement with Christian values and ethics. When Alex sends one of his sisters to a convent in upstate New York to work with the nuns there, this has very little to do with faith or the belief that she can do something meaningful for the community. It is solely meant to secure her survival, as well as his own and his other sister's, since they are left with more food. *This World We Live In*, finally, in which the protagonists of the first two books meet, extends the notion of the family beyond biological kinship, but nevertheless insists that there are people one needs to care for and people who are not one's responsibility, regardless of whether they are dying or not. "Now being a good neighbor means minding your own business" (*Life* 280), declares Miranda, and when things get tough, the only thing that counts is to save your family.

Surprisingly, Pfeffer's novels do not really suggest that this loss of larger civic solidarity and interpersonal compassion is regrettable or problematic. On the contrary, readers are led to appreciate the virtues of a self-reliant and rugged existence in a newly emerging American wilderness. This attitude is already taking shape at the end of the first book, when Miranda has learned to appreciate the basic pleasures of being alive and having food, and wonders how people, back in the old, affluent times, never seemed to realize "how precious life is" (*Life* 287). Now that she is forced to live in a state of utmost deprivation and uncertainty, she is "grateful for the good things that have happened to me this year. I never knew I could love as deeply as I do. I never knew I could be so willing to sacrifice things for other people. I never knew how wonderful a taste of pineapple juice could be, or the warmth of a woodstove . . . or the feel of clean clothes against freshly scrubbed skin" (*Life* 287). Having less and being forced to fight for one's survival, it is suggested, can lead to a more fulfilled and purposeful life.

For Alex in *The Dead and the Gone*, who lives in the decrepit urban environment of New York, things are more complicated, but he, too, realizes that in these decaying remnants of American civilization there will be no future for him and his sisters. Like the American pioneers centuries before, he decides that he must go *west*, because he has heard of places where people have food and water and everything they need. But in *This World We Live In*, which is set a year after the events of the first two books, we learn that he and Julie never made it to one of these utopian places, and that what Frederick Jackson Turner termed the frontier experience has become a lot more complicated, not least geographically. Wandering through the wilderness, Alex and Julie happen to meet Miranda's father and his wife and baby son, who are on their way back to Pennsylvania because they have been told that "there was no point" in going farther west: "Colorado, Nevada, were devastated. What survivors there were had been moved east or south" (*World* 92). The frontier of the Last Survivors series is no longer connected to westward expansion, then, but once again it is the place where "the wilderness masters the colonist" because "the environment is at first too strong for the man" (Turner 15).

Much of the plot of the third novel of the series centres on the question of who does and who doesn't count as family once Miranda's father and his new acquaintances have arrived at the house in Howell.[5] The other big question, however, is whether they should stay put and wait for the next winter, or whether it is better to move on in search of a better life elsewhere. The narrative closes with Miranda, Alex, and her father's family leaving together, "crossing Pennsylvania, making our way south to Tennessee. It will take months, but we're strong, we're all strong, and we have reason to live" (*World* 238). As a result of the dystopian conditions they live in, Miranda's new, extended family has grown and changed for the better, and even as they have lost people they love, the narrative closes with a somewhat ambiguous happy ending. As William Katerberg points out in *Future West* (2008), "frontier myths incline people to imagine the future as a return to primitive conditions" (5), and in its own way, the Last Survivors series participates in those myths and in an American tradition of utopian and dystopian writing. Like the science fiction narratives Katerberg examines, Pfeffer's novels imagine a future in which "society has been swept away by some kind of natural disaster or human-made holocaust. In the primitive conditions that ensue, survivors have been forced to start over and perhaps build a new kind of society" (Katerberg 5). What society Pfeffer's survivors will build is unclear, but there is reason to believe that it will be more attuned to the new conditions on planet Earth. At least that seems to be the vague hope of the protagonists.

In 2007 the American Library Association named *Life as We Knew It* one of the Best Books for Young Adults, and the novels in the Last Survivors series are now so frequently read in high school classrooms that they come with their own teaching guides.[6] Indeed, they seem to inspire their teenage audience to reflect critically on their lives and their current assets. The letters she receives from readers, says Pfeffer, "pretty uniformly say the positive they get out of the books is to appreciate their lives and the people they love. . . . What I'm getting from the kids is, 'I never thought to appreciate all the everyday things I took for granted'" (qtd. in Springen). A quick glance through readers'—mostly enthusiastic—comments posted online similarly suggests that the reading experience primarily makes young adults more satisfied with their current lives rather than awakening desire for a better way of being. While the fact that all of the books are marred by a number of logic and writing problems (and an American obsession with canned food) seems to have angered some young readers, the books are mostly praised for their gripping disaster scenarios and as "a very good read."[7]

All this seems to suggest that, despite its celebration of a simpler and less wasteful life, the critical potential of the Last Survivor series is rather limited. Rather than offering the opportunity for an "enlightening triangulation" (Moylan xvii), Pfeffer's novels seem to promote a greater acceptance and indeed appreciation of the status quo. As Claire Curtis has pointed out, the novels present "injustice as a fact to be accepted and adaptation to injustice as the best case scenario for moving forward" (7) rather than encouraging readers to play an active role in the shaping of a more just and sustainable world. Curtis rightly bemoans the fact that Pfeffer's novels do not offer young adult readers a space to *resist* the reality of their imaginative future world and, by extension, the inequalities and unsustainable practices of their own twenty-first-century world. The reason for this lack of critical engagement with contemporary American society might be found in the novels' relatively claustrophobic concentration on two protagonists and their kin. We learn only very little about how the rest of the world is dealing with this global disaster, and in their insistence on the need to care only for those who are near and dear to us, the novels actually discourage the recognition of the claims and needs of those who are not immediately related to us but with whom we nevertheless share the same planet. Pfeffer's nostalgic evocation of the American frontier and celebration of family solidarity stand in the way of a more critical engagement with citizenship responsibilities and the limits of solidarity and empathy in the face of ecological disaster.

From an ecocritical point of view, the choice of a non-anthropogenic cause for the disaster also takes away a lot of the books' critical potential. Eco-dystopias that put anthropogenic disasters at the heart of their stories—such as, for example, Saci Lloyd's *The Carbon Diaries 2015* (2008) and *The Carbon Diaries 2017* (2009), which imagine the mid-term effects of climate change and severe carbon rationing on the life of a London teenager and her friends and family—are in a much better position to formulate critiques of current human behaviour and potential future consequences. As the commercial success of *The Carbon Diaries* and other critical eco-dystopias demonstrates, there is considerable interest in books that dare to engage with human responsibility for our ecological future.[8] By inflicting disaster from the outside rather than making it something that humanity has brought upon itself, Pfeffer forgoes the chance to relate her critique of mindless consumer capitalism to the slowly unfolding real-world ecological disaster that is the background of her young readers' lives. What nevertheless makes the Last Survivors series an interesting object of study is the books' intense engagement with something that most contemporary teenagers give very little thought to: the fact that the earth's biosphere is a fragile and complex interactive system that is dependent on a number of delicately balanced factors. Pfeffer's achievement lies in having evoked for a twenty-first-century teenage audience how drastically a disturbance of that delicate system would affect the material and social aspects of human life, and how easily it could lead to the end of life as we know it. Unfortunately, she does not really offer them a chance to critically reflect on their own involvement in the bringing about of such a disturbance.

Notes

1 Pfeffer has made this argument on her own blog: *Susan Beth Pfeffer: Meteors, Moons, and Me.* 7 July 2008. Web. 9 Feb. 2012.
2 Interview. *Reading with Tequila.* 15 Apr. 2010. Web. 22 Sept. 2011.
3 I am taking this quotation from the *Harcourt Discussion Guide* for the novel, but it is also widely used on websites that promote the novel or offer it for purchase.
4 In the novel, safe towns are secret and highly protected communities that have food, water, fuel and all other amenities that now have become luxuries. They can be reached only by a very small and privileged elite in possession of the necessary transit papers.
5 Pfeffer originally planned to conclude the series with *This World We Live In* but is now working on a fourth book with the working title "The Shade of the Moon." For more information, see her blog http://susanbethpfeffer.blogspot.co.at/2011/04/when-shade-of-moon-meets-sleep-of-pill.html.
6 Teaching guides for the three novels are available at http://www.hmhbooks.com/lifeasweknewit/classroomresources.html.
7 This quotation from Ally's review of *Life as We Knew It* is only one example chosen from 407 customer reviews of the series currently available.
8 For a critical discussion of Lloyd's novels see my article "Hope in Dark Times: Climate Change and the World Risk Society in Saci Lloyd's *The Carbon Diaries 2015* and *2017*," in *Contemporary Dystopian Fiction for Young Adults: Brave New Teenagers*, ed. Balaka Basu, Kate Broad and Carrie Hintz (London and New York: Routledge, 2013).

Works Cited

Alaimo, Stacy. *Bodily Natures: Science, Environment, and the Material Self.* Bloomington, IN: Indiana UP, 2010. Print.
Alaimo, Stacy and Susan Hekman, eds. *Material Feminisms.* Bloomington, IN: Indiana UP, 2008. Print.

Bacigalupi, Paolo. *Ship Breaker*. New York and Boston: Little, Brown, 2010. Print.
Bloch, Ernst. *The Principle of Hope*. Basil Blackwell: Oxford UP, 1986. Print.
Boivin, Nicole. *Material Cultures, Material Minds: The Impact of Things of Human Thought, Society, and Evolution*. Cambridge: Cambridge UP, 2008. Print.
Curtis, Claire P. "Educating Desire, Choosing Justice? Susan Beth Pfeffer's *Last Survivors* Series and Julie Bertagna's *Exodus*." *Contemporary Dystopian Fiction for Young Adults: Brave New Teenagers*. Ed. Carrie Hintz, Balaka Basu, and Katherine A. Broad. London: Routledge, 2013. 85–99. Print.
Fitting, Peter. "Utopia, Dystopia, and Science Fiction." *The Cambridge Companion to Utopian Literature*. Ed. Gregory Claeys. Cambridge: Cambridge UP, 2010. 135–53. Print.
Green, John. "Scary New World." *New York Times Sunday Book Review* 7 Nov. 2008. Web. 20 Sept. 2011.
Harcourt Discussion Guide for Life as We Knew It *by Susan Beth Pfeffer*. 16 June 2008. Web. 27 Sept. 2011.
Harcourt Discussion Guide for The Dead and the Gone *by Susan Beth Pfeffer*. 2 June 2010. Web. 27 Sept. 2011.
Harcourt Discussion Guide for This World We Live In *by Susan Beth Pfeffer*. 2 June 2010. Web. 27 Sept. 2011.
Hughes, Monica. *The Guardian of Isis*. London: Hamish Hamilton, 1981. Print.
———. *The Isis Pedlar*. London: Hamish Hamilton, 1982. Print.
———. *The Keeper of the Isis Light*. London: Hamish Hamilton, 1980. Print.
———. "The Struggle between Utopia and Dystopia in Writing for Children and Young Adults." *Utopian and Dystopian Writing for Children and Young Adults*. Eds Carrie Hintz and Elaine Ostry. New York and London: Routledge, 2003. 157. Print.
Katerberg, William H. *Future West: Utopia and Apocalypse in Frontier Science Fiction*. Lawrence: U of Kansas P, 2008. Print.
Knappett, Carl, and Lambros Malafouris, eds. *Material Agency: Towards a Non-Anthropocentric Approach*. New York: Springer, 2010. Print.
Levitas, Ruth. *The Concept of Utopia*. Berne and New York: Peter Berg, 2009. Print.
Lloyd, Saci. *The Carbon Diaries 2015*. London: Hodder Children's Books, 2008. Print.
———. *The Carbon Diaries 2017*. London: Hodder Children's Books, 2009. Print.
Lowry, Lois. *The Giver*. New York: Bantam, 1993. Print.
———. "Interview with Louis Lowry, Author of *The Giver*." *Utopian and Dystopian Writing for Children and Young Adults*. Ed. Carrie Hintz and Elaine Ostry. New York and London: Routledge, 2003. 196–99. Print.
McKibben, Bill. *Eaarth: Making Life on a Tough New Planet*. New York: St. Martin's Griffin, 2011. Print.

Moylan, Tom. *Scraps of the Untainted Sky: Science Fiction, Utopia, Dystopia.* Boulder, CO: Westview, 2000. Print.

Murphy, Patrick D. "The Non-Alibi of Alien Scapes: SF and Ecocriticism." *Beyond Nature Writing: Expanding the Boundaries of Ecocriticism.* Ed. Karla Armbruster and Kathleen R. Wallace. Charlottesville: U of Virginia P, 2001. 263-78. Print.

Nash, Linda. "Agency of Nature or Nature of Agency?" *Environmental History* 10.1 (Jan. 2005): 67–69. Print.

Pfeffer, Susan Beth. *The Dead and the Gone.* New York: Harcourt, 2008. Print.

———. Interview. *Cynsations.* 2 Apr. 2008. Web. 22 Sept. 2011.

———. Interview. *Reading with Tequila.* 15 Apr. 2010. Web. 22 Sept. 2011.

———. *Life as We Knew It.* New York: Harcourt, 2006. Print.

———. "The Science of *Life as We Knew It* and *The Dead and the Gone.*" *Susan Beth Pfeffer Blogspot.* 7 July 2008. Web. 28 Sept. 2011.

———. *This World We Live In.* New York: Harcourt, 2010. Print.

Sackin, Jacob. *Iglu.* Bloomington, IN: Authorhouse, 2011. Print.

———. *Islands.* Port Orchard and Washington: Blue Works, 2008. Print.

Sambell, Kay. "Presenting the Case for Social Change: The Creative Dilemma of Dystopian Writing for Children." *Utopian and Dystopian Writing for Children and Young Adults.* Ed. Carrie Hintz and Elaine Ostry. New York and London: Routledge, 2003. 163–78. Print.

Springen, Karen. "Children's Books: Apocalypse Now." *Publishers Weekly* 15 Feb. 2010. Web. 23 Sept. 2011.

Stoutenburg, Adrien. *Out There.* New York: Viking Press, 1971. Print.

Stracher, Cameron. *The Water Wars.* Naperville: Sourcebooks Fire, 2011. Print.

Suvin, Darko. *Metamorphoses of Science Fiction: On the Poetics and History of a Literary Genre.* New Haven: Yale UP, 1979. Print.

Turner, Frederick Jackson. 1920. *The Frontier in American History.* New York: BiblioBazaar, 2008. Print.

Two Readers Reviews. "Review of *Life as We Knew It* (Last Survivors #1) by Susan Beth Pfeffer." 21 Sept. 2011. Web. 27 Sept. 2011.

Weik von Mossner, Alexa. "Hope in Dark Times: Climate Change and the World Risk Society in Saci Lloyd's *The Carbon Diaries 2015* and *2017.*" *Contemporary Dystopian Fiction for Young Adults: Brave New Teenagers.* Ed. Balaka Basu, Kate Broad, and Carrie Hintz. London and New York: Routledge, 2013. 69–83. Print.

Weyn, Suzanne. *Empty.* New York: Scholastic, 2009. Print.

"The Treatment for Stirrings"
Dystopian Literature for Adolescents

Joseph Campbell

> Children's and young adult utopias are in particular need of sustained study for two reasons. First of all, there is a long tradition of thinking of childhood itself as utopian, a space and time apart from the corruption of everyday adult life. The second reason is the unique function that utopianism and utopian writing plays in children's socialization and education.
> —Carrie Hintz and Elaine Ostry, Introduction to *Utopian and Dystopian Writing for Children and Young Adults*

In the last five years, there has been an explosion of dystopian texts intended for adolescents. Because "Young Adult" (or YA) is the predominant mode of the dystopian novel at the moment, understanding how these works fit in the discourses of adolescence is important. The label "dystopian," I propose, is an indication that the work will perform social critique in a subjunctive mode. This is especially true when considering the dystopian novel intended for an adolescent audience.

I propose that the dystopian work for adolescents explores the way subjectivity is formed in the face of a system of social pressure. Cultures watch their citizens' moves of identification, and threaten them with loss of freedom should they choose the "wrong" identification. This is how societies construct their subjects socially. I believe that we can see these functions most clearly using a framework of Foucauldian systems of surveillance and power, Burkean concepts of a subject's movements of identification, and Althusserian Ideological (ISAs) and Repressive State Apparatuses (RSAs).

This theoretical lens becomes especially important when viewing these texts within the definitions of adolescence that circulate within discourses of adolescent literature critique. Thus, this article will explain how dystopian works intended for adolescents can allow young adults to see, and perhaps critique, the web of dominant power structures in which they live by showing those webs clearly. My aim is not to present a close reading of any particular work, but instead to give the reader a lens through which to begin unpacking the work done by texts in this genre.

The Use-Value of the Genre

Dystopian literature is concerned with making the often seemingly invisible cycle of ideological subject formation clear and offers adolescents some sense of agency existing within that system. Dystopian texts, then, create social critique. We can say that:

> On the most obvious level, then, the dystopia didactically foregrounds social and political questions by depicting societies whose structures are horrifyingly plausible exaggerations of our own. Dystopian authors predominantly teach by negative example, "making the familiar strange" in order to shock and frighten readers into recognition of the dire need to question official culture [...] (Sambell "Carnivalizing" 248)

Specifically, power structures are exaggerated so as to be more easily seen by the reader. Because the dystopian text is a highly critical one, any dystopian text for young adults will come into direct conflict with the didactic impulse of society, the impulse to absorb the critical subject. "Whereas the 'adult' dystopia's didactic impact relies on the absolute, unswerving nature of its dire warning, the expression of moral meaning in the children's dystopia is often characterized by degrees of hesitation, oscillation and ambiguity" (Sambell "Presenting" 164). Fredric Jameson wants critics to consider an exploration of subjectivity as the primary thematic concern of dystopian texts (166–67). This is the most important consideration of the dystopian work: what does it do?

Dystopian texts perform social critical work—a *use-value*, to borrow Thomas O. Beebee's term—that allows the reader to question the polyvalent relationships between subjectivity and power. I maintain that in dystopian works, especially those for young adults, we see the author functioning as a cultural theorist in the subjunctive mode. The effect is often a chilling warning-by-hyperbole of what might come if we are not careful. These are works in which society is shown in totalitarian extremes. If the author's intention is to warn us of what might come, then the most logical way to examine that is in this subjunctive mode or theory—or, more specifically, theoretically informed fiction writing. Beebee writes, "I began to see genre as a set of 'handles' on texts, and to realize that a text's genre is its use-value. Genre gives us not understanding in the abstract and passive sense but *use* in the pragmatic and active sense" (14; emphasis added). It is essential that we recognize that "[...] not only literary but also extra-literary systems—political, social, religious and so on—contribute significantly to the shape of literary forms" (Dubrow 112).[1] Cultural attitudes shape genre forms, and the reverse also happens. Heather Dubrow reminds us, "[m]oreover, much like a firmly rooted institution, a well-established genre transmits certain cultural attitudes, attitudes which it is shaped by and in turn helps to shape" (4). In this way, we can see that genre is both *shaped by* ideology at the same time that it *shapes* ideology. As both Beebee and Dubrow point out, genre does a particular kind of work on the reader. Indeed, some twenty years before Beebee, Tzvetan Todorov was already working with the assumption that genre was more about relations of discourses to text than about some bound set of rules for separating the "good" from the "bad" works. He said, "In a given society, the recurrence of certain discursive properties is institutionalized, and individual texts are produced and perceived in relation to the norm constituted by that codification" (198). Each genre does a particular kind of work on the reader, just as it is worked on by the society. Dystopian texts fill a gap between what we see as our current situation and the future (Zipes ix). Again, these texts are not only critical statements, but a call to action aimed at the reader, even if that action is only to begin to think more critically about the relationships between power and subjectivity that circulate within his or her current society.

What can we say is the use-value of dystopian literature for young adults, then?

The Structure of Repression

Althusser's model of ideologic transmission from "Ideology and Ideological State Apparatuses" may be well-worn, but I believe it is still a useful way to see power enacted through discourse. Althusser says, "[i]t follows that, in order to exist, every social formation must reproduce the conditions of its production at the same time as it produces, and in order to be able to produce" (86). It is absolutely essential that we understand, Althusser tells us, that any successful society will be one that has come to recognize that, in order to remain a successful society, it must create individuals who believe it important to maintain the society in question. This ideology, along with all the others of a society, then, must be distributed or disseminated. Althusser envisions particular institutional points from which ideology is distributed: the educational system of a particular society, the religious system of a society, the predominant family structure of a particular society, etc. He also wants us to pay attention to other institutions, such as the judicial system of a particular society, and the conceptual forms (as well as types of sanctioned actions) of a particular society's policing force(s).

Althusser groups these institutions into one of two categories: those that act mostly by social force (and sometimes on the body) such as educational and religious structures, and those that act mostly on the body (and sometimes by social force) such as policing forces and judicial systems. Althusser calls these groupings the Ideological State Apparatuses and the Repressive State Apparatuses, respectively. Althusser tells us that "[t]he Repressive State Apparatus functions 'by violence' [on the body]; whereas the Ideological State Apparatuses function 'by ideology' [power enacted upon the social being]" (97). In other words, ISAs work by transmitting ideology, and RSAs enforce that ideology through means of power enacted on the body, which some interpret as violence.

We might think of this as a cycle. Envision the various RSAs inscribed as a large circle, and the ISAs inscribed as a circle within the larger RSA circle, with its lines of force flowing inward from the circumference. Thinking of the relationship this way helps us to understand that, should a subject attempt to move outside of the influence of the ISAs (ostensibly by rejecting the socialization processes inherent in interpellation in the Althusserian schema), then he or she finds him- or herself in the realm of the RSA—bodily arrested in their movement and forcefully returned to the ISA circle, likely at gunpoint. I believe that it is quite useful for us to envision the ISA/RSA relationship in this way: as a series of interrelated forces acting on the subject. Callinicos summarizes this particular aspect of Althusser this way:

> The category of the subject is therefore uniquely fitted to the purpose of ideology since the complicity of the subject and object that underlines

it gives the world a meaning *for the individual* that suppresses the mechanism of exploitation and oppression at the heart of society and the meaningless chaos at its surface. Both are abolished in a system of ideal relationships which picks out each individual, giving him a unique value by virtue of the relation that exists between him and the world under their aspect of subject and object respectively. (65–66; emphasis in original)

The subject is offered choices—should he or she reject the options given in the sphere of the ISAs, he or she becomes the concern of the RSAs. The RSAs will then attempt to move the subject, bodily, back into the sphere of influence of the ISAs. "Be a subject or else," the RSA tells the subject brought before them. Indeed, though common sense tells us that there are other options, Althusser would have us understand that being a subject to these processes is a function of language. The subject is always-already a subject: "[i]deology has always-already interpellated individuals as subjects, which amounts to making it clear that individuals are always-already interpellated by ideology as subjects" (119). Eve Wiederhold shows that:

> In an Althusserian view of language, for example, "the call" of language's law is one of interpellation. To be addressed as "a moral citizen" is not merely to be so identified but to invoke linguistic practices that make possible such identifications. We become law-abiding citizens by being interpellated within the terms of a language that makes available the very idea of "citizenship" and "morality." Hence, identifications of "good citizenship" do not reflect an existent essence of "goodness" but draw upon whatever symbols a given culture employs to describe such a quality. (131)

The subject, by the very essence of subjectivity, is an interpellated figure. Because of this, some would say that in an Althusserian view, ontological possibility within such a system is circumscribed. The subject, it would seem, is an end point of ideology with very little "power-to" agency.

To be always-already interpellated, though, makes some feel that free will has been extinguished. Althusser's structures fail in many ways to assign the agency of subjects, positing them as an end point to ideology. As Wiederhold explains, this view of Althusserian theory "implies that any image of self-determined consent is an illusion" (137).[2] Thinking of the subject as merely a point on which ideology acts is a concept that can chafe.

The Normative Pressure of Surveillance

Michel Foucault's overall project is multi-faceted. Here, I want to focus in on the part of his work that discusses how power is enacted on bodies (which he calls Discipline), and how he analyzes the mechanisms that allow this to occur (such as surveillance). Primary among those mechanisms is the concept of normative surveillance. Normative surveillance describes one of the ways that power is enacted on the bodies of subjects in institutions designed to discipline them (mental hospitals, schools, family homes, etc.). Foucault says, "[t]he perfect disciplinary apparatus would make it possible for a single gaze to see everything constantly . . . a perfect eye that nothing would escape . . ." (173). This is, then, a "disciplinary gaze." The eye he posits is normative (*Discipline* 170–79). Normalization, Foucault tells us, is the aim of power within an institution:

> the art of punishing, in the regime of disciplinary power, is aimed neither at expiation, nor even precisely at repression. . . . [I]t refers individual actions to a whole that is at once a field of comparison, a space of differentiation, and the principle of a rule to be followed . . . it measures in quantitative terms and hierarchizes . . . in short, it *normalizes*. (*Discipline* 182–83; emphasis in original)

Individuals are always under the gaze of those wielding power in institutions designed to discipline them. These individuals are measured against a set of "norms" (determined ideologically) for deviation—both above the norm and below. It is in this way, Foucault says, that "[d]iscipline 'makes' individuals; it is the specific technique of a power that regards individuals both as objects and as instruments of its exercise" (*Discipline* 170). Foucault does not theorize the disciplinary gaze as somehow separate. He says, "[t]he exercise of discipline presupposes a mechanism that coerces by means of observation; an apparatus in which the techniques that make it possible to see induce effects of power, and in which, conversely, the means of coercion make those on whom they are applied clearly visible" (171). All institutions, Foucault tells us, are engaged in the process of normalization of the subjects they contact. That is, the gaze that is always directed at the individual by those around him or her is watching for transgression against the dominant ideology.

Given this interpretation of one aspect of Foucault's work, a conflation of Foucault with Althusser seems to be possible. The notion of discipline being carried out on individuals sounds very much like ideological pressure from the ISAs.³ I say "seems" because Foucault's sense of power is quite different from Althusser's. Foucault's sense is based in the polyvalent web he speaks of, in which the subject is mobile—for Foucault, power is formative and repressive simultaneously. Althusser's sense of power is that it represses. It is for this reason that I intend to use only certain aspects of Foucault's theory in combination with certain aspects of Althusser's work, creating, in a sense, a very specific lens to look through. To be more specific, I am using Althusser's sense of the ISA/RSA system, with Foucault's sense of power as it contacts the body, as a way of thinking about how the pressures exerted by those ISA/RSA pressures work at the physical level.⁴

The Moves of Identification

We might think of Foucault's work as a bridge between the ISA and the body in terms of interpellation; if we do so, then how does the subject move within that web of power? Kenneth Burke's theory is wide-ranging but tends to focus on concepts of mankind as a symbol-using animal and how people are affected by their encounters with those symbols. In *Rhetoric of Motives,* Burke explains the functioning of rhetorical movements of unity. He says, "[i]dentification is compensatory to division. If men were not apart from one another, there would be no need for the rhetorician to proclaim their unity. If men were wholly and truly of one substance, absolute communion would be of man's very essence" (22). In Burkean rhetoric, there exists a space between subjects. Rhetorical moves create the rhetorical identifications to create an "us," a space where that distance between subjects is reduced. Suddenly, instead of two separate subjects, a "we" emerges due to some rhetorical intervention between speaker/writer and audience. Could we not also say that there is a space between subject and institution that must be addressed? Here, I will describe two specific smaller movements that overlap in the Burkean process of identification as I intend to use it: identification and scapegoating.

In Burke's theory of identification, subject A sees of subject B only what the ideology A is interpellated with will allow. Thus, to create a "we," subject A then begins the movement of self that brings him or her to combine with the part of B that he or she can see through that ideology. Burke puts it so: "[t]o identify A with B is to make A 'consubstantial' with B" (20). We must remember, of course, that A does not *become* B: the space does not collapse.

Subject A in all actuality becomes something more akin to A(B), with B denoting the part of B's subjectivity that A has come to admire and wishes to emulate. A in some ways wishes to become "simultaneously 'me' and 'not me'" (Ratcliffe 57). In order to accomplish this move, A must excise some part of self, creating an "exiled excess," as Krista Ratcliffe calls it. It is possible for that identification of "non-B-self" to become "unclean self" quite quickly in such a rhetorical ideological environment. Burke's identification system is one in which "identification does provide a place of personal agency and a place of commonality, yet it often does so at the expense of differences. As a place of common ground, Burke's identification demands that differences be bridged" (53). The danger in the move of identification that creates a "we" by excluding a "them" is, of course, that there maybe be far more similarity between the in-group and those who are shunned than appears on the surface. Instead of difference as something to be celebrated (an orientation toward diversity), it is automatically thought of as something to be overcome.

But what happens if the desire is to further the distance between subjects? Burkean theory of identification fits within another of his theoretical ideas, that of hierarchy. In Burke's concept of the scapegoat, A recognizes some aspect of B that A cannot abide, given the ideology that composes the symbol veil. Negotiation is then forbidden between the two. To attempt to see any part of B that is acceptable would be for A to soil him or herself. This forms a boundary to which A may adhere. It is fairly easy to see that movements of identification likely involve movements of power (in a sense aligning them with Foucauldian thought). As Carter says, "[t]he ladder of symbolic rank is extended to greater heights and depths. Everyone feels that there are both lower and higher rungs available. Everyone has the opportunity to locate someone toward whom it is possible to enjoy feeling superior. Few are so low that they do not fear slipping another notch" (9). What might happen to the person that is lowest on that ladder, though? We might think of that individual, the "lowest of the low" in a sense, as what Burke describes as the scapegoat. Burke says that "[t]he scapegoat . . . combines in one figure contrary principles of identification and alienation" (140). The scapegoat is the rhetorical figure that receives the blame for the current state that the "we" created by identification must endure. We might think of the scapegoat as subject C. In this case, then, in identifying with B, subject A is in some ways *dis*-identifying with subject C. The excess that A must exile, in Ratcliffe's terminology, in order to become A(B) leads to a sense of undesirability. C, then, is the subject that most embodies that exiled part of A's self. The boundary that brought the very "we" together in community now divides that community from the figure upon which all the rhetorical scorn of the community is brought. "Our" condition would be better if only "they" were punished, if you will. Or, more to the point, "we" exist because we all agree that we cannot and must not be "like them." Any contact with C, then, would sully A(B) and could cost him or her their rung on the ladder. Somewhat counter to what we may think, though, it is the sacrifice of the scapegoat (exile or, in extreme cases, death) that cleanses the community. In this way, though lowest on the social ladder, the scapegoat is powerful—all the transgressions of the community may be heaped upon the scapegoat and purged with their sacrifice.

If Burke's subject A(B) were to transgress those rhetorical/ideological boundaries and become "sullied" by contact with C, she or he might very well have her or his citizenship revoked, leaving him or her open to whatever punishment the culture she or he resides within deems fit to hand out. Worse, because of the transgression (if made public), such treatment at the hands of the RSAs might be applauded by the culture that subject A(B) formerly found him or herself within. It is a movement both internally as well as externally motivated in that way. As Karen Coats says in her exploration of Julia Kristeva's thoughts on abjection in regards to the social body, "[j]ust as we abject the unclean and improper evidences of the body's physicality in order to constitute a clean and proper body, so in the social realm we abject the unclean and improper . . . in order to constitute the boundaries of community and nation" (141).[5] The boundary between the subject who submits to social pressure and those who refuse to is something like a type of heavily policed bodily boundary. Burke's scapegoated subject C thus becomes the Kristevan abject or Agamben's *Homo sacer*, the "unclean thing," via rhetoric, both visual and otherwise, existing at the opposite end of the spectrum from the sovereign, whose body is inviolable by any means (Agamben 84).[6]

The Scapegoated, Un-Sacrificable Young Adult

Young Adulthood, like childhood, is a conceptual map laid over biological facts. Much as childhood is often theorized as a utopia that exists until adults intervene (Sands and Frank 78), adolescence is dystopian. As Peter Hollindale says, any children's author "must construct childhood from an amalgam of personal retrospect, acquaintance with contemporary children, and an acquired set of beliefs as to what children are, and should be, like" (12). It is, in that sense, ideologically constructed, as is any concept of a utopia. This conservative, pastoral-driven impulse is present in the dystopian narrative. As Hintz and Ostry explain, "[f]urthermore, adolescence frequently entails traumatic social and personal awakening. The adolescent comes to recognize the faults and weaknesses of his or her society, and rebels against it" (9). In essence, utopian writing is the predominant mode of texts intended for children because of our societal impulse to put them into a safe space, to arrest their growth. The dystopian work pervades adolescent literature because of our equally strong societal need to push the adolescent from their state of in-between-ness to a state of adulthood. Hintz and Ostry go on to assert:

> dystopia can act as a powerful metaphor for adolescence. In adolescence, authority appears oppressive, and perhaps no one feels more under surveillance than the average teenager. The teenager is on the brink of adulthood: close enough to see its privileges but unable to enjoy them. The comforts of childhood fail to satisfy. The adolescent craves more power and control and feels the limits on his or her freedom intensely. (9–10)

Adolescence is an othered subjectivity. Adolescents are pressured to conform from all sides, their identifications are watched at all times for signs of "impurity," and they are scapegoated as unclean things, ejected from the social body if they are seen to make the wrong moves of identification within the webs of ideological signifiers laid before them, such as "good citizen."

In explaining her thoughts on adolescent subjectivity, Karen Coats says,

> At the level of the social, we think of adolescence in terms of the way it, like abjection, breaches and challenges boundaries. It is an in-between time, a time when what we know and believe about children is challenged, and where what we hope and value about maturity is challenged. Adolescents are both more and less sophisticated and knowing than we want them to be. They challenge the borders of identity, trying to become adult without becoming adulterated. Striving for social recognition but not wanting to stand out, locating with specificity their status as sexual subjects and objects, seeking the terms of individuation within affiliative groupings, adolescents are intensely involved in the construction of social boundaries and in reaffirming their distance from the socially abject. (142–43)

Coats sees this time in the life of the subject as a re-eruption of Oedipal drama, as well as a time of rapid bodily change. The social conception of the child as pre-sexual is thrown into chaos as the newly emerging adolescent demonstrates undeniable movements toward sexuality. This creates a dilemma for the social body surrounding the young adult: eject the adolescent from the social order to preserve cleanliness, or accept the young adult into the order? It is at precisely that decision-making process that we can see the othered subjectivity of adolescents—they exist on the end of a web of power relations (and almost always the positions that have less power than the more accepted subjects, such as adults).

Roberta Trites, also commenting on the adolescent as other, writes:

> Indeed, adolescents occupy an uncomfortable liminal space in America. Adolescents are both powerful (in the youthful looks and physical prowess that are glorified by Hollywood and Madison Avenue; in the increased economic power of the middle-class American teenagers as consumers; in the typical scenario of teenagers succeeding in their rebellions against authority figures) and disempowered (in the increased objectification of the teenage body that leads many adolescents to perpetrate acts of violence against the Self or Other; in the decreased economic usefulness of the teenager as a producer of goods in postindustrial America; in the typical scenario of teenagers rebelling against authority figures to escape oppression). (xi)

The adolescent, in negotiating the extremely complex process of subjectivty at the hands of the ISAs, always has the choice to conform (which Foucault refers to as a Contract Oppression schema) or to rebel, thereby moving outside the ISAs and into the realm of the RSAs, where Foucault's Dominant-Oppression model takes over, and violence becomes socially viable for the state as a means to move the subject back toward the cycle of ISAs (Trites 3–7). Once more, the various discourses of power that shape our society, and the apparatuses in place to distribute those discourses, always have the adolescent under surveillance. These apparatuses are ready to apply corrective power in a continuum of force all the way from a casual verbal intervention through to violence.

In order to conceive of the work that adolescent literature does, we must come to understand it as one of these socializing discourses (Trites 22–23). The literature earmarked for adolescent readers comes into the space that

Coats theorizes, entering at the point where the social order has decided not to abject the subject, but instead to socialize it. The adolescent is told quite clearly time and time again in adolescent literature that they have but one way to remain in the social order: make identificatory moves that clearly show interest in leaving the abject subject positions behind. Coats observes that "[t]he abject characters thus act as foils and props for establishing the clean and proper identity of the normal protagonists, suggesting that one way out of abjection is the successful oedipalization of identity. Reciprocation into adult society requires leaving such figures behind" (151).

Dystopian authors create texts that show the author functioning as cultural theorist in the subjunctive mode. Dystopian fiction is a genre in which the author can readily engage contemporary social situations and theoretically project what is to come for an audience that is perhaps not always as theoretically or politically aware as an academic one. In essence, the genre is the logical extension of what is often called the slippery slope fallacy. Giorgio Agamben has said he believes that "[t]oday it is not the city, but rather the [concentration] camp that is the fundamental biopolitical paradigm of the West" (qtd. in de la Durantaye 213). Perhaps we might see, instead, that the dystopian society that so often mimics the concentration camp is the paradigm by which we can most clearly see Foucault's biopower being exercised. Hence, the dystopian literature narrative as the metaphor *par excellence* to demonstrate interpellation of the subject. Though the panopticon could be seen as the paradigm that functions within these dystopian narratives, in a sense, Agamben's paradigm of the concentration camp becomes the blueprint for the society of the narrative. The exceptional case of the suspension of law becomes the rule instead of the exception. It is in this extremist example of how a society functions that the adolescent can begin to see more clearly the webs of force and subjectivity that may be more obscured in the world outside the narrative that they occupy. Fredric Jameson says that "at best Utopia can serve the negative purpose of making us more aware of our mental and ideological imprisonment ... and that therefore the best Utopias are those that fail the most comprehensively" (xiii).

Often, when reading one of these works, we are left with a sense of unease about the future. I suggested earlier that Burkean Identification, through the social lens of the work of Althusser and Foucault, is the primary way in which the state monitors normative ideological formation of the subject in these fictions, creating whole herds of Agamben's *homo sacer*.[7] Dystopian works attempt to make this system transparent. These authors are functioning as cultural theorists showing the worst-case scenario of how the State first confines (Foucauldian surveillance) and then defines (Althusserian structures) the citizen as one that has had its (Žižekian) pre-ideological kernel bent toward accepting the suspension of its (Agambenian) sense of self-as-more-than-cattle via rhetorical structures (Burkean identification). When examining this genre we are left with a series of texts that not only show the various tactics and rhetorics the State might employ to force identification with officially sanctioned figures, but also how this same strategy is used to create figures that the subject is supposed to scapegoat.

The Treatment for Stirrings

By seeing the parallel between what happens to the protagonist of a YA dystopian novel and their own stirrings, the adolescent is given the opportunity to explore how their own culture constructs their adolescent abject, powerful-and-simultaneously-powerless subjectivity.

As Rafaella Baccolini says, "[w]e need to pass through the critical dystopias of today to move toward a horizon of hope" (521). In reaching for that horizon, the focalizer, so long infantilized by the repressive regime, moves into adolescence—a breaking away from childhood into self-reliance and responsibility. Rather than believing that hope vs. lack of hope is the primary criterion for determining if a text is utopian or dystopian, though, I instead want to point out that "[t]he assumption that in a dystopian world human beings must strive for a form of subjective agency pervades children's literature" (Bradford et al. 29). There is a reason this is the case: the primary focus of the dystopian work is just such an exploration of subjectivity. The intent is not only to explore the construction of subjectivity in the face of naked abuses of power at the hands of the ruling regime, but also to provide examples of agency in such situations. In reaching for the horizon between the infantilized subject position and the subject position with agency, the focalizer, so long infantilized by the repressive regime, moves into an adolescence—a breaking away from childhood into self-reliance and responsibility. This is what creates the term "dystopia" in these texts— the (infantilized) focalizer attempting to "outgrow" the infantilized society.

Dystopian texts intended for children and young adults show this precise metaphorization of the movement from childhood to adolescence. Trites' view of young adult fiction is that the genre functions most often as "a discourse of institutional socialization" for the adolescent (22). More often than not, the YA novel seeks to reassert the state's dominance over the individual through both repression and formation via surveillance. She further reminds us that, while some characters seem to gain power within the structure of the novel, in the end it is most often the state that gains control by normalizing the adolescent character via the narrative. These texts show the various power discourses at work on the adolescent as he or she moves from metaphoric childhood "utopia" to metaphoric adolescent "dystopia." The usefulness of this genre is that it makes the often-invisible formative discourses visible by metaphor. It shows more clearly the ways that society constructs the adolescent subject.

Notes

1 Both Jack Zipes (ix) and Carrie Hintz and Elaine Ostry (3), it should be noted, have some doubts about the use of the concept of genre to critique utopian/dystopian writing.
2 Some might ask, "What is the aim of Althusserian critique if it is no longer tied to the Marxist revolutionary trajectory?" More to the point, if ideology is always-already existent and enacted in Althusser, where does that leave the field of ideology critique? For a fascinating (but by no means exhaustive) cross-section of Althusser's critics, see Warren Montag, "'The Soul Is the Prison of the Body': Althusser and Foucault, 1970–1975," *Yale French Studies* 88 (1995): 53–77; Simon Clarke, "Althusserian Marxism," *One-Dimensional Marxism: Althusser and the Politics of Culture* (London: Allison and Busby, 1980), 7–102; Kevin McDonnell and Kevin Robins, "Marxist Cultural Theory: The Althusserian Smokescreen," *One-Dimensional Marxism: Althusser and the Politics of Culture* (London: Allison and Busby, 1980), 157–231; Alex Callinicos, *Althusser's Marxism* (London: Pluto, 1976); Terry Lovell, "The Social Relations of Cultural Production: Absent Centre of a New Discourse," *One-Dimensional Marxism: Althusser and the Politics of Culture* (London: Allison and Busby, 1980), 232–56.
3 It is important to acknowledge that Foucault himself has discouraged the conflation of his theories, based on the effects of power on the body, with Althusser's sense of State apparatuses. He says, "one of the first things that has to be understood is that power isn't localized in the State apparatus and that nothing in society will be changed if the mechanisms of power that function outside, below and alongside the state apparatuses, on a much more minute and everyday level, are not also changed" (*Power/Knowledge* 60). He says he feels that our focus should be more on "strategic apparatus" (102). We should be

looking at the strategies and tactics in which power is enacted, he feels. If there is hope for intervention, it comes from there.

4 For an informative cross-section of scholars critiquing Foucault's work, see Fabio Vighi and Feldner Heiko, *Žižek: Beyond Foucault* (New York: Palgrave, 2007); Dorrit Cohn, "Optics and Power in the Novel," *New Literary History* 26.1 (1995): 3–20; Kevin Jon Heller, "Subjectification and Resistance in Foucault," *SubStance* 25.1.79 (1996): 78–110; Neve Gordon, "Foucault's Subject: An Ontological Reading," *Polity*, 31.3 (1999): 395–414.

5 Though I am using a Lacanian-inflected concept here, I am not invoking a purely Lacanian reading of the subject.

6 In many ways, the identificatory and *dis*-identificatory movements of subject A(B) are attempts to avoid becoming what Georgio Agamben would call *homo sacer*, that subject who is stripped of the protection afforded by his/her citizenship (de la Durantaye 200–38). *Homo sacer* has fallen so low that killing him or her is no longer considered murder, and s/he is worthless for the purpose of sacrifice.

7 Please pardon the use of "herds" as it is precisely the uncaring sense of masses of animals-not-humans that I wish to reference here.

Works Cited

Agamben, Giorgio. *Homo Sacer: Sovereign Power and Bare Life.* Stanford, CA: Stanford UP, 1998. Print.

Althusser, Louis. "Ideology and Ideological State Apparatuses." *Lenin and Philosophy and Other Essays.* Trans. Ben Brewster. New York: New York Monthly Review Press, 2001. 85–126. Print.

Baccolini, Rafaella. "The Persistence of Hope in Dystopian Science Fiction." *PMLA.* 119.3 (2004): 518–21. Print.

Beebee, Thomas O. *The Ideology of Genre: A Comparative Study of Generic Instability.* University Park, PA: Pennsylvania State UP, 1994. Print.

Bradford, Clare, Kerry Mallan, John Stephens, and Robyn McCallum. *New World Orders in Contemporary Children's Literature; Utopian Transformations.* New York: Palgrave, 2008. Print.

Burke, Kenneth. *A Rhetoric of Motives.* 1950. Berkeley: U of California P, 1969. Print.

Callinicos, Alex. *Althusser's Marxism.* London: Pluto Press, 1976. Print.

Carter, C. Allen. *Kenneth Burke and the Scapegoat Process.* Norman, OK: U of Oklahoma P, 1996. Print.

Coats, Karen. *Looking Glasses and Neverlands: Lacan, Desire and Subjectivity in Children's Literature.* Iowa City, IA: U of Iowa P, 2004. Print.

de la Durantaye, Leland. *Giorgio Agamben: A Critical Introduction.* Palo Alto, CA: Stanford UP, 2009. Print.

Dubrow, Heather. *Genre*. New York: Methuen, 1982. Print.
Foucault, Michel. *Discipline and Punish: The Birth of the Prison*. 2nd ed. New York: Vintage, 1995. Print.
———. *Power/Knowledge: Selected Interviews and Other Writings 1972–1977*. Ed. Colin Gordon. New York: Pantheon, 1980. Print.
Hintz, Carrie, and Elaine Ostry. "Introduction." *Utopian and Dystopian Writing for Children and Young Adults*. Ed. Carrie Hintz and Elaine Ostry. New York: Taylor and Francis Books, 2003. 1–22. Print.
Hollindale, Peter. *Signs of Childness in Children's Books*. Stroud, UK: Thimble, 1997. Print.
Jameson, Fredric. *Archaeologies of the Future: The Desire Called Utopia and Other Science Fictions*. London: Verso, 2005. Print.
Ratcliffe, Krista. *Rhetorical Listening: Identification, Gender, Whiteness*. Carbondale, IL: Southern Illinois UP, 2005. Print.
Sambell, Kay. "Carnivalizing the Future: A New Approach to Theorizing Childhood and Adulthood in Science Fiction for Young Readers." *The Lion and the Unicorn* 28 (2004): 247–67. Print.
———. "Presenting the Case for Social Change: The Creative Dilemma of Dystopian Writing for Children." *Utopian and Dystopian Writing for Children and Young Adults*. Ed. Carrie Hintz and Elaine Ostry. New York: Taylor and Francis Books, 2003. 163–78. Print.
Todorov, Tzvetan. "The Origin of Genres." *Modern Genre Theory*. Ed. David Duff. Harlow, UK: Pearson Longman, 2000. 193–209. Print.
Trites, Roberta Seelinger. *Disturbing the Universe: Power and Repression in Adolescent Literature*. Iowa City, IA: U of Iowa P, 2000. Print.
Wiederhold, Eve. "Called to the Law: Tales of Pleasure and Obedience" *Rhetoric Review* 20.1–2 (2001). 130–46. Print.
Zipes, Jack. "Foreword: Utopia, Dystopia, and the Quest for Hope." *Utopian and Dystopian Writing for Children and Young Adults*. Ed. Carrie Hintz and Elaine Ostry. New York: Taylor and Francis Books, 2003. ix–xi. Print.

Imagining Black Bodies in the Future

Gregory Hampton

Octavia Butler's fiction is prophetic. It is a fiction that is constructed with close attention to historical facts, keen observation of current events, and deductive reasoning. The United Nations predicted that the global population would reach 7 billion in 2011, and that it will climb to 9 billion by 2050. The World Wildlife Fund speculates that to feed this new population the world will have to produce as much food in the next 40 years as it has produced in the last 8,000. The seemingly inevitable overpopulation of Earth suggests that humanity's only hope is to be scattered among the stars in search of new worlds to populate and colonize. Butler's fiction has repeatedly and prophetically predicted such a dystopian paradigm. Although her fiction makes no overt mention of the "singularity"[1] that contemporary scientists are preparing for, the colonization of the stars and the migration of humanity away from planet Earth are themes that Butler has written about for more than three decades. Her vision is unique because she has located black and brown bodies at the centre of her speculative dystopian visions of the future.

This meditation will investigate the value of understanding race beyond biological terms and will critique the employment and deployment of race by American popular culture as a metaphor to envision itself in the future. By examining the employment of race as a metaphor in narratives by Butler, as well as in James Cameron's film *Avatar*, this discussion will facilitate a better understanding of how race and racism are deployed and complicated in literature and film, as both mediums assist in demystifying American culture. I would like to suggest that discussing race in a more multifarious context might be conducive to a critical analysis of the complexities and contradictions embedded in our imaginations and employment of race. This discussion grapples with how images of black bodies are constructed in our imaginations by Butler's speculative dystopian narratives and suggests a rewriting of these images as positive and identifiable icons. Ultimately, this discussion will consider the permanence of racism and its influence on how black bodies are imagined in the future: sold to the populace as slaves and aliens, in some instances, and potentially liberated in others.

Derrick Bell's *Faces at the Bottom of the Well* comes to mind when considering the terms "future" and "race."

> Black people are the magical faces at the bottom of society's well. Even the poorest whites, those who must live their lives only a few levels above, gain their self-esteem by gazing down on us. Surely, they must know that their deliverance depends on letting down their ropes. Only by working together is escape possible. Over time, many reach out, but most simply watch, mesmerized into maintaining their unspoken commitment to keeping us where we are, at whatever cost to them or to us. (Bell v)

Whether clad in black leather, a tinted blue skin, or a glistening blue-black exoskeleton, the black body has been imprinted on the imagination of the Western world as marginalized, objectified, and subject to violence. The fiction of Butler and the blockbuster dystopian film *Avatar* have both speculated and problematized how black bodies will be imagined in the future, and how bodies defined as black literally or metaphorically will continue to struggle for subjectivity. Popular culture, including the genre of science fiction, has suggested that the faces at the bottom of the well will remain in a dark and frightening space in the collective unconscious of the American populace. The permanence of racism threatens the marginalized body even in the twenty-first century. In her article "Contemplating and Contesting Violence in Dystopia: Violence in Octavia Butler's *XENOGENESIS* Trilogy," Christina Braid notes that Butler's dystopian trilogy poses a relevant challenge to justice today with the question of why we turn to violence as an answer to conflict (Braid 51). Braid's article suggests that violence is synonymous with black bodies in most of Butler's speculative fiction. The same can be said for many contemporary science fiction films, especially *Avatar*, despite the fact that the bodies portrayed in the films may only signify literal "black bodies." In the past decade many philosophers have begun to consider film as a source of literary and philosophical analysis (Wartenberg 19).

In James Monaco's *How to Read a Film*, the semiological relationships between film and literature are defined as inextricable. Both can be understood as texts that directly reflect the aesthetic values of the society that produces them. Both film and literature represent a system of signs coded with cultural markers that shape and police the images of the society they signify. Images of marginalized bodies have been used in film and literature to construct racial, sexual, and class boundaries that continue to construct the notion of the "Other." Monaco asserts that "film has changed the way we perceive the world and therefore how we operate in it" (291). Literature has always been a medium in which society is both reflected and critiqued. If film and literature can be examined through a lens that has the ability to see into the future, or at least how society imagines the future, it becomes possible to bring into focus images of ourselves and "Others" via what is written and filmed today.

The process of reading necessarily involves elements of subjectivity, opinion, cultural bias, and social aesthetics. "Normal human beings" bring preconceived notions to all that they read and extrapolate in addition to whatever the author posits consciously or unconsciously in a text (Monaco 171). In literature, it might be assumed that the author controls what the reading audience sees and hears within the pages of a novel. This may be true to some extent, but no experienced reader is truly limited by the page. According to Monaco, "films are more or less told by their authors, too, but we see and hear a great deal more than a director necessarily intends" (54). In both literature and film "the observer [reader] is not simply a consumer, but an active—or potentially active—participant in the process" (175). Although film is not a language, the hermeneutics used to study language can be applied to the study of film. Science fiction as a literary genre is invested in the art of speculation, wondering what tomorrow will bring based on events that may have occurred in the past and are unfolding in the present. The reader's imaginative response to vivid and descriptive language is the primary tool needed to begin such speculation within the novel. Science fiction film is no different, except for the tools and technology that assist in the process of imagining the future. Sex, violence, special effects, computer-generated images (usually of marginalized bodies), time-lapse photography, and a plethora of other techniques all assist in igniting the observer's imagination. Braid defines violence as "the intentional use of physical force or power, threatened or actual, against oneself, another person, or against a group or community that either results in or has a high likelihood of resulting in injury, death, psychological harm, maldevelopment, or deprivation" (Braid 48). Braid's definition marks many of the elements that act as the most exciting components of a narrative in literature or film. As defined, violence seems to require a marginalized body of sorts, as a victim or victor. Braid notes that the discussion of violence in literature often leads to a utopian notion of justice. In other words, when violence ensues, it is usually as part of a struggle for justice, and justice is a concept often used in representation of what a utopian state should look like. "Dystopias of the 20th century teach important lessons about the role of state as regulator of violence" (Braid 49). The politics of democracy, socialism, and communism all have a presence in the texts being discussed here, but dystopian politics seem to be more overtly concerned with marginalized bodies than with Platonic notions of the political.

"The politics of film and the politics of 'real life' are so closely intertwined that it is generally impossible to determine which is the cause and which is the effect" (Monaco 292). Toni Morrison's *Playing in the Dark* asserts that racism is woven into the fabric of the American literary tradition. Therefore, it is not surprising that Monaco goes on to assert that "racism pervades American film because it is a basic strain in American history" (299). Both film and literature necessarily reflect the aesthetics of the society in which they exist. Recent scholarship supports the idea that science fiction literature and film may be an excellent location for social and racial analysis. Butler's writing of the black body is analogous to images found in several classic and contemporary science fiction films. Where contemporary films employ common stereotypical images or tropes of the extraterrestrial (something green or very black from outer space) to evoke comic relief and terror, Butler's narratives suggest a refiguring of such images to initiate questions centred on our definitions of racialism, sexuality, and humanity.

In his essay "The Conservation of Races," W.E.B. Dubois alludes to the prophetic observation that race is a social construct. As a social construct, race necessarily becomes a bendable notion or fluctuating idea. Thus, as a society changes over time its constructs change appropriately to assist in the maintenance of a particular social order. Despite the grand role that race has played in the development of American history and national identity, race is an intangible ideal used to formulate and maintain a social order. In other words, race is an intangible force with very tangible consequences.

In many respects race succeeds in transcending the boundaries of traditional Western thought, as race exists in both of Plato's realms, the real and the ideal.

Consequently, race might be thought of as a realm of its own, which might be likened to a matrix, a womb or blurred location in our imaginations, where the unreal is as concrete as the ground on which we stand and stumble. Popular culture has produced interesting and entertaining films that facilitate this notion. For example, *Avatar* (2010), directed by James Cameron, is an important social narrative that supports the notion of race as a social and commercial construct. *Avatar* had a production budget of $360 million and has yielded, to date, a worldwide gross of well over $2.7 billion.[2] As such, this film is more than a movie, it is a marker for the Western social aesthetic, speaking volumes about how America sees itself and "Others," today and in the future. The film is anchored in the genre of science fiction and the notion of dystopian speculation. In several regards, *Avatar* supports and demonstrates many of the same concepts that Butler employs in her fiction about race, colonization, sexuality, gender, and struggles for power. More importantly, it is completely dependent upon a narrative of dark bodies and their quest for subjectivity and identity. Hence, the monetary investments and yields of this commercial undertaking urgently suggest that America is consciously struggling with the value and employment of dark bodies in its imagination and reality.

The goals and objectives of this meditation are to examine the employment of race as a metaphor/euphemism in the writing of Octavia Butler and the film *Avatar*, with the intent to yield a better understanding of how race and racism are deployed and complicated in speculative narratives in literary and cinematic form; to grapple with how images of black bodies are constructed in our imaginations via literature and film; and lastly, to consider how race and racism can be used as commercial devices to influence the value of black bodies in a dystopian future.[3]

Butler's Fiction and Native Aliens

Until the characters of Octavia Butler, the black woman and her body were not located in highly visible spaces in the genre of science fiction. This is probably because science fiction had not yet been graced with a large number of black women writers or an exceptionally large reading audience of black women or men. Fortunately, the literal absence of black female bodies does not preclude their metaphorical presence. Several of Butler's narratives demonstrate how the black female body is inserted unconsciously in the minds of readers even when there is no direct mention of race or gender.

The treatment of the dark "Other" in science fiction horror films is demonstrative of how the black female has generally been situated in the imagination of American popular culture: an objectified creature focused on the reproduction of other dark bodies that present a threat to the dominant society. Cameron's narrative in *Avatar* fits well in the boundaries of a dystopian narrative in that humans are distanced from "nature" and the "normative," as well as because the engine behind the colonial space travel represented is a police state or military/corporate state promising the "good life" for its citizens based on the subjugation of an oppressed labour force provided by a marginalized female or motherland as a source of labour.

Butler's manipulation of sexuality and gender identity constructs a dialectic that employs an involved interrogation and restructuring of how the "sexual" is posited in American and African-American literary imaginations. An example of this can be found in the short story "Bloodchild," where Gan, a male protagonist, is destined to carry and give birth to the children of a non-human matriarch. The importance of Gan's situation is that his body is required to function differently from that of the ordinary human male, and it must do so with another body alien to humanity. More specifically, Butler's fiction disrupts the etiquette of the "sexual" that has been under construction by Western culture and media since the Victorian era. Such fiction attempts to dismantle the *logos* of what is acceptable and what is taboo with regards to sex as an act, and sex as a noun or body part (anatomy). Discussions of homosexuality, heterosexuality, bisexuality, bestiality, and incest are all common, and integral elements found in the project to define the body as being more than sexual and limited by its flesh. Issues of sexuality and the production of bodies are common themes in all of Butler's fiction, but nowhere are they more concentrated than in her Xenogenesis and Patternmaster series. By linking the short story "Bloodchild" to the two larger series, Butler sets an ensemble of narratives in relationship to each other vis-à-vis the representation of sexuality, gender, and reproduction, all of which are inextricable in the process of imagining racial identity. This is significant within the context of dystopian literature because Butler's fiction does not allow the oppression of marginalized bodies to go uninterrogated as a normative form of social control.

The ability of Doro and Anyanwu (main characters in the Patternmaster series) to change their sexual anatomy while maintaining some traditional gender roles and blurring others prepares the readers of Butler's Xenogenesis series for the introduction of a completely new sexual categorization and the deceptively ambiguous gender roles of the Oankali, an "alien" people known as gene traders (*Dawn* 22). By creating a third sex, Butler's fiction continues to construct "Others," but also problematizes the social definitions and roles of male and female identity. In this way the traditional understanding of dystopia is complicated. Dystopian societies commonly feature different kinds of repressive social control systems which include various forms of active and passive coercion. However, in Butler's brand of dystopian fiction the narrative is invested in challenging that coercion and moving away from any homogeneous form of social control. Sexism, racism, ageism, and class are constantly challenged by the protagonists in Butler's fiction. The discussion of the third sex entails issues of reproduction, sexual behaviour, and social hierarchies, all of which advocate a (re)examination of how sexual and gender identities are assembled and employed. These processes are further complicated in the short story "Bloodchild," where the male protagonist, Gan, exists in an alien world that deems it practical and necessary for young male humans to act as hosts for the grub-like offspring of the planet's native inhabitants, the T'lic. In "Bloodchild," the male and female gender roles are redefined drastically because the hero is forced to grapple with his inevitable impregnation, a process that places his body in jeopardy and ultimately results in the gory birthing of alien offspring.

In "Bloodchild," Butler bypasses the traditional stereotypes of black women, such as the Sapphire, the Mammy, and the Jezebel, and proceeds to the misconception that masculinity negates femininity and is the most negative trait of the black female body. Despite all of Butler's subtle and not-so-subtle suggestions that Gan is a feminine metaphor, Gan is indeed male and has possession of an easily accessible phallus—a rifle hidden in the kitchen pipes. Of course, this interpretation becomes suspect when we find that T'Gatoi uses her tail as a phallus that can sedate and kill but also has the function of bringing pleasure to those whose bodies it enters. "I felt the familiar sting, narcotic, mildly pleasant" (27). In describing his first "sexual" encounter Gan speaks of T'Gatoi's tail as though it were more than an alien appendage. Butler's text addresses the challenges of identification and ambiguity without reservation and suggests that the process of assignment of gender difference is both complicated and inextricably linked to power struggles.[4]

Avatar

The *Avatar* narrative makes little or no effort to elevate itself from stereotypes found in most tales of imperialism. I would like to suggest that the classic tale of personal survival of "man versus nature" that Cameron "thought" he was creating develops into a much more historical Walter Rodney tale of *How Europe Underdeveloped Africa* (1972) with the help of missionaries, merchants, and mercenaries (the three Ms). Rodney posits that the poor condition of contemporary African nations is due to technological, industrial, educational, military, and organization sabotage via First World capitalism and the debilitating effects of the slave trade. According to the *Avatar* narrative, friendly trade and introductions have already been established by the time the film begins. The scientists and anthropologists who seek to study and learn the way of the Na'vi in the underdevelopment of Pandora reflect the merchants and missionaries. The technologically advanced military are represented by the mercenaries that occupy the planet Pandora with the hopes of mining the planet for a mineral called "Unobtanium" in order to save Earth from an energy crisis. Cameron's film is a poorly cloaked rewrite of a very old narrative of imperialism and Western colonization of the "New World" and its indigenous peoples.

Beyond its motley wardrobe of racial and ethnic stereotypes, *Avatar*'s success at the box office and its reception by the populace are nothing less than remarkable. It may be argued that technology and the innovations of the film industry along with aggressive advertising captured the interest and the dollars of the American people, but the same explanations were given for the success of another American blockbuster, D.W. Griffith's *Birth of a Nation* (1915). It is the notion of the avatar and its employment that I find most worthy of attention. Firstly, it must be noted that the avatar is a term with a great deal of cultural and religious history. Derived from the Sanskrit word *avatāra*, which means to "descend" or "step down," the avatar has historically represented the vessel of a god come down from the heavens to visit and correct the ways of mortals. Kirsten Strayer's "Reinventing the Inhuman: Avatar, Cylons, and Homo Sapiens in Contemporary Science-Fiction Television Series" adroitly situates the contemporary employment of the term alongside its more ancient origins. Strayer notes that the avatar has been reinvented and reintroduced to the Western populace via the digital world and science fiction film and television. She cites the use of the avatar notion in films and television series as far back as *Tron* (1982) and as recent as films and series such as *Surrogates* (2009), *Dollhouse* (2009–2010), and *Battlestar Galactica* (2004–2009).

Butler's own use of the avatar motif is most evident in *Wildseed*. Doro is a sort of god to his people. He wears bodies as though they were digital images of who he needs to be at a particular moment. Doro seeks to create a body that can exist in the tangible and intangible worlds; he seeks to create a child that will represent his completion. He succeeds, with the assistance of Anyanwu, but is absorbed by his creation; the same can be said for the hero in *Avatar*, Jake Sully. Jake is voluntarily absorbed by his avatar, in order to preserve his life and to allow him to be with his love interest. Cameron's *Avatar* suggests that the future will bring a time when the black body will have even less value in the material world than it has now, but will be of a potentially much greater value in the world of gods (cyberspace). Black bodies will be amalgams of the dominant and marginalized; mixtures of the beautiful and the exotic, of the demure and the grotesque. The black bodies in the future will be perfect balances of the desired and the undesired. To be clear, Cameron objectifies black bodies in both his earlier film *Aliens* and in *Avatar*. Where the alien Queen Mother lives to reproduce, the Na'vi seem to multiply with remarkable speed, as demonstrated by their numbers in each scene, including a depiction of a Na'vi village. There is no depiction of sexual acts in either film, but the idea of a voracious sexual appetite is strongly implied.

A great deal of the literature involving discussions of sexuality seems to be characterized by tension among scholars, who pose questions in medical, legal, and popular texts about why and how the modern sexual self seems to have been first produced in the eighteenth century. Scholars such as Angela Davis, Elizabeth Fox-Genovese, John Blassingame, and Donald Bogle have all produced texts that trace the production of black female sexuality from antebellum stereotypes to contemporary visual mythologies (movie stars). In the case of the black women, the construction of a sexual self or sexual identity by a Western slave-holding society presents very little mystery. White supremacy and patriarchy constructed the sexual identity of black female bodies with the intent to oppress and control black bodies and their production in general. The vast interdisciplinary literature now being produced adopts Foucault's critique of functionalist and structuralist models of power and causality. Scholars who adhere to this critique reject a theory of history based on the premise that individuals possess pre-social inalienable rights or authentic essence (Marx's "species beings," for example) and describe instead how "disciplinary power" constitutes individual subjects (Dean 271). This type of dialectic inadvertently claims that the quest for why men did what they did begs the question of how "man" and "woman" as concepts and identities were formulated. It is with respect to these Foucauldian methodologies that Butler's provocative fiction can be transformed into an innovative and complicated theory of identity.

I would like to suggest that both "Bloodchild" and the Xenogenesis series follow a line of argumentation and theoretical assertions similar to that of historians and philosophers in a narrative that allows a step-by-step replay of the construction and employment of sexuality and sexual identities. In her narratives, Butler describes how sexuality is produced by practices and exclusions effected by disciplinary power. She reconstructs specific social practices and scenarios that exclude, marginalize, and even render unthinkable alternative forms of subjectivity and sexuality.

Gan in "Bloodchild" and Lilith in the Xenogenesis series experience an identical dilemma, as they have to choose between "authentic" humanity and something different and even more ambiguously defined than their notion of humanness. Cameron's films suggest that the black (or blue) body is permanently doomed to be objectified and oppressed by a hostile and unchanging Western aesthetic. The assertion that both literature and film seem to be making about race and racism is that as long as there is a Western aesthetic, the stain of racism will be present.

Most literary scholars will agree that "the appeal of science fiction lies in its subject: the Other"—the alien world, the stuff of dreams, the raw material from the unconscious is both the selling point and the key to longevity for the genre (Hampton 115). The element that makes Butler's fiction most notable, and the films mentioned so popular, is the fact that the bodies that are being discussed are transformed into "symbol[s] of alienation in an oppressively normative world" (Wanner 77). Placed in a book with a designation of science fiction, or on the silver screen with special effects and imaginative costumes, the terror of crossing, constructing, and deconstructing identity boundaries is manageable for most. However, facing the very real results of such phenomena has proven to be overwhelming in terms of praxis and theory. When examining the "Other," questions of the self necessarily arise. The fate of the black bodies that we imagine in the future will be dependent upon our ability to look into mirrors of our imagination and embrace the differences that we find.

Notes

1 The term "singularity" is taken from Lev Grossman's "2045: The Year Man Becomes Immortal," in *Time* magazine. In his article, Grossman comments on Raymond Kurzweil's speculations about the inevitable invention of AI (Artificial Intelligence) and its influence on humanity.
2 All of the statistics about the production costs and gross earnings for the films mentioned were obtained from the website *The Business of Movies: boxoffice.com*.
3 Henry Louis Gates suggests that "we use language in such a way as to will a sense of natural difference into our formulation" (Gates 5). For him, the term race "pretends to be an objective term of classification, when it is a dangerous trope"(9).
4 Samuel Delaney, the most prolific African-American male writer in the genre, believes that "science fiction may be the ideal genre through which to challenge traditional representations of subjectivity" (qtd. in Helford 259).

Works Cited

Appiah, Anthony. "The Uncompleted Argument: Du Bois and the Illusion of Race." *"Race," Writing and Difference*. Ed. Henry Louis Gates, Jr. Chicago and London: U of Chicago P, 1985. 21–37. Print.
Avatar. Dir. James Cameron. Fox. 2009. Film.
Bell, Derrick. *Faces at the Bottom of the Well: The Permanence of Racism*. New York: Basic Books, 1992. Print.
Blassingame, John. *The Slave Community: Plantation Life in the Antebellum South*. New York: Oxford UP, 1972. Print.
Bogle, Donald. *Toms, Coons, Mulattoes, Mammies, and Bucks: An Interpretive History of Blacks in American films*. New York: Viking Press, 1973. Print.
Braid, Christina. "Contemplating and Contesting Violence in Dystopia: Violence in Octavia Butler's XENOGENESIS Trilogy." *Contemporary Justice Review* 9.1 (Mar. 2006): 47–65. Print.
The Business of Movies: boxoffice.com. 19 Sept. 2011. Web. 4 Feb. 2012.
Butler, Octavia. *Dawn*. New York: Warner Books, 1987. Print.
——. *Bloodchild and Other Stories*. New York: Four Walls Eight Windows, 1995. Print.

Davis, Angela. *Women Race, & Class*. New York: Random House, 1981. Print.

Dean, Carolyn. "Productive Hypothesis: Foucault, Gender, and the History of Sexuality." *History and Theory* 33.3 (Oct. 1994): 271–97. Print.

DuBois, W.E.B. "The Conservation of the Races." *The Souls of Black Folk: Authoritative Text, Context, Criticism*. Ed. Henry Louis Gates, Jr. and Terri Hume Oliver. New York and London: W.W. Norton & Company, 1999. 176–83. Print.

Fox-Genovese, Elizabeth. *Within the Plantation Household: Black and White Women in the Old South*. Chapel Hill: U of North Carolina P, 1988. Print.

Gates, Henry Louis, Jr. *"Race," Writing, and Difference*. Chicago: U of Chicago P, 1986. Print.

Gould, Stephen Jay. *Mismeasure of Man*. New York: W.W. Norton and Company, 1981. Print.

Grossman, Lev. "2045: The Year Man Becomes Immortal." *Time* 21 Feb. 2011: 42–49. Print.

Hampton, Gregory. *Changing Bodies in the Fiction of Octavia Butler: Slaves, Aliens, and Vampires*. Lanham, MD: Lexington Books, 2010. Print.

Helford, Elyce. "Would you really die than bear my young?: The Construction of Gender, Race, and Species in Octavia E. Butler's 'Bloodchild.'" *African-American Review* 28.2 (Summer 1994): 259. Print.

Monaco, James. *How to Read a Film: Movies Media and Beyond*. New York: Oxford UP, 2009. Print.

Strayer, Kirsten. "Reinventing the Inhuman: Avatar, Cylons, and Homo Sapiens in Contemporary Science-Fiction Television Series." *Literature Film Quarterly* 38.3 (2010): 194–204. Print.

Tatum, Beverly Daniel. *Why Are All the Black Kids Sitting Together in the Cafeteria? And Other Conversations about Race: A Psychologist Explains the Development of Racial Identity*. Rev. ed. New York: Basic Books, 1997. Print.

Wanner, Adrian. "The Underground Man as Big Brother: Dostoevsky's and Orwell's Anti-Utopia." *Utopian Studies* 8.1 (1997): 77–89. Print.

Wartenberg, Thomas E. "Beyond *Mere* Illustration: How Films Can Be Philosophy." *Journal of Aesthetics* 64.1 (Winter 2006): 19–32. Print.

Brown Girl in the Ring as Urban Policy

Sharon DeGraw

Nalo Hopkinson's 1998 novel *Brown Girl in the Ring* describes an alternate Toronto, Canada, isolated from its suburbs and experiencing extreme urban decay. In this way, Hopkinson builds on contemporary urban trends in cities like Detroit, Michigan: urban flight, unemployment, corrupt government, gang and drug problems, and a breakdown of municipal services. At the same time, Hopkinson offers positive, mitigating reactions to these devastating trends through a reimagined Toronto. She creates urban "green spaces"; small, self-reliant, multi-ethnic communities; and prosperous local businesses. In addition, Hopkinson focuses on the role of religion for self-empowerment and community building. In these features, Hopkinson revises the technological and scientific focus of traditional science fiction and Western society more broadly. Technology is largely elided from the text, and science takes on a particularly disturbing role, as Afro-Caribbean spirituality intersects with the commercialization of body parts. Similarly, the author utilizes characterization both to critique and redeem out-of-wedlock pregnancy, single motherhood, and absentee fathers. The protagonist, Ti-Jeanne, offers a new model for science fiction heroism. Hopkinson's emphasis on Afro-Caribbean characters, culture, and language places all of the above issues in a racial nexus. Through the setting and characterization, Hopkinson acknowledges a general reality of much urban life and uses speculative fiction to warn where these trends might lead. In this way, she participates in the turn-of-the-century dystopian mood of North America. Equally important, however, is the fact that Hopkinson engages in the highly relevant political and social dialogue of urban renewal. Her empathetic, insider's perspective offers some hope of redemption. Similarly,

Ti-Jeanne models the individual growth that is necessary for positive communal change. Whereas the textual interventions of exterior forces fail or corrupt, the efforts of Ti-Jeanne and the residents of Toronto ultimately create a small, livable space of personal and communal renewal. Because of Hopkinson's dual focus on urban decay and urban renewal, Jessica Langer applies the term "anti-dystopia" to Hopkinson's text, rather than strict dystopia, and places it in the "next cycle: what comes *after* the utopia/dystopia dichotomy"; it represents "the postcolonialism to utopia/dystopia's colonialism" (185).[1]

As several critics have noted, Hopkinson modelled her apocalyptic Toronto on Detroit, Michigan.[2] Hopkinson's choice of Toronto for the setting of the text stems from her personal background in the city, but she needed a more negative model for the future apocalyptic city that she could then reimagine. For Americans, Detroit has become the dark symbol of a city gone wrong. In fact, the 2012 Science Fiction Research Association conference took place in Detroit because the topic was "Urban Apocalypse, Urban Renaissance: Science Fiction and Fantasy Landscapes." According to the SFRA conference Call for Papers (CFP),

> Detroit is at once an apocalyptic city and a Renaissance city. Over the past ten years, Detroit has suffered immensely, especially during the economic downturn and the virtual demise of the auto industry. Its apocalyptic landscape of abandoned buildings, its negative image due to high crime rates, a recently impeached corrupt Mayor, Kwame Kilpartick, and the loss of close to 300,000 people in the last census have made it the symbol of a city with a hopeless future. ("Call")

Hopkinson sets up a similar template for Toronto. First, Big Business leaves because of a trade embargo, and Toronto's economy becomes "rusted through and through," like the "Rust Belt" of the post-industrial United States, particularly the Motor City (*Brown* 4). After riots erupt, most people flee to the suburbs, and barriers are erected to keep Toronto isolated from the surrounding suburbs.[3] Subsequently, outsiders fear to enter "the Burn" (1). This common nomenclature refers to the physical devastation of the architecture and infrastructure of Toronto, as well as the spirit of its people. For example, the main character's grandfather, Rudy, is a powerful and ruthless drug lord who runs the Burn with a bloody fist. Through Rudy, Hopkinson emphasizes drug use, violent crime, and corrupt rule, particularly in correlation with black men. Hopkinson's focus on characters of African descent also references the racial segregation of Detroit and its suburbs. People of colour, crime, and urban areas are similarly linked. As a Caribbean-Canadian writer, Hopkinson's choice of Detroit, Michigan, highlights the city's widely accepted status as the worst inner city in North America.

Due to this infamy, Detroit serves as a representative dystopia in the media, making it suitable as a model for an apocalyptic Toronto. Most recently, *Time* magazine took the unprecedented step of buying a house in Detroit in 2010. The house served as a base for covering the problems of post-industrial economic collapse, white flight, racial segregation, abandoned buildings, inadequate infrastructure, failing schools, etc.[4] Artist Sean Hemmerle was assigned to take pictures of Detroit that would convey the apocalyptic nature of the city: he "sought out Detroit's derelict buildings as part of a project exploring how far America has fallen." In one of his captions, he writes: "on many occasions . . . I had the feeling I was working in a postapocalyptic environment." Abandoned industrial and transportation buildings, an isolated house, cityscapes completely devoid of people—these are the representative snapshots included in the twelve-picture collection. The pictures are in black and white in order to reinforce a setting devoid of life. When Hopkinson symbolically steals the "heart" of the urban Toronto community, through the forcible extraction of Gros-Jeanne's heart in the text, the author reworks the lifeless image of Detroit and its largely black population.

Detroit as the dystopic city that Toronto could become is evidenced also in its long history of representing urban decay in the film industry. For example, one of the "suggested topics" for the SFRA conference was "[s]et design in SF films, like Syd Mead's set design in *Blade Runner*, based in part on the Detroit skyline of the early 80s" ("Call"). Always dark, perpetually raining, composed of large, decaying structures, this urban set epitomizes the dystopic future of cyberpunk. Paul Verhoeven's 1987 portrayal of "Old Detroit" in *Robocop*, however, is the classic example of dystopic Detroit.[5] In the film, Detroit's powerful and well-connected criminal element gun down cops without consequence, so that regular law enforcement must be supplemented with a highly militarized cyborg. After much uncontrolled violence and bloodshed, the cyborg "Robocop" prevails. Robocop has become such a powerful image that plans are currently under way to place a statue of the character somewhere in Detroit (Braiker). While privately raised money will pay for the statue, much controversy has been stirred by the project

(Perkins). The image of Robocop has been infamously linked to the city of Detroit, but do the residents and leaders of Detroit want to be associated with the themes that the movie represents? No site has yet been picked, but private land will be used as a last resort if city approval is not granted (Beck).

At least one Detroit resident, Ron Williams, publicly questions such negative artistic portrayals. In addition to Hemmerle's work, Williams critiques another series by a pair of French photographers titled *Detroit's Beautiful, Horrible Decline*. He explicitly ties their pictures to the death of Detroit (including an autopsy) and labels them "vultures." In contrast, Williams suggests the work of a local artist and a more "authentic" and "respectful" view of the city. He exhorts the public to "[i]gnore the mainstream media. Detroit is not about architectural ruins. The people are reimagining their city in fresh and courageous ways and there is a lot to learn from them." Williams seeks to counter the negative, apocalyptic image of Detroit, particularly in the media, replacing it with imagination and the positive actions of urban residents. His critique of artists and the media could be applied to Hopkinson, but his replacements are similar to those of *Brown Girl in the Ring* (*Brown* hereafter). While Detroit serves as an apocalyptic model for Hopkinson's text, *Brown* also subsequently offers a model of urban renewal for the city. In this way, Hopkinson signifies on the negative image of Detroit specifically, in addition to general "ghetto" stereotypes.

Comparing *Brown* to *Robocop*, Toronto to Detroit, reveals Hopkinson's extensive revisionist agenda. Hopkinson's Toronto is as violent and dangerous as *Robocop*'s Detroit. However, Hopkinson makes several key substitutions to reimagine Toronto differently from its dystopic Detroit model. First, *Robocop* focuses on science and technology, whereas Hopkinson promotes spirituality, religion, and "magic." Hopkinson extends her technological and scientific critique through an emphasis on nature. In addition, *Robocop*'s traditional mechanized male protagonist is replaced with a marginalized young heroine. In these ways, Hopkinson takes part in key feminist and post-colonial revisions of traditional science fiction. She writes, "I saw [*Brown*] as subverting the genre, which speaks so much about the experience of being alienated, but contains so little written by alienated peoples themselves" (*Brown*). More broadly, Hopkinson challenges fundamental ideologies of patriarchal Western civilization. She illuminates the economic and political forces that drive urban decay, while offering alternatives that can lead to healing. Placing Hopkinson's Toronto and Detroit side by side brings together all the major themes of the novel, often divided by other scholarship.[6] This nexus allows for investigation of their complex intersections and highlights Hopkinson's generic transformations. In doing so, the comparison reveals *Brown* to be a valuable practical tool for urban planning and source of empowerment for personal and communal transformation.

In "Re-evaluating Suvin: *Brown Girl in the Ring* as Effective Magical Dystopia," Lee Skallerup explores how magic has become the newest wave in dystopia, replacing technology as the textual novum. The author uses Hopkinson's text as an example of this trend because "[t]he magical elements found in *Brown Girl* are impossible to ignore: they play a central role in the narrative, a central role usually reserved for science and technology" (82–83). In this context, we can see Hopkinson's magic/spirituality as the heir to *Robocop*'s technological novum. Skallerup further argues that the magical substitution is presented more positively than the traditionally "malevolent" science and technology (83). Ti-Jeanne's willingness to participate in the religious components of her Caribbean heritage allows her to triumph over evil and save her community. Throughout the text, she slowly takes on her grandmother's role as spiritual leader and healer for the Burn. Similarly, Ti-Jeanne notes that a particular area of the Burn is "safe" because "[t]he three pastors of the Korean, United, and Catholic churches that flanked the corner had joined forces, taken over. . . . They ministered to street people with a firm hand, defending their flock and their turf with baseball bats when necessary" (*Brown* 10). Hopkinson discards the traditional "technological fix" of science fiction and Western society more broadly, choosing instead to focus on the "social engineering" of religion and faith (Weinberg).

Furthermore, Hopkinson's validation of Caribbean "mythology" challenges the traditional Western, and science-fictional, distinction between fact and fiction, realism and fantasy.[7] The labels attached to Hopkinson's Caribbean spirituality reveal this tension. Is spirit possession by a Caribbean deity an element of "spirituality," "religion," "mythology," "magic," or even "scientific literacy"? The advantage to choosing spirituality and religion for the designation is an acknowledgement of the real historical presence and personal belief these ideas signify. In contrast, mythology and magic connote a break from belief, personal involvement, lived reality, and the present/future. The more recent entrance of "scientific literacies" highlights the contested nature of the debate, often between the Eurocentric academic community and indigenous people. In this case, appropriating the word "scientific" foregrounds the factual nature of this spirituality/oral history, completely collapsing the science/fantasy division.[8] Hopkinson supports this melding when she compares Gros-Jeanne's herbal medicine to the "science" practised by Haitians using "herbal lore" ("Nalo" 76). She asserts, "You can't talk about one thing people do, and then sort of hie off from the belief systems, so I didn't see it as blending genres" (76). Hopkinson's preference for the label "speculative fiction" resolves some of these literary and epistemological tensions by avoiding the science/magic dichotomy.

While each label has different connotations, they share a common critical component. Zamora and Faris, for example, note the "subversive" nature of magical realism, which has "made the mode particularly useful to writers in postcolonial cultures and, increasingly, women" (qtd. in Skallerup 69). Critic Sarah Wood stresses Hopkinson's creation of a syncretic Caribbean religion in the text, one tailored to the new Canadian context. According to Wood, this syncretic religion is one way Hopkinson "attempts to offer a localized resistance to imperialist assumptions that can be found in sf." As several critics have noted, Hopkinson does show a dark side, a misuse of the Caribbean spirituality through Rudy's obeah. However, Wood ties this misuse to Western capitalism: "[t]he correlation of Western capitalist values and the form of obeah which Rudy practices signifies a perversion of traditional Caribbean knowledge." Wood's connection largely diverts responsibility from the religion/spirituality itself and places it on Western society instead, creating more of a post-colonial critique than a religious critique. Substituting a specifically Caribbean spirituality for science and technology emphasizes post-colonialism as well. As mentioned earlier, these authorial decisions stress a revision of traditional science fiction and Western civilization more generally. Canada should be a utopian "land of promise" to a young immigrant, but Ti-Jeanne does not have this experience in inner-city Toronto. The very fact that Hopkinson creates a dystopia in a developed Western country, in the very epicentre of a major metropolitan city, becomes a post-colonial critique. Similar to Octavia Butler in her Parable of the Sower series, Hopkinson takes the "back to basics," "survival of the fittest," individualistic themes of many apocalyptic dystopias and grounds them in spirituality, ethnicity, and community.

Significantly, Skallerup asks why the focus has changed from technology to magic/spirituality. While female, coloured authors have been and still are relatively rare in science fiction, their numbers have increased in the last decade. Pioneer Octavia Butler was joined by Hopkinson and Tananarive Due, who were then joined by Nisi Shawl, Andrea Hairston, and Sherre R.

Thomas, and the list continues to grow. If such authors are making greater use of magical realism, the presence of magic will increase. Conversely, technology will be marginalized. Skallerup hypothesizes: "Perhaps this is because the technological future that we once fantasized about has arrived or is in the process of arriving. Perhaps it is because the idea of a negative future has become cliché" (71). Detroit represents the first, manifested future; *Robocop* represents the latter, negative cliché; and Hopkinson's alternate Toronto serves as a response to these dystopic contexts. The switch could mean that some people are questioning the scientific and technological focus of Western society which drove industrial urbanization and the subsequent apocalyptic environments. *Robocop* and *Blade Runner* are not appealing futures for most people.

While Hopkinson gives science and technology limited roles in *Brown Girl in the Ring*, this marginalization places even more negative emphasis on the remaining example of science and technology in the text: involuntary human organ transplantation. Hopkinson situates organ transplantation within a political, racial, and religious matrix through her choice of organ recipient and organ "donor." The powerful Premier of Ontario utilizes her connections to access a human heart, for both physical and political reasons. Because no human donor is initially found, a black market heart is acquired from the main character's grandmother, Gros-Jeanne. In the text, Gros-Jeanne serves as a positive, cohesive force in the urban community. She offers physical healing and spiritual guidance to those in need. She represents the beneficial powers of religion and Afro-Caribbean culture. However, she is seen as expendable by the politicians and their cronies. Even worse, her own ex-husband, Rudy, and the father of her grandchild, Tony, are instrumental in her murder and the acquisition of her heart for the Premier.[9] Once again, Hopkinson raises the issues of corruption, violence, drugs, and complicity in connection with black men.

Hopkinson testifies that "organ selling" was a fabrication in the 1990s, but a process known as transplant tourism or organ brokering has been gaining attention in the news recently ("Nalo" 76). In a 1998 interview, Hopkinson revealed that a so-called documentary on organ selling in the Third World initially served as inspiration for the text (76). After some research, she didn't find any truth to the human-to-human organ selling (76). Today, however, Professor Nancy Scheper-Hughes describes the horrifying new trend in which wealthy kidney buyers are connected with poor sellers in the "Third World." The organ transplants are largely unregulated, and the "free trade" relationships among the buyers, sellers, and brokers build on historical disparities. As Albert Huebner notes,

> Organs needed for the well-being of the rich are harvested from the poor, just as, under traditional colonialism, commodities like sugar, coffee, ivory, and diamonds are harvested in Third World countries and exported to developed nations. The organ trade is the "logical" 21st-century extension of hundreds of years of colonial exploitation. First appropriate labor and its fruits, then the body itself.

This is similar to the economic disenfranchisement of Gros-Jeanne and her subsequent bodily organ "appropriation." In fact, as an Afro-Caribbean, Gros-Jeanne highlights the obvious aspect of colonial exploitation that Huebner overlooks in this quote: historical slavery. Elsewhere, Huebner does explicitly compare transplant tourism to slavery generally: "The trade in organs has opened up medical and financial connections, creating a new movement of human beings that is part transplant tourism, part traffic in slaves." In the historical context of slavery, Huebner's process is revised. His "[f]irst appropriate labor . . . then the body" becomes the lengthier, appropriate the body of the slave and its labour, free the body (but not necessarily the labour), and then reclaim the body.

Afro-Caribbean women have a particularly complicated relationship to the body. In "Tananarive Due and Nalo Hopkinson Revisit the Reproduction of Mothering," Alcena Madeline Davis Rogan explores the "legacy of the past" that (non-African) black women must confront: "her status within the slavery system both as an object of property and as the hypersexualized site of the reproduction of the slavery system" (76). In this context, the appropriation of the body entails legal property, labour, sexual relations, and reproduction. The violation of Gros-Jeanne's bodily freedom and integrity intersects with this history and compounds the negativity of the act. Her body may no longer be needed for reproduction,[10] but involuntary organ transplantation is a bodily use for the twentieth century. As Rogan points out, post-slavery capitalism does not ensure black survival (76–77).

In addition, the wealthy organ buyers of transplant tourism mirror the Premier. Scheper-Hughes characterizes the buyers as "ethically obtuse, giving no more thought to dipping into the bodies of the displaced and dispossessed . . . than if they had been actual, rather than proxy, cadavers." Premier

Uttley does not question where her heart comes from, as long as her life and her political seat are saved. "'When rich people look at poor people like us . . . all they can see is a bag of parts,'" protests Laudiceia Da Silva, a contemporary Brazilian woman (Heubner). Da Silva had one of her kidneys removed involuntarily, secretly, and without any legal recourse during an operation for an ovarian cyst (Heubner). Gros-Jeanne reflects and fictionally magnifies the injustice that Da Silva experienced in real life. As economically disadvantaged women of colour, both embody the exploitation of "white capitalist patriarchy" (Rogan 76). In "Nalo Hopkinson's Urban Jungle and the Cosmology of Freedom: How Capitalism Underdeveloped the Black Americas and Left a *Brown Girl in the Ring*," Gregory E. Rutledge explores the connections between white capitalism and black exploitation. Rutledge heavily utilizes the socio-economic theory of Manning Marable to argue that "democracy and free enterprise 'are structured to deliberately and specifically maximize Black oppression'" (25).[11]

Even the medical profession reflects this connection. Scheper-Hughes describes the doctors involved with the transplants as "vultures," like the "Vultures," or ambulance technicians, from the Angel of Mercy hospital who come and take Gros-Jeanne's heart (Hopkinson *Brown* 151). The normative view of EMTs is characterized by the name Angel of Mercy, an inherently and wholly good person who works to help others. In stark contrast, Hopkinson offers "Vultures. All were wearing hooded, floor-length bulletproofs in Angel of Mercy black. Two of the men had Glocks" (151). The impersonal, practical, and rote words of the technicians jar heavily with Ti-Jeanne's impassioned grief for her grandmother. Furthermore, the Vultures offer "blood money" for Gros-Jeanne's heart, highlighting the capitalistic basis of modern medicine (153). Hopkinson's negative portrayal here references a historical legacy of distrust of the scientific and medical community by African Americans. One need only mention the Tuskegee Syphilis Study to raise the issue of active victimization, not to mention the general neglect of segregation. Gros-Jeanne's medicinal and spiritual ministrations, a prime example of "alternative medicine," are placed in stark contrast to the violent, impersonal, unethical, and exploitive portrayal of traditional Western science.

Hopkinson continues her critique of Western culture through the "recycling" of urban space in the text. For example, the spiritual use of a skyscraper revises Western capitalism and scientific positivism. In addition, the general technological and urban decay leads to more natural spaces.

Residents take up urban farming to make more appropriate use of the land. Michelle Reid discusses the "reuse of public space" in the text largely in terms of individual survival and community-focus. Placing more emphasis on her "Caribbean model of hybridity" spells out the post-colonial revision as well.[12] Hopkinson stresses the importance of (recent) immigration to urban renewal. In particular, the Caribbean immigrants have pre-existing access to natural literacies. Gros-Jeanne has an intimate knowledge of Caribbean medicinal plants, and she builds her knowledge of Canadian equivalents. In a reversal of historical Western ethnocentrism, Hopkinson illustrates how Caribbean immigrants know how to utilize natural spaces more effectively than Western natives.[13] The original Toronto residents were estranged from a pastoral existence so they built a model farm to inform the ignorant (*Brown* 34). For these residents, Riverdale farm was a "recreation space" and the Simpson House was a "façade" (34). When Gros-Jeanne and Ti-Jeanne take over the farmhouse after the Riots, they actually farm the land for food and medicine. Gros-Jeanne's relatively prosperous and positive use of the land serves as an example of urban renewal. The fact that Ti-Jeanne takes her grandmother's place on the farm at the end of the text suggests that this is a real alternative to the industrial city/rural farming dichotomy of Western civilization, as well as the barren wasteland of post-industrial, post-capitalist urban America.

In this agricultural re-appropriation, *Brown* parallels Detroit. Both cities experience significant population loss and struggle with the subsequent vacant land. Detroit has lost over half its population with the waning of the American automobile industry and white flight to the suburbs (Bury and Siegel). From a peak of 2 million in the 1950s, current estimates are for a population of only 700,000 by 2035 (Gallagher "Acres"). This tremendous population drain has created a negative housing process: houses are abandoned when they can't be sold; they become rundown and unsafe; and criminals, drug users, and the homeless make poor use of the structures. Many houses are destroyed as a result of arson by vandals, as well as fearful neighbours; accidental fires by the homeless; and electrical fires due to the aging infrastructure. A few buildings have been demolished, but resources are scarce. Recently, the drive to demolish has escalated. Current Detroit mayor Dave Bing proposed demolishing 3,000 homes in 2010, and up to 10,000 more may be on the chopping block (Bury and Siegel). The end result is large tracts of land standing vacant; single houses occupy entire blocks.[14] According to *Detroit Free Press* columnist Brian Dickerson, 40 percent of

Detroit now stands vacant; this translates to almost fifty square miles of land (Mogk and Kwiatkowski).

As a result, some remaining residents follow Gros-Jeanne's example in appropriating urban land for agriculture and reforestation. Many plant gardens in the vacant lots surrounding their homes or join others in creating larger community gardens. Inez Hobson, for example, "has lived here 60 years and gardens in the vacant lot next to her home. 'This is like the country in the city and I love it,' she said" (Bury and Siegel). Even local schools are promoting urban farming. Catherine Ferguson Academy, a school for pregnant teens and mothers, has the students "grow organic vegetables, raise fruit trees, tend to honey bees, take care of animals. The goal is to feed these families both body and soul" (Dybis). In addition, some entrepreneurs have plans to create more large-scale commercial farms. Businessman John Hantz, for example, has been working with city officials to create Hantz Farms. He hopes to plant up to 2,000 acres of land (Gallagher "Commercial"). Advocates of urban farming cite cheap, fresh produce in the "food deserts" of the inner city and a more eco-friendly distribution system (Dickerson). Studies have projected that urban farming could provide 75 percent of the vegetables and 40 percent of the fruit for Detroiters (Grimm). In addition, less obvious advantages include lessened blight and city maintenance costs, a "greater feeling of self-worth," and "economic justice" for all Detroiters (Mogk and Kwiatkowski). According to the Garden Resource Program, urban farming will also "improve our communities by connecting neighbors . . . improving property values, and reducing crime" (Grimm). These multiple nutritional and communal advantages are fictionally advocated in Hopkinson's Toronto. While not addressed in *Brown*, employment opportunities would increase with commercial farming as well.

Hopkinson's Toronto helps visualize a greener Detroit. Mayor Bing admits that Detroit is going to "go green," and that he is in the process of developing a long-term land-management plan for the city (Hackney). This includes consolidating the remaining residents in smaller areas as they face the collapse of infrastructure, from electricity to police and fire services (Hackney). According to Professor Dan Pitera, "Hopes and plans to repopulate the city and to redevelop all the city's vacant land, are unrealistic, at least for another generation. Some redevelopment deals will succeed, but realistic Detroiters should seize the opportunity to become a leaner, greener city for the 21st Century" (qtd. in Gallagher "Acres"). Ron Williams finds an ironic hope in the "disinvestment and abandonment" of Detroit because there are greater "opportunities to re-invent, re-think, re-build and re-imagine a major American city" than anywhere else. This is the process Gros-Jeanne, Ti-Jeanne, and their neighbours have begun in *Brown*. For Detroit, "Demographer Kurt Metzger envisions small urban villages connected by parks and bike paths," paralleling Hopkinson's technologically devolved natural areas (Bury and Siegel). Here we see the connection between the urban apocalypse and urban renaissance glossed in the SFRA conference CFP. *Brown* offers some fictional strategies for regeneration that seize on the opportunities for a dystopic city, like Detroit, to become the city of the future, in a more utopian sense.

The move from fiction to non-fiction reveals some potential complications for urban farming as well. For example, Dickerson raises the issue of racialized labour in Detroit. One activist compared Hantz Farms to a "plantation" (Dickerson). Hantz is white and, as he proposes to hire local workers in the future, the farm labour might be significantly black. However, Dickerson warns that "the paranoia that conflates for-profit entrepreneurs with slave-holders must give pause to anyone hoping to build a business here." These negative connections among blacks, slavery, and agricultural labour stand in contrast to Hopkinson's positive portrayal of Afro-Caribbean natural knowledge. Some of the Detroit protest seems to stem from a view of commercial farming as an invasive and exploitive "Big Business," as well. Rev. Jesse Jackson, for example, protested against commercial urban farming in Detroit because residents might be displaced (Dickerson). Restricted, non-profit urban farming generally finds support, whereas commercial farming is treated with suspicion. Because the public parks model restricts usage to entertainment, neither of the favoured "green" initiatives addresses a central concern of Detroit, Michigan, more broadly, and many North American cities: employment alternatives to industrial capitalism. Without employment initiatives, Detroit will come full circle to fully reflect Hopkinson's Toronto. Residents will have plenty of green space and perhaps some homegrown products, but no jobs or steady income. Likewise, they will be victims of criminals and drug dealers, like Rudy and Tony, who also have no other employment opportunities. Thus, some business model must be cultivated.

Hopkinson's local business model differs from the Big Business focus of Detroit. The SFRA conference CFP highlights several key areas of renewal in Detroit, most focusing on Big Business:

However, there is hope as the so called Renaissance city of the 1970s may now be experiencing a true Renaissance. New venues for the Detroit Tigers and Detroit Lions, funding obtained by Mayor Bing to raze many of the abandoned buildings, the resurgence of the auto industry along with an invitation to the film industry, and a call for repopulation of Detroit with legal immigrants by New York Mayor Bloomberg may re-establish Detroit as the major city that it could be. ("Call")

The building demolition could play into Hopkinson's focus on green spaces and urban farming, and the immigration could build more resident diversity. Major league sports teams, however, would rely more on wooing suburbanites back into the inner city for entertainment purposes. Hopkinson's portrayal of the "Strip" doesn't support this type of initiative as a primary means of meaningful renewal: "The Strip was fueled by outcity money. It was where people from the 'burbs came to feel decadent" (*Brown* 176). Hopkinson's two main examples of this "decadence" are X-rated clubs, where customers fly onto the rooftops to "get a taste of the city without ever setting foot on its streets," and a "block-long 'elite' megamall," which gives unwanted customers an "electronic jolt" (178). Such elitism, consumerism, exclusion, and immorality hardly seem a model for urban renewal; the suburbanites indulge negative appetites, while the residents get nothing positive in return.

Furthermore, in her Toronto, Hopkinson explicitly undermines the power of "big business," in contrast to small business initiatives (*Brown* 239). Rather than "providing incentives for big business to move back in and take over" at the end of the text, Hopkinson proposes "interest-free loans to small enterprises that are already there" (239–40). This strategy responds to some of the problems that have been occurring in Detroit due to an overreliance on large corporations. The auto industry has been the staple of the Motor City, but it is the epitome of Big Business. As Michigan (and the United States) has learned, the auto industry can no longer be relied upon as the sole, or even the primary contributor to a twenty-first-century economic base. When Shaun Donovan, the Secretary of the U.S. Department of Housing and Urban Development under the Obama administration, shared the new tenets of American urban development, he stressed the diversification of economies as a fundamental tool of restructuring (319). Hopkinson offers diversification through local, small business investment: Gros-Jeanne's "small private practice," Bruk-Foot Sam's bicycle repair shop

(32), and Roopsingh's roti shop (*Brown* 19). One Detroit group that seems to fit Hopkinson's small-business model and immigrant focus is Arab Americans. Spreading from the adjacent suburb of Dearborn and immigrating from abroad, Arab Americans have become a significant segment of Detroit's population. Bobby Ghosh suggests that they may be "Detroit's unlikely saviors" because they bring new residents to the city, as well as new business. Detroit gains an "economic boost from a culture that likes to start new businesses. The Arab-American community in metro Detroit produces as much as $7.7 billion annually in salaries and earnings, according to a 2007 Wayne State University study. (That amounts to more than twice Detroit's annual budget)" (Ghosh). Furthermore, many of these new businesses are small, "requiring little capital—gas stations, liquor stores and convenience shops" (Ghosh). The Arab-American community remains isolated from larger Detroit, however. In particular, an element of racial divisiveness and suspicion surfaces that is similar to the response to the Hantz Farm (Ghosh). Ghosh asks, "Are Arab merchants profiteers or pioneers?" Will they "remain at the edges of the city, at arm's length from the predominantly poor African-American population, or produce jobs and other benefits for the whole of Detroit"? In this statement, he implies that a more communal approach would be beneficial, as does Hopkinson in her text. Hopkinson creates more racially integrated groups of residents as well, although the more racially diverse composition of Toronto may play a role in this.

Hopkinson's choice of protagonist suggests that the spirit of inner-city Toronto residents is more important for renewal than Big Business investment or larger government initiatives. Hopkinson places the focus on those most interested in urban renewal—those who live there. Even when Hopkinson briefly discusses business, she foregrounds the resources and motivation of local residents via small business investment. The U.S. government has come to support a more localized strategy as well. In a 2011 speech to the Detroit Economic Club, Secretary Donovan critiqued the Washington-inspired federalism of the past and revealed a new approach: "join[ing] the Federal government with local partners in taking a pragmatic, regional approach to problem solving that supports local leadership, local resources, and local innovation" (319). For Hopkinson, renewal relies on aiding residents, rather than offering corporate perks.[15] Grassroots activism and community building transcend tourist dollars. The author conveys this message to the reader through the "conversion" of the central character. Like many readers, she begins the story indoctrinated in individualistic, narcissistic, Western techno-capitalism. She too dreams of leaving the inner-city for suburban paradise. However, as Skallerup points out, the suburbs ultimately lose their allure for Ti-Jeanne (*Brown* 76). Ti-Jeanne makes connections with fellow residents throughout the text, ultimately risking her life to rid the Burn of its criminal drug "posse" and evil overlord, her grandfather. Through Ti-Jeanne's familial connections to negative elements in society, Hopkinson emphasizes the responsibility that residents share for "cleaning up their neighbourhoods," particularly if the women enable destructive behaviour on the part of the men.[16] Ti-Jeanne complains to Tony: "'I mad at all of allyou for making me run around trying to save allyou, but allyou just digging yourselves in deeper, each one in he own pit'" (165). Despite her complaint, Ti-Jeanne ultimately moves from "imagined autonomous independence" (28) to "civic responsibility" (Michlitsch 26). At the end of the text, she replaces Gros-Jeanne as the hub of the community. She has learned the value of family, community, and spirituality. Furthermore, Hopkinson specifically creates a main character who would be insignificant within the larger power structures of Big Business or Big Government. A young, unwed black mother of low socio-economic standing holds the key to saving her community, not the CEO of a major corporation or a government official. Gretchen J. Michlitsch's article title says it all: "Breastfeeding Mother Rescues City: Nalo Hopkinson's Ti-Jeanne as Superhero."[17]

Ti-Jeanne's "superhero" status stands in stark contrast to *Robocop*'s portrayal of heroism.[18] Ti-Jeanne is the least traditionally powerful member of society; she is young, poor, female, a mother, often accompanied by her baby, from an immigrant family, and without weapons. She is disadvantaged, marginalized, and seemingly defenceless, yet she becomes empowered beyond regular humans. In contrast, *Robocop* offers a middle-aged, Anglo-American male police officer transformed into a highly weaponized cyborg; he has lost his family and primarily works alone. Robocop represents the pinnacle of Western heroism and technology, produced by Big Business, and he purges the community of all negative elements. Contrary to expectations, Ti-Jeanne rivals Robocop. Ti-Jeanne's power stems from different sources, however. Robocop's mechanized, weaponized, "masculine" power contrasts sharply with Ti-Jeanne's natural, religious, "feminine" power. Thus, Ti-Jeanne's status as "superhero" revises the Anglo, male, and technological biases of science fiction and Western society more broadly. While Hopkinson has the black female protagonists of Octavia Butler as predecessors within science fiction, such protagonists are still a very small minority in the genre. Even more damning, entire communities, societies, and worlds are portrayed without colour in speculative fiction. As many of these are futuristic conceptions, this implies the demise of people of colour and the primacy of Anglos for and in future development.[19] The original *Star Wars* represents this type of vision. *Robocop* similarly envisions Detroit almost entirely white, despite the predominantly black population. This partially deflects the negative connections between race and dystopic environment, violence, and crime. A few token black characters are also included, both on the "good" and the "bad" side, to diversify the cast. Nonetheless, the net effect is to "whitewash" the future, erasing people of colour even from their most obvious environment. Like her replacement of science with religion and technology with nature, Hopkinson replaces Robocop with Ti-Jeanne and a predominantly white cast with a predominantly black cast. Through these revisions, Hopkinson not only ensures the "survival" of blacks in the future, but also suggests that they are the foundation of the future: "As the breastfeeding mother of a newborn, Ti-Jeanne represents the creation of new life" (Michlitsch 21). A young black mother, Ti-Jeanne represents a coloured future.[20]

Ti-Jeanne's characterization also reclaims negative stereotypes for black women. Statistically, Ti-Jeanne matches an inner-city protagonist, as do Gros-Jeanne as the grandmother/head of the household and Tony as the absent father. For example, "[i]n Detroit alone, more than 3,000 pregnant teens will drop out of high school each year" (Dybis). Negative black female stereotypes in Western society specifically connect these women to dystopia. Rogan examines the negative portrayal of black mothers in American culture: "black women are scapegoated as the primary precipitators of the 'dire' state of the black American Family. The [Moynihan] report cites the high number of households headed by black women as a cause, not a symptom, of blacks' social and economic disenfranchisement" (77). Carol B. Duncan makes parallels to the negative stereotypes of the "welfare queen," "unwed mother," and "crack ho," all "images of black women as 'unfit,' 'maladjusted' and otherwise dangerous, bad mothers" (168). Even the children of such mothers become tainted within this context: "the baby that is subsequently birthed is not a symbol of rebirth, continuity and the next generation but of the reproduction of a social problem . . . for which the society will pay in monetary, psychic and other terms" (169). This resembles Ti-Jeanne's feelings of Baby as a burden through much of the text, as well as Mi-Jeanne's resentment of Ti-Jeanne when she was baby. Hopkinson acknowledges the statistical reality in the dystopic elements of Ti-Jeanne's life, but also reclaims the negative stereotypes by ultimately making Ti-Jeanne the heroine. Ti-Jeanne begins the text as a distracted parent, chafing at her maternal duties, but ends the text by bonding with her child. The promising future is symbolized by her thinking of naming Baby. Ti-Jeanne remains unwed but she has overcome her "addiction" to Tony: "Ti-Jeanne looked into his eyes, feeling none of the desperate obsession she used to have for Tony, none of the longing for him to make her life right, either. And, to her surprise, no hatred, not really. Just pity. Her heart was free" (*Brown* 246). Ti-Jeanne has learned self-control, strength, independence, and self-worth; she no longer has to rely on a man, at any cost, to feel fulfilled. Hopkinson also counters the "welfare queen" image with the self-sustainability of Ti-Jeanne and Gros-Jeanne. Nevertheless, Hopkinson doesn't glorify Ti-Jeanne's position as an unwed mother, despite her being a "superhero" in disguise; Ti-Jeanne's struggles and progress are significant.

Ti-Jeanne simultaneously represents a detailed, situated identity as an unwed black mother and "Everywoman."[21] Hopkinson highlights Ti-Jeanne's "everywoman" status in her name and mirroring of Derek Walcott's play *Ti-Jean and His Brothers* (Michlitsch 31), and we can see this element in Ti-Jeanne's association with the upwardly mobile mentality of many American readers. However, the differing cultural and generic contexts also problematize this general status. Ti-Jeanne's specific demographics contrast with the "average" American reader of science fiction, and protagonist of science fiction. By combining the specific and general elements, Hopkinson challenges stereotypes. In contrast to the marginalized identity of Afro-Caribbean immigrants and unwed mothers in American society, Hopkinson places Ti-Jeanne at the centre of the text. She wants "to make 'black women's *otherness* normal'" (Hopkinson qtd. in Ramraj 131). Hopkinson's dual focus is similar to the historical strategy of Anglo males in Western society and in sf specifically; they occupy a specific, privileged, "superior" segment of the society, while simultaneously representing the "universal."[22] In Ti-Jeanne's case, however, the purpose is to overcome prejudice and repression, rather than perpetuate them. By making Afro-Caribbean culture the norm, Hopkinson challenges the expectations and knowledge base of her non-Caribbean and non-black readers (Rutledge 31). If they rise to the challenge, they can gain "greater insight" (31).

Brown Girl in the Ring is as relevant today as a decade ago. With the recent recession, many Americans face severe economic trials and most

Americans have suffered a loss of confidence. They question the economic and political status quo and the possibility of achieving the American Dream. In a reimagined Toronto, Hopkinson's text offers a warning of where unfettered capitalism and selfish individualism will lead us, an acknowledgement of the dire economic straits that many people face, and a solution to both of these problems. Most real-world solutions attempted, or even suggested, have been massive government initiatives involving tremendous amounts of money—Wall Street and automotive bailouts, national stimulus packages, etc. Instead, Hopkinson uses her fictional Toronto to highlight an urban future different from Detroit's, one with localized, grassroots community building; a small-business focus; personal responsibility and activism; and the necessity of a more minimalistic lifestyle. Although clearly writing in the dystopic tradition, Hopkinson complicates the dystopic/utopic binary by inverting the normative "ghetto"/suburb hierarchy and "dissolving the traditional boundaries between the ideal and vilified worlds" (Skallerup 77). The protagonist works to regenerate the inner city, not escape, destroy, or completely change it. Ti-Jeanne does not leave the Burn at the end of text; she remains, in mourning, but surrounded by community members. She shows the hope in dire circumstances. In her rise from the most marginalized of characters to a "superhero," Ti-Jeanne showcases perseverance and progress. In her "everywoman" role, Ti-Jeanne serves as a model for survival. Engage in the community, look to family and faith for support and guidance, do not over-rely on science and technology for "quick fixes," and make tough decisions about personal finances and consumerism. You may not end up with the traditional American dream, but returning to your "roots" can be a sustainable alternative.

Notes

1 Ingrid Thaler posits this dual dys/utopian motif as a central element of what she labels Black Atlantic Speculative Fiction. She explores this theme in three major black female authors of speculative fiction: Octavia E. Butler, Jewelle Gomez, and Nalo Hopkinson. However, Thaler focuses on Hopkinson's subsequent text, *Midnight Robber* (2000), rather than *Brown Girl in the Ring*. Also, Thaler emphasizes the central and positive role of technology, arguing that "the cyborg body may dissolve the postcolonial high-tech utopia's need to externalize its dystopian aspects" (130).
2 See Michelle Reid, who quotes from a 2001 author interview, and Gregory E. Rutledge, who cites a note from the author.

3 This is a similar scenario to that of Warren Miller's *The Siege of Harlem* (1964).
4 See the Assignment Detroit Project at TIME.com for a list of the articles, as well as The Detroit Blog: One City. One Year. Endless Possibilities.
5 Detroit was not the filming location for the movie, however. Dallas, Texas, was the primary location and Monessen, Pennsylvania, was a secondary location ("Robocop").
6 Esther L. Jones comes closest to this type of inclusivity, bringing together spirituality and technology in the context of "transmutations" in "science fiction icons and conventions" (128). However, she foregrounds spirituality as the basis for almost all of the changes and elides the larger socio-economic connections, as the title of her dissertation would suggest.
7 Ralph Pordzik describes this post-colonial critique in *The Quest for Postcolonial Utopia: A Comparative Introduction to the Utopian Novel in the New English Literatures* (14).
8 Grace L. Dillon is a proponent of "scientific literacies," rather than mythology. I was present at an interesting conference panel where Dillon explained this perspective (International Conference for the Fantastic in the Arts 2010). See also her article "Indigenous Scientific Literacies in Nalo Hopkinson's Ceremonial Worlds."
9 Rutledge persuasively explores why inner-city black men are often complicit in the victimization of members of their own community, particularly women, the elderly, and children (25).
10 After slavery, black reproduction and offspring could be seen as a threat to white dominance.
11 Rutledge also includes some gender-specific analysis, asserting that "[f]or women, especially Black women like Ti-Jeanne, their gender compounds the formidable obstacles facing them" (25).
12 Reid analyzes Hopkinson's text in a specifically Canadian context, examining the tension between the ideal of a multicultural "mosaic" and existing "inequalities." She develops indigenous and immigrant challenges to a government-sponsored, "unity through diversity" model.
13 Reid also explores this theme in Hopkinson's 1996 short story, "A Habit of Waste."
14 For a view of this wasteland, see Sean Hemmerle's picture entitled "Former Housing Plots" in the *Time* collection. In fact, this was the photo where his caption expressed his "postapocalyptic" feeling.
15 A recent article on post-Katrina renewal supports Hopkinson's perspective: "Successful neighborhoods have rebuilt through strong grass-roots leadership and often in spite of government help, says Allison Plyer of the Greater New Orleans Community Data Center, which has tracked citywide data since Katrina" (Jervis).

16 Similarly, the Fellowship Placement Program of the Strong Cities, Strong Communities initiative places "early- to mid-career" local leaders in Wayne State University's Detroit Revitalization Fellows Program, to ensure that local leaders will be able to spearhead urban revitalization in the six cities chosen to be a part of the program (Donovan 322).

17 In a footnote, Michlitsch glosses a potential problem with the "supermom" image for black women (32). Although it places them in a highly positive light, undermining negative racial stereotypes, it can also cause undue pressure to be perfect and cause them to neglect their own care as they struggle to care for everyone around them. Similarly, one can argue that individual residents should not be primarily responsible for confronting armed, powerful, and violent criminals.

18 While Hopkinson and Verhoeven offer two vastly different protagonists and "solutions" to urban decay, they both stress the importance of individuals, responsibility for the community, and personal sacrifice.

19 This reflects a similar historical trend in Western civilization. In evolutionary theory, for example, Charles Darwin hypothesized the eventual extinction of natives and ascendancy of Anglos: "[a]t some future period, not very distant as measured by centuries, the civilized races of man will almost certainly exterminate and replace throughout the world the savage races" (Gould 417).

20 Thus, I disagree with Ruby S. Ramraj that the ultimate goal of Hopkinson's dystopian writing is to "construct a world that is truly gender blind, color blind," although I agree with the "accommodating of all beings" (138). Hopkinson's relation of a conference experience with Samuel Delany supports my view ("Nalo" 77). She elaborates: "I find that when people from other communities do get written into SF, it's with a gloss that says, 'Yes, but we're all the same.' In a way that's true, but it totally ignores the actual social issues that do make a serious difference" (77).

21 Jones also utilizes the label of "everywoman" for Ti-Jeanne, but she defines the concept in a manner that is more in line with Michlitsch: Ti-Jeanne is "everywoman" because of her "common" motherhood (133). Jones contrasts this role with Ti-Jeanne's "heroic" spirituality (133).

22 See DeGraw's *The Subject of Race in American Science Fiction* for a detailed explanation of this phenomenon.

Works Cited

Beck, Julie. "Success! The Internet Buys Detroit a Robocop Statue." *Popsci*. Popular Science, 17 Feb. 2011. Web. 26 Sept. 2011.

Braiker, Brian. "A RoboCop Statue for Detroit?" *ABC News/Entertainment*. ABCNews.com, 17 Feb. 2011. Web. 26 Sept. 2011.

Bury, Chris, and Hanna Siegel. "Detroit Has to Demolish Before It Can Rebuild." ABCNews.com. ABC News, 20 Mar. 2010. Web. 16 Sept. 2011.

"Call for Papers." *2012 SFRA Conference: Detroit.* Science Fiction Research Association, n.d. Web. 30 Aug. 2011.

DeGraw, Sharon. *The Subject of Race in American Science Fiction.* Literary Criticism and Cultural Theory series. Ed. William E. Cain. New York: Routledge, 2007. Print.

Dickerson, Brian. "Old MacDonald Is Detroit's New Bogeyman." freep.com. Detroit Free Press, 9 Sept. 2010. Web. 16 Sept. 2011.

Dillon, Grace L. "Indigenous Scientific Literacies in Nalo Hopkinson's Ceremonial Worlds." *Journal of the Fantastic in the Arts* 18.1 (2007): 23–41. Print.

Donovan, Shaun. "An Urban Economic Policy for the 21st Century." *Vital Speeches of the Day* 77.9 (Sept. 2011): 318–23. Print.

Duncan, Carol B. "Hard Labour: Religion, Sexuality and the Pregnant Body in the African Diaspora." *Journal of the Association for Research on Mothering* 7.1 (2005): 167–73. Print.

Dybis, Karen. "School's Organic Farm Inspires Film." *Detroit Blog.* Time, 28 Sept. 2009. Web. 16 Sept. 2011.

Gallagher, John. "Acres of Barren Blocks Offer Chance to Reinvent Detroit." *City Farmer News.* Detroit Free Press, 15 Dec. 2008. Web. 16 Sept. 2011.

———. "Commercial Farming to Start in Detroit with 1,000 Trees." freep.com. Detroit Free Press, 8 Aug. 2011. Web. 16 Sept. 2011.

Ghosh, Bobby. "Arab-Americans: Detroit's Unlikely Saviors." TIME.com. Time, 13 Nov. 2010. Web. 16 Sept. 2011.

Gould, Stephen Jay. *The Mismeasure of Man.* New York: W. W. Norton & Company, 1996. Print.

Grimm, Michael. "Green Detroit: From Ghost Town to Grow Town." *Allianz.* Allianz, 17 Jun. 2011. Web. 16 Sept. 2011.

Hackney, Suzette. "Bing: Strategy, Plan for Detroit Is in the Works." *Detroit Free Press.* Detroit Free Press, 12 May 2010. Web. 16 Sept. 2011.

Hemmerle, Sean. The Remains of Detroit. *TimePhotos.* Time, n.d. Web. 16 Sept. 2011.

Hopkinson, Nalo. *Brown Girl in the Ring.* New York: Aspect, 1998. Print.

———. "Nalo Hopkinson: Many Perspectives." *Locus: The Newspaper of the Science Fiction Field* 42.1 (Jan. 1999): 8+. Print.

Huebner, Albert. "Organ Snatchers; Human Body Parts Have Become a New Cash Crop." *Toward Freedom* 52.1 (30 Apr. 2004): n.p. Proquest. Web. 21 Aug. 2011.

Jervis, Rick. "Recovery in New Orleans Spotty." *Lansing State Journal* 26 Aug. 2011: 3A. Print.

Jones, Esther L. "Traveling Discourses: Subjectivity, Space and Spirituality in Black Women's Speculative Fictions in the Americas." Diss. Ohio State U, 2006. *Proquest Dissertations and Theses.* Web. 29 Dec. 2011.

Langer, Jessica. "The Shapes of Dystopia: Boundaries, Hybridity and the Politics of Power." *Science Fiction, Imperialism and the Third World: Essays on Postcolonial*

Literature and Film. Ed. Ericka Hoagland and Reema Sarwal. Jefferson: McFarland, 2010. 171–87. Print.

Michlitsch, Gretchen J. "Breastfeeding Mother Rescues City: Nalo Hopkinson's Ti-Jeanne as Superhero." *FEMSPEC: An Interdisciplinary Feminist Journal Dedicated to Critical and Creative Work in the Realms of Science Fiction, Fantasy, Magical Realism, Surrealism, Myth, Folklore, and Other Supernatural Genres* 6.1 (2005): 18–34. *Wilson Web*. Web. 24 June 2011.

Miller, Warren. *The Siege of Harlem*. New York: McGraw-Hill, 1964. Print.

Mogk, John, and Sarah Kwiatkowski. "OTHER VOICES: Urban Farming Should Take Root Here." *Crain's Detroit Business*. Crain Communications, 18 Apr. 2010. Web. 16 Sept. 2011.

Perkins, Huel. "Fundraising Goal for Detroit RoboCop Statue Met." myFOXdetroit.com. Fox Television Stations, 3 Apr. 2011. Web. 26 Sept. 2011.

Pordzik, Ralph. *The Quest for Postcolonial Utopia: A Comparative Introduction to the Utopian Novel in the New English Literatures*. Studies of World Literature in English 10. New York: Peter Lang, 2001. Print.

Ramraj, Ruby S. "Nalo Hopkinson's Colonial and Dystopic Worlds in *Midnight Robber*." *The Influence of Imagination: Essays on Science Fiction and Fantasy as Agents of Social Change*. Ed. Lee Easton and Randy Schroeder. Jefferson: McFarland, 2007. 131–38. Print.

Reid, Michelle. "Crossing the Boundaries of the 'Burn': Canadian Multiculturalism and Caribbean Hybridity in Nalo Hopkinson's *Brown Girl in the Ring*." *Extrapolation: A Journal of Science Fiction and Fantasy* 46.3 (2005): n.p. *Academic OneFile*. Web. 8 Aug. 2011.

Robocop. Dir. Paul Verhoeven. Metro-Goldwyn-Mayer, 2001. DVD.

"Robocop Filming Locations." *On Locations*. fast-rewind.com, n.d. Web. 28 Sept. 2011.

Rogan, Alcena Madeline Davis. "Tananarive Due and Nalo Hopkinson Revisit the Reproduction of Mothering: Legacies of the Past and Strategies for the Future." *Afro-Future Females: Black Writers Chart Science Fiction's Newest New-Wave Trajectory*. Ed. Marleen S. Barr. Columbus: Ohio State UP, 2008. 75–99. Print.

Rutledge, Gregory E. "Nalo Hopkinson's Urban Jungle and the Cosmology of Freedom: How Capitalism Underdeveloped the Black Americas and Left a *Brown Girl in the Ring*." *Foundation: The International Review of Science Fiction* 81 (2001): 22–39. Print.

Scheper-Hughes, Nancy. "Mr. Tati's Holiday and João's Safari—Seeing the World Through Transplant." *Body & Society* 17.2 & 3 (2011): 55-92. *Sage Publications*. Web. 21 Aug. 2011.

Skallerup, Lee. "Re-Evaluating Suvin: *Brown Girl in the Ring* as Effective Magical Dystopia." *Foundation: The International Review of Science Fiction* 104 (2008): 67–87. Print.

Star Wars. Dir. George Lucas. Twentieth Century Fox Home Entertainment, 1995. Videocassette.

Thaler, Ingrid. *Black Atlantic Speculative Fictions: Octavia E. Butler, Jewelle Gomez, and Nalo Hopkinson*. New York: Routledge, 2010. Print.

Weinberg, Alvin M. "Can Technology Replace Social Engineering?" *Science and Technology Today: Readings for Writers*. Ed. Nancy R. MacKenzie. New York: St. Martin's Press, 1995. 71–80. Print.

Williams, Ron. "Green Detroit: Why the City Is Ground Zero for the Sustainability Movement." *AlterNet*. AlterNet, 22 Apr. 2010. Web. 16 Sept. 2011.

Wood, Sarah. "'Serving the Spirits': Emergent Identities in Nalo Hopkinson's *Brown Girl in the Ring*." *Extrapolation: A Journal of Science Fiction and Fantasy* 46.3 (2005): 315–26. *Academic OneFile*. Web. 8 Aug. 2011.

PART III
Spectral Histories

Archive Failure? *Cielos de la tierra*'s Historical Dystopia

Zac Zimmer

> Right on that which permits and conditions archivization we will never find anything other than that which exposes to destruction, and in truth menaces with destruction, introducing, a priori, forgetfulness and the archiviolithic into the heart of the monument.
> —Jacques Derrida, *Archive Fever*

In the end, a whirlwind. In the end, a text. For those who have read it, these two phrases may be the most concise distillation of Gabriel García Márquez's groundbreaking 1967 novel *Cien años de soledad* (*One Hundred Years of Solitude*). Márquez's novel solidified an international aesthetic, magical realism, that came to define Latin American literature for the final third of the twentieth century. Above and beyond that term's ambivalent history within Latin American literature and literary criticism, *Cien años de soledad* stands as a classic novel of universal literature, a novel that must be part of any respectable literary canon. Yet as novels become canonical, so too do methods of reading the canon. In the case of *Cien años de soledad*, one of the most potent and enduring interpretations belongs to Roberto González Echevarría, whose *Myth and Archive: A Theory of Latin American Narrative* (1990) uses García Márquez's novel—along with a few other carefully selected texts—to construct an overarching theory of Latin American literary production from the Conquest to the present. The key concept for understanding Latin American narrative, according to Echevarría, is the *archive*.

The archive is particularly important in the understanding and interpretation of Latin American literature because of the historical circumstances at the heart of "the invention of Latin America."[1] Upon its colonization, the so-called New World—new only to sixteenth-century Europe, and simply "the world" to its indigenous inhabitants—became obsessed with creation myths, due mostly to the very *newness* attributed to its emergence. Any such creation myth, however, would have at its heart the historical foundation of the European Conquest; thus, the two seemingly opposed concepts of *history* and *myth* meld into one another in the case of Latin American narrative.

According to Echevarría's theory, the Latin American novel searches out a new myth to make the New World intelligible. *Cien años de soledad* presents the most distilled realization of that melding and searching. Márquez's novel is the archetypical archival fiction: a narrative that contains, within itself, all narratives, "a blow-up, a map of the narrative possibilities or potentialities of Latin American fiction" (Echevarría 4). That space where myth and history meet, that fictional text which contains all possible narrative permutations: that, for Echevarría, is the archive. *Cien años de soledad* becomes not only an example of Latin American narrative, but also the literal archive in which all history, and all myth, are deposited. The fact that a physical text itself—a metafictional text-within-a-text that readers suppose to be the *very text* they just finished reading—is the only object left standing after an apocalyptic whirlwind sweeps through Macondo further reinforces the centrality of the archive. The novel *becomes* archive, just as the archive finds itself *novelized*; this dynamic is at the core of Echevarría's reading of *Cien años de soledad*, and is the basis for his narrative theory.[2]

Mexican author Carmen Boullosa's 1997 novel *Cielos de la tierra* (*Earthly Heavens*) also ends with a whirlwind and a text. It is safe to say that her tale is in direct conversation with *Cien años de soledad*, as one of the characters speaks at length about the importance of García Márquez's novel in both her own and her generation's intellectual and political development. Yet Boullosa's novel differs from *Cien años* in two crucial, interrelated ways: the whirlwind that closes her novel is not apocalyptic, because the novel itself is set in a post-apocalyptic world; and Boullosa writes her novel in Mexico in the mid-1990s, in the heyday of NAFTA, the Zapatista rebellion, and Francis Fukuyama's proclaimed "end of history." Boullosa's work is, among other aspects, an extended meditation on the archive; yet, as one can imagine, the concept of the archive takes on a completely different meaning when faced with the homogenizing threat of free trade and the celebrated advent of a perpetual present.

A multi-layered text whose form directly mirrors its thematic concern about history, memory, and the archive, *Cielos de la tierra* could be described accurately as a historical novel crossed with a dystopian vision of a post-historical society. It is also a triptych of sorts, narrating three distinct yet connected tales. Estela's tale, the fulcrum, is told from 1990s Mexico. Although her story is the least developed, it frames the entire novel. Estela translates into Spanish the notebooks, originally written in Latin, of Hernando de Rivas, an indigenous student of the Colegio de la Santa Cruz de Tlatelolco. On one side of Estela's tale is Hernando's sixteenth-century narrative itself: a story of colonization and assimilation. On the other side is Lear's tale: the story of a select colony of genetically enhanced survivors of a nuclear apocalypse whose mission is to recreate Nature on an otherwise barren earth. Lear is the sole dissenter within L'Atlàntide—the name of the post-apocalyptic colony—whose mission otherwise leads them to embrace the elimination of memory and language itself.

As Boullosa's text jumps between the three temporal moments, the author weaves a meditation on Mexico in the time of NAFTA and the problems of a changing, developing, and globalizing nation. From that perspective, Hernando's story—the story of the historical Colegio de la Santa Cruz de Tlatelolco—looks back toward a previous moment of failed cultural assimilation in which religion, indigeneity, and racism played key parts. If Hernando's story grounds 1990s Mexico in the history of a failed utopia (for the Colegio advanced the ultimately frustrated dream of an educated indigenous Catholic priesthood), Lear's futuristic nightmare exaggerates and extends to the ultimate extreme many of the cultural and political fears surrounding Mexico's embrace of neoliberal globalization best exemplified by the implementation of NAFTA in 1994.

The three stories are tied together through an intergenerational project of translation, preservation, and archivization. Estela finds and translates Hernando's sixteenth-century manuscript into Spanish; Lear, in her post-apocalyptic world, discovers Estela's translation and, in turn, commits both Estela's narrative and Hernando's interpolated manuscript into the archives of a post-historical society. Lear acts against the general consensus of her L'Atlàntidean community, as they otherwise hurl themselves toward a species-altering devolution into muted, fragmented, homogeneous masses of flesh.

Thus, the key question in interpreting Boullosa's novel becomes: What happens if the globalization and neoliberalization that began to sweep through Mexico in the 1990s is successful in fully eradicating difference and particularity? What, then, of language, of history, and of memory? And if the key to understanding the Mexican future lies in the past, how does one approach a present moment that seeks to homogenize language, erase history, and install an eternal present? In other words: what does it mean to pose the question of the archive, the questions of memory—past, present, and future—in Mexico in the 1990s?

The overwhelming feeling of being lost in the midst of history is a typical one for Boullosa's readers. Although Boullosa's literary beginnings lie in the theatre, she has become best known as the author of a series of meticulously researched and energetically imagined historical novels.[3] Many of these novels address conditions of her native Mexico; others treat her adopted home of New York City. What ties them all together, even those that take place in Cervantes' Mediterranean or among the seventeenth-century pirates of the Caribbean, is an extensive process of historical research and direct quotation—at times approaching outright plagiarism—of primary-source documents.[4] Boullosa's process turns the very concept of historical fiction on its head: instead of "bringing history to life" through a fictional reimagining of historical circumstances, it is from the very same musty manuscripts—those decomposing parchments, tomes, and codices all cloistered in the archive—that Boullosa draws forth the poignant stories that form the building blocks of her narrative. Julio Ortega has described her novels as devouring all historical contexts.[5]

What, then, are the contexts consumed by *Cielos de la tierra*? The most significant, as mentioned above, is the Colegio de la Santa Cruz de Tlatelolco, the sixteenth-century college where Hernando studies Catholic theology. Like many of the characters in this section of Boullosa's novel, Hernando de Rivas has a historical model. In this case, the model is a student mentioned by Father Juan Bautista in a prologue to his *Sermonario*:

> Father Juan Bautista incorporated also a list of Indians who were graduates of Santa Cruz College and who attained prominence in the social and intellectual life of Mexico. At the head of the list is Hernando de Rivas, a native of Texcuco [sic], who during the time he was connected with the college assisted Fathers Alonso de Molina and Juan de Gaona in composing the books they wrote in the Mexican tongue. (Borgia Steck 608)[6]

The Colegio itself was the first institution of its kind in the Americas; in certain ways, its dual model of at once providing a progressive (religious) education to the local indigenous population *and* documenting/archiving pre-Columbian history and culture has yet to be matched in the Americas.[7] The original mission was to train the "best and brightest," so to speak, of the indigenous elite; the Franciscan founders of the Colegio had every intention of converting the adolescents who were originally accepted in 1536— the Colegio's first year of functioning—into priests, thus creating a class of native nobles capable of evangelizing to their fellow natives. Important names from this period of Meso-American history emerge in connection with the Colegio; indeed, the Colegio counted on the early support of Mexican Archbishop Juan de Zumárraga and Mexican Viceroy Antonio de Mendoza. After a turbulent period marked by epidemics in the mid-1540s, and increasing resistance—both from Spain and within Meso-America itself—to the idea of an Indian priesthood, the Franciscans ceded control of the Colegio to the indigenous students themselves in 1546. By the 1570s, it had essentially turned into a translation workshop and an institute for the documentation of pre-Hispanic life in Meso-America under the support of Bernardino de Sahagún and several other well-known chroniclers of the Americas (Mendieta and Bautista, first and foremost).

The Colegio, however, is not the only historical context that the novel devours. There is also the moment contemporary to the novel's composition: the Mexican 1990s. This would be, in global terms, the post-1989 moment, the neoliberal celebration of the end of the Soviet Union, the triumph of market capitalism on a global scale, and—as proclaimed by Francis Fukuyama—the "end of history." It is within this atmosphere that Mexico celebrates the quincentennial of the 1492 "discovery" of America, agrees to and implements the North American Free Trade Agreement (TLC, *tratado de libre comercio*, in Spanish), and confronts an uprising in the southern state of Chiapas. In fact, it is the Zapatistas (the EZLN: Ejército Zapatista de Liberación Nacional) who forcefully tie these seemingly disparate events together, focusing on the irony that the solidification of the *modern* (globalization, free market, neoliberalism, and specifically NAFTA) coincides with the celebration of the Spanish arrival in the Caribbean five hundred years prior.[8] Where someone like Fukuyama sees novelty and the end of history, the EZLN sees nothing but the continuity of colonial exploitation: the same old "new" thing in the New World, five centuries in the making.[9]

Even if these are the historical contexts against which the various parts of the novel unfold, the reader must not fall into the error of a rigid periodization. One critic has categorized the novel as three "historical" failed utopias (even though the final utopia, Lear's, is speculative): noble savage, modernity, and the future (corresponding to, respectively, Hernando, Estela, and Lear).[10] Although chronologically accurate, such a periodization sacrifices the continuous sense of historical violence that traverses Mexican history. Instead of separating out the three different failed utopias, it is imperative that the reader view them as cumulative, overlapping, and entwined. The violence of conquest and colonialism; the violence of uneven development and globalization; the violence of a nuclear war; the violence of the actual elimination of history: all of these respective violences intermingle, feed one another, and ultimately merge into the whirlwind that wipes language itself from the face of the planet.

Yet if the above-mentioned overlapping layers of violence culminate in the eradication of language, memory, and history, the reader must ask: what is it I am reading? This problem is not exclusively Boullosa's; it is the fundamental technical problem with post-apocalyptic narrative. If this story is told from the *other side* of the apocalypse, *after* the end of civilization, how is communication even possible? Authors of post-apocalyptic fiction—different, it must be noted, from straight apocalypse—tend toward one of two strategies: they either ignore the problem altogether, or they establish a complicated intertextuality that somehow interpolates the reader into the story.[11] In the case of *Cielos de la tierra*, the three stories—Hernando's, Estela's, and Lear's—exist within a further literary apparatus of frames and false attributions. Lear "translates" Estela's 1990s Spanish-language translation of Hernando's late-sixteenth-century Latin text; the final textual form of Lear's translation remains unclear, but she mentions a certain "kesto," which the reader supposes to be the Atlántidos' form of archive. To further complicate matters, each chapter begins and ends with Esperanto intertitles, even though the rest of the novel itself is written in Spanish. On top of these layers imminent to the three stories, there are further layers in the form of prologues.

The most perplexing of these is an "author's note," signed by one Juan Nepomuceno Rodríguez Álvarez (perhaps related to Juan Nepomuceno Álvarez, interim president of Mexico in 1855 and a leader of the Reform movement). Álvarez writes at the imminent outbreak of the global nuclear war that, one supposes, will lead to the post-apocalyptic condition in which

Lear exists. Yet in a seeming temporal contradiction, he somehow—be it prophecy or conjecture—refers to the completed text that will include the superimposition of Hernando and Lear's respective tales.

There is no neat and tidy way to resolve all of these different textual temporalities into one clear-cut narrative present, a fixed date and time in which the last and final of the text's many "authors" becomes visible as the novel's fictional narrator. The reader may experience these varied, pell-mell layers as distracting; ultimately, sorting them all out may not seem to be worth the effort. The very impossibility of chronologically temporalizing the many different interpolated voices within the novel, however, points to the larger theme of a *time out of joint*. And the text is unequivocal as to the cause of that particular malady: it is an all-encompassing violence that has set time off its hinges. The first of the several prologues and epigraphs, and the only one signed by "Carmen Boullosa," a name that coincides with the author's own, explains the conditions of possibility of the very text the reader holds in his hands:

> This violence [that gave birth to the novel] is the kind of violence that breaks things without finding anything, that tears out the roots without planting anything new, that knocks down. I pulled that violence from the air that surrounded me, because I had no idea how to avoid it. From that violence, and with it, I moved forward in the irregular and multiple way of *Cielos de la tierra*. Behind each line is the taste of destruction.[12]

The violence of which Boullosa speaks—so strong that it synesthetically permeates the flavour of each and every word—is the violence born in the destruction and forgetfulness at the heart of any archive. It is the violence that horrifies Walter Benjamin as he contemplates the accumulated treasures of history, the pile of debris that we name "progress."[13] Indeed, Lear lives among the physical manifestations of Benjaminian detritus: "Beyond the reconstructed gardens, we haven't cleaned earth's surface of its trash and rubble, so as to conserve a monument to their stupidity and clumsiness."[14] The ruined earth as monument to Historical Man's stupidity: for pessimistic Benjamin, every human monument is, at its heart, a monument to postlapsarian man's conquering brutality; in Boullosa's vision of the post-apocalyptic future, any remnant of civilization has been converted, in the wake of humanity's self-annihilation, into a *de facto* monument to barbarism. The Atlántidos only maintain humanity's archive so as to remember:

we will never again be man. Yet even that maxim is not enough for them. They proceed headlong into the annihilation of language itself: the very condition of possibility for historical man as such.

The continuity of historical violence, then, sets time out of its joint. In the wake of human society/human barbarism, the Atlántidos have decided the problem lies as much with history as with humanity. Thus, to right time *out of joint*, they adopt a strategy of the total eradication of Historical Man. Lear stands as the last remaining interlocutor capable of dialoguing with the pre-apocalyptic ancestors:

> While I lean towards the past, the rest of the inhabitants of L'Atlàntide climb towards a perpetual present and use themselves to rebuild what Historical Man strove to destroy, sublime Nature. I, for my part, do remember Historical Man, and I dialogue with him.[15]

In other words, Lear writes for an extinct species—*el hombre de la Historia*—and thus her writing slides backwards, "it runs against the hands of the clock, it disobeys the order of routine and work."[16]

Not only is Lear's position anachronistic, it is absurd. In her attempt to rupture a perpetual present she must appeal directly to a time out of joint, leading her to undertake the paradoxical goal of preserving in the archive a history written for an extinct species: *el hombre de la Historia*. L'Atlàntide is a culture of willed ignorance and forgetting carried to such an extreme that its inhabitants actually want to erase humankind's historical capacity. Only Lear dissents, firm in her belief that memory is the building block of imagination and that there is no other staircase leading from the past to the future (*Cielos* 18). Well aware of the futility of her exercise, she proceeds nonetheless with her archivization, because she realizes the species-altering implications of the total loss of history and memory:

> In all truth, the way the Atlántidos see it, that we should only pay attention to the present and the future, that it is an imperative necessity to forget the past because the past was nothing more than a series of mistakes, nothing more than the building-up of the destruction of Nature; if this were true, as they say, that one only needs to focus one's understanding on the present and the future, if this were true and it was rigorously practiced, as they ask, the erasure of the past . . . if this were brought about, Time, or whatever we understand as Time, would dissolve. We would float

in an amorphous mass in which time would not hold. The "reform of consciousness" they propose, by demanding total oblivion, would imply the very loss of consciousness itself.[17]

It is not difficult to interpret Lear's nightmare as the extreme extension of that celebrated 1990s idea of the triumphant "end of history." The most vocal representative of that position, of course, is Fukuyama, whose *The End of History and the Last Man* (1992) laid out a Hegelian-by-way-of-Kojeve argument that the empirical triumph of Western liberal democracy (notably in the former Soviet Union, but also in many parts of the post-colonial world) must be interpreted as the universalization of Western liberal democracy and, as such, the end of mankind's social and ideological evolution. *Things* will keep happening, but there will be no further paradigm shifts in human society: technocracy will replace ideology, and politics itself will become nothing more than the practical question of implementing and balancing "the twin principles of liberty and equality on which modern democracy is founded." The recognition of this fact and the acceptance of the free market economic model that supports it, Fukuyama advances, "guarantees an increasing homogenisation of all human societies, regardless of their historical origins or cultural inheritances."[18]

It is from Jacques Derrida's response to Fukuyama, his 1993 *Specters of Marx*, that I borrow the concept of *time out of joint*; and it is to this Shakespearean concept, taken from the Act 1, scene 5 exchange between Hamlet and the Ghost, that Derrida appeals to counter Fukuyama's triumphalist and facile claim of the end of history. Derrida's main contention is that, for as much as Fukuyama mobilizes the empirical fact of liberal democracy's spread, the theoretical end of history cannot account for the macroscopic empirical fact of human suffering. Derrida advances, "no degree of progress allows one to ignore that never before, in absolute figures, never have so many men, women, and children been subjugated, starved, or exterminated on the earth" (*Specters* 106). According to Derrida, Fukuyama dodges the reality of twentieth-century suffering through a philosophical "sleight of hand." Namely, Fukuyama oscillates between the ideal of liberal democracy—which Fukuyama proclaims as being an actually realized ideal in the post-1989 world—and the empirical facts: "Depending on how it works to his advantage and serves his thesis, Fukuyama defines liberal democracy here as an actual reality and there as a simple ideal. The event is now the realization, now the heralding of the realization" (*Specters* 7).

Fukuyama bandies about those facts that help his argument, and ignores those that contradict his proclaimed "good news" of liberal democracy's triumph. This very oscillation is off its hinges, and for Derrida it becomes a primary symptom of the contemporary time out of joint.

Boullosa does not precisely take a Derridean approach to critiquing Fukuyama, but she does share the deconstructionist skepticism that the question of History could ever possibly be settled. In *Cielos de la tierra*, the cause of History's untimeliness, its status as *out of joint*, is quite clear: the Atlántidos do not simply celebrate the end of history; rather, they actively attempt to bring it about. Effectively, this looks like a return to Nature, for according to the Atlántidos, Nature represent the order of all that is enduring and permanent on the planet. The fact that the concept of an enduring, permanent natural order is directly at odds with their view of the planet and Nature itself as threatened does not bother the Atlántidos in the slightest. On the contrary, in their view, Nature can only authentically be understood as *excluding* humanity: "The only memory L'Atlàntide wants to preserve is that the past drove Historical Man to despair and the destruction of Nature."[19] Thus, their primary task: the artificial recreation of authentic Nature. Lear describes how that project conflicts with her historical and archival impulse: "They say that my need to stomp through the ruins is pure folly, since we have made paradises rise up from earth's wasteland 'as if never touched by human hands,' artificial preserves that imitate what Nature was in days past."[20] The need to erase all traces of humanity literally stretches from womb to tomb, only the womb itself, in this case, is also artificial and post-human. The Atlántidos are not products of sexual reproduction. The conditions of their creation is unclear, but it appears they were grown artificially during the waning days of humanity to work as stewards and caretakers of the otherwise barren and lifeless Earth.[21] Within their artificial womb, the nascent Atlántidos were bombarded with images that featured a pre-apocalypse Earth and deliberately excluded human life. If their gestation was purely image-based and scrubbed of all reference to humanity, perhaps it is only inevitable that the Atlántidos undertake "Language Reform." One of Lear's *compañeros* describes the goals of the Reform:

> You must understand that only without language, without grammar, can we found the new man, a man who does not speak of the nasty little creature who with that same name, man, destroyed the Earth. . . .[22]

Understanding, loving language will pull you back towards the clumsy and dangerous love of things. Loving language will bind you up with man. Detach yourself from it! . . . It looks like what you want to defend, Lear, is memory. That's fine. We remember our images, but we must not keep any trace of men. Words, for instance . . .[23]

Lear does not agree. As she struggles in vain to convince her fellow Atlántidos that memory, history, and language are all bound up together in an inseparable knot, they undertake an operation that renders them voluntary sufferers of Broca's aphasia (*Cielos* 208). Literally, they are no longer physiologically able to produce language.

As her fellow Atlántidos gesture incomprehensibly to one another and degenerate to the point of cannibalism and senseless violence, Lear finds refuge in Historical Man's poetry.[24] While they are still physiologically able to communicate their disapproval, the other Atlántidos categorically reject poetry, stating that Historical Man's poets are "compañeros de la muerte" (death's companions/handmaidens). To them, this rejection is purely logical: what interest would an eternal being living in a perpetual present have in poetry?[25] In the Spanish-American context, this rejection carries a particular valance. In 1492—the same year that Columbus landed in the Caribbean, and Spain's Catholic monarchs retook Granada from the Moors and expelled the Jews from the Peninsula—Antonio de Nebrija published the first Spanish-language grammar, *Gramática de la lengua castellana*. In his dedicatory prologue to Queen Isabel, Nebrija affirms, "siempre la lengua fue compañera del imperio" ("language has always been empire's companion"; occasionally translated "language is the handmaiden of empire"). Here, then, we see another example of how Boullosa conjugates conquest, language, and memory. In the post-apocalyptic world of L'Atlàntide, death replaces empire—or, more specifically, the ruins of empire—in Nebrija's equation. And it is not mere language, but the highest realization of human language—poetry—that connects the two. The triptych of empire, language, and death becomes the constellation under which the remnants of humanity labour; l'Atlàntide itself becomes an effort to overcome each of those three points.

Lear dissents, and as the Reform unfolds, she finds herself again and again at the very limits of human language. It is in these moments that she shifts to verse. As the Atlántidos systematically disarticulate humanity from nature, Lear quotes Nicaraguan poet Rubén Darío:

> Ox that I saw in my childhood giving off steam one day
> beneath the Nicaraguan sun of blazing golds,
> in the lush hacienda, full of the harmony
> of the tropics; dove of the woods reverberating
> with the wind, with the axes, with birds and wild
> bulls, I greet you, since you are my life.[26]

Human life, for Darío, not only correlates to nature; the two are mutually definitive. The natural tableau Darío recreates in language literally *is* the poet's life. This is not the dialectic of recognition between master and slave—the Hegelian dialectic so central in Fukuyama's thesis—but rather the dialectic of the lived experience of nature: the youthful memory of a natural scene, seemingly devoid of human presence, that comes to define the life of a single human individual. But not even that: there is no escaping humanity even in this exceptionally tranquil and idyllic pastoral. The sounds of axes float among animal grunts and chirps, while the *Nicaraguan* sun is embroiled in such foolishly human ideals as nationalism. The Atlántidos do not care. They would first delete the axes and the sun from the poem for betraying an all-too-human love of *things*, and finally they would banish the poet himself for spoiling Nature with his vulgar childhood memory.

As L'Atlàntide moves farther and farther away from language, it becomes increasingly difficult for Lear to describe what is occurring around her. Finally, a whirlwind of meaningless gestures, body parts, and nonsense wipes the colony itself out of historical existence:

> In this very archive I described the importance of memory, but I did not imagine that its total loss would have this repercussion: now nothing has repercussions. My brothers, the beings who inhabit L'Atlàntide with me, have completely fallen out of time.[27]

Perhaps, for its inhabitants, L'Atlàntide ultimately realizes its mission, but for Lear, for humanity, and for the concept of history itself, it is a bitter, nearly definitive failure. Lear's tale joins Estela's and Hernando's as a narrative of defeat, of a utopian design decomposing into dystopia.

The Colegio, where Hernando's dream is resoundingly frustrated by racism and temptation, cannot make good on the promise of creating a native class of Catholic priests. In a striking example of Boullosa reworking the historical record, we see precocious American students chastised in spite of their abilities and devotion.[28] Estela's 1990s Mexico is still mired in the unresolved contradictions of the Conquest and the Colony. Estela express it in no uncertain terms: "Don't you remember the Colonial period? We came from the Colony, and we are in the Colony."[29] Not only that, but the wave of neoliberal globalization crashing over her contemporary Mexico further exacerbates the problems, as Estela observes that free trade has made it easier for her to purchase imported Gouda cheese from Europe than to eat the artisanal cheese from the southern Mexican state of Chiapas (the same state, it must be noted, that produced the Zapatista uprising).

The enduring legacy of anti-Indian racism finds a novel expression in twentieth-century Mexican radical-chic politics. Estela mourns the fact that the "indigenous question" only entered her youthful political awakening in the most superficial ways. Literally superficial: Estela and her cohort wore indigenous garments during their university *happenings*, but the question of the Indian as a political subject simply did not occur to her (*Cielos* 198). She connects this blind spot to her critical re-evaluation of García Márquez, alluded to earlier. For as much as *Cien años de soledad* redefined the political horizons of her generation—provided, of course, that "generation" is restricted to the privileged *blancos* attending university—that utopian moment was doomed to failure from the outset. As Estela understands it, the voracity unleashed by Macondo—both as fictional place and as utopian concept of a generation—ends up devouring itself. She pins this squarely on the fact that in "García Márquez's Eden the Indians are not 'actors' in the rebirth of reality."[30]

Estela's recognition of her sin of youthful enthusiasm ("I feel guilty because I sinned by dreaming") is what drives her to translate Hernando's manuscript, yet she also realizes that even her act of penance is flawed. She should be translating Hernando's Latin not into Spanish, but rather into Nahuatl. Once again, part of the blame falls on her liberal university education—in this instance, the lack of instruction in native Mexican languages.[31] Difference is the insuperable horizon that plagues Estela and dooms the Colegio. Boullosa's literary strategy is not to write a multicultural "response" or "rebuttal" to Mexican history, but rather to extend the utopian fantasy of "the same," of a smooth world that prohibits—even at the expense of dialogue itself—any and all difference, to its ultimate, disastrous, and dystopian extreme.

Three failures, although the failure of l'Atlàntide surpasses them all. The very idea, however, of overlapping and palimpsestic time attacks the heart of the end of history thesis. What Boullosa's novel brings to life is not the *end*, but the *surplus* of history. And Lear's final hope, a hope equally shared by the author and the reader, is the creation of a literary community: a triptych of three reader/writers across time, space, and world maintaining a trans-linguistic, trans-historical, trans-racial, and even trans-species dialogue. Hernando, Estela, and Lear: all three bound together in the archive, connected through the very materiality of history. Why is it, though, that this literary community only forms itself under the sign of the apocalypse? Why is it so often the case that tragedy, loss, and disaster are what snap the archival constellation into a recognizable community? Why, in other words, does Hernando's manuscript only speak to Estela in her contemporary moment of globalization and uneven development? Why does Lear only discover Estela's text in the wake of humankind's self-annihilation? Why can the only meaningful challenge to the seemingly insuperable cultural horizon of conquest and modernity come at the very limits of language, communication, and history itself?

The answer, upon first reading, looks much more pessimistic than it actually is. Just as human history is, in the Benjaminean sense, a series of disasters (because no matter how perfect the world is today, *another, better world is always possible*), human communication is a series of failures, a series of misunderstandings that approximate communication as best we can. There is great power in this realization, for it separates the so-called *hombres de la Historia* from the nihilistic Atlántidos. Instead of desiring the *elimination* of language, we actually-existing humans desire its perfection. Thus, like Lear, we reach for poetry in the most dire of circumstances. Yet we also realize a perfect language itself is impossible, at least since mythical Babel and perhaps from time immemorial.

In the face of the twin poles of communication and failure, humanity's only recourse is to try again, to attempt communication anew, to follow Samuel Beckett's categorical imperative: Try again. Fail again. Fail better.[32] Lear tries again to fail again, as does Boullosa. Not that her novel is a failure. Rather, it is a letter, written from the other side of the apocalypse we call the present, to a reader whose very survival and existence the text puts into doubt. When all else is blown away, the archive, we hope, will remain. Yet all the archive will be is a documentation of our own destruction, repeated eternally, because there is not just *one* after. As Americans, North, Central, and South, we live in a series of superimposed afters: after the conquest; after colonialism; after independence; after this revolution;

after that revolution; after this war; after that war. Perhaps, one day, there will indeed be an "after globalization," an "after neoliberalism," an "after NAFTA." And then it will be on to the next failure; but no: because we can always fail *better*. An archive of failure is not a failed archive. As long as there is some future reader, as yet unknown, there is hope.

Notes

1 In a now-classic work of post-colonial thought, Edmundo O'Gorman advanced the idea that America was never "discovered"; rather, "America" itself is a concept that was invented in the process of the European colonization of the so-called New World. See *La invención de América* (Mexico City: Fondo de Cultura Económica, 2006). O'Gorman's intellectual legacy has been carried forward by the Latin American thinkers of "coloniality"; for a broad introduction, see Mabel Moraña, Enrique Dussel, Carlos A. Jáuregui, eds., *Coloniality at Large: Latin America and the Postcolonial Debate* (Durham, NC: Duke UP, 2008).

2 It goes without saying that this presentation of Echevarría's theory is a drastic condensation and simplification; one other important characteristic of the Latin American novel for Echevarría is its seemingly self-negating relationship to its very form as *novel*. According to Echevarría, the other distinguishing fact of the Latin American novel is that it *denies* its status as a novel and adopts the tone and style of whatever archival document is culturally significant in that moment (his examples are the legal documents of Spanish conquest and administration, nineteenth-century scientific treaties, and twentieth-century anthropological investigations).

3 The best known of these novels to be translated into English thus far is *They're Cows, We're Pigs* (New York: Grove Press, 1997). For a general introduction, see Boullosa's interview with Rubén Gallo in *Bomb Magazine* 74 (Winter 2001). For a critical assessment in Spanish, refer to *Acercamientos a Carmen Boullosa*. See Durán and Reid for critical readings that focus especially on her historical fiction.

4 This is not meant as an accusation of copyright infringement, but rather an acknowledgement of Boullosa's participation in a long history of Latin American and Hispanic textual appropriation, a tradition that passes by Jorge Luis Borges and extends beyond Miguel de Cervantes.

5 "Más que antirreferencial o autorreferencial, el texto devora a los contextos con su fuerza" (Ortega 32–33).

6 Bautista's text itself reads as follows: "*Hernando de Rivas*, indio de Texcoco, que vivió en el Colegio de Tlatelolco donde cursó con gran aplicación la lengua latina y ayudó a los PP. Fray Alonso de Molina y Fray Juan de Gaona a

formar los libros que escribieron en lengua mexicana, particularmente, el 'Atre de la Lengua Mexicana,' obra de que fué autor el primero" (cited in Fernando Ocaranza, *El Imperial Colegio de Indios de la Santa Cruz de Tlaltelolco*, 27).

7   For an enthusiastic history of the Colegio, see Borgia Steck, "The First College in America: Santa Cruz de Tlatelolco," with the caveat that his reading may be too naively celebratory of the Catholic Church's motives in the New World.

8   My understanding of neoliberalism owes a debt to David Harvey, especially the introductory chapter of *A Brief History of Neoliberalism*.

9   Another important context that does not factor directly into Boullosa's novel but that indubitably exists just below the surface is the 1968 government massacre of students protesting in Tlatelolco Plaza, the actual historical site of the Colegio.

10 See Durán, "Utopia, Heterotopia, and Memory in Carmen Boullosa's *Cielos de la tierra*," an otherwise splendid article that suffers only from this one small fault.

11 Briefly, apocalyptic fiction, modelled on the New Testament's Book of Revelation, predicts and describes the coming end of the world, while post-apocalyptic fiction begins *in media res* among the ruins of a catastrophic event that has destroyed the prevailing organization of civilization. A hallmark shared by many, but not all, post-apocalyptic narratives is the absence of any direct, explicit account of the apocalyptic event itself. For more sustained reflection on apocalypse, post-apocalypse, and utopia in American narrative, see Lois Parkinson Zamora's *Writing the Apocalypse: Historical Vision in Contemporary U.S. and Latin American Fiction* (New York: Cambridge UP, 1993) and James Berger's *After the End: Representations of Post-Apocalypse* (Minneapolis: U of Minnesota P, 1999).

12 "Esta violencia [de la que nació la novela] es de las que rompen sin encontrar, arrancan sin dejar nada a cambio, y tumban. La tomé del aire, porque no supe cómo rehuirla. De ella, y con ella, avancé en la forma irregular y múltiple de *Cielos de la Tierra*. Cada línea sabe atrás de sí a la destrucción" (9).

13 See Walter Benjamin's memorable images of the historical archive as a collection of barbarisms and catastrophes in "On the Concept of History."

14 "Fuera de los jardines reconstruidos, no hemos limpiado la superficie de su basura y sus escombros, conservando un monumento a su torpeza y tontería" (*Cielos* 20).

15 "Mientras me inclino hacia el pasado, los demás habitantes de L'Atlàntide se empinan hacia un presente perpetuo y se utilizan para reconstruir lo que los hombres de la Historia se empeñaron en destruir, la sublime Naturaleza. Yo sí recuerdo al hombre de la Historia, y dialogo con él" (*Cielos* 16).

16 "avance hacia atrás, corra camino opuesto al que recorrió la aguja del reloj, llevando la contra al orden del trabajo y a la rutina, siguiéndole el paso al juego" (*Cielos* 16).

17 "De ser verdad, como se piensa ahora en L'Atlàntide, que sólo debemos atender al presente y al futuro, que es una necesidad imperiosa olvidar el pasado porque fue únicamente lección de errores, porque en él se edificó la destrucción de la Naturaleza, si fuera cierto, como se dice, que sólo hay que poner el entendimiento en el presente y el futuro, si fuera esto verdad y se practicara rigurosamente, como lo piden, al borrar el pasado, Tiempo, o lo que conocemos como tal, se disolvería. Flotaríamos en una masa amorfa donde Tiempo no tendría cabida. La reforma que proponen a nuestra conciencia, al pedir el olvido total, implicaría su pérdida" (*Cielos* 18).

18 See Fukuyama, "By Way of an Introduction" available at http://www.marxists.org/reference/subject/philosophy/works/us/fukuyama.htm. After he lays out his case of the inevitable universalization via homogenization of liberal market economics, Fukuyama then uses a Kojevean-influenced account of the Hegelian *struggle for recognition* to posit the equally inevitable universalization of liberal politics. Essentially, this amounts to the tautological universalization of the Western liberal subject: each individual, upon accepting his interpolated liberal subjecthood, will be recognized as a member of a universal class of equally valid liberal subjects. It must be noted that Fukuyama has twice updated his original hypothesis, first, in *Our Posthuman Future: Consequences of the Biotechnology Revolution* (2003), to incorporate science and technology into his post-historical equation, and then in *America at the Crossroads: Democracy, Power, and the Neoconservative Legacy* (2007), to explicitly distance himself from the most fervent boosters and implementers of his "end of history" theory.

19 "El único recuerdo que L'Atlàntide quiere conservar es que el pasado condujo al hombre de la Historia a su desaparición y a la destrucción de la Naturaleza" (*Cielos* 23).

20 "Dicen que es sólo necedad innecesaria batir mis pies entre ruinas cuando hemos conseguido alzar de la yerma tierra paraísos 'donde parece no haber llegado la mano del hombre', recintos artificiales que imitan lo que un día fue Naturaleza" (*Cielos* 24–25).

21 The exact relationship between the Atlántidos and Historical Man is also blurry; although Lear is the only one to care about humanity's history and achievements, other members are capable of citing poetry (but, it must be noted, only in the service of refuting Lear's attachment to Historical Man's cultural activity). Lear is also conscious of the irony of naming the colony L'Atlàntide, after the vanished quasi-utopian society described in Plato's dialogues *Timaeus* and *Critias*. She expands on this coincidence to comment on the general absurdity of rejecting history and memory *en masse*: "Quieren enterrar la memoria de los que nos precedieron, explicando que todos sus actos y conocimientos orillaron a la destrucción, y que los sobrevivientes debemos rehuirla. Pero todas

nuestras acciones tienden a entablar un diálogo con la civilización que existió en el tiempo de la Historia" (*Cielos* 19).

22 "Entiende que sólo sin lenguaje, sin gramática, podremos fundar un hombre nuevo, uno que no hable del dañino bicho que con ese mismo nombre destruyó la Tierra" (*Cielos* 117).

23 "Comprender, amar la lengua te regresa también al torpe y peligroso amor a la cosa. Amar la lengua te emparenta con el hombre. Despégate de ella . . . Tú [Lear] lo que pareces querer defender es la memoria. Está bien. Recordemos nuestras imágenes, pero no guardemos huella alguna de los hombres. Las palabras, para empezar . . ." (*Cielos* 114–15).

24 The theme of refuge in literature runs through the three sections of *Cielos de la tierra*. Hernando finds refuge in the Church Fathers and in his own autobiographical writing; Estela finds refuge in Hernando's manuscript and, more ambivalently, in Gabriel García Márquez's *Cien años de soledad*; beyond her poets, Lear finds refuge, of course, in Estela's translation of Hernando's diary.

25 See *Cielos* 114.

26 "Buey que vi en mi niñez echando vaho un día / bajo el nicaragüense sol de encendidos oros, / en la hacienda fecunda, plena de armonía / del trópico; paloma de los bosques sonoros / del viento, de las hachas, de pájaros y toros / salvajes, yo os saludo, pues sois el alma mía" (*Cielos* 170). Translation by Derusha and Acereda.

27 "Yo describí en este mismo archivo la importancia de la memoria, pero no imaginé que su pérdida total tuviera esta repercusión: ya nada tiene repercusión. Mis hermanos, los seres que habitan conmigo en L'Atlàntide, han escapado por completo del tiempo" (*Cielos* 322–23).

28 See *Cielos* 299–304. The scene of newly arrived priests reacting to the Colegio students' knowledge of the catechism with derision and ill will is documented in Motolinía's *Historia de los Indios de Nueva España*. See Borgia Steck, 603–604.

29 "¿No recuerdan la época de la Colonia? De la Colonia venimos, en la Colonia estamos" (*Cielos* 147). See *Cielos* 36 for the references to imported cheese.

30 "Lo que me llama la atención es que en el Edén garcíamarquiano los indios no son 'actores' de este re-nacimiento de la realidad" (*Cielos* 203). Boullosa's comments recall Chinua Achebe's now-canonical critique of Joseph Conrad's *Heart of Darkness*. See Achebe's "An Image of Africa: Racism in Conrad's *Heart of Darkness*" in the Norton edition of Conrad's *Heart of Darkness* (2005). Also available at < http://kirbyk.net/hod/image.of.africa.html>.

31 "Me siento culpable porque pequé al soñar. No soñé ni yo, ni mi generación, con un sueño que borrara la estructura suicida de nuestro pasado colonial. Yo reparo mi pena de la mejor manera: me aplico a traducir del latín al español el texto de un indio que mejor quedara de ser traducido al náhuatl, si éste se enseñara en las escuelas" (*Cielos* 204).

32 The line is from the first page of Samuel Beckett's 1983 *Worstward Ho*: "All of old. Nothing else ever. Ever tried. Ever failed. No matter. Try again. Fail again. Fail better." *Worstward Ho*, one of Beckett's final publications, explicitly addresses the theme of language's limits. It is conceivable Boullosa had this paragraph in particular in mind during the composition of *Cielos de la tierra*: "What when words gone? None for what then. But say by way of somehow on somehow with sight to do. With less of sight. Still dim and yet—. No. Nohow so on. Say better worse words gone when nohow on. Still dim and nohow on. All seen and nohow on. What words for what then? None for what then. No words for what when words gone. For what when nohow on. Somehow nohow on."

Works Cited

Anzaldo González, Demetrio. "Recordar a pesar del olvido, la alienación en *Cielos de la tierra*." *Acercamientos a Carmen Boullosa: Actas del Simposio Conjugarse en infinitivo—la escritora Carmen Boullosa*. Ed. Barbara Dröscher and Carlos Rincón. Berlin: Edition Tranvía, 1999: 210–20. Print.

Beckett, Samuel. *Worstward Ho*. New York: Grove, 1983. Print.

Benjamin, Walter. "On the Concept of History." *Selected Writings Volume 4, 1938–1940*. Ed. Howard Eiland and Michael W. Jennings. Cambridge: Harvard UP, 2003. 401–24. Print.

Borgia Steck, Francis. "The First College in America: Santa Cruz de Tlatelolco." *Catholic Educational Review* 24.8–10 (Oct. and Dec. 1936): 449–62; 603–17. Print.

Boullosa, Carmen. *Cielos de la tierra*. México: Alfaguara, 1997. Print.

Chorba, Carrie C. *Mexico, from Mestizo to Multicultural: National Identity and Recent Representations of the Conquest*. Nashville: Vanderbilt UP, 2007. Print.

Darío, Rubén. *Songs of Life and Hope. (Cantos de vida y esperanza.)* Trans. Will Derusha and Alberto Acereda. Durham: Duke UP, 2004. Print.

Derrida, Jacques. *Archive Fever: A Freudian Impression*. Trans. Eric Prenowitz. Chicago: University of Chicago Press, 1995. Print.

———. *Specters of Marx: The State of the Debt, the Work of Mourning and the New International*. Trans. Peggy Kamuf. London: Routledge, 2006. Print.

Domínguez Michael, Christopher. "*Cielos de la tierra*: Nuevo 'criollismo.'" *Acercamientos a Carmen Boullosa: Actas del Simposio Conjugarse en infinitivo—la escritora Carmen Boullosa*. Ed. Barbara Dröscher and Carlos Rincón. Berlin: Edition Tranvía, 1999: 37–42. Print.

Durán, Javier. "Utopia, Heterotopia, and Memory in Carmen Boullosa's *Cielos de la tierra*." *Studies in the Literary Imagination* 33.1 (Spring 2000): 51–65. Print.

Franco, Jean. "Piratas y Fantasmas." *Acercamientos a Carmen Boullosa: Actas del Simposio Conjugarse en infinitivo—la escritora Carmen Boullosa*. Ed. Barbara Dröscher and Carlos Rincón. Berlin: Edition Tranvía, 1999. 18–30. Print.

Fukuyama, Francis. *The End of History and the Last Man*. New York: Free Press, 2006. Print.

Harvey, David. *A Brief History of Neoliberalism*. Oxford: Oxford UP, 2005. Print.

Leon-Portilla, Miguel. "El Colegio de Santa Cruz de Tlatelolco. Temprano encuentro de humanistas españoles y sabios indígenas mexicanos." *El jaguar: su ser divino, humano y felino. Antología personal*. México: Universidad Autónoma Metropolitana, 2009. 118–33. Print.

López-Lozano, Miguel. *Utopian Dreams, Apocalyptic Nightmares: Globalization in Recent Mexican and Chicano Narrative*. West Lafayette: Purdue UP, 2007. Print.

Mathes, W. Michael. *The America's First Academic Library: Santa Cruz de Tlatelolco*. Sacramento, CA: California State Library Foundation, 1985. Print.

Ocaranza, Fernando. *El Imperial Colegio de Indios de la Santa Cruz de Santiago Tlaltelolco*. Mexico: self-published, 1934. Print.

Ortega, Julio. "La identidad literaria de Carmen Boullosa." *Acercamientos a Carmen Boullosa: Actas del Simposio Conjugarse en infinitivo—la escritora Carmen Boullosa*. Ed. Barbara Dröscher and Carlos Rincón. Berlin: Edition Tranvía, 1999. 31–36. Print.

Prado, G., Gloria M. "En el amplio espacio de los márgenes." *Acercamientos a Carmen Boullosa: Actas del Simposio Conjugarse en infinitivo—la escritora Carmen Boullosa*. Ed. Barbara Dröscher and Carlos Rincón. Berlin: Edition Tranvía, 1999. 202–209. Print.

Reid, Anna. "*Cielos de la Tierra*: ¿Utopía o Apocalipsis?" *Espéculo* 35 http://www.ucm.es/info/especulo/numero35/cielosti.html. Web. 15 Sept. 2011.

———. "The Operation of Orality and Memory in Carmen Boullosa's Fiction." *Acercamientos a Carmen Boullosa: Actas del Simposio Conjugarse en infinitivo—la escritora Carmen Boullosa*. Ed. Barbara Dröscher and Carlos Rincón. Berlin: Edition Tranvía, 1999. 181–92. Print.

———. "The Reworking of Conquest in Three Recent Mexican Novels." *(Re)Collecting the Past: History and Collective Memory in Latin American Narrative*. Ed. Victoria Carpenter. Bern: Peter Lang, 2010. 61–87. Print.

Sánchez Hernández, Diana Sofía. "Al margen: espacio de confluencia textual en *Cielos de la tierra*, novela de Carmen Boullosa." *Espéculo* 43 http://www.ucm.es/info/especulo/numero43/almargen.html. Web. 15 Sept. 2011.

Taylor, Claire. "Cities, Codes, and Cyborgs in Barmen Boullosa's *Cielos de la tierra*." *Bulletin of Spanish Studies* 80.4 (2003): 477–92. Print.

Love, War, and *Mal de Amores*
Utopia and Dystopia in the Mexican Revolution

María Odette Canivell

> Women like you are going to change this country.[1]
> —Angeles Mastretta, *Mal de Amores*

Carlos Fuentes, the Mexican novelist, essayist, and former diplomat, claims that America was born under the sign of Utopia. Long before its geographical "discovery," America was created in an "imaginary dream of the utopian search for its cities of gold, its peaceful, joyful island of Utopia . . ." (*Nueva* 18).[2] By the time explorers had disembarked on the continent, the European imaginary had granted a magical-mythical status to the New World. Anything and everything was feasible in the realm of this Promised Land, a place where "every possible utopia man could imagine could come true" (Olivero 7). Beyond the actual allure of finding gold, land, or spices, the first explorers offered Europe a "vision of the Golden Age restored on earth," paradise recovered (*Espejo* 6). Thus, this newly found Atlantis became a site upon which dreams could come true, a reminder of that happy time when humans were still dwelling in the Garden of Eden unencumbered by the trappings of mortal civilization.

For Europeans, tired of war, pestilence, cramped, filthy cities, and, with few exceptions, poor governance, the myth of the Adamic man was only possible in the New World. It was up to the chroniclers of the Americas to promote these myths and make certain their contemporaries believed their fabulous tales. From Colombus' fantastic descriptions of men with tails of monkeys (whom he punctiliously described in his letters to the Spanish Royal court) to Cortes' self-serving affirmation that the inhabitants of the

Indies were peaceful, loving souls keen on embracing the civilizing influences of Spain, Latin America was born in print as the embodiment of the ideals of perfection Europeans of the time held as true.

Two of the most common topoi in this ingeniously crafted tale were the myths of the "good savage" and the return to paradise. The reality was other. Paradise was destroyed by the European zeal to possess their version of Eden, for, as Fuentes points out ironically, "America was not the first, nor it would be the last, disorientation of the West" (*Espejo* 5). In spite of being the object of other cultures' utopian dreams, it was not until after the former Spanish colonies became independent that Latin America formulated its own utopian thought. One should note that the phrase *Latin America*, employed as a term to define a geographical, political, and historical region sharing a common language (or, rather, common Latin-derived languages), was coined in 1857 by the Colombian José María Torres Caicedo in his poem *Las dos Américas*. The region's home-born utopias, thus, had to wait until the Latin Americans found a sense of self after fighting the colonial powers for independence. Accordingly, when speaking about the Latin American utopian imaginary, two clearly identified camps emerge: *utopias for* Latin America and *utopias of* Latin America.

The first takes root in the imported millenary dreams brought to America beginning in 1492, when the unexplored continent became a medium to implement the imaginary desires of Europe's failed utopias. These Western-civilization-originated idealizations of a return to Eden were transformed, in the New World, into dystopian nightmares, destroyed by the colonial powers who turned the native American population into victims of exploitation, stealing their lands, trampling indigenous cultures, and fragmenting their sense of self. As Fuentes claims, as a result of the failure of its colonial past, "the American landmass stands perched between dream and reality, living the consequences of a divorce between the aspirations of the ideal society they want to create and the imperfect social model they actually inhabit" (*Espejo* 6). The second type of utopias for the region, the *utopias of* Latin America, are defined by the Cuban philosopher Yohanka del Rio as Latin America's social and political thought determined by the consciousness of the Latin Americans and formulated to suit the needs of its citizens. In this second type of utopian thought, Latin American authors and political thinkers try to recreate a new ideal reality to accommodate the political and social needs of their countrymen. A distinctive trait in this category, del Río continues, is the tight relationship between the social and political context and the utopia itself. As examples, one may cite the Bolivarian dream of a united Latin America, the "indigenista" movement of Chiapas, Tupac Amaru's uprising, Sandino's "Movimiento campesino," as well as the Sandinista and Mexican Revolutions.[3]

This last example is a particularly poignant case. The revolutionary ideals of the Mexican people represented (in the revolution's beginning stages) the utopian dream of the country looking forward to shedding the chains of tyranny. Most of their goals, hopes, and aspirations were quickly dashed. In a conflict lasting close to twenty years, the revolutionary leaders betrayed the confidence of their people and the principles they initially espoused, and killed (metaphorically and literally) the possibility of a strong, well-governed nation. The Mexican Revolution is a perfect paradigm of the "American anti-utopia," a dystopia characterized by "projecting as the future something already experimented in the past" (Cerutti 17). When the Mexican political elite discarded México's natural human talent (setting their political sights on Europe instead) and co-opted the failed models of other European revolutions as templates for their own national project, the failure of the political class to solve their social and political problems in situ provided the conditions for a dystopian future.[4]

Unlike the United States or Europe, where there is a clear, traceable dystopian literary tradition (particularly evident in the production of novels), Latin American writers are not as invested in writing about imagined apocalyptic scenarios, for the region suffers from *real* (rather than designed) and chronic nightmarish conditions: civil wars, despotic governments, ecological disasters.... On the contrary, while there is a clear utopian tradition beginning *after* independence (some of it, which although homegrown, is situated within the *utopias for* Latin America), exemplified in Domingo Sarmientos' *Argiropolis* and José Enrique Rodó's essay *Ariel*, the circulation of dystopian literature has been rather limited. Dystopian visions find fertile ground in industrial and post-industrial capitalists nations; they are not as common in communities where the rural encroaches on urban living, but whose main economic means of production is founded on other non-industrial revenue.

In "the South,"[5] writing history masked as fiction has been the more popular instrument of social analysis, as "novelists share the notion that, through fiction, history becomes humanized" (Borland 439), thus becoming more accessible to the reader. Still, there is a minor tradition of literary dystopias, mainly present in the genres of the novel, the short story, and plays. Among these early Latin American examples one should cite Adolfo Bioy Casares' *La Invención de Morel* (1940), a novella with clear parallels to H.G. Well's *The Island of Dr. Moreau*. Likewise, some of Jorge Luis Borges' short stories, particularly those included in *The Garden of Forking Paths* (1941) and *Fictions* (1944), and Alejo Carpentier's *The Lost Steps*[6] feature common dystopian motifs. Among female authors, Gioconda Belli's *Waslala: A Memorial of the Future* (1994) is model of a dystopian novel with an ecological message. *In the Country of Women* (2010), by the same author, can be also considered an anti-utopia. This last work, though, is tempered by a sense of humour (taken straight from *Lysistrata*) and a tongue-in-cheek attitude toward the ills befalling Latin American countries. Lastly, aspects of Nelida Piñón's *The Republic of Dreams* (1989) and Rosario Ferré's *The House on the Lagoon* (1996), two contemporary female-authored works, share with Belli a dystopian bent.[7]

Instead of the conventional apocalyptic, future-set dystopian novels, the region boasts a wide variety of utopias, which almost unfailingly turn into catastrophic failures (becoming anti-utopias in the process). Novels about them abound, as the writers in Latin America document their rise and fall systematically. Gabriel García Márquez's *The General in his Labyrinth* (1989), for example, details the botched implementation of one of the region's most famous, innovative, and homegrown utopian dreams: Bolivar's invention of a Great Latin America from Tierra del Fuego to the far North (at one point, the Venezuelan *Libertador* was planning to include all of the North, meaning the United States and Canada, in his dream of the "gran America").[8] *The War of the End of the World* (1981), by the Peruvian Nobel Prize–winner Mario Vargas Llosa, may serve to shed light on why Latin American traditional dystopian novels are few and far between. Although the title of the novel conjures visions of an apocalyptic future, the lengthy narrative is a retelling of the War of the Canudos, a conflict describing the uprising of one of the millenary nineteenth-century religious sects. This ragtag army of fanatics held the Brazilian state hostage, after defeating the army in several high-profile battles, while proclaiming the end of the world from the walls of their fortified city in the middle of the jungle. In Latin America, oftentimes, reality is more *fantastic* than what the imagination can dream of. Dystopias, in consequence, are *actually* real.[9]

In a world where a nightmarish reality trumps any fantasy the mind can conjure, it is not unusual to find writers using real events to depict a world readers might believe to be imagined, but is, unfortunately, all too true.

Mal de Amores, the 1995 novel by Angeles Mastretta, does precisely that. Referring to a real-life event (the Mexican Revolution), the Mexican novelist tells the story of a long descent into hell, one lasting close to twenty years. Like Vargas Llosa, García Márquez, or Belli, Mastretta voices a desire to deploy fiction as a conduit to analyze and discuss historical events as well as a plea to make things right—for in Latin America writers engage in nation building through their fiction while bemoaning the death of the national (and pan-national) unity Bolivar dreamt of.[10] Speaking of Colombia, but reflecting a sentiment that can certainly be applied to any other Latin American nation, Bolivar, the Venezuelan-born *caudillo*, cries on his deathbed, "the only ideas that occur to Colombians is how to divide the nation" (García Márquez, *General* 152). The history of the revolutions and internal conflicts in the region leading to civil war certainly supports Bolivar's complaint (Sendero Luminoso in Perú, the Mexican Revolution, the Cristero conflict, and the Zapatistas in México are just a few examples).[11]

A need to take the nation to task for the mistakes of the past is undoubtedly present in Mastretta's novel. Rewriting the history of her country using as a subject a period fraught with internal division, civil war, lies, and shattered dreams does not strike her readers as a coincidence, particularly coming after the NAFTA agreements and the Zapatista uprising. Challenging the conventional male point of view of the "first" Revolution in *Mal de Amores*, the Mexican novelist offers a new understanding of the events surrounding one of the first *utopias of* Latin America. Going back in time from the turbulent decades of the 1990s in México, when conditions similar to the beginning years of the Mexican Revolution were developing, the author analyzes the revolutionary project from the perspective of women, for whom this failed utopia becomes a true dystopian nightmare. Understanding what went wrong in the Revolution, the author offers, may shed light on what is happening in the Mexican nation of the now.[12]

The 1990s in México were turbulent, to say the least. In the south, the predominantly indigenous ELZN army initiated a military offensive to reclaim the use of ancestral land and political autonomy. Taking their name from Emiliano Zapata, a Mexican revolutionary leader, the Zapatistas threatened to overthrow the elected government and replace it with a socialist regime. As its name implies, the ruling PRI (Partido Revolucionario Institucional) had held power in the Mexican nation since the Revolution ended. Although claiming to espouse revolutionary ideals, the country had a level of corruption that was exceptional. Instead of a trickle-down policy, the wealth was trickling up, benefiting only the political elite. Cronyism, nepotism, a general ineptitude, and a customary misspending associated with the pre-electorate year (a ploy every PRI predecessor president had used so that voters could believe, once more, the party's "revolutionary" message) led to a financial crisis. Foreign investors, fearing another Cuba or, worse, Vietnam, pulled their money out. Local investors, in the wake of NAFTA, fretted about their competitive edge, opting to veto reinvestment of monies earned in the country and new job creation. The Mexican treasury decided not to float the Mexican peso, and was financially strapped for cash; after the forerunner in the race for president, Luis Donaldo Colosio, was assassinated (presumably on the orders of the PRI president, Carlos Salinas de Gortari, who feared he would be tried for corruption if Colosio won) a crisis of confidence damaged the banking system, causing a run on the already depleted funds of the central bank reserves. For many Mexicans, nightmarish scenarios of a second "revolution" plagued their dreams. Manifestations of social unrest and economic turmoil brought home the lesson squandered in the Mexican Revolution: seventy something years later, nothing had really changed in the nation. Writers, artists, and political theorists embraced and extolled the virtues of the Zapatistas, who seemed to offer an alternative to what many believed was the bloated corpse of the PRI. The parallels between the Zapatista uprising and the Mexican Revolution have been widely studied, but, whereas the former was at least marginally successful in terms of reminding Mexicans about due democratic process, the latter's legacy is still questionable.[13]

The Mexican revolutionary uprising was too ambitious a project. The attempt to fuse into one the somewhat liberal ideas of the bourgeoisie, the just claims of the "campesino movement," the suffragist agenda of women, the values of the conservative party, and the demands of the Church was clearly utopian. With so many cooks stirring the pot, their political and social agendas were doomed to fail. As Ramón García Resendíz claims, the Mexican Revolution might have functioned as a foundational myth of the Mexican political regime for close to sixty years, an "image of domination which the regime based its political power on, as a way to legitimize their political agenda" (144); social and political changes, however, were too little and too late coming to the nation, and the legacy of the Revolution was tainted, as the Zapatista uprising in Chiapas, at the end of the twentieth century, would prove.

Literature about the shortcomings of this failed political project abounds in México. From Mariano Azuela's early account, *Los de Abajo* (1915), to Carlos Fuentes' seminal *La Muerte de Artemio Cruz* (1962), Mexican literature and film has devoted many pages to debunking the myth. Until recently, however, the role of women in the conflict had seldom been studied.[14] For Mastretta, as a feminist and a woman, the opportunity to remedy that was hard to ignore. For the first time in their history, the Mexican Revolution offered women a change in political and social mores. Women from all walks of life embraced the promised myth of equality. Myths, though, tend to be imbued with a magical/mystical patina which, sooner or later, loses its sheen. That was the case for the women of México in the early stages of the twentieth century. As combatants in the Mexican Revolution, they supported practically every faction in the new governments (there were too many to count in the first thirty years of the twentieth century), hoping their shed blood and collective suffering would win them equal rights. These early female pioneers also sought to foster the optimal conditions necessary to bring about cultural change, hoping their newly elected politicians would desist in their belief that the primordial role for Mexican daughters was to the become the mirror image of the Virgen de Guadalupe, the sainted "mother of México."

The concept of womanhood in México is a multi-faceted proposition. The Mother/whore duality is deeply ingrained idea in the Mexican psyche, as it is reinforced (or so it is believed) by alleged historical roots.[15] The notion that the birth of the nation is a product of rape (the *malinchismo*, explored by Paz) makes it difficult for women to successfully implement a feminist agenda. The trope of the "chingada nación mexicana" is a "feminine stereotype central to Mexican constructs of femininity," thus the women of México are, at the same time, victims of rape and willing enablers of their seducers/rapists (Finnegan). As a result, the nation is metaphorically doubly "chingada." On the one hand, México suffers the actual physical rape of Malinche, the mother of the first Mexican citizen; on the other, the country is "fucked" by the alleged complicity of the women (and the nation) in its own victimization.[16]

Even without the "help" of the *willing fallen woman* archetype present in the collective Mexican imaginary, the daughters of the Mexican Revolution found it extremely difficult to reclaim their rightful place in society, for, as Nikki Craske notes, the political environment for women at the beginning of the twentieth century in México was rife with ambiguities and ambivalence. In the early 1900s, just as the forces of change were blowing over the Mexican nation, women were unable to reap their rewards. Females were placed in a twilight state where, in spite of avowed promises to the contrary, they became disenfranchised, marginalized second-class citizens who were denied many of the rights the nation afforded others. The reason for this state of affairs, Craske suggests, was that "women were being seen more as a threat to the national revolutionary project, rather than supporters and potential beneficiaries. The antipathy of revolutionary men towards women's full citizenship was despite the participation of women in the revolutionary cause" (122). In the years after the Revolution, the vital part played by women in this long-lasting armed conflict was, for the most part, buried. It is only recently that historians have been trying to highlight their contributions to the cause. The true role of the *soldaderas*, who fought in armed combat, and the achievements of the intellectual agents of the Revolution, such as Dolores Jimenez y Muro, Hermila Galindo, Elvia Carrillo Puerto (known as the Red Nun), and Juana Belén Gutierrez de Mendoza (to name just a few), was largely unknown. The *novelas de la revolución*, for example, a genre showcasing the recent history of México through the deeds of their male protagonists, had virtually no female leads.[17]

Choosing to highlight (or rather rescue from the mists of memory) the role of Mexican women during this vital historical period, and belying the conventional belief that "women are not part of the narrative of nationhood" (Thornton 217), the new feminist Mexican narrative (and, by extension, the Latin American one, Belli and Ferré, for example) has lent a voice to the oppressed, those whose achievements in the historiography of the nation have been silenced. *Mal de Amores* does precisely that. In subverting the traditional genre of the *novela de la revolución*, Mastretta creates a fascinating female revolutionary character, a woman torn between two loves, the *maderista* Daniel Cuenca and the conservative Antonio Zavalza. The book (for which the author received the prestigious prize Rómulo Gallegos) uses the lives of its fictional female character to explore dystopias and utopias in the México of the beginning of the twentieth century.

Following the traditional convention of the *novela rosa* (romance novels of a kind), Mastretta imagines a protagonist who is intelligent, extremely well educated, wealthy, beautiful, and talented. Emilia is no ordinary romance novel character, for she oversteps the boundaries of the conventional heroine of the *culebrón*. She is a doctor, a feminist, and a freedom fighter, travelling through war-torn México with her revolutionary lover. Subverting the stereotypes women occupy in female-led narratives, Mastretta creates a "dissident subject," someone deeply rooted "in the social and ideological contradiction of the affected nation" who represents the counter-discourse of the Mexican Revolution (Medeiro Lichens 300–301).[18] Although love plays a central role in the narrative, the protagonist experiences armed combat and sees first-hand the poverty and oppression her fellow women suffer.

Both as a political project and as the cause of the disagreements between Daniel and Emilia regarding the social roles women should play, the Revolution's ostensible goals grow uncertain, for women are required to be the stable centre to which their husbands return home and, at the same time, occupy the roles they vacate in war safeguarding/rebuilding the Mexican nation (Thornton 225). The daughters of México are torn between different personae, stereotypes created by the patriarchy based on the *chingada nación Mexicana* archetype. The unwitting females, in this masculine imaginary, alternate between two different submissive roles: playing the part of the Virgen de Guadalupe and that of the slave/seducer/rape victim/mother of the Mexican nation, Malinche. In such a complex cultural environment for women, the Revolution becomes an ontological impossibility: on the one hand, because it created a social environment where chaos and lawlessness reigned unchecked as, during that particular time in Mexican history, laws "were kept in a drawer, waiting to be introduced in a far distant future" (Mastretta 224)[19] and on the other, because in such a lawless universe the rights of women were swept under the rug even more, paradoxically, than in the previous despotic regime of Porfirio Díaz.[20] Tomis Kapitan claims that a dystopia may be defined as "an isolated society embodying the maximum amount of contentment and harmony, but dramatically short on justice" (268). For the women of the former Tenochtitlan, the Revolution evolves into being just that: the promise of contentment and harmony pales before the reality of injustice and isolation.

More than a historical recreation of an extremely challenging period in Mexican history, though, the novel is a literary paradigm, which the author uses to introduce a conundrum. The Mexican Revolution is at once the symbol of a utopian dream and a dystopian reality reproducing, in the future, the mistakes of the past. In the beginning years, the revolutionary uprising was seen as the vehicle for removing over thirty years of tyranny as well as the tool for creating the foundations of a modern Latin

American state. For the Mexican people, the Revolution signified México's reinsertion into the community of nations, the restoration of much needed democratic values, a social revolution, and equality for every citizen. This dream, however, was never to be fulfilled, for the ghost of war prevented any and all social changes.

Eventually, the fantasy became a living dystopia, particularly for women. Judy Maloof suggests that in the social Mexican imaginary the discourse of the Revolution was one of the master narratives fundamental to the construction of the nation (36). As a discourse, however, it became empty rhetoric, words bandied about by the different factions fighting the Revolution, who used promises as an enticement to get new recruits as cannon fodder. In *Mal de Amores*, Milagros, Emilia Sauri's aunt, is one of the first to offer to die for the revolution. As the government forces attack the revolutionary anti-election leaders in Puebla, Emilia, Josefa, and Milagros sit anxiously awaiting the news: "We should be there. Dying with them," Milagros states, to which her brother-in-law, Emilia's father, replies, "an absolute prohibition against killing a fellow human being should be the drastic principle of any coherent ethical code" (Mastretta 155–56). In *Mal de Amores*, the female protagonists take on the role traditionally associated with men, fighters willing to die for a cause, while Diego Sauri and Antonio Zavalza are seen as the peacemakers, a role usually associated with women.

Although there is a clear feminist agenda in *Mal de Amores*, Mastretta goes beyond subverting the traditional roles assigned to women to engage in nation building from the perspective of her female characters. Writing from the decade of the 1990s, when many of the ills befalling México were seen to be a revisiting of the Revolution's unsolved issues, Mastretta joined others who wondered if the Zapatistas were not the "new revolution," an opportunity to fulfill the nation's dream. Emilia, as Thornton notes, gets her name from Rousseau's *Émile*. Like him, she symbolizes an emergent "ideal citizen," a prototype of the hero who engages in healing the nation rather than killing it, and is seen as the possibility of a promising future for México. The impediment to fulfilling this personal/national destiny is the Revolution itself, for many saw the uprising as a portent of doom; "they have unleashed a tiger" (Mastretta 161), Diego Sauri confesses, and once uncaged, the wild beast can only bring pain to its people.

The relationship between the Mexicans and their turn-of-the-century Revolution, Niamh Thornton argues, parallels that of the literary characters Emilia and Daniel: they are unabashedly attracted to its/his glitter, its/

his beautiful possibilities, the alluring beauty of its/his message; in the end, however, the Revolution fails, like the "aventurero Daniel," traipsing around México leaving chaos in its wake, and all that remains are people (and Emilia herself) seeing empty promises and uncertain futures. In an echo of the Zapatista uprising, Daniel/the Revolution is the object of desire for both the female protagonist and the Mexican nation. Yet unlike the Chiapas movement, which did bring about social change and a reawakening of the nation's desire for a true democratic process, the Mexican Revolution fails in that endeavour, for "Emilia/the people are bound to him/it, but they are also the ones who suffer and must recoup the damages" (Thornton 224).

In a prescient moment, one of the secondary characters in *Mal de Amores*, a penniless Spanish encyclopedia peddler who arrives in México seduced by the promissory rhetoric of its politician to sell knowledge to the masses, tells Daniel, "you are chasing illusions," to which Emilia replies "he is [sic] been chasing illusions as long as I've known him" (Mastretta 260).[21] Parallel to the protagonists of the story, the Mexican people pursued the illusion of a better country, a better world, knowing deep in their hearts that these seemingly impossible dreams might have come true were it not for the internal incongruities (and contradictions) of the Revolution and the infighting derived from the factions wrestling for political power. The problem, Mastretta argues, is that although periods of upheaval may become the optimal time to bring about change and initiate new programs and innovative ideas, "lots of times revolutions change very little" (qtd. in Mujica). Diego Sauri, Emilia's visionary father, summarizes the authorial viewpoint: "the irony is that instead of democracy we got chaos, instead of justice, executioners" (Mastretta 268).

Just as America "was the lover one must change through violence in order to make it the *perfect* object of desire of the European mind" (Cerutti 11), México, during the Revolution, becomes the defiled victim, ravaged by one side or the other, who would rather see the nation dead than share the spoils. Emilia is the innocent onlooker, trying to make sense of this desecration. Travelling the country by train, she witnesses the hell her nation is suffering. *Revolutions are shit*, she quips, to her lover, feeling powerless to stop the madness. Inverting the utopian trope of a long journey to find paradise, Mastretta describes, through the eyes of her protagonist, a dystopian descent: the desolate countryside filled with the dead and dying, the "experience of the horror that becomes routine" (233), and the children, helpless victims to this hell on earth:

> So much horror filled [Emilia's] eyes those days that for a long time afterward she was afraid to close them and find herself again at the whim of war. . . . The train filed past a long row of hanged men, their tongues lolling out, and she hugged Daniel trying to exorcise those distorted faces, the picture of a child trying to reach the boots of his father high overhead, the doubled over body of a keening woman, the immutable trees, one after another, each with its dead man like a unique fruit in this landscape. (233–34)

Watching the pain and suffering of her people, Emilia yearns for a new country, a place where women heal, not murder, and the children need not go sick or hungry. As Carmen Rivera Villegas claims, in *Mal de Amores* Mastretta explores the "ideological and emotional Other of a woman who lives with a revolutionary hero who will not accept her right to a voice in the Revolution" (40). Had that voice been heard, children might have had a better future and the many factions fighting for power may have sat down with each other and tried to reconcile. In the impossibility of participating (politically) in the "big Revolution," Emilia and the women surrounding her (Milagros, Josefa, Dolores) are "practicing their own revolution" (Mastretta 42), changing what they can with the little support they obtain. From a hospital where holistic medicine is practised and taught to the women (Emilia), to political soirees where free love is chosen over marriage (Milagros), the female protagonists of *Mal de Amores* create, in the private space, that which the public space denies them. Although Josefa and Dolores represent somewhat more conventional views of womanhood, both are exceptionally strong female characters. The former rules the Sauri family; her husband, Diego, agrees that she acts as the *pater familias*. The latter teaches Emilia how to cope in a world of men with absent male figures. After spending time in the village with the "dark-skinned, doe-eyed women," Emilia learns "to get along on her own, to stifle what was irrelevant, to hum to herself, to mock the war, and to grapple with fate the way a plant grapples with water" (191). Living in this indigenous community of stoic, dignified women, whose understated demeanour and scarcity of material means make most people ignore them, teaches the protagonist how to address the arbitrary dictates of the patriarchal hegemony. But her time in the wealth-deprived village also helps as a way to become tutored about female empowerment and how to reconcile love and politics.

A central aspect to the novel, Rivera Villegas claims, is the binary opposition between physical love and the love for (and of) the nation. The two men in Emilia Sauri's life serve as paradigms representing the nation's paradoxical relationship with its women. Although a *maderista* by conviction, Daniel embodies the intrinsic inconsistency of a political project that while espousing (in principle) equal opportunities for women does so from a patriarchal point of view, thus hindering the intellectual, spiritual, and physical development of its members. In contrast, despite apparently conservative political views, Zavalza represents the "utopia of the intellectual *maderista* women" (Rivera 43) and promotes equal rights for both sexes. Emilia is caught in the middle. Just as she loves her country of birth and the ideals of the Revolution, Emilia loves Daniel and the political message he endorses. Like the Mexican people, however, she becomes disillusioned with the end result: a future where women are marginalized, their contributions ignored, their achievements buried.

Situating the novel in the revolutionary time, the author's very modern Sauri family nonetheless "provides a model for contemporary Mexican society" (Seminet 663), particularly that of the post-NAFTA era invested in creating a more democratic, modern Mexican nation. Establishing the parallels between the traditional national family (exemplified in the novel by Emilia's friend Sol) and juxtaposing it with the very unconventional Sauris, Mastretta creates a paradigm of a possible "different" type of Mexican family unit: the ideal, the Sauris, and the real, the actual Mexican family. In that sense, both families represent what Fuentes argued Latin American utopian thought to be: the struggle between the ideal society Latin Americans want to build and the real nightmares they have constructed, for both, real/ideal society and real/ideal family, are suffering from what Seminet terms the "lovesick malaise."

Although the name of the book stems from a Mexican bolero song (following the convention set in her first novel, *Arráncame la vida*, named after another love ballad), the title foreshadows the position of the story: a chronicle of the illness that afflicts México and Emilia, deep-rooted melancholia. This unhappiness (*desaliento*),[22] a product of the unrequited love for something (a country) or someone (Daniel), rules them in such a way that just *being* becomes unbearable; fickle, capricious, and untrustworthy as they may be, Emilia and México's lovers are still alluring, desirable, and worth fighting for. The only way to heal Emilia's/the country's heart is to rewrite the past using a different viewpoint: that of the women who were left behind in the failed revolutionary project. Restoring the Mexican nation to a "natural state" (one of the original *utopias for* Latin America), where the values the Revolution has left by the wayside are returned, will serve as a balm for the wounded heart of the nation/Emilia. Regrettably, as Georgia Seminet argues, the Revolution did not "give way to a democratic society and México continued to be ruled by authoritarian paternalistic leaders," corrupt, selfish politicians who fought tooth and nail to misrepresent what the country needed, and misruled for, what seemed to women, an eternity, using the legacy of this dystopia as their banner. The Mexican people, then, represented in fiction by the Sauri family, give voice to those "whose aspirations for democracy and peace distance them from the 'weight' and sickness of México's past." Lending words to their cry, *Mal de Amores* becomes "an exorcism of this sickness, focusing on the reconstruction of Mexican subjectivity, especially women's subjectivity" (663).

The Guatemalan Altiplano indigenous people have a tradition that comes from pre-Columbian times. In times of turmoil, or when something ails them, these Maya descendants conjure the "worry dolls," a small family of papier-maché figures made by hand. According to the local lore, if you tell these magical figurines your worries and place them under your pillow at night after confiding in them, when you wake up the next morning the magical family will have taken away your fears.[23] In the same fashion that the Guatemalan people might purge their demons (literal and figurative), Mastretta uses the written word to exorcise her (and other women's) fears. Creating an alternate story/history of the Mexican Revolution serves two purposes. In the first place, it is a way to summon the past so that the ghosts of violence and injustice can be conjured and disallowed. Second, it is a way to generate a new discourse in which women are active participants and can thus reclaim/reinvent the hope for a new future.

Notes

1 "Las mujeres como tú van a cambiar este país" (89). Translations are mine unless otherwise noted.
2 Carlos Fuentes refers in this quotation to "America" the continent. Latin Americans also consider themselves "Americans," not in the sense of citizens of the United State of America (who name themselves Americans), but as members of the entire multinational continent.

3 For more information on Latin American utopias, see Yohanka del Rio.
4 It could be appropriate, in this part of the chapter, to situate it by speaking about "formal" literature regarding Latin American dystopias and to discuss how the region sees itself vis-à-vis dystopian theorists from other traditions. By formal I mean theoretical works, rather than literary dystopias (i.e., novels, poem, etc.). I have taken a different route for, mainly, methodological reasons. As the Argentinean scholar Horacio Cerutti suggests in his seminal work *Posibilidad, necesidad y sentido de una filosofía latinoamericana*, when speaking about Latin America it is necessary to "situate" or remain metaphorically attached to Latin America's thoughts, works, and literary output. The Latin American intellectual whose "intellectual production" remains vested in the "First World" demonstrates his/her historical disorientation and the absence of a situational positioning, foregoing the possibility of claiming roots within the region. In a sense, Ceruttti reinforces Fuentes' assertion that America was not the last disorientation of the Western civilization (i.e., the First World). Our scientists, intellectuals, and thinkers (a category to which I belong) are educated within a First World context, studying its philosophies, ethics, and literary works. In that sense alone, we certainly share that "disorientation" Carlos Fuentes accuses the colonial powers of. Discussing one of the "utopias of Latin America," such as the Mexican Revolution, from within that First World theoretical framework implies a certain epistemological disconnection, particularly when Latin American utopian thought claims a deeper connection to the Latin American homegrown political and social needs, as well as a firm grounding in the praxis. The task Latin American intellectuals, artists, and writers have at hand is to avoid being/writing/situating ourselves within the Others' (in this case the Others are the First World writers and theorists) tradition and to reject the passive role of being the *topoi* of other people's utopias, for Latin Americans need to "create and postulate our own Caliban Latin American utopia, based on a Latin American philosophy and to give birth to a new America, the homeland of a new justice" (Cerutti 22).

The notion of a "Caliban" Latin America is taken from the Cuban critic Roberto Fernandez Retamar, who takes one of the early utopian Latin American works, *Ariel*, and subverts its original meaning. In *Ariel*, Rodó proposes a return to an aristocracy of the spirit, counterposing it to the "Calibanian utilitarianism" and materialistic world represented by the United States. Ariel becomes thus the spirit of culture, refinement, and individualism; this individualism, however, is not based in the search for happiness (in this case a synonym for money), but rather in the universal values of culture as reflected in the arts, literature, and a cultivation of the spirit (reminiscent of the German *geist*). Retamar, in contrast to Rodó, chooses as his symbol Caliban, but reworks the metaphor to rescue the "savage" from the hands of American imperialism. Caliban becomes the embodiment of the *mestizo* Latin American culture, a culture born of syncretism, which, even though it inherits the language from the colonial powers, uses it to curse his colonizers. As I discuss earlier in the chapter, the *utopias of* Latin America (unlike the *utopias for* Latin America) certainly reflect both Retamar and Cerutti's intent.

To close this long footnote, I believe Gabriel García Márquez summarizes best the sentiments of most Latin Americans regarding this matter. In his Nobel Prize acceptance speech, the Colombian writer states: "Poets and beggars, musicians and prophets, warriors and scoundrels, all creatures of that unbridled reality, we have had to ask but little of imagination, for our crucial problem has been a lack of conventional means to render our lives believable. This, my friends, is the crux of our solitude. And if these difficulties, whose essence we share, hinder us, *it is understandable that the rational talents on this side of the world, exalted in the contemplation of their own cultures, should have found themselves without valid means to interpret us. It is only natural that they insist on measuring us with the yardstick that they use for themselves, forgetting that the ravages of life are not the same for all, and that the quest of our own identity is just as arduous and bloody for us as it was for them. The interpretation of our reality through patterns not our own, serves only to make us ever more unknown, ever less free, ever more solitary*" (italics mine).

For further views, please see Jose Enrique Rodó, *Ariel*, and Roberto Fernandez Retamar's "Caliban Apuntes sobre la cultura de nuestra América."

5 The "South" is a concept coined by the late Uruguayan poet Mario Benedetti. Trying to find a way to distinguish the poor, non-capitalist, Third World countries from their more powerful neighbours, Benedetti plays with the geographical "name" of South in an attempt to unite in one the non-industrial, non-aligned, Third World countries, pitting them against the North (industrial, capitalist, First World, aligned Colonial powers). He does not, then, refer exclusively to Latin America and the geographical South, but rather the symbolic Third World versus First World, ex-empires versus colonies, and everything else these two last categories imply.

6 I am thinking here in particular of "The Circular Ruins," "The Library of Babel," and "The Lottery of Babylon." The imaginary planet/continent/country featured in the short story "Tlön, Ukbar and Orbius Tertius" is found to be a utopian attempt with some dystopian elements included. I should also mention that Borges' fiction has been included in every possible genre from "early magical realism" to speculative fiction. His fiction does defy any attempt at classification.

7 Although it may be argued that anti-utopias are forms of dystopias, the term anti-utopia is not used here as a synonym of dystopia, but rather in a slightly different sense. Because the *utopias of* Latin America are grounded in the praxis,

when they go wrong they become "anti-utopias" in the sense that they are the antithesis of everything the utopia stood for in the first place.
8 See María Odette Canivell's "Of Utopias, Labyrinths and Unfulfilled Dreams in *The General in His Labyrinth.*"
9 The origin of the "real maravilloso," which evolved into the magical realism *Boom*, was the ontological impossibility of hailing from a land where the real is fantastic and the fantastic real. Alejo Carpentier suggests that Latin America is a region forged in magic. When the Conquistador of Mexico, Hernán Cortés, was asked to describe to the Spanish emperor the wonders of the New World the soldier replied: "As I do not know what to call these things, I cannot express them" (qtd. in Carpentier 107). Like him, the men and women who came to populate these new lands were baffled by their limited ability to describe what they experienced. The "old language" they had grown up with was insufficient to articulate the new events they were witness to. The struggle of Latin American writers, since then, has been to find that *magic* language that can account for a reality that cannot be explained in terms of rationalism.
10 Although some Latin American writers like Guillermo Cabrera Infante have issues with the "construct" Latin America and disagree with the Bolivarian dream of one united America (speaking Spanish, obviously), the trope is revisited constantly, from Hugo Chavez's rants about "the Latin American sisterhood" (hermandad latinoamericana) to the Rodós essays I have mentioned before. See also Pablo Neruda, *Canto general*; Mario Benedetti, *El Sur también existe*; Gabriel García Márquez, *The General in his Labyrinth.*
11 For Latin-American intellectuals, writers using novels as a block toward nation building, see María Odette Canivell, "El poder de la pluma: los intelectuales latinoamericanos y la política."
12 For more information regarding this issue, see Nikki Craske, "Ambiguities and Ambivalences in Making the Nation: Women and Politics in 20th-Century México."
13 It is important to remember that the Zapatistas' call to arms came immediately after México signed NAFTA. One of their most important contributions was to force the nation to debate whether aligning itself with an "imperial power" was a good idea. Although this is more a theoretical approach to the Zapatista platform, for the parallels to the Mexican revolutionary process and the Zapatista uprising, particularly the way in which Comandante Marcos co-opts Zapata's message, see Walter Mignolo, "The Zapatista's Theoretical Revolution: Its Historical, Ethical and Political Consequences."
14 An exception is *Las Manos de Mamá*, by Nellie Campobello (1937).
15 The trope of the "chingada nación mexicana" is derived from the work of the Mexican essayist Octavio Paz. See Octavio Paz, *The Labyrinth of Solitude*; consider also, although to a lesser extent, Carlos Fuentes' *El Espejo enterrado*.

16 The *fucked* Mexican nation. Malinche, as the first mother of the Mexican mestizo, was "fucked" by Cortés, to whom she was given as tribute. Thus modern México is a product of the rape of its first "Eve."

17 Craske also notes the similarities between the situation of women in the beginning years of the Mexican Revolution and the decade of the 1990s. In both cases, the State (and the major political forces vying to gain power) promoted an agenda of equal rights using the women's claims for political gain. If the political parties were seen as progressive and modern (supporting the women's rights movement), they could garner the votes from all the women who felt disempowered by the current regimes. Although in principle the political establishment supported gendered citizenship and equality, in reality they were also promoting the traditional "stay at home," submissive role of women embodied in the Virgen de Guadalupe image. Not surprisingly, the conflicting paradox of the virgin-whore stood in the way of women's rights.

18 The "culebrón" is another name for the traditional Latin American soap operas, many of which are based on actual "novelas rosas."

19 The novel-testimony *Hasta no verte Jesús Mío*, by the Mexican author Elena Poniatowska, makes that last point quite clear. Based on the true account of an ex-*soldadera*, Josefina Bojorquez, the novel narrates the life in abject poverty, the trials and tribulations, but most importantly the marginalization of one of the "forgotten," an exceptional woman who fights for the Revolution believing in the broken promises made to these women fighters who shed blood and tears only to be cast aside at the end of the conflict.

20 See Craske.

21 The actual Spanish word is "quimera" (chimera), which I find more descriptive than "illusions" (Mastretta 348).

22 The actual Spanish word, "desaliento," is a much better descriptor for this state of being, a sadness so profound it literally robs you of the ability to breathe.

23 Perhaps it is just a tall tale for tourists, but the process of "voicing fears" has deep psychoanalytical implications.

Works Cited

Borland, Isabel Alvarez. "The Task of the Historian in *El General en su laberinto*." *Hispania* 76:3 (September 1993): 439–95. Print.

Canivell, María Odette. "Of Utopias, Labyrinths and Unfulfilled Dreams in *The General in His Labyrinth*." *The Labyrinth*. Ed. Harold Bloom and Blake Hobby. New York: Infobase Publishing, 2009. 37–45. Print.

———. "El poder de la pluma: Los intelectuales latinoamericanos y la política" [The Might of the Pen: Latin American Intellectuals and Politics]. *Asociación para el Fomento de Estudios históricos en Centroamérica*. Boletín 41, (2009): n.p.

http://afehc-historia-centroamericana.org/index.php?action=fi_aff&id=2202. Web. 8 Nov. 2011.
Carpentier, Alejo. "The Baroque and the Marvelous." In *Magical Realism: Theory, History and Community*. Ed. Lois Parkinson Zamora and Wendy Faris. Durham: Duke University Press, 2005. 89–108.
Cerruti, Horacio. Posibilidad, necesidad y sentido de una filosofía latinoamericana (divertimento etodológico). http://www.uca.edu.sv/facultad/chn/c1170/ceruttil.htm. Web. 8 Nov. 2011.
———. "Utopía y América latina." *Identidad Cultural latinoamericana: Enfoques filosóficos literarios*. Ed. Enrique Ubieta Gómez. La Habana: Problemas Cuatro, Editorial Academia. 10–52. Print.
Craske, Nikki. "Ambiguities and Ambivalences in Making the Nation: Women and Politics in 20th-Century México." *Feminist Review* 79 (2005): 116–33. Web. 18 Sept. 2011.
Del Río, Yohanka León. "Ensayo sobre la utopía." Ponencia presentada al "Diálogo Cubano-Venezolano: Globalización e interculturalidad una mirada desde Latinoamérica." Escuela de Filosofía. Universidad de Maracaibo (2000) en: http://hernanmontecinos.com/2008/03/18/ensayo-sobre-la-utopia/. Web. 1 Sept. 2011.
Fernández Retamar, Roberto. "Calibán: Apuntes sobre la cultura de Nuestra América." http://www.literatura.us/roberto/caliban2.html. Web. 7 Nov. 2011.
Finnegan, Nuala. "Reproducing the Monstrous Nation: a Note on Pregnancy and Motherhood in the Fiction of Rosario Castellanos, Brianda Domecq, and Angeles Mastretta." *Modern Language Review*. 96.4 (2001): 1006–15. Literature Resource Center. N.p. Web. 25 Apr. 2011.
Fuentes, Carlos. *El espejo enterrado*. México: Planeta, 1992. Print.
———. *La Nueva Novela Hispanoamericana*. México: Joaquín Mortíz, 1974. Print.
García Márquez, Gabriel. *The General in His Labyrinth*. New York: Knopf, 1990. Print.
———. http://www.nobelprize.org/nobel_prizes/literature/laureates/1982/marquez-lecture.html. Web. 17 Nov. 2011.
García Resendiz, Ramón. "Del nacimiento y muerte del mito político llamado Revolución Mexicana: tensiones y transformaciones del régimen político, 1914–1994." *Estudios Sociológicos* 23.67 (2005): 139–83. Web. 17 Sept. 2011.
Kapitan, Tomis. "Castañeda's Dystopia." *Philosophical Studies: An International Journal for Philosophy in the Analytical Tradition* 46.2 (1984): 263–70. Web. 16 Sept. 2011.
Maloof, Judy. "Mal de Amores un *Bildungsroman* femenino." *Revista de Literatura Mexicana* 5.11 (1999): 36–43. Print.
Mastretta, Angeles. *Lovesick*. Trans. Margaret Sayers Peden. New York: Riverhead, 1997. Print
———. *Mal de Amores*. Barcelona: Seix Barralt, 2011. Print.

Medeiro-Lichem, María Teresa. "The Dissident Subject as Protagonist in the Nation Narration of Angeles Mastretta and Elena Poniatowska." *The Boom Femenino in Mexico: Reading Contemporary Women's Writing*. Eds. Nuala Finnegan and Jane Lavery. Newcastle: Cambridge Scholars, 2010. 295–312. Print.

Mignolo, Walter "The Zapatista's Theoretical Revolution: Its Historical, Ethical and Political Consequences." *Review* 25.3 (2002): 245–75. Web. 6 Nov. 2011.

Mujica, Barbara. "Angeles Mastretta: Women of Will in Love and War." *Americas* [English Edition]. July–Aug. 1997: 36–43. *Literature Resource Center*. Web. 25 April 2011.

Olivero, Elena. Prologue in: Lozano, Alcalá May. *La Utopia Latinoamericana: Xul Solar, Matta y Lam*. Buenos Aires: Fundación Pan Klub-Museo Xul Solar, 1999. Print.

Rivera Villegas, Carmen. "Las mujeres y la Revolución Mexicana en *Mal de Amores* de Angeles Mastretta." *Letras Femeninas*. 24.1-2 (1998): 37–48. Print.

Rodo, José Enrique. *Ariel.* http://www.gutenberg.org/ebooks/22899. Web. 9 Nov. 2011.

Seminet, Georgia. "Positioned between Limits and Desire: National Reality vs. National Romance in 'Mal de Amores.'" *Hispania* 90.4 (2007): 662–71. Web. 25 April 2011.

Thornton, Niamh. "In the Line of Fire: Love and Violence in Mastretta and Belli. *Revolucionarias: Conflict and Gender in Latin American Narratives by Women*. Ed. Niamh Thornton and Par Kumaraswami. New York: Peter Lang, 2007. 217–37. Print.

Culture of Control/Control of Culture
Anne Legault's Récits de Médilhault

Lee Skallerup Bessette

The 1993 federal election in Canada was a watershed moment for the country; the Progressive Conservatives (who had signed a free-trade agreement with the United States in 1988 and had plunged the country into a recession) were unceremoniously voted out of power. The Liberal Party took control, based on a majority of seats from Ontario, but the Official Opposition was the Bloc Québécois, a separatist party consisting only of representatives from Quebec. Close behind them was the Reform Party, a conservative party based out of the western provinces. According to Alan C. Cairns, this election was "an enormously revealing glimpse of a democratic people desperately struggling for a place to stand in turbulent times when past answers no longer carry conviction" (219). The unemployment rate in Canada in 1993 was 11.5 percent and "its growing national debt . . . left it without an effective fiscal policy" (Wonnacott 140). Two consecutive Constitutional Conventions failed, causing resentment in both Quebec and the (more wealthy) western provinces (Cairns 227). The increased scope of foreign (read non-white) immigration that would come as a result of NAFTA (Weinfeld 237) was one of the reasons the Reform Party picked up so many votes and seats in the west and parts of rural Ontario (Roy 205). This uncertainty, and extreme voter reaction to it, would seem to have in part fuelled Anne Legault's dystopic imagination.

Montreal, however, was probably suffering worse than even the rest of Canada, both economically and socially. As described by Kristian Gravenor:

> [The 1990s'] first economic news announced that the city's unemployment rate had shot up into the double digits, where it would remain until near the end of the decade. Industrial jobs were being devoured by newly-enacted free trade laws. The needle trade, the city's economic cornerstone since settlers first leapt off canoes, was ravaged by new foreign competition brought on by NAFTA. The urban workforce was undergoing a painful bleaching, as blue-collar jobs disappeared, leaving a wobbly white-collar service economy to pick up the slack.

In the mid-1990s, one in four Montrealers lived below the poverty line, with unemployment holding steady at 13.4 percent (as compared to Toronto's 8.4 percent). In part because of this economic climate and the linguistic tensions, thousands of people (mostly anglophones) left Quebec.

But it wasn't just the economic climate that had Montrealers on edge. On December 6, 1989, Marc Lepine shot twenty-eight people, killing fourteen women in what is now known as the École Polytechnique Massacre. Less than three years later, on August 24, 1992, Valery Fabrikant killed four at Concordia University. A few weeks earlier, 50,000 heavy metal fans had literally torn apart the Olympic Stadium when Axl Rose refused to perform. In 1993, to celebrate the Canadiens winning the Stanley Cup, rioters caused millions of dollars in damage to downtown Montreal. Linguistic tensions were also high, with the election of a provincial majority government for the Parti Québécois in 1994 and the Referendum on Quebec Sovereignty in 1995.

Récits de Médilhault, published in 1994, was written in the shadow of this Montreal. It is a short story cycle about the interconnected lives of a handful of people living in Médilhault, a city-state that we come to recognize as Montreal. The narrative consists of thirteen interconnected short stories, told in a non-linear fashion. The use of a non-linear form to construct Legault's narrative leads to new and different questions concerning dystopias. Seizing on the "turbulent times" that Cairns describes, Legault examines questions of cultural identity, as well as economic instability, in a post-NAFTA landscape. One of the more troubling results of the 1993 federal election was the increase in the fragmentation of the population of Canada based on both geographical and economic lines, which fed into the increasing concern with national identity, culture, and cultural control. In fact, it is worth noting that many of the chief arguments made against NAFTA in Canada concerned cultural control and protection.

This social and economic uncertainty, this complex, confusing, and confused time is reflected in the structure of Legault's short story cycle. Because of the non-linear narration, we jump back and forth through time, sometimes within the same story. The characters in these stories, isolated from one another because of social and economic forces, represent the kind of isolation and fragmentation that Montreal was experiencing during the early 1990s. But was it NAFTA and the economic instability that it wrought that caused this fragmentation? Or was it possible that the type of integration that NAFTA facilitated could overcome these fissures? Legault is at best ambivalent as to the causes of both the economic and social turmoil represented in her book.

As put by René Audet, "The collection is narrated to form a whole, but the pieces remain independent, while also being reassembled by their inscription in the system of texts" (393).[1] To look at events in a isolated fashion or to try and understand them as a coherent whole, regardless of how challenging that may be, is what Legault seems to be asking us to do, both in her collection of stories and in the immediate challenges present in Montreal. Through the structure of her narrative, she points out to us that history is never linear, nor is it ever perfect: "The advantage that fragmentary literature presents in relation to History is to reveal its characteristic of incompleteness" (Lahaie and Lapalme 90).[2]

After all, events are never wholly good or bad, nor are the reasons behind economic and social conditions ever simple. Looking at Legault's critique of the economic and the social context at the time, we can begin to see her ambivalence toward NAFTA, as well as how the control of culture can lead to a further disintegration of a society. The stories will be dealt with in the order that they appear in the collection as much as possible. While each story holds a key to understanding the society that we are presented (and thus a better understanding of our own), Legault nonetheless never provides for us a clear key to understanding the world that she creates until the final story, where she provides some tantalizing hints as to where we can go moving forward.

Legault begins the short story cycle by locating it in Médilhault, "northern French city of the New World" (8),[3] formerly known as Montreal. While the setting is clear, the chronology of the story is fragmented, covering an approximate hundred-year span. We are shown the different stages and evolution of this dystopian world that affect not only Montreal, but also the whole world. The "earliest" story, "Épi," takes place in a time before an unnamed nuclear disaster, and seems to closely resemble the reader's present. Big was born "during the fifth decade of the 21st century,"[4] and she remembers a man from when she was young who remembered the École Polytechnique Massacre that occurred in 1989, and, in her memory, he is remembering the event "more than 70 years later" (8).[5] The final story, both chronologically and of the narrative, "Cent," takes place many years later, after Big has been living as a slave before finally escaping and joining a group of one hundred. Although it is never mentioned, it is not inconceivable that the story takes place when she is in her forties, thus making the timeline of the cycle approximately one hundred years.

The setting of the cycle is what Erika Gottlieb would call an "emergency dystopia," where the ruling class "find[s] an allegedly efficient solution to a crisis" (9). And the results are fairly typical of the dystopian tradition: totalitarianism (while in the story "Kiev et Kin" there is reference to a re-election party for the Protecteur, there is never a reference to an election), a walled-in protectionist city-state, the outlawing of books, screens that dispense state-approved information, a regimented class system, and the systematic persecution, exile, and execution of all those who do not follow the laws of the city-state. But what makes this narrative of particular interest is Legault's refusal to outline clearly the reasons behind this dystopian state of affairs in Médilhault, as well as her placing the reader in a state of narrative and historical confusion, mirroring the state of many of the characters in the stories, even the state of readers who would have read the story upon its release in 1994.

As the stories unfold, characters must consequently grapple with this confusion and the witholding of the reasons for this totalitarian dystopian context. In "Big," the first story of the narrative, Abigaëlle Sarrazin (Big) is immediately suffering what Erika Gottlieb identifies as the dystopian requisite "protagonist's trial" (10). But while Gottlieb suggests that "the elite's self-justification will be revealed to the protagonist at his own trial" (10), Big's captors never say a word as to why she has been captured, and, thus, we as readers are introduced immediately to the confused and conflicted times of the narrative. As we read Big's story, which is told through a series of flashbacks, we learn that she has been incarcerated for harbouring books in her family's restaurant. But the justification as to why the law banning books exists is never made explicit. Already, subverting this common characteristic of the dystopian genre has disrupted the reader's expectation of the dystopian narrative, and cast the reader and Big in confusion.

While the captors do not offer any insight into the dominant reasoning of this dystopian society, Big's family members only further the lack of clarity by offering a few conflicting theories, both economic and social. Big's grandfather, Absalon, offers the following theory concerning the control of culture as displayed on "the screens":

> Dreams, fantasies, were introduced with impunity to those who were not prepared for them! For centuries, simple people knew not to expect much, until they saw how the rich lived! Can you imagine, Big, there were organizations looking to ban violence on the screens? What about bad taste? But the violent intensity of the display of wealth spread out in front of the poor, the fact that it was in such bad taste, no one said a word about that. The poor no longer wanted to pay for the wealth of others. The rich did not want to give up anything. So everything exploded. And when it was time to remake the world, we decided that these stupid screens bring fear instead of dream. (23)[6]

Later in the narrative, her father tells Big: "The screens weren't bad, they fell into the wrong hands" (24).[7] Big also comments that "All the memories of the world were put on screens, controlled. It had been decided, in the name of the democratization of knowledge" (23).[8] There is a certain confusing irony to the idea of the "démocratisation du savoir" in a totalitarian society that tortures those who possess books. But as the reader tries to reconstruct the reasons behind the dystopian narrative, the conflicting explanations in the story make it difficult to construct a connection.

This idea of democratizing knowledge was reflected in Canadian cultural policy in the late 1980s and early 1990s. In response to NAFTA, the Canadian government often acted to "protect Canadian cultural industries with regulatory or tariff barriers" or attempted to "promote indigenous Canadian mass culture through subsidies to individual artists, or government-sponsored creation of cultural infrastructure" (Thompson 396). In his article "Canada's Quest for Cultural Sovereignty: Protection, Promotion, and Popular Culture," John Herd Thompson outlines the ways that Canada has historically tried to control and limit what Canadians can read or watch with tariffs, quotas, and other techniques. When, however, does protection become censorship? And what role does the government have in deciding what Canadians can and can't consume culturally? It is a slippery slope that is brought into being by the opposition to NAFTA, arguing for greater government control of media, the "democratization of knowledge."

The result of this attempted cultural control is a violent disintegration of community that permeates the cycle. The next story, "Épi," takes place in a time much like the reader's present, possibly allowing for readers to make that connection between the dystopian present of the narrative and their own present, as well as between the more disconnected and dehumanized aspects of our own present. In "Épi," no screen of any kind is mentioned: TV, movie, computer, or otherwise. Instead, the story concerns the brutal beating of a poet while her young medical student neighbour watches and does nothing. The medical student is described as being: "solitary, but not a recluse" (30).[9] And he is portrayed as being not at all atypical: "He saw some [of his friends], from afar, in the same situation. He called his mother once a week, saw her sparingly, like everyone in his family, as the dear woman had a gift to make everyone despise her" (30).[10] The society is portrayed as an anti-community with limited contact among friends and family, and when crisis strikes, people do not act and barely react. The dispassion displayed by the medical student is also disturbing in that he is training to be a doctor, someone who is usually associated with compassion, empathy, and a need to help his fellow man.

Through the removal of a common culture (such as books), the people become more and more isolated from one another, leading to even greater fragmentation and confusion than experienced by this solitary medical student. Marais, from "Peck," is a "quindécimvir." Explained in the story: "There were fifteen quindécimvirs, as their name illustrates, and they watched over the books" (86).[11] It is Marais who teaches Absalon, Big's grandfather, how to read. Marais also explains to Absalon why books are now accessible only through screens:

> You have looked upon these books for years, you have to know that they are from another time, right? Soon, knowledge will be accessible through the screens, and each caste will have their own version of each book, with their individual access to the screens' axial terminals. It serves no purpose for a simple artisan to read the same version of *Germinal* as I do, the same *Capital*, the same *Kamouraska*. Literature can be useful to all, but we have to be careful. We already consider books to be cryptic and it's not for nothing that their content needs to be decoded and simplified. I spend my life doing this, saving literature, protecting it from itself. You were too

young, and I myself never knew the big revolts except through word of mouth, but we can't allow ourselves to fall back into the carelessness of the past century. (85–86)[12]

Here, we have another reason for the decline of the society, which deals with the simplification of literary content, and which adds another different layer to the one presented in "Épi" and in "Big." And there are still others. Absalon's father, for instance, blames the rich for the decline (63–64). These multiple, conflicting reasons send the characters further into isolation and disconnection, far from any common culture or sense of a collective.

This desire to censor books underlines the fraught questions surrounding cultural control, and the latter's ability to neutralize the fears of those in power of a mobilized collective. For, after all, why even censor the aforementioned books to begin with? *Germinal* deals with the social realities (poverty, exploitation) of a coal mining community in northern France during the nineteenth century who eventually strike. *Capital* is Marx's dissection of the exploitative effects of capitalism. *Kamouraska* is based on an actual murder case that took place in Quebec and is fictionalized to the extent that the murder is associated with the Rebellions. All three works deal with repression (primarily economic) and its effects, and do so in a fairly obvious fashion. Why is it then that Marais feels that the books are "sibyllins" and that their contents need to be "decoded and simplified"? These books are quite explicit in their intent, and while they deserve to be studied in depth, the three works nonetheless put across a very clear message condemning oppression. But to say that the books need to be simplified? Is this a case of double-speak from Marais, or does he not understand what these books contain? And from the evidence in the text, simplified for whom? The knowledge that those in power seem to possess is shown to be limited: "nothing can be written that the powerful do not understand! They are scared of fire, of animals, of anything that is living and uncontrollable" (23–24).[13] Essentially, those in control need to "kill" the literature, simplify it, so that they can control it. The activity of censorship is not for the good of those in the lower castes, but for those in power to appease their fears. Is this why the Canadian government needs to censor culture coming from the United States?

"Rats" next reminds the reader that although these anxieties surrounding cultural control are significant, the economic factors that lead to increased isolation and fragmentation are also not to be forgotten. Two rats, one European and one North American, discuss the situation on their respective continents. We learn that life for them has become practically impossible. Because society now recycles everything and anything, there is little left for the rats to eat. Berg, the rat from the Nouveau Monde, explains, yet again, the situation as he understands it: "Nature is the thing that people dread the most because it is uncontrollable" (94).[14] We also find out that life in the Ancien Monde is just as bad as life in the Nouveau Monde, through Scip: "Don't believe it, we destroyed the forests" (92).[15] And the wars were fought for exactly the same reason, regardless of cultural affiliation:

> —Here the rich killed the poor. It's certainly less original than where you come from, where there was a proliferation of cultures, so all kinds of reasons for massacres. Here, apart from a few trifles, it took a lack of money to get people up in arms.
> —But where I'm from, too, what did you really think? Money is the root of all evil. (94)[16]

Not only do the rats have economic insight into how the disaster came about, they also go one step further by offering possibilities for being able to survive and thrive within society: getting organized and consolidating their resources:

> —Come on! Let's band together, like before.
> —In nature, there are tribes, of animals and of humans too. If you want my opinion, their salvation will be in fleeing. But fleeing is natural. We, the rats, our souls are urban.
>
> Scip got up. He had a good shiny coat, a mobile snout and shining eyes, and Berg couldn't hide the envy he was feeling. The rattus rattus had the goods in this era where sewers were rare and the heat was persistent. If they could unite, create a new race, omnivore and dwelling underground like the norvegicus, climbers and hardy like the rattus. . . . Then they could band together. . . . It wasn't impossible, all it would take would be to find some young female rats, capable of birthing six or seven times a year, like in better times.[17]

This is a revealing passage for trying to understand the utopian and dystopian implications of the narrative. In the cities, to be a citizen is to imply that one will remain an individual. But in nature, creatures band together and are able to survive. And, in contrast to the isolationist policies of the city-states, the rats suggest that interbreeding, interchange, and exchange are ways to thrive, and also that their plights are not so dissimilar. Berg is able to understand that and sees it as a way to become even more powerful. The narrative makes an interesting point that citizenship does not automatically equal community, and isolationist policies do not necessarily ensure survival. NAFTA, while seen to be a problematic agreement, is nonetheless seen here as a positive step toward cultural reconciliation. The Canadian reaction to it, which is to divide itself further, in opposition to itself, would seem to be one of the root causes of the dystopic situation described by Legault.

Lark is the central character in three stories in which he is able to travel magically in his mind to "present-day" Montreal (reinforcing the specific setting of the narrative) and engage with issues surrounding cultural survival, reconciliation, and their possible aftermaths. Lark tries to understand and explain what brought about the cataclysm, helping the reader along the way through his stories. The Montreal that he describes at first strongly resembles the Montreal shown to us in "Épi"—most people don't notice Lark because they don't want to see him: "Filled with hot liquid wax and granite pain, I pass unnoticed between them" (100).[18] In opposition, however, to this self-absorbed, isolationist view of Montreal is Lark's description of the Tams-Tams on the side of the Mountain on Sundays:

> What reigns here is a sense of liberty that is not liberty, pleasure for pleasure's sake. They are getting poorer and poorer, but they do what they want in their poverty. Their children seem happy. Will it really be their descendents who rise up in one great wave, killing and massacring before being massacred themselves, exasperated by the quest for happiness, which we had given to their ancestors precisely in the hopes of keeping them quiet? (101–102)[19]

Is it, then, the passivity of this generation, as seems to be implied in "Épi," that leads the people down the wrong path, or a rebellion against such passivity? Is it easier to imagine the population as it is described as simply *allowing* the changes that took place, or, as Lark points out, is it more difficult to imagine the population *initiating* the circumstances that allow Médilhault to evolve as it does? Lark seems to chastise the behaviour of the population, "liberty that is not liberty," but what condition do they find themselves in once the revolution/cataclysm has occurred? Who ends up being better off?

Lark, on the other hand, also discovers the world of the screens, pre-cataclysm, and finds a certain transcendant solution through its culture: "In Montreal, they have windowless temples named cinemas, deserted, like all the temples" (125).[20] And he discovers Charlie Chaplin: "I understood everything. We so effectively overwhelmed them with the idea of happiness that they ended up not having enough. . . . I understood that they had lost God. Blind faith is no match for the persistence of sight" (125–26).[21] This is the only time that organized religion is mentioned in the narrative. It seems that not only did the screens lead to the overindulgence of happiness, they also drove out the God of the Catholic Church in Quebec. Lark describes the movie theatre as being deserted, much like all the temples. Why has the society also turned away from the screens, which Lark claims have infected them with ideas of happiness? And are they empty because people instead decided to congregate together as a community at events like the Tam-Tams? Lark undercuts his own critique of the theatres: "I laughed for the first time" (126).[22] And as he points out right before his death: "It's stupid, but once you laugh, you're in less of a hurry to die" (135).[23] Culture, it seems, can transcend place and language for the better.

Is there any hope, then, for the future, any hope to escape this dystopic condition of fragmentation, isolation, and the resulting confusion? The final story, "Cent," features a group of one hundred people who are trying to make their way to the "Ancien Monde" through the Bering Strait. Their leader is Kiev, who has abandoned his privileged life: "I am the only one from power, as they say, the only tattooed one. Neither tortured, nor banished, nor escaped. One day, I left because I had had enough, because it wasn't really living, because I had known another way, because" (139).[24] Joining them in the group is Big, who has survived her captivity and is trying to move on. Along the way, they come across a group who has been slaughtered, leaving behind a large collection of books and a printing press. The group debates whether or not to bring the books and press along with them for the rest of the journey. It is Big who eventually sways them:

> I, too, was tortured and imprisoned because of books. I witnessed my father's restaurant destroyed. I saw him die and my mother too, as well as her father taken to prison. Because we all have the memory of pain, it is exactly why we cannot lose it. Alone, I would have survived with

the memory of what I had read. With others, I prefer to read something new. Who's to say that in another hundred years, our descendants, if we have any, won't want to cross the strait going the other way, and undo what we are on the verge of accomplishing? Books can do a lot of good, books can also do a lot of bad, but without them, we won't have one or the other. (153)[25]

This outlines and reiterates what Lark pointed out in his narrative: the total lack of happiness within Médilhault. Despite the intentions of those in power, life in Médilhault seems to be devoid of any kind of happiness: from those in positions of power and privilege (the quindécimvir, Kiev, the messenger who escapes her lower-caste existence in "Lena"), to the lowest forms of existence (the rats, the exiled, the prostitute in "Phar," etc.). Keeping the population ignorant does not seem to be keeping them happy, or even under control. "Cent" comes to us in the form of a journal written by Kiev. Despite his brother's protests and his own dislike of writing and literature, Kiev sees the importance of keeping a recorded history. At first, he claims to be keeping the journal in order to keep an exact account of the passage of time, but the journal that we are privy to begins each entry simply with: "Another day."[26] Writing has taken on another importance to Kiev, for the future. Kiev reclaims control over culture, over the fragmentary and unequal nature of culture and the walled-in, isolationist tendencies that the New World currently offers.

"We are at the ends of the earth. *Finis terrae*, end of the world, and it's beginning, just ahead of me. . . . Each stroke of the oars brings forth one hundred cries in unison in one common language. The end of the world is for another day" (158).[27] This is how the narrative closes, with the group of one hundred carrying the books and the printing press across the waters toward the old world. The possibility again exists, despite the dystopian society, of utopian aspirations. And how those utopian aspirations are to be achieved is one of the primary focuses of this narrative. Legault concludes that violent overthrow holds no promise of achieving utopian aspirations, nor can hope lie in those who are legitimized by the society in question.

Canada's and Quebec's response to NAFTA (fragmentation, cultural isolationism and protectionism, increased government regulation) does not seem to hold out hope for a utopian future, post-NAFTA. Instead, it takes a group of one hundred, speaking the same language, overcoming differences, and rowing together toward a new (or at least different) future.

Through both isolating themselves from the society that sought to destroy them and banding together as a new community, Legault suggests the group of one hundred as a representation of one possible (and paradoxical) way forward in "Cent." As put by Sylvie Bérard, "Legault engages in a doubly synchronic reading of the crucial disruption, a disruption destined to signal the end of our civilization and one that also allows us to experience the next one" (94).[28] As put by Kiev, if they move forward, together, the end of the world, post-NAFTA, can wait.

Notes

1 "Le recueil se narrativise pour former un tout, dont les parties demeurent indépendantes, mais qui sont resémantisées par leur inscription dans le réseau des textes"
2 "L'avantage que présente la littérature fragmentaire par rapport à l'Histoire, c'est qu'elle assume son caractère lacunaire"
3 "cité française du nord du Nouveau Monde"
4 "dans la cinquième décennie du XXIe siècle"
5 "Plus de soixante-dix ans après"
6 "Du rêve, des chimères, entrant impunément chez des gens qui n'étaient pas préparés à cela! Depuis des siècles, les gens simples savaient se contenter de peu, jusqu'à ce qu'ils voient comment vivaient les riches! Peux-tu imaginer, Big, il y avait des ligues pour bannir la violence des écrans? Et le mauvais goût? Mais la violence de cette richesse étalée chez les pauvres, le mauvais goût que cela représentait, personne ne s'est élevé contre ça. Les pauvres n'ont plus voulu faire les frais de la richesse des autres. Les riches n'ont rien voulu céder. Alors tout a explosé. Et quand il a fallu refaire le monde, on a bien veillé à ce que ces maudits écrans fassent peur au lieu de faire rêver."
7 "Les écrans n'étaient pas mauvais, ils sont tombés dans de mauvaises mains"
8 "Toute la mémoire du monde avait été écranisée, contrôlée. Il avait été décidé, au nom de la démocratisation du savoir"
9 "solitaire mais pas reclus"
10 "Il en voyait quelques-uns [de ses amis], de loin en loin, pris comme lui. Il téléphonait à sa mère une fois la semaine, le voyait peu, comme chacun dans la famille, car la chère femme avait le don de se faire détester"
11 "Les quindécimvirs étaient au nombre de quinze, comme leur nom l'indiquait, et gardaient les livres"
12 "Tu vois ces livres depuis des années, tu dois bien te douter qu'ils sont d'une autre époque, n'est-ce pas? Bientôt, le savoir sera accessible par les écrans, et chaque caste possédera sa version de chaque oeuvre, avec sa clé d'accès aux

terminaux des écrans axiaux. Il ne sert à rien qu'un petit artisan lise le même *Germinal* que moi, le même *Capital*, le même *Kamouraska*. La littérature peut être utile à tous, mais encore faut-il que ce soit avec discernement. Les livres iront dans des voutes secrètes. Déjà, on les appelle les livres sibyllins, ce n'est pas pour rien, leur contenu doit être décodé et simplifié. J'aurai passé ma vie à cela, sauver la littérature, la protéger contre elle-même. Toi, tu es trop jeune, moi-même je n'ai connu les grandes révoltes que par ouï-dire, mais nous ne pouvons pas nous permettre de revenir au laisser-aller de l'autre siècle."

13 "rien ne se peut s'écrire qui n'est pas connu des puissants! Ils ont peur du feu, des animaux, de tout ce qui est vivant et incontrôlable"

14 "La nature est ce que les gens redoutent par-dessus tout, elle est incontrôlable"

15 "Ne croyez pas ça, nous avons décimé les forêts"

16 "—Ici, les riches ont tué les pauvres. Bien sûr c'est moins original que chez vous, où il y a un foisonnement de cultures, donc toutes sortes de raisons pour massacrer. Ici, à part quelques vétilles, il n'y a eu que le manque d'argent pour faire bouger les gens."

"—Mais chez nous aussi, qu'est-ce que vous croyez? L'argent est la racine de tous les maux."

17 "—Allons donc! Mettons-nous en bande, comme autrefois."

"—Dans la nature, il y a des bandes, des animaux et des humains aussi. Si vous voulez mon idée, leur salut sera dans la fuite. Mais qui fuite dit nature. Nous les rats, nous sommes citadins dans l'âme."

"Scip se releva prestement. Il avait le poil bien gras, le museau mobile et le regard luisant, et Berg en éprouva une envie qu'il n'essaya pas de cacher. Les rattus rattus avaient la cote, en cette nouvelle ère où les égouts se faisaient rares et la chaleur persistante. S'ils avaient pu s'unir, créer une nouvelle race, omnivore et souterraine comme les norvegicus, grimpante et endurante comme les rattus. . . . Alors ils auraient pu se mettre en bande. . . . Ce n'était pas impossible, d'ailleurs, il suffisait de trouver des rates, des femelles jeunes, capables de mettre bas six ou sept fois dans l'année, comme à la belle époque."

18 "Imprégnés qu'ils sont de cirage liquéfié et de douleur granitique, au milieu d'eux je passe inaperçu"

19 "Il règne ici un singulier sentiment de liberté qui n'est pas la liberté, un loisir de faire à sa guise qui ne doit servir à rien d'autre que cela, le loisir. Ils sont de plus en plus pauvres, mais ils font ce qu'ils veulent de cette pauvreté. Leurs enfants semblent heureux. Est-ce que ce sont bien leurs descendants qui se soulèveront en une seule vague, tueront et massacreront avant d'être massacrés à leur tour, exaspérés par la quête du bonheur, qu'on avait donnée à leur ancêtres justement pour qu'ils se tiennent tranquilles?"

20 "À Montréal, ils ont des temples sans fenêtres qu'ils nomment cinémas, désertés, comme tous les temples"

21 "j'ai tout compris. On leur avait si bien injecté l'idée de bonheur, à ces gens-là, qu'ils ont fini par être en manque.... Je conçois qu'ils aient perdu Dieu. La foi aveugle ne fait pas le poids devant la persistance rétinienne"
22 "J'ai ri pour la première fois"
23 "C'est bête, quand on a ri, on est moins pressé de mourir"
24 "Je suis le seul puissant, comme ils disent, le seul tatoué. Ni torturé, ni banni, ni évadé. Un jour, je suis parti parce que j'en avais assez, parce que ce n'est pas une vie, parce que j'avais connu autre chose, parce que"
25 "Moi aussi, j'ai été torturée et emprisonnée pour des livres. J'ai vu le restaurant de mon père mis à sac je l'ai vu mourir, lui, et ma mère aussi, et j'ai vu le père de celle-ci mené au cachot.... Justement parce que nous avons tous la mémoire de la douleur, il ne faut pas la perdre. Seule, j'aurais vécu avec le souvenir de mes lectures. Avec d'autres, je préfère lire de nouveau. Qui dit que dans cent ans, nos descendants, si nous y avons, ne voudront pas refranchir le détroit dans l'autre sens, et défaire ce que nous sommes sur le point d'accomplir? Les livres peuvent faire beaucoup de bien, les livres peuvent faire beaucoup de mal, mais sans eux, nous n'aurons ni l'un ni l'autre."
26 "Un autre jour"
27 "Nous sommes aux confins du monde. *Finis terrae*, la fin de la terre, et son commencement, devant moi.... Chaque coup d'aviron nous arrache cent cris cadencés dans une langue unique. La fin du monde sera pour un autre jour"
28 "[Legault] s'engage dans une lecture doublement synchronique du bouleversement crucial, bouleversement destiné à signer la fin de notre civilisation et à laisser entrevoir la suivante"

Works Cited

Audet, René. "Le recueil de nouvelles québécois comme proto-genre (ou comment un étang de grenouilles peut bien valoir un boeuf . . .)." *La nouvelle de langue française aux frontiers de autres genres, au Moyen Âge à nos jours*. Ed. Vincent Engel and Michel Guissard. Vol. 2. Belgium: Bruylant-Academia, 2001. 387–95. *Edern Editions*. Web. 23 Jan. 2012.

Belleau, François. "Nouveau Mondes." *Lettres québécois* 77 (1995): 28–29. Print.

Bérard, Sylvie. "Nouvelles nouvelles d'ici." *XYZ: La revue de la nouvelle* 44 (1995): 89–97. Print.

Cairns, Alan. "An Election to Be Remembered: Canada 1993." *Canadian Public Policy/Analyse de Politiques* 20.3 (1994): 219–34. Print.

Dupuis, Simon. "Montréal au futur." *Solaris* 20.4 (1995): 43. Print.

Gottlieb, Erika. *Dystopian Fiction East and West: Universe of Terror and Trial*. Montreal: McGill-Queen's UP, 2001. Print.

Gravenor, Kristian. "Montreal's Lost Decade? The 1990s in Montreal, Part 1." *OpenFile Montreal*. OpenFile, 11 Oct. 2011. Web. 16 Dec. 2011.

Lahaie, Christiane and Marie-Clause Lapalme. "La culture incertaine: mémoire fragmentaire et genre nouvellier: *Récits de Médilhault* d'Anne Legault." *Mémoire et culture*. Ed. Claude Filteau and Michel Beniamino. Limoges: Presses Universitaires de Limoges, 2006. 83–90. Print.

Legault, Anne. *Récits de Médilhault*. Québec: L'instant même, 1994. Print.

Roy, Patricia. "The Fifth Force: Multiculturalism and the English Canadian Identity." *Annals of the American Academy of Political and Social Science* 538 (1995): 199–209. Print.

Thompson, John Herd. "Canada's Quest for Cultural Sovereignty: Protection, Promotion, and Popular Culture." *NAFTA in transition*. Ed. Stephen Randall. Calgary: U of Calgary P, 1995. 393–410. Print.

Weinfeld, Morton. "North American Integration and the Issue of Immigration: Canadian Perspective." *NAFTA in Transition*. Ed. Stephen Randall. Calgary: U of Calgary P, 1995. 237–51. Print.

Wonnacott, Ronald. "Canada's Interests in the NAFTA." *NAFTA as a Model of Development: The Benefits and Costs of Merging High- and Low-Wage Areas*. Ed. Richard Belous. Albany: State U of New York P, 1995. 140–44. Print.

The Sublime Simulacrum
Vancouver in Douglas Coupland's Geography of Apocalypse

Robert McGill

> Inquiring, tireless, seeking what is yet unfound,
> I, a child, very old, over waves, towards the house of maternity,
> the land of migrations, look afar,
> Look off the shores of my Western sea, the circle almost circled...
> —Walt Whitman, *"Facing West from California's Shores"*

> Vancouver is the suicide capital of the country. You keep going west until you run out. You come to the edge. Then you fall off.
> —Margaret Atwood, *Cat's Eye*

Douglas Coupland's 1998 novel *Girlfriend in a Coma* can be perplexing even for readers familiar with his other work.[1] The cast of characters is, as in his earlier fiction, a close circle of friends from the X generation that Coupland named, and the novel demonstrates his persistent interest in exploring the zeitgeist. In contrast, however, *Girlfriend in a Coma* deploys Coupland's trademark slacker realism for only the first half of the text before presenting a libidinous ghost, an assortment of miracles, and a mysterious apocalypse in which everyone on Earth suddenly falls asleep and dies—everyone, that is, but the principal characters, who are gathered together in their hometown of Vancouver. Such a turn of events might lead one to conclude that Coupland has moved into the fantasy genre and that his novel's borrowings from other apocalyptic texts mark uninspired, generic writing. In fact, these borrowings crucially facilitate a meditation on facets of apocalyptic literature and the culture that created it. In particular, *Girlfriend in a Coma* demands to be read in the context of the North American West Coast and its symbolic significance during the late twentieth century.

In that regard, Coupland's novel exists at the confluence of myth and geography. Key questions in the narrative are ones also posed by the narrator of Coupland's short story "In the Desert" in *Life After God*: "What is our history? How much a part of us is the landscape, and how much are we a part of it?" (210). For Coupland, those who constitute "us" are, quintessentially, North Americans living next to the Pacific Ocean, people who have been "raised without religion by parents who had broken with their own pasts and moved to the West Coast—who had raised their children clean of any ideology . . . at the end of history, or so they had wanted to believe" (*Life* 178). Coupland suggests that Pacific Rim inhabitants find themselves on a geo-historical margin which is also a climax point, and that they are the recipients of a mythology of time and space constructed and promoted by colonizers since the discovery of America. Coupland's interest in the legacy of the American frontier project focuses on the anxieties of these colonizers' descendants, those who had no part in the project of westward expansion but who nevertheless find themselves members of the society that the expansion shaped and whose surrounding geography both confirms and assuages their anxieties.

The first section of this paper examines the persistence of the frontier mentality in late-twentieth-century America, which carries with it the frustrations of a relentless but futile search for utopia. I argue that, as residents of the Pacific Coast, *Girlfriend in a Coma*'s characters live under the burden of a mythology that has long identified the West with the promise of an earthly paradise but that has struggled to actualize that paradise. The second section considers *Girlfriend in a Coma*'s particular representation of Vancouver and the novel's invocation of the sublime in response to the pervasive simulacra of Los Angeles. The final section argues that the novel presents an ironic apocalyptic scenario in order to break the association of utopianism with undiscovered territories and to insist instead on the importance of renewed engagements with local space. Throughout the paper, I aim to map connections between geography and literature in terms of the accreted apocalyptic valences that Coupland sees in Vancouver specifically and in the North American West Coast as a whole.

The Circle Almost Circled

A tendency to inscribe geography with temporal qualities—to give space a beginning and an end—is dramatized in *Girlfriend in a Coma*, which takes place, as the narrative's ghost, Jared, declares, "at the end of the world and the end of time" (266). This phrasing suggests that for Jared, "the world" and "time" are coterminous. Coupland's novel supports this notion insofar as it depicts the end of history from the perspective of people in Vancouver, a city that might be considered a geographic end point of North America, given its location on the Pacific coast. But the conflation of a geographic ending with a historic one is not unique to Coupland's characters. Rather, they have inherited a space-time model that equates end times with end spaces, one that imagines utopian spaces as always slipping out of reach, and that habitually situates humanity on the brink of an apocalyptic cataclysm. *Girlfriend in a Coma* insists that such utopian-apocalyptic mythology is a particular legacy of European pioneers in North America, and the novel's characters are well aware of that legacy. For instance, frequent references to train tracks—including rails formerly running through the suburban neighbourhood in which the main characters grew up—are reminders of Vancouver's position as a terminus in the colonial project of settling America, and one of those main characters, Richard, refers to "the ghosts of trains flowing nightly through my head" (15). While Vancouver's past haunts the narrative in this way from the beginning, the burden of colonization becomes more prominent after the advent of the novel's apocalyptic scenario: as its only survivors, Richard and his friends cast themselves as a new breed of pioneers while attempting to reckon with the failed utopian dreams of their forebears in North America. As Jared says, "The New World was the last thing on Earth that could be given to humankind" (238). *Girlfriend in a Coma* considers what it means to live with an awareness of that fact while situated at the edge of a continent and the end of a millennium.

The Euro-American colonial impulse to push across the continent to the Pacific has roots in archetypal myths of journeys westward. Northrop Frye argues that almost any story of travel is underpinned by a solar myth involving progress from east to west (35); when the solar myth is conflated with the biblical expulsion from Eden and the search for the Promised Land, the quest for utopia becomes decidedly a journey west. With the European landing in America, this westward-quest myth gained new geographic possibilities; Catherine Keller points out that a "new approach to space became possible," one in which "the symbolism of the new heaven and earth" became a matter of "geographic literalism" (159). With the New World seemingly rich in utopian possibility, Manifest Destiny channelled an impulse to instantiate a new Eden in the West. By 1893, Frederick Jackson Turner could go so far as to identify American identity with this impulse, claiming that the "expansion westward with its new opportunities, its continuous touch with the simplicity of primitive society, furnish the forces dominating American character" (2–3). Turner's "frontier hypothesis" has since received criticism in terms of its historical correctness, but the accuracy of the hypothesis is not so pertinent as its influence. Even if settlement did not occur in a linear westerly direction, the myth of the frontier participated in stimulating thousands of people westward well into the twentieth century. During the Great Depression, for instance, thousands fled the poverty of the Dustbowl for California, with the state's warm climate, minimal precipitation, and fertile land promising idyllic possibilities. As Reyner Banham observes, these geographic conditions have long suggested to people that California "can be made to produce a reasonable facsimile of Eden" (31). Accordingly, the state has often been explicitly or tacitly identified as a final site of utopian potentiality on Earth. Furthermore, it has been associated with a historical end point, insofar as its settlement represented a closing of the frontier. Such a conflation of history and geography was evident not least in 1992 when Francis Fukuyama notoriously announced "the end of history," referring to humanity over the course of that history as "a long wagon train strung out along a road," with the wagons all heading west and over the mountains on "one journey" and with "one destination" (228, 339).

After the apocalypse in *Girlfriend in a Coma*, one of the survivors, Linus, observes the landscape along the Northwest Pacific Coast and declares: "I guess this is what the continent looked like to the pioneers back when they first came here. . . . A land untouched by time or history. They must have felt as though they were walking headlong into eternity, eager to chop it down and carve it and convert it from heaven into earth" (238). There is an obvious irony in the pioneers' project, however: the utopian paradox is that those who equate the newness of a place with its idyllic potential doom themselves to having utopia slip away from them. Westward settlement in North America involved a celebration of newness, even the cultivation of what Charles L. Sanford calls "The American Cult of Newness" (94), but that same settlement eventually obliterated newness. In the nineteenth century, colonizers could seek further utopian possibilities by moving ever farther west, but settlement of the Pacific coast marked an arrival, symbolically speaking, at the end of the world. As Turner could point out in 1893, "never again will such gifts of free land offer themselves" (37); there were no more continental possibilities for new Edens. As Banham observes, the "Pacific beaches are where young men stop going West, where the great waves of agrarian migration from Europe and the Middle West broke in a surf of fulfilled and frustrated hopes" (24). Coupland's texts likewise evince an awareness that there are no more new worlds to which one can escape; as a chapter title for *Generation X* insists, when the apocalypse comes, "New Zealand Gets Nuked, Too" (67). And in *Girlfriend in a Coma*, the characters have a distinct sense of bearing the hopeless burden of the world's utopian dreams. As Jared says of himself, Richard, and their circle of friends, "here all of us were, living on the outermost edge of that farthest point. People elsewhere . . . expected us with our advantages to take mankind to the next level" (268). But with no possible utopian territories still to be discovered, the frontier project has long ago stalled out at the Pacific's shores.

A space that is fetishized for its newness carries with it a certain apocalyptic inevitability, given that such newness is sure to be exhausted. By 1989, Ursula K. Le Guin could diagnose North American society as suffering from just such an exhaustion, observing: "Our culture, which conquered what is called the New World, and which sees the world of nature as an adversary to be conquered: look at us now. Running out of everything" (41). Such a sense was heightened in the subsequent decade by the imminent end of the millennium, which brought with it millenarian anxiety about the end of the world. While this anxiety found its most literal expression in fears about the "Millennium Bug," it was also manifest in doomsday-scenario films such as *Deep Impact* and *Armageddon*, as well as in fiction such as *Girlfriend in a Coma*. But although Coupland's novel ostensibly identifies the apocalypse as causing an end to the possibility of newness in North America, there are hints that the apocalypse merely hyperbolizes a pre-existing situation in which, as Jared surmises, the "New World isn't new anymore" (269). In that regard, a key narrative event preceding the apocalypse takes on a particular significance: namely, the sudden awakening in 1997 of Richard's girlfriend, Karen, from her eighteen-year coma. After Karen becomes a media sensation, she finds herself facing a television interviewer who wants her "to sing the praises of the new and changed world" (164). In that moment, Karen is being asked to confirm a social valuation of the new, while her estranged perspective on the world of 1997 also promises to bring that society a renewed sense of itself.

In *Girlfriend in a Coma* and in myths of North America more generally, however, it is not just that Euro-American settlement of the West Coast exhausts the possibility of newness; it also brings with it apocalyptic possibility. This possibility is supported by mythology predating the European arrival in the New World. Frye observes that the solar myth involving a journey from east to west often involves death once the traveller reaches the horizon (35). Moreover, the seashore has the mythic status of a liminal space between stability and chaos, life and obliteration; it is both figuratively and literally a place of metamorphosis and of extinction. David Ketterer recognizes a motif of the "terminal beach" in apocalyptic narratives and explains it by observing, "just as, in Darwin's view, the transposition of life from the sea to the land allowed for the genesis of humanity, so the end of man might appropriately be envisaged as taking place 'on the beach,' to utilize Nevil Shute's title" (76).

In California, as though to compensate for this apocalyptic potentiality, there has been an impulse to live up to utopian aspirations for the place through pretence if not through actuality. Banham points to the ubiquity of facades in Californian architecture and argues that even those builders with "commercial frugality" have attempted to keep up the illusion of a grand civilization (120). The result of such efforts is what Jean Baudrillard calls "hyperreality"; he claims that America "is a utopia which has behaved from the very beginning as though it were already achieved" (28). Such a hyperreality offers not an actual utopia but, rather, a depthless mode of existence involving "perpetual simulation" in which there is a surfeit of simulacra standing in for the unachieved idyll (76). In this hyperreality, Los Angeles is the figurative capital. Banham argues that the city "has seen in this century the greatest concentration of fantasy-production, as an industry and as an institution, in the history of Western man" (124). In such a site of fantasy-production, Banham claims, "hamburger bars and other Pop ephemeridae . . . are as crucial to the human ecologies and built environments of Los Angeles as are dated works in classified styles by named architects" (22). The city's brash conflation of high art and Pop, along with its facades and simulacra, identifies it as distinctly postmodern. Its mirage of neon and glitter, its impermanence and superficiality, raise the concern that, as Baudrillard states, the "Western world ends on a shore devoid of all signification, like a journey that loses all meaning when it reaches its end" (62).

At the same time, Angelinos are acutely aware that their city's utopian geography is also apocalyptic. Banham points to the "famous slide areas, which have provided literary minds with a ready-made metaphor of the alleged moral decay of Los Angeles" (108). Ironically, these slides occurred because of excessive sculpting of the Los Angeles hills into the "reasonable facsimile of Eden" that Banham describes. Meanwhile, Joan Didion argues that when Los Angeles experiences weather, it "is the weather of catastrophe, of apocalypse" (220). She claims that such phenomena "affect the entire quality of life in Los Angeles, accentuate its impermanence, its unreliability. The wind shows us how close to the edge we are" (220–21). And Mike Davis recalls a man who once compared Los Angeles "to volcanoes, spilling wreckage and desire in ever-widening circles over a denuded countryside. It is never wise, he averred, to live too near a volcano" (14). A character in *Generation X* whose family has recently moved to Los Angeles agrees, saying: "this is *so* stupid being here because there are three earthquake faults that run right through the city. We might as well paint targets on our shirts" (35).

In *Girlfriend in a Coma*, Karen's premonitions of the impending apocalypse generate her peculiar paranoia about Richard's imminent business trip to Los Angeles, and she finds herself feeling "somewhat silly over telling Richard not to go" (200). Her feeling of irrationality is understandable given that, in the popular imagination, not just Los Angeles but the entire West Coast is susceptible to apocalyptic danger. In *Life After God*'s "The Wrong Sun," the narrator recalls with regard to an Alaskan nuclear test:

> According to the fears of the day, the blast was to occur on seismic faults connected to Vancouver, catalyzing chain reactions which in turn would trigger the great granddaddy of all earthquakes. The Park Royal shopping center would break in two and breathe fire. . . . The cantilevered L-shaped modern houses with their "Kitchens of Tomorrow" perched on the slopes overlooking the city would crumble. (96)

There is a geographic peril to being at the edge: it is always in danger of breaking away. Indeed, the characters in *Girlfriend in a Coma* are acutely conscious of their precarious position. For instance, Richard remembers an incident in which he and Jared "borrowed a golf cart from an elderly twosome and drove it through the woods, bailing out just before it ran over a small cliff" (68). Not long afterward, the narrative reveals that another character, Hamilton, has likewise fallen off a coastal cliff (81). The ride and the plunge are symbolic of the apocalyptic immanence that West Coast residents have inherited as a result of the colonial drive across the continent. *Girlfriend in a Coma* dramatizes the frustration of such stalled dynamism through repeated attention in the novel's apocalyptic scenario to paralyzed and vanished traffic. For instance, before the apocalypse begins, Pam and Hamilton—two of the eventual survivors—share a prophetic dream that includes visions of "a Houston freeway empty save for a car parked here and there" (125). Later, one of the first signs of the apocalypse to be noticed is that "there's no traffic moving anywhere" (186).

If the apocalypse's survivors in *Girlfriend in a Coma* share Fukuyama's sense of living at the end of history in a dramatically literal manner, their experiences as residents of late-twentieth-century Vancouver also signify that they are already familiar with the apocalypse's more quotidian correlative: namely, the destructive legacy of Manifest Destiny. Relatively early in the narrative, the novel hints as much when Richard and his friends walk through a railway tunnel. At the sound of an approaching train, they hurry to press themselves into ditches on either side of the tracks, and soon "a Pacific Great Western train explode[s] above in an H-bomb roar" (60). This evocation of the atomic bomb identifies the colonial push across the continent that the train represents—it is notable that it is a "Pacific Great Western" train—with cataclysmic destruction. When the physical apocalypse arrives halfway through *Girlfriend in a Coma*, it is unsurprising that the characters express little astonishment, as the event fits neatly into the view of history with which they have grown up.

Eden in a Coma

Even if California is only a simulacral utopia, it still draws people toward itself. In *Girlfriend in a Coma*, Richard refuses Karen's request that he not go on his business trip to Los Angeles, and other Canadians are also south of the border just before the apocalypse begins. Upon its commencement, however, the migration shifts northward: "Richard's parents fell asleep in a lineup trying to cross the border. Pam's parents got out of the car and walked across, but only got a half a mile or so into Canada before sleeping" (207). These journeys can be interpreted as representing yet further failed attempts to reach utopian space on the Pacific coast; indeed, *Girlfriend in a Coma* suggests that, at least in certain respects, Vancouver is a more northerly version of Los Angeles. Vancouver's ability to replicate Los Angeles and other cities is foregrounded, as Richard recognizes the presence of "the many U.S. studios shooting in their Vancouver branch plants" (75). Another character explains the city's attractiveness to the film industry by saying that "Vancouver's unique: You can morph it into any North American city or green space with little effort and even less expense" (88). This protean identity marks Vancouver as postmodern, perhaps even more so than Los Angeles, which, for all its Pop qualities, at least has a determinate ethos of superficiality and artifice.

Girlfriend in a Coma depicts Vancouver as further distinct from Los Angeles in terms of the Canadian city's topography, which resists the straightforward application of an apocalyptic mythology. Vancouver may totter on a terminal beach as Los Angeles does, but Coupland emphasizes the mountain forests to Vancouver's north and east rather than its coastal position. If Los Angeles is the city that rose out of the desert, Vancouver is the city that rose out of the rainforest, and the different ecology carries a different mythological resonance. In particular, Coupland represents that ecology as involving a north–south axis that stands in contrast with the east-west emphasis of the frontier narrative. For instance, he writes in *Polaroids from the Dead*:

> I want you to imagine you are driving north, across the Lions Gate Bridge, and the sky is steely gray and the sugar-dusted mountains loom blackly in the distance. Imagine what lies behind those mountains—realize that there are only *more* mountains—mountains until the North Pole. . . . *Here is where civilization ends; here is where time ends and where eternity begins*. (74–75)

In this passage, Coupland's depiction of Vancouver is in keeping with the notion of the sublime offered by Edmund Burke, who defines the term as that which has an "extreme of dimension," presents an idea of infinity, and "has a tendency to fill the mind with . . . delightful horror" (72). Such attributes of the Pacific Northwest are frequently apparent in *Girlfriend in a Coma*. For example, when Linus sees Mount Baker, he finds himself "thinking about time—about death, infinity, survival" (234), and the mountain's subsequent eruption is described as "gorgeous and voluptuous and *sad*" (235).

In this regard, it is notable that the characters' most common geographical position in *Girlfriend in a Coma* is an interstitial one, insofar as they occupy Vancouver's mountain suburbs, where human simulacra and the wilderness sublime impinge on each other. Richard—whose last name, Doorland, further evokes a sense of thresholds—says that in the suburbs, he and his fellow residents "have our world of driveways and lawns and microwaves and garages. Down there inside the trees... it's eternity" (150). Later in the novel, as he returns to Vancouver from Los Angeles, the airplane in which he sits "circles the city then flies over the Coast Mountains and makes lazy-eights over the pristine alps and lakes behind, a flying tour of Year Zero" (175). Not only do the "lazy-eights" and the reference to "Year Zero" evoke the Möbius strip, a symbol of infinity, but that symbol reappears when Richard and his friends spend a day "driving lazy-8's through the old neighbourhood's tangled lariat of roads" (263). As the sole living people on the planet, they find themselves occupying a space that is at once post-historical and a mythological New World, an alternative to a teleological model of history that posits the existence of end points.

A city depicted as at once simulacral and abutting on the wilderness sublime, Vancouver is peculiarly situated in *Girlfriend in a Coma*. At the beginning of the novel, as a teenage Richard skis with Karen at Grouse Mountain in 1979, he looks down upon Vancouver and sees "a shimmering city below, a city so new that it dreamed only of what the embryo knows, a shimmering light of civil peace and hope for the future" (7). Vancouver holds the promise of the New Jerusalem, the utopian city on the hill, but in the moment it is only a nascent city seen *from* the hill. Richard's mountaintop position echos that of Moses as he hears about Canaan, and that of the Joads in John Steinbeck's *The Grapes of Wrath* as they first see California, implying that Vancouver's utopian potentiality is inaccessible or illusory.[2] What is more, the city's potential is necessarily limited insofar as it is a city. As Ketterer points out, the utopian tradition has never associated cities with paradise; the "only workable concept we have of a perfected existence within human time" is the Garden of Eden, and so "the only acceptable picture of a perfected human existence during the millennium must be drawn according to pastoral conventions. There are simply no conventions appertaining to a perfect historical city that apply" (106). In that respect, it is notable that in *Girlfriend in a Coma*, Jared describes heaven as "all natural—no buildings. It's built of stars and roots and mud and flesh and snakes and birds. It's built of clouds and stones and rivers and lava. But it's *not* a building" (232). Vancouver, accordingly, is in the position of Tantalus: it is urban space that, as such, can never become a utopia, even though it strains toward such a status.

Coupland further participates in the tradition of pastoral utopianism by situating his characters' experience of paradise not only in the wilderness but also in the past. Both Richard in *Girlfriend in a Coma* and the narrator of "1,000 Years" in *Life After God* associate the mountains with an idyllic childhood. The latter writes: "Ours was a life lived in paradise.... It was the life of children of the children of the children of the pioneers—life after God—a life of earthly salvation on the edge of heaven" (273). For Richard, meanwhile, growing up meant an end to "traipsing through wilderness whenever we wanted" (57). After Karen goes into her coma, Richard suggests that she becomes a figure for others' utopian aspirations, her possible reawakening symbolic of the restitution of the idealized world that Richard identifies with his childhood—a world, he says, "of gentle Pacific rains, down-filled jackets, bitter red wine in goatskins, and naive charms" (76). For him, Vancouver itself is a utopia that has gone into a coma, a sublime possibility slumbering under the gilt of hyperreality. In that regard, it is notable that an early scene in the novel involves a suburban "house-wrecker" party that produces an apocalypse-in-miniature, as teenage attendees wantonly destroy the host's home (16). The appearance of a "lime-green lightning bolt" in the sky during the affair anticipates the global apocalypse and suggests that it has been catalyzed by the sort of destructive orientation toward the local environment that the party exemplifies (21).

The Sublime Simulacrum

Near the end of *Girlfriend in a Coma*, after the survivors have experienced a year of post-apocalyptic life without escaping the malaise that previously afflicted them, Jared announces that they have the power to undo the apocalypse, and he offers them a series of imperatives to follow once the world has been returned to its prior state. "Scrape. Feel. Dig. Believe. *Ask*," he tells them. "You're going to be forever homesick, walking through a cold railway station until the end, whispering strange ideas about existence into the ears of children. Your lives will be tinged with urgency" (272–73). Although he speaks earnestly, such instruction is problematic, given that "walking through a cold railway station until the end" is, figuratively speaking, what his friends—and their frontier-minded society—have been doing throughout the novel. The ostensibly transformed existence that he envisions for them entails the same compulsive motion that characterized colonizers' push across America. Jared even uses metaphors of pioneering, telling his friends to "clear the land for a new culture" (274). The novel's last lines have Richard thinking likewise. "We'll crawl and chew and dig our way into a radical new world," he declares. "We will change minds and souls from stone and plastic into linen and gold" (284). Despite his optimistic tone, the assertion is little more than a reiteration of colonizers' utopian fantasies, from the phrase "new world" and the metaphor of digging to the imagined production of gold. Though Coupland's characters are unable to conceive of a viable alternative to the frontier model of history, aphoristic chapter titles such as ". . . And After America?" and "Progress Is Over" ironize the characters' investments in futurity (160, 203).

Girlfriend in a Coma also ironizes the sublimity of its own post-apocalyptic Pacific Northwest landscape by recognizing that the end times scenario responsible for the emergence of that landscape is a highly conventional, culturally overdetermined one. For instance, before the apocalypse, Richard and his friends have jobs with a paranormal television show—unnamed but apparently *The X-Files*—that exposes them "day in, day out, to a constant assembly line of paranoia, extreme beliefs, and spiritual simplifications" (91). These elements of the show are phenomena that the characters themselves subsequently face with the advent of the apocalypse. Similarly, their specialty on the show is working with simulated dead bodies, work that anticipates their lives on a corpse-strewn Earth later in the novel. When the apocalypse begins, moreover, they are at work on a scene for a movie in which "only the hero survives," with the consequence that they do not even realize one of the actors is dead because he has been playing a corpse (185). When Richard becomes aware that people everywhere are dying, his mind begins "spooling out plotlines from 1970s sci-fi movies" (178), while other characters link events they are confronting to apocalyptic narratives like *The Day of the Triffids* (266). Even before the apocalypse occurs, Linus recognizes that people of his era have eschatological fantasies cobbled together from pop-culture products such as the show that employs him and his friends. He observes: "you have to take all these little bits of nothing that we're given—aliens, conspirators, angels, big government—and from them you have to construct a useful picture of the afterlife" (93). Accordingly, Philip Marchand's observation that Coupland's characters are "paper thin" seems to miss the point that their generic qualities serve to underscore how myths perpetuated by popular culture affect understandings of the world (D25). In *Girlfriend in a Coma*, the characters' self-reflexivity about pop culture encourages critical inquiry into the anxieties that such culture expresses.

Given that Coupland depicts Vancouver as offering simulacra of America's own simulacral culture, it is appropriate that the novel's characters experience what turns out to be a simulacral apocalypse, both real and unreal. Not only is the world eventually restored to its pre-apocalyptic condition, but the apocalyptic events also betray a certain telling artifice. For instance, Karen observes at one point, "The world was never meant to end like in a Hollywood motion picture—you know: a chain of explosions and stars having sex amid the fire and teeth and blood and rubies" (208). Yet that is almost exactly the form that Coupland's apocalypse takes; in fact, not long after Karen's comment, the survivors end up "tossing Krugerrands, rubies and thousand-dollar bills at each other" (211). Later, Jared concludes a visit to his friends by promising to "return when the lightning ends"; when Hamilton asks him what he means, bolts of electricity fill the sky and Jared responds, "*That* lightning, goofball" (260). In such moments, the sublime also turns out to be simulacral, undermining the characters' desires to find any simple consolation in the natural world. Moreover, such self-reflexivity about the use of the sublime in apocalyptic literature imbues the events of *Girlfriend in a Coma* with a thoroughgoing irony, establishing for the novel a critical distance on the utopian-apocalyptic mythology that Coupland associates with American culture. Vancouver becomes the site of an ironic apocalypse that encourages the interrogation of a cultural attraction to such narratives.

At the same time, repeated references in *Girlfriend in a Coma* to the wilderness as a "nowhere" recall Jean-François Lyotard's observation that the sublime resists linguistic representation and that postmodern texts, rather than trying to represent the sublime directly, aim "to impart a stronger sense of the unpresentable" (81). Jared's speech at the end of the novel similarly calls for such a renewed engagement with language and its limits. He tells his friends: "all of your living moments are to be spent making others aware of this need—the need to probe and drill and examine and locate the words that take us to beyond ourselves" (272). While the tasks of probing, drilling, and locating once more evoke the industries that brought Europeans to the West Coast, Jared is also expressing a desire for a language that expresses the inexpressible.

Meanwhile, Coupland's fiction repeatedly insists that a connection to the wilderness can soothe apocalyptic anxieties. The narrator of "1,000 Years" writes: "As long as there is wilderness, I know there is a larger part of myself that I can always visit, vast tracts of territory lying dormant, craving exploration and providing sanctity" (344). In *Girlfriend in a Coma*, Richard similarly recalls that after Karen became comatose, he and his friends retreated to a familiar nearby canyon "where the tall trees above shielded us from the wet harsh weather, and we were calmed" (31). In this regard, British Columbia's mountain ecology provides figures of endurance that suggest alternatives to the apocalypticism of the teleological westward drive. For instance, later in the novel, Richard visits riverside fish hatcheries and sees "a thousand salmon waiting to spawn, unable to swim upriver, trapped together, this clump of eggplant-purple salmon whose only wish, whose only *yearning*, was to go home" (107). While the metaphor is characteristically British Columbian, it also stands in contrast to the motif of the flight from home that, as Russell Brown has observed, is recurrent in American literature (26). The salmon's progress is upstream and inland rather than toward the Pacific, it is part of a cyclical system rather than a linear one, and—at least in Coupland's characterization—it depends upon a sense of home: that is, of a place that is not hypothetical but actualized. If the salmon that Richard sees are caught in between home and entrapment, so too are the novel's human characters in a conspicuously liminal position; in fact, Karen compares them early in the novel to "a salmon lying on a deck, one eye flat on the hot wood, the other eye looking straight to heaven" (12). The double axis here is significant, as the horizontal plane evokes the archetypal westward journeying that leads to apocalypse, while the vertical plane's association with heaven recalls the sublime monumentality of the mountains and the local geography. Rather than fixating on a single utopian direction of movement, the novel suggests the need for a more complicated process of self-location.

In that regard, it is notable that Jared's imperatives to his friends at the end of *Girlfriend in a Coma* call for incessant striving that involves questioning rather than spatial questing, not a seeking after new worlds but a renewed engagement with home. This imperative finds its literal analogue in the fact that, as Jared tells his friends, in order to return the world to its pre-apocalyptic state, they must reoccupy the same places in Vancouver they were inhabiting at the moment the apocalypse began. Hamilton responds by sarcastically calling Jared "Glinda, Good Witch of the North," and it is a notable allusion, given the utterance of the famous phrase "There's no place like home" in *The Wizard of Oz*'s own climax. *Girlfriend in a Coma* thus signals its rejection of colonial utopianism's geographic restlessness while advocating a renovation of relationships to already established places of belonging.

Earlier in the novel, Richard remembers his youthful desire to escape his everyday life, a desire that anticipates Jared's imperative to break out of habitual relations to the world. Richard recalls:

> One of my own stray childhood fears had been to wonder what a whale might feel like had it been born and bred in captivity, then released into the wild—into its ancestral sea—its limited world instantly blowing up when cast into the unknowable depths, seeing strange fish and tasting new waters, not even having a concept of depth, not knowing the language of any whale pods it might meet. (108)

Not only is the whale pod another iconic figure of the Pacific Northwest, but Richard uses it to evoke the unknown language and depths that preoccupy him. By insisting through this metaphor on the ways in which Vancouver's ecology exceeds the limits of knowledge and language, *Girlfriend in a Coma* suggests that readers might take Jared's imperative to scrape, feel, and dig as envisioning a process in which the goal is not to discover yet further spaces of utopian potentiality but rather to revise one's orientation toward local space. The novel insists that it is unnecessary to invent simulacra of utopia when there are already localities with real, immanent possibilities for wonder, if not happiness. *Girlfriend in a Coma* believes that it has found a home.

Notes

1. An earlier version of this article appeared in *Essays on Canadian Writing* 70 (2000). I am grateful to ECW Press for granting me permission to republish the article.
2. The passage also recalls Earle Birney's poem "Vancouver Lights," in which the speaker similarly looks down on Vancouver at night from a nearby mountain and meditates upon the city as a "troubling delight" (l. 11). For the speaker, Vancouver is at once a symbol of human potentiality, a mote in a sublime universe, and—given that the poem was written during World War II and reflects on the conflict—susceptible to apocalyptic possibilities.

Works Cited

Atwood, Margaret. *Cat's Eye*. 1988. Toronto: Seal, 1989. Print.
Banham, Reyner. *Los Angeles: The Architecture of the Four Ecologies*. London: Penguin, 1971. Print.
Baudrillard, Jean. *America*. Trans. Chris Turner. New York: Verso, 1988. Print.

Birney, Earle. "Vancouver Lights." *Now Is Time*. Toronto: Ryerson, 1945. 15–16. Print.

Brown, Russell. "The Road Home: Meditation on a Theme." *Context North America: Canadian/U.S. Literary Relations*. Ed. Camille R. La Bossière. Ottawa: U of Ottawa P, 1994. 23–48. Print.

Burke, Edmund. *A Philosophical Enquiry into the Origin of Our Ideas of the Sublime and Beautiful*. 1757. Ed. James T. Boulton. Oxford: Blackwell, 1987. Print.

Coupland, Douglas. *Generation X*. New York: St. Martin's, 1991. Print.

———. *Girlfriend in a Coma*. Toronto: HarperCollins, 1998. Print.

———. *Life After God*. Toronto: Pocket, 1994. Print.

———. *Polaroids from the Dead*. Toronto: HarperCollins, 1996. Print.

Davis, Mike. *City of Quartz: Excavating the Future in Los Angeles*. New York: Vintage, 1992. Print.

Didion, Joan. *Slouching Towards Bethlehem*. New York: Farrar, 1968. Print.

Frye, Northrop. *The Great Code: The Bible and Literature*. Toronto: Academic, 1982. Print.

Fukuyama, Francis. *The End of History and the Last Man*. New York: Free, 1992. Print.

Keller, Catherine. *Apocalypse Then and Now: A Feminist Guide to the End of the World*. Boston: Beacon, 1996. Print.

Ketterer, David. *New Worlds for Old: The Apocalyptic Imagination, Science Fiction, and American Literature*. New York: Anchor, 1974. Print.

Le Guin, Ursula K. *Dancing at the Edge of the World*. New York: Harper, 1989. Print.

Lyotard, Jean-François. *The Postmodern Condition*. Trans. Geoff Bennington and Brian Massumi. Minneapolis: U of Minnesota P, 1984. Print.

Marchand, Philip. "Then There Were Ten." *Toronto Star* 20 Dec. 1998: D25–26. Print.

Sanford, Charles L. *The Quest for Paradise: Europe and the American Moral Imagination*. Urbana: U of Illinois P, 1961. Print.

Turner, Frederick Jackson. *The Frontier in American History*. 1921. New York: Holt, 1962. Print.

Whitman, Walt. "Facing West from California's Shores." *Leaves of Grass*. Toronto: Bantam, 1983. 90–91. Print.

Neoliberalism and Dystopia in U.S.–Mexico Borderlands Fiction

Lysa Rivera

> The twilight years of the twentieth century bear more of a resemblance to previous centuries of barbarism than to the rational futures described in science fiction novels.
> —Subcomandante Marcos, "The Fourth World Has Begun"

If the familiar motifs of science fiction are in fact the "power tools of imperial subjects," it is worth considering how the very same tools function in the hands of imperialism's colonized subjects who, like Subcomandante Marcos, refuse to take the status quo for granted and who desire alternative frameworks for thinking about the future (Csicsery-Ronay 236).[1] Of all the subgenres within science fiction, it is the dystopia that most aggressively confronts oppressive social orders. For although dystopias project imaginary societies "considerably worse than the society in which [their] reader lived," they also contain a generative potential as they speculate, interrogate, and map possible alternatives to these hellish scenarios (Sargent 13). It is the dystopia, then, that is unquestionably germane to the task of confronting and contesting the abuses of imperial power.

    This essay examines a particular moment in the production of North American dystopias in both film and literature by looking closely at works produced in direct response to the rapid escalation of neoliberal economic hegemony, which reached its pinnacle with the ratification of the North American Free Trade Agreement (NAFTA) in 1994. Borrowing from David Harvey, I understand neoliberal economic hegemony to refer to specific social and economic conditions, including the commodification and privatization of land and labour power, "the suppression of alternative (indigenous) forms of production and consumption," and "neocolonial and imperial processes of appropriation of assets (including natural resources)," all in the service of multinational corporate capitalism (159). For clarity's sake, I will refer to these texts as post-NAFTA borderlands dystopias because they are chiefly concerned with the material realities of the U.S.–Mexican borderlands in the wake of NAFTA and because they draw on the narrative strategies of the dystopian science fiction subgenre cyberpunk to articulate these concerns.[2] After situating these texts within the context of a broader borderland narrative history, I follow with a detailed narrative analysis of one short story and one film to demonstrate the ways in which the borderland dystopia enables us to recognize how apparently novel developments in neoliberal economic hegemony are actually residual effects of colonial power in the region and must be interpreted as part of an ongoing historical continuum that, without intervention, promises to repeat the worst of colonial histories along the U.S.–Mexico border.

Following the lead of many Chicano/a literary scholars, this study assumes that a distinct borderlands genre became possible after the U.S. annexation of northern Mexico in 1848 with the ratification of the Treaty of Guadalupe Hidalgo.[3] The 1848 treaty transformed Mexicans living in northern Mexico into strangers in their own land. One may even go so far as to say that the seeds of a Chicano/a collective consciousness took root after this geopolitical transformation, which engendered a unique border culture, described famously by Gloria Anzaldúa as "a vague and undetermined space created by the emotional residue of an unnatural boundary" that is "in a constant state of transition" (25). It was this inchoate border culture that produced, by degrees, an aesthetic wholly distinct to the borderlands region. Nowhere is this argument made clearer than in Américo Paredes' landmark historical study of the *corrido* (border ballad) in *With His Pistol in His Hand*. Published in 1958, *Pistol* eloquently traces the historical development of the *corrido*, a folkloric mode of cultural production that Paredes contends emerged as a counter-narrative to white supremacist ideologies rampant in the U.S. Southwest following the 1848 Treaty of Guadalupe Hidalgo. In addition to formally analyzing the border ballad, Paredes' study adeptly argues for recognizing how the "peculiar set of conditions" in the borderlands has generated an entire literary tradition and cultural aesthetic (247). By asserting that white racial hegemony simultaneously provoked creative counter-discourse—in this case a border ballad that would eventually exfoliate into a larger border aesthetic—Paredes actually anticipates bell hooks' equally powerful claim that marginality is not simply a "site of deprivation," but also (and crucially) a "location for the production of a counter hegemonic discourse" that offers the "possibility of radical perspectives from which to see and create, to imagine alternatives, new worlds" (341).

In other words, the emergence of borderlands narratives is the formal result of site-specific political and historical conditions: the annexation of northern Mexico, the subsequent and steady industrialization of the borderlands, and, within that, the creation of a vast *fronterizo* working class, which Tom Hayden refers to as the "long-suffering 'disposables' of neoliberalism" (271).[4] Ramon Saldívar's seminal work on Chicano narrative speaks clearly to the causal relation between history and Chicano/a literary forms. "History," he argues, "cannot be conceived as the mere 'background' or 'context' for [Chicano] literature" (6). Rather, "history turns out to be the decisive determinant of the form" itself. In keeping with Saldívar's theory, I argue that another more contemporary U.S.–Mexico political treaty—namely the North American Free Trade Agreement—has animated a new trend in borderlands cultural production: namely, the post-NAFTA borderlands dystopia. What characterizes and unifies these post-NAFTA narratives is not simply that they confront the ramifications of NAFTA on borderlands culture. More poignantly, they appropriate the dystopian motifs of cyberpunk—a science fiction subgenre that emerged forcefully in the 1980s in response to late capitalism and new information technologies—to militate against the ways in which neoliberal economic policies made worse by NAFTA starve the indigenous to fatten the capitalists. In essence appropriating the cyberpunk aesthetic, these post-NAFTA borderlands texts put an entirely sombre spin on the subgenre's distinguishing imperative to "live fast, die young, and leave a highly augmented corpse" (Foster xiv).[5] They deploy the conventions of cyberpunk to dramatize the complexities of the "Fourth World," a concept that theoretically declares the utopian elimination of national borders, while in reality promoting the "multiplication of frontiers and the smashing apart of nations" and indigenous communities (Hayden 280).

Moreover, because they are decidedly speculative, these post-NAFTA borderlands dystopias are driven by a dialectic process inherent to science fiction, namely, the interplay between "estrangement and cognition" (Suvin vi; Freedman 16). Here, estrangement refers to the construction of an "alternative fictional world that, by *refusing to take our mundane environment for granted*, implicitly or explicitly performs an estranging critical interrogation of the latter" (Freedman 17). The critical edge of the genre, in other words, is actually made possible by the process of cogitating the strangeness as the speculative text "account[s] rationally for its imagined world and for the connections as well as the disconnections of the latter to our own empirical world" (18). As speculative dystopias, then, these post-NAFTA narratives defamiliarize (make strange) borderlands politics and histories to provoke a prolonged and deeper consideration of the devastating human and environmental tolls of neoliberal economic hegemony, the communications technologies that accelerate it, and the impoverished border communities that are forced to live under its so-called invisible hands. By inviting readers to rationalize the eerily familiar futures confronting them, these dystopian narratives necessitate an incisive question: *What have we as a society done to get here*? What in our collective history and our current historical moment has caused this strange, troubling, and uncannily familiar future to take shape? Readers of borderlands dystopias confront not only near and distant futures, but also how the histories of U.S.-Mexico colonial and neocolonial relations of power have provided and continue to provide the material conditions for this future.

In theorizing a distinct post-NAFTA borderlands dystopian genre, it helps to consider the concept of the "future history," a phrase John W. Campbell coined in 1941 to describe the internally consistent temporal universes in Robert A. Heinlein's dystopian Future History series. The phrase refers particularly to Heinlein's tactic of projecting a detailed timeline of the human race spanning from the author's present to the twenty-third century. Today, the phrase has come to apply generally to texts in which "the process of historical change is as important as the characters' stories" themselves" (Sawyer 491). As the phrase itself suggests, "future histories" look simultaneously forward and backward as they simultaneously construct an imaginary future and, within that, a historical backdrop *to* that future. This quality, I contend, is precisely what unifies the borderlands dystopias I examine below. Each text displays a commitment to recovering hidden colonial histories of labour exploitation along the borderlands and, in this sense, shares a deep sense of historical sensitivity and awareness. As near-future cyberpunk dystopias, however, they are also deeply attuned to the vitality of speculation and the incredible power that is obtained through constructing alternative (if imaginative) scenarios to contest oppressive political regimes. What emerges is a vibrant possibility for critique that is inherent, I argue below, in post-NAFTA dystopian borderlands, *specifically* as that possibility emerges in works that foreground historical recovery in their speculations about the future.

Mexican writer Guillermo Lavín's 1994 short story "Reaching the Shore" ("Llegar a la orilla") appears in *Border of Broken Mirrors* (*Frontera de espejos rotos*), a collection of science fiction short stories that diversely interrogate the "uncertain economy" of neoliberal capitalism as it has manifested along the U.S.–Mexico border (Schwarz and Webb ii). With contributions by both U.S. and Mexican writers, *Border of Broken Mirrors* offers a transnational sampling of borderlands dystopian literature. In their introduction, editors Don Webb of the United States and Mauricio-José Schwarz of Mexico frame the anthology as offering two perceptions of the same geopolitical terrain to give readers a multifaceted and holistic image of this politically volatile and complicated region (iv). The fact that the two editors never actually met in person, and instead collaborated through email to complete the project, suggests that in its very production the anthology implements the information technologies and transnational social relations its stories merely imagine. The collection's titular metaphor, the mirror, is entirely fitting as it underscores the primacy of multiple and, at times, fragmented perspectives in borderlands writing. As Emily Hicks argues in her important study of border writing, the border text is characteristically marked by a type of "double vision" that is the direct result of "perceiving reality through two different interference patterns" (Hicks xxii). Often retelling single historical events through multiple perspectives and in a non-linear narrative style, border writing, insists Hicks, is formally analogous to the holographic image, with both optics reflecting the collision of two "referential codes," namely the juxtaposed cultural matrices of the United States and Mexico (xxiv).[6] What make the stories in *Border of Broken Mirrors* unique is their shared use of science fiction—and dystopian narratives in particular—to dramatize and vocalize the multiplicity of perspectives along the border circa NAFTA. Mainly addressing issues relevant to immigration, free trade, white supremacy, and *mestizaje* (hybridity), *Border of Broken Mirrors* confirms the efficacy of speculative fiction to grapple with the complexities of border culture after NAFTA, a time of great economic and political uncertainty to be sure.

Lavín's portrayal of the borderlands as a space straddling different perspectives, in this case indigenous culture and U.S. industrial capitalism, finds its visual prototype in Frida Kahlo's proletariat art, specifically her Depression-era piece *Self-Portrait on the Border Between Mexico and the United States* (1932), which visualizes the borderlands as a site in which in a pre-Columbian culture must confront the presence of U.S. industrial capitalism. Adorned in a Mexican traditional Tehuana dress, Kahlo straddles both temporalities: the indigenous past and the industrialized present. She is surrounded by contrasting images of nature and technology. Verdant vegetation and images of the sun on the Mexican side are juxtaposed with skyscrapers and factory smokestacks rooted to the earth with electric cords that grow into light bulbs on the American side. At the bottom of the portrait, however, the American electrical cords merge with the Mexican roots, the two becoming indistinguishable, which suggests that the borderland is a locus of rapid modernization that is literally rooted in indigenous histories. Here, in ways similar to the post-NAFTA borderlands dystopias examined below, two different historical temporalities collide and merge into each other as the borderlands becomes a territory of futurity and history, one that speculates about an industrialized future as it simultaneously reaches back into the colonial past.

Working with similar ideas of the past and the future, "Reaching the Shore" takes place in Reynosa, a border city in the northern Mexican state of Tamaulipas. Like the sprawling "hyberborder" cities of Tijuana and Juárez, Reynosa has experienced relentless urbanization and offers hospitable real estate for hundreds of maquiladoras, large foreign-owned assembly factories that absorb cheap, unregulated Mexican labour from the nation's interior. The story centres on eleven-year-old José Paul, a *fronterizo* whose father (Fragoso) works in a maquiladora. It begins on "a special afternoon," December 24, and predominantly narrates José Paul's desire for a new, modern bicycle, clearly a symbol for social mobility insofar as "with it he could journey far beyond the Rio Bravo" to the other, more economically prosperous side of the border. It is not insignificant that the story takes place on Christmas Eve, a holiday characterized, especially in the United States, by mass consumption of commodities often manufactured on foreign soil.[7]

Although Lavín's dystopian borderlands story is set in the near future, as cyberpunk dystopias typically are, it is nonetheless rooted in labour histories familiar to the U.S.–Mexico geopolitical terrain. In fact it hearkens back to pre–Chicano Movement proletariat fiction that sought "to define and coalesce an oppositional group within the political and economic realm of American capitalism" (Shockett 65). This characteristic is most evident in the story's first sentence, which describes a maquiladora whistle "split[ting] the air exactly fifteen minutes before six p.m." (224). The whistle, likened to an authoritative "order from the team captain," spreads through the city "to tell some of the workers that their shift had ended" (224). Preceding any mention of humans in the story, the whistle becomes a metonym for American capitalism and its subordination of the human worker to the mechanical demands of the factory. Here, the human workers are mechanized, the ominous factories personified. The shrill whistle confines and controls the daily lives of the maquiladora workers, whose shifts are compared to a "long jail sentence" (225). The whistle motif is actually common in proletariat literature and, in this case, echoes other borderlands texts, most notably Américo Paredes' "The Hammon and the Beans" (1930s) and Rudolfo Anaya's *Heart of Aztlán* (1976).[8] Both narratives were written during times of Chicano political dissent, Paredes' during the "Mexican American Era," when Mexican Americans began to interact heavily with the CPUSA (Communist Party of the United States) to address migrant labour exploitation, and Anaya's, whose protagonist Clémente Chavez is a thinly veiled reference to labour activist César Chavez, during the tail end of the Chicano Movement itself. In these narratives, a whistle symbolizes U.S. economic dominance over a racially subordinated working class population. Paredes aligns the whistle with authoritative power, "like some insistent elder person who was always there to tell you it was time [to work]" (172). Similarly, the "shrill blast" of the Barelas barrio whistle in *Heart of Aztlán* signals looming disaster as well as dictating and structuring the everyday lives of the *barrio* inhabitants (25). Itself a type of whistleblowing critique of NAFTA, Lavín's story, although set in an imaginary future, thus echoes a long trajectory of labour history and the anti-capitalist borderlands literature that has militated against that history. His future history is clear: this story not only articulates a future of labour practices in a hyper-urbanized border city, it also interrogates the deep colonial relations that have led—and continue to lead—to this grim future.

Published in 1994, the story's critical target would have resonated in the minds of those opposed to NAFTA, those who understood it to be euphemistic shorthand for a new brand of colonialism and the economic exploitation of a vulnerable indigenous Mexican population. On the eve of NAFTA's signing, Mexican journalist Carlos Monsiváis criticized the Institutional Revolutionary Party's (PRI) utopian stance, exemplified by Octavio Paz's reference to NAFTA as "a chance finally for [Mexico] to be modern"

(Fox 19). In his critique, Monsiváis argued that NAFTA proponents like Paz demonstrated a failure to problematize the agreement and "take as a given that the single act of the signature liquidates centuries of backwardness and scarcity" (20). Monsiváis's articles spoke, in fact, for an overwhelming number of Mexicans—including students, progressives, and independent farmers (*campesinos*)—who believed the agreement promised neither progress nor economic harmony, but rather a new class of dependent, underpaid workers for foreign-owned factories and agricultural corporations. Critics of the agreement foresaw what it eventually would become: a renewed form of transnational capitalism that is realized in the exploitation and administration of workers and consumers through a worldwide division of labour. As one character declares in describing an "economic bloc" to young José, free trade is, in Mexico, "the cause of all problems" (227).

The transnational corporation for which Fragoso works, a U.S. "leisure company," mass produces a virtual-reality implant device known as the Dreamer, which Lavín describes as a "personalized bioconnecter" that attaches to the base of the cranium and provides cybernetic fantasies of consumption and recreation (229). The Dreamer, "the most modern and sophisticated North American technology ever," affirms the lure of the modern, which Mexican pro-NAFTA rhetorical campaigns often promised its skeptics. As someone fatally "hooked" on the idea of "progress," Fragoso economically and physically depends on the Dreamer, which is slowly destroying him and the labouring community around him (Lavín 227). Having taken on the role of a corporate "guinea pig" by volunteering to use his own body to test the quality of each computer chip, Fragoso, now a cyborg, certainly evokes a somewhat dehumanized image of the maquiladora labourer (227). Lavín thus ascribes a critical valence to the cyborg metaphor through two different uses of the idea of dependence. Fragoso is both addicted *and* attached to the computer chip, clearly a symbol of U.S. consumerism. Here we can read the cyborg body through two conceptual frames. First, the fact that the chip itself actually becomes a part of Fragoso's body by "attaching" to the base of his brain comments on the idea that maquiladora workers' bodies are in fact mechanized, mere object-bodies that are almost one with the machines they financially depend on and produce. Fragoso is also fatally *addicted* to the Dreamer and, by extension, the illusion of the American Dream. By attributing Fragoso's fatal addiction to a U.S. consumer commodity, Lavín suggests that the narcotic epidemic in the borderlands region is symptomatic of the presence and influence of

U.S. neoliberal economic dominance and not some savage Mexican predisposition to drugs and crime. In other words, by defamiliarizing "addiction" in this way, Lavín implies a scathing critique of the dangerous allure of U.S. capitalism—"leisure" always enjoyed at the expense of an invisible working class.

Through Fragoso, Lavín recasts the futuristic cyborg as a colonized subject, one whose labour is extracted by U.S. capitalism at the expense of Fragoso's very humanity. Lavín's colonized cyborg clearly departs from Donna Haraway's hopeful vision of the cyborg as that which *can* subvert the "informatics of domination," a new form of power I read as the decentralized transnational capitalism that has replaced "the comfortable old hierarchical dominations" under colonialism (161). So problematic was Haraway's sweeping claim "we are all cyborgs," even she would revise it by being "more careful to point out that [cyborgs] are subject positions for people in certain regions of transnational systems of production" (12–13). One such region, I argue, is the hyper-urbanized border city of the late twentieth century, where forms of mechanized labour really have produced the type of "cyborg labour" contemporary *fronterizo* writers imagine through science fiction. Similar to Guillermo Gómez-Peña's "ethno-cyborgs," who embody the inscription of anti-Mexican racism on the Chicano/a and Mexican body, Lavín's maquiladora cyborgs function as allegorical mechanisms for incisive socio-political critique by framing the concept of the posthuman machine-human hybrid within a narrative of colonial labour exploitation under late capitalism.

Another reading of the maquiladora body is available through Marx's early theory of labour alienation, which posits that the worker's labour is always "something alien to him," something that ultimately "becomes a power on its own confronting him" (72). In Fragoso's case the commodity produced by his labour is itself of exceptionally high quality, such that it does not actually lead to user addiction; but it is also far too expensive for the very factory workers themselves, including Fragoso. Economically unable to "buy American" (which is not truly American once one considers those whose labour produces it), Fragoso must resort to implanting a "shitty import" (228, 230). Fragoso is therefore alienated from the product of his labour. Marx additionally argues that labour estrangement manifests not only in "the worker's *relationship to the products of his labor*," but in "the act of production," or "the *producing activity* itself" (73). For Fragoso, the "producing activity" involves willingly functioning as a machine for the profit of SIMPSON BROS.: he is the corporation's "tester," whose body has quite literally become a cog in a vast machine, in this case a socket used to test high-tech commodities for U.S. consumers (229). Throughout "Estranged Labor," Marx himself frequently draws upon a human-to-non-human interface to articulate the alienation of labour and its effect on the worker, who is not only a mechanized body, but often "barbaric" and closer to "animal" than human. Stripped of his "species-being"—or his awareness of himself as a human distinguishable from animals and objects—the labourer experiences life as a subhuman at worst, a second-class citizen at best.

As its very name suggests, the Dreamer, a virtual product of empire, facilitates private fantasies of consumption, dreams that involve being able to escape the material conditions of factory life, a life whose oppressive conditions NAFTA, and neoliberal economic hegemony more generally, have dangerously aggravated. Because it offers merely the illusion of actual product consumption, however, the Dreamer underscores Fragoso's curious position of being both within and yet alienated from the global market. Uncritical notions of hybridity and borderland third-space identities are absent in Lavín's border narrative. In their place is an image of the borderlands as a site of proliferated borders and rigid socio-economic hierarchies. Despite charting the impending future of globalization, the story's representation of the borderlands is one in which the colonialist proliferation of cultural and racial hierarchies is contained within the very objects of this new consumer society as they reinforce national differences (U.S. exports versus "shitty imports"). Through this juxtaposition, Lavín is able to comment on the paradoxical coexistence of free-trade border porosity and the rigid maintenance of national borders within the borderlands communities themselves.[9]

A late-twentieth-century example of the Marxist impulses that have historically animated the broader corpus of twentieth-century Latin American science fiction and dystopian literature, "Reaching the Shore" clearly offers a timely critique of present-day capitalist hegemony in the era of free trade.[10] Yet although it cautiously peers into the future, it is deeply invested in retelling the colonial history of the borderlands region as well. Early in the story, for instance, Lavín references Juan Cortina, the nineteenth-century Mexican rebel from Tamaulipas who led two influential raids against the Texas Rangers in 1859–61. An icon of the underclass along the Rio Grande, Cortina symbolized the revolutionary spirit of indigenous *fronterizos* by defending the land rights of the Mexican Texans (*tejanas*) after the annexation of 1848. Below, Fragoso and other workers enter a "semi-deserted bar" just outside of the factory grounds:

> The cashier pointed a remote control at the wall and the sounds of the big-screen TV filled the air. The men turned toward it and protested with jeers, shouts, and threats, until the cashier changed the channel; they told him they were tired of watching Christmas movies . . . so the racket continued while the screen skipped from channel to channel. Judith's face and voice flooded the place with the ballad of Juan Cortina. (226)

Within the borderlands, this particular ballad (*corrido*) has been, and to some extent continues to be, the voice of indigenous pride and resistance. Conventionally a genre in which community is valued over individuality, the *corrido* evolves around what Américo Paredes calls "a Border man" who, with his pistol in his hand, heroically confronts white hegemonic dominance (*Pistol* 34). Lavín's reference to "The Ballad of Juan Cortina" is thus historically significant. The "earliest Border *corridor* hero" known, Juan Cortina haunts the site of the maquiladora, suggesting a temporal collapse of the neocolonial present and the colonial past (140). In other words, the dystopian future projected in "Reaching the Shore" is simultaneously an instance of colonial historical recovery and, within that, a memorial to colonial resistance.

Merging nineteenth-century political history with the twenty-first-century maquiladora capitalism, the latter functioning as "the heart of globalization's gulag," Lavín underscores the point that contemporary forms of dominance in the borderlands are an enduring extension of colonial domination and exploitation (Brennan 338). Although the narrative is set in the near future, its scope is decidedly historical as it retells the history of the "consumer-oriented economic order" that has dominated the political, cultural, and economic landscape of the borderlands region since the late nineteenth century (McCrossen 24). New transportation and information technologies, combined with a dramatic increase in foreign capitalist investment, transformed what once had been a land of scarcity into a "land of necessity," where the manufacturing of dreams and new consumer "needs" precede the actual surplus production of goods, turning the once arid terrain into a space ripe for rabid consumption and cheap labour production. For Lavín, the narrative of neoliberal hegemonic control of the borderlands' natural and human environment is not limited to developments in the late twentieth century, but stands instead as part of a deeper historical continuum and long-standing colonial relations between the north and south that Lavín's futuristic narrative both retells and contests by imagining new sinister forms of "cyborg labor" that seem (without sustained political intervention) ominously doomed to repeat history (González 176).

Drawing on similar images and motifs, U.S. Latino filmmaker Alex Rivera introduced the figure of the "cybracero" in his short film *Why Cybraceros?* (1997). Rivera's work is unique in its persistent and powerful indictment of one-sided transnational capitalism that extracts wealth and resources from indigenous and immigrant communities with little compensation, if any, in return. As Carlos Ulises Decena states, Rivera's films routinely "raise questions about immigration labour as a mobile commodity and the relationship of this commodity (and the bodies that perform it) to capital accumulation" (131). One of his earliest experiments, *Why Cybraceros?* incorporates archival footage from *Why Braceros?*, an actual promotion video produced by the Council of California Growers in the 1950s to promote cheap Mexican labour, into a short science-fictional film that effectively parodies the former by spotlighting the history of dehumanized migrant labour. In Rivera's appropriated version of the film, a "cybracero" refers to a *bracero* whose manual labour takes place in cyberspace, providing the U.S. employer with disembodied Mexican labour. "To the worker it's as simple as point and click to pick. For the American farmer it's all the labor without the worker," claims the cheerful female voice narrating the promotion video.[11] Moreover, with a montage of historical footage from the original film and Rivera's science-fictionalization of the footage, the film, like "Reaching the Shore," resonates as both a historical and a futuristic narrative. Clearly, the neologism "cybraceros" signals the convergence of a futuristic migrant labour scenario and border labour practices at mid-century, when the Bracero Program initiated rapid U.S. industrialization of the borderlands. Here, Rivera deploys the cyborg metaphor to signify the historical figure of the *bracero*, whom Ernesto Galarza described in the 1960s as "the prototype of the production man of the future," an "indentured alien" who represents "an almost perfect model of the economic man, an 'input factor' stripped of the political and social attributes that liberal democracy likes to ascribe to all human beings ideally" (*Merchants* 16).

Rivera elaborates his cybracero metaphor in the subsequent feature-length film *Sleep Dealer* (2008), a cyberpunk dystopia that projects U.S.-Mexico border culture into a nightmarish near future where most of

Mexico's indigenous population, once in control of over 80 percent of the nation's natural resources, lives in dire poverty and destitution. Like "Reaching the Shore," the film is set in a sprawling border metropolis whose futurity is actually a defamiliarized version of contemporary conditions plaguing these hyper-industrialized urban zones. *Sleep Dealer* centres on Memo, a young cybracero from the rural Mexican interior whose father, mistaken for an "aqua-terrorist" (an environmental activist of the future), is murdered by an authoritarian Mexican military regime that supports U.S. interests in Mexico's natural (including human) resources.[12] After his father's death, Memo migrates north to Tijuana to search for work to support his struggling family, whose *milpa* (small, locally owned farm) is unable to compete with corporate agriculture. In this version of the cybracero, Rivera insidiously merges the factory worker with the cyborg metaphor as Memo transports his labour through the use of computer implants ("nodes"), which reroute his physical movements to robots on the other side of the border. Similar to the cybraceros in Rivera's short film, the virtual avatars in *Sleep Dealer* provide the labour U.S. corporations need while conveniently keeping the abject Mexican body at bay. With his nodes, Memo can "connect [his] nervous system to the other system ... the global economy," a direct reference to the film's larger political context: multinational capitalism's presence in the everyday lives of *fronterizo* workers whose very livelihood is problematically reliant upon—yet altogether alienated by—the maquiladora political economy. *Sleep Dealer*, then, although projecting a decidedly futuristic vision, simultaneously recovers the deep history of labour exploitation in the U.S.–Mexico borderlands that begins and escalates with the so-called "bracero programs" of the mid-century.

Yet what aligns Rivera's film so productively with Lavín's short story is its shared tactic of emplotting a post-NAFTA borderlands landscape in a cyberpunk dystopian setting. The cyborg metaphor stands equally germane to the task of dramatizing the dystopian and dehumanizing effects of transnational capitalism (i.e., NAFTA) on the working indigenous Mexican social and individual body. One particular moment renders the parallels between the story and the film effectively. From a scene in which viewers are finally taken inside Cybertek, the maquiladora of the future, the image depicts a dark-skinned female cybracero adorned in the high-tech nodes that connect her labour to the global economic system (Figure 1).

Recalling Fragoso's cyborg body, the image conveys a scathing critique of the ways in which the demands of U.S. consumerism and capital

Figure 1. "Cybracero" from *Sleep Dealer* (courtesy of Alex Rivera).

accumulation penetrate the indigenous social, political, and, in fact, human body. Memo's voice-over narration injects a bitter dose of irony into this scene by referring to the cyberacero's labour as "the American Dream," clearly provoking the viewer to reconsider what in reality makes the so-called American dream possible: physical, embodied, but all the while invisible indigenous (or cyborg) labour.

Once in Tijuana, Memo quickly realizes that the so-called city of the future thrives on the systematic exploitation of a migrant underclass with histories similar to his own. Motivated by the murder of his father, he decides to join forces with Luz, a struggling cyber-writer who also uses "nodes" to connect to virtual space, but for the purposes of exposing the injustice brought upon the vanishing indigenous communities. Relying on the Internet to build alliances with other activists, Luz and Memo appropriate the very information technologies of the maquiladoras themselves to militate against neoliberal hegemony. They fight for the land rights of the indigenous farmworkers whose livelihoods have endured the brunt of neoliberal trade and multinational capitalism. Together, Luz and Memo conclude the film with a commitment to confront this hostile future—this veritable dystopia—in order to restore and honour the lifestyles of those who came before them, a historical narrative embodied symbolically in Memo's late father, a farmworker whose egalitarian and sustainable land use the film clearly pits against the dystopian future it imagines. While Memo, with his fascination with new technologies, does not wish to retreat entirely into his father's past (a point made early on in the film in a conversation between Memo and his father), he does desire a future that recognizes indigenous Mexican history and its core values of communal and sustainable land use. He desires, he confides, a "future with a past."

Akin to Lavín's future history, Rivera's *Sleep Dealer* demands that we, as reader/audience, simultaneously speculate and historicize in order to understand how the dystopian scenario unfolding before us can and should be apprehended through the historical contextual lens of U.S. imperial power and indigenous resistance to that power from within the U.S.–Mexico borderlands region. Just as the nineteenth-century revolutionary spirit of Juan Cortina haunted Lavín's future dystopia, so too does Rivera weave suppressed colonial histories into his own dystopian borderlands narrative. This temporal interplay is especially pronounced in the film's depiction of the "Mayan Army of Water Liberation," a paramilitary band of eco-activists who represent the film's counter-narrative to capitalist hegemony in the borderlands. In one telling screen shot, Rivera clearly establishes an allusion to the 1994 EZLN (Ejército Zapatista de Liberación Nacional) uprisings that occurred, of course, in direct response to NAFTA (Figure 1).[13]

Spectators of this image would be unable to interpret its iconic power without mentally referencing the 1994 EZLN anti-NAFTA uprisings. In an instant, Rivera is able to signify a futuristic image and a historical referent, commenting once again on the ways in which post-NAFTA borderlands dystopias are a type of "future history" that forces readers/spectators

Figure 2. The EMLA—the Ejército Mayan de Liberación Agua—as signifier for EZLN in *Sleep Dealer* (courtesy of Alex Rivera).

to read the future through the historical presence of the colonial past. Moreover, Rivera's reference to the EZLN gestures toward the possibility for counter-discourse and indigenous resistance. Just as Rivera's film itself repurposes technology to level a critique of imperial power, so too does the EZLN (and the EMLA, for that matter) appropriate new technologies like Internet communiqués to achieve the goals of so many classic dystopian characters. From Offred's secret cassette recordings in Margaret Atwood's *The Handmaid's Tale* to Lauren Olamina's subversive Earthseed diaries in Octavia Butler's *Parable of the Sower*, dystopian protagonists appropriate the oppressor's language (a veritable technology) to "recover the ability to draw on . . . alternative truths of the past and 'speak back' to hegemonic power" (Moylan 149).

These provocative post-NAFTA borderlands dystopias are similarly plagued by nightmares, *yet* they are also vibrantly speculative as they simultaneously recover the exploits of colonial history and imagine futuristic responses to those exploits. I conclude by suggesting that we read them within the context of what Tom Moylan calls "critical dystopia," a cousin of the dystopia that rejects the latter's tendencies toward hopeless resignation by offering "a horizon of hope just beyond the page" (181). Moylan situates the emergence of critical dystopia in the "hard times of the 1980s and 1990s" when the "betterment of humanity" was sacrificed to the "triumph of transnational capital and right-wing ideology" (184). Attuned to the difficulties of this time, the critical dystopia did articulate nightmare societies beleaguered by oppressive corporate-owned governments and harsh economic conditions, but it also exhibited a "scrappy utopian pessimism," a phrase Moylan uses to describe his "strong" female protagonists who, despite oppressive odds, hold fast to a relentless pursuit of a better life, a different reality, than the one before them (160). These are women "who endured the nightmare and sought out alternatives to it" (147). Butler's Parable series, for instance, does imagine a post-apocalyptic Los Angeles decimated by a devastating war and rampant corporate greed; but it also sows seeds of hope, speculation, and optimism through the figure of Lauren Olamina, the strong black female protagonist whose dreams of space travel and an alternative social structure ("Earthseed") also inform the novel's vision of the future. The critical dystopia does not entirely abandon the future, even if that future appears bleak beyond imagination. The subgenre is undeniably apocalyptic, but it can imagine "alternative socio-political" social spaces that are militantly oppositional (48). The critical dystopia therefore includes a "formal potential to re-vision the world in ways that generate pleasurable, probing, and potentially subversive responses in its readers" (43). As it pertains to post-NAFTA borderlands discourse, the critical dystopia is precisely the kind of "skeptically hopeful" work Subcomandante Marcos called for in his various Internet communiqués following the EZLN coup (Hayden 312).

The subversive potential of these narratives is made possible by their noticeably open endings, which resist closure and invite a prolonged consideration of the shape of things to come. The futures of their imaginary societies depend entirely on the thoughts and actions of a younger generation of *fronterizos*. At the end of "Reaching the Shore," the young José Paul remains uncertain whether or not he will succumb to his father's addiction to the Dreamer. "I really have to think it over," he says to himself to conclude the story, "I'll have to think it over" (234). Here, the reader cannot help but hear Lavín himself demanding the same critical thinking of his post-NAFTA readers in 1994. Young Memo and Luz in *Sleep Dealer* abandon a passive nostalgia for a lost past (Memo's father's generation) and instead opt to remain in Tijuana, the future city, to fight alongside the eco-activists the film clearly endorses. Although the border remains closed, Luz and Memo use their "nodes" to reach an international audience in order to communicate the injustices of the sleep-factories (the maquiladoras). In tempering its dystopian borderlands vision with the optimism of Luz and Memo, *Sleep Dealer*, like the EZLN movement in 1994 and the *Border of Broken Mirrors* project of the same year, speaks to the possibility for a type of reverse transnationalism that does not opt out of the post-NAFTA global economy so much as it intervenes in and appropriates it. This is a repurposed and retooled transnationalism, one that asserts the interests and voices of the disenfranchised and the invisible. It is, to conclude with Rivera himself, the very "process of becoming powerful in the context of being told to disappear" (Decena 134).

Notes

1 The following longer works offer further insight into the history of science fiction as a genre of empire and imperialism. See Patricia Kerslake, *Science Fiction and Empire* (Liverpool: Liverpool UP, 2007); De Witt Douglas Kilgore, *Astrofuturism: Science, Race, and Visions of Utopia in Space* (Philadelphia: U of Pennsylania P, 2003); John Rieder, "Fantasies of Appropriation," *Colonialism and the Emergence of Science Fiction* (Middletown: Wesleyan, 2008).

2 Throughout this paper "borderlands" refers specifically to the U.S.–Mexico geopolitical terrain of the American Southwest and northern Mexico. Here, I am prompted and inspired by the groundbreaking work of Gloria Anzaldúa, particularly *Borderlands/La Frontera* (1987), which has arguably hijacked the term "borderlands." For some readers, however, borderlands may more immediately bring to mind W.H. New's *Borderlands: How We Talk about Canada* (1998). In his own close reading of the border, New, in ways similar to Anzaldúa, grounds the term "borders" first geopolitically (as it would appear in "any modern map of Canada") and then socially, by pointing out that "in ordinary Canadian speech" the word means "one thing: the crossing-point to the continental" United States (35). Upon seeing the term "borderlands," then, Canadian readers might not think of a hemorrhaging "open wound" (Anzaldúa 25), but like New they might be reminded of an equally complex geopolitical terrain, one in which relations of "power" and "dependency" are at once omnipresent and inscrutable, like a "shrubby numbered parallel" or an "almost unseen" and "only half-appreciated edge" (New 36).

3 See Teresa McKenna (1997), Américo Paredes (1958), and Ramón Saldívar (1990).

4 A "fronterizo" refers to one who inhabits the frontier zones of either the southernmost territories of the United States or the northernmost states of Mexico. Historically, the borderlands region—home to these *fronterizos*—has experienced daily life in ways entirely detached and distanced from the urban hubs of their home nation.

5 Loyd Blankenship, cited in Tom Foster's *Souls of Cyberfolk: Posthumanism as Vernacular Theory* (2005).

6 Novels like Tómas Rivera's *y no se lo trago la tierra* (1971) and Helena María Viramontes' *Under the Feet of Jesus* (1995) exemplify this type of experimentation in border writing. In terms of content, both works address border crossings and immigration; in terms of style, both deploy unconventional narrative techniques, including multiple anonymous perspectives, flashback, and montage to represent through enactment the disjointed and disorienting experiences of migrant lives and experiences.

7 Lavín's depiction of Christmas Eve recalls "The Night Before Christmas," in Tomás Rivera's classic borderlands novel, *y no se lo trago la tierra* (1971). In this vignette Rivera recounts a harrowing Christmas Eve story from the perspective of a poor migrant family for whom the sounds and sights of the consumerist holiday bring nothing but dread, desire, and anxiety.

8 One also hears the whistle in the everyday life of Mazie, a young miner, in Tillie Olsen's *Yonnondio* (written in the 1930s, but published in 1974).

9 For an extremely insightful reading of the persistence of nationalisms in cyberpunk, a genre known for its transnational settings, see Tom Foster's

discussion of "franchise nationalisms" in *Souls of Cyberfolk* (Minnesota UP, 2005): 203–28.

10 For an overview of Marxist ideological impulses in Latin American science fiction and dystopian literature, see Andrea Bell's and Yolanda Molina-Gavilán's "Introduction" to *Cosmos Latinos: An Anthology of Science Fiction from Latin America and Spain* (Wesleyan 2003): 13–15.

11 *Why Cybraceros?* Dir. Alex Rivera (U.S. 1997).

12 All citations are from *Sleep Dealer*. Dir. Alex Rivera, Starlight Films, 2008.

13 The Zapatista Army of National Liberation (*Ejército Zapatista de Liberación Nacional*, EZLN) is a revolutionary leftist group based in Chiapas, the southernmost state of Mexico. It is the non-violent voice of an anti-globalization movement that seeks to equalize and defend the human rights and land privileges of the indigenous populations of Mexico's interior.

Works Cited

Anzaldúa, Gloria. *Borderlands/La Frontera: The New Mestiza*. 3rd ed. San Francisco: Aunt Loute, 2007. Print.

Bell, Andrea, and Yolanda Molina-Gavilán, eds. "Introduction." *Cosmos Latinos: An Anthology of Science Fiction from Latin America and Spain*. Middletown: Wesleyan UP, 2003. 7–15. Print.

Brennan, Timothy. "The Empire's New Clothes." *Critical Inquiry* 29.2 (2003): 337–67. Print.

Csiscery-Ronay, Istvan, Jr. "Science Fiction and Empire." *Science Fiction Studies* 30.2 (2003): 231–46. Print.

Decena, Carlos Ulises. "Putting Transnationalism to Work: An Interview with Filmmaker Alex Rivera." *Social Text* 24.3 (2006): 131–38. Print.

Foster, Thomas. *The Souls of Cyberfolk: Posthumanism as Vernacular Theory*. Minneapolis: U of Minnesota P, 2005. Print.

Fox, Claire. *The Fence and the River: Cultural Politics at the U.S./Mexico Border*. Minneapolis: U of Minnesota P, 1999. Print.

Freedman, Carl. *Critical Theory and Science Fiction*. Middletown: Wesleyan UP, 2000. Print.

Galarza, Ernesto. *Merchants of Labor: The Mexican Bracero Story, an Account of the Managed Migration of Mexican Farm Workers in California, 1942–1960*. New York: McNally and Loftin Press, 1972. Print.

Haraway, Donna. "Cyborgs at Large: Interview with Donna Haraway." *Technoculture*. Ed. Constance Penley and Andrew Ross. Cultural Politics 7. Minneapolis: U of Minnesota P, 1991. 1–20. Print.

———. *Simians, Cyborgs, and Women: The Reinvention of Nature*. New York: Routledge, 1991. Print.

Harvey, David. *A Brief History of Neoliberalism*. London: Oxford UP, 2007. Print.
Hayden, Tom, ed. *The Zapatista Reader*. New York: Nation Books, 2002. Print.
Hicks, D. Emily. *Border Writing: the Multidimensional Text*. Minneapolis: U of Minnesota P, 1991. Print.
hooks, bell. "Marginality as a Site of Resistance." *Out There: Marginalization and Contemporary Culture*. Ed. Ferguson et al. Cambridge: MIT Press, 1990. 341–45. Print.
Lavín, Guillermo. "Reaching the Shore." Trans. Rena Zuidema and Andrea Bell. *Cosmos Latinos: An Anthology of Science Fiction from Latin America and Spain*. Ed. Andrea Bell and Yolanda Molina-Gavílan. Middletown: Wesleyan UP, 2003. 224–34. Print.
Marx, Karl. *Economic and Philosophical Manuscripts of 1844*. Trans. Martin Milligan. Amherst: Prometheus Books, 1988. Print.
McCrossen, Alexis. *Land of Necessity: Consumer Culture in the United States–Mexico Borderlands*. Durham: Duke UP, 2009. Print.
McKenna, Teresa. *Migrant Song: Politics and Process in Contemporary Chicano Literature*. Austin: U of Texas P, 1997. Print.
Moylan, Tom. *Scraps of the Untainted Sky: Science Fiction, Utopia, Dystopia*. Boulder: Westview, 2000. Print.
New, W.H. *Borderlands: How We Talk about Canada*. Vancouver: U of British Columbia P, 1998. Print.
Paredes, Américo. "The Hammon and the Beans." *Herencia: The Anthology of Hispanic Literature of the United States*. New York: Oxford UP, 2002. 172–76. Print.
———. *With His Pistol in His Hand: A Border Ballad and Its Hero*. 11th ed. Austin: U of Texas P, 1998. Print.
Rivera, Tomas. *… y no se lo trago la tierra/And the Earth Did Not Devour Him*. Houston: Arte Publico Press. Print.
Sargent, Lyman Tower. "The Three Faces of Utopianism Revisited." *Utopian Studies* 5.1 (1994): 1–37. Print.
Sawyer, Andy. "Future History." *The Routledge Companion to Science Fiction*. New York: Routledge, 2009. 489–93. Print.
Schmidt Camacho, Alicia. *Migrant Imaginaries: Latino Cultural Politics in the U.S.–Mexico Borderlands*. New York: New York UP, 2008. Print.
Schocket, Eric. "Redefining American Proletariat Literature: Mexican Americans and the Challenge to the Tradition of Radical Dissent." *Journal of American and Comparative Culture*. 24.1–2 (Spring/Summer 2001): 59–69. Print.
Skonieczny, Amy. "Constructing NAFTA: Myth, Representation, and the Discursive Construction of U.S. Foreign Policy." *International Studies Quarterly*. 45 (2001): 453–54. Print.
Suvin, Darko. *Metamorphoses of Science Fiction: On the Poetics and History of a Literary Genre*. New Haven: Yale UP, 1979. Print.

America and Books Are "Never Going to Die"

Gary Shteyngart's Super Sad True Love Story *as a New York Jewish "Ustopia"*

Marleen S. Barr

Gary Shteyngart's *Super Sad True Love Story* positions America as a Third World country that is exploited in the manner of coffee producers who, due to the North American Free Trade Agreement (NAFTA), receive less money for their product. Shteyngart's near-future America, an exaggerated version of the country's current decline, portrays China as the world's dominant economic power. Like those adversely affected by NAFTA, Shteyngart's protagonists Lenny Abramov and Eunice Park encounter governmental power that yields escalating bureaucracy and deteriorating public-sphere conditions. Albert Brooks, the actor and director who wrote the dystopian novel *2030*, says, "I liked having more present in my future" (Schwartz SR5). So does Shteyngart.

His depiction of America's economic decline is uncannily accurate. Just before the debt ceiling almost fell, when the proud American eagle was on the verge of becoming Chicken Little, Shteyngart describes the aftermath of American economic collapse. John Schwartz, the *New York Times* national legal correspondent, comments upon Shteyngart's predictive accuracy: "Gary Shteyngart sounded like he was trying hard not to crow. Last year, he had described, in his dystopian comic novel 'Super Sad True Love Story,' a near future world in which economic chaos followed the United States' default on its debt, and Chinese creditors scolded America for its profligate ways. Now the story seemed to have an echo in real life" (Schwartz SR5).

The fictitious dystopian scenario, which is akin to America's real economic near catastrophe, is only one way in which the novel resounds.

I read *Super Sad True Love Story* as a specifically New York Jewish dystopia that is tinged with utopian elements. Margaret Atwood's "Ustopia" addresses this commingling of utopian and dystopian characteristics. She describes this term in "Dire Cartographies: The Roads to Ustopia," a piece included in her *In Other Worlds: SF and the Human Imagination*: "Ustopia is a word I made up by combining utopia and dystopia—the imagined perfect society and its opposite—because, in my view, each concerns a latent version of the other" (Atwood *Worlds* 66). In the following sections of this chapter, I explore Shteyngart's efforts to create an Ustopian "utopia embedded within a dystopia" (Atwood *Guardian* 2): (1) The Invasion of the Meta-*shiksas*:[1] Reading American Jewish Men's Heterosexual Fantasy Relationships; (2) Old Country Road, The Long Island Expressway, and Utopia Parkway as "Roads to Ustopia": Situating Real New York Roads as Ustopian Arteries; (3) Shteyngart Uses "The Language of Science Fiction": Communicating Fantastic Premises; (4) "Springtime for Hitler and Germany": Critiquing Nazism; (5) Mastering Alien Parlance: Becoming Fluent in Fantastic Language; (6) Recreating Kennedy Airport and *Fahrenheit 451*: Changing Reality and Fiction; (7) Eunice Park/Zucotti Park: Connecting a Protagonist's Surname to a Special New York City Park; (8) The "Rupture" Transcends *Tsuris* (Trouble): Envisioning Positive Aspects of the End of the World; (9) We Are All "Going To Die": Recognizing That This Statement Holds True For Everyone; (10) Hearing Survivors: Appreciating the Resiliency of Jewish Stories; and (11) Ustopia: Emphasizing the Convergence Between Atwood's and Shteyngart's Notions About Combining Utopia and Dystopia. I argue that Atwood's ideas about how "dystopia contains within itself a little utopia, and vice versa" (Atwood *Guardian* 2) are central to *Super Sad True Love Story*.

1. The Invasion of the Meta-*shiksas*: Reading American Jewish Men's Heterosexual Fantasy Relationships

Super Sad True Love Story describes a utopian version of contemporary American Jewish men's heterosexual relationships. In this male-centred utopian view of romance, Lenny, a character who closely resembles Shteyngart, could have been created by either Woody Allen or Philip Roth. As *Portnoy's Complaint* exemplifies, for Roth's generation Jewish male transgression manifested itself as romantic involvement with a blond *shiksa*. For Shteyngart's generation, dating and marrying Caucasian *shiksas* is normal, not transgressive. The present-day young Jewish male who does not want to marry a clone of his mother must now be involved in an interracial relationship, all the better if the woman practises a religion that is more exotic than Christianity. Korean Eunice Park fits the bill as the new Jewish male utopian fantasy meta-*shiksa*. Age disparity is magically erased in the Jewish male's utopian fantasy relationship scenario. Woody Allen filmed himself pursuing much younger women until the Grand-Canyon-wide age schism between him and his thirty-something love objects became too embarrassingly glaring to ignore. The fifteen-year age difference between thirty-nine-year-old Lenny and twenty-four-year-old Eunice springs from Central Casting in its echo of the twenty-five-year age difference between the female and male protagonists of Roth's *The Humbling*. Shteyngart is even more brazen in his Jewish male eradication-of-age-difference fantasy than Allen and Roth. Eunice ultimately falls for Joshie Goldmann, Lenny's boss, who is old enough to be his father. This love story's age disparity is super sad and untrue with respect to standard romantic procedure. What does the Jewish male want when imagining a utopian love story? Allen, Roth, and Shteyngart provide the answer: an inappropriately young *shiksa*. From the perspective of Jewish women, these men write dystopian love stories.

2. Old Country Road, The Long Island Expressway, and Utopia Parkway as "Roads to Ustopia": Situating Real New York Roads as Ustopian Arteries

The setting of *Super Sad True Love Story* is also at once replete with dystopian and utopian aspects pertinent to Jewish experience. Lenny's family initially resides in a Queens garden apartment before buying a house in Westbury, Long Island. The garden apartment is utopian in relation to Jewish immigrants' Lower East Side experience; the Westbury house is utopian in relation to the cramped garden apartment. Like Lenny's family, New York Jews were "movin' on up" to increasingly utopian domiciles. The Abramovs, who inhabit an excruciatingly mundane Jewish New York Location, do not make it to the affluence found in Long Island's Five Towns and Great Neck. Lenny's Queens is not the valley of ashes Jay Gatsby travels through. His family's modest Westbury house is a far cry from the north shore Long Island mansion Gatsby inhabits. Yet Westbury's very real Old Country Road is utopian in relation to the Russian old country where Shteyngart was born. When

Lenny travels from Manhattan to Westbury, he is "driving down Old Country Road, the Champs-Élysées of Westbury, past . . . the Payless Shoe Source, Petco, Starbucks. A crowd of would-be consumers still congregated around the 99 [cents] Paradise store" (Shteyngart 286). The Champs-Élysées has nothing to fear from the Champs-Élysées of Westbury. However, this Long Island thoroughfare is paradise in comparison to a dirt Russian *shtetl* path. Many Jews literally built the New York utopia/paradise; Shteyngart specifically mentions two well-known, enduring Jewish New York entrepreneurial endeavours: Waldbaum's (Shteyngart 289) food store and the large Queens housing complex known as Lefrak City (Shteyngart 285). Even though the Lefrak family real estate business was founded in France in 1883, the name "Lefrak" is pronounced "Lefwrack" in Queens parlance. Baby boomer Lefrak family members tried to re-Frenchify their name. Despite their efforts, the current Lefraks are Jewish New Yorkers, not "Le Fraques" who hail from the Champs-Élysées. Although Lefrak City is also a utopia in comparison with the Russian *shtetl* or the Lower East Side, it is another world in relation to the over-the-top opulence Donald Trump created in, for example, Manhattan's Trump Tower. In contrast to Trumpian splendour, Lenny's Queens is akin to the Jewish plebian Queens inhabited by Fran Fine, the protagonist of Fran Drescher's television sitcom *The Nanny*. Lenny is no King Kong climbing the Empire State Building. Lenny does not battle the aliens whose spaceships loom over the iconic New York skyline in *Independence Day*. Lenny is a financially secure Everyman inhabitant of his world. In the context of Russian Jews facing pogroms and Nazis murdering European Jews, being a secure Everyman Jew is a utopian success story. Lenny's ordinariness is signalled by his choice to drive on the Long Island Expressway (Shteyngart 284) rather than the Queens transportation artery that really is called Utopia Parkway. Utopia Parkway borders a Queens neighbourhood, predominantly inhabited by Jews, called Utopia. The Jewish Queens neighbourhood called Utopia is a real utopian achievement. Lenny inhabits a New York City world that is a utopian haven for Jews.

3. Shteyngart Uses "The Language of Science Fiction": Communicating Fantastic Premises

The real New York roads and neighbourhoods Shteyngart describes coincide with what Atwood calls "these not-exactly places, which are anywhere but nowhere, and which are both mappable locations and states of mind" (Atwood *Guardian* 2). Hence, despite Shteyngart's emphasis upon Lenny's real "anywhere" New York world, aspects of his milieu are "nowhere," or science-fictional. Science fiction is pertinent to *Super Sad True Love Story*'s first sentence. Lenny announces this goal in his diary: "Today, I've made a major decision: *I am never going to die*" (Shteyngart 3). Samuel Delany's notion of "the language of science fiction"—which explains how science-fictional worlds imbue ordinary language with new meanings—indicates that in Lenny's fantastic world it is possible for him to actualize his immortality assertion. Lenny is employed by a life extension company: "And yet Lenny Abramov . . . will live forever. The technology is almost here. As the Life Lovers Outreach Coordinator (Grade G) of the Post-Human Services division of the Staatling-Wapachung Corporation, I will be the first to partake of it" (Shteyngart 5). "Almost" doesn't count; the potential new technology is never invented. *Super* is not a utopia about posthuman immortals. Lenny is no posthuman Adam. His professional position merely enables him to experience a particularly Jewish super sad true love story. The relation between his Jewishness and his professional activity is never mentioned. However, his Jewishness, in a manner analogous to science fiction's impact upon meaning, imparts utopian connotation to his job description. It is ironic for a Jew to work for a life extension company. Nazis were lovers of super sad true Jewish death. In view of Hitler's extermination plan, Lenny's existence—Jewish survival—is a utopian outcome. *Super* is replete with allusions to Germany. "Grade G" humorously evokes the German obsession with classification and order. Joshie Goldmann's last name is spelled with the German double "n," like "Eichmann." "Staatling-Wapachung" resonates as New York Jewish comedian Sid Caesar's signature fake language *shtick* exemplified by attempting to combine German and Asiatic intonation. The popularity of Caesar's humour signals that New York Jews are not the alien Other.

Lenny is only a potential Superman, whose "almost" immortality is super sadly unrealized.[2] While no Superman, Lenny is a Jewish Everyman who falls in love with an acculturated Korean-American young woman. He engages in a union involving the utopian jettisoning of racial difference and discrimination. While Lenny and Eunice initially flourish together, their America exaggerates the loss of individuality and the economic decline characterizing the real contemporary America. The novel's most dystopian super sad true love story is not about the relationship between Eunice and Lenny; it is about the relationship between American readers and their love for a declining America. Americans, who readily accept the fact that they are going to die, are indoctrinated into believing that there is a viable life extension company that continuously revives America. Americans believe that America is *"never going to die."* "[A]sk what you can do for your country," said President John F. Kennedy. What Americans do for their country is to act en masse as a Borg-like citizenry whose innate heartfelt objective is to ensure that America will live forever. On September 11, 2001, ordinary citizens refused to allow a hijacked plane to crash into the Capitol Building. Americans view science fiction film images of a destroyed Capitol Building or a decapitated Statue of Liberty as culturally intolerable horror film visions. Shteyngart and his nuclear family, Russian Jewish immigrants, have themselves joined the American Borg citizenry body politic America-will-never-die brigade. Despite the very dystopian increasing lack of personal liberty and economic failure scenarios *Super Sad True Love Story* depicts, utopia ultimately prevails; Lenny's America does not die. Although the debt ceiling does crash down on Lenny's America, the "beautiful for spacious skies" do not fall and crash into the "amber waves of grain" and the "purple mountains' majesty." *Super Sad True Love Story*, then, is predominantly concerned with the decline of America, not the relationship between Eunice and Lenny.

4. "Springtime for Hitler and Germany": Critiquing Nazism

This novel also equates its use of a New York Jewish immigrant protagonist with a critique of Nazism. Staatling-Wapachung functions in utopian opposition to Nazism: "'EXCLUSIVE Immortality Assistance'? . . . You had to *prove* you were worthy of cheating death at Post-Human Services. Like I [Lenny] said, only 18 percent of our applicants qualified for our Product. That's how Joshie intended it. Hence the Intakes I was supposed to perform. . . . Hence—the whole philosophy" (Shteyngart 153). This passage's humorous indictment of Nazism places Shteyngart as his generation's standard-bearer for the humorous New York Jewish defiant response to Nazi Germany Mel Brooks expressed in *The Producers*. According to Shteyngart's version of "Springtime for Hitler and Germany" (which might be a response to Brooks' song's lyric "Germany was having trouble / What a sad, sad [super sad?] story"), the passage reminds readers that under Nazism Jews were defined as unworthy of living and only a small percentage survived—escaped becoming "Product," i.e., lampshades and soap. A "whole philosophy" describes both Post-Human Services and Nazism as Sub-Human Jewish Services. Joshie is the Hitler/architect; Lenny is the

Eichmann/functionary. *Super Sad True Love Story* is a Jewish American critique of Nazism in which Nazism fails and Post-Human Services fails. The winner: utopian Jewish *l'chaim* (to life), for Jews in particular and America in general. Shteyngart's novel positions a Jew—and all Americans—as survivors. Lenny views Joshie as father and führer: "Make Joshie Protect You— Evoke father-like bond in response to political situation. . . . Talk about what happened in the plane; evoke Jewish feelings of terror and injustice" (Shteyngart 51). When America itself is recast as survivor, "Jewish feelings of terror and injustice" become universal American feelings. When Americans, remembering the 9/11 terrorist attacks, "talk about what happened in the plane," they discuss events in which all Americans were converted into Jews targeted for extermination.

5. Mastering Alien Parlance: Becoming Fluent in Fantastic Language

Becoming fluent in the new language and fantastic premises Shteyngart creates is one of the pleasures *Super Sad True Love Story* generates. Readers encounter these pleasures in rapid-fire fashion: for example, in the humorous male-perspective fantasy about Eunice's utopian electronic panties "that snap off when you press a button in the crotch" (Shteyngart 111). Shteyngart even manages to invent new humorous dystopian aspects of New York. His subways have hilarious "business-class carriage[s]" (Shteyngart 103). Not all of his dystopian vision is funny, however: "The mandatory meeting about the Debt Crisis and the LNWI [Lower Net Worth Individuals, an example of the new terminology Shteyngart creates] protest thing in Central Park and D.C. They think the Fed may default on the dollar this year" (Shteyngart 148). In light of the debt ceiling crisis and the Occupy Wall Street initiative, Shteyngart is staggeringly prophetic, to the extent that he can be placed in the same prediction-success class as Jules Verne and Arthur C. Clarke.

As I have explained, close encounters with terms such as "LNWI" indicate that, in order to understand Shteyngart's new world's dystopian and utopian characteristics, it is necessary to master new language. The novel's first sign of the fantastic occurs as Lenny learns that when in Rome, it is wise to do what the dystopian American government says: "If you spend over 250 days abroad and don't register for Welcome Back, Pa'dner, the official United States Citizen Re-entry Program, they can send you to a 'secure screening facility' Upstate, whatever that is" (Shteyngart 7). "Welcome Back Pa'dner" is alien parlance to New York Jews, real and imagined. No reader knows exactly what happens in a "secure screening facility." Lenny can't understand "Upstate." Just as Dorothy notices that she is not in Kansas anymore, readers are aware that they are not in New York State any more: "Upstate" may not mean, for example, Albany and Syracuse any more. Ironically, language is the vehicle that transports readers into Lenny's world. They find themselves located in a place where it is normal to be functionally illiterate. Texts are relegated here to this Rolling Stones lyric: "Who wants yesterday's papers? . . . Nobody in the world" ("Yesterday's Papers"). Lenny the bibliophile is an exception; he is somebody in his world who answers this question affirmatively.

6. Recreating Kennedy Airport and *Fahrenheit 451*: Changing Reality and Fiction

Shteyngart's American dystopia is often humorously and exaggeratedly too close to American reality for comfort. For example, Lenny's advanced technology BlackBerry-esque "äppärät" device enables him immediately to know Eunice's younger sister Sally's LDL and HDL cholesterol numbers (Shteyngart 38). Due to the trend of corporate mergers on steroids, Lenny flies the unfriendly conglomerate skies of "UnitedContinentalDeltaAmerican flight 023 to New York" (Shteyngart 41). New York's Kennedy Airport is a Third World country operation where the "'security shed'" is "a strange outcropping, amidst a landscape of forlorn, aging terminals heaped atop one another like the vista of some gray Lagos slum" (Shteyngart 42). Perhaps the unkindest linguistic cut of all can be read in the description of books being thought of as things that "smell" (Shteyngart 52). In contrast, Lenny is defiant in the face of this allusion to insult. Lenny, a Jew who does not worship at the Wailing Wall in Israel, venerates the "Wall of Books" in his apartment. "I celebrate my Wall of Books. I counted the volumes on my twenty-foot-long modernist bookshelf to make sure no one had been misplaced or used as kindling by my subtenant. 'You're my sacred ones,' I told the books. . . . 'I'm going to keep you with me forever and one day I'll make you important again'" (Shteyngart 52). Lenny keeps his promise to his books; his Wall of Books, which seemingly understands English, does not experience a Humpty Dumpty Berlin Wall fall in which it is never put together again. Hence, Shteyngart creates a love story that is about books in addition to Eunice and America. Lenny, who of course is unable to time-travel to rescue Jews from the Holocaust, rescues his books from being burned as "kindling." His successful creation of a positive version of *Fahrenheit 451* provides another indication of why *Super Sad True Love Story* is ultimately more utopian than dystopian. When Lenny rescues his books, he acts as a person of the book who seems to proclaim his own individual worth by asserting this version of Descartes: I read and write therefore I am. His diary, written in standard English, not Eunice's teenage-verbiage-infused computer communication language, is the survivor. "Language, not data" (Shteyngart 53) endures. Lenny asks, "Why couldn't I have been born to a better world?" (Shteyngart 81). He himself improves his world—transforms it from dystopia to utopia—by authoring a love story about books. He never has to say he is sorry for loving reading, writing, and books.

7. Eunice Park/Zucotti Park: Connecting a Protagonist's Surname to a Special New York City Park

The very real Americans who try to improve the world through the Occupy Wall Street initiative provide a means to interpret Eunice Park's surname. *Super Sad True Love Story* clearly liberates itself from Shteyngart; the novel speaks for itself by alluding to the Occupy Wall Street movement, which transpired after its publication date. Eunice Park, who ultimately decides to care about "Political stuff" (Shteyngart 174), goes to a New York City park to engage in political protest. "The way they have it [the park] set up is pretty amazing. It's a tiny little park, but like every little bit of it is used for a purpose. . . . There's recycling of all food from garbage cans. . . . They're so organized here" (Shteyngart 174). Eunice Park describes the food preparation and organization characterizing Occupy Wall Street locale Zucotti Park.[3]

Equating "Eunice Park" with "Zucotti Park" is literary criticism that is humorously elementary. Simplistic discourse is pertinent to Eunice's world, in which people do not mature in their reading, writing, and speaking style. Eunice and her peers use social network technology to communicate in a mode appropriate only for teenyboppers; they inhabit a Peter Pan linguistic Neverland in which they never grow up. In a voice that evokes Holocaust survivors' "never again," Shteyngart and Lenny say never to this Neverland. Eunice, the protagonist of a love story partly addressed to loving text, ultimately learns to read. When preparing to evacuate Lenny's apartment, Eunice insists that "'Just the books' . . . [are] all we have room for" (Shteyngart 312). She then asks Lenny "'What do you mean?'" in regard to his letting go of her "*galaxy* of freckles . . . some *planet*-sized, others the fine floating detritus of *space*" (Shteyngart 312; italics mine). When inquiring about meaning in proximity to a wall of science fiction language, the once vacuous Eunice evokes the focus of science fiction scholars: galaxy, planet, and space. She transitions from immature linguistic banality to converting to become Lenny's fellow person of the book. She abandons being someone who "never really learned how to read text. . . . Just to scan them for info" (Shteyngart 277).

8. The "Rupture" Transcends *Tsuris* (Trouble): Envisioning Positive Aspects of the End of the World

Eunice and Lenny are forced to become refugees because America implodes when the currency fails; the "Rupture" ensues (Shteyngart 271). The end of the American world "Rupture" is not the Evangelical Christian "Rapture." The word "Rupture" replacing "Rapture" is applicable to a specific example of Jewish artistic endeavour: Philip Roth, in *Operation Shylock*, explains that Jews were enraptured when New York Jewish songwriter Irving Berlin wrote "White Christmas" and "Easter Parade"—songs that remove Christ from Christmas and Easter. Berlin, according to Roth, made it possible to substitute snow and bonnets for Christ. In this vein, Shteyngart removes Christ from the end of the world—ruptures Christ away from the Evangelical Christian Rapture end of the world vision. When he creates a Jewish-perspective utopian societal calamity scenario, he indicates that "book rescue" shares much in common with Berlin's Christ "*frei*" snow and bonnets. The disruption of education is a major post-Rupture calamity: "the teachers aren't getting paid. . . . No school" (Shteyngart 271). Despite the temporary setback of his being reduced to refugee status, Lenny's Wall of Books—no ghetto wall that encloses Jews and their particular cultural production—triumphs. Lenny's diary and Eunice's messages are identified as having been "published in Beijing and New York two years ago" (Shteyngart 327). Words—both highbrow and bastardized—are survivors.

Words transcend Dickensian *tsuris* and rise to the occasion of meeting Lenny's once upon a former time seemingly fantastic utopian great expectations for them: "When I wrote these diary entries so many decades ago, it never occurred to me that *any* text would *ever* find a new generation of readers" (Shteyngart 327). Shteyngart positions the life of the mind and texts as things that fell apart. Nazis tried to relegate Jews to the same super sad end. Like the debased texts Shteyngart describes, the debased Jews survived. Some concentration camp inmates were able to engender new generations of Jews. Members of new Jewish generations created Waldbaum's, Lefrak City—and *Super Sad True Love Story*.

9. We Are All "Going to Die": Recognizing That This Statement Holds True for Everyone

New generations of Jews were born in New York and created New York Jewish parlance. A native speaker of this new dialect—which is as distinct as Eunice's young adult teenybopper speak—might immediately discern that Joshie Goldmann's immortality business endeavour is doomed to fail. Language indicates that his efforts are not to be taken seriously. "Joshie" resonates as the name of a cute young Jewish summer camp counsellor—not a trustworthy septuagenarian businessman.[4] (Ditto for "Bernie" Madoff. Would consummate successful entrepreneur New York Mayor Michael Bloomberg ever dream of calling himself Mikey?) When Shteyngart chose the name "Joshie," he indicated that failed immortality is readily discernible.

But it is not dystopian. Lenny's initial bravura assertion that he is never going to die morphs into "'We're all going to die'" (Shteyngart 328). Immortality fails because you can't fool Mother Nature, and that is a good thing. "Our genocidal war on free radicals proved more damaging than helpful, hurting cellular metabolism, robbing the body of control. In the end, nature simply would not yield" (Shteyngart 329). Life is a story. Like individual books, individual lives need to have a "The End." Individual Jews and all individual Americans are all going to die. Shteyngart indicates that the same does not hold true for Jews as a people and America as a country.

He stresses that immortality is achieved through art, not technological innovation. The story of Eunice and Lenny becomes a tale retold in the form of a play. An actress cast as Eunice "launched into a fairly accurate rendition of a spoiled pre-Rupture California girl while her friend hastened to appropriate the luckless Abramov" (Shteyngart 330). The novel's last line speaks to the first line's utopian immortality hope and implies that this hope can be achieved after all: "Their silence, black and complete" (Shteyngart 331). The rest of death is not black and complete silence; art, the play, is the thing to enable authors to become immortal. Eunice and Lenny are "launched" toward immortality via the science-fictional "video spray of my diaries" (Shteyngart 330), a new technology that does not jettison the content of books. Juxtaposing communication technology with art and life and words can yield immortality for individual writers. Textual art is never going to die.

10. Hearing Survivors: Appreciating the Resiliency of Jewish Stories

After the actress who plays Eunice articulates "a long-winded critique of America" (Shteyngart 331), Lenny thinks, "*America's gone*" (Shteyngart 331). He silences the actress by authoring a false story: "They're [many characters in *Super Sad True Love Story*] dead. I lied. 'They didn't survive'" (Shteyngart 331). But the characters do, in fact, survive. Lenny Abramov and Eunice Park are never going to die; text immortalizes them. America is not dead either. American democratic ideals—despite NAFTA and George W. Bush, etc.—are alive and well and lived in Zucotti Park. Eunice Park *was* in Zucotti Park; Shteyngart's story about her is super true. Shteyngart has written a super sad true dystopian love story about Lenny and Eunice, books, and America. The story has a utopian happy ending. Despite the vicissitudes Lenny and Eunice face, Lenny and Eunice and books and America are "*never going to die.*"

The detailed story that constitutes the lie Lenny authors reveals this super truth: "And I laid out a scenario for the final days of Lenny Abramov and Eunice Park more gruesome than any of the grisly infernos splashed on the walls of the neighboring cathedral" (Shteyngart 331). Cathedrals and the Holocaust are examples of Christian-constructed reality that exclude Jews as authors of their own subjectivity. These Christian master narratives do not completely silence Jewish stories. Some Jewish refugees were hidden by Christians in Christian religious edifices. Not all Jews succumbed to the final days Rupture final solution Nazi scenario of gruesome and grisly inferno. The Italians Lenny addresses see "a tableau of olive tress and grain fields, arrested by winter, dreamed of a new life" (Shteyngart 331). The olive trees and the grain fields are fantastic in that they can dream. As fantastic as it seemed at the time, Jewish concentration camps inmates could also dream; they could imagine the peace symbolized by olive trees and grain fields. Arrested by winter/Hitler, they dreamed of a new life—and for some survivors springtime for Hitler was actualized. (American G.I. Mel Brooks, who encountered Jewish survivors when he liberated a concentration camp, like Irving Berlin, writes songs—creates Jewish textual art.) Add living hills to the dreaming trees and fields. Jewish refugees experienced springtime for Hitler when they emigrated to, for example, Forest Hills, Queens. The hills of Forest Hills, Queens were (and, in ever fewer instances, still are) alive with the sound of World War II–era surviving Jews. I heard them. I grew up and learned to speak there.

Upon arrival in New York, Shteyngart heard them too. He encountered European Jews who remade themselves as Americans. Shteyngart, a new Russian Jewish New York American, imagines a new near future utopian Russian: the "gorgeous five-year-old kid, a Russian adoptee already an expert at Mandarin and Cantonese . . . [who tried] to mimic the funny English words" (Shteyngart 330). Shteyngart's declining America rings true; his description of English in decline is still fictitious. The point is that the importance of the word—not the dominance of a particular language—is what matters. Linguistic change is a part of Jewish survival/transformation. Shteyngart writes in English, not Russian. The Lefraks speak English, not French. The Jewish Holocaust survivors who emigrated to Queens now speak English, not continental European languages. Shteyngart gives Lenny's grammatically correct English and Eunice's teenybopper English equal attention and space.

11. Ustopia: Emphasizing the Convergence Between Atwood's and Shteyngart's Notions about Combining Utopia and Dystopia

Is *Super Sad True Love Story* optimistic or pessimistic? Albert Brooks, in describing his novel *2030*, provides an answer: "Of the book, he said, 'People ask is this optimistic or pessimistic?' Mr. Brooks, whose work is rarely sunny but shows tremendous heart, suggested that the answer should be obvious. 'Hey! We're still here! We're still functioning'" (Schwartz SR5). When creating a new generation's twenty-first-century version of Mel Brooks' New York Jewish utopian humorous response to dystopian catastrophe, Shteyngart says the same thing. And so does Atwood:

Historically, Ustopia has not been a happy story. High hopes have been dashed, time and time again. The best intentions have indeed paved many roads to Hell. Does that mean we should never try to rectify our mistakes, reverse our disaster-bent courses, clean up our cesspools or ameliorate the many miseries of many lives? Surely not: if we don't do maintenance work and minor improvements on whatever we actually have, things will go downhill very fast. So of course we should try to make things better, insofar as it lies within our power. But we should probably not try to make things perfect, especially not ourselves, for that path leads to mass graves. We're stuck with us, imperfect as we are; but we should make the most of us. Which is about as far as I myself am prepared to go, in real life, along the road to Ustopia. (Atwood *Guardian* 2)

Ultimately, in the America Lenny and Eunice inhabit, people try to rectify mistakes and reverse disaster-bent courses. They make things better, not perfect. We're stuck with an imperfect America. Jewish immigrants, in real life, chose to travel along the road to Ustopian America. American roads—Shteyngart's and Lenny's Old Country Road, Long Island Expressway, and Utopia Parkway, for example—are not paths that lead to mass graves for Jews. In America, Jews are able to participate in making the most of the imperfect American us. We love our opportunity—even if it is not perfect. This sentiment forms the crux of why *Super Sad True Love Story* is a Jewish-American Ustopia.

Newly American New York Jew Gary Shteyngart himself exemplifies New York Jewish immigrants' Ustopian super sad/happy true story. Michiko Kakutani notes that "while Mr. Shteyngart's descriptions of America have a darkly satiric edge, his descriptions of New York are infused with a deep affection for the city that is partly nostalgia for a vanished metropolis (in other words, Gotham as we know it today) and partly an immigrant's awestruck love for a place mythologized by books and songs and movies, by everyone from F. Scott Fizgerald to Frank Sinatra" (Kakutani C1). *Super Sad True Love Story* is at once dystopian and utopian because Shteyngart at once depicts a dystopian America and a utopian New York. Add Mel Brooks and Irving Berlin to Kakutani's "F. Scott Fitzgerald" and "Frank Sinatra"; Shteyngart makes New York come alive with Jewish culture. Fitzgerald's Gatsby finds his Jewish version in the great writers Lenny and Shteyngart whose books are "*never going to die.*" Shteyngart has fallen in "awestruck love" with New York—and this novel is his love story about New York.

He came to New York. He saw and loved Waldbaum's and Lefrak City. He conquered the New York literary establishment. Shteyngart and his semi-autobiographical super sad true love story exemplify this super happy fact: Hey!—the Jews and the book and New York and America are still here and still functioning!

L'chaim!

Notes

1 I recognize that this section title is unusual in regard to standard academic language. My deviation from typical scholarly tone is characteristic of my writing style. Brooks Landon comments on my style in his blurb for my book *Feminist Fabulation: Space/Postmodern Fiction*: "What I found so remarkable about this book is that it hit home in a way I associate with fiction more than with criticism; its power reminded me of the fiction of Kathy Acker, Angela Carter, and Joanna Russ." I *love* writing scholarly prose in a manner that combines scholarly writing with fiction writing. Everyone, of course, does not have a positive response to my academic prose style. I, in unapologetic response, do not think that all scholarly articles need to be written in a cookie-cutter mode. In other words, in a way that brings Erich Segal's *Love Story* to bear upon the tone I use to communicate my interpretation of *Super Sad True Love Story*, "love means never having to say you're sorry."
2 Superman was created by Jewish immigrants Jerome Siegel and Joe Shuster. Stan Lee, the Jewish inventor of Spider-Man, resided in Forest Hills, a Queens neighbourhood that is walking distance from Lefrak City.
3 It is interesting to compare Shteyngart's vision with Zucotti Park reality: "The makeshift kitchen has fed thousands of protesters each day.... [I]t has developed a cuisine not unlike the Occupy Wall Street movement itself: free-form, eclectic, improvisatory and contradictory.... At any moment, scores of cucumbers might be dropped off, and the volunteers, like contestants on 'chopped,' have to improvise a quick use for them.... Platters and utensils are washed on site. The soapy runoff slides in a gray-water system that's said to draw impurities out through a small network of mulch-like filters.... [P]eople know where the good Dumpsters are" (Gordinier 1).
4 *Heeb Magazine* editor Joshua Neuman, referring to the role Ben Stiller plays in *Tower Heist*, discusses the relationship between the name Josh and the concept of youthfulness: "Stiller's character, Josh Kovacs, got me thinking about the prolonged childhood that characters named Joshua or Josh have had on the big screen. Long used as a signifier for youth and vulnerability, finally there is a big screen representation worthy of a name of such Biblical proportions" (Neuman *Heeb*).

Works Cited

Atwood, Margaret. "Dire Cartographies: The Roads to Ustopia." *In Other Worlds: SF and the Human Imagination*. New York: Doubleday, 2011. 66–98. Print.

———. "The Road to Ustopia." *The Guardian* 14 Oct. 2011: 2. Print.

Barr, Marleen S. *Feminist Fabulation: Space/Postmodern Fiction*. Iowa City: University of Iowa Press, 1992. Print.

Bradbury, Ray. *Fahrenheit 451*. New York: Simon and Schuster, 1967. Print.

Brooks, Albert. *2030: The Real Story of What Happens to America*. New York: St. Martin's, 2011. Print.

Gordinier, Jeff. "Want to Get Fat on Wall Street? Try Protesting." *New York Times* 12 Oct. 2011: D1. Print.

Independence Day. Dir. Roland Emmerich. Fox. 1996. Film.

Kakutani, Michiko. "Love Found Amid Ruins of Empire." *New York Times* 26 July 2010: C1. Print.

The Nanny. Perf. Fran Drescher, Charles Shaughnessy, and Daniel Davis. CBS. 1993–99. TV series.

Neuman, Joshua. "No More Joshing Around." *Heeb* 4 Nov. 2011. Web. 4 Feb. 2012.

The Producers. By Mel Brooks, Thomas Meehan, and Doug Besterman. Dir. Susan Stroman. Perf. Nathan Lane and Matthew Broderick. St. James Theater, New York. 2001–2007. Performance.

Rolling Stones. "Yesterday's Papers." *Between the Buttons*. Comp. Mick Jagger and Keith Richards. Decca, 1967. LP.

Roth, Philip. *The Humbling*. Boston: Houghton Mifflin, 2009. Print.

———. *Operation Shylock: A Confession*. New York: Vintage, 1994. Print.

———. *Portnoy's Complaint*. New York: Random House, 1969. Print.

Schwartz, John. "Novelists Predict Future with Eerie Accuracy." *New York Times* 3 Sept. 2011: SR5. Print.

Segal, Erich. *Love Story*. New York: Harper & Row. 1970. Print.

"Springtime for Hitler." Lyrics by Mel Brooks. Music by John Morris. *The Producers*. By Mel Brooks, Thomas Meehan, and Doug Besterman. Dir. Susan Stroman. Perf. Nathan Lane and Matthew Broderick. St. James Theater, New York. 2001–2007. Song.

Tower Heist. Dir. Brett Ratner. Universal. 2011. Film.

In Pursuit of an Outside
Art Spiegelman's In the Shadow of No Towers *and the Crisis of the Unrepresentable*

Thomas Stubblefield

For the first hundred years of their existence, comics functioned as an art form whose abbreviated shelf life rivalled the ephemerality of modern media such as television or radio.[1] Born out of the nineteenth-century "circulation wars," their serial format was aimed at transforming the casual reader into the regular customer and as such betrayed not only an incompleteness at the level of narrative, but a material disintegration that fuelled the urgency of their consumption. However, as the form has gained credence among collectors, scholars, and artists in the last several decades, the planned obsolescence of yellowing newsprint has given way to a new sense of permanency. The emerging "graphic novel" not only jettisoned the serial format (a transformation that can be traced back to the arrival of the comic book in the early 1930s) but also enjoyed high-quality printing (and correlative high prices) alongside a more sophisticated mode of address.[2] Despite the shift from "disposable pulp to acid free archival paper" that has accompanied the elevation of the art form in recent years, an enduring connection to the medium's prehistory appears at least partially to determine the medium's cultural position (Wolk 10). At least, this seems to be the implication of the unique status that the graphic novel assumed in the wake of 9/11.

Posed somewhere between the immediacy of news and the afterwardness of art, the graphic novel in the wake of the 9/11 appeared to offer an intermediary or safe space in which as of yet unresolved questions of representation could safely be worked out. Indeed, while Hollywood and the major television networks observed an extended taboo against representing the event, this heterochronic medium seemed all but preoccupied with the disaster.[3] Less than three months after 9/11, a veritable wave of publications on the disaster hit the shelves. These included *9-11Emergency Relief*; *Heroes: The World's Greatest Super Hero Creators Honor the World's Greatest Heroes 9-11-2001*; *After 9/11: America's War on Terror*; as well as Dark Horse and DC Comics' release of a two-volume set on 9/11 which featured some of the most prominent artists working in the field.[4] Of these works, none is as exemplary of the impasses of representation that this unique position afforded the graphic novel as Art Spiegelman's *In the Shadow of No Towers* (2004).

Marianne Hirsch has described Spiegelman's work in terms of a larger trajectory of the visual culture of 9/11 that encapsulates both the "impossibility of seeing and the impossibility of not looking" (1212). This paradox manifests in the text in terms of a confusion between first-hand experience and the mediated memories of the media, an unstable relationship between textual and visual elements, as well as a pervasive play between presence and absence that informs the graphic aspect of the work. The challenges that these elements pose to the artist/narrator are presented in a way that merges the creative process with the disaster itself. As such, the dystopia presented in *In the Shadow of No Towers* concerns not only the event and its aftermath, but also the author's struggle to translate his experience of the disaster into graphic narrative form. This struggle centres on two interrelated dynamics: the encroaching images of the media that serve to confuse the boundaries of personal and collective experience, and the unavailability of the "unrepresentable" as a viable visual strategy in the twenty-first century. Margaret Atwood has claimed that both utopia and dystopia contain latent versions of their opposites (66). However, in extrapolating this discourse to the creative process, Spiegelman's work can be seen as positing an interruption between the utopian aspirations of its opposite and thereby reaffirming Fredric Jameson's insistence on "disjoining" the concepts from one another altogether (55). In these terms, the larger impasse that the work chronicles speaks to the unavailability of a utopia to come within the post-9/11 dystopia. This condition enacts a "crisis of the representation" that differs drastically from its postwar counterpart in that representation no longer proves inadequate but unavoidable, so much so that the image appears bound to dramatize a co-opting of individual experience and, more broadly, the outside of representation.

Experience Becomes Image: The Artist as Spectator

That trauma studies would prove to be a primary lens through which scholars have read Spiegelman's work is hardly unexpected. Not only does each new disaster seem to breathe life into this critical idiom, the work's specific character (its abrupt shifts in location, point of view and style, atavistic re-experience of the past, and overall ontological rootlessness) bears all the classic symptoms of the Freudian constellation. This knee-jerk reaction, though productive in its own right and even indirectly referenced by the work itself, has nonetheless served to de-emphasize the reflexive character of the text and thereby obscure a crucial discourse. Taking into consideration what can only be called the work's obsession with its own creation, an obsession that at times takes on the dimensions of the disaster itself, suggests that these same attributes might just as easily be read as the product of a historically specific conflict of representation. From this perspective, the threat to the stability of the symbolic order that structures the work is issued not only by the unassimilability of the disaster itself, but, perhaps more pressing from the standpoint of the creative process, by the absorption, even co-opting of the experience of the event by the images of the media. As this latter process shares many of the same surface features as trauma, its relative scarcity in scholarship is understandable. As *In the Shadow of No Towers* suggests, both dynamics are engaged in absorbing the utter incomprehensibility of first-hand experience, and in the process undermine the first-person perspective of the witness.

On the first page of the work, Spiegelman establishes the narrator's perspective on the events of 9/11 as the structuring agent of the work: "I live on the outskirts of Ground Zero and first saw it all live—unmediated" (1). However, with the television keeping him awake at night with conspiracy theories and camera crews swarming his Manhattan neighbourhood, it is not long before the reader senses a slippage in the authenticity of this perspective. On the following page, the author reiterates his intent to "sort out the fragments of what I'd experienced from the media that threatened to engulf what I actually saw" (2). However, this text bubble is positioned underneath a static-laced image whose 4:3 aspect ratio conjures an anachronistic televisual frame, while at the same time the untenable viewing position of the image betrays the presence of a zoom lens. As Patrick M. Bray describes it, the grid-like quality of the image's static also bears the influence of a more contemporary regime of images. He explains:

> The computerized illustration, which repeats dozens of times throughout the book, calls attention to itself as visually different from the surrounding hand drawn comics. At the same time, within the image itself, its own status as the representation of a lived memory is undermined by the exaggerated size of its pixels, which guarantee the readability of the image's technological origin. The fleeting memory of the moment just before the collapse of the north tower, a memory threatened by the devastating force of media images, can only be represented by an image that . . . offers a vision of disintegration (of the tower and of memory). (15)

Reaffirming the contamination of the narrator's "unmediated" access, two frames later we see the author sitting mesmerized in front of a television as an airplane smashes into the side of the screen. The cathartic blending of lived experience and image (two realms that the author has promised to keep separate) that this scene visualizes is echoed in the work's recurring dynamic of materialization, whereby non-visible and/or unrepresentable phenomena are mobilized by the media's images of the event. As the seeming immateriality and instability of memory give way to a static and legible narrative in these instances, the work, as Anne Whitehead puts it, "make[s] visible the inscription of 9/11 into state organized acts of commemoration and the rhetoric of war" (234).

Describing the scene in which Spiegelman confesses to not actually seeing but hearing the jet collide with the World Trade Center, Marianne Hirsch notes that "the word-image 'roarrrrrrrr!!' almost covers the statement about not seeing, occluding it to the point of near illegibility. *Not seeing* becomes *visible* and even *audible*, as graphic as the absent towers." Following the logic of trauma, Hirsch regards this transformation as a reflection of the way in which "words, images, and word-images work together to enact the impossibility of seeing and the impossibility of not looking" (1213). However, so much of the work seems to suggest the exact opposite trajectory, namely, the uncanny ability of experience to succumb to the visible and manifest in graphic form. Rather than a negation of the image, this manifestation of the non-visible within the frame speaks to its hyper-visualization, a process by which even non-visible sensation achieves visual form. The dystopic position of the narrator/artist comes about as a result of the intersection of the unrepresentability of the disaster and the quest to somehow preserve this quality in the graphic novel itself with the hyper-visualization of the same event, which occurs at the hands of the media.

The intrusion of this process of becoming-image into Spiegelman's project is driven home by the objectification of the most crucially invisible aspect of the image, the frame. At the top of page two, as the author describes the sensation of trauma ("time stands still . . . I see that awesome tower, glowing as it collapses"), the frames gradually turn as the eye moves from left to right, eventually forming two burning towers at the end of the sequence. As the incomprehensibility of this reactivated moment transmogrifies into an iconic image, the impossibility of the traumatic experience literally takes shape. Katalin Orbán understands this emphasis on materiality in terms of Alois Reigl's notion of "memories of tactile surface" (76). By foregrounding the object quality of a memory, such phenomena essentially introduce a material trigger that instantiates the "near" of subjective experience so as to banish the "distant view" that is to some degree inherent to the illusionistic plane of images. However, in the context of *In the Shadow of No Towers* this process does not return sensory experience, but rather speaks to its reification by the image.

Historically, the frame, as a materialization of Alberti's famous theorization of the image as a "window onto a world," turns upon invisibility (54–55). This is especially so in the context of the graphic novel, where seriality is often interrupted by actions and words that bleed outside of the frame in order to signify intensity and/or to create non-linear chronologies. In short, the frame is both an invisible cue, whose presence precludes the outside and thereby bolsters the fictitious world inside, and a boundary to be transgressed, often to mark the subjectivity of experience. The closing of the frame that the above sequence illustrates demonstrates a larger unavailability of the event to inscription. It is telling in this respect that the end result of this transformation is often canonical images of the event whose impersonal and "objective" quality gives them the air of history, while at the same time they preclude the narrator's own experience of the event.

This opposition between material presence as both the domain of subjective experience and the residue of the ossifying tendency of the historical record manifests most acutely in the design of the book itself. Certainly, the tangible presence of the book does prompt an individual experience and, as Orbán points out, the images themselves reinforce this quality through their play with depth and texture (75). Frames are stacked on top of one another and the text is layered on top of the entire layout. Indeed, on page four the entire layout almost mimics a table upon which photographs and handwritten notes have been spread. While these attributes might serve to re-interject the here and now of reading so as to foreground the subjectivity of the reading experience, the sheer girth of the work seems to almost parody such interventions. Despite its having only seventeen full-page plates, the volume's exceptionally thick pages create the impression of a much larger work. Turning the page for the first time, the reader feels as if they are the butt of a joke, as the book they hold more closely resembles a clandestine "hollow book" whose pages have been cut out to hide valuables or incriminating evidence than a graphic novel.

Throughout this dialogue, the opposition between incomprehensible subjective experience and legible narrative is tilted toward the latter. As this "intrusion" appears to displace experiential knowledge of the event, the self-assuredness of the author's initial declaration gives way to an admission of non-seeing. Eventually, he describes being "haunted now by images he didn't witness . . . images of people tumbling to the streets below . . . especially one man (according to a neighbor) who executed a graceful Olympic dive as his last living act" (6). As Katalin Orbán points out, it is telling that Spiegelman does not "fabricate the visual record" of this event and instead relies upon a verbal description that is based only on hearsay (73). Rather than the unassimilability of trauma, this non-seeing is the remainder of the media's translation of memory into narrative, a presentation of the event, which has destabilized the parameters of image, memory, and rememberer. Accordingly, the original distinction that the narrator makes between his events and those presented on television no longer holds, as memory now appears always already prosthetic. The dystopia that this realization presents for the artist who continually seeks to rescue lived experience from the image is further magnified by his recourse to the unrepresentable, a constellation that once served to summon an outside to representation but which proves untenable for the artist/narrator.

The Outside and the Image: The Unrepresentable as Historical Trope

> The extermination of the Jews of Europe is as accessible to both representation and interpretation as any other historical event.
> —Saul Friedlander, "Introduction" in *Probing the Limits of Representation*

> I do not think that the Holocaust, Final Solution, Shoah, Churban, or German genocide of the Jews is any more unrepresentable than any other event in human history.
> —Hayden White, *"Historical Emplotment and the Problem of Truth"*

The cover of *In the Shadow of No Towers* presents one of the earliest artistic interpretations of 9/11. Originally published on the cover of *New Yorker* magazine on September 24, 2001, the image features what at first glance seems to be a monochromatic black surface. Only by tilting the work ever so slightly or by placing it in bright light can the shadows of the two towers be made visible. Most immediately, this play between presence and absence visualizes the lingering afterimage of the towers that the Manhattan skyline, and indeed the collective imaginary itself, now seemed to contain. At the same time, the image signalled what would soon become a resurgence of the unrepresentable. From Hollywood's unofficial ban on disaster films to the art world's self-imposed silence, the "most photographed disaster in history" most often appeared in the aftermath of the event as a silent but reverent non-image. As Bray points out, Spiegelman's cover "crystallizes the [ensuing] tension between the overwhelming presence of media images [from that day] and the absence revealed by a shadow image" (15).

Gauging the depth of this internal opposition within both the visual culture of the disaster in the wake of 9/11 and Spiegelman's own work requires that the unrepresentable be understood as a historically specific constellation rather than a transcendental outside to representation. While in the aftermath of the Holocaust illustrating the inadequacy of representation may have appeared to preserve the unfathomability of the event, such a strategy has undergone a radical transformation in recent years. Suffice it to say that Adorno's original prohibition on poetry and the expectation of a necessary failure of the image it engendered has largely been undermined by popular culture. From *Sophie's Choice* (1982) to *Schindler's List* (1993), Hollywood has not only sidestepped the taboo but in fact wed the event to the image in an intimate fashion, especially for those born after the war. Recognizing that the unassimilable quality of the event does not necessarily preclude representation in the contemporary sphere, scholars such as Hayden White, Saul Friedlander, and Andreas Huyssen have recently declared the Holocaust to no longer be unrepresentable (66).

As Derrida's critique of the void in Daniel Libeskind's Jewish Museum suggests, recourse to absence as an aesthetic strategy can no longer be considered in terms of a contemplation of the ineffable, but rather seems to introduce a kind of nostalgic emptiness that lacks the productivity that was ascribed to its postwar instantiation.[5] Derrida illustrates this shift by comparing architectural articulation of absence in Libeskind's museum with the refusal of closure that one finds in the Platonic *chora*. Whereas the latter functions as "a place that precedes history and the inscription of Forms," Libeskind's evocation of a historically determined visual trope presents a space that is already "circumscribed" by the history it claims to destabilize (92). As such, this space largely fails to materialize as a future-oriented potentiality, but rather comes to illustrate what Leo Bersani calls "the susceptibility of all potential being to nothingness—as if potentiality could itself *fail to take place* . . . could tilt the universe backward into the void" (169).

The contradictory status of this motif in the contemporary sphere is illustrated on page three of the *In the Shadow of No Towers* as the narrator describes his father's attempts to convey the horrors of Auschwitz. In recounting this event (itself a representation), the narrator suddenly appears as a character from the author's earlier work *Maus*, while his cigarette and first-person narration retain the figure's identity as Spiegelman. The transformation is emblematic of a larger chain of associations which have come to destabilize the image: the smoke from the concentration camp merges with the toxic air of lower Manhattan, which in turn slips into the cigarette smoke that fills the frame. Overseeing this chain of casual associations is the originary trauma, which Spiegelman tells us his father could describe only as "indescribable" and which subsequently appears as shadows of the present event. Such sequences illustrate what Kristiaan Versluys describes as the text's "transmission of trauma . . . far beyond the immediate circumstances" (983). At the same time, they evoke the paradox of this trope in contemporary visual culture. They embody the fragmentary perceptions of an event that exceeds representation while simultaneously establishing the event as wholly representable, one that can be conjured by a well-established back history of images, which in this case the author himself has helped to establish. However, it is not simply the author's previous work that creates this latter dynamic, but also the pervasive references to Cold War science fiction films of the 1950s and '60s, gas mask public service announcements, and billboards for Hollywood disaster films, all of which present the unrepresentable as anything but.

This unending flow of historical images undercuts the linearity of the narrative and in this way reproduces the dislocation that occurs with trauma's reactivation of past events.[6] The subsequent collapse of time whereby the original event returns "without having lost any of its freshness" is in fact referenced throughout the text itself ("time stands still at the moment of trauma . . . trauma piles on trauma") (2, 5). To this extent, the work continues a trajectory begun in *Maus*, which, in recounting the father's tale of the Holocaust, presents the past's intrusion on the present in terms of what Andreas Huyssen describes as a "cross-cutting of past and present [which] points . . . to how this past holds the present captive, independently of whether this knotting of past into present is being talked about or repressed" (71). However, aside from the creative impasse it creates, this reactivation seems at some more primary level safely contained within the image. Indeed, the fact that trauma itself appears as one of the cultural references to which the author resorts to convey the anxiety of the event and its aftermath suggests a kind of assimilation into symbolic discourse. From this perspective, the suddenness and lack of explanation that accompany the appearance of these images from the past testify as much to the iconic quality of the author's earlier work and the other visual references as the reactivation of the past.

The artist's goal to convey the incomprehensibility of the event is in some sense sabotaged by the realization of the historical determinedness of this category. Rather than a pure outside, which safely suspends the symbolic, such a trope has been thoroughly coded and as such internalized by the image. The work thus forms the very shadow that the title references. The sense of remove built into the word "shadow" combined with the "no" forms a double negative, which reiterates the visual presence of this missing thing, a presence that is canonized and historically specific. The unrepresentable as a transcendental category therefore proves unavailable in the midst of this hyper-visualization, a fate that ensures the absorption of the narrator's very work into the narrative that it so desperately seeks to evade.

Spiegelman's attempts to preserve the incomprehensibility of the event end only in anxiety and frustration ("despair slows me down"), which ultimately renders the artist passive. We see him asleep at his drawing table, while Bush and Osama battle it out in the foreground. Confirming the utter passiveness of the artist in the face of this political struggle, a "Missing" poster for Spiegelman's brain hangs in the background.

Conclusion: Rebuilding Narrative, Rebuilding Nation

In the last several decades, the Holocaust has moved from a position of unrepresentability epitomized by Adorno's prohibition on poetry and the crisis of representation in postwar art to a recognizable visual trope. This newfound representability of the atrocity speaks to a larger transformation whereby events once deemed outside the confines of representation have proven less resistant to the image under the "visual turn." This shift was reinforced by 9/11, the reception of which, though incomprehensible at almost every level of the experience, could certainly not be described in terms of the same melancholic acknowledgement of the failure of representation that characterized the experience of the Holocaust or Hiroshima. Rather, the event was from the beginning saturated with presence as images endlessly presented the collisions and subsequent collapse of the Towers from almost every imaginable angle. Indeed, to speak of the failure of the image in such a context is not only to disregard the hyper-mediation of the disaster, but to overlook a primary intent of the attack, which itself was directed at and made for the image.

The excessive representation and the apparent "failure" that it prompts in Spiegelman's work testify to the near immediate transformation of the event into a "national trauma" as a means to mobilize the general public for war. The dissolution of the singular perspective that the work dramatizes not only illustrates the always already prosthetic quality of media and its relation to memory, it subtly suggests the ways in which this formative power can be used to produce collective experiences and identities so as to justify larger narratives of aggression. Summarizing this progression, Kaplan explains that "trauma produces new subjects . . . the political-ideological context within which trauma occurs shapes their impact . . . [and in the end it] is hard to separate individual and collective trauma" (1). In the mobilization toward war, which began almost immediately, the individual testimony was absorbed into such collective framings in order to forge the other as such and in the process provide the condition of possibility for war. The violence of the event is then reproduced by a larger process, by which the bloodless and often anonymous images of 9/11 become historical record. Registering an encroaching objectification of the image and a correlative unsustainability of an outside to representation, Spiegelman's work conveys the drama of resistance and assimilation to the narrative of "9/11" which was formed within and by the image. The dystopia of the event bleeds into the process of representation itself, both of which acknowledge the limitlessness of the image at the same time they expose its vulnerability.

Notes

1. As Rebecca Zurier describes, "Most accounts trace the invention of the modern comic strip to the Sunday humor sections, which were developed as ammunition in the circulation wars waged in the 1890s by the American newspaper tycoons Joseph Pulitzer and William Randolph Hearst. Entertaining characters, reappearing each Sunday, ensured that loyal readers would buy the paper week after week, providing a steady audience for advertisers" (98).
2. While there is a great deal of uncertainty as to when the first graphic novel arrived, the first self-described graphic novels emerged in the mid-1970s. Examples include *Bloodstar* (1976) by Richard Corben and *Red Tide* (1976) by Jim Steranko.
3. As Spiegelman explains: "The only cultural artifacts that could get past my defenses to flood my eyes and brain with something other than images of burning towers were old comic strips; vital, unpretentious ephemera from the optimistic dawn of the 20th century" ("Disaster Is My Muse").
4. This preoccupation continued in the years that followed as works such as *The 9/11 Report* (2006) and *American Widow* (2008) continued this head-on look at the traumatic events of that day.
5. Citing a pervasive fear of "aesthetic pollution" that pervades postwar art and architecture, Brett Ashley Kaplan points out that even the initial connection between monumentality and Fascism was shaky at best. Not only did the conception of, for example, Speers's monumental architecture predate the Nazi regime by at least a century, but there was considerable disagreement within the party over the proper form of Nazi art. In fact, many, including Goebbels, were sympathetic to Modernist design despite its eventual demonization in the Degenerate Art Exhibition and other venues. Nonetheless, as Kaplan points out, postwar visual culture continues to operate from the assumption that monumentality is inherently fascistic and for this reason often sabotages its own attempts at history in the process (152).

6 See E. Ann Kaplan's discussion of the way in which 9/11 dredged up memories of the air raids in London during World War II in "9/11 and 'Disturbing Remains'" in *Trauma Culture: The Politics of Terror and Loss in Media and Literature* (Newark, NJ: Rutgers UP, 2005).

Works Cited

Alberti, Leon. *On Painting*. New York: Penguin Books, 2005.
Arnold, Andrew D. "Disaster Is My Muse." *Time* 3 Sept. 2004. Web. 2 Feb. 2012.
Atwood, Margaret. *In Other Worlds: SF and the Human Imagination*. New York: Nan A. Talese, 2011. Print.
Bersani, Leo. "Psychoanalysis and the Aesthetic Subject." *Critical Inquiry* 32 (Winter 2006): 161–74. Print.
Bray, Patrick. "Aesthetics in the Shadow of No Towers: Reading Virilio in the Twenty-First Century." *Yale French Studies* 114 (2008): 4–17. Print.
Derrida, Jacques. "Response to Daniel Libeskind." *Research in Phenomenology* 22 (1992): 88–94. Print.
Friedlander, Saul. "Introduction," in *Probing the Limits of Representation*. Ed. Saul Friedlander. Cambridge, MA: Harvard U Press, 1992, 2–3. Print.
Hirsch, Marianne. "Collateral Damage." *PMLA* 119:4 (2004): 1209–15. Print.
Huyssen, Andreas. "Of Mice and Mimesis." *New German Critique* 81 (Autumn 2000): 65–82. Print.
Jameson, Fredric. *Seeds of Time*. New York: Columbia UP, 1994. Print.
Kaplan, Brett Ashley. *Unwanted Beauty: Aesthetic Pleasure in Holocaust Representation*. Champaign, IL: U of Illinois P, 2007. Print.
Kaplan, E. Ann. *Trauma Culture: The Politics of Terror and Loss in Media and Literature*. Newark, NJ: Rutgers UP, 2005. Print.
Orbán, Katalin. "Trauma and Visuality: Art Spiegelman's *Maus* and *In the Shadow of No Towers*." *Representations* 97:77 (Winter 2007): 57–89. Print.
Spiegelman, Art. *In the Shadow of No Towers*. New York: Pantheon, 2004. Print.
Versluys, Kristiaan. "Art Spiegelman's *In the Shadow of No Towers*: 9/11 and the Representation of Trauma." *MFS Modern Fiction Studies* 52:4 (Winter 2006): 980–1003. Print.
White, Hayden. "Historical Emplotment and the Problem of Truth." In *Probing the Limits of Representation*, Ed. Saul Friedlander. Cambridge, MA: Harvard UP, 1992. 52. Print.
Whitehead, Anne. *Memory*. New York: Routledge, 2004. Print.
Wolk, Douglas. *Reading Comics: How Graphic Novels Work and What They Mean*. Jackson, TN: Da Capo Press, 2007. Print.
Zurier, Rebecca. "Classy Comics." *Art Journal* 50:3 (1991): 98–103. Print.

Homero Aridjis and Mexico's Eco-Critical Dystopia

Adam Spires

Founder of the Group of 100,[1] a prominent environmental protection organization, writer Homero Aridjis is one of Latin America's leading environmental activists, with numerous achievements to his credit in defence of Mexico's natural heritage, most notably his successful campaign to safeguard the annual monarch butterfly migration in his home state of Michoacán. This activism very much informs and is reflected within his poetic, dramatic, and fictional work. Owing to Aridjis' determined lobbying against logging companies and local officials, the monarch's wintering grounds were finally declared a nature reserve. To struggle against multinational corporations and the collusion of local governments is standard for environmentalists, but in Mexico the challenges they face are intensified by the country's subordination to economic pressures from the North, a relationship satirized in the time-honoured expression "Poor Mexico: so far from God, and so close to the United States." Indeed, since its independence from Spain in 1821, Mexico has ceded territory and economic sovereignty to the United States and, increasingly, to other countries of the Global North.

The imbalance of power and influence within the North–South divide becomes all the more onerous for environmentalists like Aridjis in this era of global neoliberalism when free markets take precedence over the welfare of local habitats in developing countries. The signing of the North American Free Trade Agreement (NAFTA) presents a case in point. Aridjis had lobbied to have the monarch butterfly adopted as the official symbol of NAFTA, which would have been a compelling reminder to respect sound environmental practices in all three countries traversed by the butterfly during the round-trip migrations of its life cycle. It was a noble idea befitting what was to be dubbed the "greenest trade agreement in history" (Roberts and Thanos 56) insofar as NAFTA would pioneer an environmentalist side agreement, and establish a governing body to manage environmental affairs: the Commission for Environmental Cooperation (CEC).[2] Unfortunately, nothing came of Aridjis' idea and, worse yet, the monarch population suffered precipitous declines in the years that followed, and disruptions to their migratory patterns remain a growing concern.

Illegal logging still occurs in the nature reserve but the more immediate cause of the butterfly's dwindling numbers has been identified as agricultural practices in Canada and the United States, where genetically modified crops and herbicides are used in tandem to eradicate milkweed, the monarch's primary source of food and nesting grounds. From the foregoing, the monarch reminds us of the risks associated with free trade agreements and the anonymity of environmental responsibility. For Aridjis, it is clear that his victory on the local front has proven insufficient. Like free trade, environmental issues do not stop at borders. Any additional victories that Aridjis stands to achieve in the name of Mexican conservation will require that his efforts grow in proportion to the portentous global economy. It is a monumental task befitting an activist who has devoted his entire career to championing just causes: from environmentalism to defending human rights and freedom of expression.

Importantly, this direct public engagement is mirrored in his literary works, where Aridjis equally resists and questions the imperatives and environmental repercussions of the Global North within Mexico. The author of over thirty titles, Aridjis has also conveyed his vision of environmental justice through a corpus of poetry, drama, and fiction that captures half a century of his growing apprehension of the modern age. In this respect, literature has proven a worthwhile medium for engagement with an adversary that is as ethereal as it is universal: namely, globalization. More specifically, in his two novels, *The Legend of the Suns* (1993) and *Who Do You Think of When Making Love?* (1995), Aridjis is situated within a specific Mexican literary claiming of dystopia, one that critiques Mexico's attempts to modernize in order to meet the demands of global capital. Dystopia becomes the vehicle for writing about an immediate local context, one in which the cyclicism of the environment and of indigenous mythology are sacrificed for the linearity of capital progression. It is only in the apocalyptic conclusion of this narrative of erasure, amid the ruins, that the reimagining can begin.

Development: Mexico's El Dorado

Arguably the greatest challenge that Aridjis addresses in his writing is the drive to catch up with other industrialized nation-states, a mindset that has governed Mexican policy for over a century. In the late nineteenth century, Porfírio Díaz—who converted the country into the so-called "mother of foreigners, and stepmother of Mexicans"—was determined to modernize Mexico according to models of progress imported from Europe. Under his dictatorship, a simulacrum of modernity was fostered in the capital city, while social inequities were ignored in the countryside where the Mexican peasantry (the *campesinos*) and indigenous communities lived under a feudal system of often foreign-owned landed estates. The injustice was enough to spark a revolution.[3] Though an agrarian reform under President Cárdenas (1934–40) would later see land redistributed via the *ejido* system,[4] by the 1950s, the Green Revolution and the modernization of agriculture was beginning to threaten subsistence farming with an ever-encroaching commercial sector. The result was an unprecedented exodus from rural towns, heading either to the northern border and beyond, or straight to Mexico City.

By the time President Salinas ratified NAFTA, he had already enacted Article 27, ending the *ejido* system that had been enshrined in the constitution, effectively paving the way for a new era of privatizations. For NAFTA critics, the would-be utopia of Mexican modernity was equated with unsustainable urban growth, a border abandoned to the predation of the maquiladora industry,[5] PRI totalitarianism[6]—notorious for electoral fraud, corruption, and violence—and both *campesinos* and indigenous communities living in squalor, fearful of land expropriation by foreign companies. NAFTA was supposed to protect Mexico from another debt crisis. It did not. More economic crises would follow. NAFTA supporters promised economic growth and an ensuing trickle-down effect to the lower classes, not the islands of high-tech wealth surrounded by seas of poverty that characterize the burgeoning maquiladora sector. The upsurge in remittances is ample testimony that globalization does not enrich Mexicans but, rather, displaces them. NAFTA was supposed to safeguard the environment but, as critics point out, spending on environmental protection dropped by nearly

50 percent following NAFTA and, not surprisingly, every major environmental problem in Mexico has since worsened (Roberts and Thanos 59). For the growing number of Mexicans already marginalized by the country's integration into global capitalism, it was clear that NAFTA would only accelerate the country's perilous race to the bottom.[7]

Accordingly, Subcomandante Marcos—Mexico's postmodern defender of social justice—chose NAFTA's inaugural day for his army of indigenous insurgents, the Zapatistas, to take up arms in protest. In anticipation of NAFTA's fallout, they were asserting their human and territorial rights in the name of Zapata, the 1910 revolutionary. For the indigenous peoples of Chiapas, and the rural peasantry nation-wide, NAFTA was equated with nothing less than a return to the nineteenth-century Porfiriato.

Mexico's unmanageable economic burden is symptomatic of a trend that sees other underdeveloped countries in Latin America hastening to modernize in order to participate in the global economy. They are the nation-states that are left unfinished, still a long way from achieving the prosperous, capitalist democracies that they have been promised by the myth of development. How a mere free trade agreement should close the gap between a developing nation like Mexico and its northern neighbours is incomprehensible. Even the phrase "developing nation" is a misnomer, as it has come to suggest an evolutionary certainty toward a final result of material progress when, in actuality, the pursuit of prosperity in developing nations remains as elusive as the conquistador's search for El Dorado (de Rivero 72). In Mexico, the rich continue to get richer, while poverty has not abated. At best, Mexico has achieved "buffer state" status, a subordinate role ratified by NAFTA, and stabilized, when necessary, by financial bailouts (de Rivero 44).

Echoing José Martí's historic warning against the "false erudition" (138) of European colonizers, Homero Aridjis has consistently argued that the very concepts of global capitalism and development do not match Mexico's nature in the first place. For Aridjis, they are foreign ideals, imposed by the superpowers of the West, whereas Mexico is a country with a pre-Columbian—read pre-Western—cultural heritage. In effect, the indigenous past and Mexico's relationship to nature in many ways remain the round hole for modernity's square peg. It is only through the complicity of local elites who stand to gain, and unscrupulous governments—from the Porfiriato to Salinas—that Western ideologies have come to dominate Mexican affairs, much to the detriment of the lower classes and the environment. For impoverished *campesinos* and indigenous groups, in particular, environmentalism is not just about protecting nature; rather, it means having access to protected nature: clean water, fertile land, and forest resources. As these rudiments of rural life diminish under the advance of agribusiness and other so-called progressive forms of development, Mexico City and northern border towns swell with ever increasing numbers of displaced migrants, tipping the scales to record levels of poverty and environmental degradation. Indeed, the deficiencies stemming from Mexico's economic ambitions are many, and they have been sufficiently distressing to warrant the taking up of a genre new to Mexican writers: the dystopian novel.

The Mexican Dystopia and Eco-Criticism

Aridjis is part of a larger trend on the part of Mexican writers to employ the dystopian novel for addressing the aftermath of global integration. There is an unambiguous cause-and-effect relationship between NAFTA and the emergence of the Mexican dystopia. In López-Lozano's chronicle of this genre in Mexico, he draws a parallel between the angst provoked in Mexico by globalization and the dehumanizing effects of the industrial revolution that stirred the fears conveyed in the original European dystopias a century earlier (1). That NAFTA was signed at the time of the quincentenary—five hundred years after the first contact between Europeans and *indios*—is a bitter irony that stages a recurring dystopian motif: the erasure of the indigenous past by the technocratic future. In Mexico, the dystopian genre is thus calibrated *a priori* as a post-colonial eco-critique that views the Western paradigm of modernity as a thinly veiled strategy of neocolonial exploitation. Consequently, in the five novels that López-Lozano identifies as the canon of Mexican dystopias, there is a common thread that runs through each of them in their repositioning of the meaning of modernity measured against the conquest of both indigenous peoples and nature. These novels include: *Christopher Unborn* (1987) by Carlos Fuentes; *The Rag Doll Plagues* (1992) by Alejandro Morales; *The Legend of the Suns* (1993) and *Who Do You Think of When Making Love?* (1995) by Homero Aridjis; and *Heavens on Earth* (1997) by Carmen Boullosa.[8] As López-Lozano affirms, "written under the shadow of NAFTA, these dystopian novels engage the theme of Mexico's pattern of development, revisiting images of science fiction to depict the potentially disastrous impact of globalization on the environment and on the indigenous peoples of the Americas" (4). It bears mentioning here that eco-criticism is a standard motif of the dystopian genre, by no means particular to Mexican literature. Having emerged in response to the rise of the machine and humankind's resultant alienation in urban slums, for over a century dystopias have brought to light our detachment from nature and, by extension, from our natural instincts, hence the collective nature-deficit disorder that tends to characterize dystopian societies. Moreover, dystopias commonly extrapolate from distressing trends in urban growth to envision a global civilization that has exceeded the planet's carrying capacity. At length, that human culture must be recalibrated to ensure a sustainable symbiosis with its natural habitat is a tenet held by both environmentalists and skeptics of the modern age. These are two schools of thought that come to a confluence in the better part of dystopian fiction.

In such classic dystopias as Yevgeny Zamyatin's *We* (1924), Aldous Huxley's *Brave New World* (1932), and George Orwell's *Nineteen Eighty-Four* (1949), for example, the representation of how the state controls the relationship between humans and nature is key. What varies in this theme is the novelist's foresight into how or why the future might lead to such unnatural worlds. For this reason, it is particularly noteworthy that the portrayal of nature in the canon of Mexican dystopias is consistent through all five novels. Fuentes, Morales, Aridjis, and Boullosa all fashion their nightmarish societies around the same perceived threat to Mexico's well-being, specifically, pollution. What is more, the cause to which environmental crisis is attributed is also consistent throughout the five novels: Mexico's injudicious pursuit of modernity. There are thus critical differences that surface between the Mexican dystopia and the European classics of the genre. In contrast to the literary technique of "defamiliarization" (Booker 19) that characterizes the latter—exemplified by ambiguous settings in the remote future with only vague nuances to orient readers to familiar points of reference—what sets the Mexican dystopia apart is the immediacy of a local crisis. Written in NAFTA's wake, these novels extrapolate specifically from Mexico's economic turmoil in order to project an already recognizable environmental aftermath. Another distinction pertains to how the dystopia of Mexico's future is weighed against the indigenous past, when a cosmology centred on nature worship was suppressed by a supposedly more advanced world view. As a barometer of Mexico's future, it is indeed a compelling prophecy that four different novelists should converge on the pivotal signing of a free trade agreement in order to warn of the impending environmental consequences, and that they should evoke the indigenous past as an implicit countercultural discourse.

The story of *Christopher Unborn*, by Carlos Fuentes, opens on the polluted beaches of Acapulco, where the fetal narrator is conceived. During the nine chapters of his gestation, he bears witness to the ravages of the Mexican landscape as a result of his country's blind pursuit of progress, best exemplified in state-sponsored slogans: "CITIZENS OF MEXICO: INDUSTRIALIZE. YOU WON'T LIVE LONGER BUT YOU WILL LIVE BETTER" (23). As Christopher approaches full term, he fears that the environment will redirect his genetic course, that he will mutate before birth since he has been exposed to so much pollution: "that's all there is here: rubbish, decomposition, mountains of garbage, an implacable circle of garbage, a chain of garbage, linked by a network of plastic and rags. . . . If I'm not the son of my genes, then must I be the (bastard) son of the environment" (462). Such is the danger awaiting the next generation born in "Makesicko City" (76).

In a similar fashion, Alejandro Morales depicts a future when pollution and poverty are so prevalent in Mexico City that *pepenadores* (garbage pickers) undergo a genetic mutation, just as Fuentes' narrator had feared. It is a mere evolutionary adaptation to a changing environment. Like Fuentes, Morales calls attention to nature's influence on our epigenetics, on how our genes can either be activated or go dormant, depending largely on the health of our natural surroundings. It is a process that, over time, can lead to enduring variations. As Morales foresees it, Mexico's poorest are afforded an evolutionary advantage from this genetic shift, only to find themselves exploited once again by Euro-Americans who require life-saving blood transfusions from "MCMs" (Mexico City Mexicans) to survive the ecological plagues of the future. Analogous to modernity's destruction of nature, injustices committed in the colonial past are evoked in this novel to frame the Mexican labourer's history of subservience. It is the mid-twenty-first century, and though NAFTA has developed into one political body (The Triple Alliance), the imbalance in human rights between North and South has not changed. Mexico's poor are still consumed north of the border like an imported commodity.

Similar to Morales' novel, Carmen Boullosa's dystopia is structured within three time frames: the colonial past, the late twentieth century, and the post-apocalypse. Hundreds of years into the future, the Earth is uninhabitable as the result of a disastrous ecocide. The few survivors inhabit "L'Atlàntide," a community made up of spheres floating in the sky. As in the novels by Fuentes and Morales, Boullosa's characters, the dystopian heroines, include anthropologists and archaeologists who bring out the indigenous past for the purpose of diagnosis and commentary on the dystopian future. L'Atlàntide is depicted as humanity's rise to perfection through technological advance. However, the pursuit of progress heedless of past mistakes that should have taught us our *natural* place in the world leads to humanity's ultimate degeneration: infanticide, cannibalism, and, in the end, extinction.

Ultimately, this binary model that portrays nature and indigenous heritage as the victims of enduring colonial ambition is best represented by Homero Aridjis, as one might expect given his illustrious profile as Mexico's most renowned environmentalist and an outspoken human rights advocate. His task as a writer, as he words it, "is to tell the stories of this planet and to express an ecological cosmology that does not separate nature from humanity" (Russell 66).[9] It is evident in his two dystopian novels that this "ecological cosmology" is aligned with the *indio*'s reverence of nature, as recorded in Aztec mythology. Herein lies his riposte to the errant utopian ideals of the West that continue to wreak havoc on his country. Aridjis reminds us that "Mexico" is derived from "Mexica"—meaning "Aztec"—and that long before Tenochtitlán came to be known as "Mexico City," the Aztecs prophesied that when the fifth sun came to the end of its cycle, the city would crumble. For Aridjis, the extremes of Mexico's environmental crises are a sign that the prophecy of the fifth sun is coming to fruition.

The Eco-Apocalypse: Mexico, 2027

Aridjis' novels *The Legend of the Suns* and its sequel *Who Do You Think of When Making Love?* recount simultaneous stories that take place in the year 2027, a generation after NAFTA. The intrigue of the first involves a quest to recover a missing page from a sacred codex of Aztec lore. If the protagonist succeeds, the goddess of the sixth sun will restore balance between humans and nature. In the sequel, the narrator, "Yo Sánchez," treks across an apocalyptic urban landscape with her friends, relating her life story. Distressed by the violence and pollution that surround them, they press on against the backdrop of a foreboding climate of uncertainty. In effect, it is this background setting of Mexico City's chaos that presages the main lines of reasoning of both novels while, as López-Lozano argues, their respective plots serve more "as the pretext for Aridjis's examination of Mexico's projected post-NAFTA future, a future in which political corruption and the destruction of nature have called into question the goals of global industrialization" (179). Aridjis puts forward no curative measures for this calamity. On the contrary, for the Mexico City of the near future it is too late. However, this is not to say that all is lost. Instead, nature is reborn once Western paradigms of progress and development run their course, ushering civilization to its apocalyptic end.

One of the more compelling points made in these novels pertains to how nature's collapse leads to the erosion of society. Consistent through both stories, social decay is measured in terms of the widespread violence against Mexico City's most vulnerable, primarily the street children who are sold to the sex trade or to the black market for the extraction and sale of vital organs. Such depravity accentuates both the looming insecurity of dystopia and the hubris of political tyranny. Ruthless power is wielded by President Huitzilopochtli of the timeless PRI—satirized as the PRC, "Partido Revolucionario de la Corrupción"[10]—and by police chief General Tezcatlipoca. As their names suggest, they are, in essence, wicked Aztec gods who battle one another for supremacy, indifferent to the resultant upheavals. Hyperbole gives this dystopia a satirical tone, evoking a seemingly fatalistic attitude toward the mainstays of political corruption, violence, and overpopulation. To attest to a culture on the wane, bereft of any humane values, marginalized children are showcased on dystopia's front lines, depicted in an array of atrocities within public view and juxtaposed with familiar landmarks. The faceless, nameless multitude ambles on, leaving its footprints in the freshly fallen ash, apathetic to injustice and to their city on the brink of collapse, "not because of natural disasters, but rather, the inept and corrupt hand of man" (Aridjis, *La leyenda* 143).[11] In the reckless haste to industrialize, Mexico has ironically created living conditions that regress to colonial times, illustrating that, in developing countries, economic globalization proves counterproductive. Infrastructure is derelict and sewage runs through streets lit by torches during perpetual blackouts. Even language bears the mark of digression, Americanized to a Spanglish that accommodates the market economy.

Posited throughout this inauspicious portrayal of the future, frequent references to an environmental crisis corroborate the argument that when nature perishes, culture follows. Humankind's vital bond to nature is staged at the opening of *The Legend* when the protagonist, Juan de Góngora, perceives that the "gradual loss of earth, air, and water around him was the loss of his own self" (17).¹² Pollution becomes the next generation's natural habitat. The sky has taken on a life of its own, like a toxic grey amoeba, and the only rain that falls is ash and metallic particles, requiring a new vocabulary to describe the smog that has permanently replaced weather patterns: "Here people used to talk about the February dust storms, the downpours in May, October's moon and the chills of December. Now they were talking about floating particles, thermal inversions, and ozone concentrations" (42).¹³ Air pollution has reached a critical extreme but the water crisis is worse yet. In both novels, the city is portrayed as a suffering body dying of thirst, and, to underscore modernity's failure to manage this vital resource, the misery of millions without water is contrasted to the earthly paradise of ancient Tenochtitlán, a veritable Atlantis in the eyes of the astonished conquistadors, a city floating on water. The reader witnesses this vision vicariously through Juan de Góngora, who, unlike the automaton masses, remembers that his environment "had not always been that unbreathable immensity that made your eyes water and scratched your throat but rather, a luminous valley covered with glimmering lakes and ever-lasting greenery" (15).¹⁴ Ultimately, that a city once permeated by fresh water should suffer such devastating drought where the only flow is raw sewage incites a "vile reminiscence of what was once the Venice of the Americas" (19).¹⁵

Environmental catastrophe is thus the central conflict against which Aridjis deploys the common dystopian motif of an ancient manuscript that, though unlikely to resolve the conflict, promises to shed light on its origins. Guided by the descendant of *Coatlicue* (Aztec goddess), if Juan de Góngora can recover the missing page of the codex and decipher its archaic signs, then the past may reveal itself in order to illuminate the future. By weighing this mythological intrigue—coupled with sporadic dialogues in Náhuatl¹⁶—against the modern city, Aridjis generates a poignant contrast that polarizes our perception of a pre-colonial utopia brutally destroyed by a post-colonial dystopia. It is both a condemnation of Mexico's ambition to imitate Western models of progress and a mockery of the political elite's illusion that Mexico controls its own future. To challenge these assumptions, Aridjis envisions the natural world, presided over by primeval gods, as the real force at work behind Mexico's fate. By dispensing with the Aztecs' religious cosmology and their reverence of nature in order to abide instead by imperialist hegemony, what Mexico has achieved is nothing more than the acceleration of its own annihilation. Accordingly, Aridjis brings his moralizing tale to an unambiguous denouement. Destroyed by an earthquake,

Mexico City lies in ruins while, sacred and symbolic, the city's sister volcanoes, Popocatépetl and Iztac Cíhuatl, reappear on the horizon as the shroud of contaminated skies begins to lift.

Ever the environmentalist, early in the sequel—*Who Do You Think of When Making Love?*—Aridjis stages a cameo appearance for the now iconic monarch butterfly: "I hadn't seen them since my childhood. Disoriented, they flew among the graves and dead trees, perhaps in search of water. One of them, like the survivor of a biological extinction, a ghost from migrations past, out of place and time, lit in María's hair" (25).[17] There is, however, no water to be found. As mentioned earlier, the sequel runs concurrently with the first story, foregrounding the same environmental woes. The "One day without a car" initiative is replaced in 2027 with a "One day without breathing" (200)[18] program: a sardonic about-face from the earlier efforts to reduce motor vehicle emissions. As in the first novel, indigenous children linger in the background of the toxic metropolis as easy targets for sexual exploitation or extermination by police brigades responsible for ridding the city of undesirables. There are frequent references to rape and the child sex trade as evidence that the devaluation of the peso has ushered in an equal measure of "human devaluation" (228).[19] Here, again, Aridjis overlaps nature's collapse with society's ensuing debauchery and collective state of alienation. This correlation is brought to the fore by the protagonist's own estrangement from the natural world of the past: "In many parts of the nation they were declaring environmental emergencies that were becoming permanent.... I felt defenseless against the onerous fantasy of our age, defenseless against that heartless sprawl that was replacing the world of my ancestors, and forming a strange reality where familiar objects slowly became the cold inventions of some anonymous technology" (179).[20] It is indeed this sense of anonymity that renders globalization unassailable to any opposition. Thus, unlike the rebellious protagonist from *The Legend*, "Yo Sánchez" remains submissive, resigned to a dystopian fate: "I'm an urban animal, uprooted from nature, that breathes polluted air and drinks contaminated water, and that's how I'll die" (165).[21]

If, in the first novel, it is the contrasting Aztec imagery of Tenochtitlán that stands dystopia in relief, here, in the sequel, the more prominent technique is via simulacrum: dystopia's feeble attempt to mask an impending doom. For instance, the ubiquitous "Circe"—a system of interactive telescreens—has effectively steered attention away from the local crises.[22] Broadcasting "the happiest times of our History"[23] (188), the screen "had converted human beings into thinking pigs [who] pass the hours and the years asleep with their eyes open, devouring the images and sounds" (176).[24] Life experience is thus replaced by electronic sensation. Nature, too, is simulated throughout the city, concealing the ecocide with plastic trees, and with rubber dolphins swimming in artificial lakes. They are dystopia's synthetic surrogate for Mother Nature. And to emulate prosperity, historic buildings are demolished so that props inspired by more modern cities can be erected in their stead. Once again, language, the very essence of cultural identity, conforms to economic pressures, as citizens are prompted to learn to "speak correctly [at the] Spanglish School" (235).[25] Clearly, the impetus behind these new values stems from Mexico's commitment to imitate progress, and to project the facade of a productive integration into the global economy. As expected, to accentuate the country's moral failings, only the novel's protagonists perceive the perverse contradictions of Mexico's admission into the new world order, leading them to question the validity of erasing the sacred past in the interest of pursuing economic growth: "we've replaced the high priests with accountants, the shamans with economists, the wizards with lawyers" (218).[26] Finally, the seismic tremors that ripple through the sequel, like an aftershock from the previous novel, culminate in the same catastrophic earthquake. It is the end of the fifth sun, and of Mexico City. As in the first novel, the destruction of dystopia heralds the era of the sixth sun, and the rebirth of nature, bringing this dystopian duet to a dramatic and eco-critical close. Confused by the fiery blaze of destruction, birds long absent from the dystopian metropolis return to the setting and begin to sing, mistaking the crimson glow of the apocalypse for the breaking of a new dawn.

The Sun, the Moon, and Walmart

Thus, Aridjis' novels evidence a predominant theme of the Mexican dystopia: the disownment of the parents of today's Mexico, who have sold out to foreign investment, and the replacement of them with indigenous ancestry conjured from the distant past. Dystopian fiction, by its nature, is a vehicle of social criticism designed to disturb, but not necessarily to set forth any solutions. The sacred indigenous past is evoked not to augur hope for what Mexico could be but, rather, to parody what it has become. Though the countercultural discourse of indigenous ethics may hold a tempting moral appeal inasmuch as it implies a superior, ecology-based set of guiding principles, at no point do these dystopian novels digress into the realms of the New Age or Neopagan movements that advocate a *tabula rasa* return to nature and to indigenous ways. In his 1971 treatise *Tiempo mexicano*, Carlos Fuentes concluded plainly on this point, "imposible Quetzalcóatl, indeseable Pepsicóatl" (39), meaning that a return to indigenous culture under the god Quetzalcóatl is simply impossible. Nevertheless, a culture grounded in consumer values that worships the almighty dollar, presided over by Pepsicóatl, is equally undesirable. If the following, more recent Walmart scandal at Teotihuacán is any indication, then Mexico can only expect a protraction of Pepsicóatl's imperious reign.

This scandal is an example of the immediate context that is presaged in Aridjis' texts. The year 2027, the setting of his dystopian novels, is not a random projection. According to the Aztec calendar, 2027 marks the next pilgrimage to Teotihuacán—an archaeological site located fifty kilometres north of Mexico City—for the ritualistic relighting of fires to pay tribute to the sun. In 2004, however, Teotihuacán came under the spotlight as the meeting place, not for religious ceremonies, but for commercial pursuits. In spite of zoning laws, widespread news coverage, and public outcry, Walmart de México succeeded in opening a store within the protected archaeological zone of what the Aztecs called "the city of the gods," not far from the stately Pyramids of the Sun and Moon. Such a brazen violation of indigenous patrimony raised the ire of protesters on both sides of the border, frustrated with the deference shown by local officials to the commercial giant. Residents also bemoaned the encroachment of U.S. consumer values, "united by a fear that Wal-Mart was inexorably drawing Mexico's people away from the intimacy of neighborhood life, toward a bland, impersonal 'gringo lifestyle' of frozen pizzas, video games and credit card debt" (Barstow and von Bertrab 18). Regrettably, even in ancient Teotihuacán, poor Mexico remains so far from the gods, and so close to the United Sates. The message here is unnervingly clear: if Walmart can build at Teotihuacán, it can build anywhere.

In his op-ed piece, "The Sun, the Moon and Walmart," Aridjis, who is accustomed to being offered bribes and/or death threats whenever his environmental campaigns thwart the advance of big business, argues that corruption from inside the system is as much to blame as external factors. Free trade agreements may attract multinational companies to Mexico, but it is internal corruption that allows them to break the rules once they get there. Such is the case with the multiple Walmart scandals in Mexico, involving an estimated total value of $24 million in bribes for fraudulent building permits (Aridjis, "The Sun, the Moon and Walmart" 1). It is a challenge to imagine how even the most staunch adherents to global neo-liberalism might spin the scenario at Teotihuacán into anything resembling progress. Nevertheless, there is an inherent contradiction in the notion of progress itself that Aridjis calls to our attention. It stems from a view of history as teleological, as a steady advance toward an improved final cause. Conversely, Aridjis' novels, informed by Aztec history, remind us that, like the laws of nature, mythological time is cyclical, not linear, and that the indigenous legacy of mythology is inextricable from Mexico's future. For this reason, the dystopian city that encroaches on nature and marginalizes indigenous peoples supposedly to liberate Mexicans through economic development must be sacrificed so that a new generation, imbued with an environmental conscience, can take its place.

Notes

1 The Group of 100 was founded by Aridjis in 1985. It consists of prominent artists and intellectuals devoted to environmental protection in Mexico and throughout Latin America. Under Aridjis' leadership, they have succeeded in legislating protection for sea turtles, grey whales, and wildlife sanctuaries. Also owing to their efforts, stricter regulations were implemented to reduce motor vehicle emissions in Mexico City.
2 The CEC (Commission for Environmental Cooperation) is headquartered in Montreal, and operates in Canada, Mexico, and the United States.
3 The Mexican Revolution was a decade-long civil war that began in 1910. Its most notable figures include the dictator Porfírio Díaz—whose thirty-five years of rule are referred to as the "Porfiriato"—and the two revolutionaries: Pancho Villa and Emiliano Zapata.
4 The 1917 Constitution abolished the colonial *encomienda*, a feudal structure of land holdings. Under the *ejido* system, land was expropriated from *haciendas* (landed estates) by the Mexican government, and allocated to peasant farmers for communal use.
5 The "maquiladora belt" refers to the assembly plants or in-bound factories situated on the Mexican side of the United States border. Maquiladoras were developed originally in the 1960s from a Border Industrialization Program but can now be found throughout Mexico.
6 The Revolution gave rise to the Mexican Constitution of 1917, and the Partido Revolucionario Institucional (Institutional Revolutionary Party) known more commonly as the "PRI," that held power until the general election of 2000.
7 The phrase "race to the bottom" refers to the current socio-economic trend whereby governments of developing countries reduce labour and environmental standards in the interest of attracting the business of multinational companies.

8 Only the novels by Fuentes and Morales are available in English. The titles of the novels by Aridjis and Boullosa (cited in this study) are translations. Their Spanish titles are *La leyenda de los soles* (1993) and *¿En quién piensas cuando haces el amor?* (1995) by Aridjis; and *Cielos de la Tierra* by Boullosa.
9 "La tarea de los poetas y hombres santos es contar las historias de este planeta y expresar una cosmología ecológica que no separe a la naturaleza de la humanidad."
10 "Partido Revolucionario de la Corrupción" translates as the "Revolutionary Party of Corruption."
11 "ruinas contemporáneas no producidas por los desastres naturales sino por la mano inepta y corrupta del hombre."
12 "la pérdida gradual de suelo, de aire y de agua a su alrededor era la pérdida de su propio yo."
13 "Antes aquí las gentes platicaban de las tolvaneras de febrero, de los aguaceros de mayo, de la luna de octubre y de los fríos de diciembre, ahora hablan de las partículas suspendidas, de las inversiones térmicas y de las concentraciones de ozono."
14 "ésta no siempre había sido esa inmensidad irrespirable que hacía llorar los ojos y raspaba la garganta, sino un valle luminoso cubierto de lagos resplandecientes y verdores inmarcesibles."
15 "reminiscencias viles de lo que un día fue la Venecia americana."
16 The language of the Aztecs, Náhuatl, along with its variations, is spoken today by over a million Nahua people, who live primarily in central Mexico.
17 "No las veía desde mi infancia. Desorientadas anduvieron entre las tumbas y los árboles muertos, quizás en busca de agua. Una de ellas, como sobreviviente de la extinción biológica y como fantasma de migraciones pasadas, fuera de lugar y de tiempo, se posó en el pelo de María."
18 "Hoy no circula" and "Hoy no Respire."
19 "las devaluaciones humanas"
20 "En muchas partes de la nación se declaraban emergencias ambientales que se convertían en permanentes. . . . Yo me sentía inerme ante la fantasía abrumadora de mi época, inerme ante ese orbe desalmado que suplantaba el mundo de mis ancestros y conformaba una realidad ajena en donde los objetos familiares se convertían poco a poco en las invenciones frías de una tecnología anónima."
21 "Soy un animal urbano, desarraigado de la naturaleza, que respira aire contaminado y bebe agua poluta, y así moriré."
22 The son of a Greek father and Mexican mother, Aridjis' interest in ancient worlds also extends to Greek mythology, hence the reference to "Circe," the enchantress who could transform her enemies into animals.
23 "Los tiempos más alegres de la Historia."

24 "la Circe de la Comunicación había convertido a los seres humanos en puercos mentales. El prójimo puto y caníbal pasaba las horas y los años dormido con los ojos abiertos devorando las imágenes y los sonidos."
25 "Speak con Propiedad: Escuela de Spanglish."
26 "Hemos reemplazado a los sacerdotes por los contadores, a los chamanes por los economistas, a los magos por los licenciados."

Works Cited

Aridjis, Homero. *¿En quién piensas cuando haces el amor?* Mexico D.F.: Alfaguara, 1995. Print.

———. *La leyenda de los soles*. Mexico D.F.: Fondo de Cultura Económica, 1993. Print.

———. "The Sun, the Moon and Walmart." *New York Times* 30 April 2012: 1–3. Web. 17 Apr. 2013.

Barstow, David, and Alejandra Xanic von Bertrab. "How Wal-Mart Used Payoffs to Get Its Way in Mexico." *New York Times* 17 Dec. 2012: 1–21. Web. 17 Apr. 2013.

Booker, M. Keith. *The Dystopian Impulse in Modern Literature: Fiction as Social Criticism*. Westport: Greenwood, 1994. Print.

Boullosa, Carmen. *Cielos de la Tierra*. Mexico D.F.: Alfaguara, 1997. Print.

De Rivero, Oswaldo. *The Myth of Development: Non-Viable Economies and the Crisis of Civilization*. 2nd ed. London: Zed Books, 2010. Print.

Fuentes, Carlos. *Christopher Unborn*. Trans. Alfred MacAdam. New York: Farrar, Straus and Giroux, 1989. Print.

———. *Tiempo mexicano*. Mexico D.F.: Editorial Joaquín Mortiz, 1971. Print.

Huxley, Aldous. *Brave New World*. Middlesex: Penguin, 1960 [1932]. Print.

López-Lozano, Miguel. *Utopian Dreams, Apocalyptic Nightmares: Globalization in Recent Mexican and Chicano Narrative*. West Lafayette: Purdue UP, 2008. Print.

Martí, José. "Our America." *The America of José Martí*. Trans. Juan de Onís. New York: Noonday, 1968. 138–152. Print.

Morales, Alejandro. *The Rag Doll Plagues*. Houston: Arte Publico, 1992. Print.

Orwell, George. *Nineteen Eighty-Four*. Middlesex: Penguin, 1954 [1949]. Print.

Roberts, J. Timmons, and Nikki Demetria Thanos. *Trouble in Paradise: Globalization and Environmental Crises in Latin America*. New York: Routledge, 2003. Print.

Russell, Dick. "Homero Aridjis y la ecología." *La luz queda en el aire: Estudios internacionales en torno a Homero Aridjis*. Ed. Thomas Stauder. Frankfurt: Vervuert Verlag, 2005. 65–81. Print.

Zamyatin, Yevgeny. *We*. Ed. Michael Glenny. London: Jonathan Cape, 1970 [1924]. Print.

PART IV
Emancipating Genres

Lost in Grand Central
Dystopia and Transgression in Neil Gaiman's American Gods

Robert T. Tally, Jr.

> Shadows present, foreshadowing deeper shadows to come.
> —Herman Melville, *"Benito Cereno"*

Dystopia never appears all at once. One does not stumble upon the "bad place" out of the blue, like an island in the middle of the sea. Rather, one slowly apprehends that she or he has been living there all along. Famously, some dystopias emerge from the attempts to form some sort of utopian society (as in the notorious visions of Yevgeny Zamyatin's *We*, George Orwell's *Nineteen-Eighty-Four*, or Aldous Huxley's *Brave New World*), but more often the dystopian aura envelops a reality that has simply proceeded along in its quotidian ways. One goes about one's everyday life and work, while as time passes noting this or that odd occurrence that might be a sign; a creeping suspicion evolves toward certainty, a gloomy presentiment congeals into visible shape, and dystopia appears, right here and right now, where it has been for a while. Like a shadow, suggestive of simultaneous absence and presence, the gathering darkness of dystopia colours our perception of the world, even when we cannot be sure it is really there at all.

If "dystopia became the dominant literary form" of the twentieth century (Sargent 29), it is at least partly because of a pervasive dystopian mood or anxiety that increased its momentum throughout that era. By the beginning of the 1990s, in the United States as elsewhere, clouds congregated on the horizon, and the final decade of the twentieth century brought with it a deep sense of foreboding and unease. The triumphal rhetoric that accompanied the "end of the Cold War," spectacularly represented by the fall of the

Berlin Wall in December 1989, was inflated by the optative mood of early criers for a "borderless world" of free trade, globalization, and multiculturalism (see Ohmae, for example). At the same time, however, these very victories appeared to augur greater calamity, as the aftermath of the crumbling Soviet Bloc brought not only new freedoms but intense sectarian violence, war, even genocide; the economic *glasnost* and burgeoning world market provided hitherto unimagined productivity and wealth, but also bred greater economic instability, transforming communities and restructuring world views. If the industrial age had already created the conditions under which "all that is solid melts into air, all that is holy is profaned, and man is at last compelled to face with sober sense his real conditions of life and his relations with his kind" (Marx and Engels 207), then the postmodern moment of multinational capitalism and global finance in the final years of the twentieth century compounded this situation immeasurably. This generalized unease and social malaise characterized the public mood during the debates over the passage of the North American Free Trade Agreement (NAFTA) in the early 1990s, as the promise of fluid, cross-border movements of goods and services was necessarily tempered by a nameless fear of the radical, likely unforeseeable transformations such free trade would engender or entail.

Neil Gaiman's 2001 fantasy novel *American Gods*[1] explores the sorts of anxieties that typify the NAFTA era. *American Gods* offers a portrait of "U.S. Culture in the Long Nineties" (to use Phillip Wegner's phrase in *Life Between Two Deaths, 1989–2001*), and it dramatizes the era's dystopian atmosphere by highlighting the role of transgression or transgressivity: movement, border-crossing, illicitness, and indeterminate danger. Although most readers would place *American Gods* in the genre of fantasy, rather than utopian or dystopian literature, Gaiman's use of the fantastic mode—more specifically, his blend of fantasy and realism—helps to vivify the dystopian narrative in the novel.[2] Gaiman's fantasy thus provides a more visceral, though less overt critique of the contemporary scene, while also maintaining a pervading spirit of ambiguity and vague menace. The ominous suspicion of a potential conspiracy amplifies the unease, and the inability to map the shifting landscape and one's place in it becomes the most persistent form of existential anxiety for North Americans at the end of the millennium. In *American Gods*, the dystopian moment of the post-NAFTA United States is illustrated in the transgressive movement of its tenebrous hero in his attempt to make sense of the "bad place" he inhabits. In the conclusion of the narrative, the dystopian condition and the method by which to counteract it coalesce into a single conception, that of transgression itself.

As Hank Wagner, Christopher Golden, and Stephen R. Bissette argue in their *Prince of Stories: The Many Worlds of Neil Gaiman*, "*American Gods* is a novel that only Gaiman could have written.... The novel reflects his deep fascination with and love for his adopted country, but also subtly reflects its harshness, and strangeness, and flaws" (331). In an interview appended to the text of *American Gods*, Gaiman describes the tortuous paths he took in first conceiving, then writing the novel, which he labels "a contemporary American phantasmagoria." At that point, he is speaking strictly as a writer of imaginative fiction, and the twists and turns involve his many abortive attempts to create a protagonist (who will become Shadow), latch onto a novelistic concept, orchestrate multiple movements, flesh out the other characters, and so on. But pointedly, Gaiman's own peripatetic biography asserts itself in subtle ways in how he imagined this book. A descendant of Polish Jewry, whose ancestor emigrated to England from the Netherlands, Gaiman grew up in England, began his career in London,[3] and moved to Minnesota in 1992. In response to the question in the same interview of how his life and work have changed now that he lives in the United States, Gaiman refers to his early comic book series *The Sandman* and replies: "I wrote about America a lot in *Sandman*, but it was a slightly delirious America—one built up from movies and TV and other books. When I came out here I found it very different from the country I'd encountered in fiction, and wanted to write about that. *American Gods* was, in many ways, my attempt to make sense of the country I was living in" (n.p.). Even at this personal level, then, *American Gods* represents the perspective of the transgressor, the border-crosser, who moves into a foreign domain while retaining a hybrid identity (old and new, native and foreign, etc.). America appears as both a real and an imaginary place, or perhaps, in Edward Soja's appropriately hybridized notion, a *real-and-imagined* space (see *Thirdspace*, 11–12), in which the author represents both the mental and material spaces of the place simultaneously. *American Gods* is in some respects Gaiman's attempt to map the spaces of his newly adopted but still foreign territory: a stranger *at home* in a strange land.[4]

Such transgressivity animates the whole of *American Gods*, which is, if nothing else, a story of immigrants, border-crossers, travellers from afar. The foundational concept of the novel is that those people who immigrated to the United States brought their gods with them as they traversed oceans and national boundaries. Moreover, the old gods native to that North American soil remain, and Gaiman duly records aspects of Native American or First Nations myths and religions, as when Shadow encounters a deity like Whiskey Jack (Wisakedjak), the Buffalo Man, or the Thunderbird. What is more, the gods carried over by the transients and settlers are not necessarily the same as those left behind in their old worlds. In the novel's postscript, for instance, Shadow meets an Odin character rather different from the Wednesday he had worked for in the United States; these two (and many others, of course) are the "same" god, but they are also imbued with a different character specific to their current time and place. Such characteristics, like their powers *as* gods, derive from the force of belief on the part of those who worship them. A god is only as powerful as the belief in him or her that the faithful maintain, and "gods die once they are forgotten" (514).[5] Retaining many aspects of their immortal identities, these gods also take on new forms in the changing society; Cairo (pronounced "KAY-ro"), Illinois, home to several Nile Delta deities, is not Cairo, Egypt, after all. America, which one character claims "has been Grand Central for ten thousand years or more" (196), is a metaphysical free-trade zone in which fluid economies of belief alter the social landscape of the continent. Displaced from their native soil, put into circulation in a spiritual marketplace, subject to metaphysical competition from new and more powerful objects of faith, the gods experience a kind of perpetual crisis. Beliefs, like goods and services, are also subject to the vicissitudes of international trade.

It follows that, if the old gods are given life through the faith of their believers, new believers will engender new gods who will be nourished by the power of their adherents. In *American Gods*, we find a haughty cadre of young, powerful deities, some displaying open disdain for the ancient gods. The new American gods include "gods of credit card and freeway, of Internet and telephone, of radio and hospital and television, gods of plastic and of beeper and of neon. Proud gods, fat and foolish creatures, puffed up with their own newness and importance" (137–38). A large part of the drama in *American Gods* comes down to a putative war between the old and the new gods, between gods on the brink of extinction, eking out some meager existence at the furthest margins of their former glory (like poor Bilquis, Queen of Sheba, whose erotic powers are reduced to the prostitute's wiles in the quest for worshippers), and those thrilling to the ecstatic rush of their novel and seemingly limitless power (like the gods of television and computers). Upon this unstable ground, the apparent plot of *American Gods* unfolds.

And, yet, this is not really the main narrative in the novel. Rather, as is hinted at by the many coin-tricks and confidence games in the text, the metaphysical war is a diversion, a sleight-of-hand ploy to distract attention from the much more powerfully dystopian theme in the novel. *American Gods* is a fable of transgression, and transgressivity is eventually disclosed to be not only the state of things in the dystopian, end-of-the-millennium United States, but also the means by which to navigate the spaces of dystopia. America, which in so much of its nationalist ideology, going all the way back to the earliest settlements, had been conceived as a utopia, is fundamentally dystopian. In *American Gods*, the state of transgressivity within the United States is a dialectical reversal of the utopian prospects of transgressive movements across porous national and social boundaries. With its tenebrous hero Shadow winding his way around the continental United States on his odyssey to find himself, the novel's mood is anxious and foreboding, consistent with Peter Fitting's view that the dystopian mood is "a sense of a threatened near future" (140), but without the science fiction projection of a future tense at all. *American Gods* is set very much in the present, and the otherworldly aspects of that present are not technological but, in the language of Darko Suvin, metaphysical (Suvin 61). But the dystopian mood is quite fitting as the action seems to be leading up to Ragnarök, the *Götterdämmerung*, and the final doom of all creation. Amid the gloom, the utopian impulse to carve out new spaces of liberty unfolds as a dystopian confrontation between the new and old, which reveals the country to be "a bad place for gods" (586). "Bad place" is, after all, what the very word *dystopia* means, but the dystopia in *American Gods* will have more to do with the movements of the shadows than with the twilight of the gods.

American Gods is ultimately about transgression. The word has, from its Latin root, the meaning of a "step across" and a specifically spatial sense. As Bertrand Westphal notes in *Geocriticism*, "Among the Romans, one transgressed when passing to the other side of a boundary or a river.... The *transgressio* could also be an infraction: one does not cross a boundary without departing from the norm. But the Romans did not give priority to that sense of the word" (41–42). The foundational conceit of *American Gods* (i.e., that gods and legends accompany their believers who cross into new territories) requires this image of transgression, and the primary narrative trajectory, Shadow's circuitous travels that ultimately lead him to his own identity, repeatedly enacts Shadow's boundary-crossing. However, the more modern meaning, with its moral valences, is also pertinent. Not only is Shadow a shady figure (ahem) with a criminal past, engaged in continuing illicit activity in abetting Wednesday's swindles, but the narrative's generalized lawlessness, the sense that all characters are somehow operating outside or only on the margins of the national *nomos*, and the almost constant allusions to trickery, illusion, and deception, mark *American Gods* as a transgressive text in even the less than literal sense. Indeed, most transgressive of all is the novel's clever insinuation that transgressivity is itself an essential constitutive feature of America, the grounds upon which dystopia discloses itself as dystopian. Shadow's transcontinental itinerary merely traces some of the contours of the transgressive space that is the dystopian United States at the end of the twentieth century.

The novel announces its theme of transgression from the start. In the opening pages, the protagonist is completing his prison sentence, time served for a crime he most certainly did commit, so the commonplace definition of transgression is established as a theme even before Shadow's peripatetic movements begin. He is released from prison early because his wife has died; as he discovers later, she died in a car crash while performing a sex act upon Shadow's best friend and business partner, as the "transgressions" begin to pile up in the novel. (His wife proves more faithful in the liminal, living-death existence she maintains after her funeral, as she frequently comes to his aid throughout the narrative.) With no one to return home to, he agrees to work for a mysterious stranger he meets on an airplane, a Mr. Wednesday, who we soon discover is Odin, the All-Father of Norse mythology. True to the multiple meanings of *transgression*, Shadow follows Wednesday as he engages in a series of illegal or morally questionable activities, all while travelling to different places to meet with odd persons (who are themselves the avatars of various deities). These movements are punctuated by a few layovers in which Shadow is able to pause, and the reader is able to gain greater insight into the overall scheme of things. First, in his time with the Egyptian deities (working as undertakers) in Cairo, Illinois, Shadow discovers the breadth and depth of the metaphysical free-trade zone that is North America. Then, in the town of Lakeside, Wisconsin, Shadow experiences a sort of utopian space outside of the flows of commerce and history; in the end, he discovers the dark secret behind the town's timelessness and resistance to change. Finally, in his suspension—literally, as he is hanging by ropes from the World Tree—between life and death, Shadow discovers his own origins and identity, and prepares himself (and the reader) for the final conflict between the new and old gods, a battle that turns out to be little more than an elaborately orchestrated confidence game. At the conclusion of this apocalyptic ruse, Shadow returns to Lakeside, where he helps to return that anomalous site to the spatiotemporal flux of American dystopia, before eventually moving on farther, "transgressing" beyond those national borders, to Iceland, and thence... beyond.

An additional, fascinating feature of *American Gods* is its use of brief interludes labelled "Coming to America" or "Somewhere in America," which depict scenes of immigrants and their gods finding and, in some respects, creating themselves in the New World spaces. We learn that Mr. Ibis, the Egyptian deity and Illinois undertaker, is the author of these vignettes. In addition to breaking up the narrative trajectory of Shadow's journey, these scenes (most of which do not bear directly or at all on that plotline) help to populate the American world with gods, legends, and folkloric figures, as well as showing the ways in which strangers in this strange land long for the connections to their ancient gods even as they experience the wonders of a brave new world. Yet the punctual interventions that these episodes provide help to colour the entire world of *American Gods*, demonstrating both the ongoing desire for an evanescing tradition and the transformative force of movement and displacement. The dystopia of America is thus tied to its utopian aspects. In "Coming to America," the horrors of transgression, of crossing over the borders, are mitigated by the old spirits, but a new god—first and foremost, the mythical entity that is "America" itself—tortures the past and shapes it into something barely recognizable. In these "Coming to America" passages, the admixture of transgression and dystopia is dramatized, and the reader's pause in these moments makes the headlong rush of the Shadow narrative more meaningful.

"This country has been Grand Central for ten thousand years or more" (196). Early in the book Mr. Ibis, who provides so much background information to Shadow and to the reader, asserts the astonishing proposition that voyagers over several millennia have travelled to and around North America, leaving their remains and establishing their gods upon this new soil. According to Ibis, the city of Cairo, Illinois, was once a trading post, visited by people of the Nile Delta over 3,500 years ago. Indeed, a kind of free trade is the basis for all of these improbable—Ibis calls them "impossible"—voyages to America, which include those of the aboriginal race of Japan, the Ainu, 9,000 years ago, of Polynesians to California two millennia later, of the Irish during the Dark Ages, of the Welsh and the Vikings, of West

African traders in South America, of Chinese adventurers exploring the Oregon coastline, of Basque fishermen tending their nets off the coast of Newfoundland in the eighth century, and so on. The primitive conditions of transoceanic travel were no impediment. As Ibis continues in his lecture, "My people, the Nile folk, we discovered that a reed boat will take you around the world, if you have the patience and enough jars of sweet water" (198). What mattered was not technology or transportation, but goods and services to trade. "You see, the biggest problem with coming to America in the old days was that there wasn't a lot here that anyone wanted to trade" (198). But after Columbus, so the story goes, the traffic within this Grand Central becomes heavier, as the North American trade zone expands. With all this movement and circulation, the long-hidden dystopian character of place creeps into view as well.

As another incarnation of Odin notes late in the novel, America "is a good place for men, but a bad place for gods" (586). There are several reasons why this may be, and one lies in the formulation itself. If it is a "good place" (or *eutopia*) for humans, then it may be because America favours the present, the material, the novel, the living, and the mortal; as visitors have long known, whether Alexis de Tocqueville or Jean Baudrillard, Americans have little open regard for the traditions of the past, the intellectual sphere, or—notwithstanding (or, perhaps, owing to) the profoundly potent forms of religious observance and zeal—matters of spirit. These play small roles in the public spaces of the national culture in the United States, although, as its literature frequently reveals, such ideas become quite powerful in the dream world of America. *American Gods* also makes great use of dreams, as omens, portents, or merely vistas into times and places not always available to the waking mind. The shadowy and liminal sphere of that space between conscious thought and unconscious flows provides yet another figure of transgression in *American Gods*.

Another reason why America may be a "bad place" (or *dystopia*) for gods is that "America" is itself a kind of religious artifact, a totem or myth, an imaginary construct that natives and immigrants alike must imbue with divine substance and bow down before. Whether in the old Puritan rhetoric of the "city on a hill" or a New Jerusalem, or in the providential decree of a Manifest Destiny, or even more strongly perhaps in a twentieth-century America as a utopian space of freedom in a world beset by totalitarianism or terror, the entity known as "America" becomes something to be "believed in" (see Tally). As far back as 1693, Cotton Mather suggested that the early pilgrims had hoped to find Thomas More's Utopia, but ended up creating one instead, and this vision colours the national rhetoric even in the twenty-first century. Indeed, even the critics of United States policies often launch their criticism from this quasi-religious and utopian view of America as a place of freedom, bemoaning the "fact" that America is not living up to its purported mission. What gods could be more powerful than this mythic, national deity who can unite all parties arrayed along its political spectrum under this divine banner? In this, the utopianism of America is also its most dystopian feature, as the dissatisfaction with a failure to be utopia is felt more strongly than anything else.

Thus, in its own somewhat apolitical way, *American Gods* launches its own critique of the condition of the United States' national identity as a technological and political pseudo-utopia, one that welds together individual freedom, economic opportunity, and collective harmony. Shadow's apparent disgust with several of the new gods (such as the god of television, who appears as Lucille Ball in *I Love Lucy* and offers to show him "Lucy's tits" [176]) registers his indifference to these modern achievements that are supposed to make the New World superior to the Old. *American Gods* is not utopian, then, but it is not really anti-utopian either, and the distinction between dystopia and anti-utopia ought to be made. As many critics have argued, dystopia (rather like utopia, in fact) is fundamentally critical. Even in offering what seems an ambiguous or bleak image of the threatened near future, dystopian narratives are not really critiques of utopian schemes so much as critiques of the *status quo* itself. Often, in dystopian narratives, the future disaster is extrapolated from a present condition, and the critical edge of the text lies in its ability to identify and challenge the state of things. Fitting notes that the "critique of contemporary society expressed in the dystopia implies (or asserts) the need for change; the anti-utopia is, on the other hand, explicitly or implicitly a defense of the status quo" (141). Similarly, Tom Moylan has introduced the concept of "critical dystopia" to emphasize how, "[f]aced by the delegitimation of Utopia and the hegemonic cynicism of Anti-Utopia," certain recent dystopian texts "do not go easily toward that better world [of utopia]. Rather, they linger in the terrors of the present even as they exemplify what is needed to transform it" (Moylan 198–99). In *American Gods*, the dystopian mood of the millennial moment is suffused with a sense of movement and change, transgressions that simultaneous render the present both a "bad place" and a site of possibility.

Some readers might legitimately object that *American Gods* is not exactly a dystopian novel, and since it is not likely to be confused with utopian fiction either, the traditional association or binary opposition between utopia and dystopia is not entirely apt. However, Jameson's description of a key, categorical difference between the two genres indicates the degree to which *American Gods* might be called a dystopian text. Tacitly drawing upon Georg Lukács's distinction between narration and description, Jameson observes that "dystopia is generally a narrative, which happens to a specific subject or character, whereas the Utopian text is mostly nonnarrative." Jameson goes on to posit that, in general, whereas the utopian text "does not tell a story at all" but "describes a mechanism," "the dystopia is always and essentially what in the language of science fiction is called a 'near-future' novel: it tells the story of an imminent disaster—ecology, overpopulation, plague, drought, the stray comet or nuclear accident—waiting to come to pass in our own near future, which is fast-forwarded in the time of the novel" (*Seeds of Time* 56). Assiduously narrative even in its few descriptive scenes, *American Gods* certain fits the bill here, with Shadow's own personal story dominating the plot even as the broader depiction of a dystopian America at spiritual war provides the necessary context.

More fantasy than any other genre, Gaiman's novel enables the reader to detect a dystopian aura inherent in the otherworldly, yet real, America presented through Shadow's tale.[6] Peter Paik, in his exploration of the apocalyptic science fiction of certain recent comic books or graphic novels, argues in part that the combination of realism and fantasy in such works makes possible a clearer rendering of the dystopian conditions of the present moment and offers the possibility of imagining other conditions. "It is perhaps only such a fantastic realism that is at present capable of opening up a critical space for reflection between the alternatives of an enlightened obedience to a devouring and deteriorating beast and a headlong embrace of fate that masquerades as a godlike freedom" (Paik 22). Gaiman's fantastic realism in *American Gods*, while not as openly political as that employed in many other dystopian texts, nevertheless clears room for this "critical space for reflection" of the shifting social relations of the late-1990s' United States.

The events in Lakeside, Wisconsin, offer one allegorical example. After the apparently climactic scene at Rock City, Shadow returns to Lakeside to uncover the town's secret. From time immemorial, each year a child had gone missing, and it is presumed that many are runaways or possibly victims of kidnapping. Shadow discovers the terrible connection between such a regular misfortune and the annual "klunker" raffle, where everyone in town participates in guessing the date and time in which an old car will break through the melting ice and fall to the bottom of the lake. In each klunker's trunk, a dead child sinks beneath the water annually, in what amounts to a macabre ritual. Hinzelmann, the old man in charge of the raffle, turns out to be an Old World kobold, a totemic spirit who re-enacts the yearly child-sacrifice in order to protect the town. Hinzelmann had hinted that the "good town" survived the insidious advances of economic turbulence through "hard work" (277), but in the end Shadow sees how this tiny utopian space was artificially created by a magic that, with Hinzelmann's death, no longer has power. As he tells Lakeside's police chief, "this town is going to change now. It's not going to be the only good town in a depressed region anymore. It's going to be a lot more like the rest of this part of the world. There's going to be a lot more trouble. People out of work. People out of their heads. More people getting hurt. More bad shit going down" (573). In other words, Lakeside will re-enter history, re-enter the late-twentieth-century's post-NAFTA world of economic uncertainty and dystopia.

A one-man (or one-kobold) scheme is not exactly a conspiracy, but the idea of some well-organized and often nefarious conspiracy to explain how all of these odd and threatening circumstances came to be is itself of pervasive feature of the late twentieth century. In addition to the diffuse millenarian paranoia, the old-fashioned fears of one-world governments and Big Brother accompanied some of the louder, if marginal, debates over the passage of NAFTA in 1994, for example. The idea that the mysteriously swirling, seemingly unfathomable conditions affecting our everyday lives may be explicable in terms of some conspiracy is a paradoxically comforting thought. If nothing else, the vast conspiracy would explain the inexplicable, putting a face, albeit an evil face, on the vague insecurities. *American Gods* is also suffused with various notions of false consciousness, if not in the strictly ideological sense, then in the more diffuse meaning attached to discovering that one is being "fooled." Illusions permeate the text, whether in the form of Shadow's good-natured sleight-of-hand magic and coin tricks, Wednesday's petty cons or his larger "two-man con" executed with the aid of Low Key (or Loki), or the menacing "men in black" agents of those vicious new gods. Of these latter mysterious figures, with names like Wood, Stone, Town, and World, the goddess Easter (or Eostre) explains: "They exist because everyone knows they must exist" (309). As Jameson has suggested in reference to conspiracy films, such a grand scheme may be one of the few ways in which individuals can imagine the global totality that is now the horizon of their existence; conspiracy then functions as a kind of allegorical or cognitive map by which individuals can imagine collective action at all (see Jameson, *The Geopolitical Aesthetic*). In *American Gods*, the elaborate confidence game pulled off by Wednesday and Loki is revealed in the end as a means of explaining Shadow's entire life, but this is also the moment at which he both fulfills his destiny and moves on. Again, the dystopia is transgressive, in both positive and negative senses.

Shadow himself, as well as the image of the shadow more generally, becomes the indistinct but defining feature of the transgressive dystopia in *American Gods*. Shadow is a liminal figure, assiduously occupying a space *in-between*, straddling presence and absence, here and there, life and death, and so forth. As in Herman Melville's deliberately ambiguous deconstruction of the black-and-white narrative in "Benito Cereno," the shadows (which are, after all, a mixture of black and white) only foreshadow deeper shadows to come. The conclusion of *American Gods* does not offer a clean victory for one side over the other, since the entire battle was a complicated con. Shadow in the final pages continues his wanderings, now in Reykjavik, where he does not really intend to stay, but nor does he intend to return to America or to go to some other particular place. The novel's final line—"He walked away and he kept on walking" (588)—suggests further transgression, perpetual motion, but no fixed state.

Movement, displacement, relocation, translation, and above all transgression provide the conceptual underpinnings of the dystopian phantasmagoria that is *American Gods*. As I have argued, the transgressive dystopia of *American Gods* is also positive, insofar as transgressivity itself becomes the *status quo*. This is certainly not the *eutopian* state of happiness, nor is it a *outopian* or nonexistent no-place. Rather, it is the "bad place" in which we move, struggle, and live. The state of transgressivity, which is also the state of dystopia, is the condition of our historical being itself, and no otherworldly Ragnarök can impose celestial meaning upon things. The shadowy, inconclusive or open-ended ending allows for mere continuation or radical changes with no discernible clue, beyond Shadow's own personal revelations, of the new America about to emerge in the next millennium. The metaphysical free trade zone of "Grand Central" continues unabated, presumably, and the cosmopolitan Shadow continues his uncertain wandering. *American Gods* leaves us in the dystopia we were already in, but in the novel's attention to the transgressivity, both a distinctive feature of the

American dystopia and a means of understanding and thereby also transforming it, perhaps, we see that other spaces are not only still possible, but we are already shaping them by our border-crossing movements.

Notes

1. All references to *American Gods* are to the edition listed in the Works Cited. This essay was written prior to the publication of *American Gods: Tenth Anniversary Edition* in 2011.
2. Although all could be characterized as *fantasy* in a broad sense, Gaiman's novels range widely over various literary and marketing genres, partaking of both gritty realism and fanciful romance, and frequently operating within the subgenres of children's literature, horror, mystery, and so on. For instance, *Good Omens* (1990), co-authored with Terry Pratchett, was a comic end-of-the-world mystery, as a demon and an angel rush to avert Armageddon. *Neverwhere* (1996), which began life as a BBC miniseries before Gaiman turned his script into a novel, blends fairy-tale characters, such as Puss in Boots, with a somewhat realistic cityscape of present-day London. *Stardust* (1998) is an enchanting fairy tale in its own right. *American Gods* (2001) was followed by *Anansi Boys* (2005), a sort of sequel in that it is set in the same world, but which does not necessarily follow from the events of *American Gods*. His many children's books—although Gaiman does not always agree that they are meant for children exclusively—include *Coraline* (2002) and *The Graveyard Book* (2008), the latter a sort of reimagining of Rudyard Kipling's *The Jungle Book*, in which an orphaned child is raised by ghosts, rather than wild animals. Thus, although the fantastic *mode* pervades Gaiman's entire corpus, Gaiman's work resists generic pigeonholing.
3. Gaiman's early career reveals the breadth of his interests, as well as the rollercoasting fortunes of a would-be professional writer. His first books include a pop "biography" of the band Duran Duran, a critical study of Douglas Adams' *Hitchhiker's Guide to the Galaxy* series, and a co-authored work of comedic fantasy, *Good Omens* (with Terry Pratchett). Beginning in 1989, his immensely well-respected comic book series *The Sandman* began its run of seventy-five issues.
4. Gaiman includes, by way of preface, a "Caveat, and Warning for Travelers," in which he writes: "While the geography of the United States of America in this tale is not entirely imaginary—many of the landmarks in this book can be visited, paths can be followed, ways can be mapped—I have taken liberties. Fewer liberties than you might imagine, but liberties nonetheless" (n.p.).
5. The same principle is evident in a number of key intertexts, among which I mention only Terry Pratchett's *Small Gods*, where the more powerful the belief, the more powerful the god. In that novel, a formerly mighty deity is shocked to

discover himself almost utterly powerless, since—even though the society of his purported believers is essentially a theocracy—he has only one faithful follower.

6 In *Archaeologies of the Future*, Jameson makes the case for a clear distinction between fantasy and science fiction (or utopia), but I argue that the radical alterity of both enable similar critical programs, even where the methods are demonstrably different.

Works Cited

Fitting, Peter. "Utopia, Dystopia, and Science Fiction." *The Cambridge Companion to Utopian Literature*. Ed. Gregory Claeys. Cambridge: Cambridge UP, 2010. 135–53. Print.

Gaiman, Neil. *American Gods*. New York: Harper Perennial, 2001. Print.

Jameson, Fredric. *Archaeologies of the Future: The Desire Called Utopia and Other Science Fictions*. London: Verso, 2005. Print.

——. *The Geopolitical Aesthetic: Cinema and Space in the World-System*. Indianapolis and London: Indiana UP and the British Film Institute, 1992. Print.

——. *Postmodernism, or, the Cultural Logic of Late Capitalism*. Durham: Duke UP, 1990. Print.

——. *The Seeds of Time*. New York: Columbia UP, 1994. Print.

Marx, Karl, and Friedrich Engels. "The Manifesto of the Communist Party." *The Portable Karl Marx*. Ed. Eugene Kamenka. New York: Penguin, 1983. 203–41. Print.

Melville, Herman. "Benito Cereno." *The Piazza Tales and Other Prose Pieces, 1839–1860*. Ed. Harrison Hayford, Alma A. MacDougall, G. Thomas Tanselle, et al. Evanston and Chicago: Northwestern UP and the Newberry Library, 1987. 46–117. Print.

Moylan, Tom. *Scraps of the Untainted Sky: Science Fiction, Utopia, Dystopia*. Boulder: Westview Press, 2000. Print.

Ohmae, Kenichi. *The Borderless World: Power and Strategy in the Interlinked Economy*. Rev. ed. New York: HarperCollins, 1999. Print.

Paik, Peter Y. *From Utopia to Apocalypse: Science Fiction and the Politics of Catastrophe*. Minneapolis: U of Minnesota P, 2010. Print.

Pratchett, Terry. *Small Gods*. New York: Harper, 1992. Print.

Sargent, Lyman Tower. *Utopianism: A Very Brief Introduction*. Oxford: Oxford UP, 2010. Print.

Soja, Edward W. *Thirdspace: Journeys to Los Angeles and Other Real and Imagined Places*. Oxford: Blackwell, 1996. Print.

Suvin, Darko. *The Metamorphoses of Science Fiction: On the Poetics and History of a Literary Genre*. New Haven: Yale UP, 1979. Print.

Tally, Robert T., Jr. "'Believing in America': The Politics of American Studies in a Post-National Era." *The Americanist* XXIII (2006): 69–81. Print.

Wagner, Hank, Christopher Golden, and Stephen R. Bissette. *Prince of Stories: The Many Worlds of Neil Gaiman*. New York: St. Martin's Press, 2008. Print.

Wegner, Phillip E. *Life Between Two Deaths, 1989–2001: U.S. Culture in the Long Nineties*. Durham: Duke UP, 2009. Print.

Westphal, Bertrand. *Geocriticism: Real and Fictional Spaces*. Trans. Robert T. Tally Jr. New York: Palgrave Macmillan, 2011. Print.

Which Way Is Hope? Dystopia into the (Mexican) Borgian Labyrinth

Luis Gómez Romero

> This is the weirdest thing that has soared from the whole American continent: A perfect knot, a blind machine, a Borgian labyrinth.[1]
> —La Barranca, "Reptil"

Prelude: Stories from the Borgian Labyrinth

My homeland, Mexico, and indeed Latin America as a whole, invokes the delirious tasks undertaken by Ts'ui Pên in Jorge Luis Borges' celebrated "El Jardín de Senderos que se Bifurcan." The story describes Ts'ui Pên, a Chinese astrologer who devoted his final years to the composition of a novel more populous than the fabled *Hung Lou Meng* and the construction of a labyrinth in which all men and women would sooner or later lose their way. Ts'ui Pên is murdered before completing the novel—he leaves behind what seems to be a confusing collection of wavering drafts—and the labyrinth is never found. Eventually, however, the reader learns that Ts'ui Pên accomplished his goal in the vast, intricate, and apparently unfinished novel depicting a world in which all possible outcomes of an event occur simultaneously, each one itself leading to further possibilities. Readers of the novel can make no sense of it precisely because the forking paths of Ts'ui Pên's labyrinth are not placed in space, but in time. And so it is with Latin America: a historical labyrinth erected upon antique and new stories of oppression and inequality that seem to stretch from the sixteenth century right into the twenty-first.

The stories told in Latin America recurrently mirror the perplexing, chaotic, and troubled history of its dwellers. Accordingly, the evolution of Latin American dystopian literature cannot be adequately explained with just the critical elements provided by political and literary theories. More powerful and eloquent images are required to address the many voices summoned up in Latin American realities: the centennial resignation of the aboriginal peoples, the decaying but still animated arrogance of the conquerors' inheritors, the resented discourses on the colonial past that conflict the *mestizo* identity, and the pathologies of globalized capitalism overlapping a living system of Baroque mores. Above and behind these voices—challenging them, destabilizing them, sometimes even overcoming them—parallel speeches of resistance struggle to open new spaces for conceiving the possibility of a yet unrealized emancipated and fair society. An apt metaphor for understanding Latin America might be found in music: the cadence of its stories is itself polyphonic, beat provided by dramatic but paradoxically coexisting fluctuations in its historical *tempo*. If Ts'ui Pên had ever been interested in music, Latin America could have inspired his final symphony.

In a celebrated Nobel Prize lecture, Gabriel García Márquez praised Latin America as an "immense homeland of haunted men and historic women, whose unending obstinacy blurs into legend" (516). As one of the main cultivators of Latin American magical realism, García Márquez eulogized the impassioned fantasy of Latin American daily life and its impact on storytelling. *Ut pictura poesis*: supposedly, those who undergo quotidian miracles are prone to create marvellous stories. García Márquez nonetheless also acknowledged the devastation to the enchanted Latin American realms wrought by the unbridled madness of vicious dictatorships, interventionism of all sorts on the part of colonial and post-colonial powers, poverty, and ignorance. The narrative problem of Latin Americans, García Márquez claimed—in view of "the immeasurable violence and pain of our history"—has always been "a lack of conventional means to render our lives believable" (517–18).

I cannot think of a better reading strategy to address contemporary Latin American literature and, more specifically, Mexican dystopian narratives of the last fifteen years. Dissimilar realities raise dissimilar stories: Mexican dystopian literature, though influenced by the Anglo-American tradition, has developed unique "site-specific" features. This essay intends to outline a theoretical approach to a groundbreaking Mexican variant of dystopian storytelling whose origin can be traced to a recent work of novelist Carlos Fuentes: *La Silla del Águila* (2002).[2] According to María del Rosario Galván, the novel's protagonist, Mexico's history is nothing but a large episode of "bloodstained rivers . . . ravines used as cemeteries and . . . unburied corpses" in the "desolate landscape of injustice that is the holy scripture of our Latin American land" (15). Her view is not the whole story of Mexico, however. A new ingredient has been added to this bleak mixture: a persistently yearned for and easily jeopardized democracy.

The fragility of Mexican democracy has decisively influenced dystopia as a genre of speculative fiction focused on the possible outcomes of the oppressive and unjust—though unexamined—historical tendencies entrenched in our daily life. The radical (and quite violent) changes that Mexico has undergone since the defeat of the PRI (Partido Revolucionario Institucional) in the 2000 presidential election certainly represent a major challenge for Mexican dystopian narratives, which have been forced to seek alternate ways to assess and criticize the current social and political system. By focusing on the conflicts and antinomies of Mexican ongoing realities, Fuentes opened a uniquely realistic path of dystopian ideological contestation to the repeated betrayal of the Mexican people's inveterate dreams of deliverance and egalitarianism. Along with a few authors who have addressed from a dystopian standpoint the current situation of Mexico,[3] Fuentes constituted an authentically contemporary Mexican narrative subgenre: the realistic dystopia.

Fugue: *La Silla del Águila*, or, The Erring Hopes of Mexico

Even in Fuentes' early works an attentive reader can detect a symptomatically utopian "nostalgia of the future" (Befumo Boschi and Calabrese). Fuentes unswervingly denounced the forgery of Mexican emancipating ideals by holding a dialectic critical view of Mexico's history. As Claude Fell notes, Fuentes' narrative is imbricated in three different levels that, *grosso modo*, epitomize Latin American cultural discourses: utopia, represented in the continent's idyllic imagery of good savages; epic, rarely intruded upon by the upheavals of history; and myth, whose temporal unworldliness allows a permanent re-enactment of the past (151). Fuentes' stories consistently illustrate the historical deception inscribed in this cyclical time when the present is superimposed upon the unsolved grievances of the past and consequently projects a shadow of denied justice over the future.

Two obsessions define Fuentes' storytelling: Mexico (Delden 261) and the present as a mirror image of the past (Faris 299–314). *La Silla del Águila*, delving deeply into Mexican iconography, maintains both narrative strands. Literally, "*la silla del águila*" means "the eagle's chair." Yet, the "*silla*" that is the leitmotif of the story is not a simple chair since it is particularized by its possessor: "*el águila*." *La Silla del Águila* is therefore *The Eagle's Throne*, that is, the seat of the Mexican Republic's most cherished symbol: the eagle standing over the prickly pear while devouring a snake, which, according to the Aztec legend, pointed to the place chosen by the indigenous gods to build Mexico City. For a long time the eagle was not merely an abstraction, but a living reality incarnated in Mexico's sexennial strong man (*never* a woman): the president of the Republic. Fuentes' novel is a witty political satire on this subject. As César León, a fictional former president, explains, the Aztec emperor was called *Tlatoani*, a Nahuatl name meaning "Lord of the Great Voice." León declares as a political dogma that, like the ancient Aztec emperors, a Mexican president "must prove from the very moment he takes his seat in the Eagle's Throne that there is only one voice in Mexico: his own" (89).

Some historical context seems to be needed in order to explain the peculiarities of Mexican political culture. In Mexico the very idea of an open election was put into practice only about twelve years ago when the PRI was finally defeated by Vicente Fox, the presidential candidate of the PAN (Partido Acción Nacional), the conservative party. Previously, elections were held periodically but were either shrewdly or unashamedly manipulated by the governing oligarchy. The division of powers and the federal system were preserved in the current laws, but state governors, legislators, and the judiciary were actually selected and controlled by the president (Carpizo 190ff.; Cosío Villegas 22–35). Civil liberties and individual rights were integrated into Mexican constitutional principles, but essential elements of political freedom were abridged in the daily practicalities of political life. Though it is true that this phenomenon of simulated democracy was repeated, in various forms, throughout the Hispanic world, in no country except Mexico did it assume the lasting features of a paternal dictatorship exercised by a series of eleven six-year administrations (from 1934 to 2000) led by the same political party, the aforementioned PRI (Krauze).

In Fuentes' novel, the Mexican *ancien régime* is called a "hereditary republic" (90) and, most outstandingly, a "*dictablanda*" (52, 224). This Spanish expression, which has been recurrently used in Mexico to define the sustained hegemony of the PRI, is meant to be a pun on the word *dictadura* (dictatorship). The wisecrack consists in opposing *blanda* (soft) to *dura* (hard): a *dictablanda* is a dictatorship that is not ultimately callous in every circumstance. Thus, the craftily humorous tone of *dictablanda* is definitely lost in English as it can only be drearily translated in the phrase "soft dictatorship." The semantic potential of the term *dictablanda* is richer, however, as it expresses two peculiarities of Mexican twentieth-century politics: firstly, that the PRI did not owe its nearly seventy unbroken years in office to mere force, but also to a peculiar corporative political organization that was soundly based in clientelism and corrupted policies; secondly, that each president really appointed his successor because he could not be re-elected.

The key pieces of the political system were basically two: the PRI and the president (Cosío Villegas 21). One party ruled everything, and one man ruled that party by simply pointing out his successor. The inheritor of the leaving president was colloquially called *"tapado"* ("covered one" or "hidden one") before his official recognition as the PRI's candidate. "The *tapado*," writes Carlos Monsiváis, was "the ghost of the coming presidency, the spectre that would be materialized in absolute power" over a devastating "absence of citizens" (18). The result of the candidate election was *"el destape"* ("uncovering" or "stripping off"), his being brought into the open by *"el dedazo"* ("the point of the big finger," i.e., the presidential choice). Given the outright administrative and governmental significance of the president, succession itself was always at the heart of Mexican political imagery. As one particularly cold-blooded character in *La Silla del Águila* states, "when it comes to Mexican politics, we shed our skin every six years" (119).

"Sufragio efectivo/No reelección" ("effective suffrage/no re-election") is a Mexican political mantra hilariously quoted by a parrot in Fuentes' novel (220). This slogan actually appeared in every official Mexican document, as if to enforce such constitutional rule by the pervasive repetition of its key idea (just as parrots do). Mexican political life had its own vernacular logic: while the president changed every six years, the PRI reigned without cease. The PRI's candidates were almost always voted to whichever office they aspired to, even if electoral fraud was required to accomplish it. Among the most upsetting features of the PRI's regime was its overwhelming cynicism: suffrage was chiefly ineffective despite the solemn avowal reproduced in each and every official document.

Fuentes' novel approaches from a pessimistic perspective the problem of whether the Mexican transition to democracy has outlived the successional fiends of the past. *La Silla del Águila* is temporally situated after the historic change that occurred in 2000. Fuentes imagines that the PRI *took back* the presidency in 2006, and two subsequent six-year terms have transpired since then. The action takes place in 2020: once again, the PAN has won the election. Condoleezza Rice is president of the United States and she has just invaded Colombia. In an unusual act of protest the honourable—but indolent and indecisive—Mexican President Lorenzo Terán has openly called for the withdrawal of U.S. troops from Colombian territory and has prohibited the importation of Mexican oil into the United States unless OPEC prices are paid. Rice responds by blacking out all Mexican means of electronic communication. Without telephones, faxes, email, computers, Internet, and satellites, Mexican politicians retreat into letter writing and audiotapes as they race for positions of power at the beginning of a struggle to put a new president in the Eagle's Throne. Terán has hardly been in the office for two years, but everyone is already looking toward the elections of 2024. Terán is a member of the PAN, but the PRI's long-standing ways have survived the alternation of political elites.

The plot is invigorated by the early fading of Teran's political power. Apart from his sudden act of defiance, Terán does almost nothing except die in the middle of his term, making succession the *only* question there is for almost every character: two scheming ex-presidents, a loyal counsellor in Teran's administration, multiple power-hungry and thieving cabinet members, shrewd would-be presidents, wary generals, murderous police chiefs, various political bosses, and a raft of drudges and lovers. Each of these characters represents a parodical archetype of Mexican politics: the Corrupt One, the Technocrat, the Self-Denying Patriot, the Sexual Temptress, and the Bloodthirsty Military, among others (Rosenberg).

Such is the narrative frame that structures *La Silla del Águila* as a delightfully old-fashioned epistolary novel that echoes Choderlos de Laclos' *Les Liaisons Dangereuses*. The reading experience of *La Silla del Águila* is therefore quite disconcerting: the reader is situated in an imaginary future that is disturbingly similar to the present, while, at the same time, the distant past of Laclos' intriguing Marquise de Merteuil is recreated in a contemporary Mexican style, incarnated in María del Rosario Galván. Fuentes' heroine writes the book's first letter to her younger *protégé*, Nicolás Valdivia. "With me," she confides, "everything is political, even sex" (9). She presides over the political education of Valdivia, stating from the very beginning that "political fortune is one very long orgasm" (17). She has little interest in

Nicolás as a romantic figure. María simply takes advantage of his interest in her in order to wield him as an instrument to pave the way for her preferred candidate and long-standing lover, Bernal Herrera, by purging the cabinet of her arch-nemesis, the "fawning, contemptible, despicable" (48) chief of staff, Tácito de la Canal.

Once the scenario for the story is settled, we do not hear much more about the invasion of Colombia, or indeed about anywhere in the world except the backstage of Mexican power. With formidable satirical mastery, Fuentes unfolds simultaneously multiple bizarre conspiracies: an ex-president's scheme for his return to power, a foiled military takeover, a financial scandal, countless love affairs, multiple assassinations, and even a mysterious political prisoner. The wide democratic public sphere and the civil society, however, seem to be ominously absent. We learn early in the novel about three unsettled strikes—respectively performed by students, workers of a factory funded by Japanese venture capital, and plundered peasants—that endure unsolved until the end without any major consequences. Where are the outraged citizens deprived of communication technologies? Where are the riots and the looming revolution? Fuentes' tragicomic gentry are apparently afforded far too much indulgence in which to pander to their own agendas.

Fuentes' critics have interpreted this narrative omission as a significant misunderstanding of the development of Mexican politics after the PRI was overpowered in the 2000 election. Christopher Domínguez Michael, for example, reproaches Fuentes' depiction of Mexico, calling it "congenitally incapable of generating a democratic society" because "the uses, abuses, and customs of the 71-year PRI regime will forever taint the nation's future, like an oil spill." Instead of rendering the transformation of Mexican society, Domínguez Michael argues, Fuentes refuses to acknowledge it (85). Tina Rosenberg similarly observes that, by preserving the presidential succession mainly as an insiders' game, Fuentes lingers on the authoritarian dominion of the PRI, thereby showing his writing is "out of touch" insofar as it has been "reluctant to adapt to a country whose political direction and literary opportunities disappoint him."

My reading of *La Silla del Águila* differs. Fuentes' storytelling strategy is clever, insightful in ways his critics do not discern. The PRI profited from the general disappointment about the ineffective administrations of the PAN and slowly recovered positions in almost every region of the country. The 2012 presidential election resulted in the PRI's victory. Enrique

Peña Nieto, 57th president of Mexico, has revived the party's old practices as a proven path for heading to political success.[4] The ageless evils of the Mexican presidential succession have not been averted at all during the last decade. The power concentrated in Mexico's presidential office is still available only to those who have been initiated in the intriguing ways of the economic and political oligarchy.

In such a context, Fuentes' genius resides in showing his readers that the Eagle, like the emperor of Hans Christian Andersen's tale, is obscenely naked. The truth about the schemers who covet the Eagle's throne is that they are ridiculous because they essentially remain blind to the most basic of Mexican realities. While their names evoke a glorious past—Tácito, Cícero, Séneca, and, of course, César—their ambitions compromise the survival of their unfortunate object of desire: Mexico. Nicolás Valdivia dreams of emulating his *tocayo* (namesake) Niccolò Machiavelli (107, 322), but tragically decides to ignore the people he is plotting to rule. The absence of the Mexican people in *La Silla del Águila* underlines the deep injustice (and impending threat) of a government deserting its needs.

In a key scene, María del Rosario Galván has an ephemeral glimpse of the truthful setting of her quest for power. Near the end of the novel she writes a letter to Bernal Herrera in which she recalls their Down Syndrome child, whom they have not only put away in an institution but whose existence they actually deny. She acknowledges that, though it seemed largely reasonable to conceal their son from their political enemies in order to "construct a better country over the ruins of the cyclically devastated Mexico" (359), both of them in fact "stopped being parents to one little boy" because they thought they would "become godparents to a whole country" instead (360). "How cold, how clever we were," she confesses. "Together we decided that fighting for power was less painful than fighting for a child" (359). The boy, as Michael Wood suggests, hints at the hidden Mexico, pictured as permanently deniable (67). Galván, however, quickly catches herself and returns to courtesan conspiracies: her final letter to Herrera declares a will to surrender to the "slow suicide" that lurks in Mexican politics (408). Only Cícero Arruza, the spiteful chief of the Federal Police, perceives the unrest of 70 million Mexican "kids" under the age of twenty. "Look at them," Arruza demands of the Minister of Defence, Mondragón von Bertrab, "they wanted to be engineers, lawyers, fat cats. Look at them now, they're driving taxis, delivering pizzas, working as cinema ushers or making a living by parking other people's cars, they're broken people who were meant to become something better, and now they have been abandoned to their rotten wretchedness." Anticipating the danger personified in these young underdogs, Arruza asks his addressee: "What can our seventy million *chamacos* [kids] look forward to?" (126-27).

Fuentes does not directly answer this question in *La Silla del Águila*. Those 70 million anonymous men and women, however, reappear in *La Voluntad y la Fortuna* (2008), another of his recent dystopian works.[5] The story is told in this case by Josué, a victim of Mexico's ubiquitous violence who introduces himself as "the thousandth severed head so far this year in Mexico . . . one of the fifty beheaded victims this week, the seventh today and the only one in the past three and a quarter hours" (12).[6] In his last moments of consciousness, Josué ruminates that many of those frustrated young men and women, still subjected to the cruel law of "survival by a wink," have opted for a "Hugoesque world of mischievous crime" that at least provides them with the pride of a "fierce independence" based on the unbroken and furious mockery of the established powers (396). Jericó—Josué's friend, mentor, accomplice, and rival—likewise diagnoses that they only await their opportunity "to ruin somebody" or "to take revenge on somebody," to get what they deserve, what was denied to them either "by injustice, wickedness, envy, inequality" or the "youthful millionaires" and the "corrupt politicians." They are battered and marginal human beings who look ahead for someone to tell them: "Take the pistol I'm going to give you, take the Uzi, take the club, the bludgeon, the lasso . . . make lists . . . who do you want to ruin, who do you want to pay for their faults?" They are, in short, motivated by an anger incited by a hope too often denied. We should not be surprised if they are enthusiastic about the terrible promise spread by Jericó among Mexico City's downtrodden masses: "Personal vendettas are allowed" (402-403).

In the meantime, María del Rosario Galván tells Nicolás Valdivia of her augury: he will become president of Mexico. Far away, a character known as "el Personaje" (or as "the Old Man under the Arches") sits all day in a café in the main square of Veracruz drinking coffee, dispensing aphorisms, and conspiring. "*Plus ça change, plus c'est la même chose*," he advises Valdivia. The Old Man appreciates this rule of Mexican politics and, correspondingly, declares with compact and eloquent wisdom: in Mexico, "we've stood wide-eyed, not knowing what to make of democracy. From the Aztecs to the PRI, we've never played that game here" (222-23). He knows how to survive among the sharks of the Mexican oligarchy: in order to keep his privileges, the Old Man must ensure that the rules of the presidential succession remain mostly untouched under the appearance of democratic reform. Unfortunately, his personal concerns blind him to the growing weariness of the Mexican people. While the ruling oligarchy—personified by Fuentes in the Old Man, Galván, Valdivia, and their sidekicks—denies this reality, the country has gradually been transformed into a living dystopia.

Grave: Tocqueville's Curse or, the Land where Reality is Darker than Dystopia

A good number of passages of Alexis de Tocqueville's *De la Démocratie en Amérique* provide an instructive assessment of Mexican political life since the country obtained its independence from Spain in 1827. Tocqueville observes that Mexican people replicated the constitution and the federal system of the United States. He also notices that while Mexicans "borrowed the letter of the law," they were seemingly unable to capture the spirit that had inspired it. On this basis, Tocqueville describes Mexico alternately as "the victim of anarchy" or "the slave of military despotism" (I: 269). The future he predicts for the country is rather negative: Mexico, Tocqueville states, would be prevented for a long time from occupying a "high rank" among the nations of the world given its general "uncivilized state," the deep "corruption of its mores," and the widespread "misery" of its people (I: 277).

Tocqueville's rough diagnosis of Mexican politics has not lost its topicality. It is as though Tocqueville cast a curse over Mexico; the authoritarian regime has been dismantled not by democratic institutions, but by rampant criminality. Almost 50,000 people have been murdered since 2006, after former President Felipe Calderón took office and threw the federal police and the army against the drug cartels.[7] Life in Mexico has turned into a hazard bounded by the vicious arbitrariness of the state and that of the powerful cartels controlling the lucrative drug trade and other illicit businesses, such as extortion and human trafficking.[8] Once again, as Tocqueville anticipated, despotism has been followed by anarchy. This perverse fluctuation between tyranny and lawlessness[9] is the drama of Mexico's brand-new democracy. It is also a major challenge for the dystopian imagination. Does anybody need to be advised about the perils and pitfalls that may plunge incautious wanderers into hell once all its demons have been released? Even a hasty glance over recent events that have caught the attention of international media immediately makes evident the uneasy intersection between Mexican realities and the wildest grim worlds ever dreamt by the most pessimistic of dystopian authors: in Mexico, reality is the harshest competitor for dystopian fiction.

How can dystopian narratives address realities that seem more consistent with Batman's Gotham City, including its crooked law enforcement agencies and wild super-villains, than with a contemporary state respectful of the rule of law? As a literary genre, dystopia expresses a concern for warning its readers about the most dreadful socio-political tendencies rooted in the present that, if continued, could turn our lives into a nightmare. In order to achieve this, dystopian fictions represent dark potential futures that generate the opportunity for a cognitive encounter, firstly, with the worst social and political features of our own times and, secondly, with what might be done to prevent the dreadful advent of the dystopian society. Thus, we can fairly ask ourselves about the relevance of dystopia in face of this ghastly Mexican actuality.

Interlude: The Perplexities of Dystopian Fiction in (Our) Times of Cholera

My experience as an immigrant has allowed me to learn that some of the lucky citizens from the richest nations of the world—including the United States and Canada, Mexico's partners in the North American Free Trade Agreement—look at my convulsed homeland with confident petulance, as an exotic bloodthirsty country conveniently separated from their national realities by two oceans and the cruel Sonoran Desert. Why should any of them care about Mexico, when the violence unleashed by the drug prohibition is kept so far away from their neighbourhoods and backyards?[10] Today, as in the late years of the nineteenth century, the most comfortable reading of Tocqueville's analysis about Mexico can be summarized in the hideously biased judgment heard by young José Vasconcelos in the small American school of Eagle Pass, Texas: "Mexicans are a semi-civilized people." Vasconcelos, Mexico's most important educational reformer of the twentieth century, as well as the first opposition candidate, was tricked in a fraudulent presidential election just after the Partido Nacional Revolucionario (National Revolutionary Party—PNR), the primal version of the PRI, was founded (Skirius). In his memoirs, Vasconcelos claims he stood up and shouted: "We had the printing press before you did!" (33). I certainly do not share Vasconcelos' nationalist pride, but I am still aware of

Joseph Conrad's enduring warning: even London was once "one of the dark places of the earth" (19). Wherever political institutions are constructed over flawed bases, dystopia is likely to emerge.

Paradoxically, the present actualization of dystopia has exposed its weaknesses as a narrative genre. The very conditions necessary to dystopian fiction are emperilled not only in Mexico, but in several seemingly hopeless locations all around the world. Dystopia has widely taken possession of the "real" world, even exceeding its traditional domains in Africa, Asia, and Latin America.[11] These days, dystopian realities have returned forcefully to the core of the Western powers in the form of a titanic economic crisis that has resulted not only in the collapse of large financial institutions, the failure of several businesses, and repeated downturns in stock markets around the world, but also in massive unemployment and a fatal blow to the residual foundations of the welfare state.

Fredric Jameson has frequently been quoted for having observed that the "ultimate subject-matter of Utopian discourse" consists in "its own conditions of possibility as discourse" ("Of Islands and Trenches" 21). Jameson states, moreover, that literary utopias actually mirror our "constitutional inability to imagine Utopia itself," which is not due "to any individual failure of imagination" but is the result "of the systemic, cultural and ideological closure of which we are all in one way or another prisoners" ("Progress Versus Utopia" 153). Jameson's disquieting argument here may be summarized by saying that utopian texts show our incapacity to envision alternatives beyond our historical horizon: we can only conceive what is already embedded in our epoch, its ideologies, beliefs, and assumptions. Dystopia seems to face a similar problem now. Once a privileged index for the anxieties of the twentieth century—destructive use of science and technology, conditioned obedience, limited freedom, crumpled individuality, or unrestrained state surveillance, among others (Hillegas 3)—and a clever discursive means for calling attention to and identifying what needed to be changed in our society (Moylan, *Scraps of the Untainted Sky* xi–xvii), dystopian narratives have reached a cultural breaking point now.

Utopia and dystopia share the general vocation of utopianism that Lyman Tower Sargent embodies under the general label of "social dreaming" (3). The specific formal strategies of literary utopias and dystopias, however, are distinctly different. The traditional utopian text characteristically conveys an alternative world to the reader by means of a travelogue consisting in the perambulation of a voyager throughout the utopian society, vividly interspersed with his or her questionings and comments to a local guide (Moylan, *Demand the Impossible* 36–37). In contrast, the typical dystopian text does not appeal to a dislocating narrative device in order to provoke estrangement: it simply opens right in the midst of a nightmarish world that appears to be far worse than that of the reader (Sargent 9). The protagonist is already immersed in a polity deeply pierced by social and political wickedness. As Raffaella Baccolini and Tom Moylan note, however, the storyline then develops a counter-narrative "as the dystopian citizen moves from apparent contentment to an experience of alienation and resistance" ("Dystopia and Histories" 5). Dystopia represents in this way a conflict between a narrative of hegemonic order and a counter-narrative of resistance personified in a singular misfit or a discontented social class and its eventual allies. Dystopia remains consequently an open literary form: the resistant dissenters can either prevail or be crushed by the established power structures. In both cases, the dystopian discourse is made possible by a chilling view of our probable future that distances us from the present and transforms it, regardless of whether the alienated protagonist is finally victorious or defeated, in a moment of possibility that, paraphrasing Darko Suvin, reconciles the principle of reality with the principle of hope because social and political evils are always historically contingent and thus historically reversible (*Positions* 80–83).[12]

The crisis of dystopia is rooted in the breakdown of our capacity for hope. Generally speaking, hope regards the world as a *laboratorium possibilis salutis*, as an ongoing process in which our final salvation or perdition has not yet been decided (Bloch, "Kann Hoffnung enttäutsch warden?" 392). Dystopia needs hope, both as a cognitive basis that rouses awareness of the fact that the current social and political system is contingent and as an ethical principle that makes us, as readers, responsible for seizing the opportunity to resist the advent of an oppressive and unjust future. If the dystopian society turns out to be either our unavoidable fate or the best of all possible worlds, then dystopian fiction is useless.

The tragic resistance of Winston Smith or John "The Savage" against the extreme injustice of dystopian societies has been precluded today by two parallel anti-utopian discourses: on one hand, the well-known existential nihilism that deems human life pointless and deprived of moral value (Carr); and on the other, the latest authoritarian forms of shallow optimism that have imposed a peculiar practice of self-deception generally called "positive thinking" as a normative means to achieve personal health, happiness, and prosperity (Ehrenreich). In short, even from a dystopian standpoint our collective imaginations have been confined in what Roberto Mangabeira Unger calls the "dictatorship of no alternatives" (*The Left Alternative* 1–11). Imagining a way out of the present craziness of exploitation, degradation of civil and political liberties, ecocide, and global usury has become increasingly difficult, either because political commitment is considered a useless sacrifice for an irrelevant emancipation or because *wishful thinking* has been transformed into the ultimate expression of utopia itself.

Nonetheless, the practicality of dystopian realities is *precisely* what makes dystopian fiction more necessary than ever. Carlos Fuentes appears to have found a narrative formula for addressing our present dystopian perplexities. The most effective discursive method for Mexican (and probably worldwide) contemporary dystopian narrative can be epitomized in a political proverb unearthed from Mexico's recent authoritarian past by "La Pepa" Almazán, one of the many archetypical voices in the choral cast of *La Silla del Águila*: "You have to be Beelzebub if you want to triumph over Satan" (142).

Larghissimo Lamentoso: Mexican Realistic Dystopia

Ernst Bloch situates the principle of concrete utopia within real historical possibilities and tendencies that have not yet been actualized (*Das Prinzip Hoffnung* 1:224ff.). *Concrete utopia* stands for a present and significant expression of hope that anticipates the future by bringing it about. If we accept this premise for utopia, we may legitimately extend it to dystopia, which encapsulates similar dialectical tendencies. Real fear, despair, and alienation transform dystopia into a tangible force. *Concrete dystopia* thus designates specific moments, events, institutions, and systems that actually represent and accomplish organized forms of violence and subjugation (Varsam 208–209).

In most of his last work, Carlos Fuentes' storytelling went beyond concrete dystopia by providing the genre with a realistic streak, beginning with *La Silla del Águila* and continuing with *Todas las Familias Felices* (2006), *La Voluntad y El Destino*, and *Adán en Edén* (2009). The darkening Mexico Fuentes presents to us is only slightly different from the actual one, as a nightmare dreamt within a nightmare. We must nonetheless admit that such a realistic trait may seem oxymoronic when attributed to dystopian fictions, whose discursive basis depends heavily on estranged narrative strategies. Following Darko Suvin, we can constructively distinguish between two main forms of literary prose: the *naturalistic* that painstakingly reproduces textures, superficies, and relations that can be authenticated by our senses; and the *estranged* that displaces a given event or object, situating it in an imaginary frame outside the known reality ("On the Poetics of the Science Fiction Genre" 374-75). By means of estranged representation, we are able to recognize an object or a situation but, at the same time, we lose our familiarity with it. Utopias and dystopias can be properly classified as estranged narratives.

Can a narrative be at the same time realistic and estranged? We must answer affirmatively to this question for two reasons. Firstly, in historical terms, the great utopians have been also great realists: they possess, as Frank E. Manuel and Fritzie P. Manuel observe, "an extraordinary comprehension of the time and place in which they are writing and deliver themselves of penetrating reflections on socioeconomic, scientific, or emotional conditions of their moment in history" (28). Secondly, Fuentes' work precisely proves that imagination is not alien to reality, addressing in this way the core of Roberto Unger's profoundly revolutionary and utopian plea: "we must be visionaries to become realists" (*Democracy Realized* 74). The striking similitude between the fictional Mexico in Fuentes' work and its real counterpart potentiates the cognitive substratum and the ethical appeal of dystopian fiction. Fuentes' realistic dystopias effectively warn readers about the horrifying proximity of a definitively deformed future. Today is the last call for Mexico: indifference or procrastination for a personal commitment with solid and reliable democratic institutions would simply be suicidal.

Epilogue, or, *Furioso*: The Explosive Unsteadiness of the Prickly Pear

Utopia frequently finds its way through the margins of dystopia, as in the final footnote of Jack London's *The Iron Heel*, the appendix on the principles of newspeak in George Orwell's *Nineteen Eighty-Four,* or the concluding historical notes of Margaret Atwood's *The Handmaid's Tale*. In the case of Carlos Fuentes' *La Silla del Águila* such open utopian possibility resides, as Michael Wood has suggested (67), in the novel's epigraph, referred to the main theme—by Manuel Esperón and Ernesto Cortázar—of a 1972 movie musical called *Me he de comer esa tuna* (*I Have to Eat That Fruit of the*

Prickly Pear): "L'águila siendo animal / Se retrató en el dinero. / Para subir al nopal / Pidió permiso primero." ("The Eagle, being an animal / Had itself pictured on money. / It asked for permission, however, / Before perching on the prickly pear.") As I have stated before, the eagle's throne of the book's title is clearly the lofty seat of presidential power. Yet, it is also a thorny plant. The Mexican eagle may hold a snake in its mouth, as in the legendary image of the founding of Mexico City, but to do so it must acknowledge its dangerous and uncomfortable position over a prickly pear, especially if it has not asked for permission to stand there. What will finally cause the downfall of the intriguing courtesans that swarm *La Silla del Águila*, the implication goes, is the denied reality of Mexico itself: the rage of 70 million *chamacos* against the backdrop of long centuries of poverty, injustice, and unfulfilled dreams.

Notes

I want to express my earnest gratitude to Brett Josef Grubisic, whose painstaking editing of the first drafts of this essay honestly contributed to improving my work.

1 "Esta es la cosa más extraña que ha surgido en todo el continente americano: Es un nudo perfecto, una máquina ciega, un laberinto borgiano." All translations are mine unless noted otherwise.
2 The English translation (by Kristina Cordero) was published as *The Eagle's Throne* in 2006.
3 For example, Roberto Bolaño in *2666* (2004) or Rodrigo Plá and Laura Santullo in the screenplay of *La Zona* (2007).
4 During his political campaign, for example, Peña Nieto performed the staged spectacle of unanimous support to the party's contender known as "*la cargada*" (the bandwagon), in which the so-called followers have been previously bribed with (depending on their status) trinkets (for example, T-shirts, caps, or key chains), promises of free meals, or even the prospect of a public appointment (Zamarripa).
5 This novel was translated to English by Edith Grossman and published as *Destiny and Desire* in 2011.
6 Mexican drug cartels presently use spectacular exhibitions of violence—from depositing severed heads in town squares to mutilating corpses or hanging them from overpasses—in order to propagate terror among their rivals and Mexico's general population (see González Rodríguez).
7 See Presidencia de la República, and Camarena, "La Violencia del 'Narco' ha causado casi 50.000 víctimas."

8   See Human Rights Watch.
9   For ample evidence of wide-ranging and ongoing atrocities, see reportage by Archibold, Camarena, Robles, Aristegui, Jiménez, Granados Chapa, Baranda, Guerrero Gutiérrez, and Juárez.
10 I admit my statement implies an oversimplification of the complex social realities and political ideologies behind drug policies. The effects that the international hysteria over drugs have had in Mexico and other countries of Latin America, however, demand an urgent revision of the current drug regulations that largely follow the lead of the United States, which frequently do not focus on health or addiction at all, but express instead bigotry and deep-rooted class and social fears. See Manderson, *From Mr. Big to Mr. Sin*, and "Symbolism and Racism in Drug History and Policy."
11 For a recent account on the present worldwide dystopian realities, see World Economic Forum (specifically, the section titled "Seeds of Dystopia," 16-19).
12 See also Baccolini, "Finding Utopia in Dystopia," 177-86.

Works Cited

Archibold, Randal. "Arson Kills 40 at a Casino in the North of Mexico." *New York Times*, 26 Aug. 2011: A11. Print.

Aristegui, Carmen. "Veracruz." *Reforma*, 23 September 2011: Opinión 13. Print.

Atwood, Margaret. *The Handmaid's Tale*. 1985. London: Vintage, 1996. Print.

Baccolini, Raffaella. "Finding Utopia in Dystopia: Feminism, Memory, Nostalgia and Hope." *Utopia Method Vision: The Use Value of Social Dreaming*. Ed. Raffaella Baccolini and Tom Moylan. Oxford and Berne: Peter Lang, 2007. 159-89. Print.

Baccolini, Raffaella, and Tom Moylan. "Introduction: Dystopia and Histories." *Dark Horizons: Science Fiction and the Dystopian Imagination*. Ed. Raffaella Baccolini and Tom Moylan. New York and London: Routledge, 2003. 1-11. Print.

Baranda, Antonio. "Anuncian Protección a Planteles Educativos." *Reforma*, 7 Oct. 2011: Nacional 10. Print.

——. "Suman Ya 34 Mil 612 Muertos." *Reforma*, 13 Jan. 2011: Nacional 6. Print.

Befumo Boschi, Liliana and Elisa Calabrese. *Nostalgia del Futuro en la Obra de Carlos Fuentes*. Buenos Aires: Fernando García Cambeiro, 1974. Print.

Bloch, Ernst. *Das Prinzip Hoffnung*. 1954-59. 3 vols. Frankfurt am Main: Suhrkamp, 1977. Print.

——. "Kann Hoffnung Enttäuscht Werden?" *Gesamtausgabe: Literarische Aufsätze*. Vol. 9. Frankfurt am Main: Suhrkamp, 1985. 16 vols. 385-92. Print.

Bolaño, Roberto. *2666*. Barcelona: Anagrama, 2004. Print.

Borges, Jorge Luis. *El Jardín de Senderos que se Bifurcan*. Buenos Aires: Sur, 1942. Print.

Camarena, Salvador. "La Violencia del 'Narco' Ha Causado Casi 50.000 Víctimas en México Desde 2006." *El País*, 13 January 2012: Internacional 6. Print.

———. "Los Maestros de Acapulco se Rebelan Contra la Extorsión." *El País*, 28 September 2011: Internacional 7. Print.

———. "Los Narcos Dejan 35 Cadáveres en una Avenida de Veracruz." *El País*, 22 September 2011: Internacional 8. Print.

Carpizo, Jorge. *El Presidencialismo Mexicano*. 1978. 18th ed. Mexico: Siglo XXI Editores, 2004. Print.

Carr, Karen L. *The Banalization of Nihilism: Twentieth-Century Responses to Meaninglessness*. Albany: State U of New York P, 1992. Print.

Conrad, Joseph. *Heart of Darkness: Complete, Authoritative Text with Biographical, Historical, and Cultural Contexts, Critical History, and Essays from Contemporary Critical Perspectives*. 1903. 3rd ed. Ed. Ross C. Murfin. Boston: Bedford/St. Martin, 2011. Print.

Cosío Villegas, Daniel. *El Sistema Político Mexicano: Las Posibilidades de Cambio*. Mexico: Joaquín Mortiz, 1972. Print.

Delden, Maarten van. "*Agua Quemada* de Carlos Fuentes: La Nación como una Comunidad Inimaginable." *Carlos Fuentes Desde la Crítica* 261–76. Print.

Domínguez Michael, Christopher. "Mexico's Former Future." Rev. of *La Silla del Águila*, by Carlos Fuentes. *Foreign Policy* 141 (Mar.–Apr. 2004): 84–85. Print.

Ehrenreich, Barbara. *Bright-Sided: How Positive Thinking Is Undermining America*. New York: Picador, 2009. Print.

Faris, Wendy B. "El Regreso del Pasado: El Quiasmo en los Textos de Carlos Fuentes." *Carlos Fuentes Desde la Crítica*: 299–316. Print.

Fell, Claude. "Mito y Realidad en Carlos Fuentes." *Carlos Fuentes Desde la Crítica*: 145–53. Print.

Fuentes, Carlos. *Adán en Edén*. Madrid: Alfaguara, 2010. Print.

———. *La Silla del Águila*. 2002. Madrid: Punto de Lectura, 2007. Print.

———. *La Voluntad y la Fortuna*. Madrid: Alfaguara, 2008. Print.

———. *Todas las Familias Felices*. Madrid: Alfaguara, 2006. Print.

García-Gutiérrez, Georgina, ed. *Carlos Fuentes Desde la Crítica*. Mexico: Taurus, 2001. Print.

García Márquez, Gabriel. "Conferencia Nobel 1982: La Soledad de América Latina." *Les Prix Nobel/The Nobel Prizes 1982*. Ed. Wilhelm Oderberg. Stockholm: Nobel Foundation, 1983. Rpt. in *El Ensayo Hispanoamericano del Siglo XX*. Ed. John Skirius. 5th ed. Mexico: Fondo de Cultura Económica, 2004. 515–19. Print.

González Rodríguez, Sergio. *El Hombre sin Cabeza*. Barcelona: Anagrama, 2009. Print.

Granados Chapa, Miguel Angel. "Escuadrón de la Muerte." *Reforma*, 3 Oct. 2011: Opinión 13. Print.

———. "Tragedia y Ridículo en Veracruz." *Reforma*, 9 Oct. 2011: Opinión 11. Print.
Guerrero Gutiérrez, Eduardo. "Violencia y Mafias." *Nexos* 33.405 (2011): 55–59. Print.
Hillegas, Mark. *The Future as Nightmare: H.G. Wells and the Anti-Utopians*. London: Oxford UP, 1967. Print.
Human Rights Watch. *Neither Rights Nor Security: Killings, Torture and Disappearances in Mexico's "War on Drugs."* New York: Human Rights Watch, 2011. Print.
Huxley, Aldous. 1932. *Brave New World*. London: Vintage, 2004. Print.
Jameson, Fredric. "Of Islands and Trenches: Naturalization and the Production of Utopian Discourse." *Diacritics* 7.2 (1977): 2–21. Print.
———. "Progress Versus Utopia; or, Can We Imagine the Future?" *Science Fiction Studies* 9.2 (1982): 147–58. Print.
Juárez, Alfonso. "Desalojan a Docentes Policías en Acapulco." *Reforma*, 13 Oct. 2011: Nacional 8. Print.
Jiménez, Benito. "Reivindica Grupo Matanza de 35." *Reforma*, 27 Sept. 2011: Nacional 7. Print.
Krauze, Enrique. "Mores and Democracy in Latin America." *Journal of Democracy* 11.1 (2000): 18–24. Print.
La Zona [The Zone]. Dir. Rodrigo Plá. Screenplay by Rodrigo Plá and Laura Santullo. With Daniel Giménez Cacho, Carlos Bardem, and Maribel Verdú. Morena Films et al., 2007. Print.
London, Jack. *The Iron Heel*. 1907. Chicago, IL: Lawrence Hill Books, 1980.
Manderson, Desmond. *From Mr. Big to Mr. Sin: A History of Australian Drug Laws*. Melbourne: Oxford UP, 1993. Print.
———. "Symbolism and Racism in Drug History and Policy." *Drug and Alcohol Review* 18.2 (1999): 179–86. Print.
Manuel, Frank and Fritzie Manuel. *Utopian Thought in the Western World*. Oxford: Basil Blackwell, 1979. Print.
Monsiváis, Carlos. "La Era del PRI y sus Deudos." *Letras Libres* 20 (2000): 16–22.
Moylan, Tom. *Demand the Impossible: Science Fiction and the Utopian Imagination*. New York and London: Methuen, 1986. Print.
———. *Scraps of the Untainted Sky: Science Fiction, Utopia, Dystopia*. Boulder, CO: Westview Press, 2000. Print.
Orwell, George. *Nineteen Eighty-Four*. 1949. London: Penguin, 2000. Print.
Presidencia de la República. "Base de Datos de Fallecimientos Ocurridos por Presunta Rivalidad Delincuencial." *Presidencia de la República*. Web. 28 Sept. 2011.
Robles, Osvaldo. "'Vendo Quesos de Oaxaca.'" *Reforma*. 1 Sept. 2011: Nacional 6. Print.

Rosenberg, Tina. "All the Presidential Schemers: What Carlos Fuentes Misunderstands about Mexican Politics." *Slate*. 1 May 2006. Web. 20 Dec. 2011.

Sargent, Lyman Tower. "Three Faces of Utopianism Revisited." *Utopian Studies* 5.1 (1994): 1–38. Print.

Skirius, John. *José Vasconcelos y la Cruzada de 1929*. Spanish trans. Félix Blanco. Mexico: Siglo XXI, 1978. Print.

Suvin, Darko. "On the Poetics of the Science Fiction Genre." *College English*, 34: 3 (1972): 372–83. Print.

———. *Positions and Presuppositions in Science Fiction*. Kent, OH: Kent State UP, 1988. Print.

Tocqueville, Alexis de. *De la Démocratie en Amérique*. 1835–1840. 4 vols. Paris: Pagnerre, 1848. Print.

Unger, Roberto Mangabeira. *Democracy Realized: The Progressive Alternative*. London: Verso, 1998. Print.

———. *The Left Alternative*. London: Verso, 2009. Print.

Varsam, Maria. "Concrete Dystopia: Slavery and Its Others." *Dark Horizons*. 203–23. Print.

Vasconcelos, José. *Ulises Criollo*. 1935. Ed. Claude Fell. Paris: ALLCA XX, 2000. Print.

Wood, Michael. "The Power of the Prickly Pear." Rev. of *The Eagle's Throne*, by Carlos Fuentes. *New York Review of Books*. 54.10 (2007): 66–67. Print.

World Economic Forum. *Global Risks 2012: Insight Report*. 7th ed. Geneva: World Economic Forum, 2012. Print.

Zamarripa, Roberto. "Revive Peña al viejo PRI." *Reforma*. 28 Nov. 2011: Nacional 1. Print.

Dystopia Now

Examining the Rach(a)els in Automaton Biographies *and* Player One

Kit Dobson

> It's too bad she won't live, but then again, who does?
> —*Blade Runner*

> More than iron, more than lead, more than gold I need electricity.
> I need it more than I need lamb or pork or lettuce or cucumber.
> I need it for my dreams.
> —Racter, *The Policeman's Beard Is Half-Constructed*

Why open with *Blade Runner* and computer-generated poetry in a post-NAFTA paper on dystopias and the topic (in)security? My first epigraph is a statement made by the character Gaff in one of the final scenes of Ridley Scott's iconic 1982 film *Blade Runner* about the character Rachael, a Nexus-6 replicant, an artificially intelligent robot who is virtually indistinguishable from the humans around her. My second is from the first book of poetry composed by a computer, published in 1984. Two books recently published in Canada—Larissa Lai's *Automaton Biographies* and Douglas Coupland's *Player One: What Is to Become of Us*—restage aspects of *Blade Runner* and, in particular, the character Rachael, in order to query the present world in the context of computerization. Lai quotes Gaff's words directly in her book (40). My chapter will investigate these two restagings in order to argue for a view of Canada that is, today, becoming its own dystopia as the country aligns itself increasingly with transnational neoliberal politics. This chapter will approach the importance of understanding dystopic spaces through a comparison with Canadian apocalyptic visions before approaching the character Rachael through, first, *Blade Runner* (and the novel that spurred the film) and then Lai's and Coupland's visions in order to understand the limits of what it means to be human, ultimately ending with a consideration of the significance of security regimes in Canada today. This final reading will be grounded in the recently developed Nexus card, a regulatory process designed to facilitate security clearance for the privileged, one that marks ways in which today's neoliberal world marks some humans as being more fully human than others.

First, then, why dystopia as a site for such investigations? The contributors to this book all offer their particular takes on the idea (some in more depth than I can go into here); for me, the term begins in a straightforward sense, but then takes on additional significance in a post-1994 environment under the North American Free Trade Agreement (NAFTA). In the first instance, I am interested in the textbook definition: M.H. Abrams gives us the notion that a dystopia is "a very unpleasant imaginary world in which ominous tendencies of our present social, political, and technological order are projected in some disastrous future culmination" (218). This definition of an "ill-place" or a "bad-place," to give the term a more etymological definition, differentiates it from the idea of the utopia in more ways than one. The notion of utopia comes, of course, most famously from Thomas More's 1516 book of the same name, and, it is frequently noted, is defined in particular through its etymology as a "no-place"; it is a place so idyllic that it cannot exist. The dystopia is therefore not only the reverse of the utopia, a place that has taken on a nightmarish form. The dystopia is also potentially possible in ways that the utopia may not be. It could exist, whereas a utopia, by etymological definition, cannot. In Canada, the discourse of dystopia in literature is dominated by references to Margaret Atwood, and her visions of the dystopic have very much been nightmare imaginings of the not-too-distant future. Her novels *The Handmaid's Tale* (1985), *Oryx and Crake* (2003), *The Year of the Flood* (2009), and *MaddAddam* (2013) predominate any given search that one might do on the topic, while her recent book *In Other Worlds: SF and the Human Imagination* (2011) is a consistent point of reference for many critics. My desire in this chapter is, in part, to broaden considerations of the dystopic beyond the Atwoodian because the term is more flexible than a focus on Atwood allows. In my reading, Lai's and Coupland's works offer generative understandings for the dystopic in Canada that might extend the dominant conversation thus far.

Flexibility is needed in part because the dystopia needs to be considered in contrast to the idea of the Apocalypse. According, for instance, to Slavoj Žižek, in his 2010 book *Living in the End Times*, "the global capitalist system is approaching an apocalyptic zero-point" (x). Žižek sees the Four Horsemen of the Apocalypse embodied in "ecological crisis, the consequences of the biogenetic revolution, imbalances within the system itself . . . and the explosive growth of social divisions and exclusions" (x), and he reads the contemporary world according to the five stages of grief (denial, anger, bargaining, depression, and acceptance). What is particularly striking in Žižek's book—aside from its range—is this focus on the Apocalypse, a notion that is useful for understanding Canadian literature as well. Marlene Goldman, tracing the idea of the Apocalypse in Canadian writing, has argued that "the apocalyptic paradigm pervaded Canadian literature from its beginnings" and that, specifically, this paradigm focuses on a vision of "the 'old world' being replaced by the new" (3). Apocalypse, Goldman notes, requires both "a transformative catastrophe and a subsequent revelation of ultimate truth" (4). Its Canadian incarnation, she argues, "refuses to celebrate the destruction of evil and the creation of a new, heavenly world." Instead, she finds, Canadian "works highlight the devastation wrought by apocalyptic thinking on those accorded the role of the non-elect" (5). It is important to note, too, the temporal dimension: "the idea of apocalypse," Goldman states, "falls under the general category of eschatology, the teaching of 'the last things'" (14). Time is a key aspect of the apocalyptic: the end may be now in this vision, but the second focus, upon the afterlife or the world to come, pushes this vision toward the future, leaving it deferred. In either an Atwoodian dystopic or Canadian apocalyptic vision, the diagnosis of the present comes through a vision of the future. To propose to look for a dystopia that is ever closer to the present, as I am doing here, then, is to suggest a simultaneous reading of the future and the now. This temporal move is increasingly relevant in an ever more dystopic era, in which NAFTA and subsequent agreements facilitate the negotiation of increasingly synchronous cross-border arrangements, security regimes, and data sharing used to police the boundaries of citizenship and the human.

Given these cross-border arrangements, it is important to think about these temporal issues across national divides, bringing international influences to Canadian conversations. Such temporal questions are also important when examining *Blade Runner*. Like George Orwell's *1984*, a novel whose date has now long since passed, *Blade Runner* is catching up with itself. Ridley Scott's film version opens by announcing the setting of the film: it takes place in Los Angeles in 2019. The date would have been more remote in 1968, of course, when Philip K. Dick published the novel *Do Androids Dream of Electric Sheep?*, which was transformed into *Blade Runner* in 1982. In Dick's novel, the Earth has been largely evacuated following World War Terminus, except for those declared unfit for colonizing other planets. On Earth, androids known as replicants are illegal; especially feared is the new Nexus-6 variety, which cannot be reliably detected through the complicated eye scans used on previous models. Rick Deckard, played by a young Harrison Ford in the film, and other bounty hunters chase down and "retire"—kill—them. The film takes on much of the tone and structure of Dick's novel while it abandons many of the contextual elements of the book: it is a bleak, pared down world in Scott's version. The film is a vexed one, with at least four distinct versions in circulation, and it divides viewers as to whether the protagonist of the film, Deckard, is himself a replicant.

Perhaps the most enduring character from Dick's novel and from *Blade Runner*, however, is Rachael, played by Sean Young in the film. Rachael at first appears to be an employee of the Tyrell Corporation, the company responsible for the manufacture of the Nexus-6 and other replicants. She learns in the course of the film that she is a replicant, and is therefore doomed to suffer the four-year lifespan of her kind. While Deckard battles with and retires four Nexus-6 replicants who have come back to earth in order literally to "meet their maker," Dr. Eldon Tyrell, so that they might increase their lifespans, he also engages in an affair with Rachael. Rachael's early lack of knowledge of her own inhumanity points to that, in turn, of the characters in the film. While those who appear to be human in the film are concerned with the purity of their species, they are perhaps the least "human" of the beings displayed: solitary, depressive, and socially anaesthetized, their environment is one that it is hard to imagine fighting for. The replicants, on the other hand, are deeply emotional and form lasting bonds with one another—or they are childlike and immature, according to Eldon Tyrell. By the film's end, the replicants are shown to the viewers to be in the light (literally and metaphorically)—the replicant leader Roy Batty is shown backlit by a clear halo of light behind his head as he dies—while the humans are enshrouded in the dank, penumbral world that they have created. Rachael, as she is violently seduced by Deckard, is humanized, recognizes the danger to her, and flees with him at the film's end.

One clear framework for investigating the role of Rachael in the film falls within the discourse of the notion of the cyborg, written about so persuasively by Donna Haraway in "The Cyborg Manifesto" and in all of the scholarship that has followed from that piece. Indeed, Haraway mentions Rachael directly in her manifesto, several years before either the 1992 "Director's Cut" or the 2007 "Final Cut" of the film was released: as she puts it, "the replicant Rachael in the Ridley Scott film *Blade Runner* stands as the image of cyborg culture's fear, love, and confusion" (178). The cyborg remains a useful frame of reference here because, in Haraway's terms, it "can suggest a way out of the maze of dualisms in which we have explained our bodies and our tools to ourselves" (181). That is, the nature/culture dichotomy is here undone: while the dichotomy typically is used to oppose humans-as-culture to everything-else-as-nature, the role of the human is reversed in *Blade Runner*; humans become the natural order against which the cyborg-as-culture seems to align itself. Yet here, too, the cyborg is cast as being outside of the domain of the human; it does not fit this dualistic paradigm and is therefore to be eliminated. That Rachael, however, gains our sympathies through her affective pull demonstrates the falsity of the divide and pushes the human to—and possibly beyond—its limits.

This disruption of the human moves from a distinct moment in the near future to a more ambiguous temporality—yet a clear locus within the geographies of Canada—in the works of Larissa Lai and Douglas Coupland; in many respects, the divide between the present and the future is suspended in both authors' accounts. Lai's 2009 book of poetry *Automaton Biographies* is an intelligent voicing of the limits of the human and the self. Broken into four parts, each investigates what it means to exist in the then, the now, and the future: the opening part, "rachel," is written in the voice of Sean Young's character, and therefore set in the future; the second part, "nascent fashion," dismantles our contemporary state of war; part three, "ham," is written in the voice of the chimpanzee of the same name, the first chimpanzee sent into space, in 1961, and is therefore set in the past; while part four, "auto matter," is presented as semi-autobiographical research on the present, largely set in the Vancouver that Lai inhabits. It is a book of disruptive, enjambed poetics that questions the human and beyond. It is this particular query that drives my interest in Lai's work.

Lai's engagement with *Blade Runner* in *Automaton Biographies* extends her previous work. Her first novel, *When Fox Is a Thousand*, contains explicit reference to the film. This novel moves between the story of the T'ang dynasty poet Yu Hsuan-Chan and the contemporary haunting of Artemis Wong by the figure of the fox in Vancouver, challenging the constructions of gender and race in the contemporary world. In an interview, Lai stated that she hopes that her "narratives open questions—about race, about class, about gender for sure, but also about being human, about ethics, about action" (qtd. in Morris "sites" 23). Her use of *Blade Runner* enables these themes to be explored. In an early scene in *When Fox Is a Thousand*, the characters Eden and Artemis watch the film. The scene, which focuses on Artemis' reactions to the violence of the film, and especially the use of eyes, prompts critic Robyn Morris to read the novel through the film. Indeed, Morris notes, Lai's use of *Blade Runner* in her first novel "is integral to her interrogation of a white hegemonic gaze that seeks to simultaneously possess, and dispossess, a specifically Chinese Canadian self" ("Re-visioning" 70). Lai also makes explicit use of *Blade Runner* in her short story "Rachel," a text that, critic Michelle Reid notes, allows Lai to open "up many disjunctions between . . . the novel and film source-texts" that she uses—that is, between the work of Philip K. Dick and Ridley Scott (354). Lai's engagement with the film, then, is sustained and deep.

Lai's second novel, *Salt Fish Girl*, Morris notes, continues "the dialectic between *Fox* and *Blade Runner*" ("Re-visioning" 81). Set in the near future in the Pacific Northwest, *Salt Fish Girl* follows the story of Miranda Ching, juxtaposing her story with that of the Chinese creator figure Nu Wa. The Pacific Northwest in this novel is bleak, broken into fortified corporate compounds and the "Unregulated Zone," largely made up of the ruins of Vancouver. As the novel unfolds, Miranda becomes involved with a woman named Evie. Evie is, it turns out, a clone, one who is also made up, in part, of fish DNA—"point zero three percent *Cyprinus carpio*—freshwater carp" (158). Evie's narrative provides a sustained parallel with *Blade Runner*, as Evie finds herself in search of a better understanding of her father, Dr. Rudy Flowers, the scientist who created her and her fellow clones, who are used in sweatshop labour. This search runs parallel to the replicants' search for their creator in Ridley Scott's film. More pressing still, however, is the parallel interest in the cyborg. Critics Diana Brydon and Jessica Schagerl term Evie "a literalization of Donna Haraway's cyborg" (37), and, indeed, the clones—named Sonias—who work in the sweatshops literally interrogate the boundaries of the human. As rebellion begins to foment among them, they begin writing subversive messages on the soles of sneakers, which leave legible prints behind. The first of these begins with the question "What does it mean to be human?" (237). These prints, left in the ground on which the shoes tread, provides a geo-specific site for the cyborg within a dystopic vision of Canada.

Lai's interest in *Salt Fish Girl* rests, more broadly, in the dystopic near future. As Rita Wong puts it, "Lai projects a futuristic scenario that traces the logic of contemporary capitalist relations" in that book (111). That is, the logic in this novel is contemporary, while the setting is futuristic. Lai is well aware of this dynamic movement between the present and the future in her writing: describing her novel, she notes that although a variety of "futuristic" events—she lists genetic modification, the criminalization of migrant labourers, simulacra of reality like the town of Celebration, U.S.A., and so on—may be "happening now," "for some reason, it seemed that a futuristic idiom could handle it better" ("Future Asians" 171–72). Why might this be the case? What does Lai's futuristic setting enable? As in *Blade Runner*, for one, it enables aspects of the present order to be interrogated and challenged. Joanna Mansbridge argues that Lai takes "the global as a site of conflict wherein individual and national origins are constructed through the abjection of feminized and racialized bodies" (123). Witnessing and unpacking this construction enables it to be queried and disrupted. Women's bodies become a site of contestation, of control, one where the state asserts itself and demonstrates its power at the level of the biopolitical. Tara Lee's analysis of *Salt Fish Girl*, for instance, exemplifies this disruption. Lee writes that the cyborg body is thoroughly enmeshed in capital, leading to questions as to "whether agency is possible for a body so entrapped in a system of commodification and consumption" (94). She finds, however, that Lai's narrative provides a means of witnessing how "the body can break out of its passivity" as Evie and Miranda uncover the machinations of Dr. Flowers (94). Paul Lai similarly contends that "[Larissa] Lai's embrace of messy origins and futures inevitably disrupts generic categories, offering a hybrid future that questions assumptions of scientific progress and Western modernity" (184). Similarly, Pilar Cuder-Domínguez argues that Lai's work questions "the representation of Asian women's subjectivity, challenging standards of both gender and genre" (127). Or, in the words of Eleanor Ty, Lai's novel uses a structure that is useful "to express lesbian desire, as well as to critique technological advances such as cloning, the genetic modification of food, and the exploitation of Third World women's labor by large corporations" (90). For readers of Lai's previous work, then, the possibilities expressed through *Blade Runner*, the cyborg, and the dystopic enable her to expose and disrupt the category of the human itself, especially in its sexual and racial encodings.

Lai's work in *Automaton Biographies* pushes this process of disrupting the human further. In a review of the book in *Quill & Quire*, Mark Callanan suggests one of the virtues of Lai's investigation: "Lai's meditations on a post-human world," he writes, "proceed with an unsettling machine-like efficiency stripped of human vitality" (n.p.). Reviews of her book have been, in general, quick to observe the move toward the posthuman or non-human, but how, exactly, this effect is achieved with Rachel bears study (note that Lai, like Coupland, drops the second "a" in Rachael, which Philip K. Dick uses in his writing). There is a great deal of linguistic depth to Lai's writing: direct quotations from the film, when they occur, tend to be offset in italics (like the motto of the Tyrell Corporation, "*more human than human*" (13), which is also, of course, the chorus of the well-known, *Blade Runner*–referencing White Zombie song of the same name from 1995). Rachel, as the speaker of her portion of the book, focuses on Deckard, the "policeman" to whom she repeatedly refers. This focus is one of the moves that humanizes her, alongside the fact that she dreams. In dreaming, she seems at once to achieve both consciousness and the unconscious: "i dream insect hatching," she notes in Lai's version (17). The reference is to both the film and to Dick's novel, which returns to the question "Do androids dream?" (161). It appears that they may well, and at this moment the human/inhuman dichotomy, privileging the human, fails anew. That she dreams insects hatching rather than dreaming *of* them suggests that she brings them into being, more immediately than humans might. Rachel's dream world intersects, moreover, with the waking world, her syntax blurring distinctions between states of consciousness and the unconscious:

> i half my memory
> what's past is polaroid
>
> i collect water in ditches
> my body ticks out
> its even rhythm too flawless
> for birth
>
> i athena my own sprouting
> this knowledge colds me
> in my ice-fringed room
> my asian fits this frost

i owl my blink
slow stare i thought was mine
father given

my heart exudes a kind of love
a kind of mourning. (16)

Significant in these lines is Rachel's practice of verbing her nouns; nouns and adjectives like "half," "athena," "cold," and "owl" become verbs here, with the jarring effect of creating an artificial syntax that mimics the overly formal, well-coiffed expression worn by her character in the film, but that also expands the range of language, into and with the natural world from which humans separate themselves. Viewers can tell that she is a replicant simply through her framing in the film; that she does not know this fact from the outset is surprising, and suggests the instability of self-knowledge. In this passage, it is the unconscious dimension of Athena's story, her sprouting from the head of Zeus, who does not know that she resides within, that Lai foregrounds. The film invites this link between Rachel and Athena: in Los Angeles in 2019, animals have largely died off from an unknown cause; the Tyrell Corporation houses an artificial owl that Deckard encounters in his first meeting with Rachael. The owl, of course, is Athena's symbolic animal, bringing to mind her birth, as well as the "blink" of its eyes and hers, the blink that she thinks is her own until she learns that her "father," Eldon Tyrell, gave it to her in her manufacture. The manufacture of her eyes, which the film depicts as being made by a stereotyped Asian man in an ice-cold room, is particularly important. Eyes reappear throughout the film, not only in the artificial owl's blink, or simply in the repeated images of eyes, but also in the Voigt-Kampff test that Deckard and others like him administer to suspected replicants in order to test their humanity.

That Rachel is not a human does not, however, lead her to feel inferior in Lai's rendition; quite the reverse. The world that she inhabits is distinctly dystopic to her:

the future we sight still
in shot wounds
foreign coil
wrings dystopia
from others we mark contagious
from sound by eye. (24)

Rachel's present is the future, self-consciously so, and it is an acknowledged failure. The failure, however, is not hers, but that of the humans around her:

> i rank my anger
> rail against this solitude
> was a princess with perfect clothes
> beloved daughter of a new elysium
> our flawless manufacture
> had shed earth's dirt
> imperfection's disease toil filth. (30)

Lai's Rachel, then, sees herself as representing the future, a better future than that which the humans around her are able to offer. The world is bleak, and it drags her down into its depths. The possibility that Rachel might, in fact, be an improvement upon the very flawed human species is something that the text offers. Nevertheless, her Rachel "mourn[s her] purity / in guilt in fear" (31), recognizing the way in which her "perfect construction" is an instrument that can be used by the humans around her.

The humans who surround the character Rachel in Douglas Coupland's *Player One: What Is to Become of Us* are a similar source of consternation. The works of Lai and Coupland may be far apart in terms of aesthetics and politics: Lai writes complex, multi-layered texts that resist dominant narrative structures in order to interrogate the formation of identity, while Coupland frequently presents readers with highly accessible, witty stories about the ironies of life under late capitalism. The existing scholarship on Coupland notes an ongoing search for utopic spaces in, for instance, the western end of North America in *Girlfriend in a Coma* (McGill 49), or a lament for the failure of history—and the possibilities therein—in his breakout novel *Generation X* (Lainsbury). Coupland's frequent intergenerational complaint about the abandonment of youth by those who were supposed to be in charge can be seen to parallel, in some ways, the challenge of father figures in both *Blade Runner* and Lai's novels, yet the tone is sharply different. The most extensive study of Coupland to date, written by Andrew Tate, suggests that Coupland's writing occupies "a perplexing hinterland between . . . optimism" and "everyday, apocalyptic paranoia" (162). He is a documenter, in many ways, of aspects of the contemporary Zeitgeist, and publicly embraces his role as such.

Coupland's *Player One*, his "novel in five hours," is remarkable, though, within his output for its variation from his established patterns of discussing contemporary ennui: it is formally unusual, given its five-part segmentation, and it was written as the 2010 CBC Massey Lectures, a lecture series that attempts to engage Canadians on key contemporary issues. That said, the novel nevertheless includes many familiar Couplandisms, and, in some cases, direct references to his previous works. One notable Couplandism is the "Future Legend" at the end of the book, a series of definitions of future-oriented words. Among these is not merely the posthuman, defined by Coupland as "whatever it is we become next" (236)—but also the "trans-human"—"whatever technology made by humans that ends up becoming smarter than humans" (244). Coupland's version of the trans-human, in turn, raises a further question, which he labels the "trans-humane conundrum": "if technology is only a manifestation of our intrinsic humanity, how can we possibly make something smarter than ourselves?" (244). The novel does not answer this question, but it is only mildly sympathetic toward the humans who are bypassed by the post- or trans-human future. Set in a sort of perpetual present that relies on many contemporary pop culture references, but also in the near future, the book revolves around five characters stuck in a seedy cocktail lounge near Pearson International Airport in Toronto during a sudden, massive, and unexplained spike in global oil prices, leading to rapid social collapse. The five characters—Karen, a desperate single mother; Rick, a downtrodden bartender; Luke, an embezzling pastor; Rachel, who is here transformed into a blonde but is in other respects very similar, in terms of character, to Rachael in *Blade Runner*; and a semi-present speaker simply called Player One—struggle to survive, trapped within the lounge.

The movement between the post- and the trans-human in Coupland's novel is witnessed in particular through Rachel, as well as through the disembodied voice of Player One. Player One is presented as the online avatar of Rachel, but also appears to be separate from her, a possibly trans-human electronic self protruding into our world. Rachel, on the other hand, is arguably to be aligned with the posthuman. *Globe and Mail* reviewer Catherine Bush finds Rachel to be paradoxically the "most compelling" of the book's characters as a result of her failing attempt to be human. Rachel describes herself in predominantly medical terms, stating that she has "multiple structural anomalies in [her] limbic system that affect [her] personality," as well as "prosopagnosia, which is an inability to tell faces apart," and a lack of "subjective qualities like humour and irony" (40–41). Additionally, she describes her brain as having lesions that create "tone-blindness" and that strip her "speech of inflection and tone," as well as "autism-related facial recognition blindness syndrome," "autistic spectrum disorder . . . problems with inhibition and disinhibition, as well as mild OCD" (96–97). She describes her conditions differently to various characters in the lounge, and many of her abilities appear to be connected. She notes that her "sequencing abilities are in the top half percentile" and she knows pi to over a thousand digits (97). She is simultaneously frightening and compelling to those around her. Luke finds that

> this cool Hitchcock blonde is a living, breathing, luscious, and terrifying terminal punctuation mark on [his] existence, a punctuation mark along the lines of *This is the New Normal, Luke, and guess what—it's left you out in the weeds, and you pastor, reverend, good sir, have outlived your cultural purpose and . . . are a chunk of cultural scrap metal, not even recyclable at that.* (27; italics in original)

Luke cannot decide whether she is "genuinely alien" or "the desired end product of an entire century's eugenic efforts at physical perfection," leaving the human species behind (30). Rachel's father sees her as "a robot . . . working in the garage eighteen hours a day," the space where she breeds mice for scientific testing (33). In response, Rachel has come to the lounge in order to "bear children and thus prove to the world her value as a human being" (33). She has spent her youth trying "to make herself human" by researching "what makes humans different from all other creatures" (34) and by undergoing what the book refers to as "normalcy training" (41). Rachel provides a clear demonstration of the limits of what can be accommodated within the category of the human, as she only marginally fits the rubric that the world provides for her.

In contrast, the human world of the novel is far from compelling. Rachel thinks that "neurotypical people are an endless source of puzzles" (74). Karen, thinking about her recent flight to Toronto, notes that "your body isn't even a body—it's an ecosystem" (3), one that she finds unappealing. Ultimately, the human is very meagre within this system: "only her DNA is actually *her*," she realizes, and it would amount to "a fine powder maybe the size of an orange" if the rest of her ecosystem were to be removed (4). An additional character, named Bertis—madman sniper and son of the phony self-improvement guru Leslie Freemont, who visits the lounge just as the crisis begins—accuses the characters of being "a depressing grab bag of pop culture influences and cancelled emotions, driven by the sputtering engine of the most banal form of capitalism" (136), a sentiment with which Rachel agrees.

Why, then, does Rachel wish to be human? At the end of the day, and beyond Rachel's desire to prove her father wrong (which would upend humanity's patriarchal structure from a posthuman perspective), Coupland's writing falls back on metaphysics and the unconscious in order to ground its characters: Player One states that "humans have souls and machines have ghosts" (42); they remain different, and the soul—especially Rachel's—is highly valued by the novel. Rachel notes that she has never had a dream that she can remember, because "dreams are for normal people" (160). But, like the status of dreams in *Blade Runner* as a seeming guarantee of existence—a guarantee that is, however, undercut in that film—Rachel's humanity is seemingly proven in the "vision" that she has of crawling through empty suburbs, and in which she comes as a prophet of the "Third Testament" (170). In this vision, she declares that "fiction and reality have married" and that "what we have made now exceeds what we are" (171). The dream, in confirming her humanity, signals at the same time a move toward a future that is, in the terms of the Tyrell Corporation, more human than human: we have made things that exceed ourselves. Karen, similarly, suggests that "we *can* change into something else, even if it's something we don't understand" (196). Rick is unsure: Rachel, he thinks, is "genetically advanced or genetically flawed, depending on how you [look] at her" (202). In the final movement of the book, Rachel is shot by Bertis and dies, her voice merging with her avatar Player One. Her final reckoning is possibly Nietzschean, as she provides a sidelong glance at the über-Menschen whom we may become: "in a thousand years," she thinks, "electively mutated post-humans will look back at us with awe and wonder" (211). Simultaneously, however, she will miss the earth; the novel's ending is therefore highly ambivalent. This ambivalence suggests that while humankind is deeply flawed, it is also affectively compelling in itself, that it remains a locus for desire that cannot quite be abandoned yet.

Throughout this paper, I have been investigating the limits of the human through the character of Rach(a)el in her multiple incarnations. Ultimately, the human condition appears to be baffling to Coupland's Rachel; it is angering to Lai's Rachel, who recognizes the flaws of the human and her own implication in its workings; and it is destructive to Ridley Scott's Rachael, as her failure to fit the nature/culture dichotomy will lead to her demise. In all of these visions, it is humankind that is deeply flawed: Rachael's flaw is her lack of flaws. To return to the idea of peace and (in)security with which I began, I want to note the ongoing relevance of Rachael's character, particularly as adapted by Lai and Coupland. When we contemplate these texts, written in contemporary Canada, we should note that these dystopic visions reflect directly upon the myriad ironies and failures of our world, both in Canada and beyond. The present and future collapse not only textually; increasingly, the future is now. That the futurism of the present affects the world of "security" in which we live is only reinforced by one of the recent border synchronization plans created by the U.S. Department of Homeland Security and the Canada Border Services Agency: the Nexus card. Whether or not this recently introduced security measure self-consciously refers to *Blade Runner*'s Nexus model replicants is uncertain; however, the parallels are worth noting. The iris-scanning technology that this card uses in order to expedite border crossings highlights the markers that we, as human animals, rely upon to differentiate ourselves not only from the explicitly non-human animal world, but also, and increasingly, from those people who, as in Judith Butler's *Precarious Life*, are not recognized or recognizable within the terms that our society is today creating. With the Nexus card—just one example among many—our borders organize us into certifiably "good" citizens who qualify for expedited service, or as the undistinguished masses shuffling through the regimes of post-9/11 security to which we are, by now, more or less accustomed, or have been brutalized into accepting as the new normal. This ranking and differentiating brings me back to Rachael, to the humanized figure who is excluded for one reason or another, who is designated for "retirement," and whose humanity is constantly challenged in, for instance, Deckard's administration of the eye-scanning Voigt-Kampff test on her. Our notions of security, illuminated by the character of Rachael, revolve around such classificatory systems, and thereby maintain the increasingly dystopic state of affairs under which we live today.

Acknowledgements

Many thanks to Erin Wunker, who provided invaluable feedback on a draft of this paper. Thanks also to the British Association for Canadian Studies Annual Conference at the University of Birmingham in 2011, where an early version of this paper was delivered.

Works Cited

Abrams, M. H. *A Glossary of Literary Terms*. 6th ed. Fort Worth: Harcourt Brace, 1993. Print.

Blade Runner. Dir. Ridley Scott. Warner Bros., 1982. DVD.

Brydon, Diana, and Jessica Schagerl. "Empire Girls and Global Girls: A Dialogue on Spaces of Community in the Twentieth Century." *Moveable Margins: The Shifting Spaces of Canadian Literature*. Ed. Chelva Kanaganayakam. Toronto: TSAR, 2005. 27–45. Print.

Bush, Catherine. "The End of the Story." Review of *Player One: What Is to Become of Us*, by Douglas Coupland. *Globe and Mail*. 22 Oct. 2010. Web. 23 Feb. 2011.

Butler, Judith. *Precarious Life: The Powers of Mourning and Violence*. London: Verso, 2004. Print.

Callanan, Mark. Review of *Automaton Biographies*, by Larissa Lai. *Quill & Quire* Dec. 2009: n.p. Web. 23 Feb. 2011.

Coupland, Douglas. *Generation X: Tales for an Accelerated Culture*. New York: St. Martin's Press, 1991. Print.

———. *Girlfriend in a Coma*. Toronto: HarperCollins, 1998. Print.

———. *Player One: What Is to Become of Us*. Toronto: Anansi, 2010. Print.

Cuder-Domínguez, Pilar. "The Politics of Gender and Genre in Asian Canadian Women's Speculative Fiction: Hiromi Goto and Larissa Lai." *Asian Canadian Writing Beyond Autoethnography*. Ed. Eleanor Ty and Christl Verduyn. Waterloo: Wilfrid Laurier UP, 2008. 115–31. Print.

Dick, Philip K. *Do Androids Dream of Electric Sheep?* New York: Ballantine, 1968. Print.

Goldman, Marlene. *Rewriting Apocalypse in Canadian Fiction*. Montreal: McGill-Queen's UP, 2005. Print.

Haraway, Donna. "A Cyborg Manifesto: Science, Technology, and Socialist-Feminism in the Late Twentieth Century." *Simians, Cyborgs and Women: The Reinvention of Nature*. New York: Routledge, 1991. 149–81. Print.

Lai, Larissa. *Automaton Biographies*. Vancouver: Arsenal Pulp Press, 2009. Print.

———. "Future Asians: Migrant Speculations, Repressed History & Cyborg Hope." *West Coast Line* 38.2 (2004): 168–75. Print.

———. "Rachel." *So Long Been Dreaming: Postcolonial Science Fiction and Fantasy*. Ed. Nalo Hopkinson and Uppinder Mehan. Vancouver: Arsenal Pulp Press, 2004. 53–60. Print.

———. *Salt Fish Girl*. Toronto: Thomas Allen, 2002. Print.

———. *When Fox Is a Thousand*. 2nd ed. Vancouver: Arsenal Pulp Press, 2004. Print.

Lai, Paul. "Stinky Bodies: Mythological Futures and the Olfactory Sense in Larissa Lai's *Salt Fish Girl*." *Melus* 33.4 (2008): 167–87. Print.

Lainsbury, G. P. "*Generation X* and the End of History." *Essays on Canadian Writing* 58 (1996): 229–40. Print.

Lee, Tara. "Mutant Bodies in Larissa Lai's *Salt Fish Girl*: Challenging the Alliance Between Science and Capital." *West Coast Line* 38.2 (2004): 94–109. Print.

Mansbridge, Joanna. "Abject Origins: Uncanny Strangers and Figures of Fetishism in Larissa Lai's *Salt Fish Girl*." *West Coast Line* 38.2 (2004): 121–33. Print.

McGill, Robert. "The Sublime Simulacrum: Vancouver in Douglas Coupland's Geography of Apocalypse." *Essays on Canadian Writing* 70 (2000): 252–76. Print.

More, Thomas. *Utopia*. Ed. George M. Logan and Robert M. Adams. Cambridge: Cambridge UP, 1989. Print.

Morris, Robyn. "Re-visioning Representations of Difference in Larissa Lai's *When Fox Is a Thousand* and Ridley Scott's *Blade Runner*." *West Coast Line* 38.2 (2004): 69–86. Print.

———. "'sites of articulation'—an interview with Larissa Lai." *West Coast Line* 38.2 (2004): 21–30. Print.

"Nexus." *Canada Border Services Agency*. 28 Jan. 2011. Web. 23 Feb. 2011.

Orwell, George. *1984*. Harmondsworth: Penguin, 1954. Print.

Racter. *The Policeman's Beard Is Half-Constructed*. New York: Warner Books, 1984. Print.

Reid, Michelle. "Rachel Writes Back: Racialised Androids and Replicant Texts." *Extrapolations* 49.2 (2008): 353–67. Print.

Tate, Andrew. *Douglas Coupland*. Manchester: Manchester UP, 2007. Print.

Ty, Eleanor. *Unfastened: Globality and Asian North American Narratives*. Minneapolis: U of Minnesota P, 2010. Print.

White Zombie. "More Human Than Human." *Astro-Creep: 2000*. Geffen, 1995. CD.

Wong, Rita. "Troubling Domestic Limits: Reading Border Fictions Alongside Larissa Lai's *Salt Fish Girl*." *BC Studies* 140 (2003–2004): 109–24. Print.

Žižek, Slavoj. *Living in the End Times*. London: Verso, 2010. Print.

The Romance of the Blazing World
Looking Back from CanLit to SF

Owen Percy

In the last four decades Margaret Atwood has gone from the Queen of CanLit—trying in 1972 to articulate the "national habit of mind" (13) of 30 million Canadians in *Survival: A Thematic Guide to Canadian Literature*—to the planet's reigning "doyenne of dystopia" (Grubisic "Astounding" par. 1) in her exploration of our here-and-now world's speculative and futuristic others. In novels like *The Handmaid's Tale* (1985), *Oryx and Crake* (2003), and *The Year of the Flood* (2009), Atwood plots her own vision of a planet and a civilization overrun by corporate and ecological malfeasance and blind(ing) greed. More recently, with the publication of her non-fiction study *In Other Worlds: SF and the Human Imagination* in 2011, she aspires to collect and articulate the theses of the increasingly unquantifiable field of science fiction (SF) through a process of intelligent taxonomy and convincing conviction. Like *Survival*, *In Other Worlds* is as undeniably fruitful and provocative as it is frustrating, broad, impossible, and terrifying. In her introduction, though, Atwood makes sure to cover her tracks and to establish her parameters clearly: "*In Other Worlds* is not a catalogue of science fiction, a grand theory about it, or a literary history of it. It is not a treatise, it is not definitive, it is not exhaustive, it is not canonical. It is not the work of a practising academic or an official guardian of a body of knowledge" (1). It is, rather, a subjective examination of the kind of literature that has come most clearly to define the *ennui*, *malaise*, and anxious *je ne sais quoi* of the decades around and since the North American Free Trade Agreement (NAFTA). If it is true that "[o]f recent years, [North] American society has moved much closer to the conditions necessary for a takeover of its own power structures by an anti-democratic and repressive government" (Atwood, *In Other Worlds* 90), then Atwood's focus in *In Other Worlds* is on the kind of writing, according to Bruce Sterling, that "simply makes you feel very strange; the way that living in the late twentieth century makes you feel, if you are a person of a certain sensibility" (qtd. in Atwood, *In Other Worlds* 8). Atwood is. And she assumes that we are as well—the "certain sensibility" being that of general anxiousness about our civilizational being-in-the-world as the world itself begins to crumble in the form of its economic, political, and cultural institutions.

This essay, after Atwood, will examine the prophetic promises of two early, generically foundational SF texts as they have been reinterpreted in two contemporary CanLit novels that follow the Atwoodian shift from survival in/as CanLit to survival in/as planetary civilization writ large. Ronald Wright's *A Scientific Romance* (1997) and Michael Murphy's *A Description of the Blazing World* (2011) construct their own shadowy versions of the future on the abandoned foundations of other worlds conceived of by SF writers who have come before them. Both texts are postmodern novels about the reliability of text and documentation, the act of writing as a means of fending off mortality, loneliness, and silence, and the always-impending collapse of the institutions that we still hold dear as natural, neutral, authoritative, and objective, despite all evidence to the contrary since the early to mid-twentieth century. Wright argues in his 2004 CBC Massey Lectures, *A Short History of Progress*, that, in the current civilizational moment, "[o]ur practical faith in progress has ramified and hardened into an ideology . . . [that] is blind to certain flaws in its credentials" (4), and that "the engine of capitalism" (123) has in fact culminated in what Zsuzsi Gartner has more recently recognized as "the chaos of capitalism run amuck [sic]" (4); that is, the era of materialistic Jamesonian late capitalism embodied by transnational and neoliberal economic initiatives like NAFTA and its kin. Tellingly, in her 2008 Massey Lectures *Payback: Debt and the Shadow Side of Wealth*, Atwood herself explores the millennia-old historical and cultural roots of the current global economic crises born of the "opening" of the markets since the 1970s, undoubtedly informing her discussion of what she calls "economic SF"—texts that "have as their central focus the production and distribution of goods and the allocation of economic benefits among various social classes" (*In Other Worlds* 63). It should be noted here that Wright and Murphy do not proffer "economic SF" texts at all—they imagine what we might call "post-economic SF," as the worlds they (re)construct imply the culmination and collapse of civilizational systems—of economy, of class, of government—altogether, emerging directly from our collective refusal to recognize the warnings of each of their respective SF source-worlds. Both *A Scientific Romance* and *A Description of the Blazing World* acknowledge and meditate on, albeit in different ways, our collective failures to learn and prosper from the speculations of earlier writers who have already imagined the other-worldly futures upon which we seem increasingly to be verging because of our blinding belief in the stability of our markets and institutions.

A Scientific Romance takes its cue and its narrative vehicle from H.G. Wells' *The Time Machine*. Wright's protagonist is David Lambert, an Oxford-educated archaeologist suffering from bovine spongiform encephalopathy (BSE, or mad cow disease) in the last days of 1999. Lambert comes into possession of a mysterious letter claiming to be from the late Wells' solicitors, inviting its reader to a clandestine meeting at midnight on the crest of the twenty-first century. Lambert goes to the appointed meeting place and discovers Wells' own unlikely gift to the future: a functional time machine that sends Lambert five hundred years into *his* future to wander a tropical, desolate, and deserted England. As Lambert comes to realize and understand the inevitable end to the history, culture, and civilization from which he has travelled, he also begins to recognize the implications of his escape from it, and from his responsibility as a former citizen of the here-and-now in which we must read the book. The diptych narratives of *A Description of the Blazing World* present readers with even more Wellses with which to reckon: a troubled teenage boy struggling with the disappearance of his war-correspondent father is sent to spend the summer with his arch-nemesis older brother in Toronto. Then, in the midst of the major blackout of August 2003, the boy stumbles across a copy of Margaret Cavendish's 1666 utopian fantasy novella *A Description of a New World, Called the Blazing World* (henceforth just *The Blazing World*), widely considered to be one of the first works of science fiction in English. He takes to the streets with his tape recorder to document what he is certain is "the coming Super Death" (Murphy 120)—an apocalypse that will birth a Cavendishian new world that might in fact blaze with the natural enlightenment of a new civilization that has learned from its historical other's mistakes.

These two novels set themselves in the *aporia* between our recognizable and contemporary here-and-now and the terrifyingly recognizable other worlds that might follow what they both see as our impending civilizational implosion—"our own planet in a future" (Atwood, *In Other Worlds* 5). Both novels, too, position themselves in urgently declining millennium-era presents in order to consider the comfort and confidence with which we have been living in spite of the warnings issued to us by *The Time Machine* and *The Blazing World*—foundational texts in the SF genre. *A Scientific Romance* and *A Description of the Blazing World* proffer, in this respect, a kind of textual "syncreticity" (Ashcroft, Griffiths, and Tiffin 14) that does not resist or refuse their canonical precedents but redraws our attention to the prophetic possibilities of the source texts themselves. They portray the potential future others of our own contemporary civilizational environments by, in fact, looking backwards into the distorted mirrors of what Atwood might call Wellsian and Cavendishian "ustopias." According to Atwood, the term "ustopia"—a *portmanteau* of "utopia" and "dystopia"—signifies "the imagined perfect society and its opposite" on the assumption that "each contains a latent version of the other" (*In Other Worlds* 66). And although, again in shades of *Survival*, "Atwood's coinage of 'ustopia' is presented as though the last half century of scholarship about dystopian literature never happened" (Grubisic "Margaret Atwood" par. 3), the term's elasticity of signification allows it to stand simply for the concept of a geographical and/or temporal "elsewhere" (Atwood, *In Other Worlds* 71). Like the very ustopic fictions by Wells and Cavendish that their speculations draw upon, *A Scientific Romance* and *A Description of the Blazing World* are the "diaries and journals left by the literary descendants of Robinson Crusoe in the hope that someone in the future may read them" (Atwood, *In Other Worlds* 73). They insist, though, in a way their source texts do not, that the ustopic future is urgently, irrefutably *now*, and that we must address its potentialities if we are to survive it at all.

Both novels engage Atwood's dystopic doctrine of conceiving of the here-and-now world in terms of the here-and-soon, and both inherently demonstrate our arrogant civilizational defiance of Wells' and Cavendish's earlier prophetic prognostications by reinscribing them as monstrous distortions of our (post-NAFTA) present. In their rewritings, Wright and Murphy are not themselves Wellsian or Cavendishian; they do not propose new possibilities for the future, or, really, escapism from the mundane realities of our post-millennium present—what Wright believes to be "our last chance to get the future right" (*A Short History* 132). In fact, they threaten to deny the future altogether; they turn our attentions again to those who have come speculating before us in order to underline the relative inertia of our civilizational and socio-cultural progress, and to our wilful ignorance of SF's earlier generic warnings against our self-styled and capital-driven progress toward so-called enlightenment. In other words, the novels "extrapolate imaginatively from current trends and events to a near-future that's half prediction, half satire" (Ursula LeGuin qtd. in Atwood, *In Other Worlds* 5) and craft satires, both of the texts and the worlds that have come before theirs, and of the dystopias that they have bred. They are fictions that urge us, in fact, to speculate *against* fiction itself, that is, narratives that draw upon *The Time Machine* and *The Blazing World* in order to demonstrate their continued urgent relevance to the crisis-laden present and the possible futures of our other worlds if these visions were to become, horrifyingly, non-fictional.

In borrowing H.G. Wells' canonical time machine for his own fiction, B.C.-based Richard Wright directly invokes the history and generic connotation of the scientific romance—a genre that flourished in the Victorian era and came to refer predominantly to the work of British writers who used the veil of fiction to speculate upon the potentiality of science, technology, and the future. According to Wright himself, the genre "had two modern descendants: mainstream science fiction, and profound social satire set in nightmare futures" (*A Short History* 122). Despite receiving a relatively rocky initial reception in 1895, H.G. Wells' *The Time Machine* has proven itself to be the most important scientific romance of its (or any other) generation in the British tradition. In it, according to Margaret Drabble, Wells "foresaw the annihilation of our species" and "the inevitable death of our planet" ("Introduction" viii, xix) resulting from the ultimate triumph of capitalistic Darwinian logic. Upon arrival in the year 802,701 A.D., Wells' nameless Time Traveller initially seems to have stumbled upon a utopian society comprised of diminutive, serene, intellectually simple beings living in an apparent Golden Age wherein there are "no hedges, no signs or proprietary rights, no evidences of agriculture; the whole earth had become a garden" (29), and where the creatures—the Eloi—seem to "spen[d] all their time in playing gently, in bathing in the river, in making love in a half-playful fashion, in eating fruit and sleeping" (40). Indeed, the Eloi world seems initially to be a "social paradise" wherein humanity and nature have achieved harmony and humankind is "engaged in no toil . . . nor economical struggle" because "all that commerce which constitutes the body of our world, was gone" (30). But what first seems like the perfect *culmination* of Darwinian evolution soon begins to show traces of its dystopic other as night falls over the Eloi. A second race of beings, the Morlocks, emerge from their subterranean homes in order to terrorize and hunt the passive Eloi, fattened and unable to protect themselves thanks to their labourless evolutionary triumph (which Drabble attributes to "humanity ha[ving] reached a state of tragic degeneracy because at one point it achieved such a level of material comfort that it lost the need to fight for survival" [xiv]). Unsurprisingly, Wells' Time Traveller sees in this relationship a class allegory mirroring the "social difference between the Capitalist and the Labourer" wherein the "Haves pursu[e] pleasure and comfort and beauty, and below ground the Have-nots, the Workers, [get] continually adapted to the conditions of their labour" (46–47) before they begin, literally, eating the rich. Wells' alarming 1895 vision, then, was of "a real aristocracy, armed with a perfected science and working to a logical conclusion the industrial system of today" (*The Time Machine* 47). That is, Wells' horrifying ustopia contains in it at once the seeds of injustice, degradation, and collapse of industrial civilization that the story's narrator acknowledges as "only a foolish heaping that must inevitably fall back upon and destroy its makers in the end" (87), and is itself erased under a frightening ice age witnessed as the Time Traveller later moves several million years further into the future.

Wells himself, reflecting on his novella in 1931, demonstrated a much more hopeful attitude toward the future of civilization than his predecessors might be said to have adopted from *The Time Machine* when he admitted to having been informed by the "dreadful lies about the 'inevitable' freezing up of the world—and of life and mankind with it" told to him by *fin de siècle* geologists and scientists who believed at the time that "[t]he whole game of life would be over in a million years or less" ("Preface" 417). How strange it would seem to a late-Victorian reader, then, to have us consider Wells an idealistic optimist today.

In *A Scientific Romance*, Wright's David Lambert arrives "After London" in the year 2500 A.D. to "the fox heat of a rainforest. . . . A new heaven, a new earth" (77) in his city now overrun by the ecosystems of the tropics but completely devoid of living humanity. England's rivers have "reclaimed their surface rights" (134), the "sea-level has risen several metres . . . widening the Thames estuary by a mile or so" (77–78), and thick rainforest vegetation obscures most discernible landmarks in the former hub of the Western world. At first, in fact, Lambert hopes against hope that he has landed in what might now be a national park or nature preserve because of the complete and eerie absence of the thriving, bustling London he left. But London is not devoid of life itself; in fact, Lambert soon discovers that it is "spread out below [him] like a promised land" (110) and that the "instinctual clamour of the forest—a skiffle of buzzing, scarping, belching, and sharp cries" relays nature's message to (old) London's (new) last human resident: "*Your* city has been dead for centuries" (97; emphasis added). Being an archaeologist, then, Lambert spends much of his time in speculation about how this civilization—his civilization—came to its end, how "[c]ycles have changed from ice to heat or vice versa not in millennia, but in *decades*" (88), and how London itself became a tropical Eden. There are enough standing buildings, he believes, "to rule out a bang. But what sort of whimper?" (111). So what happened? "Warming, obviously, as many foresaw. But for the reasons they foresaw? Or something else, something for which we can't be blamed: an asteroid smacking the planet in the chops; or the world relapsing like a malaria patient into its old sweat and chills?" (Wright, *A Scientific Romance* 87).

And herein lies the crux of *A Scientific Romance* as a dystopic speculation about the world on our current civilization's doorstep: Where Wells is content to imagine a future world whose evolutionary lines are drawn very clearly, Wright employs a protagonist whose vision is less stable and whose consciousness is less secure in its assumptions of how his new here-and-now came to be. In other words, Wright has Lambert asks Wells' rhetorical questions literally, to us, his readers, fumbling toward whatever whimper is set to fade us into civilizational silence. Most notably, Wright plants the seeds of doubt about the globalization and "free-ness" of our current markets, culture, and economic perspective in the deafening silences that wake Lambert from his slumber in the abandoned Tower of London:

> Again and again the enormity of where I am crashes down, stripping me naked in this ancient monument, my home. And the next thought: what chance that the rest of the world is any different? The civilizations of the past were local, feeding on particular ecologies. While one fell, another rose elsewhere. But ours has wrapped itself around the world, its very scale and complexity making it uniquely vulnerable to any global change. It isn't hard to see the droughts and floods, the failed harvests, the end of trade, the refugees, the desperate measures to control the starving. (97)

The world gone to seed here is in fact recognizably our world in ruins—a ustopia in its marked otherness from the gold standard by which we live today, and one in which Lambert's out-loud speculations necessarily fall on deaf ears while his textual ones must resonate into our own here-and-now, still lingering in the *before* before the ustopic fall.

The legacy that Lambert brings with him to his new world (from our here-and-now) is a damning one; he suffers from BSE (though there are suggestions it might in fact be HIV), he is unprepared for the power of the sun (81), and despite befriending an affectionate puma whom he names Graham (101) he is terrified of his solitude. In fact, his very presence in London in the year 2500 A.D. is owing only to his willingness to attempt the impossible as a means of potential suicide out of a world—our world—that has nothing but suffering and hopelessness to offer him. If Lambert's new world is not itself civilizationally dead, though, neither is it empty or devoid of the traces of its old self. In stumbling upon what he assumes to be a landfill, he reflects upon the inevitable legacy of *stuff* that the twentieth century has left to its ustopic future:

> All those *things* . . . Zamfir recordings, yo-yos, xylophones, weedkillers, video games, train sets, televisions, stereos, snuff films, rocket silos, railways, pinball tables, one-armed bandits, oil refineries, nuclear piles, motorhomes, milk cartons, lipsticks, lawnmowers, lava lamps, Kleenex holders, Jacuzzis, hula-hoops, houseboats, gravy boats, golf carts, footballs, fondue sets, drinks trolleys, cameras, bottles, beds, airliners—all those splendid Things that made up the sum of the world, which we had to keep on making and buying to keep ourselves diverted and employed—were just garbage-to-be. Ripped, smelted, sucked, blown from the raddled earth; turned into must-haves, always-wanteds, major advances, can't-do-withouts. And *pouf!* a decade later, a season later, it's ashamed-to-be-seen-in, clapped out, white elephant, obsolete, *infra dig*, inefficient, passé, and away it goes to the basement or the bushes or the ditch or the bottom of the sea. . . . Our final century has left more of a mess than our previous million years. (160–61)

Lambert the archaeologist is left to wander the former motorways of England (turfed conveniently and exclusively with what he believes to be a species of weed-choking "*Übergras*" [173] called Ecolawn that had been in development by "Big Oil and Briggs & Stratton" [142] at the moment of his departure from the twentieth century) and to dig through the detritus of the future, guided only by his own speculations, sparse documents, and overpass graffiti—"civilization's last comment on itself" (155)—scrawled on the decaying infrastructure of England and charting a spotty history suggestive of our end times: we learn, at the very least, of seasonal evacuations of London (136) before a definitive "moment of abandonment" (131), likely in the face of a major global military conflict that led to the final rise of a corporatocracy (evidenced by documents that treat the Land Rover Corporation as a kind of government body and evidence that health care had become little more than privatized euthanasia) that facilitated, we assume, the end of civilization itself.

Or at least civilization as Lambert (and we) knew/know it. Lambert's journey north to the shores of present-day Loch Ness proves to him that he is not alone; he falls into the unfriendly clutches of the Macbeth clan—a tribe of around five thousand "survivors" genetically modified (ostensibly Africanized) to deal with the warmer climate but living in primitive, barbaric, and seemingly "Neolithic" (203) conditions. Lambert is taken hostage and treated as a supernatural signifier delivered to the clan from the mythical *beyond* beyond their own unwritten maps of consciousness. The village, replete with "wafting Chaucerian smells [of] ageing meat and offal; urine, straw, and dung" (215), is also itself littered with the detritus of the materialistic twentieth century—the clan decorates their hall with shiny compact discs, they revere a very familiar plastic golden arch as a war trophy won from the Macdonald clan, and the women wear bottle-caps as earrings—which is explained to its inhabitants through a roughly memorized (for literacy is nearly extinct) sermon by the dreadlocked clan leader Angus Kwame Macbeth. His own version of the future's Book of Genesis consists primarily of a poorly memorized version of our own Chapter 24 of the Book of Isaiah:

> Behold, the Lord maketh the earth empty, and maketh it waste, and turneth it upside down, and scattereth abroad the inhabitants thereof. The land shall be utterly emptied, and utterly spoiled; for the Lord hath spoken this word. The earth mourneth and fadeth away, the world languisheth and fadeth away, the haughty people of the earth do languish. The earth also is defiled under the inhabitants thereof; because they have transgressed the laws, changed the ordinance, broken the everlasting covenant. Therefore hath the curse devoured the earth, and they that dwell therein are desolate: therefore the inhabitants of the earth are burned, and few men left. In the city is left desolation, and the gate is smitten with destruction. For thou hast made of a city an heap; of a defenced city a ruin. (228)

When Macbeth discovers Lambert's literacy, though, the time traveller quickly becomes a commodity for his ability to explain the clan's heretofore muted documents and artifacts. Lambert's near-fatal mistake comes when the increasingly affable Macbeth asks him to explain the concept of civilization itself during one of their conversations. Panicking because of his own recent revelations, though, Lambert indirectly "hint[s] at cycles of plunder and collapse" (259) aloud, wisely keeping his actual conclusions about human progress to himself (and us):

> Civilization is plumbing
> Civilization requires slaves
> Civilization is gunpowder, printing, and the Protestant religion
> Civilization is arranging the world so you needn't experience it
> Civilization is the gradual replacement of men by things
> Civilization is living beyond your means
> Civilization results in deserts
> Civilization dies as easily from irony as from debauchery (259)

Lambert's reflective honesty, however suppressed, is clearly coloured by the travelling that he has done across centuries and the evidence that he now has of civilization's self-immolation upon the altar of unchecked materialism. Lambert is literally crucified as a cursed Saviour the next day, escaping only thanks to the secret scheming of his friend Mailie, who arranges for him to be pulled off the cross and secreted to a waiting sailboat which he steers silently across the Loch to safety in the *beyond* outside of the clan's reach. Humbled and disheartened, Lambert gradually makes his way back to London to recover the Wells device and depart the year 2500 (and the narrative of *A Scientific Romance*) for the unknown shores of his next future world. Unlike Wells, Wright realizes that time travel can only move toward the future—one cannot return to alter the past—so Lambert's disappearance into the oblivion of tomorrow comes to stand for the silence that *A Scientific Romance* threatens us with unless we begin to ask ourselves the here-and-now questions that, for Lambert, can only be rhetorical.

In his canonical updating, Wright agrees to speculate in a way that his predecessors did not: the natural world—tropically overgrown or otherwise—will not be the source of our civilizational collapse, but will instead bear its brunt with constancy. Humanity's curse after NAFTA is not to survive against the malevolent natural world CanLit *Survival*-style, but to survive ourselves, with our own provocations of that world, and our material-driven exploitations of it in the name of progress and civilization. Even Wright's Lambert, who at first seems to inhabit a lush and self-repairing Eden, acknowledges of his old world that "[o]ne thing seems clear enough: nature didn't clobber us, except in self-defence. There was no *deus ex machina*, no cosmic foot. . . . Shall we go for the 'great villain' school of historical blame, or must we concede that the enemy of the people was the people? How many politicians were willing to tell the world that four billion, or six billion, or ten could never live the California dream?" (288–89). Still, the crux and thrust of this imaginative fiction lies not in its prognostications and admonishments, but in its probing speculations *about* and *as* a future.

Michael Murphy's *A Description of the Blazing World* also speculates upon this world's potential futures, albeit in a much different register than that of Wright's *A Scientific Romance*. On the eve of the so-called Northeast Blackout of 2003 in which upwards of 60 million North Americans lost power due to a major overload, the Greater Toronto Area experienced cascading power failures that lasted anywhere between three and ninety-six hours. One of Murphy's protagonists—fourteen-year-old Morgan Wells from "Nowhereville, NS" (18), in "shithole Toronto," "the world's dumbest city" (Murphy 64, 161) to spend the summer with his despised older brother—discovers a copy of Margaret Cavendish's 1666 novella *A Description of a New World, Called the Blazing World* in his brother's apartment while searching for candles in the dark. The young Morgan, reared on Choose-Your-Own-Adventure novels and in constant search of meaning in what angstily seems to him to be a meaningless world, believes the book itself and the circumstances by which it comes to him to be significant: "I wouldn't go so far as to say I thought I was receiving a message from beyond the grave or anything, but it seemed strange to me that on the day when the power went out, when everyone in the whole city thought the world was about to end, I'd found a book that seemed to be about the world coming to an end. The world burning up" (Murphy 78). Although the blackout fails to deliver on its seeming apocalyptic promise, it sparks a morbid sense of foreboding about the state of post-NAFTA civilization that uses Cavendish's original Blazing World as its ustopic template.

In fact, Cavendish's enigmatic proto-feminist and proto-science-fiction tale is not in and of itself apocalyptic, despite all of its blazing. The narrative follows, to quote the young Morgan's paraphrasing, "this woman, this super hot Lady with a capital L, who gets kidnapped by some foreigner for sex slave purposes" (51), but who stumbles into a literal other world at the North Pole after her captors die of exposure in the Arctic weather, because, thanks to a combination of Restoration-era geographical uncertainty and pure fictional imagination, "the Poles of the other World, joining to the Poles of this, do not allow any further passage to surround the World that way; but if any one arrives to either of these Poles, he is either forced to return, or to enter into another World" (Cavendish 155–56). The woman is quickly met by a variety of gentle, intelligent, and fantastical hybrid creatures (Bear-men, Bird-men, Fish-men, Worm-men) who whisk her away to the Emperor's golden city (itself called Paradise) where she is immediately married to the Emperor and named Empress of all the Blazing World. As her first order of imperial business, she insists on understanding her new civilization—a world in which the sun, moon, and stars shine extraordinarily brightly, thus prompting the world's pejorative descriptor (167). The Empress enlists her new subjects in an exhaustive survey of physical, metaphysical, scientific, biological, philosophical, and religious questions about the Blazing World in order to establish its characteristics. The Empress is able to establish some general facts about her own seemingly utopian society—that "the men were of several complexions, but none like any of our World . . . there was but one language in all that world, nor no more than one Emperor, to whom they all submitted with the greatest duty and obedience, which made them live in a continued peace and happiness, not acquainted with other forreign [sic] wars, or home-bred insurrections" (160), and that they enjoyed political and religious harmony and unanimity. In doing so the Empress establishes a speculative world that has its clear and recognizable precedent in the England of Cavendish's own day. The Empress, though, grows wary of the arrogance of the scientific prognostications made by her servants with the help of both telescopes and microscopes, and she ultimately concludes, in order to "satirize the arrogant opinions of modern philosophers who claim that mankind has superior powers of observation, especially when aided by the technology of a microscope" (Bowerbank and Mendelson 31–32), that "Natures [sic] Works are so various and wonderful, that no particular Creature is able to trace her ways" (Cavendish 185). There are several reasons that this aspect of Cavendish's text is historically, sociologically, and epistemologically remarkable, not the least of which is the vehemence with which she concludes her treatise (after a lengthy militaristic foray back into her own world). In her "Epilogue to the Reader," Cavendish proffers an Atwoodian buffer against her inevitable detractors:

> [I]n the formation of these Worlds, I take more delight and glory, then ever *Alexander* or *Caesar* did in conquering this terrestrial world. . . . I have made my *Blazing-world*, a Peaceable World, allowing it but one religion, one Language, and one Government; yet could I make another World . . . if any should like the World I have made, and be willing to be my Subjects, they may imagine themselves such, and they are such; I mean, in their Minds, Fancies or Imaginations; but if they cannot endure to be subjects, they may create Worlds of their own, and Govern themselves as they please . . . (251)

This is an invitation that Murphy willingly accepts in his reimagination of what *The Blazing World* (and the Blazing World) might promise in the new millennium, and one that his own text demands of us anew.

Appropriately, mid-blackout Toronto does become a kind of blazing world for its millions of inhabitants (Morgan included) with the newly observed brightness of the nighttime stars (Murphy 65, 66, 92, 169) and the suddenly "moon-shiny-night[s] . . . the first in decades" (67) in the city. This blazing aside, though, discovering the Cavendish book proves to be especially provocative for the teen's overactive imagination; as a boy who frequently fantasizes about all of the ways he might die over the course of a typical day, Morgan is immediately able to draw connections between his plight and that of Cavendish's Empress: "I was in a new world, a hostile environment, a humid garbage town full of strange creatures. [Cavendish's] story reminded me of being downtown. Of seeing so many people from so many places looking so lost" (Murphy 52). Tellingly, and in direct defiance of his sister-in-law who has warned him about E. coli and tainted beef, young Morgan is "trying to decide between a regular burger and a cheeseburger in the Eaton Centre food court when the lights flickered, then went out" (42). Upon evacuating the mall, young Morgan makes his way to Union Station in the blinding heat in a suddenly frozen cityscape that invokes the chaos of 9/11 New York City:

> The sidewalks were choking. Rivers of people. The subway was shut down, there were stranded commuters everywhere, briefcases and book-bags floating along the surface of the city. I've never seen that many bodies all in one space. All drowning. The traffic lights were out. The bodies, the cars, the metalized air. No one knew what was happening. (43)

Young Morgan's "terror alert [goes] from yellow to orange" (48) as he makes his way to his brother's home "thinking about weapons of mass destruction and the Middle East" (44). By the time he arrives, Morgan's overactive imagination has concluded, irrefutably, that "[t]he blackout was clearly only the beginning. A test. . . . First take the power out, see what happens. Wait a day or two. Then cut the power off for good before sending in the nukes. It seemed so obvious. We'd be picking the flesh off our faces before the week was up. I knew it" (71). Among other things that Morgan suddenly "knows" upon uncovering the Cavendish book is that he must produce and preserve a record of the end-of-days, "[s]omething to leave behind for future archaeologists, something they could find three hundred and thirty-seven years after civilization as we know it had disappeared off the face of the earth" and after "the men in hazmat suits [had] comb[ed] through the smoking ruins of Toronto, a place still radioactive and crawling with subhuman winged creatures, airborne zombies, drooling, slobbering Torontonians desperate for a taste of human meat" (87). The young Morgan's record, though unlike Cavendish's, would be "[n]ot about a new world, but a world about to be no more. A dead world. . . . The nuclear power plants all Chernobyling at once, sending clouds of Black Death from one city to the next. The Great Lakes turning toxic in a half-second, bubbling and seething with biochemical diseases" (87).

Murphy's *A Description of the Blazing World* endows its protagonist with the stifling burden of materialistic modernity wherein the Eaton Centre—"the mall that is one thousand malls, the A/C island at the heart of this hellhole city" (193)—becomes the his last refuge and escape: "the only place in Toronto that lets me forget I am in Toronto" (193). He has, it seems, given up. Unlike Wright's tenacious protagonist, young Morgan is settling in for what is surely coming for him: the horrible fictional fact of tomorrow. Wright's David Lambert has not, against all odds, given up. Looking back— to us, his readers—he still wonders if twentieth-century capitalism and civilization's track record of greed and self-destruction could have been/ might still be tempered:

> Could it have gone another way? Is the Good Samaritan always a bad economist? Was capitalism—that "machine for demolishing limits"—a suicide machine? . . . [W]ere all human systems doomed to stagger along under the mounting weight of their internal logic until it crushed them? And I think of the Maya temples reaching higher and higher as the jungle

died by the stone axe. And I think of Easter Island, and even there—where the limits must have been plain to anyone—the last tree came down to put up the last colossus, the rains washed the soil to the sea, the people starved and ate each other, and there was no escape because without wood there's no canoe. (*A Scientific Romance* 167–68)

Both Wright and Murphy reinvigorate what they recognize in Wells and Cavendish as the nebulous and fleeting frailty of human existence on the planet, as well as our contradictory confidence in our own supremacy over both the space and time of our here-and-now. Wright's mature speaker recognizes that the promise (and premise) of Wells' original scientific romance is one of survival and evolutionary disaster resulting from the perfect functioning of epistemological, scientific, and economic systems of late modernity—*A Scientific Romance* revises this thesis into a postmodern ustopic world that does not allow us to get that far and that does not allow our here-and-now world to exist but in buried, mute fragments silenced by the planet itself. Lambert's acknowledgement that "[e]ven if our peculiar gifts were ultimately fatal, nature will make the best of the mess we've left behind" (306) is mirrored awkwardly by young Morgan's final adolescent apocalyptic vision of our civilizational insignificance: "When the great plague comes we'll rot from the guts to the skin until there's nothing left but corpses crumbling in the corners of rooms, floating bloated in the ocean, rotting slowly in the sand. We're dead. We're a fraction of a second. We were never here" (Murphy 234). That Morgan's *Blazing* visions never come to fruition proves superficially disappointing to him as he heads back to Nova Scotia to start school again, but the terrifying promise that Cavendish's ustopic text makes sparks in him an awareness of the fragility and artificiality of the air-conditioned world of late-capitalist Toronto, and makes visible the spectre of its own impending decimation. There is, apart from the fictional, no other world from which we might escape when this one begins to blaze.

In *A Short History of Progress*, Wright notes that "[o]ne of the dangers of writing a dystopian satire is how depressing it is when you get things right" (122). In the decade that he took to craft *A Scientific Romance* into the postmodern masterpiece that it was to become, Wright himself witnessed what we might consider the clearest marker of the urgency of the novel's plea: when he began crafting the narrative he intended Lambert's impending death from BSE to be a "wild extrapolation" (*A Short History*

122) of fictional licence—a fantastic exaggeration born of the then-muted speculations about the severity and scale of what was to become the global BSE crisis. By the time the novel was complete, though, several British citizens had died of the disease, and the narrative's fictional thrust had become a terrifyingly real present. That is to say, then, the seeds and traces of the for-now-imaginary futures of both *A Scientific Romance* and *A Description of the Blazing World* exist today. They *are* the ustopias of the future; other worlds that are speculatively here-and-soon. And as the crumbling of our late-capitalist and post-NAFTA institutions continue to sow the hypothetical seed for the archaeologists of the future who might harvest our ruins centuries from now, Wright and Murphy leave their texts as warnings about repeating history, reconsidering "progress," and rereading the promises of science fiction as a genre. Neither the time travel of Wells and Wright, nor the wild, blazing geographies of Cavendish and Murphy, are the point of their speculative or imaginative fictions—they are, we might assume, the fictions themselves. *What* they speculate upon—our world returned Edenic in our civilizational absence, the fiery culmination of our socio-economic suicide in an apocalyptic flash—remain the urgent and prescient threads seeded in SF's master-narratives: reminders that, in the words of Carl Jung, "[t]hat which we do not bring to consciousness appears in our lives as fate" (qtd. in *In Other Worlds* 15). Novels like *A Scientific Romance* and *A Description of the Blazing World* deny the very concept of fate when it comes to their ustopias and their projections of our futures. They remind us, we hope, of the promise—not the sentence—of the future by trying to scare us straight with speculation. More importantly, both Wright and Murphy recognize the value that Sylvia Bowerbank and Sara Mendelson attribute to Cavendish's *The Blazing World*: they "urge us to consider whether new worlds and new natures are waiting to be discovered by those readers with bold imaginations" (34). So when Atwood wonders why we still insist on preserving, revisiting, and retelling the stories in the face of the great unknown tomorrow by asking, "Do we tell them to show off our skills, to unsettle the complacent audience, to flatter rulers, or, as Scheherazade the Queen of Storytelling did, to save our own lives?" (41), we might answer "yes" to all. But let us hope, then, that like David Lambert, we might let these novels, in their imaginative prophesying, do the same for us as we wade into our yet-to-be-written futures.

Works Cited

Ashcroft, Bill, Gareth Griffiths, and Helen Tiffin. *The Empire Writes Back: Theory and Practice in Post-Colonial Literatures*. 2nd ed. London: Routledge, 2002. Print.

Atwood, Margaret. *In Other Worlds: SF and the Human Imagination*. Toronto: McClelland & Stewart, 2011. Print.

———. *Survival: A Thematic Guide to Canadian Literature*. Toronto: Anansi, 1972.

Bowerbank, Sylvia and Sara Mendelson. "Introduction." *Paper Bodies: A Margaret Cavendish Reader*. Ed. Sylvia Bowerbank and Sara Mendelson. Peterborough: Broadview, 2000. 9–34. Print.

Cavendish, Margaret. *A Description of a New World, Called the Blazing World*. 1666. *Paper Bodies: A Margaret Cavendish Reader*. Ed. Sylvia Bowerbank and Sara Mendelson. Peterborough: Broadview, 2000. 151–251.

Drabble, Margaret. "Introduction." *Three Science Fiction Novels* by H.G. Wells. Toronto: Knopf/Everyman, 2010. vii–xix. Print.

Gartner, Zsuzsi. "A Few (Hundred) Words from the Editor." *Darwin's Bastards: Astounding Tales from Tomorrow*. Ed. Zsuzsi Gartner. Vancouver: Douglas & McIntyre, 2010. 1–6. Print.

Grubisic, Brett Josef. "Astounding Tales." Review of *Darwin's Bastards* edited by Zsuszi Gartner. 2 May 2010. *Ottawa Citizen*. Web. 20 Feb. 2012.

———. "Margaret Atwood: A Dedicated Rummager with Eclectic Tastes." Review of *In Other Worlds* by Margaret Atwood. 3 Nov. 2011. *Vancouver Sun*. Web. 20 Feb. 2012.

Murphy, Michael. *A Description of the Blazing World*. Calgary: Freehand, 2011. Print.

Wells, H.G. Preface. *The Time Machine*. 1931. *Three Science Fiction Novels* by H.G. Wells. Toronto: Knopf/Everyman, 2010. 415–18. Print.

———. *The Time Machine*. 1895. *Three Science Fiction Novels* by H.G. Wells. Toronto: Knopf/Everyman, 2010. 3–87. Print.

Wright, Ronald. *A Scientific Romance: A Novel*. 1997. Toronto: Vintage, 1998. Print.

———. *A Short History of Progress*. CBC Massey Lectures. Toronto: Anansi, 2004. Print.

"It's not power, it's sex"
Jeanette Winterson's The PowerBook *and Nicole Brossard's* Baroque at Dawn

Helene Staveley

Both Jeanette Winterson of London, England, and Nicole Brossard of Montreal, Canada, play seriously with reading and sex in their texts. Querying arbitrary distinctions such as those between reality and fiction, theory and narrative, the authentic and the artificial, texts by Winterson and Brossard interrogate distinctions between writing and reading as well. In particular, Winterson's *The PowerBook* (2000) and Brossard's *Baroque at Dawn* (1995; trans. 1997) reverse the conventional relationship between writer and reader. Where sex and seduction are invoked as analogies for the writer-text-reader relationship, especially within metafiction, the writer is often constructed as a seducer who exercises her skills and wiles to bring her target, the reader, to the point of willing surrender. But by recasting their model-reader figures as their seducers—not their writer-protagonists—Winterson and Brossard invert the relationship and privilege the reader's role in the production of texts. Both *The PowerBook* and *Baroque at Dawn* are constructed as texts-in-process that are shaped and moulded by the desires of seducing model readers; the texts-in-process in their turn model uncertain utopias, idyllic possible worlds undermined by dystopic conditions. The utopian desires that subtend both texts are explicitly dialogical, interactive, and erotic, holding out hope for a new world free of phallocratic contaminants. Winterson's writing "I" composes romantic stories online for her lover, a married woman; one of Brossard's two writer-protagonists tries to replenish the ocean's literary significance at the request of her fan.

In each case it is the interests of a seducing reader that direct the parameters of the embedded fictions. This reader is no longer a somewhat gullible person whose submission to a stronger authorial will brings her to relinquish arbitrary notions of "virtue" or value, of fact, reality, and credibility. She is already predisposed toward suspending her disbelief, and willing to embrace fiction as fact, in what she recognizes as a necessary precondition of the narrative process. It is this savvy and seasoned reader who paradoxically introduces to the narratives both utopian and dystopian energies and facilitates their idiomatic rendering in powerfully sexualized terms. In Winterson and Brossard it is the reader figure, not the writer, who takes the initiative in the process of constructing a text. Her engagement in this process helps produce an ontologically disparate narrative whose intersecting realities swell and pulsate with mutually sympathetic sensuality, promising to burst the bounds of the fictional and flood the terrain of the actual.

While Winterson in particular often resists being categorized as a lesbian writer, theorists and critics have placed both her texts and Brossard's within this context. In *Archaeologies of the Future* (2005), Fredric Jameson founds his intensive investigation of utopian writing on the premise that "[the] fundamental dynamic of any Utopian politics (or of any political Utopianism) will therefore always lie in the dialectic of Identity and Difference, to the degree to which such a politics aims at imagining, and sometimes even at realizing, a system radically different from this one" (xii). Theorizations of the complex identities of LGBTQ individuals and communities play intensively with the identity and difference dialectic Jameson references, and utopian writing in particular, according to José Esteban Muñoz in *Cruising Utopia: The Then and There of Queer Futurity* (2009), resonates powerfully in queer reading and writing practices: "We have never been queer, yet queerness exists for us as an ideality that can be distilled from the past and used to imagine a future. The future is queerness's domain. Queerness is a structuring and educated mode of desiring that allows us to see and feel beyond the quagmire of the present. The here and now is a prison house. We must strive, in the face of the here and now's totalizing rendering of reality, to think and feel a *then and there*" (1).

Muñoz follows Ernst Bloch in valorizing utopian thinking that, if abstract, still "pose[s] a critical function that fuels a critical and potentially transformative political imagination" and, if concrete, is "relational to historically situated struggles, a collectivity that is actualized or potential" and that articulates "the hopes of a collective, an emergent group or even a solitary oddball who is the one who dreams for many. Concrete utopias are the realm of educated hope" (3). For Muñoz, hope can be a critical methodology and a hermeneutics as well as a state of mind, and hope for the transformation of human society toward universal acceptance underpins the writing of Winterson and Brossard. In a sentence that Brossard has repeated in several of her works, she writes, "For me the word *lesbian* is laden with an existential flavour and fervour that derive from our faculty for dreams, imagination, utopia" ("Fragments" 23). Rather than constructing the fabulous spaces of science fiction or fantasy, Winterson and Brossard situate their narrative worlds in the context of the actual world, in Winterson's case moving between London and Paris and visiting extant romantic narratives such as the story of Lancelot and Guinevere, and in Brossard's case moving between Buenos Aires, Rimouski, the ocean, and Montreal, with worlds bending back on themselves through a proliferation of writers and readers—Brossard herself makes a cameo appearance within *Baroque at Dawn*. Whatever queer or lesbian utopia emerges within their texts must be possible in reality. Both writers make such utopia desirable through their metafictional deployment of the trope of the romantic relationship, specifically the romantic relationship between a reader who seduces and a writer who succumbs.

To identify reader as seducer and writer as seducee inverts conventional constructions of agency and passivity, production and consumption, femininity and masculinity, and of the sexual experience that is the ubiquitous analogy for all of these and more. In so doing, Winterson and Brossard engage in a project of critique with which feminists have been perhaps especially engaged: the questioning of a thought process that erects arbitrary binaries and dichotomies. On one side, both the seducer and the seduced are women and both narratives participate in a lesbian erotic economy; on the other, the relative aggressiveness or authority of the writer and reader figures is reversed. This revisitation of well-trodden territory also revisits the feminist project of theorizing sexuality. In the 1970s and '80s, theorists including Luce Irigaray and Hélène Cixous distinguished female sexuality from male sexuality, constructing women's erogenous zones as multitudinous and shifting, and women's orgasm as relating to a uniquely female economy of inexhaustible giving. Both of these positions pit "feminine" multiplicity and excess against what they see as a more restrictive phallocentric pattern of arousal, tumescence, friction, and release, or a rigidly masculine "debit versus credit" economy.[1] While this provides an alternative to the phallocentric equivalence between the pattern of male genital climax and plot resolution by making room for alternative points of bliss, it remains an essentializing alternative because it reinforces distinctions between the genders while sidestepping what is held in common.

Jean Baudrillard's *Seduction* (1979; trans. 1990) reinstates these problems by distinguishing the seducer's practices and pleasures from the seductress's and the male's resistances and vulnerabilities from the female's. Yet it also establishes common ground between male and female pleasure. Baudrillard cites a passage by Vincent Descombes:

> What seduces is not some feminine wile, but the fact that it is directed at you. It is seductive to be seduced, and consequently, it is being seduced that is seductive. In other words, the being seduced finds himself in the person seducing. What the person seduced sees in the one who seduces him, the unique object of his fascination, is his own seductive, charming self. (Descombes *L'Inconscient Malgré Lui*; qtd. in Baudrillard, 68)

Seduction is a viscerally compelling experience for both participants because it affirms and validates individual subjectivities whether or not that subjectivity is a temporary disguise assumed by the seducer. Baudrillard contends that the seducer identifies in the "seducee" (or "subject of seduction") signs of vulnerability and of attraction, then incorporates those signs into her own image and reflects them back to the writer. Once the projected vulnerability, sensual attraction, and desire of both parties are "harmonized" by being telegraphed by the seducee and reflected back by the seducer, all that remains is for the seducer to fan the flames of the desire that seems to have sprung up so spontaneously. Baudrillard formulates the actual sexual experience as anticlimactic because the exchange that has pretended to be about affection and validation is actually about power for both participants.

The only truly orgasmic moment for Baudrillard's seducer is the moment of her target's mental surrender. This presumes that the sexual experience is always already agonistic, founded on a competitive economy of triumph and defeat, victor and victim, shallow consumer and vapid product. In "Animal Sex: Libido as Desire and Death," Elizabeth Grosz (1995) reconfigures these power politics that underlie physical sexuality. In her construction, the physical proximity and sensual contact of consensual sex are appealing and even addictive experiences whether or not the adrenalin rush of competition is involved.

> Libidinal desire, the carnal caress, desire as corporeal intensification . . . is an interchange with an other whose surface intersects its own. It is opened up, in spite of itself, to the other, not as passive respondent but as co-animated, for the other's convulsions, spasms, joyous or painful encounters engender or contaminate bodily regions that are apparently unsusceptible. It is in this sense that we make love to worlds: the universe of an other is that which opens us up to and produces our own intensities; we are placed in a force field of intensities that we can only abandon with libidinal loss and in which we are enervated to become active and willing agents (or better, agencies). (290)

Orgasm becomes an experience wherein the "borders" of the subject "blur, seep, liquefy, so that, for a while at least, it is no longer clear where one organ, body, or subject stops and another begins" (290). Narrative can also be constructed as a charged node of interaction between narrator and narratee or as the dynamic encounter between writer and reader; narrative here resembles the charged node of orgasmic interaction in that both are connected to the experience of mutual permeability. In *Volatile Bodies: Toward a Corporeal Feminism* (1994), Grosz works toward a framework that accommodates both the "interior dimensions of subjectivity" and "the surface corporeal exposures of the subject to social inscription" (188), positing "a model which insists on (at least) two surfaces which cannot be collapsed into one and which do not always harmoniously blend with and support each other; a model where the join, the interaction of the two surfaces is always a question of power" (189). Resembling a Möbius strip, this model is powerful because it "has the advantage of showing that there can be a relation between two 'things'—mind and body—which presumes neither their identity nor their radical disjunction, a model which shows that while there are disparate 'things' being related, they have the capacity to twist one into the other" (209–10).

In the case of the text-sex analogy, narrative has the potential to twist its disparate narrators and narratees into one another, to vex power's binaries—dominance-submission, oppression-resistance, victor-victim—by presenting them as distinct but still indistinguishable. This analogy is heightened in Winterson and Brossard by the utopian fantasy of an eroticized narrative encounter that diverts agonistic negotiations for power. Here the limens of subjectivity are overstimulated and distended until distinctions between controller and controlled, seducer and seduced, reader and writer, consumer and producer evaporate in the onrush of jouissance. Some possible textual experiences that promote the idyllic "seeping together" of reading and writing subjects could include: an intensification of ideas or images to the point of overdetermination within a text; felicitous but unforeseen links between disparate ontological levels within a narrative; or what Roland Barthes calls the sensation of being read by the text. Readerly orgasm blurs together reading subject and writing subject, consumer and producer, seducer and seduced.

Partly a reader can be said to seduce simply by reading a text—by selecting one title from among many that promise to satisfy her readerly appetites. The reader desires to find herself or her needs adequately represented in a world outside her own consciousness, and by supplying an appreciative audience for the writer, the seducing reader recodes as an "attraction" the writer's answering vulnerability, which has already been confirmed by the fact that a text is available to be read. When she is being seduced by her reader, the writer is brought to recognize that she has the power to fulfill a particular need for resolution between related ways of thinking. This resolution is apprehended as quasi-sexual in part because of the escalating tension of unknowables (which characters will fail or succeed? will the plot twist? which systems of imagery will inflect the fiction most interestingly?). The writer-seducee also has the power to validate the magnetic seducing reader, whose openly desiring gaze has already refigured her in her own eyes, transforming weakness into strength.[2] The yearning, feigned or otherwise, that the reader-seducer expresses for her target seems to give the writer-seducee the power to interpolate her into a different order, or perhaps into the differently signifying order of the fictional world the writer, in thrall to the reader, is in the process of representing as potentially utopian. It remains the seducer's choice, however, to accept or reject the seducee's interpolating call, to read herself in the terms offered by the writer.

Winterson's *The PowerBook* conflates these issues of sex and seduction with issues of production and consumption by using Iserian model readers and model writers who are involved sexually with each other. Meanwhile, the complexities of *The PowerBook*'s proliferating fictional worlds make them read as though they are in conversation with each other, particularly since they are largely framed in terms of an exchange of emails. This dialogism establishes Winterson's narrative as initiating a utopian critique of a dystopian culture that understands romance as necessarily agonistic.

M. Keith Booker asserts that utopian literature is a recognizably "important means by which any culture can investigate new ways of defining itself and of exploring alternatives to the social and political status quo" because utopian literature "critically examine[s] both existing conditions and the potential abuses that might result from the institution of supposedly utopian alternatives" (3). Winterson's *The PowerBook* fantasizes a no-win, no-lose romantic game of perpetual flux without diminishment; however, this idyll is destabilized by a dystopian reality that prefers its games of love in zero-sum form.

The model-reader figure in Winterson's *The PowerBook* is the married woman whose affair with "I," the writer, provides the underlying premise for the novel. "You," the reader, is consistently represented as the seducer. The novel opens above a store called Verde's, a *topos* whose connection to the imagination is suggested by its stock of costumes and disguises (3); this is where the writing "I" constructs her narratives. Like any shy wallflower at a ball, the writing "I" waits passively for the first few pages for "you" the reader to enter and initiate the relationship. As the narrative progresses through a number of discrete diegetic levels, it becomes clear that "you" the reader has already taken the initiative "in the real world" as well as in the nebulous cyberworld where you-the-reader and the writing "I" interact. At the first meeting between "you" and "I" in Paris, "you" makes the first personal confession of weakness by explaining her fear of surprise (33–34), introduces the topic of sex, and initiates then escalates physical contact (35ff.). In what she later characterizes as begging (108), "you" actively pleads for sexual interaction. "Come to bed with me." / "Now?" ["I" asks]. / "Yes now. It's all I can offer. It's all I can ask" (55). "You" makes her need for sexual interaction clear and suggests that "I" is the only person who can fill this need, even though "you" has another ready alternative in the form of her husband.

In the framing narrative, which is set above Verde's at night near a computer and which details online communication between the pair, "you" the reader-seducer guides the course of both the framing and embedded narrative/s by granting and withholding approval from the writing "I." "You" even specifies which narrative form she wants, requesting a romance instead of the bawdy and picaresque fabliau about Ali and the tulips that the writing "I" has produced (25–26). The writing "I" complies, producing a courtly romance about Lancelot and Guinevere (67–74), Dante's near-Gothic romance of Paolo and Francesca (123–29), an historical romance about mountaineer George Mallory and his beloved Mount Everest (149–52), and a quasi-autobiographical romance about an orphan raised in the Muck Midden (137–46; 193–96). These embedded fables span the gamut of the romance form, representing doomed love on the one hand and the emergence of the protagonist as hero as discussed by Northrop Frye on the other. Separated physically from "you" the reader-seducer, the writing "I" consistently seeks approval and validation from "you," shaping the embedded love narratives to please "you"—and to remind "you" of the passion "you" aroused.

The embedded narratives in Winterson's *The PowerBook* play with the interdependence of lovers. The text's model lovers, "you" and "I," reader and writer, are made up of each other, distinct but inseparable. Kim Middleton Meyer writes about Winterson's construction of loving pairs: "No longer an object to be controlled, [the love object] here has agency and can affect as well as be affected by the narrator"; "in her own right" she is "materially attached and yet conceptually whole" (219). In one embedded romance the writing "I" writes herself as Lancelot; she writes "you," the reader, as Guinevere.

> Your marrow is in my bones. My blood is in your veins. Your cock is in my cunt. My breasts weigh under your dress. My fighting arm is sinew'd to your shoulder. Your tiny feet stand my ground. In full armour I am wearing nothing but your shift, and when you plait your hair you wind it round my head. Your eyes are green. Mine are brown. When I see through your green eyes, I see the meadows bright with grass. When you creep behind my retina, you see the flick of trout in the reeds of the lake.
>
> I can hold you up with one hand, but you can balance me on your fingertips.
>
> I am not wounded unless you wound me.
>
> I am not strong unless you are my strength. (69–70)

In androcentric texts, terms such as these could signal a victor-victim relationship of possession and consumption, but here the writing "I" and the reading "you" are equally possessing and possessed, consuming and consumed. By extension neither reader nor writer holds ultimate control over the text, which consequently remains a text in process, to adapt Linda Hutcheon's phrase: a text whose content is polyvalent because it remains in flux, and whose "meaning" will thus always escape a definitive reading.

The intertwining of reader and writer in *The PowerBook* foregrounds Winterson's postmodernist practice of questioning and eliding dichotomies. The elisions begin early as the lovers, identified mainly by the pronouns I, you, and she, remain nameless except for obvious pseudonyms: Lancelot, Guinevere, Paolo, Francesca. Even physical descriptions are minimal, confined mostly to hairstyle and taste in clothing. Similar techniques are used in popular romances to let readers easily "enter" the character of the protagonist or, as Janice Radway (1984) writes, "to project themselves into the story, to become the heroine, and thus to share her surprise and slowly awakening pleasure at being so closely watched by someone who finds her valuable and worthy of love" (568–69). In its condition as wish-fulfillment strategy, the mass-market romance that Radway discusses parallels the wish-fulfillment strategy on which, as Fredric Jameson (2005) argues, utopian narratives are founded. Readers, Radway asserts, vicariously experience the heroine's "success at drawing the hero's attention to herself, at establishing herself as the object of his concern and the recipient of his care" (582). The process is anything but random or ingenuous. Radway's romance readers have very rigid reading tastes but return repeatedly to writers who produce texts that model fictional worlds they can like. Readers endorse such worlds emotionally, but also financially by paying the purchase price. Purportedly responding to the emotional endorsement, writers facilitate further reader endorsement by restricting characterization to a very few traits that readers see as desirable in romance heroines and heroes (565; 576–77). Apparently based on such indefinables as taste and the quality of emotional response, the process masks itself as a "natural" or "intuitive" one, even a point of vulnerability, but clearly can also be seen as sheer calculation. As Baudrillard writes, "*To seduce is to die as reality and reconstitute oneself as illusion. It is to be taken in by one's own illusion and move in an enchanted world*" (69; italics in original).

Winterson's minimal delineation of character, then, seems calculated to foreground the responsiveness of the writing "I" to the seductive attentions of the reader; it helps to ease the reader's "entry" into the fictional world from the actual world, or to produce the illusion that the boundaries of the fictional world are permeable and have expanded to embrace the reader. This illusion of permeability is intensified by the illusion that the model writer is directly addressing the actual reader through direct addresses such as: "Undress. / Take off your clothes. Take off your body. Hang them up behind the door. Tonight we go deeper than disguise" (4). The intense proximity or even intimacy of reader-seducer and writer-seducee within the fictional world generates desire. While the minimalist characterization in *The PowerBook* is so extreme that it parodies such Harlequin romance conventions, the parodic tone itself foregrounds and intensifies the empathy among reader, character, and writer that is one of the foundations of romance narratives (Radway 569).

Early on in *The PowerBook*, "you" the reader says she prefers structures without cladding, like the Eiffel Tower; she tries to live without cladding in her work, her life, and her body (34–35). Cladding, then, accentuates boundaries and disparities while it disguises foundations. In contrast, open structures seem accessible and honest, displaying an undisguised congruity of design and function. A parallel commitment to a life free of shell and ornament is what the seduced writing "I" comes to value in "you" the reader and in herself:

> In your face, in your body, as you walk and lie down and eat and read, you have become the lineaments of love. When I touch you I touch something deeper than you. This touches something in me otherwise too sunk to ever recover. (188)

Sex expands the terms of love:

> Sex between women is mirror geography. The subtlety of its secret—utterly the same, utterly different. You are a looking-glass world. You are the hidden place that opens to me on the other side of the glass. I touch your smooth surface and then my fingers sink through to the other side. You are what the mirror reflects and invents. (174)

The reader provides for the writer access to both similarity and alterity; but those "exquisite attributes of variation" (214) can produce an illusion of friction, a tension that yearns for release.

Winterson's *The PowerBook* employs this blurring as part of its overt utopian narrative strategy, as suggested by the Lancelot-Guinevere passage explored earlier. The text's embedded romances conflate coition and narrative climax after the male narrative paradigm, because each ends in loss or death shortly after desire is consummated. Yet they also work toward simulating multiple successive orgasms, in part through structural and linguistic repetition. Since the narrative structure intertwines levels and experiences by echoing structures, names, motifs, and linguistic patterns, the interconnecting surfaces of the ontologies are easily recognizable. As the tensile surfaces of the ontologies expand and contract with the ebb and flow of each other's resonances, they seem to achieve a kind of cosmic textual orgasm. The narrative structure of *The PowerBook* seems to hold forth a hope that a utopian ideal is realizable even while the particular relationship that gives rise to that hope falters and fails, and even while the fictional worlds it represents emerge as dystopian, as "imaginative extension[s] of those conditions and systems into different contexts that more clearly reveal their flaws and contradictions" (Booker 3). Additionally, all levels of the narrative are infused with eroticism simultaneously, so that the various fictional worlds are characterized as electrically sexually aware—individually and collectively.

Another case in point, the intricately enfolding structure of Québécoise Nicole Brossard's *Baroque at Dawn* is as erotically energized as that of *The PowerBook*. The opening narrative frame, "Hotel Rafale," begins with a replete Cybil Noland lying between the legs of her lover, La Sixtine, before beginning a new round of lovemaking. The scene charges with erotic energy both characters and every activity they undertake inside or outside the bedroom. Walking through the streets of Buenos Aires, playing tango music, drinking wine, and everything else the lovers do remains suggestive, even when echoed by other characters in other places and at other textual levels. Now erotically overdetermined, these activities help make arcs and folds of the narrative structure while they bring with them their erotic charge.

Erotic "awareness" within a text can be amplified by mutually caressing, recursive narrative folds and superimpositions that model sexual desire.[3] Susan Knutson claims in *Narrative in the Feminine* (2000) that Brossard's characters meet their own needs independently of an androcentric economy. Like Sappho's community of women on Lesbos, Brossard's women engage communally in learning and idea-sharing in order to increase the group's understanding (Knutson 115–21), and they do so whether they are in Buenos Aires, in Rimouski, Quebec, in London, or on a ship on the open sea. In this way Brossard's women bond together and strengthen each other to counteract a poisonous patriarchy, and where erotic interaction occurs it generally amplifies this strength. Fredric Jameson writes in *Archaeologies of the Future* that "The view that opens out onto history from a particular social situation must encourage such oversimplifications; the miseries and injustices thus visible must seem to shape and organize themselves around one specific ill or wrong. For the Utopian remedy must at first be a fundamentally negative one, and stand as a clarion call to remove and to extirpate this specific root of all evil from which all the others spring" (12). In Brossard's novels, patriarchal and phallocentric culture functions as that specific root of all evil. Within the utopian project of continual growth, it is understood that no single meeting of the community members will produce "the ultimate epiphany"; the community's idea-sharing is a process that will grow organically and indefinitely.

While Brossard was raised in privilege within the urban centre of Montreal, she was still raised within the province's then distinctly parochial culture. Compared to English-speaking Canada, which tended to be less Catholic, Quebec in the middle of the twentieth century continued to be dominated by Roman Catholic ideologies that subjugated women, a situation that was especially limiting for women who lived in the isolation of the province's rural areas. As Alice A. Parker writes in *Liminal Visions of Nicole Brossard* (1998), "Femininity in Québec signified passivity and self-sacrifice in the service of others. Suffrage did not come for women in Québec (1940) until a generation after the rest of Canada (1917), and liberation (getting out of the house, access to jobs, control of their bodies, and articulation of desire through a process of re-education and re-vision) was not possible until the 1960s and 70s" (18). According to Parker, "For women like Brossard who became adults in the sixties and early seventies, the groundswell of liberation movements in Europe and North America, along with the analytical tools provided by French thought—existentialism, structuralism and poststructuralisms—as well as the creative boost of *modernité* and postmodernist work were appreciable aids in cultural interrogation and redefinition" (31). Brossard's valorization of the critical utopian potential made available by travelling and by inhabiting cosmopolitan communities emerges through her representation of urban spaces as sites of successful attempts to "[t]o reclaim the body by rewriting it," "to invalidate the old programs, to design new code or strategies for re-education and revaluation" (Parker 29). This also means reclaiming desire, and reclaiming lesbian desire, as a means of perpetuating utopian change.

Brossard's project is to cause actual change in the thought processes of her readers; she hopes "to produce or change consciousness" (Knutson 130) in those who read her texts by stimulating their cortical functions. Her triptych structures, her construction of characters who experience change through interacting sexually and socially with women, and her graphically erotic *scènes blanches* (white scenes) are all techniques that are central to this process, and repetition of event units is itself a technology to effect cortical transformation. Brossard's textually holographic representations of woman in the process of changing emulate "the interaction of wave fronts [that] produces awareness, intention, emotion, motivation, and desire—all Brossardian motifs" (Knutson 131). Jennifer Wawrzinek discusses "Brossard's belief that writing and speaking the female body offers a way to 'break down the oppressive structures of the patriarchal system and to establish a space—discursive, sexual and social—for and between women outside that system'" (72; Annamarie Jagose qtd.). Louise H. Forsyth likewise notes,

> Words are means to produce sharing among real writers and readers—along with textual and virtual ones—as they work together like creatively engaged translators to make meanings out of personal experiences and collective lives. As [Alice] Hunter shows . . . Brossard has adopted and sustained a writing project which is nothing less than a dynamic, experimental and creative process for the never-ending re-invention of the world and of life itself, making imaginative use of words—freed of their conventional, deadwood meanings and placements—in ever-renewed ways of speaking and writing. (36)

Brossard's poems, ficto-theoretical narratives, and essays are insistently utopian, to the point that "Brossardian utopianism" is a topic of discussion among scholars, being founded on her faith in the twin transformational powers of writing and reading and the transformational will of feminists, lesbians, and their allies. In this her texts participate wholeheartedly in what Jameson calls Utopian Fancy: "Where the Utopian Imagination does flourish, it does so in the former space of Utopian Fancy, namely in the attempt to imagine a daily life utterly different from this one, without competition or Care, without alienated labor or the envy and jealousy of others and their privileges" (32). By constructing her ficto-theoretical narratives on principles that model the permeability, even malleability of reality and fiction, Brossard works toward generating concrete, positive change within the mind of the reader—a change which her reader-seducer has already desired to achieve through the writer-seducee, as indicated by her willingness to begin and finish reading the narrative.

Like her earlier texts, *Picture Theory* and *Le Désert Mauve*, Brossard's *Baroque at Dawn* divides easily into the three parts of a triptych structure.

The first segment, "Hotel Rafale," is about Cybil Noland and her sexual and romantic relationship with La Sixtine. The second segment holds three chapters called "Rimouski," "Buenos Aires," and "The *Dark* Future"[4] (English and italics in original). This embedded section of the triptych comprises the most substantial and "complete-seeming" but also distinctly dystopian narrative. It constructs a second Cybil Noland who is pursued by her fan, Occident DesRives, who wants her to produce a text about the ocean with computer image artist Irène Mage. The third frame of the triptych, "One Single Body for Comparison," contains no proper names at all but follows a virtually archetypal publicity tour in Montreal for a writer and translator, both nameless, and an untitled text. This writer, who may or may not be the ambiguous "Hyde Park woman" who has appeared to both Cybils (23–26, 42, 111, 181),[5] keeps the journal of the tour which forms *Baroque at Dawn*'s third and final frame.

The fictionality of each third of the triptych is affected by the other thirds in succession. "Hotel Rafale," the opening frame situated in a hotel in Buenos Aires, adheres to basic novelistic conventions like verisimilitude and linear progression, so that both its truth-value and its fictionality seem commensurate with those of any other fiction. In the second section, embedded-Cybil, who begins in Rimouski, insistently constructs both La Sixtine and framing-Cybil[6] as characters in a narrative she is producing. "Hotel Rafale" now seems to be a fragment of a novel written by this second Cybil; accordingly, its truth-value seems to diminish while its fictionality increases. The triptych's final third, the publicity tour for the Hyde Park writer and her translator, codes the writing "I" or Hyde Park woman as more real or "actual" than both (fictional) Cybils. Her narrative follows the form of excerpts from a private journal, recording subjective impressions with little attempt to accommodate a reader outside herself. The reality effect of a narrative written in journal form is exceptionally pronounced because journals generally seem less mediated by aesthetic concerns than are literary narratives, apparently abjuring formal progressive literary conventions like plot, characterization, setting, imagery.

In Brossard's text the reality effect of "One Single Body for Comparison,"[7] the closing frame set entirely within a cosmopolitan Montreal, trumps the "realities" of both preceding narratives. Viewed retrospectively from the standpoint of "One Single Body for Comparison," the comparative status of the fragmentary "Hotel Rafale" as fictional or actual artifact becomes indifferent, even irrelevant, while the more finished and elaborate second embedded narrative about the ocean voyage with Irène and Occident seems almost exaggeratedly artificial. It is now possible to read the triptych's centre section as a novel within a novel: one fiction embedded whole and complete between two halves of a framing "real-world" (or realer-world) narrative, a technique Brossard has already employed in *Le Désert Mauve* (1987). Since Brossard strategically resists conventional characterization and closure in her writing practice, the artificiality of the second, central section amplifies its negative status as dystopian narrative: dystopian due to the interference of masculine influences dividing women from each other and themselves. The negative potential of this dystopian world is carefully bracketed and contained by the opening and closing frames, and its ontological status is implicitly coded as irredeemably fictional. Its presence within the narrative establishes a negative example of a phallocratic situation to be avoided even while it transforms the utopian dream into a dialogic situation. Jameson writes, "But what in literature or art remains an irreconcilable existence of so many absolutes, on the order of the various religions, becomes in the Utopian tradition a Bakhtinian dialogue or argument between positions which claim the stats of the absolute but are willing to descend into the field of struggle of representability and desire in order to win their case and convert their readership" (143). And yet the dialogue also effects an interpenetration of the three ontologies that is intricately sensual, suggesting worlds that enfold, caress, and embrace each other in a relationship predicated on mutual compromise, and recalling both the *scène blanche* between framing-Cybil and La Sixtine in the opening pages of the narrative and Grosz's image of orgasmically intersecting worlds.

Like Winterson's *The PowerBook*, Brossard's *Baroque at Dawn* presents model writers and readers. There are multiple model writers. One, or possibly both, of the two Cybil Nolands write;[8] there are two different Nicole Brossards, one who writes the novel *Baroque at Dawn* and one who, as an author admired by Cybil (124–27), is fictionalized within the text; and there are the nebulous unnamed writer figures known as the "Hyde Park woman" and/or the "Covent Garden woman" (it is not clear whether or not they are the same character). These nominally different writer-women become increasingly indistinct until it is difficult to tell which one is writing the other, and indeed the distinction becomes more immaterial each time one writer thinks of the other and blurs the boundaries between their fictional spheres—both the ones they write and the ones they inhabit. It matters more that women collectively are rethinking and rewriting the world than that any single woman should either take responsibility or receive credit. The proliferation of writer-figures strains the boundaries between "fictional" and "actual," vexing the construction of any reality effect and promoting the concept that actual concrete change can be catalyzed within a fiction. The seducing reader may indeed have died as reality and reconstituted herself as illusion, but Brossard's liminal and holographic narrative offers her a means of rebirth as a new kind of person in a new kind of utopian reality.

Far outnumbered by writers, the most easily identifiable model reader in *Baroque at Dawn* is Occident DesRives. She neither writes, illustrates, nor designs the book, but like the reading public whose reading interests, cash outlay, and mere existence are crucial to literary production, she does provide the parameters, the funding, and the means of executing the project. Interestingly, when Occident is inspired by Cybil's name to discourse on the five sibyls of Classical times, she observes that "Each holds a book in her hand, except for the youthful Delphic sibyl who is holding the rolled end of a papyrus scroll" (trans. Claxton 134).[9] Occident constructs the sibyls as holding books that are apparently complete volumes to be read rather than manuscripts to be written, making the sibyls readers more than writers, that is, interpreters and communicators of signs and portents. As a reader, Occident prioritizes the reading function, describing the sibyls in a way that suggests how she might read herself: as a powerful oracle capable of deciphering mysterious messages and passing them on. As model-reader Occident herself is magnetic, dictatorial, and enigmatic, staying largely in the background until her death moves her to the forefront. But at the same time, Occident comes to be read as iconic of this section's dystopianism, as if she bears in her body and mind the scars of living as a woman in a world explicitly hostile to women and women's utopian potential, as signalled by the vivid "pink scar"[10] on her face. In one telling event, she pressures her creative collaborators Cybil and Irène to attend a screening of pornographic films held by the ship's all-male crew, a situation that Cybil in particular finds extremely offensive (161–65). Almost immediately after Occident's death, Brossard's text moves out of the realm of the fictive altogether and into "One Single Body for Comparison," whose ontology throws off conventions of fictionality to mimic a less mediated actuality.

Meanwhile, erotic interaction is strangely suppressed in the embedded dystopian narrative. Writer embedded-Cybil and reader Occident do not have an affair at all, and while Cybil and Irène do engage erotically with each other once each at Rimouski, at Buenos Aires, and on board the ship so resonantly named "Le Symbole," these encounters unfold off-page. The erotic resonance that builds up around framing-Cybil and La Sixtine in "Hotel Rafale" seems to have a stronger impact on embedded-Cybil than her affair with Irène. Her preoccupation with her "character" La Sixtine gradually outstrips her anxiety about the literary conventions she thinks she has violated by importing a character with her own name into her text (55–56, 62).[11] Eventually both Cybils seem equally in love with the fictional musician regardless of the incommensurability of fictional and actual worlds, so that the text's erotic charge undulates among both fictionalized and quasi-actual versions of writer, reader, musician, and illustrator figures. Their worlds rub against each other, producing interpretive jouissance at unexpected times in unusual places as motifs, discursive threads, characters, actions, and insights echo from plane to plane.

What Brossard works toward in her narrative structure is echoed by her model readers and writers. In the narrative embedded in the centre of the triptych, embedded–Cybil Noland is already immersed in producing a number of texts when Occident approaches her. Concerned that the ocean is being depleted of its literal and figurative value, Occident, coded as hypnotically but jarringly attractive despite (or because of?) her scarred face, hopes that the collaboration between embedded-Cybil and Irène will help change received ideas about the ocean and replenish its earlier, rich levels of significance. They correspond by letter, and Cybil, enchanted with the style and content of Occident's letters, "[plays] hard to get" (trans. Claxton 52).[12] Occident discusses representations of the ocean by Verne, Melville, Conrad, da Vinci, and Cousteau, seductively implying that Cybil's book will "fit" into that company.[13] She clinches the seduction by offering Cybil "all the freedom you could wish. [. . .] I want heart, I want your passion" (trans. Claxton 51–52).[14]

But ironically the ship, called "Symbol," is a phallocracy: the ship is crewed by men, access to the ocean is mediated by men, and even forceful Occident finds it politic to defer to the men. Embedded-Cybil and Irène are virtually imprisoned for the first five days on board, since the newly tyrannical Occident, whose demeanour until now had seemed courting or seductive, restricts them to the library to study male-authored texts and movies about the ocean (135–36). Later, Cybil and Irène experience immersion in the ocean only through an instructional virtual-reality program on diving produced by three men, the brothers Demers. Despite being surrounded by it, Cybil and Irène can access the actual ocean only from the deck, which seems contrary to the reason for the voyage. Although Irène, who herself makes art of computer graphics, takes to the virtual-reality technology easily, Cybil feels disconcertingly, frighteningly overstimulated by the experience of realities superimposing themselves on each other, and her mounting ambivalence toward the project intensifies (174–75). She cannot rest or write, and the women with whom she is to build a creative community and replenish the ocean's symbolic resonance do not meet her needs. The frustration she experiences at these severe restrictions does, however, eventually bring Cybil the vivid dreams that fuel her writing, which Occident asserts was part of her plan all along:

> If dreaming means being there without being there, you must agree that I made you dream beyond anything you ever hoped for. [. . .] It's not in my power to free the dark forces holding you on shore. I have never questioned your freedom of expression. [. . .] An artist must be able to turn everything to account, including the deadwood that hinders the coming of thoughts. (trans. Claxton 186)[15]

By voicing her intention to nudge her writer-seducee toward unfamiliar levels of courage and resourcefulness, and toward new ways of reading and writing the world, Occident begins to utter an idea that is affirmed by the wider universe when a siren figure called "Voice" (trans. Claxton 187)[16]—composed of writer Cybil, illustrator Irène, and reader Occident—appears and urges Cybil to produce a cosmically female text by blending disparate unknowns:

> You will write this book in the midst of night, mingling your shadow with the shades, uniting the dead with the living, and all the necessary words with your overabundance of desire. [. . .] You will seek out every one of those voices, the high and the low whose tones you hear even now, the recitative, the modulated strains of anxiety and fear, the cries of joy and pleasure, the enigmatic whisperings, the amorous murmurs in the pale light of morning. [. . .] Your ear you will place to the mouths of loud-voiced, angry women, fearless of the crudity and gravity of their words. You will kiss Occident on her ugly pink scar, shuddering with her in the memory of time. You will teeter above the abyss and the water, and live in your vertigo. (trans. Claxton 187)[17]

By conjoining the figures of the writer, the artist, and the reader, the Voice, a quasi-hallucinatory vision seen by Cybil, Irène, and Occident but whose "reality" is otherwise unclear, bodies forth their inescapable interdependence. Evoking the interacting ontologies of the orgasmic narrative, and articulating a utopian dream within a dystopian ontology, this intensely sensual description conjures its addressee, Cybil, not only to engage with a multiplicity of worlds, but to inhabit her own vertigo, to relinquish her accustomed boundaries and embrace the dizzying disequilibrium of other actualities.

Because Occident, along with Irène and La Sixtine, is named specifically by the Voice, the seducing reader seems integral to this cosmic project. But mere hours later the asthmatic Occident dies aboard the "Le Symbole," ironically unable to breathe the sea air, and while she later regrets it (198), Cybil permits the men to exclude her from the death-scene (195–96). Merging the end of the tale with its beginning, Cybil describes her stay at a hotel and her efforts to write the text demanded of her by Occident and the Voice, an activity that receives her intense concentration and hard work. The hotel itself is ornate but empty and offers no meaningful interaction with other guests. Anticlimax, disappointment, and futility attend the end of "The *Dark* Future": Cybil is deprived of access not only to the seducing reader, but also to the artist, the ocean, the Voice, and the many worlds they hold. While the triptych's framing narratives and fictional worlds hover at the limens of Cybil's embedded world, the gaps they offer to fill are not those that Cybil experiences; for the moment even the writing seems unpromising to her, and the prospect of another seducing reader seems remote.

Embedded at the heart of *Baroque at Dawn* and woven through with ambivalence, this tale seems exceptionally dystopic even for Brossard, who in *Le Désert Mauve* and elsewhere has used dystopic figures to counterpoint utopic potential. Brossard herself points out, in conversation with Louise Forsyth, her penchant for positioning a male character as an "oppositional figure" in her narratives (Brossard 2005, 26–27, 28), as Wawrzinek establishes in her analysis of Longman in *Le Désert Mauve*; as a character, Longman is specifically evocative of nuclear physicist Robert Oppenheimer and those who worked with him on developing the nuclear bomb, so that he stands for perverse mass destruction, and he seems directly responsible for the murder of Angela Parker, the protagonist's love interest. In *Baroque at Dawn* there are few named male characters. They are almost entirely absent in the opening and closing frames, but they are present in groups and clusters in the central embedded narrative, facilitating an interlude of hallucinatory violence during a shore visit when Cybil's host explains first the War Measures Act, then the Vietnam war to her (116–18); his placement of Montreal, her home city, within a context of global violence further weakens Cybil, who has lost faith in her ability to write only pages earlier—ironically, in the middle of a lively conversation with Irène and Occident (111). Later, at Occident's death-scene, when the men intervene and separate her from Cybil and Irène they seem almost to hasten the death of this reader-seducer and are the occasion of Cybil's lasting sense of guilt. The brothers Demers are also in charge of the virtual-reality technology that alienates Cybil from her contracted project, so that men form a stultifying presence at virtually every point that could open into utopia for a more beneficially situated Brossardian writer-protagonist.

In Brossard's writing, sex often functions as a metaphor for total commitment, openness, and loving support, a communication that is beyond language, but even sexuality seems exceptionally subdued here. Sexual interaction refuses to become an occasion for Brossardian joyous sharing at this core of the triptych because it remains implicit, occurring strictly off-page between Cybil and Irène in Rimouski, in Buenos Aires, and on board "Le Symbole." Nevertheless, Cybil's status as a fictional product and the reader's role as a consumer remain able to energize each other. Pronouns that are multivalent rather than restrictive promote this reciprocal dynamic through a linguistic chiasmus. The Cybil who makes the ocean voyage is usually written in the third person feminine, but like Winterson's two lovers she cycles through the first- and second-person pronouns as well. "I" is both Cybil and the reader, "you" is both Cybil and the reader; the reader is as "responsible" for the text's dystopic bent as character/narrator/writer, and experiences the blurring of boundaries between fictionality and actuality as intensely as does Cybil.

Although Brossard has been described as determinedly utopic, she does employ dystopic figures to foreground forces that undermine and diminish women's strength, and in *Baroque at Dawn*, she forms her narrative around a dystopic core—a novel about "the volcano of violence erupting in cities" (trans. Claxton 15).[18] Describing this violence requires words "that turn one's stomach, turn one's head to suffering, to people and their progeny who thirst for vengeance" (trans. Claxton 16).[19] Brossard codes this dystopic fictional world as a possible but non-actual world—a situation that can still be resisted—by confining it to the 150-page core. The more optimistic framing narratives suggest alternatives by foregrounding the communication, intellectual contact, and loving emotions shared among framing-Cybil and La

Sixtine in "Hotel Rafale," and by the writing "I" and those who experience the touch of her texts in "One Single Body for Comparison."

The closing segment, "One Single Body for Comparison," is in the voice of the nameless journal writer who is on a publicity tour in Montreal with her nameless translator. Translators in Brossard resemble alchemists of language whose twinned expertise in reading and writing grants them unique positions within the text (see Knutson). This translator expresses her admiration of the way in which the writing "I" uses "a holographic haze to heighten the impression of presence and strangeness. And the sudden illusion of power you give. Power to touch, caress perhaps. . . . Yet every time one suspects an absence, a void, the words turn into ripe fruits bursting with energy. Ah yes, you have caught me off guard at times" (trans. Claxton 209).[20] The writing "I" muses: "*Ah yes* has stayed in my mind as an expression of joy, a kind of eagerness for the raw pleasure of life, for the pleasure of a goal in life. . . . *Ah yes* on her lips brought me back a pleasure from days gone by. Like, at the time, a series of little capers low in the belly giving the world harmonious proportions, a cheerful manner . . ." (trans. Claxton 209).[21]

An involuntary expression of pleasure, of ecstatic assent, "Ah yes" is mutually recognized by seducer and seducee as the performative sign of orgasm reached. "Ah yes" confirms that their caresses have blended the reading-seducing subject with the writing-seduced subject, conferring presence, strangeness, power, energy. In "One Single Body for Comparison," this writing "I" has published a book and is writing a journal, is surrounded by seducing readers and partnered with a translator; all elements of a Brossardian utopia are again in place, answering and soothing the anguished dystopian utterance of the central narrative.

In Winterson's *The PowerBook* and Brossard's *Baroque at Dawn*, the planes of narrative operate as super-sensitized and dynamic liminal sites that offer means of transposing and thereby blending dichotomized subjectivities. During erotic interaction, the skins of lovers can seem less to limit where one lover begins and the other ends than to elide the differences between one body's sensations and the other's. This elision makes of both skins a single liminal Möbius strip, sensitively responding to external stimuli with inner electricity, merging "the other" into "the same." The sensual frictions between skins also temper and modulate the grievous wounds of the dystopian experience of agonistic love, of being seduced by a fickle or fatally compromised reader whose zero-sum approach to relationships aims at mutual obliteration instead of at the mutual re-creation at stake in an aleatory and utopian love. Winterson's *The PowerBook* ends on a bittersweet note of nostalgia, a wistful and impossible desire that this blending could extend beyond the duration of the erotic encounter. Through the medium of hologrammatic narrative, Brossard's *Baroque at Dawn* works toward making this ability to blend a more permanent quality by effecting a cortical change in the seducing reader; the dystopic embedded narrative emphasizes that there is a profound need for change in the way that subjectivities interact. These texts suggest that as long as distinctions arise between victor and victim, producer and consumer, reader and writer, actuality and fictionality, seducer and seducee, the only power is the power to oppress; however, when these dichotomies seep together, the blending itself becomes a dynamic power to effect change. Winterson's writing "I" declares:

> In this space which is inside you and inside me I ask for no rights or territories. There are no frontiers or controls. The usual channels do not exist. This is the orderly anarchic space that no one can dictate, though everyone tries. This is a country without a ruler. I am free to come and go as I please.... Most of us try to turn this into power. We're too scared to do anything else. But it isn't power. It's sex. (175)

Winterson and Brossard work toward removing both literary production and seduction from that realm of power politics, which constructs the writer as victor and the reader as victim of the seduction process, and reshape both as catalyzed and catalyzing agents of utopian change. Freed from the dystopian power to oppress, text and sex do not patronize or limit. Instead, they provide options to repressive ideologies; they open channels of communication; they constellate, transmute, energize. The reader's seducing eye recognizes and nourishes the writer who can refigure her way of reading the world, who can expand the ability of her "skin" to accommodate other subjectivities that complement and extend her perception of the world she inhabits. If, as Occident contends, "artists can change blocks of fiction into currents of thought" (trans. Claxton 75),[22] then it is up to readers to complete the transmutation from fiction to thought to reality.

Acknowledgement

Earlier versions of this paper were delivered to the Association of Canadian College and Universtity Teachers of English at the May 2004 Congress in Winnipeg, were published in *English Studies in Canada* (30:4, December 2004), and formed part of my doctoral dissertation. Many thanks to all who helped shape this article through their valuable questions, comments, and suggestions, especially to my dissertation supervisor, Noreen Golfman, and to the editorial team at *ESC*.

Notes

1 Luce Irigaray and Hélène Cixous are among these feminists; Roland Barthes, Peter Brooks, and Robert Scholes are some of their masculinist counterparts.
2 Anne McMillan (1988) notes that the main power held by the sexually embattled heroine of Gothic romance is the power of her transforming gaze. This gaze sees beneath the sinister Byronic hero's ambiguous exterior to the good man underneath who is waiting to be redeemed by the heroine.
3 The thought is suggested by Alice A. Parker, who describes *Baroque at Dawn* as the most emphatically "invaginated" of Brossard's texts. Following Derrida, she describes textual invagination as a term that "refer[s] to structures that enfold, re-fold, and superimpose themselves" (234 n. 16).
4 "Le futur *dark* (English and italics in original).
5 The Hyde Park woman, like Winterson's lovers, has a bare minimum of identifying characteristics and experiences, which makes her an exceptionally enigmatic figure. She has a red raincoat and an apartment in London that overlooks Hyde Park and holds one or two books by Beckett, and which is where she writes; she also visits the British Museum, where she purchases the Beckett books. On page 90, she seems simply to be another embedded fictional character because Irène describes encountering her in a passage of a book written by the second Cybil some years ago. But the writing "I" who writes the journal about the publicity tour in "One Single Body for Comparison" concretely recalls the view of Hyde Park and the visit to the museum as being within her own experience (221, 255), not shared vicariously through the medium of a narrative. She is also differentiated from the Cybil of the embedded narrative who is a Montréalaise: her publisher provides a hotel room for her in Montreal; presumably this would not be necessary if she actually lived in Montréal. As such, she grows organically into an autonomous character from seeds planted in two quasi-fictional ontologies, so that she seems to be the closest thing to an "actual" hologram that this narrative offers. This helps explain the almost obsessive attention that attends her abrupt appearances and disappearances.
6 Identifying the two Cybil Nolands as embedded-Cybil and framing-Cybil may be a somewhat awkward expedient but it is necessary. If the figures are not distinguished from one another, it can seem that embedded-Cybil somehow "is" framing-Cybil when this is far from true. The two Cybils are very different characters with different experiences; they are commensurate only in their name and their passion for La Sixtine. Framing-Cybil is written to be sexually open: her sex scene is explicit, suggesting she has nothing to hide even

from other ontological levels. She seems confident: she does not feel the need to secure La Sixtine's affections by relating her life story. She is constructed as mature, possibly wise, and possibly the initiator of the relationship with La Sixtine (this last is not detailed within the text, but Irène's characterization closely resembles framing-Cybil's, and Irène does take the initiative with embedded-Cybil). In contrast, embedded-Cybil is sexually reticent: even her non-sexual fantasies can be repressed and anxious, especially where fish and oceans are involved, and her erotic encounters with Irène are never represented on the page. She seems suspicious of others, especially Occident, and continually requires explanations and reassurance; and she tends to react to the presence and actions of others rather than taking the initiative. Further, embedded-Cybil is embedded into the dystopic narrative of the triptych.

7 "Un seul corps pour comparer" (and throughout).
8 Framing-Cybil is never identified concretely as a writer, but Brossard privileges writing women so strongly and consistently that it seems safer to assume that she is than otherwise.
9 "[t]outes tiennent un livre à la main, sauf la sybille de Delphes . . . dont la main se referme sur la partie enroulée d'un papyrus" (140). All notes supplying the original French are from the Hexagone edition of *Baroque d'aube*. In-text parenthetical references that do not cite Claxton as translator refer to the Hexagone edition.
10 "balafre rose"
11 The problem of importing an "actual world" name into a fictional world does preoccupy embedded-Cybil considerably, but the paradox seems to balance itself in "Buenos Aires." Embedded-Cybil is in a cemetery near the tomb of Eva Peron when she notices the approach of "*les deux femmes*" (113; italics in original). The two approaching women are not concretely identified at this point, but the use of italics suggests that embedded-Cybil experiences heightened anxiety or excitement at their proximity. The geographic setting has already been outlined, of course, in "Hotel Rafale," where La Sixtine tells framing-Cybil about her visit to the same cemetery with the admiral's wife (34–35); thus the italics seem to refer to the fact that "*les deux femmes*" both are and are not the young musician and her friend. The fictional world and the actual world seem to "haunt" or invade each other. This co-presence of mutually impossible realities accentuates the arbitrariness of the borders that separate the two worlds and models how easily they interpenetrate each other, which is entirely consistent with Brossard's larger project of effecting change in the actual world through the texts that she writes.
12 "se laissait courtiser" (59)
13 These writers are all white men who can be read as espousing the imperialist, or at least androcentric, values of a bygone era. I read this as contributing to the dystopic bent of this narrative. It is virtually impossible to discern Occident's

agenda: does she wish to reinscribe on the public consciousness the figure of the ocean as devouring mother or seductive killer that prevailed in Early Modern culture? Or would she be willing to consider a more neutral or even gynocentric revision of that significance? She dies before the question even rises to the surface of the text, let alone becomes resolved. Neither do Irène and Cybil take up the question to any great extent, leaving the issue troublingly, dystopically open.

14 "la latitude de vos désirs. . . . [J]e veux des émotions, votre intensité" (59).
15 "Si rêver signifie être là sans y être, convenez que je vous ai fait rêver au-delà de toute espérance. . . . Il ne m'appartient pas de libérer en vous les forces obscures que vous retenient au quai. Je n'ai jamais mis en cause votre liberté d'expression. . . . Une artiste doit savoir faire de feu de tout bois y compris du bois mort que entrave la venue des pensées" (189).
16 "La Voix"
17 "Tu écriras ce livre, au milieu de la nuit, mêlant ton ombre aux ténèbres, liant les morts et les vivants, tous les mots nécessaires et le trop vaste du désir. . . . Tu iras toutes les chercher ces voix dont tu entends les hautes et les basses, la mélopée, le modulé de l'angoisse et de la peur, les cris de joie et de plaisir, les chuchotements énigmatiques, le murmure amoureux au matin clair. . . . Ton oreille tu appuieras sur la bouche de femmes à la voix forte et coléreuse sans craindre la verdeur et la gravité de leurs propos. Tu embrasseras Occident sur son malheur de balafre rose, frissonant avec elle dans la mémoire du temps. Tu garderas l'équilibre au-dessus de l'abîme et de l'eau, vivras dans ton vertige" (190–91).
18 "le volcan de violence qui déferle dans lesles" (23).
19 "font tourner l'estomac, font tourner la tête du côté de la souffrance, du côté des êtres et de leur descendance avide de vengeance" (24).
20 "un flou holographique pour aviver l'impression de présence et d'étrangeté. Et soudain l'illusion que vous donnez de pouvoir. Toucher, caresser peut-être. . . . Pourtant chaque fois qu'on soupçonne une absence, un vide, ils se transforment en grenades d'énergie. Oh! oui vous m'avez surprise" (213).
21 "*Oh! oui* m'est resté dans la tête comme une expression de joie, une sorte d'empressement à guetter le plaisir brut de la vie. . . . *Oh! oui* entre ses lèvres m'a fait retrouver un plaisir ancien. Comme à l'époque une série de petites ruades au bas du ventre et le monde se met à prendre des proportions harmonieuses, des allures gaies . . ." (213; italics in original).
22 "les artistes transforment les blocs de fiction en courants de pensée" (83).

Works Cited

Baudrillard, Jean. *Seduction*. Paris: Editions Galilée, 1979. Trans. Brian Singer. New York: St Martin's Press, 1990. Print.

Brossard, Nicole. *Baroque at Dawn*. Trans. Patricia Claxton. Toronto: McClelland & Stewart, 1997. Print.

———. *Baroque d'aube*. Montréal: L'Hexagone, 1995. Print.
———. "Fragments of a Conversation. *Nicole Brossard: Essays on Her Works*. Ed. Louise Forsyth. Guernica: Toronto, 2005. 19–33. Print.
———. *Le Désert Mauve*. Montréal: L'Hexagone, 1987. Print.
———. *Picture Theory*. Montréal: Éditions de l'Hexagone, 1982, 1989. Trans. Barbara Godard. Montréal: Guernica Editions, 1991. Print.
Forsyth, Louise. "To Write: In the Feminine Is Heavy With Consequences." *Nicole Brossard: Essays on Her Works*. Ed. Louise Forsyth. Guernica: Toronto, 2005. 34–51. Print.
Grosz, Elizabeth. "Animal Sex: Libido as Desire and Death." *Sexy Bodies: The Strange Carnalities of Feminism*. Ed. Elizabeth Grosz and Elspeth Probyn. New York: Routledge, 1995. 278–99. Print.
———. *Volatile Bodies: Toward a Corporeal Feminism*. Bloomington: Indiana UP, 1994. Print.
Hutcheon, Linda. *The Canadian Postmodern: A Study of Contemporary English-Canadian Fiction*. Toronto: Oxford UP, 1988. Print.
Jameson, Fredric. *Archaeologies of the Future: The Desire Called Utopia and Other Science Fictions*. Verso: London, New York, 2005. Print.
Knutson, Susan. *Narrative in the Feminine: Daphne Marlatt and Nicole Brossard*. Waterloo: Wilfrid Laurier UP, 2000. Print.
McMillan, Ann. "The Transforming Eye: *Lady Oracle* and Gothic Tradition." *Margaret Atwood: Vision and Forms*. Ed. Kathryn Van Spanckeren and Jan Garden Castro. Carbondale: Southern Illinois UP, 1988. 48–64. Print.
Meyer, Kim Middleton. "Jeanette Winterson's Evolving Subject: 'Difficulty into Dream.'" *Contemporary British Fiction*. Ed. Richard J. Lane, Rod Mengham, and Philip Tew. Cambridge: Polity, 2003. 210–25. Print.
Muñoz, José Esteban. "Introduction: Feeling Utopia." *Cruising Utopia: The Then and There of Queer Futurity*. New York: New York UP, 2009. 1–18. Print.
Parker, Alice A. "In the Beginning Is Desire." *Liminal Visions of Nicole Brossard*. New York: Peter Lang, 1998. 17–40. Print.
———. *Liminal Visions of Nicole Brossard*. New York: Peter Lang, 1998. Print.
Radway, Janice. "The Readers and Their Romances." *Reading the Romance*. 1984. Print.
Warhol, Robyn R., and Diane Price Herndl, eds. *Feminisms: An Anthology of Literary Theory and Criticism*. New Brunswick, NJ: Rutgers UP, 1991. 551–92. Print.
Wawrzinek, Jennifer. "Translation as Erotic Surrender: Nicole Brossard's Radical Other in *Le Désert Mauve*." *Ambiguous Subjects: Dissolution and Metamorphosis in Postmodern Culture*. Amsterdam: Rodopi, 2008. 57–87. Print.
Winterson, Jeannette. *The PowerBook*. 2000. London: Vintage, 2001. Print.

Another Novel Is Possible
Muckraking in Chris Bachelder's U.S.! and Robert Newman's The Fountain at the Center of the World

Lee Konstantinou

Dystopia When?

Over the last decade, Anglo-American novelists have increasingly turned to the genre of dystopia to explore themes of militarism, environmental risk, media manipulation, and global economic exploitation. Notable dystopian novels include Max Barry's *Jennifer Government*, Richard K. Morgan's *Market Forces*, M.T. Anderson's *Feed*, and Paolo Bacigalupi's *The Windup Girl*, as well as popular young adult dystopias, most prominently Suzanne Collins' *Hunger Games* trilogy, which imagines a future North America where a gladiatorial tribute system takes on the logic of reality television. Even novelists who don't typically write science fiction have gotten into the dystopia business, with more or less apocalyptic overtones. One thinks immediately of Matthew Sharpe's *Jamestown*, Jim Crace's *The Pesthouse*, Gary Shteyngardt's *Super Sad True Love Story*, Margaret Atwood's *Oryx and Crake* and *The Year of the Flood*, Cormac McCarthy's *The Road*, Kazuo Ishiguro's *Never Let Me Go*, David Mitchell's *Cloud Atlas*, Colson Whitehead's *Zone One*, as well as quasi-surrealist dystopias such as George Saunders' *The Brief and Frightening Reign of Phil* and Joshua Cohen's *Witz*. These "new maps of hell," to borrow the memorable title of Kingsley Amis' classic 1960 study of science fiction, are literary snapshots of the future, fallen to pieces, that either serve as warnings about where Utopian political aspirations might lead or encode an author's tentative hopes for a better future. Fredric Jameson would call the former category—for example,

Orwell's *1984*—"anti-Utopias," reserving the prestigious term "dystopia" only for works that include Utopian hopes alongside political criticism (*Archaeologies* 198–99). Whether we categorize them as "anti-Utopias" or "dystopias," all the texts listed above attempt to sublimate fears inspired by contemporary technological, political, and economic crises into art. The popularity of dystopia raises an important, seemingly simple question: If contemporary life is so bad, why do novelists focus on the future rather than criticize the present in some more direct fashion?

Given that many of these dystopias satirically extend the logic of neoliberalism, why can't we find realist fiction about contemporary political and economic crises? Though definitions differ, I will adopt David Harvey's description of neoliberalism as "a theory of political economic practice that proposes that human well-being can best be advanced by liberating individual entrepreneurial freedoms and skills within an institutional framework characterized by strong private property rights, free markets, and free trade" (2).[1] Over the last forty years, neoliberalism has yielded stark results globally. Even in the United States, the presumed beneficiary of such policies, wages for lower income brackets have remained stagnant or decreased, accompanied by an explosion of working hours and borrowing to maintain living standards, supporting Harvey's suggestion that neoliberalism is not only a political-economic theory but a "project to restore class power" (62). Neoliberalism's damaging effects have been noted not only by leftists, but increasingly by Keynesian liberals. Larry Bartels, who can hardly be called a radical, has characterized the political economy of the present era (in the United States) as a "New Gilded Age," a "retrogression of historic scope," with little prospect for change in the near future (13). Even outside the United States, there has been a marked rise in inequality since the mid-1980s in almost all OECD countries, including relatively egalitarian societies such as Norway and Denmark ("Growing Income Inequality in OECD Countries"). These dire circumstances reinforce the urgency of my question: Where might we find literary *economic* protest in a non–science fictional mode today? The original Gilded Age[2] spawned a rich tradition of protest in the subsequent Progressive Era, the naturalism of Crane, Norris, and Dreiser, the muckraking fiction of Upton Sinclair, David Graham Phillips, and the American novelist Winston Churchill. This tradition was enriched in the 1930s by a diversity of new genres, such as "new realism, dynamic realism, magic realism, social surrealism, proletarian surrealism, epic theatre [and] revolutionary symbolism," as Michael Denning documents in *The Cultural Front* (121).

In the 1960s and 1970s, metafiction and postmodernist fiction refurbished the tradition of protest fiction, participating in the era's broader cultural and social movements, in many cases targeting the military-industrial complex and the white-collar economy. Even in an age of affluence, economic issues were central in important novels such as William Gaddis' *J R* (1975). Today, literary writers rarely incorporate political and economic themes into their fiction. The former diversity of political literary genres has atrophied.

This essay asks why, and examines two recent novels that offer answers. Though there are other genres that this essay might have investigated, I am interested in the fortune of the muckraking novel, the *ne plus ultra* of partisan fiction.[3] My first example, Chris Bachelder's 2006 novel *U.S.!: Songs and Stories*, is a work of metafiction that also paradoxically celebrates the muckraking tradition. Robert Newman's 2003 novel *The Fountain at the Center of the World*, meanwhile, revives muckraking literary strategies in order to attack water privatization in Mexico and to dramatize the protests at the 1999 World Trade Organization Ministerial Conference in Seattle. Both novels reconsider the tradition of muckraking for the New Gilded Age, albeit in different ways, and with different degrees of enthusiasm. Though we shouldn't equate muckraking with political fiction *tout court*, or deny the Lukácsian possibility of finding political significance in seemingly nonpolitical realist novels, *U.S.!* and *The Fountain at the Center of the World* have much to teach us about contemporary literary culture.

Liberalism, Objectivity, and Muckraking

Jonathan Franzen's *Freedom* begins with news, or rather with a double disavowal of the news: "The news about Walter Berglund wasn't picked up locally—he and Patty had moved away to Washington two years earlier and meant nothing to St. Paul now—but the urban gentry of Ramsey Hill were not so loyal to their city as not to read the *New York Times*" (3). The triple negative of Franzen's first sentence maps the social world of Ramsey Hill with startling economy. On the one hand, Walter's public meltdown at a press conference isn't picked up in local newspapers. He simply isn't important enough to merit attention in St. Paul. On the other hand, residents of Ramsey Hill, where Walter and Patty once lived, fancy themselves to be world citizens, which means, of course, that they read the *New York Times*, the ultimate metonym for their aspiring urbanity. Franzen's narrator, it seems, mocks Ramsey Hill residents for exposing their provinciality through their conflation of knowledge of the news with worldliness. Not only are they not cosmopolitans, they're naive enough to think that subscribing to the *New York Times* might make them so. And yet, isn't *Freedom* itself a novel of the news? Hasn't it been lavishly praised for depicting a sweeping social portrait of the American 2000s, immediately negating the central premise of this essay?[4] Hasn't it been praised in this way by the *New York Times*, the paper of record, which leads one to suspect that Ramsey Hill's urban gentry would eagerly read *Freedom*? Indeed, *Freedom* features characters attacking George W. Bush, skewers neoconservative ideology, depicts the outrageous corruption of Iraq War subcontracting, and focuses on the devastating effects of mountaintop removal mining, all while showing the difficulties of environmental activism.

Despite all this, Franzen would insist that his novel is anything but a novel of the news. In one of his most important essays, "Why Bother?," he disowns his previous drive to "Address the Culture and Bring News to the Mainstream." He rejects the spirit of his first two novels (*The Twenty-Seventh City* and *Strong Motion*) in favour of his new "desire to write about the things closest to [him], to lose [himself] in characters and locales [he] loved" (95).[5] For much the same reason, he also rejects injecting politics into fiction. "I am a fiction writer," he explains in an interview with Chris Connery. "I'm political only as a citizen, not as a novelist." To be political as a novelist is dangerous because "your art's in danger of becoming illustrative or didactic—in some sense, an act of bad faith." In a startling reversal, within only a few sentences, Franzen also claims that fiction is "a liberal project" and that "[w]hen Jane Smiley uses the phrase 'the liberal novel,' she basically means 'the novel, period.' The form is well suited to expanding sympathy, to seeing both sides. Good novels have a lot of the same attributes as good liberal politics. But I'm not sure it goes much further than liberalism" (qtd. in Connery 46). It would be easy to accuse Franzen of self-contradiction. After all, he wants the novel to be a non-political vehicle for aesthetic pleasure, while also associating it with the prestigious political name of liberalism. Yet to dismiss Franzen would be a mistake, leading us to miss that his position is part of a long tradition, embodying the same paradox, that promotes the liberal value of good fiction.

A compressed reminder of this tradition clarifies Franzen's view. There is, of course, the American liberal interpretation of Bakhtin, which celebrates dialogism or heteroglossia as the novel's official ideology; according to this view, dialogism is also a political bulwark against a "mistaken attachment to systems," which Bakhtin calls "theoretism" or "monologism," and which one set of his interpreters calls "semiotic totalitarianism" (Morson and Emerson 28).[6] Though we would hardly be tempted to think of him as a carnivalesque figure, Lionel Trilling expresses a similar sentiment about the powers of the novel. In "Reality in America," an essay written against the literary critic V.L. Parrington, Trilling juxtaposes the crass reductionism of Theodore Dreiser with the subtle complexity of Henry James. According to Trilling, James' complexity both avoids the mind-denying tendency of Dreiser's leftist politics and constitutes a politics that more aptly approaches our multivalent political reality than naturalism does. For Trilling and other mid-century intellectuals, the liberalness of the novel stood in opposition to radical politics, sociology, and deterministic social theory. The liberalness of the novel was reaffirmed yet again by Richard Rorty, who claimed that one's ironic aesthetic preferences are a purely private matter but also that the novel is better than philosophy at enlarging human sympathy and producing a vicarious fellow feeling among readers.[7] Great novels teach us what it might feel like to suffer in another's shoes, even someone whose "final vocabularies" are very different from our own. Advocates of the liberal novel describe liberalism as a specific ideological alternative to dogmatic political positions—for Rorty, the theological certainties of metaphysics; for Trilling, the undialectical grossness of radical literature; for some of Bakhtin's interpreters, an oppressive semiotic totalitarianism; and for Franzen, the mania for using fiction as a vehicle for conveying information about Systems, a sin he attributes not only to canonical postmodernists but also to contemporary novelists, such as Richard Powers. These writers paradoxically posit not only that the novel essentially is liberal but also, when discussing non-liberal novels, that the novel ought to be liberal. The foil of the liberal novel is usually the radical novel, committed art, the didactic novel, naturalism, activist fiction, or muckraking fiction. Though Franzen may personally agree with Walter Berglund's political opinions, his responsibility as a novelist requires him to subordinate his beliefs to the novel's essential dialogism. News is in *Freedom*, then, despite the fact that it is not a novel of the news.

Muckraking fiction, by contrast, aspires to give us news. Indeed, the very term "muckraking" arose from the intersection of journalism and fiction. When, in 1906, he denounced the "Man with the Muckrake, who could look no way but downward," Teddy Roosevelt had in mind Upton Sinclair's *The Jungle* and David Graham Phillips' journalistic exposé of

Senate corruption and graft, which appeared in the Hearst-owned magazine *Cosmopolitan* (Miraldi 26). By Roosevelt's account, the muckraker was the sort of man who is perniciously "fixed on carnal instead of on spiritual things," who "refuses to see aught that is lofty, and fixes his eyes with solemn intentness only on that which is vile and debasing," a refusal that makes him "one of the most potent forces for evil" in the Republic (58, 59).[8] Muckraking threatened to enflame "the brutal greed of the 'have-nots,'" to inspire "violent emotionalism," and to empower "the wild preachers of unrest and discontent" (62, 64). Typically associated with Progressive Era reform movements, turn-of-the-century socialist fiction, and partisan journalism published in venues such as *McClure's*, *Collier's*, and *Cosmopolitan*, the term muckraking survives today in contemporary journalistic debates, but has largely disappeared among novelists. Discussing philosophical debates among journalists, Robert Miraldi explores muckraking (from the Progressive Era to today) in terms of its difference from objective journalism. Miraldi identifies objective journalism with the idea that "readers and listeners can best make up their minds about public policy issues when they are given verifiable 'facts'" that are "delivered by independent, neutral observers . . . who provide for the reader competing versions of the 'truth'" (15). More substantively, drawing on the classic work of sociologist Gaye Tuchman, Miraldi outlines the "strategic rituals" that journalists aspiring toward objectivity deploy. Stories that seek to satisfy "the profession's unwritten tests of objectivity" value government documents and sources above others; cite evidence only when it is clear that "someone else is responsible for the facts, words, or opinions" presented; attribute every presented fact to someone other than herself, often to a point where the reporter and her opinions are rendered invisible; frame every story around some recent event or "newspeg"; and structure every story as an "inverted pyramid," with the most important information in the lede and the least important information at the end, so that editors can easily cut stories (16–17). Against what we might call the poetics of objective journalism, contemporary muckraking stories "are compilations of documented fact that lead to an indictment—of individuals or institutions," works that emphasize the first-person situatedness of the reporter, that focus on long-term research rather than newspegs, and that do not attempt to conceal the opinion of the writer (18).

Miraldi symptomatically omits fiction from his account, defining muckraking as "journalism, not literature" even as he discusses Progressive

Era novelist-journalists (18). While a systematic study of contemporary muckraking fiction has yet to be written, it should be clear that the aspiring raker of muck faces strikingly different opponents in the fields of journalism and literature. Whereas contemporary muckraking journalism opposes claims of objectivity, literary muckraking claims to speak about "reality"—to be more objective—in a way that liberal literature can't or won't. In an interview, Bachelder suggests:

> The blind spot of classical liberalism is that it does not see itself as a position.... It wants to be a container for all positions, not a position itself.... The novel fits well into the liberal ideology—it's a space where competing views can be dramatized. The author does not (*should* not—this is ethical) have an agenda. She does not advance a position. Pedophilia is complicated! Let's see this from all the angles. I'm interested in Chekhov with regard to our contemporary notions of art. He was among the first to say that the author should not have a point of view. He valued ambiguity, complexity, mystery. This is our notion of high literary art, while Sinclair's notion has declined. It's barely art. (email interview)

While contemporary activist journalists, such as Michael Pollan, Barbara Ehrenreich, and Naomi Klein, differentiate themselves from objective reporters, contemporary political novelists, such as Bachelder and Newman, struggle against the hegemony of literary liberalism. Understood this way, muckraking fiction, we will see, is as much a formal as a historical or social category. Indeed, if, as Cecelia Tichi argues, muckraking aspires to "radically change people's minds," the novels under consideration here might be regarded as failures (1). Neither *U.S.!* nor *Fountain* has changed many minds or altered our public discourse about neoliberalism, though phenomena such as Occupy Wall Street might be regarded as an activist response to similar political-economic circumstances. The fact, nonetheless, that these novels try to change minds is significant in itself, and the formal means by which they make this attempt differ from muckraking journalism. Contemporary muckraking novelists openly present their political views; embrace political-economic topicality; foreground the ideological views of their characters over other characteristics; and seem to hope that novels will inspire real-world political activity. In short, *U.S.!* and *Fountain* imagine a non-liberal political mission for fiction; they make economic class a primary narrative concern; and they place fiction and news in closer proximity than the liberal tradition would allow. Rather than run away from providing "social news" or displaying political partisanship, these novels embrace such goals. A different kind of novel, they seem to argue, is not only possible, but also crucially necessary.

U.S.! and Them

Chris Bachelder's strange second novel, *U.S.!*, attempts to revive muckraking realism for an era that has, to put it mildly, lost interest in the genre. The novel tells the story of the American left's attempts to resurrect Upton Sinclair. This is, in the world of the novel, a literal resurrection. Upon each revival, Upton[9] earnestly writes muckraking novels that address the problems of the day, books with titles such as *Bombs Away!*, *More Oil!*, *Safe Drinking Water! A Novel*, and *Arms for Hostages!* The publication of these political novels, though largely ignored by the American reading public, so enrages the American right that the resurrected Upton is continually assassinated, only to be resurrected again in an endlessly repeating cycle. Upton's assassins become major celebrities, and upon each resurrection, they compete to be the first to murder the writer again. On the one hand, the assassination plots of *U.S.!* recall the actual history of muckraking, specifically the career and 1906 assassination of Pulitzer journalist and novelist David Graham Phillips. On the other hand, the novel—published exactly a hundred years after Phillips' murder—builds its bleak central joke atop the fact that someone like Upton Sinclair would need to be literally resurrected for anything like a left novelistic tradition to be revived in the twenty-first-century United States. What would it be like, *U.S.!* asks, to live in a world where political novels could motivate murder? Bachelder programmatically lays out his reasons for exploring this question in an October 2004 article in *The Believer*, which takes the form of an annotation of a *Harper's*-style graph, featuring facts about Sinclair's uses of the exclamation point in his novel *Oil!* "Exclamation points as ammunition," Bachelder writes in his telegraphic annotation, suggesting that the exclamation point might be a tool of political art, part of a "poetics of class war" ("A Soldier"). For Bachelder, the exclamation point becomes both the formal expression of Sinclair's embarrassing political sincerity and, in its typographic gaucheness, a sign of why it is difficult to revive his example in the present.

In order to embrace Sinclair's enthusiasm, Bachelder must, like Franzen, reject aspects of his earlier commitment to metafiction and postmodernism.

In his *Believer* essay, Bachelder disavows his first novel, *Bear v. Shark*, which satirizes American political and media culture by imagining a dystopian near-future world in which Las Vegas has seceded from the United States and is hosting a virtual-reality duel between a computer-generated bear and shark at the Darwin Dome. This first novel fails, Bachelder declares, because it is unable to keep up with the ruthless pace and self-parodying tendencies of American reality. "[W]e are actually living in an age when satire is increasingly untenable," Bachelder concludes, "because satire relies on clear distinctions between real and absurd, and between core and surface, and those are not distinctions we can easily make anymore" ("A Soldier"). In wishing that the novel had the vitality to keep up with its society, Bachelder participates in the postmodern tradition that the critic James Wood has denounced as "hysterical realism" and that Franzen abandoned after the publication of his first two systems novels. And yet, in growing weary with his own postmodern irony, Bachelder takes his cue less from Wood and Franzen than from David Foster Wallace and the writers associated with Dave Eggers' various literary enterprises (McSweeney's Books, *McSweeney's Quarterly Concern*, and *The Believer*). That is, Bachelder breaks with postmodernism not at the level of goal—the critique of things as they are—but rather at the level of strategy. Postmodern fiction was once useful for novelists but has now lost its power. It follows that the task of the post-postmodern novelist shouldn't be to remove all traces of political content and "social news" from fiction but rather to invent new, more effective ways of injecting news, politics, and critique into the novel.

Despite his belief in the need for a politicized post-postmodern novel, Bachelder is ambivalent about his own efforts. It's true, he writes, that contemporary fiction has "turned inward: into the suburbs, into the house, into the mind. The canvas has gotten small. We still of course have a few straight-up political writers . . . but by and large it seems that we have done little to expand and develop this tradition." And yet, Bachelder's postmodern irony has left him too skeptical to trust in politically motivated fiction. "I'm not ambivalent about the cruel and crumbling empire, but I am ambivalent about how to engage it artistically. I'm ambivalent about Upton, who on one hand was a tireless, courageous class hero, and on the other hand was a poor writer, an egomaniac, a gullible freak, and a bad father" ("A Soldier"). Paradoxically, Bachelder wants to reanimate the literary tradition that Sinclair represents but seems to accept the liberal critique of naturalism and muckraking fiction. He is unable to imagine the possibility of a well-written update to Sinclair's brand of muckraking fiction. One suspects that his problem isn't really a question of style—someone of Bachelder's talent could easily write sentences better than Sinclair's—but rather the drive to rake muck in the first place. Bachelder's solution to the problem that Sinclair poses resembles John Barth's solution to the "exhaustion" of the novel in 1967. Instead of solving the political problem, finding a way to reanimate Sinclair's literary legacy with better sentences, Bachelder turns a postmodern novelistic form against itself, foregrounding the need to find a successful version of post-postmodernism.

In the 200-page first part of *U.S.!*, the "Resurrection Scrapbook," Bachelder presents primary source documents from the world of his novel. These documents include amazon.com reviews of Upton's books (there aren't many), Upton's journal entries, transcripts of television interviews with Upton assassins, a syllabus for a course that Upton teaches—called "English 684! Advanced Fiction Writing (Or Literature as a Class Weapon)"—short vignettes featuring nameless starry-eyed leftists devoted to resurrecting Upton, transcripts of voice-mail messages, haikus written in Upton's honour, jokes told at his expense, among other genres and types of documents. There is even a section called "The Camera Eye," after Dos Passos' sections of the same name in the *U.S.A. Trilogy*, which is another important reference point for Bachelder. The overall portrait of Upton that emerges is of a writer who is almost universally reviled, with the exception of a small cadre of leftist supporters. In *U.S.!*, an anonymous (fictional) review of Upton's (fictional) novel *Pharmaceutical!* describes the book as a "criminally unbalanced tirade against the pharmaceutical industry" that utterly fails as art:

> One does end up sympathizing with [the protagonist] Harold, though not for the reasons that Sinclair intends. Harold's great conflict is not that he is trapped within a ruthless economic system, but that he is trapped within a ruthless novel, a structure infinitely more dehumanizing, rigid, and predetermined than the capitalism it denounces. The wonderful thing about America is that you always have a shot, while the dreadful thing about a Sinclair novel is that you don't. (14–15)

Bachelder cleverly inserts the critique of partisan fiction into his own attempted political novel, as though to inoculate *U.S.!* from the charge that he is as unreflecting as Sinclair. In this fictive review, which recalls Wood's polemic against hysterical realism, the fictional reviewer creates an analogy between determination in fiction and determination in the economy. As many actual liberal literary critics have done before him, this critic claims that the aesthetic failure of the radical novel can be found in its deterministic view of life. Fiction that denies the reality of socioeconomic mobility must therefore fail aesthetically. It is important to note that Bachelder does not necessarily disagree with this fictional reviewer's aesthetic assessment of Sinclair. In addition to describing Sinclair as "a poor writer, an egomaniac, a gullible freak, and a bad father," he laments that "[t]he end of *The Jungle* (the socialist pamphlet part)" is "almost unreadably bad" ("A Soldier"). And yet, it is clear that Bachelder does not agree with the reviewer's assessment of American reality. America is not a place where "you always have a shot."

Despite these reservations, the second part of *U.S.!* dramatizes the power of Upton's fiction to change lives. Titled "The Greenville Anti-Socialist League Fourth of July Book Burning," Part 2 is a self-contained novella about Upton's inadvertent visit to the GASL's annual event, which features the burning of *A Movable Jungle!* The second part shifts from primary source fragments to continuous realist narrative, describing the arrangement of the burning and Upton's journey to Greenville. The novella reaches its narrative climax when the naive and well-meaning young organizer of the book burning, Stephen, accidentally picks up a copy of *A Movable Jungle!* and reads it. Bachelder describes what happens next this way: "Stephen had only slept three hours, and when he awoke, on the floor with the novel on his chest, he found that nothing in his life was the same. He felt that the book had been a strange dream and that he was still trapped within it" (268). Stephen's unexpected development of political consciousness has inconclusive effects. His transformation does indirectly prevent Upton from being successfully killed by the assassins who have gathered in Greenville to murder him, and yet the novella ends with the haunting image of children "permitted to stay up late for this one special night, [who] waved sparklers and danced wildly around the pyre of burned books," suggesting that one boy's political awakening can hardly mollify the enduring power or appeal of the American right (298). What is noteworthy about this novella is that even though, at the level of form, it uses realist narrative codes, at the level of content it remains fantastic, as any rendition of a resurrected Upton Sinclair must. It's not hard to imagine that the transforming power of literature is just as much a fantasy as the possibility of bodily resurrection. Readers, moreover, never learn anything about the content of *A Movable Jungle!* Even if the power of Upton's writing to transform lives were more than a fantasy, *U.S.!* itself doesn't have the journalistic density of Sinclair's actual fiction. It is a novel about muckraking, not a muckraking novel.

The reader is left in a paradoxical situation. If the fact that "the world is crappy (not existentially, but socio-politically . . .)" requires the novelist somehow to address that crappiness; and yet, if Sinclair's writing (his "poetics of class war") is as "unreadably bad" as his critics and Bachelder accuse it of being; and finally, if the postmodern tradition turns out to be little more than "making fun of everything and standing for nothing"—what should the post-postmodernist novelist be doing ("A Soldier")? We get a partial answer from Albert, a character also known as The Last Folksinger, the son of Upton, whose death, which Upton learns about telepathically, marks the emotional climax of *U.S.!*: "Albert knew that art must not turn its back on the world. He felt deeply that art—his songs—must address inequity and cruelty and suffering. What was required, he knew, was a poetics of engagement. And yet what was also required was that Journey song, you know the one" (261). The phrase "poetics of engagement" comes from E.L. Doctorow. "Every writer knows how dangerous it can be [to write about one's political convictions] in terms of doing something good," Doctorow explains in an interview. "But I'm rethinking the whole thing. In view of the emergency—I think it *is* an emergency—is some kind of new aesthetic possible that does not undermine aesthetic rigor? A poetics of engagement" (qtd. in Morris 64). Writing of Doctorow, Fredric Jameson famously elucidates "the paradox that a seemingly realistic novel like *Ragtime* is in reality a nonrepresentational work that combines fantasy signifiers from a variety of ideologemes in a kind of hologram" (*Postmodernism* 22). *U.S.!* reverses the terms of this description. As though trying to get around Jameson's denial of the possibility of political realism (outside science fiction), Bachelder tries to get at reality not through Doctorow-style realism but through the very holographic "fantasy signifiers" that Doctorow is accused of creating in lieu of realism. Bachelder hopes to find a way back to partisan realism, without denying the difficult obstacles posed by aesthetic liberalism and postmodernism.

Where Is the Centre of the World?

Bachelder rejects Franzen's assumption that the novel is intrinsically liberal but also wants to reject the postmodernist critique of realism; and yet, as we have seen, Bachelder finds himself unable to find a way to move forward.

That is, *U.S.!* is less the sort of novel that Bachelder wishes that he could write—a novel composed in terms of a "poetics of engagement"—than a novel outlining the difficulty of writing such a novel in the present, at least for him. The stand-up comic and activist Robert Newman offers a different perspective on the same problem. Whereas *U.S.!* metafictionally recollects the power of muckraking without wholly adopting the narrative strategies associated with that tradition, Newman's *The Fountain at the Center of the World* actually tries to rake the muck of neoliberal globalization and to imagine alternatives to it. Newman dismisses the view that realism is always a code word for liberalism and tacitly contends that it is still possible to tell realist political stories, even in the era of multinational capitalism.

Fountain is a novel concerned with the political battle over water privatization in Mexico and the 1999 protests at the World Trade Organization Ministerial Conference in Seattle. Newman tells this political story through the entwined lives of two brothers, separated at a young age and reunited when the younger brother develops what seems to be myelogenous leukemia, which turns out instead to be the incurable "chagas disease," a disease that "feeds on the blood of the poor" (130). After their mother dies, an English couple adopts the younger brother, who is given the name Evan Hatch; the older brother, Chano Salgado, is raised by family members in Mexico. Evan becomes a public relations professional working for Poley Bray Communications, while Chano becomes a disillusioned activist whose wife is murdered as a result of her political work. The novel's third major character is Chano's son Daniel, who is sent to Costa Rica after Chano is imprisoned and mistakenly thought to have died. The contrast between the brothers—their starkly different political views, their different positions in global relations of power—drives the novel's plot. A full account of the Dickensian twists of *Fountain* is impossible here. Newman takes us from London to Tamaulipas to Costa Rica to the deck of a container ship to Seattle, portraying a vast and dazzling global network of characters and organizations. What is most striking about the novel is the style Newman employs to narrate political-economic interconnection and complexity. Newman sketches the contours of the capitalist world-system through his rendition of the brothers' ideological perspectives. Evan and Chano imagine power relations in remarkably similar ways, albeit with their political conclusions reversed. The critic Suman Gupta observes "a certain common ground" between the brothers because "the two are looking at the screen of people (the *demos* in democracy) from opposite sides" (21).

Not only do the novel's characters see the world in similar, if ideologically flipped, terms, but the novel's third-person narrator constantly intervenes in the main narrative, editorializing, giving readers reams of relevant information. These factual interventions operate formally as interruptions in the novel's diegesis, sometimes to a level that recalls the genre of "faction" that the muckraker David Graham Phillips is famous for inventing. Early in the novel, for example, we learn in a parenthetical aside that Chano's wife "(. . . never called him Chano, the short form of Mariano)" (10), and on the next page we are informed that "Tamaulipas, the northeasternmost state of Mexico, is a land of dead rivers" (11). These relatively minor interruptions—parenthetical explanations designed to orient a reader unfamiliar with Mexican geography and nicknames—pepper Newman's prose. Newman interjects numerous descriptions into his narrative: of public relations strategies, the details of global trade agreements, bomb-making methods, techniques for enduring tear gas, among others. A critic like James Wood would condemn this style for breaking the suspension of disbelief required of great novelistic art and for elevating information above characterization. Newman, by contrast, consciously makes managing information, weaving fact into the fabric of fiction, an operative element of his novelistic craft. Whereas, in the mainstream literary novel, facts are supposed to be filtered through specific and distinct points of view, Evan and Chano are distinguished less by their voices and styles of consciousness than by their ideological commitments and political disagreements. Whereas the liberal literary tradition conceals necessary research, the novel that Newman writes paints an openly partisan and information-rich portrait of the world-system.

Even chapters narrated from the teenage Daniel's point of view insert news and dense descriptions of global interconnection. Early in the novel, the Mexican fishing fleet has been grounded because it is no longer compliant with American legal mandates following the passage of the "Dolphin Death Act." Because the fleet is grounded, Daniel is able to crew for a Costa Rican fishing boat that is making its way to Mexico, which immediately takes advantage of the economic opening, fearing that the Mexicans will not be landlocked for long. "[T]he Dolphin Death Act coincided with strange events," we are told:

> At first no one saw the connection. But on the Frankfurt Eurex and in London Bridge City, on the Dow Jones and Tokyo Nikkei, the numbers

were going up and down and all around and no one knew why. Green screens howled like amps wailing feedback from an undiscovered electrical source. All was confusion until, with an apologetic cough, the U.S. Drug Enforcement Agency stepped forward and explained.

The Mexican trawler fleet, said the DEA, is the Cali cartel's fishing fleet of choice, the preferred delivery service to export cocaine to the Docks of Bologna, Rotterdam, and Liverpool, which was why finance houses that had long handled these high-yield, see-no-evil blind trusts suddenly had burst condoms in the belly. Thus the Mexican fishing fleet was to get a rapid dolphin-friendly refit and its grounding was, in the event, to last only ten days. (26)

Though it appears in a chapter focalized through his perspective, this description bears no relation to Daniel's consciousness or to any facts about the world that he would know. The homogeneity of capitalist value—represented by the high mobility of "see-no-evil" drug money—and the interconnections of the world economy find a formal analog at the level of the sentence. Metaphors, like "burst condoms in the belly," seem to come straight from Newman, or at least a narrator who has done the same research that he has. Interestingly, Newman does not only reserve his arguably monological style to represent the capitalist economy; he also uses it to portray the anti-WTO Seattle protests and alternative-globalization protests more generally, which have often been described as a "movement of movements" to give a sense of their size and political heterogeneity. The Seattle alternative-globalization protests were—somewhat like Occupy Wall Street and its offshoots—based on an affinity group model, loosely affiliated organizations, each of which had its own agenda, united through the governing body of a spokescouncil, which operated according to a consensus model. This mode of organization is often seen as a postmodern solution offered by alternative-globalization movements to global capitalism.

In a fine ethnography of the 2001 protest at the Summit of the Americas meeting in Quebec City, David Graeber goes so far as to align the radical puppeteers present at the protest to the Bakhtinian tradition of carnival, suggesting that the tactic is a "tacit [attack] on the principle of hierarchy itself" (503). Graeber's invocation of Bakhtin suggests both the continuities and breaks with liberal thought that any radical protest novel of the present moment must negotiate. Like liberalism, the new radical movements attempt to satisfy multiple, competing, often very different desires via designated deliberative procedures; against the liberal tradition, alternative-globalization protesters reject the market as the specific deliberative mechanism of arriving at these collective decisions in the sphere of the economy. For liberals, the carnival looks a lot like a marketplace; Graeber's anarchist version of the carnival more resembles a spokescouncil. Whatever we think of the political efficacy of radical puppetry, it is noteworthy that Newman's strategy for representing both the global hierarchies of multinational capitalism and the anti-hierarchical but heteroglossic politics of counter-globalization movements relies on a consistently flat descriptive style. This might suggest that the heteroglossia of actual movements need not find a formal analog in novelistic heteroglossia. Or, more provocatively, it might suggest that the muckraking tradition and monological style are necessarily linked. I have been making a case for the latter view. Specifically, I would argue that Newman's flatness of style originates in his apparent rejection of the idea that political information should be delivered to the reader only through the consciousness of his characters, which is an analog of the muckraking journalist's rejection of the objective journalist's insistence on not speaking in her own voice. Like Newman, Bachelder rejects the idea of filtering political facts through the focalizing consciousness of characters, and thus in his novel presents a large array of primary-source documents alongside an unmarked monological narrative voice. Newman, meanwhile, firmly chooses the path of muckraking, and the evidence of his novel suggests that this option is anything but "unreadably bad."

Toward a Non-Liberal Novel

In his review of *The Corrections*, James Wood means to malign Jonathan Franzen when he says that the novel is "a kind of glass-bottomed boat through which one can glimpse most of the various currents of contemporary American fiction" (201). Franzen's focus on character is laudable, while "[a]ll the rest is 'social news' and may be turned off, as it deserves" (209). In the world of literary reviewing, there is always a critic ready to expose trace amounts of news, information, and partisanship in literary fiction. Foregrounding heteroglossia, differentiating between and rounding out characters, writing your identity, achieving mutual understanding across chasms of difference—these are the dominant values of contemporary Anglo-American literary culture. It has not been my goal in this essay to condemn liberal fiction or determine the true purpose of the novel. I don't believe any authoritative or general statements can be made on this question. It's perfectly possible to enjoy—and celebrate—both *Freedom* and *The Fountain at the Center of the World*. Rather, a simple question has driven my inquiry. As economic inequality accelerates, as transnational corporations grow in power, as elites are increasingly identified as part of a highly mobile cosmopolitan "Superclass"—what Samuel P. Huntington pejoratively and from a nakedly nationalist perspective called "Davos Man"—the great mainstream of Anglo-American literary production remains locked in what we might as well call the Franzen Orthodoxy. Only the paraliterary world of science fiction has ignored this orthodoxy in any systematic way. Even modest literary attempts to relate individuals to large social structures and collectives—as we find, say, in the fiction of Richard Powers—are often treated as out of bounds. Why?

My conclusions are necessarily tentative. I think we must reject the argument that global politics as it now exists is, in some sense, unrepresentable or impossible to get at using old forms, as though representing global power relations was once upon a time some simple matter. The evidence of these books, especially *The Fountain at the Center of the World*, suggests that we should regard this argument with great skepticism. We must also, for similar reasons, be suspicious of any suggestion that there are not really contemporary political movements for radical fiction writers to connect to. The flourishing of political documentary, non-fiction, and memoir—not to mention the existence of alternative-globalization movements, powerful oppositional responses to the American War on Terror, and now Occupy Wall Street—suggest that the lacuna I am noting is specifically located in the field of literary fiction.

The forgotten origin of the term "muckraking" suggests that the institutional division of journalism and fiction might offer some measure of explanation for this gap. Whereas novelists once cut their teeth as journalists, as Shelly Fisher Fishkin has observed, today, writers more often do their apprenticeships in creative writing programs, or write in an environment shaped by program aesthetics. In what Mark McGurl has called "the program era," the aesthetic ideology of the M.F.A. degree goes well beyond the program, encompassing professional reviewing culture, influencing the global publishing field, and shaping careers that unfold outside academia. And as McGurl notes, science fiction is markedly outside the system—it is "only minimally represented in the creative writing program establishment" (405)—which might explain why literary authors, disturbed by the present, are turning to the genre as a way of addressing political themes. The ultimate paradox of *U.S.!* is that Bachelder, who went through the creative writing system, subscribes enough to its aesthetic ideology that he cannot directly write the muckraking novel he wants to write, but must displace the writing of such fiction to a future moment. Newman, meanwhile, came to fiction after previous careers as a stand-up comic and a political activist. *Fountain* also suggests a final explanation for the relative absence of muckraking novels today. Corporate publishers, in the United States and elsewhere, largely do not support the genre. Published by Verso in the U.K., and Soft Skull Press in the United States, *Fountain* had a hard time finding its way into print. The rejection letters it elicited reportedly took the form of "five-page, single-spaced screeds about the book's politics"; Newman's U.S. publisher, Richard Nash of Soft Skull, quips that "[i]f the big corporate publishers didn't act like big corporate publishers, we'd never have gotten Rob's book" (qtd. in Charle). How science fiction manages to avoid these concerns will have to be the topic of future research. Further research will also be needed to quantify more precisely the full range of output of mainstream literary publishing, as well as to develop better literary-sociological models to account for why a genre like muckraking could once have been so widespread and so popular, but is currently, despite its enduring aesthetic power, stuck in the grave.

Notes

I'd like to thank Sam Cohen, Linda Kauffman, and Peter Mallios for their helpful comments on previous drafts of this chapter. I'd also like to thank members of the audience at the 2011 ASAP/3 Conference in Pittsburgh for their responses to an early version of this argument. Finally, I owe a great debt to Chris Bachelder for answering my many questions about his inspiring novel.

1. One definitional question here concerns the relationship of classical liberalism to neoliberalism. On this question, the development economist Ha-Joon Chang provides a useful distinction: "Neo-liberal economics is an updated version of the liberal economics of the 18th-century economist Adam Smith and his followers. . . . Neo-liberal economists support certain things that the old liberals did not—most notably certain forms of monopoly (such as patents or the central bank's monopoly over the issue of bank notes) and political democracy. But in general they share the old liberals' enthusiasm for the free market" (13).
2. The term "Gilded Age" itself has a literary origin, arising from the title of Mark Twain's 1873 novel of the same name, which he co-authored with Charles Dudley Warner.

3 I will not, for instance, be discussing David Simon's *The Wire*, which Walter Benn Michaels calls "the most serious and ambitious fictional narrative of the twenty-first century so far," "like a reinvention of Zola or Dreiser for a world in which the deification of the market is going out rather than coming in." I will also not be discussing documentaries, non-fiction, memoir, or other directly journalistic genres.

4 Sam Tanenhaus, the editor of the *New York Times* Book Review, wrote, "Jonathan Franzen's new novel, 'Freedom' . . . is a masterpiece of American fiction. . . . Once again Franzen has fashioned a capacious but intricately ordered narrative that in its majestic sweep seems to gather up every fresh datum of our shared millennial life." And yet, despite being impressed by Franzen's sweep, Tanenhaus concludes this way: "Walter, groping toward deliverance, mourns 'a fatal defect in his own makeup, the defect of pitying even the beings he most hated.' But of course it is no defect at all. It is the highest, most humanizing grace. And it cares nothing about power." The review's final emphasis falls, unsurprisingly, on characterization and the non-relation of the novel's ambitious sweep to the aspiration for power.

5 For Franzen's view of the failure of postmodernism, see "Mr. Difficult," originally published in *The New Yorker* and then reprinted in *How to Be Alone*.

6 Morson and Emerson define semiotic totalitarianism as "the assumption that everything has a meaning relating to the seamless whole, a meaning one could discover if only one had the code. This kind of thinking is totalitarian in its assumption that it can, in principle, explain the totality of things; it is semiotic (or cryptographic) in its approach to all apparent accidents as signs of an underlying order to which the given system has the key" (28). For a critique of Morson and Emerson's interpretation of Bakhtin, see Hirschkop.

7 For a thoughtful analysis of Rorty's paradoxical claims about the relationship of cultural politics and "real" politics, see Robbins 127–47. At times, Rorty seems committed to reviving patriotic discourse in the service of reconstructing the Old Left; on other occasions, Rorty celebrates aesthetic liberal autonomy from public life in ways that recall Cold War liberalism.

8 Roosevelt drew the figure of the muckraker from John Bunyan's *The Pilgrim's Progress*.

9 In this chapter, I use "Upton" to refer to the character in Bachelder's novel and "Sinclair" to refer to the historical person, Upton Sinclair.

Works Cited

Amis, Kingsley. *New Maps of Hell: A Survey of Science Fiction*. New York: Harcourt, Brace, 1960. Print.

Bachelder, Chris. Email interview. 6 Dec. 2011.

———. "A Soldier Upon a Hard Campaign." *The Believer* Oct. 2004. Web. 31 Oct. 2011.

———. *U.S.!: Songs and Stories*. New York: Bloomsbury, 2006. Print.

Bartels, Larry. *Unequal Democracy: The Political Economy of the New Gilded Age*. Princeton: Princeton UP, 2008. Print.

Chang, Ha-Joon. *Bad Samaritans: The Myth of Free Trade and the Secret History of Capitalism*. New York: Bloomsbury, 2008. Print.

Charle, Suzanne. "Write On." *American Prospect*, 8 Mar. 2004. Web. 31 Oct. 2011.

Connery, Chris, and Jonathan Franzen. "The Liberal Form: An Interview with Jonathan Franzen." *boundary 2* 36.2 (2009): 31–54. Print.

Fishkin, Shelley Fisher. *From Fact to Fiction: Journalism and Imaginative Writing in America*. Oxford: Oxford UP, 1988. Print.

Franzen, Jonathan. *Freedom*. New York: Farrar, Straus and Giroux, 2010. Print.

———. "Mr. Difficult." *How to Be Alone*. New York: Picador, 2003. 238–69. Print.

———. "Why Bother?" *How to Be Alone*. New York: Picador, 2003. 55–97. Print.

Graeber, David. *Direct Action: An Ethnography*. Oakland, CA: AK Press, 2009. Print.

"Growing Income Inequality in OECD Countries: What Drives It and How Can Policy Tackle It?" *OECD Forum on Tackling Inequality*. OECD, 2 May 2011. Web. 31 Oct. 2011.

Gupta, Suman. *Globalization and Literature*. Cambridge: Polity Press, 2009. Print.

Harvey, David. *A Brief History of Neoliberalism*. New York: Oxford UP, 2007. Print.

Hirschkop, Ken. *Mikhail Bakhtin: An Aesthetic for Democracy*. Oxford: Oxford UP, 2000. Print.

Jameson, Fredric. *Archaeologies of the Future: The Desire Called Utopia and Other Science Fictions*. London: Verso, 2007. Print.

———. *Postmodernism, or, The Cultural Logic of Late Capitalism*. Durham: Duke UP, 2001. Print.

McGurl, Mark. *The Program Era: Postwar Fiction and the Rise of Creative Writing*. Cambridge, MA: Harvard UP, 2009. Print.

Michaels, Walter Benn. "Going Boom." *Bookforum* Feb./Mar. 2009. Web. 30 Dec. 2012.

Miraldi, Robert. *Muckraking and Objectivity: Journalism's Colliding Traditions*. Santa Barbara, CA: Greenwood Press, 1990. Print.

Morris, Christopher D. *Conversations with E.L. Doctorow*. Jackson: UP of Mississippi, 1999. Print.

Morson, Gary, and Caryl Emerson. *Mikhail Bakhtin: Creation of a Prosaics*. Palo Alto: Stanford UP, 1990. Print.

Newman, Robert. *The Fountain at the Center of the World*. Brooklyn, NY: Soft Skull Press, 2004. Print.

Robbins, Bruce. *Feeling Global: Internationalism in Distress*. New York: New York UP, 1999. Print.

Roosevelt, Theodore. "The Man with the Muck-Rake." In *The Muckrakers*. Ed. Arthur Weinberg and Lila Weinberg. Champaign: U of Illinois P, 2001. 58–65. Print.

Rorty, Richard. *Contingency, Irony, and Solidarity*. Cambridge: Cambridge UP, 1989. Print.

Tanenhaus, Sam. "Peace and War." *New York Times* 19 Aug. 2010. Web. 31 Oct. 2011.

Tichi, Ceclia. *Exposés and Excess: Muckraking in America, 1900/2000*. Philadelphia: U of Pennsylvania P, 2004. Print.

Trilling, Lionel. "Reality in America." *The Liberal Imagination*. New York: NYRB Classics, 2008. 3–21. Print.

Wood, James. "Jonathan Franzen and the 'Social Novel.'" *The Irresponsible Self: On Laughter and the Novel*. New York: Farrar, Straus and Giroux, 2004. 195–209. Print.

ABOUT THE CONTRIBUTORS

Marleen S. Barr is known for her pioneering work in feminist science fiction and teaches English at the City University of New York. She has won the Science Fiction Research Association Pilgrim Award for lifetime achievement in science fiction criticism. Barr is the author of *Alien to Femininity: Speculative Fiction and Feminist Theory*, *Lost in Space: Probing Feminist Science Fiction and Beyond*, *Feminist Fabulation: Space/Postmodern Fiction*, and *Genre Fission: A New Discourse Practice for Cultural Studies*. Barr has edited many anthologies and co-edited the special science fiction issue of *PMLA*.

Gisèle M. Baxter has taught in the English Department at the University of British Columbia in Vancouver since 1997. Her teaching/research interests include dystopian/post-apocalyptic texts, the Gothic inheritance in literature and popular culture, children's/young adult fiction, and British Modernism.

Lee Skallerup Bessette has a Ph.D. in Comparative Literature from the University of Alberta. Her research interests include Caribbean literature in French and English, as well as speculative fiction and translation. She has published on Nalo Hopkinson and Dany Laferrière. Dr. Skallerup Bessette is currently an Instructor of English at Morehead State University, Kentucky.

Joseph Campbell has a doctorate in Literature for Children and Adolescents from Illinois State University. His research focuses are science fiction (both SF intended for adults as well as SF intended for an adolescent audience), dystopian literature (both YA and otherwise), and graphic novels. He teaches English as well as Gender Studies at Casper College in Wyoming.

María Odette Canivell is a Guatemalan-born Associate Professor of English at James Madison University in Harrisonburg, Virginia. Her publications range from the novels *María Isabel* (1995) and *La Historia de Hans Zimmermann* (2000) to scholarship, including *El poder de la pluma: Los escritores y la política* (2012), *Marketing Myths: On Heroedom, Intellectual Imperialism, and the Construction of National Symbols* (2012), and "Don Quijote's Woes: Challenges in Teaching *Don Quijote* in Translation" (2010).

Sharon DeGraw teaches the history of science and science fiction at Michigan State University in East Lansing, Michigan. Race, post/colonialism, and science fiction are her primary research areas. Her book, *The Subject of Race in American Science Fiction*, was published by Routledge in 2007. In addition, she has published articles on Octavia Butler, Doris Lessing, and Tobias S. Buckell.

Kit Dobson is a faculty member in the Department of English at Calgary's Mount Royal University. He is the author of *Transnational Canadas: Anglo-Canadian Literature and Globalization* (Wilfrid Laurier UP, 2009), co-author with Smaro Kamboureli of *Producing Canadian Literature: Authors Speak on the Literary Marketplace* (Wilfrid Laurier UP, 2013), editor of *Please, No More Poetry: The Poetry of derek beaulieu* (Wilfrid Laurier UP, 2013), and co-editor with Áine McGlynn of *Transnationalism, Activism, Art* (U of Toronto P, 2013).

Luis Gómez Romero joined the School of Law at the University of Wollongong in June 2013. Prior to this, Luis developed a postdoctoral research project at the Institute for the Public Life of Arts and Ideas (IPLAI) at McGill University (2011–2012). In 2009, Luis finished his Ph.D. in jurisprudence at the Universidad Carlos III de Madrid with a dissertation titled "Fantasy, Dystopia, and Justice: Harry Potter's Saga as an Instrument for Teaching Human Rights."

Richard Gooding is a lecturer in Arts Studies in Research and Writing and the Department of English at the University of British Columbia in Vancouver, where he teaches children's literature and writing. He has published on the early novel, eighteenth-century literature and medicine, and children's and young adult literature.

Brett Josef Grubisic is the author of *The Age of Cities* and *Understanding Beryl Bainbridge*; he co-authored (with David L. Chapman) *American Hunks: The Muscular Male Body in Popular Culture, 1860–1970* and co-edited (with Andrea Cabajsky) *National Plots: Historical Fiction and Changing Ideas of Canada*. *This Location of Unknown Possibilities*, his second novel, will be published in 2014. He teaches at the University of British Columbia in Vancouver.

Gregory Hampton is an Associate Professor of African American Literature and the Director of Graduate Studies in the Department of English at

Howard University in Washington, D.C. He has published articles in various academic journals and is the author of *Changing Bodies in the Fiction of Octavia Butler: Slaves, Aliens, and Vampires* (2010), the first monograph of literary criticism invested in examining the complete body of fiction produced by Octavia Butler. His principal research areas are African American speculative fiction and marginalized bodies.

Lee Konstantinou is an Assistant Professor in the English Department at the University of Maryland, College Park. He wrote the novel *Pop Apocalypse* and co-edited (with Samuel Cohen) the collection *The Legacy of David Foster Wallace*. He is completing a literary history of irony called *Postirony: Countercultural Fictions from Hipster to Coolhunter*, which is under contract with Harvard University Press.

Annette Lapointe holds a Ph.D. in English from the University of Manitoba (2010) and teaches at Grande Prairie Regional College in northern Alberta. Her primary research areas are constructions of gender and contemporary science fiction. She has published two novels: *Stolen* (2006) and *Whitetail Shooting Gallery* (2012).

Tara Lee holds a Ph.D. in English Literature from Simon Fraser University, and teaches at the University of British Columbia in Vancouver. Her teaching and research interests include techno-scientific studies, critical race theory, and minority Canadian literature.

Robert McGill is an Assistant Professor in the Department of English at the University of Toronto, where he teaches Canadian Literature and Creative Writing. He is the author of *The Treacherous Imagination: Intimacy, Ethics, and Autobiographical Fiction* (2013), and of two novels, *The Mysteries* (2004) and *Once We Had a Country* (2013). He has also published articles on authors such as Margaret Atwood, Alice Munro, Flannery O'Connor, and Elizabeth Smart.

Carl F. Miller (Ph.D., University of Florida) is an Assistant Professor of English at Palm Beach Atlantic University in Florida, where his primary research interests are in twentieth-century comparative literature, critical theory, and children's literature. He has other recent publications on the influence of the Cold War on the 1980s graphic novel, the significance of philosophical ethics in Dr. Seuss's *Horton Hears a Who!*, and the cultural capital of pop music in Bret Easton Ellis's *American Psycho*.

Owen Percy holds a Ph.D. in English from the University of Calgary. His research and teaching focus on Canadian literature, literary culture, genre theory, and poetics. He is a Professor of Communication and Literary Studies at Sheridan College in Brampton, Ontario.

Sharlee Reimer is a Ph.D. candidate in the Department of English & Cultural Studies at McMaster University in Hamilton, Ontario. Her dissertation focuses on gender nonconformity, race, and nation in contemporary Canadian literatures.

Lysa Rivera is an Associate Professor at Western Washington University, where she teaches Chicano/a literature, African American literature, and American Cultural Studies. Her work has appeared in *MELUS*, *Film Philosophy*, *Science Fiction Studies*, and *Aztlán: The Journal of Chicano Studies*. She currently serves on the editorial board for *FemSpec*. She teaches and writes in Bellingham, Washington, where she lives with her husband and their son.

Adam Spires is an Associate Professor of Spanish and Latin American Studies at Saint Mary's University in Halifax, Nova Scotia. His published works include critical analyses of dystopian fiction in Latin America with a primary interest in the portrayal of marginalization in Acadia and Aztlán. His current research is focused on the representation of environmental issues in the Mexican dystopia.

Helene Staveley teaches English at Memorial University in St. John's, Newfoundland, where she earned a Ph.D. in the study of play and game elements in contemporary Canadian narrative, especially Margaret Atwood, Nicole Brossard, Gail Scott, Thomas King, and Lisa Moore. She has also published on the memoir form and is incorporating Canadian children's narrative into her academic interests.

Paul Stephens grew up in Coquitlam, British Columbia, and now lives in Brooklyn, New York. His articles have appeared in *Digital Humanities Quarterly*, *Postmodern Culture*, *Contemporary Literature*, and *Social Text*. He is the author of *The Poetics of Information Overload: From Gertrude Stein to Conceptual Writing* (University of Minnesota Press, 2014), and is editor of the journal *Convolution*. He teaches at Columbia University in New York.

Thomas Stubblefield is an Assistant Professor in Art History at the University of Massachusetts, Dartmouth. His research interests include: the visual culture of disaster, cultural memory, and theories of photography. Recent publications include "Do Disappearing Monuments Simply Disappear? The Counter-Monument in Revision" in *Future Anterior* and "Two Kinds of Darkness: Jean-Luc Nancy and the Community of Cinema" in *The Canadian Journal of Film Studies*. His book *Visual Culture of Disaster, 9/11 and the Spectacle of Absence* is forthcoming in 2014 from Indiana University Press.

Robert T. Tally, Jr., is an Associate Professor of English at Texas State University. His books include *Fredric Jameson: The Project of Dialectical Criticism, Poe and the Subversion of American Literature, Spatiality (The New Critical Idiom), Utopia in the Age of Globalization, Kurt Vonnegut and the American Novel*, and *Melville, Mapping and Globalization*. The translator of Bertrand Westphal's *Geocriticism*, Tally is the editor of *Geocritical Explorations: Space, Place, and Mapping in Literary and Cultural Studies* and *Kurt Vonnegut: Critical Insights*, and he serves as the general editor of the Palgrave Macmillan book series *Geocriticism and Spatial Literary Studies*.

Hande Tekdemir is an Assistant Professor of English in the Western Languages and Literatures Department at Bogazici University, Turkey. Her research interests include the modern English novel, post-colonial studies, urban theory and literature, and detective fiction. Her most recent publication is an article titled "Magical Realism in the Peripheries of the Metropolis: A Comparative Approach to *Tropic of Orange* and *Berji Kristin: Tales from the Garbage Hills*" that appeared in *The Comparatist*.

Janine Tobeck is an Assistant Professor of English at the University of Wisconsin–Whitewater, and studies post-1945 American fiction. Her article "Discretionary Subjects: Decision and Participation in William Gibson's Fiction" appeared in *Modern Fiction Studies*, and she has also published articles on Flannery O'Connor and Clarice Lispector.

Alexa Weik von Mossner is Assistant Professor of American Studies at the University of Klagenfurt in Austria and an Affiliate at the Rachel Carson Center for Environment and Society at the University of Munich. She is the co-editor, with Christoph Irmscher, of a special issue on "Dislocations and Ecologies" of the *European Journal of English Studies on Dislocations and Ecologies* (2012) and the editor of *Moving Environments: Affect, Emotion, Ecology, and Film* (Wilfrid Laurier UP, 2014).

Zac Zimmer is Assistant Professor of Spanish at Virginia Tech in Blacksburg, Virginia. He received his Ph.D. from the Department of Romance Studies, Cornell University. His research explores questions of literature, aesthetics, politics, and technology in Latin America. His current project, tentatively titled *First Contact*, is a comparative study of Latin American science fiction and narratives of the sixteenth-century conquest of the Americas.